Dear reader,

WE'RE BAAAAACK! We have a freaking sequel!! You guys!! I can't begin to explain how surreal all of this continues to be, and it's all thanks to you! You came out and supported *After* so hard that the entire world noticed, and YOU made *After* the biggest indie film of 2019!! It's also because of you that we won a People's Choice Award and THREE Teen Choice Awards! You are simply the best community in the entire world.

We get to see another chapter of Hessa's story in *After We Collided*, and we listened to your feedback from *After* and made this movie with you in mind. I hope you love it the same way you love this book (or at least close :P). I love you all, and I'm so excited to go on another journey with you as the world sees *After We Collided*. I can't wait for more. ;)

For now, thank you for everything, and as a little thank-you, I've written a chapter that SO many of you have asked for. <3 If you haven't read the entire series, BEWARE OF THE HUGE, GIGANTIC SPOILER THAT THE CHAPTER WILL BE FOR YOU. And if you're not new here, enjoy. <3

Anna

AFTER
WE
COLLIDED

Also available from Anna Todd

THE AFTER SERIES
After
After We Collided
After We Fell
After Ever Happy
Before

THE LANDON SERIES
Nothing More
Nothing Less

STANDALONES
Imagines
The Spring Girls
The Brightest Stars

AFTER
WE
COLLIDED

ANNA TODD

GALLERY BOOKS

New York   London   Toronto   Sydney   New Delhi

G

Gallery Books
A Division of Simon & Schuster, Inc.
1230 Avenue of the Americas
New York, NY 10020

The author is represented by Wattpad.

First Gallery Books trade paperback edition November 2014
This paperback edition first published 2020

GALLERY BOOKS and colophon are registered trademarks
of Simon & Schuster, Inc.

For information about special discounts for bulk purchases,
please contact Simon & Schuster Special Sales at 1-866-506-1949
or business@simonandschuster.com.

The Simon & Schuster Speakers Bureau can bring authors
to your live event. For more information or to book an event,
contact the Simon & Schuster Speakers Bureau at 1-866-248-3049
or visit our website at www.simonspeakers.com.

Interior design by Davina Mock-Maniscalco
Cover design by Damonza
Cover image © Julian Walter/Offset

Printed and bound by CPI Group (UK) Ltd, Croydon, CR0 4YY

10 9 8 7 6 5 4 3 2 1

Library of Congress Cataloging-in-Publication Data is available.

ISBN 978-1-9821-7382-1
ISBN 978-1-4767-9255-2 (ebook)

To every single person reading this,
with so, so, so much love and gratitude

AFTER
WE
COLLIDED

prologue

HARDIN

I can't feel the icy concrete under me or the snow settling over me. I can feel only the hole that was ripped through my chest. I'm kneeling helplessly, watching as Zed pulls out of the parking lot with Tessa in the passenger seat.

I couldn't have imagined this—never in my wildest fucking dreams would I have thought that I'd feel this type of pain. The sting of loss, I've heard it called. I haven't had anything or anyone to cherish, never felt the need to have someone, to make them completely mine, I haven't wanted to hold on to someone so fiercely. The panic—the complete and utter fucking panic of losing her—wasn't planned. None of this was. It was supposed to be easy: sleep with her, get my money and my bragging rights over Zed. Pretty cut-and-dried. Only it didn't happen that way. Instead, the blond-haired girl in the long skirts who obsessively makes long to-do lists crept her way inside of me until, slowly, I fell for her so hard that I couldn't believe it. I didn't realize just how much I loved her until I was vomiting into a sink after showing my fucked-up friends the proof of her stolen virginity.

I hated it, hated every moment of it . . . but I didn't stop.

I won the bet, but I lost the only thing that has ever made me happy. And along with that, I lost every ounce of goodness she made me see in myself. As the snow soaks into my clothes, I want to blame my father for passing his addiction on to me; I want to blame my mum for staying with him for too long and helping create such a fucked-up child; I want to blame Tessa for ever speaking to me. Hell, I want to blame everyone.

But I can't. *I* did this. I ruined her and everything we had.

But I'll do whatever it takes to make up for my mistakes.

Where is she going now? Is it someplace where I'll ever find her?

chapter one

TESSA

It took longer than a month," I sob as Zed finishes explaining how the bet came to be made. I feel sick to my stomach, and I close my eyes to get some relief.

"I know. He kept coming up with excuses and he kept asking for more time and he'd lower the amount he was supposed to get. It was weird. We all just thought he was obsessed with winning— like to prove a point or something—but now I get it." Zed stops talking for a second, and his eyes scan my face. "It was all he talked about. Then, that day when I invited you to the movies, he flipped out. After he dropped you back off, he totally flipped shit on me and said I had to stay away from you. But I just laughed it off, because I thought he was drunk."

"Did he . . . did he tell you about the stream? And the . . . other stuff?" I hold my breath as I ask. The pity in his eyes answers me. "Oh my God." I put my hands over my face.

"He told us everything . . . I mean *everything* . . ." he says in a low voice.

I stay quiet and turn off my phone. It hasn't stopped vibrating since I left the bar. He has no right to be calling me.

"Where's your new dorm?" Zed asks, and I notice we're near campus.

"I don't live in a dorm. Hardin and I . . ." I can barely finish my sentence. "He convinced me to move in with him, just a week ago."

"He *didn't*," Zed gasps.

"He did. He's so beyond . . . he's j-just . . ." I stutter, unable to come up with a fitting word for his cruelty.

"I didn't know it was going this far. I thought once we saw the . . . you know, the proof . . . he'd be back to normal, seeing a different girl every night. But then he disappeared. He's barely come around us at all, except the other night he showed up at the docks and was trying to get Jace and me to agree not to tell you. He offered Jace a shitload of money to keep quiet."

"Money?" I say. Hardin couldn't be lower. The space inside Zed's truck grows smaller with each sickening revelation.

"Yeah. Jace laughed it off, of course, and told Hardin he would keep his mouth shut."

"And you didn't?" I ask, remembering Hardin's busted knuckles and Zed's face.

"Not exactly . . . I told him that if he didn't tell you soon, I would. He didn't like that idea, obviously," he says, and waves at his face. "If it makes you feel any better, I do think he cares about you."

"He doesn't. And if he does, it doesn't matter," I say, and lay my head against the window.

Every kiss and touch have been shared among Hardin's friends, every moment on display. My most intimate moments. My only intimate moments aren't mine at all.

"Do you want to come back to my place? I don't mean that in a pushy or creepy way. I just have a couch you could stay on until you . . . figure things out," he offers.

"No. No, thank you. Can I use your phone, though? I need to call Landon."

Zed nods at the phone resting on the console, and for a moment my mind wanders to thoughts of how things would be different if I hadn't blown Zed off for Hardin after the bonfire. I would never have made all of these mistakes.

Landon answers on the second ring, and just like I knew he

would, he tells me to come right over. Granted, I haven't told him what's up, but he's just so kind. I give Zed Landon's address, and he stays quiet for most of the drive across town.

"He's so going to come after me for taking you anywhere but to him," he finally says.

"I would apologize for being in the middle of this . . . but you guys did this to yourselves," I say honestly. I do pity Zed slightly, because I believe he had much better intentions than Hardin did, but my wounds are too fresh to even think about that right now.

"I know."

"If you need anything, call me," he offers, and I nod before climbing out of the car.

I can see my breath coming out in front of my face in hot spurts through the cold air. I can't feel the cold, though. I can't feel anything.

Landon is my only friend, but he lives at Hardin's father's house. The irony of this is not lost on me.

"IT'S REALLY COMING DOWN out there," Landon says as he rushes me inside. "Where's your coat?" he scolds playfully, then flinches when I step into the light. "What happened? What did he do?"

My eyes scan the room, hoping that Ken and Karen aren't downstairs. "That obvious, huh?" I wipe under my eyes.

Landon pulls me into his arms, and I wipe my eyes again. I no longer have the strength, physical or emotional, to sob. I'm beyond that, so far beyond it.

Landon gets me a glass of water and says, "Go up to your room."

I manage to smile, but some perverse instinct leads me to Hardin's door when I reach the top of the stairs. When I realize it, the pain that is so close to breaking back through stirs even more forcefully, so I quickly turn and go into the room across the hall. Memories of running across the hall to Hardin that night I heard him screaming in his sleep burn within me as I open the door. I sit awkwardly on the bed in "my room," unsure what to do next.

Landon joins me a few minutes later. Sitting next to me, he's close enough to show concern, yet far enough to be respectful, as is his way.

"Do you want to talk about it?" he asks kindly.

I nod. Even though repeating the whole saga hurts worse than finding out about it in the first place, telling Landon feels almost liberating, and it's a comfort to know that at least one person didn't actually know about my humiliation the entire time.

Listening to me, Landon is as still as stone, to the point that I can't read what he's thinking. I want to know what this makes him think of his stepbrother. Of me. But when I finish, he immediately jumps up with an angry energy.

"I can't believe him! What the hell is wrong with him! Here I thought he was becoming almost . . . decent . . . and he does— *this*! This is so messed up! I can't believe he would do this to you, of all people. Why would he ruin the only thing he has?"

As soon as Landon finishes speaking, his head snaps to the side.

And then I, too, notice it: footsteps rushing up the staircase. Not just footsteps, but heavy boots slamming against the wooden steps in a frenzy.

"He's here," we both say, and for a split second I actually consider hiding in the closet.

Landon looks at me with a very adult seriousness on his face. "Do you want to see him?"

I shake my head frantically, and Landon moves to close the door just as Hardin's voice slices right through me.

"Tessa!"

Just as Landon reaches out his arm, Hardin bursts through

the doorway and blows past him. He stops in the middle of the room, and I stand up off the bed. Not used to this sort of thing, Landon stands there, stunned for a moment.

"Tessa, thank God. Thank God you're here." He sighs and runs his hands over his hair.

My chest aches at the sight of him and I look away, focusing on the wall.

"Tessa, baby. I need you to listen to me. Please, just . . ."

I stay silent and walk toward him. His eyes light with hope and he reaches out for me, but when I continue past him, I catch the hope extinguishing in him.

Good.

"Talk to me," he begs.

But I shake my head and stand next to Landon. "No—I'll never be talking to you again!" I shout.

"You don't mean that . . ." Hardin steps closer.

"Get away from me!" I scream as he grabs my arm.

Landon steps between us and puts his arm on his stepbrother's shoulder. "Hardin, you need to go."

Hardin's jaw clenches and he looks back and forth between us. "Landon, you need to get the fuck out of the way," he warns.

But Landon stands his ground, and I know Hardin well enough to know that he's weighing his options, whether it's worth punching Landon right now, in front of me.

Seeming to have decided against it, he takes a deep breath. "Please . . . give us a minute," he says, trying to keep his calm.

Landon looks at me and my eyes plead with him. He turns back to Hardin. "She doesn't want to talk to you."

"Don't you fucking tell me what she wants!" Hardin screams and his fist connects with the wall, cracking and denting the drywall.

I jump back and begin to cry again. *Not now, not now*, I silently repeat to try to manage my emotions.

"Go, Hardin!" Landon shouts just as Ken and Karen appear at the doorway.

Oh no. I shouldn't have come here.

"What the hell is going on?" Ken asks.

No one says anything. Karen looks at me with sympathy, and Ken repeats his question.

Hardin glares at his father. "I'm trying to talk to Tessa, and Landon won't mind his own damn business!"

Ken looks at Landon, then at me. "What did you do, Hardin?" His tone has changed from worried to . . . *angry*? I can't quite put my finger on it.

"Nothing! Fuck!" Hardin throws his hands in the air.

"He messed everything up, is what he did, and now Tessa has nowhere to go," Landon states.

I want to speak; I just have no idea what to say.

"She has somewhere to go, she can go home. Where she belongs . . . with me," Hardin says.

"Hardin has been playing Tessa this entire time—he did unspeakable things to her!" Landon blurts out, and Karen lets out a gasp, stepping over to me.

I utterly shrink. I've never felt so naked and small. I didn't want Ken and Karen to know . . . but it may not make much of a difference, since after tonight they surely won't really want to see me again.

"Do you want to go with him?" Ken asks, interrupting my downward spiral.

I shake my head meekly.

"Well, I'm not leaving here without you," Hardin snaps. He steps toward me, but I cringe away.

"I think you need to go, Hardin," Ken surprises me by saying.

"Excuse me?" Hardin's face is a deep shade of red that expresses what I can only describe as *rage*. "You're lucky I even come here to your house—and you dare to kick me out?"

"I've been very happy with how our relationship has grown, son, but tonight you have to go."

Hardin throws his hands into the air. "This is bullshit, who is *she* to you?"

Ken turns to me, then back to his son. "Whatever you did to her, I hope it was worth losing the only good thing you had going for you," he says and then drops his head.

I don't know if it was the shock of Ken's words, or just that he'd hit a point where all the rage peaked and flowed out of him, but Hardin just stills, looks at me briefly, and marches out of the room. We all remain quiet while we listen to him walk down the stairs at a steady pace.

When the sound of the front door slamming cuts through the now-quiet house, I turn to Ken and sob, "I'm so sorry. I'll go. I didn't mean for any of this to happen."

"No, you stay as long as you need. You're always welcome here," Ken says, and both he and Karen hug me.

"I didn't mean to come between you," I say, feeling terrible for the way Ken had to kick his son out.

Karen grabs hold of my hand and gives it a squeeze. Ken looks at me with exasperation and weariness. "Tessa, I love Hardin, but I think we both know that without you, there isn't anything to come between," he says.

chapter two

TESSA

I stayed in as long as I could, letting the water roll over me. I wanted it to clean me, reassure me somehow. But the hot shower didn't help me relax like I had hoped. I can't think of anything that's going to calm the ache inside of me. It feels infinite. Permanent. Like an organism that's come to live within me, but also like a hole growing steadily larger.

"I feel terrible about the wall. I offered to pay for it, but Ken refuses to let me," I tell Landon as I brush out my wet hair.

"Don't worry about that. You have a lot going on." Landon frowns and rubs his hand across my back.

"I can't comprehend how my life came to this, how I ever got to this point." I stare ahead, not wanting to meet my best friend's eyes. "Three months ago, everything made sense. I had Noah, who would never do something like this. I was close with my mother and I had this idea of how my life would be. And now I have nothing. Literally nothing. I don't even know if I should go to my internship anymore because Hardin will either go there, or he'll convince Christian Vance to fire me just because he can." I grab the pillow on the bed and grip the material hard in my fist. "He had nothing to lose, but I did. I let him take everything from me. My life before him was so simple and decided. Now . . . after him . . . it's just . . . after."

Landon looks at me with wide eyes. "Tessa, you can't give up your internship; he's taken enough from you. Don't let him take that, please," he practically pleads. "The good thing about this afterlife without him is that you can make it whatever you please, you can start all over."

I know he's right, but it isn't that simple. Everything in my life is tied to Hardin now, even the paint on my damn car. He somehow became the string that held everything in my life together, and in his absence I'm left with the rubble that once was my life.

When I relent and give Landon a halfhearted nod, he smiles a little and says, "I'll let you get some rest." He hugs me and starts to leave.

"Do you think this will ever stop?" I ask, and he turns around. "What?"

My voice almost a whisper: "The pain?"

"I don't know . . . I'd like to think it will, though. Time heals . . . *most* wounds," he answers and gives me his most comforting half smile, half frown.

I don't know if time will heal me or not. But I do know that if it doesn't, I won't survive.

WITH HEAVY-HANDED INTENT, yet enacted with his unfailing politeness, Landon forces me out of bed the next morning to make sure I don't miss my internship. I take a moment to leave a note of thanks to Ken and Karen, and to apologize again for the hole Hardin put in their wall. Landon is quiet, and keeps looking over at me as he drives, trying to give me encouraging smiles and little slogans to remember. But I still feel terrible.

Memories begin to creep into my mind as we pull into the parking lot. Hardin on his knees in the snow. Zed's explanation of the bet. I quickly unlock my car, jumping inside to get away from the cold air. When I get into my car, I cringe at my reflection in the rearview. My eyes are still bloodshot and rimmed with dark circles. Bags have swollen up under them, completing the horror-movie look. I will definitely need more makeup than I thought.

Going to Walmart, the only nearby store open at this hour, I buy everything I need to mask my feelings. But I don't have the strength or the energy to make a real effort on my appearance, so I'm not sure I look much better.

Case in point: I arrive at Vance, and Kimberly gasps when she sees me. I try to muster a smile for her, but she jumps up from her desk.

"Tessa, dear, are you okay?" she asks frantically.

"Do I look that bad?" I shrug weakly.

"No, of course not," she lies. "You just look . . ."

"Exhausted. Because I am. Finals took a lot out of me," I tell her.

She nods and smiles warmly, but I can feel her eyes on my back the entire walk down the hall to my office. After that, my day drags on, no end in sight, it seems, until late morning, when Mr. Vance knocks at my door.

"Good afternoon, Tessa," he says with a smile.

"Good afternoon," I manage.

"I just wanted to touch base with you and let you know how impressed I am with your work so far." He chuckles. "You're doing a better and more detailed job than many of my *actual* employees."

"Thank you, that means a lot to me," I say, and immediately the voice in my head reminds me that I only have this internship because of Hardin.

"That being the case, I would like to invite you to the Seattle conference this coming weekend. Often these things are pretty boring, but it's all about digital publishing, the 'wave of the future' and all that. You'll meet a lot of people, learn some things. I'm opening a second branch in Seattle in a few months, and I need to meet a few people myself." He laughs. "So what do you say? All expenses would be paid and we'll leave Friday afternoon; Hardin is more than welcome to come along. Not to the conference but to Seattle," he explains with a knowing smile.

If only he really *knew* what was going on.

"Of course I would love to go. I really appreciate your invitation!" I tell him, unable to contain my enthusiasm and the immediate relief that, finally, something decent is happening to me.

"Great! I'll have Kimberly give you all the details, and explain how to expense things . . ." He rambles on, but I wander off while he does.

The idea of going to the conference soothes my ache slightly. I will be farther away from Hardin, but on the other hand, Seattle now reminds me of when Hardin wanted to take me there. He has tainted every aspect of my life, including the entire state of Washington. I feel my office getting smaller, the air in the room getting thicker.

"Are you feeling okay?" Mr. Vance asks, his brow lowers in concern.

"Uh, yeah, I just . . . I haven't eaten today and I didn't sleep much last night," I tell him.

"Go ahead and go home, then, you can finish what you're doing at home," he says.

"It's okay—"

"No, go on home. There are no ambulances in publishing. We'll manage without you," he assures me with a wave, then strolls off.

I gather my things, check my appearance in the bathroom mirror—yup, still pretty horrible—and am about to step into the elevator when Kimberly calls my name.

"Going home?" she asks and I nod. "Well, Hardin's in a bad mood, so beware."

"What? How do you know?"

"Because he just cussed me out for not transferring him to

you." She smiles. "Not even the tenth time he called. I figured if you wanted to talk to him, you would have on your cell."

"Thank you," I say, silently grateful she's as observant as she is. Hearing Hardin's voice on the line would have made the aching hole in me grow that much more quickly.

I manage to make it to my car before breaking down again. The pain only seems to get worse when there are no distractions, when I'm left alone with my thoughts and memories. And, of course, when I see the fifteen missed calls from Hardin on my phone and a notice that I have ten new messages, which I won't read.

After pulling myself together enough to drive, I do what I've been dreading to do: call my mother.

She answers on the first ring. "Hello?"

"Mom," I sob. The word feels odd coming out of my mouth, but I need the comfort of my mom right now.

"What did he do?"

That this has been everyone's reaction shows me just how obvious the danger of Hardin was to everyone, and how oblivious I've been.

"I . . . he . . ." I can't form a sentence. "Can I come home, just for today?" I ask her.

"Of course, Tessa. I'll see you in two hours," she says and hangs up.

Better than I thought, but not as warm as I had hoped for. I wish she were more like Karen, loving and accepting of any flaw. I wish she could just soften up, just long enough for me to feel the solace of having a mother, a loving and comforting one.

Pulling onto the highway, I shut my phone off before I do something stupid, like read any of those messages from Hardin.

chapter three

TESSA

The drive to my childhood home is familiar and easy, requiring little thought on my part. I force myself to let out every scream—literally, as in screaming as loud as I possibly can and until my throat is sore—before I arrive in my hometown. I find this is actually much harder to do than I thought it would be, especially since I don't feel like yelling. I feel like crying and disappearing. I would give anything to rewind my life to my first day of college; I would have taken my mother's advice and changed rooms. My mother had worried about *Steph* being a bad influence; if only we'd realized it would be the rude, curly-haired boy that would be the problem. That he would take everything in me and spin it around, tearing me into tiny pieces before blowing on the pile and scattering me across the sky and beneath his friends' heels.

I have only been two hours away from home this whole time, but with everything that's happened, it feels so much farther. I haven't been home since I started school. If I hadn't broken up with Noah, I would have been back many times. I force my eyes to stay focused on the road as I pass his house.

I pull into our driveway and practically jump out of my car. But when I get to the door, I'm not sure if I should knock. It feels strange to do so, but I don't feel comfortable just walking inside either. How can so much have changed since I left for college?

I decide to just walk inside, and I find my mother standing by the brown leather couch in full makeup, a dress, and heels. Everything looks the same: clean and perfectly organized. The only difference is that it seems smaller, maybe because of my time at Ken's house. Well, my mother's house is definitely small and unappealing from the outside, but the inside is decorated nicely, and my mother always did her best to mask the chaos of her marriage with attractive paint and flowers and attention to cleanliness. A decorating strategy she continued after my dad left, because I guess it had become habit by that point. The house is warm and the familiar smell of cinnamon fills my nostrils. My mother has always obsessed over wax burners and has one in every room. I take my shoes off at the door, knowing that she won't want snow on her polished hardwood floors.

"Would you like some coffee, Theresa?" she asks before hugging me.

I get my coffee addiction from my mother, and this connection brings a small smile to my lips. "Yes, please."

I follow her into the kitchen and sit at the small table, unsure how to begin the conversation.

"So are you going to tell me what happened?" she asks bluntly.

I take a deep breath and a sip of my coffee before answering. "Hardin and I broke up."

Her expression is neutral. "Why?"

"Well, he didn't turn out to be who I thought he was," I say. I wrap my hands around the scalding-hot cup of coffee in an attempt to distract myself from the pain and prepare myself for my mother's response.

"And who did you think he was?"

"Someone who loved me." I'm not sure who I thought Hardin was other than that, on his own, as a person.

"And now you don't think he does?"

"No, I know he doesn't."

"What makes you so sure?" she asks coolly.

"Because I trusted him and he betrayed me, in a terrible way." I know I'm leaving out the details, but I still feel the strange need to protect Hardin from my mother's judgment. I scold my-self for being so stupid, for even considering him, when he clearly wouldn't do the same for me.

"Don't you think you should have thought about this possibil-ity before deciding to live with him?"

"Yes, I know. Go ahead and tell me how stupid I am, tell me that you told me so," I say.

"I did tell you, I warned you about guys like him. Men like him and your father are best to stay away from. I'm just glad it's over with before it really even began. People make mistakes, Tessa." She takes a drink from her mug, leaving a pink lipstick ring. "I'm sure he'll forgive you."

"Who?"

"Noah, of course."

How does she not get this? I just need to talk to her, to have her comfort me—not push me to be with Noah again. I stand up, looking at her, then around the room. *Is she serious? She can't be.* "Just because things didn't work out with Hardin doesn't mean I'm going to date Noah again!" I snap.

"Why doesn't it? Tessa, you should be grateful that he's will-ing to give you another chance."

"What? Why can't you just stop? I don't need to be with anyone right now, especially not Noah." I want to rip my hair out. Or hers.

"What do you mean, especially not Noah? How can you say that about him? He's been nothing but great to you since you were kids."

I sigh and sit back down. "I know, Mother, I care about Noah so much. Just not in that way."

"You don't even know what you're talking about." She stands up and pours her coffee down the drain. "It's not always about love, Theresa; it's about stability and security."

"I'm only eighteen," I tell her. I don't want to think that I'd be with someone without loving them just for the stability. I want to be my own stability and security. I want someone to love, and someone to love me.

"Almost nineteen. And if you aren't careful now, no one will want you. Now go fix your makeup, because Noah will be here any minute," she announces and walks out of the kitchen.

I should have known better than to come here for comfort. I would have been better off sleeping in my car all day.

AS PROMISED, NOAH ARRIVES five minutes later, not that I've bothered to fix my appearance. Seeing him walk into the small kitchen makes me feel even lower than I have so far, which I didn't think was possible.

He smiles his warm perfect smile. "Hey."

"Hey, Noah," I respond.

He walks closer and I stand up to hug him. He feels warm, and his sweatshirt smells so good, just like I remember. "Your mom called me," he says.

"I know." I try to smile. "I'm sorry that she keeps bringing you into this. I don't know what her problem is."

"I do. She wants you to be happy," he says, defending her.

"Noah . . ." I warn.

"She just doesn't know what really makes you happy. She wants it to be me, even though it's not." He gives a little shrug.

"I'm sorry."

"Tess, stop apologizing. I just want to make sure you're okay," he assures me and hugs me again.

"I'm not," I admit.

"I can tell. Do you want to talk about it?"

"I don't know . . . are you sure that's okay?" I can't bear to hurt him again by talking about the guy I left him for.

"Yeah, I'm sure," he says and pours himself a glass of water before sitting across from me at the table.

"Okay . . ." I say and tell him basically everything. I leave out the sex details, since those are private.

Well, they *aren't*. But to me they are. I still can't believe that Hardin told his friends everything that we did . . . that's the worst part. Even worse than showing the sheets is the fact that after telling me that he loved me, and making love, he could apparently turn around and make a mockery of what had happened between us in front of everyone.

"I knew he was going to hurt you, I just had no idea how bad," Noah says. I can tell how angry he is; it's strange to see this emotion on his face, given how calm and collected he normally is. "You're too good for him Tessa; he's scum."

"I can't believe how stupid I was—I gave up *everything* for him. But the worst feeling in the world is loving someone who doesn't love you."

Noah grabs his glass and twists it in his hands. "Tell me about it," he says softly.

I want to smack myself for saying what I just said, saying it to him. I open my mouth, but he cuts me off before I can apologize.

"It's okay," he says and reaches out to rub his thumb over my hand.

God, I *wish* I did love Noah. I would be much happier with him, and he would never do something like Hardin did to me.

Noah catches me up on everything I've missed since I left, which isn't much. He's going to go San Francisco for college instead of WCU, which I find I'm grateful for. At least one good thing came out of my hurting him: it gave him the push he needed to get out of Washington. He tells me about what he's researched on California, and by the time he leaves, the sun has fallen, and I realize that my mom has stayed in her room during his whole visit.

Stepping out to the backyard, I wander to the greenhouse where I spent most of my childhood. As I stare through my reflection in the glass and into the little structure, I see that all its plants and flowers are dead, and it's generally a mess, which feels fitting at the moment.

I have so many things to do, to figure out. I need to find somewhere to live and find a way to get all of my stuff from Hardin's apartment. I was seriously considering just leaving everything there, but I can't. I have no clothes except the ones I've been keeping there and, most importantly, I need my textbooks.

Reaching into my pocket, I turn my phone on, and within seconds my inbox is full and the voicemail symbol appears. I ignore the voicemails and quickly scan the messages, only looking at the sender. All except one are from Hardin.

Kimberly wrote me: Christian said to tell you to stay home tomorrow, everyone will be leaving at noon anyway since the first floor needs to be repainted, so stay home. Let me know if you need anything. xx.

Having the day off tomorrow is a huge relief. I love my internship, but I'm beginning to think I should transfer out of WCU, maybe even leave Washington. The campus isn't big enough for me to be able to avoid Hardin and all of his friends, and I don't want the constant reminder of what I had with Hardin. Well, what I thought I had.

By the time I go back inside the house, my hands and face are numb from the cold. My mother is sitting in a chair reading a magazine.

"Can I stay tonight?" I ask her.

She looks at me briefly. "Yes. And tomorrow we'll figure out how to get you back into the dorms," she says and goes back to her magazine.

Figuring I'll get no more from my mother tonight, I go up to my old room, which is exactly the way that I left it. She hasn't changed a thing. I don't bother removing my makeup before bed. It's hard, but I force myself to sleep, dreaming of when my life was much better. Before I met Hardin.

My phone rings in the middle of the night, waking me. But I ignore it, briefly wondering if Hardin's able to sleep at all.

THE NEXT MORNING all my mother says to me before leaving for work is that she'll call the school and force them to let me back into the dorms, in a different building far from my old one. I leave, intending to head to campus, but then decide to go to the apartment, taking the exit to the road that leads there and driving quickly to keep from changing my mind.

At the complex, I scan the parking lot for Hardin's car, twice. Once I'm sure he isn't around, I park and hurry across the snowy lot to the door. By the time I get to the lobby, the bottoms of my jeans are soaked and I'm freezing. I try to think of anything except Hardin, but it's impossible.

Hardin must have really hated me to go to this extreme to ruin my life and then to move me into an apartment far from anyone I know. He must be pretty proud of himself right now for causing me this much pain.

As I fumble with my keys before unlocking the door to our place a tidal wave of panic crashes over me, nearly knocking me the ground.

When will it stop? Or at least decrease?

I go straight to the bedroom and grab my bags from the closet, roughly shoving all my clothes in them without care. My eyes flicker to the bedside table, where a small frame stands, displaying the picture of Hardin and me smiling together before Ken's wedding.

Too bad it was all fake. Leaning across the bed, I grab it and throw it against the concrete floor. It shatters into pieces and I jump over the bed, grab the photo, and rip it into as many pieces as I can, not realizing that I'm sobbing until I choke on my own breath.

I grab my books, piling them into an empty box, and, instinctively, Hardin's copy of *Wuthering Heights*; he won't miss it, and, honestly, I'm owed it, after what he's taken from me.

My throat is sore, so I go into the kitchen and grab a glass of water. I sit down at the table and allow myself a few minutes to pretend that none of this has happened. To pretend that instead of my having to face the future days alone, Hardin will be home from class shortly, and will smile at me and tell me he loves me, that he missed me all day. That he will lift me onto the counter and kiss me with longing and love—

The clicking of the door startles me out of my pathetic daydream. I jump to my feet as Hardin walks through the door. He doesn't see me, since he's looking over his shoulder.

At a brunette in a black sweater dress.

"So this is it . . ." he begins, and then stops when he notices my bags on the ground.

I'm frozen as his eyes travel around the apartment and then over to the kitchen, where they widen in shock at seeing me.

"Tess?" he says, as if he's not sure that I actually exist.

chapter four

TESSA

I look like hell. I'm in baggy jeans and a sweatshirt, yesterday's smeared makeup, and tangled hair. I look at the girl standing behind him. Her curly brown hair is silky and cascades in loose waves down her back. Her makeup is light, and perfect, but then, she's one of those women who doesn't need it to begin with. Of course she is.

This is humiliating and I wish I could sink into the floor, disappearing out of the beautiful girl's sight.

When I reach down to pick one of my bags up off the floor, Hardin seems to remember the girl is there and turns around to face her.

"Tessa, what are you doing here?" he asks. As I wipe at the makeup around my eyes, he asks his new girl, "Can you give us a minute?"

She looks at me, then nods and goes back into the building hallway.

"I can't believe you're here," he says and walks into the kitchen. He removes his jacket, which makes his plain white T-shirt ride up and reveal the tanned skin of his torso. The ink there, the twisted, angry branches of the dead tree on his stomach, taunt me. Calling out to be touched. I love that tattoo, it's my favorite that he has. Only now I see the parallel between him and the tree. Both unfeeling. Both alone. At least the tree has hope to bloom again. Hardin does not.

"I . . . I was just leaving." I manage to say. He looks so perfect, so beautiful. Such a beautiful disaster.

"Please just let me explain myself," he begs, and I notice the dark circles under his eyes are even more prominent than mine.

"No." I reach for my bags again, but he grabs them from me and drops them back onto the floor.

"Two minutes, that's all I'm asking for, Tess."

Two minutes is too long to be here with Hardin, but this is the closure I know I need in order to move on with my life. I sigh and sit down, trying to hold back any noise that would betray my neutral expression. Hardin is clearly surprised, but quickly takes the seat across from me.

"You sure moved on fast," I say quietly, lifting my chin toward the door.

"What?" Hardin says, then seems to remember the brunette. "She works with me; her husband is downstairs with their newborn daughter. They're looking for a new place, so she wanted to see our . . . the layout."

"You're moving?" I ask.

"No, not if you'll stay, but I don't see the point in staying here without you. I'm just going over my options here."

Something in me is slightly relieved, but then immediately a more defensive part of me notes that just because he isn't sleeping with the brunette doesn't mean he won't be sleeping with someone else soon. I ignore the twinge of sorrow that comes along with Hardin talking about moving out, even though I won't be here when he does.

"You think I would bring someone back here to our apartment? It's only been two days—is that how you think of me?"

He has some nerve. "Yes! Of course it is—now!"

When I nod viciously at this, pain flashes across his face. But after a moment he just sighs in defeat. "Where did you stay last night? I went to my father's and you weren't there."

"My mother's."

"Oh." He looks down at his hands. "Did you guys work everything out?"

I stare directly into his eyes—I can't believe he has the nerve to ask me about my family. "That's no longer any of your business."

He starts to reach out to me, but stops. "I miss you so much, Tessa."

I lose my breath again, but remember how good he is at twisting things around. I turn away. "Sure you do."

Despite the whirlwind of my emotions, I won't allow myself to come undone any further in front of him.

"I do, Tessa. I know I fucked up big-time—but I love you. I need you."

"Just stop, Hardin. Save yourself the time and energy. You aren't fooling me, not anymore. You got what you wanted, so why not just stop?"

"Because I can't." He reaches for my hand, but I jerk away. "I love you. I need you to give me a chance to make this up to you. I need you, Tessa. I need you. You need me, too—"

"No, I don't actually. I was fine before you came into my life."

"Fine isn't *happy*," he says.

"Happy?" I scoff. "And what, am I happy now?" How dare he try to claim he makes me happy.

But he did make me happy. So happy, once.

"You can't sit here and tell me that you don't believe that I love you."

"I know you don't, it was all a game to you. While I was falling in love with you, you were using me."

His eyes well up with tears. "Let me prove to you that I love you, please. I'll do anything, Tessa. Anything."

"You've already proved enough to me, Hardin. The only reason I'm even sitting here right now is because I owe it to myself to listen to what you have to say so I can move on with my life."

"I don't want you to move on," he says.

I let out a harsh breath. "This isn't about what *you* want! This is about how you *hurt me*."

His voice sounds small, and cracks. "You said you'd never leave me."

I don't trust myself when he's like this. I hate the way his pain rules me, making me irrational. "I said I wouldn't leave you if you didn't give me a reason to. But you *did*."

Now it makes perfect sense to me why he was always worried about me leaving. I thought it was his own paranoia about being good for me, but I was wrong. So wrong. He knew once I found out I would run. I should be running right now. I made excuses for him because of the things he went through as a child, but now I'm beginning to wonder if he was lying about that, too. About all of it.

"I can't do this anymore. I trusted you. Hardin, I trusted you with every fiber of my being—I depended on you, I loved you, and you were using me all along. Do you have any idea how that makes me feel? That everyone around me was mocking me and laughing behind my back, including you, the person I trusted the most."

"I know, Tessa, I know. I can't begin to tell you how sorry I am. I don't know what the fuck was wrong with me when I brought up the bet in the first place. I thought it would be easy . . ." His hands shake as he pleads with me. "I thought you would sleep with me and that would be the end of it. But you were so headstrong and so . . . intriguing that I found myself thinking of you constantly. I would sit in my room and try to plot ways that I could see you, even if it was just to fight with you. I knew it wasn't just a bet anymore after that day at the stream, but I couldn't bring myself to admit it. I was battling with myself, and I was worried about my reputation—I know that's fucked up, but I'm trying to be honest. And when I told everyone about the things we did, I didn't tell them what we were actually doing . . . I couldn't do that to you, even in the beginning. I would just make up shit that didn't actually happen, and they bought it."

A few tears fall from my eyes and he reaches across to wipe them. I don't move away fast enough and his touch burns my skin. It takes everything in me to not lean into his palm.

"I hate to see you this way," he mutters. I close my eyes and reopen them, desperate for the tears to stop. I stay quiet as he continues: "I swear, I started telling Nate and Logan about the stream, but I found myself getting irritated, jealous even, over the idea of them knowing what I did with you . . . how I made you feel, so I told them that you gave me . . . well, I just made shit up."

I know that him lying about what we did is no better than telling them the truth, not really. But for some reason I feel some relief that Hardin and I are the only people who really know what happened between us, the real details of our moments together.

Which isn't good enough. And then again, he's probably lying right now—I can never tell—and here I am already quick to believe him. *What the hell is wrong with me?*

"Even if I believed you, I can't forgive you," I say. I blink away my tears and he puts his head in his hands.

"You don't love me?" he asks, looking at me between his fingers.

"Yes. I do," I admit. The truth of my confession weighs heavily between us. He lowers his hands, staring at me in a way that makes me regret my admission. It's true, though. I love him. I love him too much.

"Then why can't you forgive me?"

"Because this is unforgivable, you didn't just lie. You took my virginity to win a bet—and then showed people my blood on the sheets. How could anyone forgive that?"

He drops his hands and his bright green eyes look desperate. "I took your virginity because I love you!" he says, which only makes me shake my head vigorously, so he continues. "I don't know who I am without you anymore."

I look away. "This wasn't going to work anyway, we both know that," I tell him to make myself feel better. It's hard to sit across from him and watch him in pain, but at the same time my sense of justice means that seeing him in pain eases mine . . . somewhat.

"Why wouldn't it work? We were doing great—"

"Everything we had was based on a lie, Hardin." And because his pain has given me a sudden feeling of confidence, I say, "Besides, look at you and look at me." I don't mean it, but the look on his face when I use his biggest insecurity about our relationship against him—though it kills something inside me—also reminds me that he deserves it. He's always been worried about how we look together, that I'm too good for him. And now I've thrown it in his face.

"Is this about Noah? You saw him, didn't you?" Hardin asks and my mouth falls open at his audacity. His eyes shine with tears and I have to remind myself that he did this. He ruined everything.

"Yes, I did, but that has nothing to do with it. That's your problem—you go around doing whatever the hell you want to people, not caring about the outcome, and you expect everyone to just be okay with it!" I shout and stand up from the table.

"No, I *don't*, Tessa!" he yells, and I roll my eyes. At that, he pauses, then stands and looks out the window, then back at me. "Okay, yes, so maybe I do. But I really do care about you."

"Well, you should have thought about that when you were bragging about your conquest," I say steadily.

"My conquest? Are you *fucking serious* right now? You aren't some conquest of mine—you're everything to me! You're my breath, my pain, my heart, my life!" He takes a step toward me. What's makes me the saddest is that these are the most touching words that Hardin has ever said to me, but he's screaming them.

"Well, it's a little too late for that!" I scream back. "You think you can just—"

He catches me off guard by wrapping his hand around the back of my neck and pulling me to him, crashing his lips to mine. The familiar warmth of his mouth nearly brings me to my knees. My tongue is moving along with his before my mind catches up to what's happening. He moans in relief and I try to push him away. He grabs my wrists in one hand and holds them on his chest as he continues to kiss me. I keep struggling to get out of his grip, but my mouth continues to move along with his. He backs up and pulls me with him until he's against the counter, and his other hand reaches out to the side of my neck, holding me still. All of the pain and heartache inside me begin to dissolve and I relax my hands in his. This is wrong but so right.

But wrong.

I pull away and he tries to reconnect our lips, but I turn my head. "No," I say.

His eyes soften. "Please . . ." he begs.

"No, Hardin. I need to go."

He lets go of my wrists. "Go where?"

"I . . . I don't know yet. My mother is trying to get me back into a dorm."

"No . . . no . . ." He shakes his head, his voice becoming frantic. "You live here, don't go back into the dorms." He runs his hands through his hair. "If anyone should, it's me. Just please stay here so I know where you are."

"You don't need to know where I am."

"Stay," he repeats.

If I'm being completely honest with myself, I want to stay

with him. I want to tell him that I love him more than I want to breathe, but I can't. I refuse to get pulled back in and be that girl who lets guys do whatever the hell they want to her.

I pick up my bags and say the only thing that will keep him from following. "Noah and my mother are waiting, I have to go," I lie and walk out of the door.

He doesn't follow, and I don't let myself turn around to see the pain he's in.

chapter five

TESSA

When I get to my car I don't cry like I had assumed I would. I just sit and stare out the window. The snow sticks to my windshield, blanketing me inside. The wind around the car is chaotic, picking up the snow and swirling it, completely sheltering me. With each flake of snow coating the glass, a barrier between the harsh reality and the car is formed.

I can't believe that Hardin came to the apartment while I was there. I had hoped to not see him. It did help, though, not the pain but the situation in general. At least now I can try to move on from this disastrous time in my life. I want to believe him and that he does love me, but I got into this situation by believing him. He could just be acting like this because he knows he doesn't have control over me anymore. Even if he does love me, what would that change? It wouldn't take back everything he did, it wouldn't take back all the jokes, the terrible bragging about the things we did, or the lies.

I wish I could afford that apartment on my own, I would stay there and make Hardin leave. I don't want to go back to the dorms and get a new roommate—I don't want a community shower. Why did it all have to start with a lie? If we'd met in some different way, we could be inside that apartment right now, laughing on the couch or kissing in the bedroom. Instead, I'm in my car alone with nowhere to go.

When I finally start the car, my hands are frozen. Couldn't I be homeless in the summer?

I feel like Catherine again, only not my usual *Wuthering Heights* Catherine. This time Catherine in *Northanger Abbey* is who I relate to: shocked and forced to make a long journey alone. Granted, I'm not making a seventy-mile journey from Northanger after being dismissed and embarrassed, but still, I feel her pain. I can't decide who Hardin would be in this version of the book. On one hand, he's like Henry, smart and witty, with a knowledge of novels as great as mine. However, Henry is much kinder than Hardin, and that's where Hardin is more like John, arrogant and rude.

As I drive through town with nowhere to go, I realize that Hardin's words had a bigger impact on me than I would like to admit. Him begging me to stay almost put the pieces back together just to break them again. I'm sure he only wanted me to stay to prove that he could. It's not like he's started calling and texting again since I drove away.

I force myself to drive to campus and take my last final before winter break. I feel so detached during the exam and it feels impossible that everyone on campus could be so clueless about what I'm going through. A fake smile and small talk can hide the splitting pain, I suppose.

I call my mother to check on the status of getting into a new dorm, only to have her mumble "no luck" and quickly hang up the phone. After driving aimlessly for a bit, I find myself a block away from Vance and realize it's already five in the evening. I don't want to take advantage of Landon by asking him to stay at Ken's house again. I know he wouldn't mind, but it's not fair of me to put Hardin's family in the middle of this, and honestly that house holds too many memories. I couldn't stand it. I pass a street lined with motels and pull into the lot of one of the nicer-looking ones. I suddenly realize that I've never actually stayed at a motel before, but it's not like I have anywhere else to go.

The short man behind the counter looks friendly enough as

he smiles at me and asks for my driver's license. A few short minutes later he's handing me a key card and a slip of paper with
a Wi-Fi code. Getting a room is much easier than I thought it
would be—a little expensive, but I don't want to stay someplace
cheap and risk my safety.

"Down the sidewalk and make a left," he informs me with a
smile.

I thank him and head back out into the blistering cold and
move my car to the spot next to my room so I don't have to carry
my bags.

This is what I've come to because of that thoughtless, egotistical boy: I am someone staying in a motel, alone, all my belongings stuffed frantically into bags. I am someone who has no one to
lean on instead of someone who always had a plan.

Grabbing some of my bags, I lock my car, which looks like
junk compared to the BMW next to me. Just as I think my day
could not get any worse, I lose my grip on one of my bags and
drop it onto the snowy sidewalk. My clothes and a few books topple out onto the wet snow. I scramble to pick them up with my
free hand, but I'm afraid to see which books they are—I don't
think I can take my favorite possessions being ruined alongside
me, not today.

"Here let me help you, miss," a man's voice says as a hand
reaches down to help me. *"Tessa?"*

Shocked, I look up to see blue eyes and a concerned face.
"Trevor?" I say even though I know it's him. I stand upright and
look around. "What are you doing here?"

"I'd ask you the same thing." He smiles.

"Well . . . I'm . . ." I take my bottom lip between my teeth.

But he saves me from having to explain myself. "My plumbing went haywire, so here I am." Bending down, he gathers some
of my stuff and hands me a soaked copy of *Wuthering Heights*
with a raise of his brow. Then he hands me a couple of wet sweat-

ers and *Pride and Prejudice*, saying ruefully, "Here . . . this one's in bad shape."

And like that, I know the universe is playing a sick joke on me.

"I somehow knew you would be into the classics," he tells me with a friendly smile. He takes the bags from me and I give him a nod of thanks before sliding in the key card and opening the door. The room is freezing, so I go over to the heater immediately and turn it all the way up.

"You would think for how much they charge here they wouldn't worry about their electric bill," Trevor says and sets my bags on the floor.

I smile and nod in agreement. I grab the clothes that fell onto the snow and put them over the shower curtain rod. When I come back into the main room, there's an awkward silence with this person I barely know in this room that isn't really mine. "Is your apartment nearby?" I ask, to bring some life into the space.

"House. But yeah, it's only about a mile away. I like to be close to work, so I know I won't ever be late."

"That's a good idea . . ." It sounds like something I would do.

Trevor looks so different in casual clothes. I have only ever seen him in suits, but here he's wearing snug blue jeans and a red sweatshirt, with his hair messy where it's usually perfectly gelled.

"I think so, too. So are you alone?" he asks and looks at the ground, obviously uncomfortable prying.

"Yeah. I'm alone." I mean that in more ways than he knows.

"I'm not trying to be nosy, I was just asking because your boy-friend doesn't seem to like me much." He half laughs and wipes his black hair from his forehead.

"Oh, Hardin doesn't like anyone—don't take it personally." I pick at my nails. "He isn't my boyfriend, though."

"Oh, sorry. I just assumed he was."

"He was . . . sort of."

Was he? He said he was. But then, Hardin said a lot of things.

"Oh, sorry again. I just keep saying all the wrong things." He laughs.

"It's okay. I don't mind," I tell him and unpack the rest of my bags.

"Do you want me to go? I don't mean to intrude." He half turns toward the door, as if to show his offer is genuine.

"No, no, you can stay. If you want, of course. You don't have to," I say too quickly.

What is wrong with me?

"It's settled, then, I'll stay," he says and sits down on the chair next to the desk. I look for a place to sit myself, and eventually decide on the edge of the bed. I'm pretty far away from him, which makes me realize how spacious the room really is.

"So, how are you liking Vance so far?" he asks, his fingers tracing patterns on the wooden desk.

"I love it. It's so much more than I ever expected. It's literally my dream job. I hope to get hired on after I graduate."

"Oh, I think you'll be offered a position there well before then. Christian is very fond of you—that manuscript you turned in last week was all I heard about at lunch the other day. He says you have a good eye, and from him that's a huge compliment."

"Really? He said that?" I can't help but smile. The action feels odd and unwelcome but also comforting all at once.

"Yeah, why else would he invite you to the conference? Only the four of us are going."

"Four of us?" I ask.

"Yeah. Me, you, Christian, and Kim."

"Oh, I didn't know Kim was going." I hope desperately that Mr. Vance didn't only invite me because he feels obligated due to my relationship with Hardin, his best friend's son.

"He wouldn't be able to go a weekend without her," Trevor teases. "Because of her office management skills, of course."

I give a little smile. "I can see that. So why are you going?" I ask, and then mentally slap myself. "I mean why are you going, since you work in finance, don't you?" I try to clarify.

"No, I get it, you bookies don't need the human calculator around." He rolls his eyes, and I laugh, really laugh. "He's opening a second office in Seattle shortly and we're going to a meeting with a potential investor. Also, we'll be scouting locations, so he needs me to make sure we get a good deal, and Kimberly to make sure whatever building we like functions with our work flow."

"Are you into real estate, too?" The room is finally warm, so I take my shoes off and tuck my feet underneath me.

"No, not at all, but I'm good with numbers," he brags. "It'll be a good time, though. Seattle is a beautiful city. Have you been?"

"Yeah, it's is my favorite city. Not that I have a lot to choose from . . ."

"Me either; I'm from Ohio, so I haven't seen much. Compared to Ohio, Seattle is like New York City."

I find myself genuinely interested in knowing more about Trevor. "What made you come to Washington?"

"Well, my mother passed away my senior year of high school and I just had to go. There's just so much more to see, you know? So I promised her right before she died that I wouldn't spend my life in that dreadful town where we lived. The day I got accepted to WCU was the best and worst day of my life."

"Worst?" I ask.

"She passed away that same day. Ironic, isn't it?" He gives a wan smile. The way only half of his mouth turns up is lovely.

"I'm sorry."

"No, don't be. She was one of those people that didn't belong here with the rest of us. She was too good, you know? My family got to have more time with her than we deserved, and I wouldn't change a thing," he says. He gives me full smile and gestures at me. "What about you? Are you going to stay here forever?"

"No, I always wanted to move to Seattle. But lately I've been thinking of going even further," I admit.

"You should. You should travel and see everything you possibly can. A woman like you shouldn't be kept in a box." He must notice some odd look on my face, because he quickly says, "Sorry . . . I just mean you could do so much. You have a lot talents, I can tell."

But I wasn't bothered by what he said. Something about the way he called me a woman makes me happy; in my life, I've always felt like a child because everyone treats me like one. Trevor is only a friend, a new friend, but I'm really glad to have his company on this terrible day.

"Have you had dinner?" I ask.

"Not yet. I was debating whether or not to order a pizza, so I don't have to go back into that blizzard." He laughs.

"We could split one?" I offer.

"Deal," he says, with the kindest look I've seen in a long time.

chapter six

HARDIN

My father has the stupidest expression on his face; it always happens when he tries to look authoritative, like now, with his arms crossed as he stands filling his front doorway.

"She isn't going to come here, Hardin—she knows you'll find her."

I fight the urge to knock his teeth down his throat. Instead, I rake my fingers through my hair, flinching slightly when my knuckles twinge. The cuts are deeper than usual this time. Punching the drywall did more damage to my hands than I thought. It's nothing compared to how I feel inside. I never knew this type of pain existed; it's so much worse than any physical pain I could cause myself.

"Son, I really think you should give her some space."

Who the fuck does he think he is?

"Space? She doesn't need space! She needs to come home!" I yell. The old woman next door turns to look at us, and I raise my arms at her.

"Please don't be rude to my neighbors," my dad warns me.

"Then tell your neighbors to mind their own damn business!" I'm sure the old gray-hair heard *that*.

"Goodbye, Hardin," my father says with a sigh and closes the door.

"Fuck!" I yell and pace back and forth on the porch a few times before finally going back out to my car.

Where the hell is she? As mad as I am, I'm worried as hell about her. Is she alone, or afraid? Oh course, knowing Tessa, she isn't afraid at all; she's probably going over the reasons she hates me. Actually, she's probably writing them down. Her need to be in control of everything and her stupid lists used to drive me crazy, but now I long to see her scribbling the most irrelevant things. I would give anything to watch her chew on her full bottom lip in concentration, or see that adorable scowl take over her sweet face, even one more time. Now that she's with Noah and her mother, the small chance I thought I had is gone. Once she's reminded why he's better for her than me, she'll be his again.

I call her again, but her phone goes straight to voicemail for the twentieth time. Goddammit, I'm such a fucking idiot. After driving around for an hour to every library, every bookstore, I decide to go back to the apartment. Maybe she'll show up, maybe she'll show up . . . I know she won't.

But what if she does? I need to clean up the huge mess I made, and buy some new dishes to replace the ones that I smashed against the walls, just in case she comes home.

A MAN'S VOICE BOOMS through the air, and vibrates my bones: "Where are you, Scott?"

"I saw him leave the bar. I know he's here," another man says.

The floor is cold when I climb out of bed. At first I thought it was Daddy and his friends, but now I don't think it is.

"Come out, come out wherever you are!" the deepest voice yells, and there's a massive crash.

"He isn't here," my mummy says as I reach the bottom of the stairs and can see everyone. My mum and four men.

"Ohhh, look what we have here," the taller man says. "Who knew Scott had such a bangin' wife." He grabs my mum by the arm and pulls her off the couch.

She grabs at her shirt desperately. "Please . . . he isn't here. If he owes you money, I'll give you all I have. You can take anything in the house, the television maybe . . ."

But the man only sneers at her. "A television? I don't want a damn television."

I watch her struggle to shake free of him, almost like a fish I caught once. "I have some jewelry—not much, but please—"

"Shut the fuck up!" another man says and smacks her.

"Mum!" I yell and run into the living room.

"Hardin . . . go upstairs!" she shouts, but I'm not leaving my mummy with these bad men.

"Get out of here, you little shit," one of them tells me, pushing me so I land hard on my butt. "See, bitch, the problem is that your husband did this," he snarls, pointing to his head, where I see a massive gash across his bald scalp. "And since he isn't here, the only thing we *want* is *you*." He smiles, and she kicks her legs at him.

"Hardin, baby, go upstairs . . . Now!" she yells.

Wait, why is she mad at me?

"I think he wants to watch," the injured man says and pushes her onto the couch.

I jolt awake and sit up.

Fuck.

They keep coming, every night worse than the last. I got so used to them not coming that I could sleep. Because of her, it was all because of her.

But here I am at four in the damn morning with bloody sheets from my busted knuckles and a killer headache from my nightmares.

I close my eyes and try to pretend she's really here, and hope that sleep will come.

chapter seven

Tess, baby, wake up," Hardin whispers as he touches his lips to the soft skin just under my ear. "You look so beautiful when you're waking up."

I smile, pulling him by his hair to meet my eyes. I brush my nose against his, and he chuckles.

"I love you," he says and presses his lips to mine.

Only I can't feel them. "Hardin?" I question. "Hardin?"

But he fades from my side—

I snap my eyes open and am thrown back into reality. The strange room is pitch black, and for a second I forget where I am. And then it comes to me: a motel room. Alone. I grab my phone off the bedside table and see it's only 4 a.m. I wipe the tears from the corners of my eyes and close my eyes to try to get back to Hardin, even if it's only in a dream.

WHEN I FINALLY wake up again, it's seven. I step into the shower and try to enjoy the hot water as it relaxes me. I blow-dry my hair and do my makeup; today is the first day I feel like looking decent. I need to get rid of this . . . *mess* that's inside of me. Not knowing what else to do, I take a page from my mother's book and paint a perfect face on in order to bury what's inside.

When I'm finished, I look well rested somehow and actually really nice. I curl my hair and dig my white dress out of my bag, and cringe. Good thing this room has an iron. It's cold, too cold for this dress, which doesn't quite reach my knees, but I won't be outside long. I choose some plain black flats and set them on the bed with the dress.

Before I get dressed, I repack my bags so they're more orderly. I hope my mother calls with some good news about the dorms. If not, I'll have to stay here until she does, which will drain what little money I have, and fast. Maybe I should just look into getting my own place. I might be able to afford something small close to Vance.

I open the door to find the snow mostly melted under the morning sun. Thank goodness. Just as I unlock my car door, Trevor walks out of his room two doors down from mine. He's wearing a black suit and a green tie; he looks so put together.

"Good morning! I would've helped you get those, you know," he says when he sees I'm carrying my bags.

Last night, after we ate pizza, we watched a little television and shared stories of college. He had a lot more stories than me since he's already graduated, and while I really enjoyed hearing about what my college experience could have—and should have—been like, it made me a little sad, too. I shouldn't have been going to parties with people like Hardin. I should have found myself a small but true group of friends. It would've been so different, so much better.

"Did you sleep well?" he asks and pulls a set of keys out of his pocket. With a click, the BMW engine starts. Of course, the BMW is his.

"Your car starts itself?" I laugh.

He holds up his key. "Well, this thing starts it."

"Nice." I smile a little sarcastically.

"Convenient," he counters.

"Extravagant?"

"A little." He laughs. "But still very convenient. You look lovely today, as usual."

I put my bags in the back of my car. "Thank you, it's freezing out," I say and get into the driver's seat.

"See you at work, Tessa." he says and climbs into his BMW.

Despite the sun, it's still cold, so I quickly thrust my key into the ignition and turn it to start up the heater.

Click . . . click . . . click . . . is my car's only response.

Frowning, I try again, and get the same thing.

"Can I get a freaking break!" I say aloud and hit my palms against the steering wheel.

For a third time I try to start my car, but of course nothing happens, not even the clicking this time. I look over, thankful that Trevor's still here. His window rolls down, and I can't help but laugh at my own misfortune.

"Do you think you could give me a ride?" I ask and he nods.

"Of course. I think I know where you're going . . ." He laughs, and I climb out of my car.

I can't help but turn my phone on during the short drive to Vance. Surprisingly, I have no new texts from Hardin. I have a few voicemails, but I don't know if they're from him or my mother. Choosing not to listen to them just in case, I instead text my mother and ask her about the dorms. Trevor drops me off at the door so I don't have to walk in the cold, which is really thoughtful of him.

"You look refreshed," Kimberly says with a smile as I walk in and grab a donut.

"I feel a little better. Sort of," I say and pour myself a cup of coffee.

"Are you ready for tomorrow? I can't wait to get out of here for the weekend—Seattle has amazing shopping, and while Mr. Vance and Trevor have their meetings we'll find some fun stuff to do. Is . . . um . . . have you talked to Hardin?"

It takes me a second, but I decide to tell her. She'll probably find out anyway. "No. Actually, I moved my stuff out yesterday," I say and she frowns.

"I'm sorry, girl. It'll get easier as time goes by."

God, I hope she's right.

MY DAY GOES faster than expected, and I finish this week's manuscript early. I'm excited to go to Seattle, and I hope that I can get my mind off Hardin, even if it's only for a little bit. Monday is my birthday, which I'm not looking forward to it at all. If things hadn't gone downhill so quickly, I'd be on my way to England with Hardin on Tuesday. I don't really want to spend Christmas with my mother either. Hopefully I'll be back in the dorms by then—even if they'll basically be empty—and then maybe I can think of a good enough reason to not show at my mother's. I know it's Christmas, and that's terrible of me, but I'm not exactly in a holiday mood.

My mother texts me as my day is winding down, saying that she hasn't heard back about the dorm. *Great.* At least I only have one more night until the Seattle trip. Shuffling around from place to place is not fun at all.

As I'm getting ready to leave for the day, I remember I didn't drive to work myself. I hope Trevor hasn't already left.

"See you tomorrow, we'll meet here, and Christian's driver will take us to Seattle," Kimberly tells me.

Mr. Vance has a driver?

Of course he does.

When I step off the elevator, Trevor is sitting on one of the black couches in the lobby; the contrast of the black couch, black suit, and his blue eyes is very appealing.

"I wasn't sure if you needed a ride or not, and I didn't want to bother you in your office," he tells me.

"Thank you, I really appreciate it. I'm going to call someone about my car when I get back to the motel." It's slightly warmer than it was this morning but still freezing outside.

"I can wait with you if you want. My plumbing is fixed now,

so I won't be staying at the motel again, but I'll wait with you if you—" He stops talking suddenly and his eyes go wide.

"What?" I ask and follow his eyes to see Hardin standing by his car in the lot and staring angrily at Trevor and me.

The breath has been knocked out of me once again. How does it keep getting worse?

"Hardin, what are you doing here?" I ask, storming toward him.

"Well, you don't answer my calls, so I didn't have much of a choice, did I?" he says.

"I didn't answer for a reason, you can't just show up to my job!" I yell back.

Trevor looks uncomfortable and intimidated by Hardin's presence, but he stays next to me. "Are you okay? Let me know if you're ready."

"Ready for what?" Hardin's eyes are wild.

"He's taking me back to the motel since my car wouldn't start."

"Motel!" Hardin raises his voice.

Before I can stop him, Hardin has his hands on Trevor, gripping the collar of his suit as he slams him against a red truck.

"Hardin! Stop! Let him go! We didn't stay together!" I explain. Why I'm explaining myself to him is beyond me, but I don't want him to hurt Trevor.

Hardin lets go of Trevor's clothing but stays in his face.

"Back off of him, now." I grab Hardin's shoulder and he relaxes slightly.

"Stay away from her," he spits, his face only inches from Trevor's.

Trevor looks pale, and once again I've brought someone else into this mess that doesn't deserve to be.

"I'm so sorry," I tell Trevor.

"It's okay, do you still need a ride?" he asks.

"No, she doesn't," Hardin answers for me.

"Yes, please," I say to Trevor. "I just need a minute."

Like the gentleman that he is, he nods and goes over to his car to give us space.

chapter eight

TESSA

I can't believe you're staying at a motel." He runs his hand over his hair.

"Yeah . . . neither can I."

"You can stay at the apartment, I'll stay back at the frat house or something."

"No." Not happening.

"Please don't be difficult." He rubs his hand across his forehead.

"Difficult? You aren't serious! I shouldn't even be talking to you right now!"

"Would you just calm down? Now, what's wrong with your car? And why was that guy staying at the motel?"

"I don't know what's wrong with my car." I groan. I'm not answering him about Trevor, it's none of his business.

"I'll take a look at it."

"No, I'll call someone. Just go."

"I'll follow you to the motel." He nods toward the road.

"Would you just stop?" I growl and Hardin rolls his eyes. "Is this some sort of game to you, to see just how far you can push me?"

He takes a step back as if I pushed him. Trevor's car is still here, waiting for me.

"No, that's not what I'm doing. How could you even think that after everything I've done?"

"Exactly, I do think that because of *everything you've done,*" I say, almost laughing at his choice of words.

"I just want you to talk to me. I know we can work this out," he tells me. He's played so many games with me since the beginning that I can't tell what's real.

"I know you miss me, too," Hardin says, leaning against his car. His words stop me in my tracks. So arrogant.

"Is that what you want to hear? That I miss you? Of course I miss you, but you know what? It's not actually you that I miss, it's who I thought you were, and now that I know who you really are, I want nothing to do with you!" I yell.

"You've always known who I really am! I've been me all along, you know that!" he shouts back. Why can't we ever just talk without yelling at each other? He makes me crazy, that's why.

"No, I don't know that; if I knew that I . . ." I stop myself before I admit that I want to forgive him. What I want to do and what I know I should do are two totally different things.

"You what?" he asks. Of course he would try and coerce me to continue.

"Nothing, you need to go."

"Tess, you don't know what it's been like the last few days for me. I can't sleep, I can't even function without you. I need to know there's a chance we could—"

I interrupt him before he can finish.

"What it's been like for *you*?" How can he be so selfish?

"What do you think it's been like for me, Hardin? Imagine how it feels to have your life completely ripped apart within hours! Imagine how it feels to be so in love with someone that you give them everything, only to find out it was all a game, a bet! How do you think that feels!" I take a step toward him, my hands moving frantically between us. "How do you think it feels to lose my relationship with my mother over someone who could give less of a shit about me! How do you think it feels to be staying in a goddamn motel room? How do you think if it feels to try to move on from this when you keep showing up everywhere! You just don't know when to stop!"

He doesn't say anything, so I continue my rant. Part of me feels like I'm being too harsh on him, but he betrayed me in the worst way and he deserves it.

"So don't you sit here and tell me that it's been hard for you because you did this! You fucking ruined everything! Just like you always do, so you know what? I don't feel sorry for you . . . Actually I do. I feel sorry for you because you will never be happy. You will be alone for the rest of your life, and for that I feel sorry for you. I'll move on, find a nice man who'll treat me the way you should have, and we'll get married and have children. I will be happy."

I'm out of breath after my long speech, and Hardin is looking at me with red eyes and an open mouth.

"You know the worst part of all of this? It's that you warned me, you said you would ruin me and I didn't listen." I try desperately to stop my tears, but I can't. They fall mercilessly down my face, and my mascara runs, burning my eyes.

"I'm . . . I'm sorry. I'll go," he says in a low voice. He looks completely and utterly defeated, the way I wanted him to look, but it doesn't give me the satisfaction that I thought it would.

I maybe could have forgiven him in the beginning if he'd have told me the truth, even after we slept together, but instead he hid it from me, offered people money for their silence, and tried to trap me by making me sign the lease with him. My first time being intimate with someone is something I will never forget, and he's ruined that.

I rush over to Trevor's car and jump inside. The heat is on, blasting at my face, mixing with my hot tears. Trevor stays quiet and I'm thankful yet again for his silence as he drives me to the motel.

By the time the sun goes down, I force myself to take a hot shower, too hot. The look on Hardin's face as he backed away from me and got into his car is etched in the back of my mind. I see his face every time I close my eyes.

My phone hasn't rung once since he left. I had this silly, naive idea that we could work. That despite our differences and his temper . . . well, both of our tempers . . . we could make it work somehow. I'm not sure how I manage to fall asleep, but I do.

THE NEXT MORNING I'm a little anxious about going on my first business trip and begin to panic. Plus I forgot to get someone to fix my car. I look up the nearest mechanic and call them. I'll probably have to pay them extra to keep my car for the weekend, but that's the least of my worries right now. I don't mention it to the friendly man who answers in the hopes they just won't bother charging me for it.

I get myself ready, curling my hair and putting on more makeup than usual. I choose a navy-blue dress that I haven't worn yet, something I bought because I knew Hardin would love the way the thin material hung on my curves. The dress itself isn't revealing at all; the hem reaches just below my knees and the sleeves go halfway down my arm. But the way it fits makes it look really good on me.

I hate that everything makes me think of him. As I stand in front of the mirror, I imagine how he would be looking at me in this dress, the way his pupils would dilate and he'd lick his lips before pulling his lip ring between his teeth while he watched me adjust my hair one last time.

A knock on the door brings me back to reality.

"Ms. Young?" A man in a blue mechanic's uniform asks when I open the door.

"That's me," I say and pull open my purse to grab the keys. "Here, it's the white Corolla," I say as I hand them to him.

He looks behind him. "White Corolla?" he asks, confused.

I step outside. My car is . . . gone.

"What the . . . Okay, let me call the front desk and see if they had my car towed for leaving it here yesterday." What a great way to start my day.

"Hello, this is Tessa Young, room thirty-six," I say when the front desk guy answers. "I think you had my car towed?" I'm trying to be nice, but this is really frustrating.

"No, I didn't," he replies.

My head is spinning. "Okay, well then, my car must have been stolen or something . . ." If someone took my car, I am beyond screwed. It's almost time for me to leave.

"No, your friend came and got it this morning."

"My friend?"

"Yeah, the one with . . . all the tattoos and stuff." He says it quietly, as if Hardin could actually hear him.

"What?" I know what he said, but that's all I can think to say.

"Yeah, he came with a tow truck this morning about two hours ago," he says. "Sorry, I thought you knew—"

"Thanks." I groan and hang up. Turning to the man before me, I say, "I am so sorry. Apparently someone has already had my car taken to another mechanic. I didn't know; I'm sorry for wasting your time."

He smiles and assures me that it's okay.

After my fight with Hardin yesterday, it slipped my mind that I needed a ride to work today. I call Trevor to let him know, and he tells me that he already asked Mr. Vance and Kimberly to swing by and pick me up on their way. After thanking him, I hang up and pull back the curtain on the window. A black car pulls into the lot and stops in front of my room. The window rolls down and I see Kimberly's blond hair.

"Good morning! We're here to save you!" she announces with a laugh when I open the door. Smart and kind Trevor, always thinking ahead.

The driver gets out and with a tip of his cap grabs my bag and stashes it in the trunk for me. When he opens the back door, I see two seats that face each other. On one, Kimberly pats the leather, inviting me to sit next to her. On the other, Mr. Vance and Trevor look at me with amused expressions.

"Ready for your weekend getaway?" Trevor asks with a wide smile.

"More than you can imagine," I reply and get into the car.

chapter nine

TESSA

As we pull out onto the highway, Trevor and Mr. Vance return to what appears to be a deep conversation about price per square foot on a new building in Seattle. Kimberly nudges me with her elbow and then mimics their talking with her hand.

"Those boys are so serious," she says. "So, Trevor said something happened to your car?"

"Yeah. I have no idea what," I say, trying to keep a light tone, which is easier with Kimberly's friendly smile. "It wouldn't start yesterday, so I called someone to fix it. But Hardin already had someone come get it."

She smirks. "Persistent, isn't he?"

I sigh. "I guess so. I just wish he would give me a little time to process all of this."

"Process what?" she asks. I forget that she doesn't know about the bet, my humiliation, and I certainly don't want to tell her. She only knows that Hardin and I broke up.

"I don't know, just everything. I have so much going on right now, and I still don't have anywhere to live. I feel like he isn't taking this as seriously as he should. He thinks he can just play puppeteer with me and my life. He thinks he can just show up and say sorry and all will be forgiven, but that's not how it works. Not anymore at least," I huff.

"Well, good for you. I'm happy you're standing up for yourself," she says.

I'm just glad she isn't asking for details. "Thank you. Me, too."

I really am proud of myself for standing up to Hardin and not just giving in, but at the same time I feel terrible for what I said to him yesterday. I know he deserved it, but I can't help but think, *What if he does care as much as he claims?* But even if somewhere deep down he does, I just don't think it's enough to ensure he doesn't hurt me again.

Because that's what he does: he hurts people.

Changing the subject, Kimberly says excitedly, "We should go out tonight right after the last talk. On Sunday those two will be in meetings all morning, so we'll do some shopping then. We'll go out tonight, and maybe Saturday night, too. What do you think?"

"Go out where?" I laugh. "I'm only eighteen."

"Oh, please. Christian knows a lot of people in Seattle. If you're with him, you can get in anywhere." I love the way her eyes light up when she speaks of Mr. Vance, even though he's already right next to her.

"Okay," I say. I've never been "out" before. I've been to the few parties at the frat house, but I haven't ever been to a night-club or anything even close.

"It'll be fun, don't worry," she assures me. "And you should definitely wear that dress," she adds with a laugh.

chapter ten

HARDIN

You will be alone for the rest of your life, and for that I feel sorry for you. I'll move on, find a nice man who'll treat me the way you should have, and we'll get married and have children. I will be happy.

Tessa's words keep playing over and over in my head. I know she's right, but I so desperately don't want her to be. I had never minded being alone until now—now I know what I'm missing.

"You in?" Jace's voice breaks through my muddled thoughts.

"Uh, what?" I ask. I almost forgot that I was driving.

He rolls his eyes and takes a hit from his joint.

"I asked if you were in. We're going to Zed's."

I groan. "I don't know . . ."

"Why not? You need to stop being such a pussy. You're moping around like a fucking baby."

I glare at him. If I had gotten any sleep last night, I'd reach across and choke him. "I am not," I say slowly.

"You so *are*, dude. You need to get wasted and laid tonight. I'm sure there'll be some easy girls there."

"I don't need to get laid." I don't want anyone but her.

"Well, come on, drive over to Zed's. If you don't want to get laid, then at least come have a few beers," he says.

"Don't you ever want to do more?" I ask and he looks over at me like I've grown horns.

"What?"

"You know, doesn't it feel like it's getting old just partying and hooking up with different girls all the time?"

"Whoa, whoa—this is worse than I thought. You got it bad, man!"

"No, I don't. I'm just saying. Doing the same old shit all the time gets old."

He doesn't know how enjoyable it is to lie in bed and make Tessa laugh, he doesn't know how fun it is to hear her ramble on about her favorite novels, to have her swat at me when I try to grope her. It's much better than any party that I've ever been to or will ever go to.

"She really did a number on you. That's some shit, isn't it?" He laughs.

"No, she didn't," I lie.

"Sure . . ." He throws the remainder of his joint out of my car window. "She's single, though, right?" he asks, and when I grip the wheel he laughs even harder. "I'm just fucking around, Scott. Just wanted to see how pissed you would get."

"Fuck off," I grumble, and to prove a point, I turn on the back road to Zed's.

chapter eleven

TESSA

The Four Seasons in Seattle is the nicest hotel I have ever seen. I try to walk slowly to take in all the beautiful details, but Kimberly practically drags me onto the elevator and down the hall, leaving Trevor and Mr. Vance in her wake.

Stopping in front of a door, she says, "Here's your room. After you unpack, we'll meet in our suite to go over the itinerary for the weekend, even though I already know you've already done this. You should change, because I really think you should save that dress for tonight when we go out." She winks and strolls off down the hall.

The differences between my hotel from the last two nights and this one are vast. One painting from the lobby here probably costs more than what they spent decorating an entire room at the other place. The view from my window is incredible. Seattle is such a beautiful city. I can easily imagine myself living here, in a high-rise apartment with a job at Seattle Publishing, or even Vance Publishing, now that they're opening an office here. That would be amazing.

After I hang up my clothes for the weekend, I change into a black pencil skirt and a lilac shirt. I'm excited about the conference, but nervous about going out. I know I need to have some fun, but it's all new to me and I still feel empty from the damage Hardin has caused.

By the time I get to Kimberly and Mr. Vance's suite, it's two thirty. I'm anxious because I know we should be downstairs in the banquet room by three.

Kimberly greets me warmly when she opens the door and leads me inside. Their suite has its own living room and a separate sitting room. It looks bigger than my mother's entire house.

"This is . . . wow," I say.

Mr. Vance laughs and pours himself a glass of what looks like water. "It's okay."

"We ordered some room service so we can all eat a little something before we head downstairs. It should be here any minute," Kimberly says, and I smile and thank her. I didn't realize how hungry I was until she mentioned food. I haven't eaten at all today.

"You ready to be bored out of your mind?" Trevor asks as he appears from the sitting room.

"It won't be boring to me." I smile and he laughs. "I may not want to leave this place," I add.

"Me either," he admits.

"Same," Kim says.

Mr. Vance shakes his head. "That could be arranged, love." He puts his hand on her back and I look away from the intimate gesture.

"We should just bring the main office here and all move!" Kimberly jokes. At least I think she's joking.

"Smith would love Seattle." Mr. Vance says.

"Smith?" I ask, then I remember his son from the wedding and blush. "Sorry, your son, of course."

"It's okay—it's an odd name, I know." He laughs and leans into Kimberly. It must be so nice to be in a loving, trusting relationship. I envy Kimberly this, a shameful envy, but envy nonetheless. She has a man in her life who obviously cares for her and would do anything to make her happy. She's so lucky.

I smile. "It's a lovely name."

After eating, we head downstairs, and I'm thrown into a large conference room full of people who love books. It's heaven.

"Network. Network. Network," Mr. Vance says. "It's all about networking." And for the next three hours he introduces me to almost every single person in the room. The best part is that he doesn't introduce me as his intern and he treats me like an adult. They all do.

chapter twelve

HARDIN

Well well well, look who it is," Molly says and rolls her eyes when Jace and I walk into Zed's apartment.

"Drunk and pregnant already?" I say to her.

"So? It's past five," she says with an evil grin. I shake my head at her right as she says, "Have a shot with me, Hardin," and grabs a bottle of brown liquor and two shot glasses off the counter.

"Fine. One," I say, and she smiles before filling up the small glasses.

Ten minutes later, I find myself looking through the photo gallery on my phone. I wish I'd have let Tessa take more pictures of us together so I would have more to look at now. God, I do have it bad, like Jace said. I feel like I'm slowly losing my mind, and the most fucked up part is, I don't care how crazy I'm being as long as it helps me get closer to her again.

I will be happy, she said. I know I didn't make her happy, but I could. At the same time, it isn't fair for me to keep bothering her. I got her car fixed because I didn't want her to have to worry about doing it herself. I'm glad that I did, because I wouldn't have known she was going to Seattle if I hadn't called Vance to make sure she'd have a ride to work.

Why wouldn't she tell me? That prick Trevor is with her right now when I should be. I know he likes her, and I could see her falling for him. He's exactly what she needs, and they're a lot alike. Unlike her and I. He could make her happy. The thought pisses me off and makes me want to slam his head through a window . . .

But maybe I need to give her space and give her a chance to be happy. She made it clear yesterday that she can't forgive me.

"Molly!" I call from the couch.

"What?"

"Bring me another shot." And even without looking at her, I can feel her victorious smile fill the room.

chapter thirteen

TESSA

That was so amazing! Thank you so much for bringing me along."
I'm practically gushing at Mr. Vance as we all step into the
elevator.

"It was my pleasure really, you're one of my best employees.
Intern or not, you're very bright. And please, for the love of God,
call me Christian, like I told you already," he says with a fake
gruffness.

"Yes, okay. This was beyond incredible, Mister . . . *Christian*.
It was great hearing everybody talk about their thoughts on digital
publishing, especially since it will only continue to grow and is so
convenient and easy for readers. This is huge, and the market just
keeps expanding . . ." I ramble.

"True, true. And tonight we helped Vance Publishing grow
a little more—imagine how many new customers we'll get when
we've fully optimized our operations," he agrees.

"Okay, are you two done?" Kimberly teases and wraps her arm
through Christian's. "Let's get changed and hit the town! This is
the first weekend in months that we've had a sitter." She pouts
playfully.

He smiles down at her. "Yes, ma'am."

I'm glad that after his wife passed away Mr. Vance—I mean
Christian—got a second chance at happiness. I look over at
Trevor and he gives me a small smile.

"I need a drink," Kimberly says.

"Me, too," Christian says. "Okay, so everyone meet in the

lobby in thirty minutes, and the driver will pick us up out front. Dinner's on me!"

When I get back to my room, I plug in my curling iron so I can touch up my hair. I brush dark powder over my eyelids and look in the mirror. The powder looks heavy for me, but not too heavy. I line my eyes with black liner and add some blush to my cheeks before fixing my hair. The navy dress I wore this morning looks even better now, with my darker makeup and fuller hair. I wish Hardin . . .

No, I don't. I don't, I repeat to myself and slip on my black heels. I grab my cell phone and purse before leaving the room to meet my friends . . . *are* they my friends?

I don't know, but I feel like Kimberly is, and Trevor is very kind. Christian's my boss, so that's a little different.

In the elevator, I text Landon to tell him that I'm having a great time in Seattle. I miss him, and I hope we can still remain close even if Hardin and I aren't together anymore.

When I step out of the elevator, I spot Trevor's black hair near the entrance. In his black dress pants and cream sweater, he reminds me of Noah a bit. I take a second to admire how handsome he looks before I make my presence known. When his eyes find me, they go wide, and he makes a noise between a cough and a squeak. I can't help but laugh a little as his cheeks flush.

"You look . . . you look beautiful," he says.

I smile and say, "Thank you. You don't look so bad yourself."

His cheeks redden. "Thanks," he murmurs. It's an odd thing to see him off balance like this. He's usually so calm and collected.

"There they are!" I hear Kimberly call.

"Wow, Kim!" I say and wave my hand over my face, like I'm dispelling some illusion. She looks stunning in a red halter dress that only reaches halfway down her thighs. Her short blond hair is pin straight, making her look sexy, yet classy at the same time.

"I have a feeling we'll be fighting men off all night," Christian says to Trevor, and they both laugh as they escort us out to the sidewalk.

At Christian's instruction, the car takes us to a really nice seafood restaurant, where I have the most delicious salmon and crab cakes, and where Christian tells us all sorts of hilarious stories about his days in publishing in New York. We all have a great time, and Trevor and Kimberly tease him a little, since he has a good sense of humor about everything.

After dinner, the car takes us a short distance to an all-glass three-story building. Through its windows I watch hundreds of flashing lights illuminate swaying bodies, creating a fascinating mix of lights and darks across limbs and bodies. It's not far off from what I envisioned a club would be like, though much larger and with a lot more people.

As we get out, Kimberly grabs my arm. "We'll go to a more laid-back place tomorrow—some of the guys from the conference wanted to come here, so here we are!" She laughs.

The very large man guarding the door holds a clipboard in his hands and is clearly controlling access to the inside. A line of expectant partygoers fills the entire sidewalk and reaches around the corner of the street.

"Will we have to wait long?" I ask Trevor.

"Oh no." He chuckles. "Mr. Vance doesn't wait."

I soon see what he means when Christian whispers something to the bouncer and the big man moves the rope to let us through immediately. I'm a little dazed when I walk in, with music pounding and lights dancing across the massive smoke-filled space.

I'm pretty sure I'll never understand why people like to pay to get a headache and inhale synthetic smoke while grinding on strangers.

A woman in a short dress leads us up some stairs to a small

room with thin curtains for walls. Within are two couches and a table.

"This is a VIP section, Tessa," Kimberly tells me as I look around with curious eyes.

"Oh," I answer simply and follow their lead by taking a seat on one of the couches.

"What do you usually drink?" Trevor asks me.

"Oh, I don't usually," I answer.

"Me either. Well, I like wine, but I'm not much of a drinker."

"Oh no, *you* are drinking tonight, Tessa. You need it!" Kimberly says loudly.

"I—" I start to say.

"She'll have a Sex on the Beach, and so will I," she tells the woman.

The hostess nods, and Christian orders a drink that I've never heard of and Trevor orders a glass of red wine. No one has yet questioned whether I'm of legal age or not. Maybe I look older than I am, or maybe Christian is known well enough here that people don't want to upset his company by asking.

I have no idea what a Sex on the Beach is, but I prefer not to showcase my ignorance. When the woman returns, she hands me a tall glass with a piece of pineapple and a small pink umbrella sticking out of the top. I thank her and quickly take a sip through the straw. It 's really very good, sweet but with a little kick of bitterness as I swallow.

"Good?" Kim asks, and I nod, taking another long drink.

chapter fourteen

HARDIN

A w, come on, Hardin. One more," Molly says in my ear.

I haven't decided yet if I want to get drunk. I've already had three shots, and I know if I take another, I *will* be drunk. On the one hand, getting as plastered as I can and forgetting about everything that's going on sounds nice. But on the other hand, I need to be able to think clearly.

"Do you want to get out of here?" Molly says, slurring her words.

Molly smells like pot and whiskey. Part of me wants to take her into the bathroom and fuck her, just because I can. Just because Tessa is in Seattle with fucking Trevor and I am three hours away sitting on a couch half fucking drunk.

"Come on, Hardin, you know I can make you forget all about her," she says and scoots onto my lap.

"What?" I ask her as she wraps her arms around my neck.

"Tessa. Let me make you forget her. You can fuck me until you can't even remember her *name*." Her hot breath touches my neck, and I pull away from her.

"Get off me," I say.

"What the fuck, Hardin?" she snaps, her ego obviously wounded.

"I don't want you," I say harshly.

"Since when? You didn't have a problem fucking me *all those other times*."

"Not since . . ." I start to say.

"Not since *what*?" She jumps up off the couch, swinging her arms around wildly. "Since you met that *stuck-up bitch*?"

I have to remind myself that Molly is a female—and not the actual demon she acts like—before I do something stupid. "Don't talk about her like that." I stand up.

"It's true, and now look at you. You're like a fucking lost puppy over some Virgin Mary–turned–skank who obviously doesn't even want you!" she yells, laughing or crying. Those things tend to look almost the same on Molly.

I clench my fists as Jace and Zed appear next to her. Molly puts a hand on Jace's shoulder. "Tell him, guys. Tell him that he's a fucking snore ever since we outed him to her."

"Not we. *You*," Zed corrects her.

She glares at him. "Same thing," she says, and he rolls his eyes.

"What's the problem?" Jace asks.

"Nothing," I answer for her. "She's just upset because I won't fuck her needy ass."

"No—I'm pissed because you're an *asshole*. No one wants you around anyway. That's why Jace told me to tell her in the first place."

All I see is red. "He what?" I say through my teeth. I knew Jace was a dick, but I thought for sure it was Molly's jealousy that drove her to reveal everything to Tessa the way she did.

"Yeah, he told me to tell her. He had it all planned: I was going to tell her right in front of you after she had a couple drinks, then he was going to chase after her and comfort her while you were crying like a fucking baby." She laughs. "What was it that you said, Jace? You were going to 'fuck her brains out'?" Molly says, using her claws to make air quotes.

I take a step toward Jace.

"Hey, it was just a joke, man—" he starts to say.

If I'm not mistaken, a smirk plays on Zed's lips as my fist connects with Jace's jaw.

I feel nothing on my knuckles from the repeated blows to Jace's face; my anger overpowers everything as I climb on top of him to continue my assault. Images of him touching Tessa, kissing her, undressing her flash through my mind, making me hit him harder. The blood on his face only pushes me on, making me want to hurt him as much as I possibly can.

Jace's black-framed glasses lie broken and shattered next to his bloody face as strong hands pull me off him.

"Come on, man! You're going to kill him if you don't stop!" Logan yells in my face, snapping me back to reality somewhat.

"If any of you have anything to fucking say to me, say it now!" I yell to the group I had once considered friends, or the closest things I had to such.

Everyone stays silent, even Molly.

"I mean it! If anyone says another fucking word about her, I won't hesitate to take each and every one of you motherfuckers down!" I take one last look at Jace, who is struggling to get up off the floor, and walk out of Zed's apartment into the cold night.

chapter fifteen

TESSA

These taste so good!" I practically yell at Kimberly as I suck down the remainder of my fruity drink. I greedily shift the straw around the ice to try to get as much as I can out of the glass.

She beams. "Want another?" Her eyes are a little red, but she's still composed, whereas I feel funny and light.

Drunk. That's the word I'm looking for.

I nod eagerly and find myself tapping my fingertips on my knees to the beat of the music.

"Are you feeling okay?" Trevor laughs when he notices.

"Yeah, I feel really good actually!" I yell over the music.

"We should dance!" Kimberly says.

"I don't dance! Well, by *don't* I mean *can't*, not to this type of music anyway!" I've never danced the way the people inside the club are dancing, and usually I would be *terrified* of joining them. But then the alcohol buzzing in my veins gives me courage like never before. "Fudge it—let's dance!" I exclaim.

Kimberly smiles, then turns and gives Christian a kiss on the lips, lingering longer than normal. Then in a flash she stands up and hauls me off of the couch, pulling me out toward the crowded dance floor. As we pass a railing, I look down and see the two stories below us filled with people dancing. Everyone looks so lost in their own world it's intimidating and intriguing at the same time.

Of course, Kimberly moves expertly, so I close my eyes and just try to let the music take control of my body. I feel awkward, but I just want to fit in with her; I have nothing else.

After I've danced through an unknown number of songs and two more drinks, the room begins to spin. I excuse myself to head for the bathroom, grabbing my purse on the way and pushing through endless sweaty bodies. I feel my phone start vibrating in my bag, so I dig it out. It's my mother; no way I'm answering that—I'm way too drunk to talk to her right now. When I hit the bathroom line, something makes me scroll through my inbox, and I immediately frown at the realization that Hardin hasn't texted me.

Maybe I should see what he's up to?

No. I can't do that. That would be irresponsible and I would regret it tomorrow.

The flashing lights bouncing off the walls are starting to get to me as I wait in line. I try to concentrate on my phone screen, hoping the feeling goes away. When the door to one of the stalls finally opens, I bolt in and lean over the toilet, waiting for my body to decide whether to get sick. I hate this feeling. If he were here, Hardin would bring me water, he would offer to hold my hair back.

No. No, he wouldn't.

I should call him.

Realizing I won't be sick, I exit the little room and go to the sink area. Hitting a couple of buttons on my phone, I place it between my shoulder and cheek and tear a paper towel from the dispenser. I place it under a faucet to wet it, but the water doesn't come until I wiggle the towel around the sensor; I hate these automatic sinks. My eyeliner has run a little, and I look like a different person. My hair is wild and my eyes are bloodshot. After the third ring, I hang up and set my phone on the edge of the sink.

Why the hell isn't he answering? I ask myself, and right then my phone starts to vibrate, almost falling into the water, which makes me laugh. I have no idea why, but I find it amusing.

Hardin's name appears on the screen, and I swipe my wet finger across the screen. "Harold?" I say into the phone.

Harold? Oh Lord, I drank way too much.

Hardin's voice sounds funny and breathless when it comes through. "Tessa? Is everything okay? Did you call me?"

God, his voice is heavenly.

"I don't know—does your caller ID say that I did? Because if so, there's probably a good chance it was me." I laugh as I say this.

His tone changes. "Have you been drinking?"

"Maybe," I squeak and toss the makeshift wipe into the trash.

Two drunken girls enter the area and one of them trips over her own feet, making everyone laugh. They stumble into the largest stall, and I focus my attention back on my phone call.

"Where are you?" Hardin asks harshly.

"Oh, calm down, would you?" He always tells me to calm down, so now it's my turn.

He sighs. "Tessa . . ." I can tell he's angry, but my head's too fuzzy to care. "How much did you drink?" he asks.

"I dunno . . . like five. Or six. I think," I answer and lean against the wall. The cold tile feels amazing on my hot skin through the thin material of my dress.

"Five or six what?"

"Sexes on the Beaches . . . *we* never had sex on the beach . . . That could have been fun," I say with a smirk. I wish I could see his stupid face right now. Not stupid . . . *beautiful*. But stupid sounds better right now.

"Oh God, you're *trashed*," he says. Somehow I know that he's running his fingers through his hair. "Where are you?" he asks again.

I know it's immature, but I reply, "Somewhere you're not."

"Obviously. Now tell me. Are you at a nightclub?" he barks.

"Oooh . . . someone is a grumpy gills." I laugh.

Clearly he can hear the music in the background, so when he threatens, "I can easily find out where you are," I sort of believe him. Not that I care.

The words are out before I can stop them: "Why didn't you call me today?"

"What?" he asks, clearly thrown off by my question.

"You didn't try to call me today." I sound pathetic.

"I didn't think you wanted me to."

"I don't, but still."

"Well, I'll call you tomorrow," he says calmly.

"Don't get off the phone yet."

"I'm not . . . I was just saying that I'll call you tomorrow, even if you don't pick up," he explains and my heart leaps.

I try to sound neutral. "Okay." *What am I doing?*

"So now can you tell me where you are?"

"Nope."

"Is Trevor there?" His tone is serious.

"Yeah, but Kim is, too . . . and Christian." I'm defending, though I don't know why.

"So this was the plan, then? To take you to the conference and get you wasted and take you to a fucking club?" He raises his voice. "You need to go back to your hotel. You aren't used to drinking and now you're out and Trevor—"

I hang up before he can finish. Who does he think he is? He's lucky that I even called him, drunk or not. What a buzzkill.

I need another drink.

My phone vibrates repeatedly, but I press ignore each time. *Take that, Hardin.*

I find my way back to our VIP section and ask the cocktail waitress for another drink.

"Are you okay?" Kimberly asks. "You look pissed."

"Yeah, I'm fine!" I lie and down my drink as soon as the waitress brings it. Hardin is such a jerk, he's the reason that we aren't together, and he has the nerve to try to yell at me when I call him? He could be here with me right now if he hadn't done what he did. Instead, Trevor is. Trevor, who is very sweet and very handsome.

"What?" Trevor smiles at me when he catches me staring.

I laugh and look away. "Nothing."

After I finish another drink and we talk about how great tomorrow will be, I stand back up. "I'm going to dance again!" I call to them.

Trevor looks like he wants to say something, maybe even offer to come with me, but his cheeks flame and he stays quiet. Kimberly looks like she's had enough and waves me off, but I don't mind going out there on my own. I find my way to the middle of the dance floor and start to move. I probably look ridiculous, but it feels good to enjoy the music and let everything else go, like my drunken phone call to Hardin.

After about half a song, I sense a tall figure behind me, near me. I turn to find a pretty cute guy in dark jeans and a white shirt. His brown hair is shaved into a buzz cut, and his smile is handsome enough. He's no Hardin, but then, no one is.

Stop thinking about Hardin, I remind myself as the man puts his hands on my hips and says close in my ear, "Can I join you?"

"Um . . . sure," I reply. But really it's the alcohol that's speaking for me.

"You're very beautiful," he says, then turns me around, closing the gap between us. He pushes up against my back, and I close my eyes, trying to imagine that I'm someone else. A woman who dances with strangers in a club.

The beat to the second song is slower, more sensual, which makes my hips move slower. We turn to face each other, and he brings my hand to his mouth and touches his lips to my skin. His eyes meet mine and the next thing I know he has his tongue in my mouth. My heart screams for me to push him away, almost gagging at the unfamiliar taste of him. But my brain, my brain says something entirely different: *Kiss him to forget about Hardin. Kiss him.*

So I ignore the sick feeling in my stomach. I close my eyes and move my tongue across his. I've kissed more guys in my three months at college than I have in my whole life. The stranger's hands move to my back and inch down farther.

"Do you want to come back to my place?" he says as our mouths disconnect.

"What?" I heard him, but something in me hopes that by saying what I say I can erase that question.

"My place, let's go," he slurs.

"Oh . . . I don't think that's a good idea."

"Oh, it's a good idea." He laughs. The multicolored lights strobe across his face, making him look odd and much more threatening than before.

"What makes you think I would go home with you? I don't even know you!" I shout over the music.

"Because you were just all over me and *loved it*, you dirty girl," he says like it's obvious, and not offensive.

Just as I prepare myself to scream at him, or knee him in the crotch, I try to calm down and think clearly for a second. I was just grinding on this guy, and then I kissed him. *Of course* he's going to want more. What the hell is wrong with me? I just made out with a stranger in a club—this is not me.

"I'm sorry, but no," I say and walk away.

When I get back my group, Trevor looks like he's about to fall asleep on the couch. I can't help but smile at his adorableness.

Is that even a word? God, I drank too much.

I take a seat and grab a bottled water out of the ice bin on the table.

"Have fun?" Kimberly asks me, and I nod.

"Yeah, I had a great time," I say, despite what happened a few minutes ago.

"Are you almost ready, honey? We have to get up early," Christian says to Kim.

"Yup. I'm ready when you are." She runs her hand up his thigh. I look away and feel my cheeks flush.

I poke Trevor. "Are you coming or are you going to sleep here?" I tease.

He laughs and sits up straight. "I haven't decided, this couch is comfortable. The music so soothing . . ."

Christian calls the driver, who says he'll be here in a few minutes. We all get up and decide to walk down the spiral staircase that runs along one side of the club. At the first-floor bar, Kimberly orders one last drink, and I debate whether to have another while we wait, but realize I've had enough. If I have another, I might pass out, or throw up. Neither of which I want to do.

When Christian gets a text, we all move toward the exit. I welcome the cold air on my hot skin, thankful there is only a light breeze as we climb into the car.

It's almost three in the morning when we get back to the hotel. I'm drunk and starving. After raiding my minifridge and eating almost everything inside, I stumble over to the bed and plop down without even removing my shoes.

chapter sixteen

TESSA

"Shhhrrrrut up," I grumble when an obnoxious noise pulls me from my drunken slumber. It takes me a few seconds to realize the noise isn't my mother yelling at me for something, but rather someone banging on my door.

"God, I'm *coming*!" I shout and stumble my way to the door.

But then I stop and glance at the clock on the desk: it's almost four in the morning. *Who the hell could that be?*

Even in my drunken state, my mind begins to race with sharp fear. What if it's Hardin? It's been over three hours since I drunk-dialed him, but how would he find me? What will I say to him? I'm not ready for this.

When the pounding recommences, I throw all my thoughts aside and swing the door open, preparing for the worst.

But it's just Trevor. Disappointment stings in my chest, and I wipe at my eyes. I feel just as drunk now as I did when I lay down.

"Sorry for waking you, but do you have my phone?" he asks.

"Huh?" I say and back into the room so he can enter. When the door swings shut behind him, we're engulfed in relative darkness, the only light being from the city outside my window. I'm too drunk to find the light switch, though.

"I think our phones got switched. I have yours and I think you grabbed mine by accident." He holds my phone out in his palm. "I was going to wait until the morning, but yours just wouldn't stop ringing and ringing."

"Oh" is all I say, I walk over and open my purse. Sure enough, Trevor's phone is sitting on top of my wallet.

"I'm sorry . . . must have grabbed yours in the car," I apologize and hand it to him.

"It's okay. I'm really sorry for waking you up. You're the only girl I know who looks just as beautiful when she wakes up as she did—"

A loud banging at the door cuts him off, and the sudden noise infuriates me.

"*What the hell is this?* Party in Tessa's room?" I yell and stomp to the door, ready to yell at whatever hotel employee is likely here to reprimand me for the noise Trevor made, ironically by making more noise than he did.

Just as I reach for the door, the noise gets even louder, which shocks me into stillness. I then I hear it: "Tessa! Open this damn door!" Hardin's voice booms through the air, as if no barrier at all stood between us. A light flips on behind me, and I see Trevor's face pale with real fear.

Hardin finding him in my room won't go over well, regardless of what was really going on.

"Hide in the bathroom," I say, and Trevor's eyes widen.

"What? I can't hide in the bathroom!" he exclaims, and I realize how ridiculous that idea is.

"*Open the fucking door!*" Hardin yells again, and then he starts kicking it. Repeatedly.

I look at Trevor again before opening the door, trying to memorize his handsome face before Hardin mutilates it.

"I'm *coming!*" I yell and open the door halfway to find a fuming Hardin, dressed in all black. My drunk eyes wander, and I notice that instead of his thick boots, he's wearing plain black Converses. I've never seen him in any shoes except his boots. I like these new shoes . . .

But I'm getting distracted.

Hardin pushes the door open and blows right by me, going for Trevor. Luckily, I grab his shirt and manage to stop him, somehow.

"You think you can get her drunk and come into her fucking hotel room!" Hardin screams at him and tries to surge forward. I know he isn't trying as much as he could because in that case I would surely be on the floor, not holding him by his thin shirt. "I saw that light flip on through the peephole—what were you two doing alone in the dark here!"

"I wasn't . . . I—" Trevor begins.

"Hardin, stop it! You can't go around beating people up!" I shout and tug at his shirt.

"Yes . . . I can, though!" he growls.

"Trevor," I say. "Go back to your room so I can talk some sense into him. I'm sorry for his crazy-ass behavior."

Trevor almost laughs at my word choice, but one look from Hardin silences him.

Hardin turns to me as Trevor leaves the room. " 'Crazy-ass behavior'?"

"Yes, crazy! You can't just show up here and barge into my room trying to beat my friend up."

"He shouldn't have been in here. Why was he in here? Why are you still dressed? And fuck, where did that dress come from?" he says, eyeing my body.

I ignore the heat stirring in my belly and focus on my indignation.

"He came to get his phone because I took it by accident. And . . . I can't remember any of the other questions you just asked," I admit.

"Well, maybe you shouldn't have drunk so much."

"I'll drink what and why and how and when I want. Thank you."

He rolls his eyes. "You're annoying when you're drunk." He flops down on the wingback chair.

"You're annoying when you're . . . *everything*. And who said you could sit down?" I huff, crossing my arms.

Hardin looks up at me with those brilliant green eyes. God, he looks so hot right now. "I can't believe he was in your room."

"I can't believe *you're* in my room," I counter.

"Did you fuck him?"

"*What?* How *dare* you even ask me that!" I shout.

"Answer the question."

"No, you asshole. Of course I didn't."

"Were you going to—do you want to?"

"Oh my God, Hardin! You're insane!" I shake my head and pace between the window and bed.

"Well then, why are you still dressed?"

"That doesn't even make sense!" I roll my eyes. "Besides, it's none of your business who I have sex with. Maybe I did have sex with him—maybe I had sex with someone else?" The corners of my mouth threaten a smile, but I force a straight expression as I say slowly, "You will never know."

My words have the intended effect, and Hardin's face turns dark, animalistic. "What did you just say?" he barks.

Oh, this is much more fun than I thought it would be. I like being drunk around Hardin because I say things without thinking—things that I *mean*—and everything seems funny.

"You heard me . . ." I say, and move to stand over Hardin. "Maybe I let the guy at the club take me into the bathroom."

"Maybe Trevor took me on this bed," I say and casually look back at the bed over my shoulder.

"Shut up. Shut up now, Tessa," Hardin warns me.

But I laugh. I feel empowered, strong—and I feel like ripping Hardin's shirt off of him. "What's wrong, Hardin? Don't like the idea of Trevor's hands all over my body?" I don't know if it's Hardin's anger, the alcohol, or the fact that I miss him, but without letting myself overthink my actions, I climb onto his lap on the chair. My knees rest on either side of his thighs. Completely taken aback by my action, if I'm not mistaken, he's shaking.

"W-what are you . . . what are you doing, Tessa?"

"Tell me, Hardin, do you like the idea of Trev—"

"Stop it. Stop saying that!" he begs and I oblige.

"Oh, lighten up, Hardin, you know I wouldn't do that."

I wrap my arms around his neck. The nostalgic feeling that washes over me at being in his arms almost takes my breath away.

"You're drunk, Tessa," he says and tries to remove my arms from around him.

"So . . . I want you," I say, surprising both of us.

I decide to shut my thoughts off, the logical ones, anyway, and grab two fistfuls of his hair. Oh, how I've missed the way it feels between my fingers.

"Tessa . . . You don't know what you're doing. You're wasted," he says.

But there's no conviction behind his voice.

"Hardin . . . stop overthinking this. Don't you miss me?" I say against his neck, sucking lightly. My hormones have completely taken over, and I don't know that I've ever wanted him so badly.

"Yesss . . ." he hisses as I suck harder, sure to leave a mark. "I can't, Tess . . . please."

But I refuse to stop and instead rock my hips on his lap, making him groan.

"No . . ." he whispers and grips his large hands on my hips, stopping my movements.

I snap and glare at him. "You have two options here: you fuck me or you leave. You decide."

What the hell did I just say?

"You'll hate me tomorrow if I do this while you're in this . . . state," he says and looks into my eyes.

"I already hate you," I say, and he flinches from my words. "Sort of," I add more softly than I mean to.

He loosens his grip on my hips, allowing me to move. "Can we at least talk about this all first?"

"No, stop being such a Debbie Downer." I groan and rub myself against his leg.

"We can't do this . . . not like this."

Since when does he have morals? "I know you want to, Hardin, I can feel how hard you are for me," I say in his ear.

I can't believe the dirty words falling from my drunken lips, but Hardin's mouth is a deep pink, and his eyes are wide, almost black.

"Come on, Hardin, don't you want to bend me over this desk? Or the bed? The sink? So many possibilities . . ." I whisper up close and gently bite his earlobe.

"Fuck . . . Okay. Fuck it," he says and wraps his hands in my hair, pulling my mouth to his.

The moment Hardin's lips touch mine, my body ignites. I moan into his mouth and am rewarded with an equally feverish sound from Hardin. My fingers thread through his hair and tug harder, not able to control myself or my need for him. I know he's holding back and it's driving me crazy. My hands move from his hair down to the hem of his black T-shirt, gripping the fabric and pulling it up and over his head. The second the kiss breaks, Hardin leans back slightly.

"Tessa . . ." he pleads.

"Hardin," I counter and run my fingertips over his ink. I've missed the way his hard muscles strain against his skin, the way the intricate black ink swirls and decorates his perfect body.

"I can't take advantage of you," he says but then moans as I swipe my tongue over his bottom lip.

I let out a derisive little chuckle. "Just stop talking."

As my hand reaches down to palm him through his jeans, I know that he can't resist me, which pleases me more than it should. I never thought I would be in a situation with Hardin where I'd have all the control; it's amusing, really, the way we've switched roles.

He's so hard and so turned on, I climb off of him and reach for his zipper.

chapter seventeen

HARDIN

My mind's racing and I know how wrong this is, but I can't help it. I want her, need her. Long for her. I have to have her—and she gave me an edict to either leave or fuck her, so there is no way I'm leaving her if those are my options. The words that came out of her mouth sounded so unnatural, so strange . . .

But so hot.

Her small hands reach down to unbutton and unzip my jeans. When my belt hits my ankles, I shake my head. I'm not thinking clearly; I'm not thinking rationally. I'm wasted, completely gone for this usually sweet, now wild woman that I love more than I can stand.

"Wait . . ." I say again, not really wanting her to stop, but the good part of me wants to at least put up a little fight to ease the guilt it feels.

"No . . . no waiting. I've waited enough." Her voice is soft and teasing as she pulls my boxers down and grips me in her hand.

"Fuck, Tessa . . ."

"That's the idea. Fuck. Tessa."

I can't stop her. Not even if I wanted to. She needs this, needs me. And drunk or not, I am selfish enough to take it if this is the only way I can have her wanting me.

She drops to her knees in front of me and takes me into her mouth. When I look down at her, she looks up at me, batting her lashes. Fuck, she looks like an angel and the devil at once, so sweet and so goddamn dirty as she works her tongue around me, swirling and flicking.

She pauses with my cock next to her face and asks with a smirk, "You like me like that?"

I almost come from her words. I nod, unable to speak, as she swallows me again, hollows her cheeks, and sucks harder, taking more of me into her sweet mouth. I don't want her to stop, but I need to touch her. To feel her. "Stop," I beg and gently push her back by her shoulder. She shakes her head and tortures me by moving her head up and down at a dangerous speed. "Tessa . . . please," I moan, but I feel her laugh, a deep vibration that rumbles through me until, luckily, she stops just before I'm about to come down her throat.

She smiles and wipes her now swollen lips with the back of her hand. "You just taste so good."

"Fuck, where did this dirty mouth of yours come from?" I ask her as she gets up off of her knees.

"I don't know . . . I always think these things. I just never have the balls to say them," she says and moves toward the bed.

I almost laugh from her saying "balls." It's so unlike her, but tonight she's in charge and she knows it. I can tell she's enjoying this, having me at her complete and utter mercy.

This dress she has on is enough to break any man. The way the fabric clings to her every curve, every dip in her flawless skin, is the sexiest thing I've ever seen. That is, until she pulls it over her head, tossing it at me playfully. I can literally feel my eyes straining to pop out of my head when I take her body in. The white lace of her bra is barely holding her full breasts inside, and her matching panties are bunched up on one side, revealing the soft skin between her hip and pubic bones. She loves to be kissed there, even though I know she's embarrassed by the thin, almost transparent white lines on her skin. I have no idea why; she is flawless to me, marks and all.

"Your turn." She smiles and lets her heels hit the bed before she falls backward onto the mattress.

I've been dreaming of this since the day she left me. I didn't think it would ever come, and now that it's happening, I know that I need to pay attention to every detail because it probably won't happen again.

I must pause a little bit too long because she cocks her head up and looks at me with a raised brow. "Do I need to start myself?" she teases.

Christ, she's insatiable right now.

Instead of answering, I join her on the bed. I sit next to her legs and she impatiently tugs at her panties. I move her hands away and pull them down for her.

"I've missed you so much," I say, but she just grabs my hair and pushes my face down where she wants it. I shake my head but give in, pressing my lips against her. She whines and squirms under my tongue as I pay extra attention to her most sensitive bud. I know how much she loves this. I remember the first time I touched her, she had asked, "What is that?"

Her innocence was and still is such a turn-on for me.

"Oh my God, Hardin," she moans.

I've missed that sound. Normally I would say something about how wet she is, how ready, but I can't find any words. I'm too consumed by her noises and her hands gripping the sheets from the pleasure I'm giving her. I slip one finger inside of her, sliding in and out, and she whimpers.

"More, Hardin, please, more," she begs, and I give her what she wants. I circle and curl both fingers inside of her before pulling them out and giving her my tongue. I notice her legs stiffening, the way they always do when she's close. I pull back to watch my fingers rub over her, quickly from side to side, and she screams—literally screams my name—as she comes all over my fingers. I stare at her, taking in every detail, the way her eyes screw shut, the way her mouth forms an almost perfect O, the way her chest and cheeks flush a light pink as she goes through her orgasm. I love her; fuck, do I love her. I can't help but slide my fingers into my mouth after she finishes. She tastes so good, and it's something I hope I can remember when she leaves me again.

The rapid rising and falling of her chest distracts me and her eyes fly open. Her beautiful face holds a huge grin, and I can't help but smile as she hooks her finger to tell me to come closer.

"Do you have a condom?" she asks wickedly as I lean over her.

"Yeah . . ." I answer. A frown takes over the smile, and I hope she doesn't think too much into this. "It's just a habit," I admit truthfully.

"Don't care," she mumbles and looks over at my jeans on the floor. She sits up and grabs them, digging in the pockets until she finds what she's looking for.

I reluctantly grab the foil packet and hold her gaze. "You're sure?" I ask for the twentieth time.

"Yes. And if you ask again, I will go down to *Trevor's* room with *your* condom," she barks.

I lower my eyes at her. She's ruthless tonight, but I can't imagine her with anyone but me. Maybe because it would kill me. My heart begins to race as I picture her with that faux-Noah, my blood heating and my temper rising.

"Have it your way, then, he'll be—" she starts to say, but I cut her off by placing my hand over her mouth.

"Don't you dare finish that," I growl at her and feel her lips pull into a smile beneath my hand. I know this isn't healthy, her antagonizing me this way and me fucking her while she's drunk, but it seems neither of us can help it. I can't deny her when I know she wants me, and there's the chance . . . the small chance that if she's reminded of what we have together she'll give me another shot. I remove my hand from her mouth and tear open the condom. As soon as I roll it on, she climbs onto my lap.

"I want to do it this way first," she insists, gripping my length before she lowers herself onto me. I let out a sigh full of defeat and pleasure as she rolls her hips against mine. She moves herself slowly in circles, creating the sweetest rhythm. The shape of her body, the perfect fullness of her curvy hips, is mesmerizing and so fucking sexy as she rides me. I know I won't last long; I have been deprived for too long. The only relief I've gotten lately is from myself while imagining it was her.

"Talk to me, Hardin, talk to me like you used to," she whimpers and wraps her arms around my neck, pulling me closer to her. I hate the way she says "used to" like it was really so long ago.

I lift off the bed slightly to meet her movements and bring my mouth to her ear. "You like when I say filthy things to you, don't you?" I breathe and she moans. "Answer me," I say, and she nods her head yes. "I knew you did—you try to act all innocent, but I know better." I nip at her neck. My self-control has diminished and I suck her skin harshly, making sure to leave a mark. For fucking Trevor to see. For everyone to see.

"You know I'm the only one who can make you feel like this . . . you know no one else can make you scream the way I can . . . no one knows exactly where to touch you," I say and reach down and rub her where our bodies join. She's soaking, my fingers glide easily over the moisture.

"Oh God . . ." she purrs.

"Say it, Tessa, say that I'm the only one." I rub her clit in tighter circles and move my hips to thrust into her while she continues moving on her own.

"You are." Her eyes roll back in her head. She's so lost in her passion for me and I'm joining her.

"I'm *what*?"

I need to hear her say it, even if she's lying. My desperation for her terrifies me. I grab her hips and flip us over, me hovering over her, and she shrieks as I pound into her harder than ever before. My fingers dig into her full hips. I need her to feel me, feel all of me, and I need her to love the way I claim her. She's mine and I'm hers. Her soft skin is glistening with sweat, and she looks absolutely delicious. Her breasts move rhythmically with my force, and her eyes roll back in her head.

"You're the only one . . . Hardin . . . the only . . ." she says, and I watch her bite her lip, grab at her face, and then at mine. I watch her come completely undone beneath me . . . and it's beautiful. The way she lets go of everything as she comes is too damn perfect. Her words are all I needed to find my own release, and she rakes her nails down my back. The sting is welcomed, I love the passion between us. I lean up, bringing her body with me, resting her on my lap so she can ride me again. My arms wrap around her back, and her head falls onto my shoulder as I lift my hips off of the bed. My cock moves in and out of her at a steady pace as I spill into the condom with a groan of her name.

I lie back with my arms still wrapped around her body, and she sighs when I run my fingers over her forehead, pushing her sweat-soaked hair from her face. Her chest rises and falls, rises and falls, comforting me.

"I love you," I tell her and try to look at her, but she turns her head and touches a finger roughly to my lips.

"Shhh . . ."

"I can't just shhh . . ." I roll her off and say softly, "We need to talk about this."

"Sleep . . . up in three hours . . . Sleep . . ." she mumbles and wraps her arm around my waist.

Her holding me feels better than the sex we just had, and the idea of sleeping in the same bed as her thrills me, it has been too long. "Okay," I say and kiss her forehead. She flinches slightly, but I know she's too exhausted to fight me.

"I love you," I tell her again, but when she doesn't say anything else, I soothe myself by deciding she's already fallen asleep.

Our relationship or whatever this is has done a complete turnaround in just one night. I have suddenly become everything I was terrified of being, and she has complete control of me. She could make me the happiest man on earth, or she could crush me with one word.

chapter eighteen

TESSA

The song of my phone alarm breaks into my sleep like a dancing penguin. Literally, my dream-mind incorporates it as a dancing penguin.

But that pleasant fantasy doesn't last long. I wake up a little more, and my head immediately begins to pound. When I try to sit up, I am weighed down by something . . . someone.

Oh no. Memories of dancing with some creepy guy flood my mind. Panicked, I snap my eyes open . . . to find instead the familiar tattooed skin of Hardin sprawled across me. He has his head on my stomach and an arm wrapped around me.

Oh my God. What the hell?!

I try to push Hardin off without waking him, but he groans and slowly opens his eyes. He closes them again and lifts himself off of me, untangling our legs. I jump off the bed, and when he opens his eyes again, he doesn't say anything but just watches me like I'm some sort of predatory animal. The image of Hardin thrusting into me relentlessly and me calling out his name plays through my thoughts. *What the hell was I thinking?*

I want to say something, but, honestly, I have no idea what. I am freaking out inside, having a total meltdown. As if sensing my struggle, he climbs off the bed, taking the sheet with him and wrapping it around his naked body. Oh my God. He sits in the chair and looks up at me, and I realize I'm only wearing my bra. Instinctively, I squeeze my legs together and sit back on the bed.

"Say something," he instructs.

"I . . . I don't know what to say," I admit. I can't believe this happened. I can't believe Hardin is here, in my bed, naked.

"I'm sorry," he says, and his head falls into his hands.

My head is pounding from the excessive alcohol I consumed only hours ago and the fact that I slept with Hardin last night. "You should be," I mutter.

He tugs at his hair. "You called me."

"I didn't tell you to come here," I retort. I haven't decided how to handle this. I haven't decided if I want to fight with him, to kick him out, or to try to handle this like an adult.

I get up and head for the bathroom, his voice traveling with me as I do. "You were drunk and I thought you were in trouble or something, and Trevor was here."

I turn on the shower and look into the mirror. On my neck is a deep red bruise. Freaking hell. As I run my fingers over the sensitive mark, my mind travels to Hardin's tongue on my skin. I must still be a little intoxicated, because I can't think straight. I thought I was moving on, and yet here is my heartbreaker in my room, and here I am with a massive hickey on my neck like some wild teenager.

"Tessa?" he says and enters the bathroom as I step into the hot water. I stay quiet as the scalding water rinses off my sins. "Are you—" His voice cracks. "Are you okay with what happened last night?"

Why is he acting so weird? I would've expected a cocky smirk and at least five "you're welcome's" the second his eyes opened.

"I . . . I don't know. No, I'm not okay with it," I tell him.

"Do you hate me . . . you know even more than before?"

The vulnerability laced through his voice tugs at my heart, but I need to stand my ground. Everything about this situation is a mess; I had just started to get over him. *No you didn't*, my sub-conscious mocks, but I ignore her.

"No. It's about the same," I say.

"Oh."

I rinse my hair one last time and give a little prayer that the shower water will rehydrate me out of a hangover.

"I didn't mean to take advantage of you, I swear it," he says as I turn the shower off. I grab a towel off of the small rack and wrap it around me. He is leaning in the doorway in only his boxers, his chest and neck littered with red spots of his own.

I'm never drinking again.

"Tessa, I know you're probably angry, but we have a lot to talk about."

"No, we don't. I was drunk and called you. You came here, and we had sex. What else is there to talk about?" I'm trying to stay as calm as I can. I don't want him to know the effect that he has on me. That last night had on me.

Then I notice the raw skin on his knuckles. "What happened to your hands?" I ask. "Oh my God, Hardin—you beat Trevor up, didn't you!" I yell, then wince from the shooting pain in my head.

"What? No, I didn't." He raises his hands in defense.

"Then who?"

He shakes his head. "It doesn't matter. We have more important things to talk about."

"No, we don't. Nothing has changed." I open my makeup bag and pull out the concealer. I begin applying it to my neck generously while Hardin stands behind me silently.

"This was a mistake, I shouldn't have even called you," I finally say, annoyed when the third layer of concealer doesn't cover the spot.

"It wasn't a mistake, you obviously missed me. That's why you called."

"What? No, I called because . . . because it was an accident. I didn't mean to."

"You're lying."

He knows me too well. "You know what? It doesn't matter

why I called," I snap. "You didn't have to come here." I grab the eyeliner and begin applying it, thick.

"Yes, I did. You were drunk and God knows what could have happened."

"Oh, like what? I could have slept with someone who I shouldn't have?"

His cheeks flare. I know I am being harsh, but he should have known better than to sleep with me when I was so drunk. I rake my hairbrush through my wet hair.

"You didn't give me much of a choice, if you remember," he says equally harshly.

I remember, I remember climbing onto his lap and grinding myself against him. I remember demanding he have sex with me or leave. I remember him telling me no and to stop. I'm humiliated and horrified at my behavior, but maybe worst of all, I am reminded of the first time I kissed him and he claimed I'd thrown myself at him.

Anger boils inside me and I throw my brush against the counter with a loud clatter. "Don't you dare try to blame this all on me, you could have said no!" I shout.

"I did! Repeatedly!" he shouts back.

"I had no idea what was going on, and you know it!" I half lie. I knew what I wanted; I'm just not willing to admit it.

But he begins repeating my dirty words from last night— " 'You just taste so good!' " " 'Talk to me like you used to!' " " 'You're the only one, Hardin!' "—and it pushes me over the edge.

"Get out! Get out now!" I yell and go grab my phone to check the time.

"You weren't telling me to get out last night," he says cruelly.

I turn to face him. "I was doing just fine before you even came here. Trevor was here," I say, because I know how mad it will make him.

But he surprises me by laughing. "Oh, *please*, you and I both know Trevor isn't enough for you. You wanted me, only me. You still do," he scoffs.

"I was drunk, Hardin! Why would I want you when I can have *him*?" I instantly regret the words.

Hardin's eyes flash with either pain or jealousy, and I take a step toward him.

"Don't," he says, holding his arm out. "You know what—that's fine. He can fucking have you! I don't even know why I came here. I should have known you would act like this!"

I try to keep my voice down before someone calls in a complaint, but I'm not sure I'm able to pull that off. "Are you kidding me? You come here and take advantage of me and have the nerve to insult me?"

"Take advantage of you? You took advantage of me, Tessa! You know that I can't say no to you—and you kept pushing and pushing!"

I know he's right, but now I'm pissed off and humiliated by my aggressive behavior last night. "It doesn't matter who took advantage of who—all that matters is that you are leaving and not coming around me again," I say with finality, then turn the blow dryer on to muffle his comeback. Within seconds, he's ripped the blow-dryer cord—and nearly the outlet—from the wall.

"What the hell is wrong with you?" I yell and plug it back in. "You could have broken that!"

Hardin's so infuriating—*what the hell was I thinking, calling him?*

"I'm not leaving until you talk to me about all of this," he huffs.

Ignoring the pain in my chest, I tell him, "I already told you, we have nothing to talk about. You hurt me, and I can't forgive you. End of story." As much as I try to fight it, deep down I love having him here. Even if we're fighting and yelling at each other, I've missed him so much.

"You haven't even tried to forgive me," he says, his voice much softer.

"Yes, I *have*. I have tried mentally to get over this, but I can't. I can't trust that this isn't still part of your game. I can't trust you won't hurt me again."

I plug my curling iron in and sigh. "I need to finish getting ready."

When I turn the blow dryer back on, he disappears from the bathroom, and I hope he leaves. The small part of me that hopes he's sitting on the bed when I come out is an idiot. She isn't the rational part of me. She's the naive, ridiculous girl who fell in love with a boy who is the furthest thing from what she needs. Hardin and I will never work, I know that. I just wish she did, too.

I curl and style my hair, making sure that it will cover Hardin's mark on my neck. When I walk out of the bathroom to gather my clothes, Hardin *is* sitting on the bed, and that stupid girl rejoices a little. I grab my light red bra and panties out of my bag and slip them on without removing my towel. When I drop the towel, Hardin gasps, then tries to hide it with a cough.

As I slip a dress over my head, I feel like I'm being pulled toward him by an invisible string, but I fight it and grab my white dress out of the closet. I feel strangely comfortable around him right now, considering our situation. Why is this all so confusing and consuming? Why does it have to be so complicated? And most importantly why can't I just get over him and move on?

"You really should go," I say quietly.

"Do you need help?" he asks when I struggle with zipping the dress.

"No . . . I'm fine. I've got it."

"Here." He stands up to walk over to me. We are walking this fine line between love and hate, anger and calm. It's strange and surely toxic for me.

I lift my hair, and he zips my dress, taking longer than he

should. I feel my pulse quicken and scold myself for allowing him to help me.

"How did you find me?" I ask him just as soon as the thought enters my mind.

He shrugs like he didn't just stalk me across the state. "I called Vance, of course."

"He gave you my room number?" I'm not pleased at the idea.

"No, the front desk did." He gives a little smirk. "I can be very persuasive."

That the hotel would do that doesn't make me feel any better. "We can't do this . . . you know, you making jokes and acting all friendly," I say and step into my black heels.

He grabs his pants and starts putting them on. "Why not?"

"Because it's not good for either of us to be around the other."

He smiles, those evil dimples coming out. "You know that's not true," he says casually and puts on his T-shirt.

"Yes, it is."

"No."

"Will you please just go?" I beg.

"You don't mean that, I know you don't. You knew what you were doing when you let me stay."

"No, I didn't," I whine. "I was intoxicated. I didn't know what I was doing at all last night, from kissing that guy to letting you in."

Immediately, I snap my mouth shut. I did not just say that out loud. But by the way Hardin's eyes pop and his jaw clenches, I know that I did. My headache multiplies by ten and I want to slap myself.

"Wh-wh-what? What did you . . . what did you just say?" he growls.

"Nothing . . . I . . ."

"You *kissed* someone? Who?" he asks, his voice strained as if he just ran a marathon.

"Someone at the club," I admit.

"Are you serious?" he breathes. And when I nod, he explodes. "What the—what the *actual fuck*, Tessa? You kiss some guy at a fucking club, then have sex with me? Who *are* you?" He runs his hands over his face. If I know him as well as I think I do, he's getting ready to break something.

"It just happened, and we aren't even together." I try to defend myself, but only make myself sound worse.

"Wow . . . you are unbelievable. My Tessa would never kiss a fucking stranger at a club!" he barks.

"There is no 'your' Tessa," I tell him.

He just shakes his head no over and over and over again. Finally he stares deep into my eyes and says, "You know what? You're *right*. And just to let you know, while you were kissing that guy? I was fucking Molly."

chapter nineteen

TESSA

I was fucking Molly. I was fucking Molly. I was fucking Molly. I was fucking Molly. I was fucking Molly. I was fucking Molly. I was fucking Molly. I was fucking Molly. I was fucking Molly. I was fucking Molly. I was fucking Molly. I was fucking Molly.

Hardin's words echo in my head over and over long after he's slammed the door and marched out of my life forever. I try to calm myself down before having to go down to meeting everyone.

I should have known Hardin was toying with me, I should have known that he was still messing around with that skank. Hell, he was probably sleeping with her the whole time he was "dating" me. How could I be so stupid? I almost believed him last night when he said he loved me—I was thinking, why else would he drive all the way to Seattle? But the answer really is: because he's Hardin and he does things like that to mess with me. He always has and always will. Confusing me is this guilt I feel for blurting out that I kissed that guy, and the way I basically blamed Hardin for last night when I know I wanted it just as much as he did. I just don't want to admit that to him, or to myself, not really.

Thinking of him and Molly together makes my stomach churn. If I don't eat something soon, I'll vomit. Not only from my hangover but from Hardin's confession. Molly, of all people . . . I despise her. I can picture her, with her stupid smirk, knowing that her sleeping with Hardin again would torture me.

These thoughts circle around me like vultures until, finally, having pulled myself back from the abyss of a total breakdown, I dot the corners of my eyes with a tissue and grab my purse. In the elevator I nearly lose it again, but by the time I reach the bottom floor, I've regained control.

"Tessa!" Trevor calls from the other side of the lobby. "Good morning," he says as he hands me a cup of coffee.

"Thank you. Trevor, I'm so sorry for Hardin's behavior last night—" I start.

"It's okay, really. He's a little . . . intense . . . ?"

I almost laugh, but the thought of doing this makes me nauseous again. "Um, yeah . . . *intense*," I mumble and take a sip of my coffee.

He looks at his phone then tucks it back into his pocket. "Kimberly and Christian will be down in a few minutes." He smiles. "So . . . is Hardin still here?"

"No. And he won't be coming back." I try to sound like I could care less. "Did you sleep well?" I ask in attempt to change the subject.

"Yeah, but I was worried about you." Trevor's eyes travel to my neck, and I move my hair to cover where my mark maybe is showing.

"Worried? Why?"

"Can I ask you something? I don't want to upset you . . ." His tone is cautious, and it makes me a little nervous.

"Yeah . . . go ahead."

"Has Hardin ever . . . you know . . . he hasn't ever hurt you, right?" Trevor looks at the ground.

"What? We fight a lot, so, yeah, he hurts me all the time," I answer and take another gulp of the delicious coffee.

He looks up at me sheepishly. "I mean *physically*," he mutters.

I snap my head to the side to look at him. He didn't just ask me if Hardin puts his hands on me? I cringe at the thought. "No! Of course not. He would never do that."

I can tell by the look in Trevor's eyes that he doesn't mean to offend me. "I'm sorry . . . he just seems so violent and angry."

"Hardin is angry, and sometimes violent, but he would never, ever hurt me like that." I feel an odd wave of anger toward Trevor for accusing Hardin of such a thing. He doesn't know Hardin . . . but then again, neither do I, apparently.

We stand in silence for a few minutes, and I ponder that until I spot Kimberly's blond hair coming toward us.

"I really am sorry. I just think you should be treated much better," Trevor says quietly right before the others join us.

"I feel like shit. Absolute shit." Kimberly groans.

"Me, too—my head is killing me," I agree as we all walk down a long corridor toward the conference center.

"You look so good, though. I, on the other hand, look like I just crawled out of bed," she says.

"You do not," Christian says and kisses her forehead.

"Thank you, babe, but your opinion is quite biased." She laughs and then rubs her temples.

Trevor smiles and says, "Looks like we won't be going out tonight." Everyone readily agrees.

When we arrive at the conference, I go straight to the breakfast bar and grab a bowl of granola. I eat it much faster than I should, and I can't seem to shake Hardin's words from my mind. I wish I had at least kissed him once more . . . No, I *don't*. I must still be drunk.

The seminars go by quickly, and though Kimberly groans as the keynote speaker's voice booms far too loudly through the room, come the lunchtime break my headache is almost completely gone.

Noon. Hardin would be back home by now, probably with Molly. He probably drove straight to her place just to spite me. Have they already slept together in our room? I mean, our *old* room? In the bed that was meant for us? When I remember the way he touched me and moaned my name last night, my body is replaced by hers. All I can see is Hardin and Molly. Molly and Hardin.

"Did you hear me?" Trevor asks and takes a seat next to me.

I smile apologetically. "Sorry, I was out of it."

"I was wondering if you want to grab dinner tonight since everyone's staying in." I look into his shining blue eyes, and when I don't immediately answer him, he stutters, "I-if you don't . . . want to, that's okay, too."

"Actually, I would love to," I tell him.

"Really?" he breathes. I can tell he thought I would turn him down, especially after Hardin's behavior toward him.

For the next four hours of talks, I let it warm my heart that Trevor would still want to take me out even after being threatened by my crazy ex.

"THANK GOODNESS THAT'S OVER. I need *sleep*," Kimberly groans as we get into the elevator.

"Looks like you're just not as young as you used to be," Christian teases, and she rolls her eyes and leans against his shoulder.

"Tessa, tomorrow we'll go shopping in the morning while these two are at meetings," she says and closes her eyes.

Which sounds great to me. As does a nice quiet dinner in Seattle with Trevor—in fact, it sounds *amazing* after my wild night with Hardin. I'm a little uneasy about my behavior this weekend already, kissing a stranger, basically forcing Hardin to have sex with me, and now going to dinner with a third guy. But the last of these is the most benign, and at least I know there won't be anything physical involved.

Not for you, sure, but for Hardin and Molly . . . my subconscious throws in.

Man, she is getting on my nerves.

At my door, Trevor stops and says, "I'll come get you at six thirty, is that okay?"

I answer him with a smile and a nod and go inside to the scene of the crime.

I was going to try to take a small nap before my dinner with Trevor, but I end up taking another shower instead. I feel dirty from the events of last night, and I need to rewash Hardin's scent from my body. This time two weeks ago, I had thought everything would be so different right now, with Hardin and me getting ready to visit his mother in London for Christmas. Now I don't even have anywhere to live, which prompts the thought that I need to call my mother back. She called me multiple times last night.

After I get out of my shower, I start reapplying my makeup and hit her number.

"Hello, Theresa," she says in a clipped tone.

"Hey, sorry I didn't call you back last night. I'm in Seattle for that publishing conference, and we were talking to clients later over dinner."

"Oh, that's right. Is he there?" she asks, and I'm a little stunned she would even ask me that.

"No . . . Why do you ask?" I say as nonchalantly as possible.

"Because he called here last night trying to find out where you were. I don't appreciate you giving him this number—you know how I feel about him, Theresa."

"I didn't give him the number—"

"I thought the two of you ended things?" she interrupts.

"We did. I did. He probably just needed to know something about the apartment, or something," I lie. He must have been really desperate to get hold of me if he called my mother's house. That thought hurts and pleases me at the same time.

"Speaking of which, we can't get you into a dorm until Christmas break is over, but since you'll be off of work and school for the week, you can just come here."

"Oh . . . okay," I agree. I don't want to spend my break at my mother's, but what choice do I have?

"I will see you Monday. And, Tessa, if you know what's good for you, you will stay far away from that boy," she says and hangs up.

Spending a week at my mother's house will be hell; I don't know how I lived there for eighteen years. Honestly, I never realized how bad she was until I got a taste of freedom. Maybe since Hardin is leaving the country Tuesday, I can stay in that motel for two more nights and go to the apartment while he's gone. As much as I don't want to ever go there again, it is still my name on the lease, and it's not like he would ever know.

Scrolling through my phone, I see that I have no new messages or calls from him, though I knew that I wouldn't. I can't believe he would sleep with Molly and throw it in my face like that. The worst part is that if I hadn't blurted out that I kissed someone else, he would have never told me. Just like with the bet that started our "relationship." And that means I just can't trust him.

I finish getting myself ready, deciding upon a plain black dress. My days of woolen, pleated skirts seem so long ago. I apply another layer of concealer to my neck and wait for Trevor to come. True to his nature, he knocks on the door at exactly six thirty.

chapter twenty

HARDIN

I stare at my father's massive house, unable to decide whether or not to go inside.

Karen has decorated the outside with too many lights, mini Christmas trees, and what appear to be dancing reindeer. The blow-up Santa in the yard twists with the wind in a way that seems to mock me as I climb out of my car. Pieces of ripped-up airline tickets blow around the seat before I close the door.

I will have to call and make sure I can get a credit for the un-used tickets, otherwise I just blew two grand. I probably should just go alone and escape this dreadful state for a while, but for some reason, going home to London doesn't sound as appealing with Tessa not coming along. I'm grateful that my mum was okay with coming here instead. She actually seems excited to come to America.

As I ring my father's doorbell, I try to come up with an excuse as to why the hell I am here. But before I can conjure something, Landon appears.

"Hey," I say as he opens the door wider for me to come inside.

"Hey?" he questions.

I dig my hands into my pockets, unsure what to say or do.

"Tessa isn't here," he says and walks toward the living room, indifferent to my presence.

"Yeah . . . I know. She's in Seattle," I say, following a few feet behind him.

"So . . ."

"I . . . um . . . well, I came to talk to you . . . or my dad, I mean Ken. Or your mum," I ramble on.

"Talk? About what?" He takes the bookmark from the book he's holding and begins to read. I want to snatch the book from his hands and toss it into the fire, but that won't get me anywhere.

"Tessa," I say quietly. My fingers fiddle with my lip ring as I wait for him to burst into laughter.

He looks at me and closes his book. "Let me get this straight . . . Tessa doesn't want anything to do with you, so you're here to talk to me? Or your father, or even my mother?"

"Yeah . . . I guess . . ." God, he's irritating. This is embarrassing enough.

"Okay . . . and what exactly do you think I can do for you? I, personally, don't think Tessa should ever speak to you again, and I honestly figured you would have moved on by now."

"Stop being a dick. I know I fucked up—but I love her, Landon. And I know she loves me. She's just hurt right now."

Landon takes a deep breath and rubs his chin with his fingers.

"I don't know, Hardin. What you did is pretty unforgivable. You humiliated her and she trusted you."

"I know . . . I know. Fuck, don't you think I know that?"

He sighs. "Well, seeing as you showed up here to ask for help, I'd say you get how messed up this whole situation is."

"So what do you think I should do? Not as her friend, but as my . . . you know, my father's stepson?"

"You mean stepbrother? Your stepbrother." He smiles. I roll my eyes and he laughs. "Well, has she talked to you at all?" he asks.

"Yeah . . . I actually went to Seattle last night, and she let me stay with her," I tell him.

"She *what*?" He is clearly surprised.

"Yeah, she was drunk. I mean *really* drunk, and she practically *made* me fuck her." I notice his sour expression at my choice of words. "Sorry . . . she made me sleep with her. Well not *made me,* because I wanted to, I mean how could I say no . . . she's just . . ." *Why am I even telling him this?*

He waves his hands in the air. "Okay! Okay! I get it, jeez."

"So anyway, then this morning I said some shit that I shouldn't have said because she told me she kissed someone else."

"Tessa kissed someone?" he asks, disbelief clear in his voice.

"Yeah . . . some guy at a fucking nightclub." I groan. I don't want to think about that again.

"Wow. She really is pissed at you," he says.

"I. Know."

"What did you say to her this morning?"

"I told her that I fucked Molly yesterday," I admit.

"Did you? You know . . . have sex with Molly?"

"No, God no." I shake my head.

What the hell is going on here that I am having some twisted heart-to-heart with Landon, of all people?

"Then why did you say that you did?"

"Because she angered me." I shrug. "She kissed someone else."

"Okay . . . so you said that you slept with Molly, who you know Tess despises, just to hurt her?"

"Yeah . . ."

"Good idea." He rolls his eyes.

I wave his snarky movement away with a strong hand. "Do you think she loves me?" I ask, because I have to know.

Landon snaps his head up, suddenly serious. "I don't know . . ." He's a terrible liar.

"Tell me. You know her better than anyone, except me."

"She loves you. But because of how you betrayed her, she's convinced that you never loved her," Landon explains.

It breaks my heart all over again. And I can't believe I'm asking for his help, but I need it. "What can I do? Will you help me?"

"I don't know . . ." He looks up at me with uncertainty, but he must see my desperation. "I guess I can try to talk to her. Her birthday is tomorrow—you know that, right?"

"Yeah, of course I know that. Do you have plans with her?" I ask him. He better not.

"No, she said she's going to stay at her mother's house."

"Her mother's house? Why? When did you talk to her?"

"She texted me about two hours ago, and what else is she supposed to do? Stay at a motel by herself on her birthday?"

I choose to ignore his last question. If I'd just kept my cool this morning, she might have possibly let me stay another night with her. Instead, she's still in Seattle with fucking Trevor.

I hear footsteps coming down the stairs, and my father's body appears in the doorway a moment later. "I thought I heard your voice . . ."

"Yeah . . . I came to talk to Landon," I lie. Well, it's half the truth; I was going to talk to whoever I saw first.

I'm pathetic.

He looks surprised. "You did?"

"Yeah. Um, also, Mum is coming Tuesday morning," I tell him. "For Christmas."

"That's great to hear. I know she misses you," he tells me.

My first instinct is to think of a comeback, some remark about how shitty a father he is, but I simply don't feel like it.

"Well, I'll leave you two boys to talk," he says and walks back to the stairs. "Oh, and Hardin?" my father says when he's halfway up.

"Yeah?"

"I'm glad you're here."

"Okay," I state. I don't know what else to say. My dad gives me a tight smile and continues up the stairs.

This whole day is a fucking mess. My head hurts. "Well . . . I guess I'm going to go . . ." I say to Landon, and he nods.

"I'll do what I can," he promises as I walk to the door.

"Thanks." And when we both stand awkwardly in the door-way, I mumble, "You know I'm not going to like hug you or some shit, right?"

As I walk out the door, I hear him laugh and shut the door.

chapter twenty-one

TESSA

"Big plans for Christmas?" Trevor asks.

I raise one finger to tell him to wait a moment while I savor this bite of ravioli. The food here is excellent, and I'm no foodie, but I imagine this has to be a five-star restaurant.

"Not really. Just going to my mother's house for the week. You?"

"I'm doing some volunteer work at this shelter, actually. I don't really like to go back to Ohio. I have a few cousins and aunts, but since my mother passed, there isn't much there for me," he explains.

"Oh, Trevor, I'm sorry about your mother. But that's very kind of you, to volunteer." I smile sympathetically and take the last piece of ravioli into my mouth. It tastes as good as the first bite, but this revelation about Trevor makes me enjoy the food a little less while making me appreciate the dinner even more. Is that strange?

We talk for a while longer, and enjoy an amazing flourless chocolate cake with a caramel topping for dessert. Afterward, when the waitress brings our check, Trevor pulls out his wallet.

"You aren't one of those women who demands to pay half of the bill, are you?" he teases.

"Ha." I laugh. "Maybe if we were at McDonald's."

He chuckles but doesn't say anything. Hardin would have made some stupid sarcastic remark about how my comment had set feminism back fifty years.

Seeing that a light rain-snow mix has resumed, Trevor tells me to wait inside while he calls a cab, which is very considerate of him. A few moments later he waves at me through the glass, and I rush to get inside the warm cab.

"So what made you want to get into publishing?" he asks as we head back to the hotel.

"Well, I love to read—it's all I do. It's the only thing that interests me, so it was just a natural career choice for me. I would love to become an author sometime in the future, but for now I love what I get to do at Vance," I tell him.

He smiles. "That's the same with me and accounting. Nothing else interests me either. I've known from a young age that I would do something with numbers."

I despise math, but I just smile as he continues to talk about it. "So do you like to read?" I ask when he finishes and we pull up at the hotel.

"Yeah, sort of. Mostly nonfiction."

"Oh . . . why?" I can't help but ask.

He shrugs. "I just don't really care for fiction." He hops out of the cab and holds a hand out for me.

"How can you not?" I ask and take his hand to get out. "The best thing about reading is to escape from your life, to be able to live hundreds or even thousands of different lives. Nonfiction doesn't have that power—it doesn't change you the way fiction does."

"Change you?" He raises his brow.

"Yes, change you. If you aren't affected somehow, even in the slightest bit, you aren't reading the right book." As we pass through the lobby, I look at the great artwork on the walls. "I would like to think that every novel I've read has became a part of me, created who I am, in a sense."

"You're very passionate!" He laughs.

"Yeah . . . I guess I am," I say. Hardin would agree with me, we would carry on this conversation for hours, possibly even days.

We ride the elevator in relative silence, and when we step off, Trevor walks a half step behind me down the hall. I'm exhausted and ready to go to sleep even though it's only nine.

Trevor smiles when we reach the door to my room. "I had an amazing time with you tonight. Thank you dining with me."

"Thank *you* for the invitation." I smile back.

"I really enjoy spending time with you; we have a lot in common. I would love to see you again." He waits for my response, then clarifies: "Outside of the work setting."

"Yeah, I would like that," I say.

He takes a step toward me, and I freeze. His hand reaches up and rests on my hip and he leans into me.

"Um . . . I don't really think this is the right time," I squeak.

His cheeks flame in embarrassment, and I feel terribly guilty for declining his advance.

"Oh, I understand. I'm sorry. I sh-shouldn't have . . ." he stutters.

"No, it's okay. I'm just not ready for that . . ." I explain, and he smiles.

"I understand. I'll let you go now. Good night, Tessa," he says and walks away.

As soon as I enter my room I let out a deep breath that I hadn't realized I was holding in. I step out of my shoes, debating whether or not to undress or just lie down. I'm tired, so tired. I decide to lie down while deciding, and within minutes I'm out.

THE ENTIRE NEXT DAY with Kimberly flies by, and we do more gossiping than shopping.

"How was your night last night?" she asks me.

The woman filing my nails perks her head up nosily, and I smile at her. "It was nice, Hardin and I went to dinner," I say, and Kimberly gasps.

"Hardin?"

"Trevor. I meant Trevor." I would smack myself in the forehead if I weren't getting a manicure.

"Hmm . . ." Kimberly teases me, and I roll my eyes.

After our manicures we find a department store. We look at a lot of different shoes, and I see some stuff I like, but nothing I really want to buy. Kimberly buys several tops with an enthusiasm that tells me she *really* likes shopping.

As we pass by the men's department, she pulls a navy button-up shirt off the rack and says, "I think I'll get Christian a shirt as well. It's fun because he hates when I spend money on him."

"Doesn't he . . . you know, have a lot?" I ask, hoping not to sound too nosy.

"Oh yes. Shitloads. But I like to pay for myself when we go out. I'm not with him for his money," she says proudly.

I'm glad that I met Kimberly. Aside from Landon, she's my only friend now. And I've never really had a lot of female friends, so this is a little new for me.

Despite that, when Christian calls and arranges for the car to pick us up, I'm glad. I've had an amazing time here in Seattle, but it's been a horrible time as well. I sleep the entire drive back home and have them drop me back off at the motel. To my surprise, my car is there, parked where it had been before.

I pay for two more nights and text my mother to tell her I'm sick, and that I suspect it's food poisoning. She doesn't respond, so I turn on the television after getting into my pajamas. There is nothing, literally nothing, on, and I would rather read anyway. I grab my car keys and go out to the car to get my bag.

When I open my car door, something black catches my eye. An e-reader?

I pick it up and pull the small Post-it note off the top. *Happy Birthday—Hardin*, it reads. My heart swells, then tightens. I never liked the idea of portable reading devices. I prefer to hold a book in my hands. But after the conference this weekend, my opinion has slightly changed. Besides, it'll make it easier to carry around submissions for work without having to waste all that paper printing them out.

Still, I grab Hardin's copy of *Wuthering Heights* off the floorboard and go back to my motel room. When I turn the device on, I immediately smile, then sob. On the home screen there is a tab named *Tess*, and when I tap it with my finger, a long list of every novel Hardin and I have discussed, bickered over, or even laughed about appears.

chapter twenty-two

TESSA

When I finally wake up, it's two in the afternoon. I can't remember the last time I slept past eleven, let alone later than lunch, but I forgive myself by taking into account that I stayed up until four reading and browsing through Hardin's wonderful gift. It is so thoughtful, too thoughtful, the best gift I've ever received.

Grabbing my phone off the nightstand, I check my missed calls. Two from my mother, one from Landon. A few "Happy Birthday" messages clog my inbox, including one from Noah. I've never been that into birthdays, but I don't exactly love the idea of being alone today either.

Well, I won't be alone. Catherine Earnshaw and Elizabeth Bennet are much better company than my mother.

I order a crapload of Chinese food and stay in my pajamas the entire day. My mother is irate when I call her and tell her that I'm "sick." I can tell that she doesn't believe me, but honestly, I don't care. It's my birthday, and I can do whatever I choose to do, and if what I choose to do is lie in bed with takeout and my new toy, then that's what I'll do.

My fingers try to pull up Hardin's number a few times, but I stop them. No matter how wonderful his present was, he still slept with Molly. Whenever I think he couldn't possibly hurt me worse, he does. I begin to think about my dinner with Trevor on Saturday. Trevor, who is so nice and so charming. He says what he means, and he gives me compliments. He doesn't yell at me, or annoy me. He has never lied to me. I never have to guess what he's thinking or how he's feeling. He's smart, educated, successful, and he volunteers at shelters on holidays. He's so perfect, compared to Hardin.

The problem is that I shouldn't be comparing him to Hardin. Trevor is a little boring, yes, and we don't share the same passion for novels that Hardin and I do, but we also don't share a damaged past.

The most infuriating thing about Hardin is that I actually love his personality, rudeness and all. He's funny, witty, and can be so sweet when he wants to be. This gift is messing with my head—I need to remember what he has done to me. All the lies, the secrets, and most all the times he's fucked Molly.

I text Landon back to thank him, and within seconds he responds asking for the address of my hotel. I want to tell him not to drive all the way here, but I also don't want to spend the remainder of my day completely alone. I don't get dressed, but I do slip on a bra under my shirt and read some more, waiting for Landon to arrive.

An hour later, he knocks at the door, and when I open it, his familiar, warm smile makes me smile in return and he pulls me into his arms.

"Happy Birthday, Tessa," he says into my hair.

"Thank you," I say and hug him tighter.

He lets me go and sits at the desk chair. "Do you feel any older?"

"No . . . well, yes. I feel like I've aged ten years in the last week."

He gives me a small smile but doesn't say anything.

"I ordered takeout—there's plenty left if you want some," I offer.

Turning, he grabs the white Styrofoam container and a plastic fork from the desk. "Thanks. So is this what you're doing all day?" he teases.

"Sure is." I laugh and sit cross-legged on the bed.

As he chews, Landon looks past me and raises a brow. "You got an e-reader? I thought you hated them."

"Well . . . I did, but now I kind of love them." I pick up the device and admire it. "Thousands of books right at my fingertips! What could be better?" I smile and tilt my head to the side.

"Well, nothing says happy birthday like buying yourself a gift," he says with his mouth full of rice.

"Actually, Hardin got it for me. He left it in my car."

"Oh. That was nice of him," he says with a peculiar tone.

"Yes, very. He even put all these wonderful novels on there and . . ." I stop myself.

"So what do you think about it?" he asks.

"It confuses me even more. He does these incredibly kind things sometimes, but he does the most hurtful things at the same time."

He smiles and waggles the fork while he says, "Well, he does love you. Unfortunately, love doesn't always go hand in hand with common sense."

I sigh. "He doesn't know what love is." I start scrolling through the list of romantic novels, and note that common sense is not something usually seen in any of these stories.

"He came to talk to me yesterday," he says, causing me to drop my gift onto the mattress.

"*What?*"

"Yeah, I know. It surprised me, too. He came looking for me, his dad, or even my mother," he says, and I shake my head.

"Why?"

"To ask for help."

Worry builds inside of me. "Help? With what? Is he okay?"

"Yeah . . . well, no. He asked for help with *you*. He was completely distraught, Tessa. I mean, he came to his father's house, of all places."

"What did he say?" I can't picture Hardin knocking on Ken's door to ask for relationship advice.

"That he loves you. That he wants me to help him persuade you to give him another chance. I wanted you to know; I don't want to keep things from you."

"I . . . well . . . I don't know what to say. I can't believe he came to you. To anyone, really."

"As much as I hate to admit it, he isn't the same Hardin Scott that he was when I first met him. He even joked about hugging me." He laughs.

I can't help but join him. "He did *not!*" I don't know how I feel about any of this, but that thought is definitely funny. When I stop laughing, I look at Landon and dare to ask, "Do you really believe that he loves me?"

"Yes, I do. I don't know if I think you should forgive him, but if there's one thing I'm certain of, it's that he does love you."

"It's just that he lied to me, made me a *joke*—even after he told me he loved me, he still went and told them all what happened between us. Then, as soon as I begin to think I could possibly consider trying to move past that, he sleeps with Molly." Tears prick my eyes, and I grab the water bottle on the nightstand and take a drink in an attempt to distract myself.

"He didn't sleep with her."

I look over at him. "Yes, he did. He told me he did."

Landon puts the food container down and shakes his head. "He just said that to hurt you. I know that's not much better, but you two are both known to fight fire with fire."

Looking at Landon, the first thing I think is that Hardin is *good*. He even has his stepbrother believing his lies. The second thing I think is: *But what if Hardin didn't actually sleep with Molly?* Absent that, could I move toward forgiving him? I had my mind made up that I never would, but I can't seem to shake that boy.

As if the universe is mocking me, my phone lights up with a message from Trevor that says Happy Birthday, Beautiful.

I send him a quick thanks, then say to Landon, "I need more time. I don't know what to think."

He nods. "Fair enough, so what are you doing for Christmas?"

"This." I gesture to the empty takeout box and e-reader.

He grabs the remote. "You aren't going to go home?"

"This is more of a home than my mother's house," I say and try not to think about how pathetic I am.

"You can't just stay in a hotel alone on Christmas, Tessa. You should come to our place. I think my mother got you a few things before . . . you know."

"My life went down the drain?" I half laugh and he nods playfully.

"Actually, I was thinking that since Hardin is leaving tomorrow, I would stay at the apartment . . . just until I get into the dorms, which hopefully will be before he returns. If not, then I can always come back to this lovely abode." I can't help but joke about how ridiculous of a situation I'm in right now.

"Yeah . . . you should do that," Landon says with his eyes focused on the television.

"You think? What if he shows up or something?"

He still doesn't take his eyes from the screen but agrees. "He'll be in London, right?"

"Yeah. You're right. My name is on the lease, after all."

Landon and I watch television and talk about Dakota leaving for New York. He's considering transferring to NYU next year if she decides to stay out there. I'm happy for him, but I don't want him to leave Washington—not that I tell him that, of course. Landon stays until nine, and after he leaves I curl onto the bed and read until I fall asleep.

* * *

THE NEXT MORNING I get ready for my return to the apartment. I can't believe I'm actually going back there, but I don't have many options. I don't want to take advantage of Landon, I definitely don't want to go to my mother's, and I'll run out of money if I stay here. I feel guilty for not going to my mother's, but I don't want to listen to her snide comments all week. I still may go there for Christmas, but not today. I have five days to decide.

Once my hair is curled and my makeup is done, I put on a long-sleeved white shirt and dark jeans. I want to stay in my pajamas, but I need to go to the store to get some food for the next few days. If I eat whatever food Hardin has in the apartment, he'll know I was there. I pack my few belongings in my bags and hurry to my car, which, to my surprise, has been vacuumed and smells faintly of mint. Hardin.

It starts to snow as I make my way to the grocery store. I buy enough food to last me until I decide what I want to do on Christmas. As I wait in line to check out, my mind wanders to what Hardin would have gotten me for Christmas. My birthday gift was so thoughtful, who knows what he'd have came up with. I hope it would be something simple, not expensive.

"Are you going to move up?" a woman's voice barks from behind me.

When I look up, the cashier is waiting impatiently with a scowl on her face. I didn't notice the line moving or disappearing in front of me.

"Sorry," I mumble, placing my groceries on the belt.

My heart begins to race as I pull into the parking lot of the apartment. What if he hasn't left yet? It's only noon. I look frantically around the lot, and his car is gone. He probably drove himself to the airport and left his car there.

Or Molly drove him.

My subconscious doesn't know when to shut up. Once I determine that he isn't here, I park and grab the groceries. The snow is coming down harder and covers the cars around me in a thin layer. At least I'll be in the warm apartment soon. When I reach the door, I take one last breath before unlocking the door and stepping inside. I really love this place—it's so perfect for us . . . for him . . . or me, separately.

When I open the cabinets and fridge, I'm surprised to find them stocked full of food. Hardin must have gone shopping in the last few days. I shove the food that I bought wherever it will fit and head back down to get my belongings.

I can't stop thinking about what Landon said. I'm floored by the fact that Hardin would go to anyone for advice, and that Landon professed to think Hardin loves me—a fact that I've known but buried and locked away for fear it would give me hope. If I allow myself to admit that he loves me, it will only make all of this worse.

As soon as I get back into the apartment, I lock the door and put my bags in the room. I take out most of my clothes and hang them up so they won't be too wrinkled, but using the closet that was intended for Hardin and me only makes the knife inside of me twist once again. He only has a few pairs of black jeans hung up on the left side. I have to force myself not to hang up his T-shirts, they are always slightly wrinkled, although somehow he still manages to look perfect. My eyes travel to the black dress shirt hanging sloppily in the corner, the shirt he wore to the wedding. I hastily finish my task and walk away from the closet.

I make myself some macaroni on the stove and turn on the television. I turn the volume up so that I can hear an old episode of *Friends* that I have seen at least twenty times, and go into the kitchen. I speak along with the characters as I load the dishwasher; I hope Hardin hasn't noticed, but I can't stand to have dishes in the sink. I light a candle and wipe off the counters. Before I know it, I'm sweeping the floor, vacuuming the couch, and making the bed. Once the entire apartment is clean, I do a load of my laundry and fold the clothes Hardin had left in the dryer. Today is actually the most peaceful and calm day that I've had in the last week. That is, until I hear a set of voices and watch in slow motion as the lock turns.

Shit. He's here, again. Why does he always show up at the apartment when I'm there! Hopefully it's just that he gave an extra key to one of his friends to check on the place . . . Maybe it's Zed with a girl? *Anyone but Hardin—please, let it be anyone but Hardin.*

A woman I've never seen before steps through the doorway, but I somehow instantly know who she is. The similarities are undeniable, and she is beautiful.

"Wow, Hardin, this flat is beautiful," she says, her accent just as thick as her son's.

This. Is. Not. Happening. I'm going to look like a complete psychopath in front of Hardin's *mom*—with my food in the cabinets, my clothes in the washer, and the entire apartment cleaned from top to bottom. I stand completely frozen and panicked as she looks up at me.

"Oh, my goodness! You must be Tessa!" She smiles and rushes over to me.

As Hardin steps through the doorway, he cocks his head to the side and drops her floral-print luggage from his hands. The surprise on his face is beyond evident. I tear my eyes from him and focus on the woman coming toward me with open arms.

"I was so disappointed when Hardin said you'd be out of town this week!" she gushes and wraps her arms around me. "What a cheeky boy, fibbing just to try and surprise me!"

What?

She puts her hands on my shoulders and pulls me to look at her. "Oh, you are so lovely, look at you!" She squeals and hugs me again.

I stay silent and hug her once more. Hardin looks terrified and extremely caught off guard.

Join the club.

chapter twenty-three

TESSA

As his mother hugs me for the fourth time, Hardin finally mumbles, "Mum, let's give her a little space. She's a bit shy."

"You're right, and I'm sorry, Tessa. I'm just so happy to finally meet you. Hardin has told me so much about you," she says warmly. I feel my cheeks flame as she steps back and nods in acknowledgment. I'm surprised she even knows that I exist—I would have figured he would have kept me a secret, as usual.

"It's okay," I manage to say through my horror.

Mrs. Daniels smiles brightly and looks over at her son, who says, "Mum, why don't you grab a drink of water in the kitchen for a minute?" When she leaves, Hardin comes over to me with gentle movements. "Can . . . I, um . . . talk to you in the bedroom for a mo-moment?" he stammers.

I nod and glance toward the kitchen before following him into the bedroom that we once shared.

"What the hell?" I say quietly as I close the door.

Hardin winces and sits on the bed. "I know . . . I'm sorry. I couldn't tell her what happened. I couldn't tell her what I did."

"Are you here . . . you know, to stay?" His voice holds more hope than I can bear.

"No . . ."

"Oh."

I sigh and run my fingers through my hair, a habit I picked up from Hardin, I suspect. "Well, what am I supposed to do?" I ask him.

"I don't know . . ." he says with a long sigh. "I don't expect you to go along with it or anything . . . I just need a little time to tell her."

"I didn't know you would be here either, I thought you were going to London."

"I changed my mind, I didn't want to go without . . ." He trails off, and pain is evident in his eyes.

"Is there a reason why you didn't tell her that we aren't together?" I don't know if I want to hear his answer.

"She was just so happy that I found someone . . . I don't want to ruin that for her."

I recall Ken telling me that he never thought Hardin was capable of being in a relationship, and he was right. However, I do not want to ruin Hardin's mother's time here. I certainly don't say what I say next for his sake: "Okay. You can tell her whenever you are ready. Just don't tell her about the bet." I look down, thinking that his mom knowing the details of how her son ruined his first and only love would surely hurt her.

"Really? You're okay with her thinking we're together?" He sounds more surprised than he should be. When I nod, he lets out a deep breath. "Thank you. I thought for sure you'd call me out right in front of her."

"I wouldn't do that," I say and mean it. No matter how angry I have ever been at Hardin, I wouldn't damage his relationship with his mother. "I'll just finish my laundry, then go. I thought you weren't going to be here, so I figured I'd stay here instead of that motel." I shrug uncomfortably. We've been in the bedroom a little too long.

"You don't have anywhere to go?"

"I could go to my mother's. I just really don't want to," I admit. "The motel isn't bad, just a little expensive." This is the most civil conversation Hardin and I have had in the past week.

"I know you won't agree to stay here, but I could give you some money?" I can tell he's afraid of my reaction to his offer.

"I don't need your money."

"I know, I just thought I would offer." He stares at floor.

"We better go back out there." I sigh and open the door.

"I'll be out in a second," he says softly.

I don't like the idea of going out there to face his mother alone, but I can't stay in the small space of this bedroom with Hardin. I take a deep breath and leave the room.

When I enter the kitchen, she looks over at me from where she stands at the sink. "He isn't upset with me, is he? I didn't mean to crowd you." Her voice is so sweet. A total contrast to her son's.

"Oh no, of course not. He was just . . . going over a few things about this week," I lie. I have always been a terrible liar, so I usually avoid it at all costs.

"Okay, good. I know how moody he can be." She smiles with such warmth that I can't help but smile back.

I pour my own glass of water to calm my nerves, and she begins to speak as I take a sip. "I still can't wrap my head around how beautiful you are. He told me you were the most beautiful girl he's ever seen, but I thought he was exaggerating."

Less gracefully than the most beautiful girl a boy's ever seen would do, I spit my water back into my glass. *Hardin said what?* I want to ask her to verify that, but instead I just take another sip of water to mask my embarrassing reaction.

She laughs. "Honestly, I thought you would be covered in tattoos and have green hair or something."

"No, no tattoos for me. Or green hair." I laugh and feel my shoulders begin to relax.

"You're an English major like Hardin, right?"

"Yes, ma'am."

"Ma'am? Call me Trish."

"I actually have an internship at Vance Publishing, so my class schedule is kind of weird. And right now we're on break."

"Vance? As in Christian Vance?" she asks. I nod. "Oh, I haven't seen Christian in at least . . . ten years." She looks down at the glass of water in my hands. "Hardin and I actually lived with him for a year after Ken . . . Well, never mind, Hardin doesn't like when I spout off at the mouth." She chuckles nervously.

I didn't know that Hardin and his mother stayed with Mr. Vance, but I knew that he was very close with him, closer than he would be if Christian were only his father's friend.

"I know about Ken," I say to Trish in an attempt to ease her discomfort, but then I immediately worry that I've implied I know about what happened to *her*, and I worry I've upset her.

So when she replies, "You do?" I try to hedge a little and follow up with, "Yeah, Hardin has told me . . ."

But when Hardin appears in the kitchen I stop, and I have to admit I'm happy for the intrusion.

He raises a brow. "Hardin has told you what?"

My tension goes through the roof, but to my surprise, his mother covers, saying, "Nothing, son, just some girl talk," and walking over to him and wrapping her arm around his waist. He pulls away slightly, as if out of instinct. She frowns, but I get the feeling this is a normal interaction between them.

The dryer beeps, and I take that as my cue to exit the room and finish up my laundry so I can get out of here, fast.

I pull my warm clothes from the dryer and sit on the floor in the small laundry room to fold them. Hardin's mother is so sweet, and I find myself wishing that I could have met her under different circumstances. I don't feel anger toward Hardin; I have been angry long enough. I feel sadness, and a longing for what we could have been.

After I'm done with my clothes, I go to the bedroom to repack my bags. I wish I hadn't hung any clothes in the closet or put food in the kitchen.

"Do you need some help, dear?" Trish asks me.

"Um, I was just getting my things ready to go to my mother's for the week," I reply, figuring I might as well just go there since the motel is expensive.

"You're leaving today? Right now?" She frowns.

"Yeah . . . I told her I would come for Christmas." For once I want Hardin to come into the room to help me talk my way out of this.

"Oh, I was hoping you would stay at least a night. Who knows when I'll be able to see you again—and I would love to get to know the young woman who my son has fallen in love with."

And suddenly something in me wants to make this woman happy. I don't know if it's because of my mistake about saying I knew about Ken and her, or because of the way she covered for me in front of Hardin. But I do know I don't want to overthink this, so I silence my inner voice and just nod, and say, "Okay."

"*Really?* You'll stay? Just one night, then you can go to your mum's house. You don't want to be driving through that snow anyway." She wraps her arms around me and hugs me for the fifth time today.

At least she'll be here to be a buffer between Hardin and me. We can't fight if she's here. Well, I won't fight, at least. I know this is probably . . . certainly the worst idea, but Trish is hard to say no to. Just like her son.

"Well, I'm going to take a quick shower. I had a long flight!" She smiles broadly and heads out.

I sink down onto the bed and close my eyes. This is going to be the most awkward, painful twenty-four hours of my life. No matter what I do, I always seem to end up back where I started, with him.

After a few minutes I open my eyes to find Hardin standing in front of the closet with his back to me. "Sorry, I didn't mean to bother you," he says when he turns back around. I sit up. He is being so strange, apologizing every other word. "I see that you cleaned the apartment," he says softly.

"Yeah . . . I couldn't help it." I smile, and so does he. "Hardin, I told your mom that I would stay tonight. Only tonight, but if that's not okay, I'll go. I just felt bad because she's so nice, and I couldn't say no, but if that makes you uncomfor—"

"Tessa, it's fine," he says quickly, but then his voice shakes when he adds, "I want you to stay."

I don't know what to say, and I don't understand this strange turn of events. I want to thank him for the present, but there is just too much going on inside of my head.

"Did you have a nice birthday yesterday?" he asks.

"Oh, yeah. Landon came by."

"Oh . . ." But then we hear his mother in the living room, and he moves to go. He stops before walking through the door and turns to me. "I don't know how I'm supposed to act."

I sigh. "Me either."

At that, he nods, and we both get up to join his mother in the other room.

chapter twenty-four

TESSA

When Hardin and I enter the living room, his mother is sitting on the couch with her wet hair pulled into a bun. She looks so young for her age, so stunning. "We should rent some movies, and I'll make dinner for all of us!" she exclaims. "Don't you miss my cooking, dumpling?"

Hardin rolls his eyes and shrugs. "Sure. Best cook ever."

This couldn't possibly be more awkward.

"Hey! I'm not that bad." She laughs. "And I think *you* just talked yourself into being chef tonight."

I shift uncomfortably, unsure how to behave around Hardin unless we're together or fighting. This is an odd place for us, though I suddenly realize this is a pattern of ours: Karen and Ken had been under the impression that we were dating before we actually were.

"Can you cook, Tessa?" Trish asks, breaking my thoughts. "Or is it Hardin, too?"

"Um, we both do. Maybe more 'preparing' than cooking, really," I answer.

"I'm glad to hear that you're taking care of my boy, and this apartment is so nice, too. I suspect Tessa does the cleaning," she teases.

I'm not "taking care of her boy," since that's what he's missing out on for hurting me the way he did. "Yeah . . . he's a slob," I answer.

Hardin looks down at me with a small smile playing on his lips. "I'm not a slob—she's just too clean."

I roll my eyes. "He's a slob," Trish and I say in unison.

"Are we going to watch a movie or pick on me all night?" Hardin is pouting.

I sit down before Hardin does so I don't have to make the uncomfortable decision about where to sit. I can see him eyeing the couch and me, silently deciding what to do. After a moment, he sits right next to me, so I feel the familiar heat from his proximity.

"What do you want to watch?" his mother asks us.

"It doesn't matter," Hardin replies.

"You can choose." I try to soften his answer.

She smiles at me before choosing 50 First Dates, a movie I'm sure Hardin will hate.

And right on cue, Hardin groans as it begins. "This movie is old as shit."

"Shhh," I say, and he huffs but stays quiet.

I catch him staring at me several times while Trish and I laugh and sigh along with the movie. I'm actually enjoying myself, and for a few moments I almost forget everything that has happened between Hardin and me. It's hard not to lean into Hardin, not to touch his hands, not to move his hair when it falls onto his forehead.

"I'm hungry," he mumbles when the movie ends.

"Why don't you and Tessa cook, since I had such a long flight?" Trish smiles.

"You're really milking this long-flight thing, aren't you?" he says to her.

She nods with a wry smile that I've seen on Hardin's face a few times.

"I can cook, it's okay," I offer and stand up. I walk into the kitchen and lean against the counter. I grip the edges of the marble countertop harder than necessary, trying to catch my breath. I don't know how long I can do this, pretend that Hardin didn't destroy everything, pretend that I love him. *I do love him, I am miserably in love with him.* The problem is not my lack of feelings toward this moody, egotistical boy. The problem is that I've given him so many chances, always dismissing the hateful things that he says and does. But this time it's too much.

"Hardin, be a gentleman and help her," I hear Trish say, and I rush over to the freezer to pretend like I wasn't having a mini breakdown.

"Um . . . I can help?" His voice carries through the small kitchen.

"Okay . . ." I answer.

"Popsicles?" he asks, and I look at the object in my hands. I had meant to grab chicken, but I was distracted.

"Yeah. Everyone likes Popsicles, right?" I say, and he smiles, revealing those evil dimples of his.

I can do this. I can be around Hardin. I can be nice to him, and we can get along.

"You should make that chicken pasta that you made for me," I suggest.

His green eyes focus on me. "That's what you want to eat?"

"Yes. If it's not too much trouble."

"Of course not."

"You're being so weird today," I whisper so our houseguest doesn't hear.

"No, I'm not." He shrugs and steps toward me.

My heart begins to race as he leans in. As I move to step away, he grabs the door to the freezer and pulls it open.

I thought he was going to kiss me. What the hell is wrong with me?

We cook dinner in almost complete silence, neither of us knowing what to say. My eyes watching him the entire time, the way his long fingers curl around the base of the knife to chop the chicken and the vegetables, the way he closes his eyes when the steam from the boiling water hits his face, the way his tongue swipes the corners of his mouth when he tastes the sauce. I know that observing him like this isn't conducive to being impartial, or healthy in any way, but I can't help it.

"I'll set the table while you tell your mom it's ready," I say when it's finally done.

"What? I'll just call her."

"No, that's rude. Just go get her," I say.

He rolls his eyes but obeys anyway, only to return seconds later, alone. "She's asleep," he tells me.

I heard him, but I still ask, "What?"

"Yeah, she's passed out on the couch. Should I just wake her up?"

"No . . . She had a long day. I'll put some food away for her so whenever she gets up she can eat. It's sort of late anyway."

"It's eight."

"Yeah . . . that's late."

"I guess." His voice is flat.

"What is with you? I know this is uncomfortable and all, but you are being so *weird*," I say as I put food on two plates without thinking.

"Thanks." he says and grabs one before sitting down at the table.

I grab a fork from the drawer and opt to stand at the counter to eat. "Are you going to tell me?"

"Tell you what?" He grabs a forkful of chicken and digs in.

"Why you're being so . . . quiet and . . . nice. It's weird."

He takes a moment to chew then swallow before he answers. "I just don't want to say the wrong thing."

"Oh" is all I can think to say. Well, *that's* not what I expected to hear.

He turns the tables on me then. "So why are *you* being so nice and weird?"

"Because your mother is here and what happened, happened—there's nothing I can do to change it. I can't hold on to that anger forever." I lean against the counter on my elbow.

"So what does that mean?"

"Nothing. I'm just saying that I want to be civil and not fight anymore. It doesn't change anything between us." I bite my cheek to keep my eyes from tearing up.

Instead of saying anything, Hardin stands up and throws his plate into the sink. The porcelain splits down the middle with a loud crack that causes me to jump. Hardin doesn't flinch or even turn back around as he stalks off to the bedroom.

I peer into the living room to make sure that his impulsive behavior hasn't woken up his mother. Fortunately, she's still asleep, her mouth slightly open in a way that makes her resemblance to her son all the stronger.

As usual, I'm left to clean up the mess that Hardin made. I load the dishwasher and put away the leftovers before wiping down the counter. I'm exhausted, mentally more than physically, but I need to take a shower and go to bed. But where the hell am I going to sleep? Hardin is in the bedroom and Trish is on the couch. Maybe I should just drive back to the motel.

I turn the heat up a little and switch off the light in the living room. When I walk into the bedroom to get my pajamas, Hardin is sitting on the edge of the bed, his elbows on his knees and his head in his hands. He doesn't look up, so I grab a pair of shorts and a T-shirt and panties from my bag before exiting the room. As I hit the doorway, I hear what sounds like a muffled sob.

Is Hardin crying?

He isn't. He couldn't be.

On the off chance that he is, I can't leave the room. I pad back to the bed and stand in front of him. "Hardin?" I say quietly and try to remove his hands from his face. He resists, but I pull harder. "Look at me," I beg.

The breath is knocked out of me when he does. His eyes are bloodshot and his cheeks are soaked with tears. I try to take his hands in mine, but he jerks away. "Just go, Tessa," he says.

I've heard him say that too many times. "No," I say and kneel down between his opened legs.

He wipes his eyes with the back of his hands. "This was a bad idea. I'm going to tell my mum in the morning."

"You don't have to." I've seen him let out a few tears before, but never full-on, body-shaking, tears-streaming-down-his-face crying.

"Yeah, I do. This is torture for me to have you so close but so far. It's the worst possible punishment. Not that I don't deserve it, because I know I do, but it's too much," he sobs. "Even for me." He draws in a deep, desperate breath. "When you agreed to stay . . . I thought that maybe . . . maybe you still cared for me the way I do for you. But I see it, Tess, I see the way you look at me now. I see the pain I've caused. I see the change in you because of me. I know that I did this, but it still kills me to have you slip through my fingers." The tears come much faster now, falling against his black T-shirt.

I want to say something—anything—to make this stop. To make his pain go away.

But where was he when I was crying myself to sleep night after night?

"You want me to go?" I ask, and he nods.

His rejection hurts, even now. I know I shouldn't be here, we shouldn't be doing this, but I need more. I need more time with him. Even dangerous, painful time is better than no time. I wish I didn't love him, that I had never met him.

But I did. And I do love him.

"Okay." I swallow and stand up.

His hand grips my wrist to stop me. "I'm sorry. For everything, for hurting you, for everything," he says, goodbye thick in his tone.

As much as I resist this, I know deep down that I'm not ready for him to give up on me. On the other hand, I'm not ready to easily forgive him either. I've been in a constant state of confusion for days, but today takes the cake.

"I . . ." I stop myself.

"What?"

"I don't want to go," I say so low that I'm not sure he even heard me.

"What?" he asks again.

"I don't want to go. I know I should, but I don't want to. Not tonight at least." I swear I can see the pieces of the broken man in front of me slowly come back together, one by one. It's a beautiful sight, but terrifying deep in my soul, too.

"What does this mean?"

"I don't know what it means, but I'm not ready to find out either," I say, hoping to be able to get at this feeling by talking about it.

Hardin looks at me blankly, his earlier sobs nowhere to be find. Robotically, he wipes his face with his shirt and says, "Okay. You can sleep on the bed, I'll take the floor."

As he grabs two pillows and the throw blanket from the bed, my mind can't help but entertain the thought that maybe, just maybe, all those tears were for show. Still, somehow I know that they couldn't have been.

chapter twenty-five

TESSA

Tucked like I am under our comforter, the thought that keeps going through my mind is that I never, ever would have thought I'd witness anything like that from Hardin. He was so raw, so vulnerable, as his body shook with tears. I feel like the dynamic between Hardin and me is constantly shifting, so that one of us is always gaining an upper hand over the other. Right now, I would be the one in control.

But I don't want to be. And I don't like this dynamic. Love shouldn't be such a battle. Besides, I don't trust myself to be in control of what happens between us. Up until a few hours ago I had it all figured out, but now, after seeing him so shaken up, my mind is muddled and my thoughts clouded.

Even in the darkness, I can feel Hardin's eyes on me. When I let out the breath I realized I was holding, he quickly asks, "Do you want me to turn the television on?"

"No. If you want to, you can, but I'm okay," I answer.

I wish that I had grabbed my e-reader so I could read until I fell asleep. Maybe observing the ruination of Catherine and Heathcliff's lives would make mine seem easier, less traumatic. Catherine spent her whole life trying to fight her love for that man, on and off until the day she begged for his forgiveness and claimed she could not live without him—only to die hours later. I could live without Hardin, couldn't I? I won't spend my entire life fighting this. This is only temporary . . . Right? We won't bring ourselves and others misery because of our stubbornness and hard heads, right? I'm bothered by the uncertainty of this parallel, especially since it means I start comparing Trevor to Edgar. I don't know how to feel about this. It's awkward.

"Tess?" my very own Heathcliff calls, wresting me away from my thoughts.

"Yeah?" I croak.

"I didn't fuck . . . *sleep with* Molly," he says, as if correcting his foul language makes the statement any less shocking.

I stay silent, partly stunned by him talking about this, partly because I want to believe him. But I can't allow myself to forget that he's a master of deception.

"I swear it," he adds.

Oh, well, if he "swears" it . . . "Why did you say that, then?" I ask harshly.

"To hurt you. I was just so mad because you said you kissed someone, so I just said the thing that I knew would hurt you the most."

I can't see Hardin, but somehow I know that he's lying on his back, his arms crossed, hands under his head, staring at the ceiling. "Did you really kiss someone?" he asks before I can respond.

"Yeah," I admit. But when I hear the suction of a deep breath, I try to soften the blow by adding, "Only once."

"Why?" His voice is cool yet heated. It's a strange sound.

"I honestly have no idea . . . I was mad because of how you were acting on the phone, and I had way too much to drink. So I danced with this guy, and he kissed me."

"You danced with him? Danced how?" he asks.

I roll my eyes at Hardin's needing to know every detail of what I do, even when we aren't together. "You don't want me to answer that."

His words thicken the air between us again. "Yes, I do."

"Hardin, we just danced like people do at a club. Then he kissed me and tried to get me to go home with him." I stare at the blades on the ceiling fan. I know that if we keep talking about this, they will eventually be forced to stop, unable to cut through the tension.

I try to change the subject. "Thank you for the e-reader. It was very thoughtful."

"He tried to get you to go home with him? Did you?" I hear him shuffling, giving me an indication that he's now sitting up.

I remain flat against the mattress. "Do you even have to ask that? You know I would never do that," I snap.

"Well, I never thought you would be kissing and dancing at a club either," he barks.

After a few beats of silence I speak. "I don't think you want to get started on the unexpected."

The blankets shuffle again, and I can feel him right next to me. That voice is right next to me. "Tell me, please tell me, that you didn't."

He sits down on the bed next to me and I move away from him. "You know I didn't. I saw *you* later that night."

"I need to hear you say it." His voice is harsh but pleading. "Say that you only kissed him once and you haven't spoken to him since."

"I only kissed him once and I haven't spoken to him since," I repeat, only because I know he desperately needs to hear the words.

I keep my eyes focused on the swirl of ink poking out from the low collar of his shirt. Having him on the bed soothes me and burns me all at once. I can't stand the internal battle I'm stuck in the middle of.

"Is there anything else I should know?" he asks softly.

"No," I lie. I am not telling him about the date with Trevor. Nothing happened and it's none of Hardin's business. I like Trevor, and I want to keep him safe from the time bomb that is Hardin.

"You sure?"

"Hardin . . . I don't really think you're in the position to be hounding me," I say and look into his eyes. I can't help it.

"I know," he surprises me by saying.

When he moves off of the bed, I try to ignore the emptiness that takes me over.

chapter twenty-six

HARDIN

Today has been hell. A hell that I welcomed with open arms, but hell all the same. I never expected to see Tessa when I came home from the airport. I had come up with a simple lie: my girlfriend wouldn't be available because she'd be out of town all week for Christmas. My mum had whined a little but didn't ask too many questions or push my story. She had been so thrilled—and surprised, really—that I had a woman in my life. I think her and my father both expected me to be alone my entire life. Then again, so did I.

I find it amusing, in a twisted way, that I can't go a second without thinking of this girl, when up until three months ago I wanted to be alone. I never knew what I was missing, and now that I found it, I can't let it go. It's only her, though; no matter what I do, I can't shake her.

I tried to stop, tried to forget about her, tried to move on . . . and it was a disaster. The perfectly nice blonde that I took out Saturday night wasn't Tessa. No one would ever be. Sure, she looked like her, even dressed like her. She blushed when I cursed and seemed a little afraid of me throughout our dinner. She was nice enough, yeah, but she was boring.

She was missing that fire that Tess has—she didn't scold me for my foul language, she didn't even say anything when I put my hand on her thigh in the middle of dinner. I knew she only agreed to go out with me to fulfill some fucked-up bad-boy fantasy before church the next morning, but that's okay, because I was using her, too. I was using her to fill the void of Tessa. To distract me from Tessa being in Seattle still with fucking Trevor. The guilt I felt when I moved in to kiss her was overwhelming. I pulled away, and the embarrassment was clear on her innocent face—I practically ran to my car, leaving her stranded at the restaurant.

I sit up further and look at the sleeping girl that I am desperately in love with. Seeing her in our apartment with her clothes in the washer, the apartment clean, and even her toothbrush in the bathroom . . . it gave me a little bit of hope. But then again, you know what they say about hope.

I'm still holding on to the sliver that exists, the small chance that she may forgive me. If she woke up now, she would surely scream at the sight of me standing over her as she sleeps.

I know I need to take it down a few notches. I need to give her a little space. This behavior and these feelings are so exhausting, so overwhelming to me, and I have no fucking idea how to deal with them. But I *will* figure this out—I have to fix all of this. I push a loose strand of her soft hair from her face and force myself away from the bed, back to my pile of blankets, on the concrete floor, where I belong.

Maybe I'll be able to sleep tonight.

chapter twenty-seven

TESSA

When I wake up, I'm momentarily confused by the brick ceiling above me. It's strange to wake up here after staying in hotels for the past week. When I climb out of bed, the floor is clear, with the blanket and pillows piled next to the closet. Grabbing my toiletry bag, I head to the bathroom.

I hear Hardin's voice from the living room: "She can't stay today, Mum. Her mother is expecting her."

"Couldn't we have her mom come here? I would love to meet her," Trish responds.

Oh no.

"No, her mother is . . . not very fond of me," he says.

"Why not?"

"She doesn't think I'm good enough for Tessa, I guess. And maybe because of how I look."

"How you look? Hardin, don't you ever let anyone make you feel insecure. I thought you loved your . . . style?"

"I do. I mean, I don't give a shit what anyone thinks. Except Tessa."

As my mouth falls open, Trish laughs. "Who are you, and where is my boy?" Then, with real happiness in her voice, she says, "I can't even remember the last conversation we had where you didn't curse me out, it's been years. This is nice."

"Okay . . . okay . . ." Hardin groans and I giggle while imagining Trish trying to hug him.

* * *

AFTER MY SHOWER I decide to get myself all the way ready before leaving the bathroom. I'm a coward, I know, but I need a little more time before I put on a fake smile for Hardin's mother. It's not exactly a fake smile . . . *And that's part of the problem*, my subconscious reminds me. I had a really nice time yesterday, and I slept better than I have all week.

Once my hair is curled to near perfection, I pack my toiletries back into my small bag. There's a light tap on the door. "Tess?" Hardin asks.

"I'm finished," I respond and open the door to find him leaning against the door, wearing long gray cotton shorts and a white T-shirt.

"Not to rush you or anything, but I really have to piss."

He gives me a small smile and I nod. I try not to notice the way his shorts hang on his hips, making the cursive writing that's inked onto his side even more visible under the white T-shirt.

"I'm going to get dressed, then be on my way," I tell him.

He looks away, focusing on the wall. "Okay."

I go to the bedroom, feeling terribly guilty about lying to his mother and leaving so soon. I know she was so excited to meet me, and here I am leaving on her second day.

Deciding on my white dress, I put on my old black tights underneath since it's too cold without them. I probably should just put on jeans and a sweatshirt, but I love that the dress gives me a strange sense of confidence, which is something that I need today. I pack my clothes back into my bags and place the hangers back in the closet.

"Do you need some help?" Trish says from behind me. I jump, dropping the navy dress that I wore in Seattle.

"I was just . . ." I fumble.

Her eyes examine the half-empty closet. "How long are you planning on being at your mother's?"

"Um . . . I . . ." I'm a really terrible liar.

"Looks like you're going to be gone for a while."

"Yeah . . . I don't have many clothes," I squeak.

"I was going to see if you wanted to do some shopping while I was here; maybe if you come back before I leave, we can go?"

I can't tell if she believes me or if she suspects that I don't ever plan on returning here. "Yeah . . . sure," I lie again.

"Mum . . ." Hardin says in a low voice as he enters the room. I notice his frown as his eyes take in the empty closet, and hope that Trish isn't observing her son the way that I am.

"Just finishing packing," I explain, and he nods. I zip the last bag and look at him, completely unsure what I should say.

"I'll take your bags down for you," he says, grabbing my keys from the dresser and disappearing with my things.

As he leaves, Trish's arms wrap around my shoulders. "I'm so glad that I got to meet you, Tessa. You have no idea what it means to me as a mother to see my only child this way."

"What way?" I manage to ask.

"Happy," she replies and my eyes begin to sting.

If this is happy Hardin to her, I don't want to see her usual Hardin.

I say my final goodbye to Trish and prepare to leave the apartment for the last time.

"Tessa?" Hardin's mother says plainly. I turn around to face her once more.

"You'll come back to him, won't you?" she asks, and my heart sinks. I get the feeling she means more than coming back after Christmas break.

I don't trust my voice. So I just nod and quickly exit.

When I reach the elevator, I turn around and head to the

stairs to avoid seeing Hardin. I wipe the corners of my eyes and take a deep breath before walking out into the snow. When I reach my car, I notice that the windshield has been cleared of snow and the engine is running.

I DECIDE NOT TO CALL my mother to tell her that I'm on my way. I don't feel like talking to her right now. I want to use this two-hour drive to try to clear my head. I need to make a mental list of the pros and cons of being with Hardin again. I know how stupid I am for even entertaining the thought—he has done terrible things to me. He has lied to me, betrayed me, and humiliated me. So far, on the cons list we have the lies, the sheets, the condom, the bet, his temper, his friends, Molly, his ego, his attitude, and him destroying my trust.

On the pros list I have . . . well . . . I have the fact that I love him. That he makes me happy, makes me feel stronger, more confident. That he usually wants the best for me, unless, of course, he's the one doing the damage in his reckless way . . . The way he laughs and smiles, the way he holds me, the way he kisses me, the way he hugs me, the way I can tell he is changing for me.

I know my pros list is full of small things, especially compared to the large negatives, but the small things are the most important, right? I can't decide if I'm completely insane for even thinking about forgiving him, or if I'm doing what love dictates. Which will guide me best in love—my feelings or my mind?

As much as I try to fight it, I can't stay away from him. I never have been able to.

This would be a good time to have a friend to talk to, a friend that has been in this type of situation before. I wish I could call Steph, but she lied to me the whole time, too. I would call Landon, but he's already told me his opinion, and sometimes a woman's point of view is better, more relatable.

The snow is thick and the wind is strong, nudging at my car on the deserted roads. I should have just stayed in the hotel—I have no idea what possessed me to come here. Still, despite some scary moments, the drive goes much quicker than I thought it would, and before I know it, my mother's house looms before me.

I pull into her neatly shoveled driveway, and after three knocks she finally opens the door, wearing a robe, her hair wet. I can count the times in my life that I've seen her without her hair and makeup done on one hand.

"What are you doing here? Why didn't you call?" she fires off, as unfriendly as ever.

I step inside. "I don't know; I was driving through the snow and didn't want to be distracted."

"You still should have called so I could have been ready."

"You don't need to be ready, it's only me."

She huffs. "There is never an excuse to look like a slob, Tessa," she says with a tone as if she's telling *me* about *my* current state. I almost laugh at her ridiculous comment, but I decide against it.

"Where are your bags?" she asks.

"In my car, I'll get them later."

"What is that . . . that dress you are wearing?" Her eyes scan my body and I smile.

"It's for work. I really like it."

"It's way too revealing . . . but the color is nice, I suppose."

"Thanks. So how are the Porters?" I ask. I know bringing up Noah's family will distract her.

"They're great. They miss seeing you." As she goes into the kitchen she says casually over her shoulder, "Maybe we should invite them over for dinner tonight."

I cringe and scurry after her. "Oh, I don't think that's a good idea."

She looks at me, then pours herself cup of coffee. "Why not?"

"I don't know . . . it would be awkward for me."

"Theresa, you have known the Porters for years. I would love for them to see you now that you have an internship as well as going to college."

"So you basically want me to show off?" The thought annoys me. She only wants to have them over so she can have another thing to brag about.

"No, I want to show them the things that you've accomplished. It's not showing off," she snaps.

"I really would rather not."

"Well, Theresa, this is my house, and if I want to invite them, I will. I'm going to finish getting myself presentable, and then I'll be back." And with a dramatic turn, she leaves me in the kitchen alone.

I roll my eyes and walk back to my old bedroom. Tired, I lie down on the bed and wait for my mother to finish her extensive beautification rituals.

"THERESA?" MY MOTHER'S VOICE wakes me up. I don't even remember falling asleep.

I lift my face up from where it was resting on Buddha, my ancient stuffed elephant, and say a disoriented "Coming!"

I drowsily get to my feet and wobble down the hall. When I reach the living room, Noah is sitting on the couch. Not the entire Porter clan, as my mother had threatened, but this does wake me up.

"Look who stopped by while you were napping!" my mother says, smiling her fakest smile.

"Hey," I reply, but am really thinking, *I knew I shouldn't have come here.*

Noah waves a slight hand at me. "Hey, Tessa, you look great."

Of course, I have no problem with Noah at all—I care for

him deeply, like a family member. But I need a break from everything going on in my life, and him being here only adds to my guilt and pain. I know it isn't his fault and it's not fair for me to be short with him, especially when he's been so kind throughout our whole breakup.

My mother leaves the room, and I pull my shoes off and sit down on the couch, opposite Noah. "How's your break going?" he asks.

"Good, yours?"

"Same. Your mom said you went to Seattle?"

"Yeah, it was great. I went with my boss and some coworkers."

He nods excitedly. "That's awesome, Tessa. I'm happy for you—you're really doing the publishing thing!"

"Thank you." I smile. This isn't as awkward as I thought it would be.

After a moment, he looks down the hall where my mother disappeared, then leans in close. "Hey, so, your mom has been so tense since Saturday. I mean more than usual. How are you doing with all of this?"

I scrunch up my brows. "What do you mean?"

"The whole thing with your dad?" he says slowly like I know what he's talking about.

What? "My dad?"

"She didn't tell you?" He looks down the empty hall. "Oh . . . Don't tell her I told—"

Before he can finish, I'm on my feet and storming down the hallway to her room. "Mother!"

What the hell about my dad? I haven't seen or heard from him in eight years. The way Noah was acting kind of solemn . . . *Did he die?* I don't know how I'd feel about that.

"What about Dad?" I raise my voice as I burst into her room. Her eyes go wide but she composes herself quickly. *"Well?"* I shout.

She rolls her eyes. "Tessa, you need to lower your voice. It is nothing, nothing that you need to worry about."

"That's not for you to decide—tell me what's going on! Is he dead?"

"Dead? Oh no. I would tell you if he was," she says and drops a hand as if to pooh-pooh me.

"Then what is it?"

She sighs and looks at me for a second. "He's moved back. Not too far from where you are now, but he won't be contacting you, so don't you worry about it. I took care of it."

"What does that even *mean*?" I don't have enough space in my head for all of this crap with Hardin, and now my absentee father is moving back to Washington. Now that I think about it, I didn't know he moved away in the first place. I only knew he wasn't around *me*.

"It doesn't mean anything. I was going to tell you when I called you Friday night, but since you couldn't be bothered to pick up the phone, I handled it myself."

I was too drunk to answer that night—thank goodness I didn't. I could have never handled this wasted. I can barely handle it now.

"He isn't going to bother you, so wipe that sad look off of your face and get ready, we're going to do some shopping," she says, too indifferently.

"I don't really want to go shopping, Mother. This is sort of a big deal to me, you know."

"No, it isn't," she says, full of annoyance and venom. "He hasn't been around for years. He still won't be around now, nothing has changed." She disappears into her closet, and I realize there's no use arguing with her.

I walk back to the living room, grab my phone, and put my shoes on.

"Where are you guys going?" Noah asks.

"Who knows," I say and walk out into the chill air.

I wasted all this time coming here, two hours of driving in the snow just to have her be a complete witch . . . no, *bitch*. She's a complete *bitch*. I wipe the snow off my windshield with my arm; a terrible idea, since it only freezes me further. Climbing inside the car, I clench my rattling teeth as I start the engine and wait for it to heat up somewhat.

As I drive, I scream, repeatedly calling my mother every foul name I can think of. When I've exhausted my voice, I try to figure out what to do next, but memories of my father flood my mind, and I can't concentrate on anything. Tears soaking my cheeks, I grab my phone off the passenger seat.

In a few seconds, Hardin's voice booms through the small speaker. "*Tess?* Are you okay?"

"Yeah . . ." I start, but my voice betrays me and I choke on a sob.

"What happened? What did she do?"

"She . . . can I come back?" I ask, and he lets out a deep breath.

"Of course you can, baby . . . Tessa." He corrects himself, but I find myself wishing we hadn't.

"How far are you?" he asks.

"Twenty minutes," I cry.

"Okay, do you want to stay on the phone?"

"No . . . it's snowing," I explain and hang up.

I shouldn't have left in the first place. It's ironic that I'm running to Hardin despite everything he has done.

Far too long later, when I pull into the parking lot, I'm still crying. I wipe my face the best I can, but my makeup streaks and dirties my face. When I step out into the snow, I see Hardin standing by the door covered in snow. Without thinking, I run over and wrap my arms around him. He steps back, obviously thrown off by my affection, but then he wraps his arms around me and lets me cry into his snow-covered sweatshirt.

chapter twenty-eight

HARDIN

Holding her for the first time in what seems like a lifetime is better than I could even begin to describe. Physical relief floods through me when she runs into my arms—I never expected this to happen. She has been so distant, so cold lately. I don't blame her, but fuck if it hasn't hurt.

"Are you okay?" I ask into her hair.

She nods her head up and down against my chest but continues to cry. I know she isn't okay. Her mother probably said some shit to her that she shouldn't have. I knew this would happen, and honestly, the greedy part of me is glad for whatever she did. Not because she hurt Tessa, but because it meant my girl ran to me for comfort.

"Let's go inside," I say.

She nods but doesn't let go of me, so I force myself to release my arms from her and walk us both inside. Her beautiful face is marked with black streaks and her eyes and lips are swollen. I hope she didn't cry the whole drive.

As soon as we step into the lobby, I pull out the scarf I brought down and wrap it around her head and ears, making a soft purple bundle around her beautiful face. She must be cold only wearing that dress. That dress . . . I would normally go into an extended fantasy about peeling the thin fabric off her. But not today, not while she's like this.

She lets out the cutest hiccup and pulls the scarf over her

head. Her blond hair sticks up out of the side in a big knot, making her look even younger than usual.

"Do you want to talk about it?" I take the small chance to ask her when we step off the elevator and walk down to our . . . the apartment.

She nods, and I unlock the door. My mum is sitting on the couch and worry spreads across her face as she takes in Tessa's appearance. I shoot her a warning glare, hoping she'll remember the promise she made to not bombard Tessa with questions about her return. Mum tears her eyes from Tessa and looks at the television, feigning indifference.

"We're going to go into the room for a little while," I announce, and my mum nods. I know it's driving her crazy not being able to talk, but I won't have her making Tessa feel any worse by prying.

As we go, I pause at the thermostat in the hallway to turn the heat up, since I know she's freezing. When I step into the room, Tessa's already sitting on the edge of the bed. Unsure of how close I'm allowed to get, I wait for her to say something.

"Hardin?" she says in a weak voice. The hoarse tone of her voice tells me she *had* been crying the whole drive, and it makes me feel worse for her.

I go stand in front of her and she surprises me again by grabbing hold of my T-shirt and pulling me to stand between her legs. This is more than her mum saying some rude shit.

"Tess . . . what did she do?" I ask as she starts crying again, smearing her makeup on the bottom of my white shirt. I could give a shit about the mess; if anything, it will give me a reminder of her when she leaves again.

"My dad . . ." she croaks, and I go rigid.

"Your dad?" If he was there . . . "Tessa, was he there? Did he do something to you?" I ask her through my teeth.

She shakes her head no, and I reach down to lift her chin up, forcing her to look at me. She's never quiet, even when upset. That's usually when she's the most vocal.

"He moved back here—but I didn't even know he left. I mean, I guess I did, but I never thought about it. I never thought about him."

My voice is not as calm as I mean for it to be when I ask, "Did you talk to him today?"

"No; she did, though. She said he isn't going to come near me, but I don't want her making that choice for me."

"You want to see him?" All of the things she has told me about this man have been negative. He was violent, often smacking her mum around in front of her. Why would she want to see *him*?

"No . . . well, I don't know. But *I* want to be the one to decide." She dabs at her eyes with the back of her hand. "Not that he would even want to see me . . ."

The instinct to hunt this man down and make sure he doesn't come near her takes over, and I have to talk myself down before I do something stupid and brash.

"I can't help but think, what if he's like *your* dad?"

"What do you mean?"

"What if he's different now? What if he doesn't drink anymore?" The hope in her voice breaks my heart . . . well, what's left of it.

"I don't know . . . that usually doesn't happen," I tell her honestly. I see the way her mouth turns down at the ends, so I continue: "But it could. Maybe he's different now . . ." I don't believe it, but who am I to extinguish her hope? "I didn't know you had any interest in him."

"I don't . . . well, I didn't. I'm just angry because my mother kept it from me . . ." she says, and then, between bouts of wiping her nose and face against my shirt, she tells me the rest of what happened. Tessa's mother is the only woman who would reveal the return of her alcoholic ex-husband and then promptly mention going shopping. I keep my mouth shut about Noah being there even though it pisses me off. That kid just won't seem to go away.

Finally she looks up at me, a bit calmer. She seems much better than she was when she ran to me in the parking lot, and I would like to think that's because she's here with me. "It's okay that I'm here, right?" she asks.

"Yeah . . . of course. You can stay as long as you need to. It is your apartment, after all."

I try to smile, and surprisingly she returns the gesture before wiping her nose on my shirt again. "I should have a dorm room next week."

I nod; if I speak, I'll end up pathetically begging her not to leave me again.

chapter twenty-nine

TESSA

I walk to the bathroom to remove the makeup from my face and pull myself together. The warm water washes away all evidence of my eventful morning, and I'm actually glad to be back here. Despite everything that Hardin and I have been through, I'm glad to know that I still have a safe place to land with him. He is the only constant in my life; I remember him saying that to me once. I wonder if he meant it then.

Even if he didn't, I believe that he feels that way now. I just wish he would tell me more about how he feels. Seeing him break down yesterday was the most emotion that I've seen out of him since we met. I just want to hear the words behind the tears.

I go back into the bedroom to find Hardin setting my bags down on the floor. "I went down and got your stuff," he informs me.

"Thank you, I really hope I'm not intruding," I tell him and bend down to grab some sweats and a T-shirt. I have to get out of this dress.

"I want you here, you know that, don't you?" he says quietly. I shrug and he frowns. "You should know that by now, Tess."

"I do . . . it's just that your mother is here, and here I am bringing all this drama and crying," I explain.

"My mum is glad that you're here, and so am I."

My chest swells, but I change the subject. "Do you guys have anything planned today?"

"I think she wanted to go to the mall or something, but we can go tomorrow."

"You can go, I can keep myself entertained." I don't want him to cancel plans with his mother when he hasn't seen her in over a year.

"No, it's fine, really. You don't need to be alone."

"I'm fine."

"Tessa, what did I just say?" he growls and I look up at him. He seems to have forgotten that he doesn't get to decide things for me anymore. No one does.

He softens and corrects himself. "Sorry . . . you stay here. I'll go shopping with her."

"Much better," I say and try to fight my smile.

Hardin has been so gentle, so . . . *afraid* the last few days. Even if he was wrong to push me, it was kind of nice to see he's still himself.

I go into the closet to change my clothes, and just as I lift the dress over my head, he taps on the door. "Tess?"

"Yes?" I say.

After a beat he asks, "You'll be here when we get back?"

I snort. "Yeah. It's not like I have anywhere else to go."

"Okay. If you need anything, call me," he says; the sadness in his voice is clear.

A few minutes later I hear the front door close and I emerge from the bedroom. I probably should have gone with them so I wouldn't be here alone with my thoughts. I already feel lonely. After watching television for an hour, I am beyond bored. Periodically my phone buzzes and my mother's name flashes on-screen. I ignore her entirely and wish Hardin would come back already. I grab my e-reader and start to read to pass the time, but I can't stop looking at the clock.

I want to text Hardin and see how much longer they'll be, but instead I decide to make dinner to pass the time. I go into the kitchen to decide what to make, something that takes a while but is easy. Lasagna it is, then.

Soon it's eight, then eight thirty, and by nine I'm already thinking again that I'll text him.

What the hell is wrong with me? One fight with my mother and suddenly I'm back to clinging to Hardin? If I'm honest with myself, I know that I never truly stopped clinging to him. Even though I don't really want to admit it, I know that I'm not ready for a life without Hardin. I'm not going to jump into anything wholesale with him, but I'm exhausted from battling myself all the time over him. As terrible as he has been to me, I'm even more miserable without him than I was when I found out about the entire bet. Part of me is irritated at myself for my lack of strength, but another part can't deny how resolved I felt when I came back today. I still need a little time to think, to see how everything goes with us being around one another. I'm still so confused.

Nine fifteen. It's only nine fifteen when I finish setting the table and cleaning up the mess I made in the kitchen. I'll text him, just once, a simple Hey, how's it going? just to check on him. It's snowing, so I'm only texting him to check on him, you know, for safety reasons.

Just as I pick up my phone, the front door opens. I set my phone down covertly as Hardin and his mom enter.

"So, how was shopping?" I ask him at the same exact time that he says, "You made dinner?"

"You first," we both say and laugh.

I hold up one hand and inform him and Trish, "I made dinner. If you already ate, that's fine, too."

"It smells so good in here!" his mother says as she surveys the tableful of food. Immediately she drops her bags and drops into a seat at the table. "Thank you, Tessa dear. That mall was dreadful, all the last-minute Christmas shoppers filled the place. Who waits until two days before Christmas to get their gifts?"

"Um, *you*," Hardin answers and pours himself a glass of water.

"Oh, hush," she scolds and picks off the end of a breadstick to pop into her mouth.

Hardin sits down next to his mother, and I take the chair across from her. Over dinner Trish talks about the shopping horrors they experienced and how a man was tackled by security guards for trying to steal a dress from Macy's. Hardin swears that the dress was for the man himself, but Trish rolls her eyes and continues with the outlandish tale. I realize that the meal I prepared is actually quite good—better than usual—and almost the entire pan of lasagna is gone by the time the three of us finish. I had two servings myself—that's the last time I'll go all day without eating.

"Oh, we bought a tree," his mom says suddenly. "Just a small one, but you two have to have a tree in your place—especially your first Christmas together!" She claps her hands and I laugh.

Even before everything fell apart, Hardin and I had never talked about getting a Christmas tree. I had been so distracted by moving in, and just by Hardin in general, that I nearly forgot about the holidays altogether. Neither of us had taken any interest in Thanksgiving—him for obvious reasons and me because I didn't want to spend it at my mother's church, so we ordered pizza and hung out in my dorm room.

"That's okay, right?" Trish asks, making me realize I haven't responded.

"Oh yeah, of course it is," I tell her and look at Hardin, who is just staring at his empty plate.

Trish takes over the conversation again and I'm grateful. After a few more minutes she announces, "Well, as much as I'd love to stay awake with you party animals, I must get my beauty sleep." Thanking me again and putting her plate into the sink, she bids us good night before leaning down to kiss Hardin on his cheek. He groans and moves away, so her lips barely brush his skin, but she seems pleased with the small amount of contact. She wraps her arms around my shoulders, placing a kiss on the top of my head. Hardin rolls his eyes, and I kick him under the table. After she disappears I stand up and put away the few remaining left-overs.

"Thanks for making dinner. You didn't have to," Hardin tells me, and I nod before we both head into the bedroom.

"I can sleep on the floor tonight since you did last night," I offer, even though I know he wouldn't actually let me sleep on the floor.

"No, it's fine. It's actually not so bad," he says

I sit on the bed, and Hardin takes the blankets from the closet and lays them on the floor. I toss him two pillows, and he gives me a small smile before unbuttoning his jeans. *Oh, I definitely should look away*. I don't exactly want to, but I know that I should. He pulls his black jeans down and steps out of them. The way his muscles move on his tattooed stomach as he bends down has me unable to look away, reminding me just how attracted I am to him, despite my anger. His black boxers cling to his skin, and his head snaps up to look at me. His face, hard and concentrated on mine, only feeds my trance. His jawline is so sharp, so intriguing. He's still staring.

"Sorry," I say, and jerk my head to the side, my cheeks flaring in humiliation.

"No, I'm sorry. Just a habit, I guess." He shrugs and pulls a pair of cotton pants from the dresser.

I keep my eyes on the wall until he says "good night, Tess" and flicks the light off. I can practically hear the smirk in this tone.

I'M AWOKEN BY A SHARP SOUND and stare at the ceiling, I can barely see the blades of the fan moving through the darkness.

Then I hear it again, Hardin's voice. "No! Please!" he whimpers.

Shit, he's having one of his nightmares. I jump out of bed and kneel down beside his thrashing body.

"No!" he repeats, much louder this time.

"Hardin! Hardin, wake up!" I say into his ear and shake his shoulders.

His shirt is soaked with sweat and his face twisted as he opens his eyes, sitting up immediately. "Tess . . ." he breathes and pulls me into his arms.

I rub my fingers through his hair before bringing my hand down to his back. I gently run my hands up and down his back, my nails barely grazing his skin.

"It's okay," I tell him over and over again, and he hugs me tighter. "Come on, let's go to bed," I say and stand up. Holding on to my T-shirt, he climbs into the bed with me.

"Are you okay?" I ask him when he lies down.

He nods and I pull him closer to me. "Do you think you could get me some water?" he asks.

"Of course. I'll be right back."

I turn on the lamp before climbing back out of the bed, then try to keep as quiet as possible so as not to wake Trish. But I get to the kitchen, she's already there.

"Is he okay?" she asks.

"Yeah, he's okay now. I'm just getting him some water," I say to her and fill up a glass in the sink. When I turn back around, she pulls me into a hug and kisses my cheek.

"Can we talk tomorrow?" she asks.

Suddenly I'm too nervous to speak, so I just nod, which makes her smile, though she sniffles as I walk off.

Back in our room, Hardin looks slightly relieved when I return and thanks me as he takes the water from my hand. He gulps down the entire glass while I watch him and join him back on the bed. I can see how uneasy he is, likely from the nightmare, but I know part of it is because of me.

"Come here," I tell him and see the relief in his eyes as he scoots his body toward mine, and I wrap my arms around him and put my head on his chest. It feels just as comforting to me as I imagine it does to him. Despite everything he has done, I feel like home in this flawed boy's arms.

"Don't let me go, Tess," he whispers and closes his eyes.

chapter thirty

TESSA

I wake up sweating. Hardin's head is on my stomach, and his arms are in a bear hug around me. Surely his arms must be numb from my body weight. His legs are intertwined with mine, and he's snoring lightly.

Taking a deep breath, I carefully lift my hand to brush his luscious hair from his forehead. I feel like I haven't touched his hair in so long, but in reality it's only been since Saturday. My mind replays the events in Seattle like a movie as I run my fingers through his soft mess of hair.

His eyes flutter open, and I jerk my hand away quickly. "Sorry," I say, embarrassed to be caught in the act.

"No, it felt good," he says, his voice thick from sleep.

After gathering himself and breathing against my skin for a moment, he lifts himself up from me—too soon—and I wish I hadn't touched his hair so he would still be asleep, holding me.

"I have some work to do today, so I'll be going to town for a little while," he says and grabs a pair of black jeans from the closet. He grabs his boots and slips them on quickly. I get the feeling that he's rushing out of here.

"Okay . . ." *What?* I thought he'd be happy that we slept together, and that we held each other for the first time in a week. I thought something would have changed—not completely, but I thought maybe he could see that my resolve was wearing down, that I was a few steps closer to reconciling with him than I was yesterday.

"Yeah . . ." he says and twists his eyebrow ring between two fingers before pulling the white T-shirt over his head and grabbing a black one from the dresser. He doesn't say anything before he exits the room, leaving me confused once again. Of all the things I expected to happen, him running out like this wasn't one of them. What work could he possibly have to do right now? He reads manuscripts, the same as I do—only he has much more freedom to work from home, so why would he want to do it today? The memory of what Hardin was doing the last time he had to "work" makes my stomach turn.

I hear him talking to his mother briefly before the front door opens and closes. I plop back onto the pillows and kick my feet in a childish manner. But hearing the siren song of caffeine, I finally climb out of bed and pad out into the kitchen to make some coffee.

"Good morning, sweetie," Trish chirps as I pass where she sits at the counter.

"Good morning. Thank you for making coffee," I say and grab the freshly brewed pot.

"Hardin said he had some work to do," she says, though it really sounds like she's asking, not telling.

"Yeah . . . he said something about that," I reply, unsure what else to say.

But she seems to ignore that and says, "I'm glad he's okay after last night," her voice full of worry.

"Yeah, me, too." Then, without thinking, I add, "I shouldn't have made him sleep on the floor."

Her brows knit together in question. "He doesn't have the nightmares when he isn't on the floor?" she asks carefully.

"No, he doesn't have them if we . . ." I trail off, stirring the sugar into my coffee and trying to think of a way to talk myself out of this.

"If *you're* there," she finishes for me.

"Yeah . . . if I'm there."

She gives me a hopeful look that—so I'm told—only a mother can give when talking about her children. "Do you want to know why he has them? I know he'll hate me for telling you, but I think you should know."

"Oh, please, Mrs. Daniels." I swallow. I don't really want to hear her tell me that story. "He told me . . . about that night." I swallow when her eyes widen in surprise.

"He *told* you?" she gasps.

"I'm sorry, I didn't mean to just say it that way. And the other night, I thought you knew . . ." I apologize and take another drink of coffee.

"No . . . no . . . Don't apologize. I just can't believe he told you. Obviously you knew about the nightmares, but this . . . this is astounding." She dabs her eyes with her fingers and smiles a smile straight from the heart.

"I hope it's okay. I'm so sorry for what happened." I don't want to intrude on their family secrets, but I also have never had to deal with anything like this before.

"It's more than okay, Tessa dear," she says and begins full-on sobbing. "I'm just so happy he has you . . . They were so bad—he would scream and scream. I tried to send him to therapy, but you know Hardin. He wouldn't speak to them. At all. As in not one word, he would just sit there and stare at the wall."

I set my mug down on the counter and wrap my arms around her.

"I don't know what it was that made you come back yesterday, but I'm glad that you did," she says into my shoulder.

"What?"

She pulls back and gives me a wry expression and dabs at her eyes. "Oh, honey, I'm old, but not that old. I knew something was going on between the two of you. I saw how surprised he was to see you when we arrived and I could tell something was off when he said you weren't going to make it to England."

I had a feeling that she was onto us, but I didn't know how transparent we were to her. I take a big gulp of my now lukewarm coffee and consider this.

Trish tenderly grabs on to my other arm. "He was so excited . . . well, as excited as Hardin gets . . . to bring you to England, and then a few days ago he said you were going out of town, but I knew better. What happened?" she asks.

I take another drink and make eye contact with her. "Well . . ." I don't know what to tell her, because *Oh nothing, your son just took my virginity as a part of a bet* doesn't exactly feel helpful right now.

"He . . . he lied to me" is all I say. I don't want her to be upset with Hardin, and I don't really want to get into all of it with her, but I don't want to completely lie either.

"A big lie?"

"A massive lie."

She looks at me then like I'm a landmine. "Is he sorry?"

Talking to Trish about this is strange. I don't even know her, and she's his mother, so she'll feel inclined to take his side no matter what. So I reply delicately, "Yeah . . . I think he is," and drain the rest of my coffee.

"Has he said that he is?"

"Yeah . . . a few times."

"Has he shown it?"

"Sort of." *Has he?* I know he broke down the other day, and he's been calmer than usual, but he hasn't actually said what I want to hear.

The older woman looks at me, and for a moment I really fear what her response is going to be. But then she surprises me by saying, "Well, as his mother, I have to put up with his antics. But you don't. If he wants you to forgive him, then he needs to work for it. He needs to show you that he'll never again do anything like whatever it is that he did—and I figure it must have been a pretty big lie if you moved out. Try to keep in mind that emotion is not a place he goes to often. He's a very angry boy . . . *man* now."

I know the question sounds ridiculous—people lie all the time—but the words tumble out before my brain can process them: "Would you forgive someone for lying to you?"

"Well, it would depend on the lie, and how sorry they were. I will say that when you allow yourself to believe too many lies, it's hard to find your way back to the truth."

Is she saying I shouldn't forgive him?

She taps her fingers on the counter lightly. "However, I know my son, and I can see the change in him since the last time I saw him. He's changed the last few months, so much, Tessa. I can't even tell you how much. He laughs and smiles. He even engaged in conversation with me yesterday." Her smile is bright despite the serious subject. "I know that if he lost you he would go back to how he was before, but I don't want you to feel obligated to be with him because of that."

"I don't . . . feel obligated, I mean. I just don't know what to think." I wish I could explain the whole story to her so I could have her honest opinion. I wish my mother was as understanding as Trish seems to be.

"Well, that's the hard part, you have to be the one to decide. Just take your time and make him work it, things come easily to my son, they always have. Maybe that's part of his problem, he always gets what he wants."

I laugh because that statement couldn't be more true. "That he does."

I sigh and go to the pantry and grab a box of cereal. But Trish interrupts my plan by saying, "How about you and me get dressed and go get some breakfast and do some girl things? I could use a haircut, myself." She laughs and shakes her brown hair back and forth.

Her sense of humor is nice, just like Hardin's is, when he allows it to show. He's more raunchy, yes, but I see where he gets his humor.

"Great. Let me just take a shower first," I say and put back the box.

"Shower? Its snowing outside, and we'll be getting our hair washed anyway! I was going to just wear this." She gestures to her black tracksuit. "Throw on some jeans or something, and let's go!"

This is so different than if I was going anywhere with my mother. I would have to have ironed clothes, my hair curled, and makeup on—even if we were just going to the grocery store.

I smile and say, "Okay."

In the bedroom, I grab a pair of jeans and a sweatshirt from the closet, then pull my hair into a bun. Slipping on my Toms, I head to the bathroom and quickly brush my teeth and splash cold water on my face. When I join Trish in the living room, she's ready and waiting by the door.

"I should leave Hardin a note or text him," I say.

But she smiles and pulls me toward the door. "That lad will be fine."

AFTER SPENDING THE REST of the morning and the majority of the afternoon with Trish, I feel much more relaxed. She is kind, funny, and great to talk to. She keeps the conversation light and has me laughing almost the entire time. We both get our hair done, and Trish adds bangs, daring me to do the same, but I refuse with a smile. I do, however, let her talk me into buying a black dress for Christmas. I have no idea what I'm doing for Christmas, though. I don't want to intrude on Hardin and his mother, and I haven't bought any presents or anything. I think I may take

Landon up on the invitation to his house. It seems a little too much to spend Christmas with Hardin when we're not together. We're in this alien in-between stage: we aren't together, but I'd been feeling like we were getting closer to each other until he left this morning.

By the time we return to the apartment, Hardin's car is in the lot, and I start to feel nervous. When we get up to the apartment, we find him sitting on the couch with papers spread out across his lap and the coffee table. He has a pen between his teeth and looks deep into whatever it is that he's doing. Working, I suspect, but I have only actually seen him work a few times in the months I've known him.

"Hello, son!" Trish says in a cheery voice.

"Hey," Hardin responds flatly.

"Did you miss us?" she teases, and he rolls his eyes before gathering up the loose pages and shoving them into a binder.

"I'll be in the bedroom," he huffs and stands from the couch.

I shrug at Trish, then follow Hardin into our bedroom.

"Where'd you guys go?" he asks and sets down his binder on the dresser. A page falls out, and he quickly shoves it back inside, closing the tab with a snap.

I sit on the bed with my legs crossed. "To breakfast, then we got haircuts and did some shopping."

"Oh."

"Where did you go?" I ask him. He looks down at the floor before answering.

"To work."

"Tomorrow is Christmas Eve. I'm not buying that," I say with a tone that tells me Trish must have worn off on me.

His green eyes blaze at me. "Well, I don't really care if you're not *buying that*," he says in a mocking tone and sits down on the opposite side of the bed.

"What's your problem?" I snap.

"Nothing. I don't have a problem." His walls are up; I can feel them guarding him.

"Obviously you do. Why did you leave this morning?"

He runs a hand through his hair. "I already told you."

"Lying to me isn't going to help anything, that's what got you . . . us into this mess in the first place," I remind him.

"Fine! You want to know where I was? I was at my dad's!" he shouts and stands up.

"Your dad's? Why?"

"Talking to Landon." He sits down on the chair.

I roll my eyes. "I believed the work story more than this."

"I was. Go on and call him, if you don't believe me."

"Okay, and what were you talking with Landon about?"

"You, of course."

"What about me?" I raise my hands in front of me.

"Just everything. I know you don't want to be here." He looks over at me.

"If I didn't want to be here, I wouldn't be."

"You have nowhere else to go, I know you wouldn't be here if you did."

"What makes you so sure? We slept in the bed together last night."

"Yeah, and you know why—if I hadn't had a nightmare, you wouldn't have agreed to it. That's the only reason you did, and the only reason you're talking to me now. Because you feel sorry for me." His hands are shaking, and his eyes are piercing. I can see the shame behind the green.

"It doesn't matter why it happened." I shake my head at him. I don't know why he always jumps to these conclusions. Why is it so hard for him to accept that he is loved?

"You feel sorry for poor Hardin who has nightmares and can't sleep in a fucking bed alone!" His voice is too loud, and we have company.

"Stop yelling! Your mom is in the other room!" I yell back.

"Is that what you two did all day . . . talk about me? I don't need your fucking pity, Tess."

"Oh my God! You are so frustrating! We did not talk about you, not in that way. And for the record, I do not feel sorry for you, I wanted you in that bed with me regardless of your dreams." I cross my arms.

"Sure," he barks.

"This isn't about how I feel; it's about how you feel about yourself. You need to stop feeling sorry for yourself, if anything," I say equally harshly.

"I don't."

"Seems like it. You just started a fight with me for no reason. We should be moving forward not backward."

"Moving forward?" His eyes meet mine.

"Yeah . . . I mean may-maybe," I stutter.

"Maybe?" He smiles.

And he's so happy all of a sudden—he's grinning like a small child on Christmas. He was just fighting with me, his cheeks flushed in anger. And strangely, I feel most of my anger evaporating as well. The control that he holds over my emotions terrifies me. "You are insane, literally," I tell him.

He gives me a killer smirk. "Your hair looks nice."

"You need to be medicated," I tease, and he laughs.

"I wouldn't argue there," he responds.

And I can't help but laugh with him . . . Maybe I'm just as crazy as he is.

chapter thirty-one

TESSA

Our moment together is interrupted when my phone vibrates and dances across the dresser. Hardin grabs it for me, looks at the screen, and says, "Landon."

Taking the phone from him, I answer, "Hello?"

"Hey, Tessa," Landon says. "So, my mum wanted me to call and see if you were coming over for Christmas?"

His mom is so nice. And I bet she makes a great Christmas spread. "Oh . . . yeah, I'd love to. What time should I be there?" I reply.

"Noon." He laughs. "She's already started cooking, so if I were you, I wouldn't eat anything until then."

"I'll start fasting now," I joke. "Anything I should bring? I know Karen's a much better cook than me, but I could make something—dessert, maybe?"

"Yeah, you can bring a dessert . . . and also . . . I know this is awkward, and if you aren't comfortable with it, then that's okay." His voice lowers. "But they want to invite Hardin and his mum. But if you and Hardin aren't getting along—"

"We are. Sort of," I interrupt. Hardin raises his brow at my reply, and I give him a nervous smile.

Landon lets out a little breath. "Super. If you could just pass the invite along, they would really appreciate it."

"I will," I assure him, and then something occurs to me. "What should I get them, giftwise?"

"No, no—nothing! You don't have to bring gifts."

I keep my eyes on the wall and try not to focus on Hardin's steady gaze on me. "Okay, sure. But I'm bringing gifts, so what should it be?"

Landon sighs good-naturedly. "Stubborn as always. Well, my mum likes her kitchen, and Ken would go for a paperweight . . . or something."

"A paperweight?" I snort. "That's a dreadful gift."

He laughs. "Well, don't get him a tie, because I did." Then he groans. "Well, let me know if you need anything between now and then. I have to go help clean the house," he says and hangs up.

When I put my phone down, Hardin immediately asks, "You are going there for Christmas?"

"Yeah . . . I don't want to go to my mother's," I say and sit on the bed.

"I don't blame you." He rubs his chin with his index finger. "You could stay here?"

I pick at my fingernails on my lap. "You could . . . come with me."

"And leave my mum here alone?" he scoffs.

"No! Of course not, Karen and your dad want her to come . . . Both of you."

Hardin looks at me like I'm crazy. "Yeah, right. And why would my mum want to go there with my father and his new wife?"

"I . . . I don't know, but it could be nice to have everyone together."

Really, though, I'm not sure how exactly that would go, largely because I don't know what type of relationship Trish and Ken have now, if they have one at all. It's also not my place to try to bring everyone together—I'm not part of their family. Heck, I'm not even Hardin's girlfriend.

"I don't think so." He frowns.

Despite everything going on between Hardin and me, it would

have been nice to spend Christmas with him, but I understand. It would have been hard enough to convince Hardin to go to his father's house for the holiday anyway, let alone with his mother.

Because part of my brain likes a problem to solve, I start thinking that I need to get gifts for Landon and his parents, maybe something for Trish as well. But what? I should go now, really—it's already five, which only leaves a bit tonight and then tomorrow, Christmas Eve. I have no idea whether or not I should get something for Hardin; actually, I'm pretty sure I shouldn't. It would be awkward to give him a present when we're in this strange in-between place.

"What is it?" Hardin asks of my silence.

I groan. "I have to go to the mall. This is what I get for being homeless on Christmas," I tell him.

"I don't think bad planning has anything to do with you being homeless," he teases. His smile is small but his eyes are bright . . .

Is he flirting with me? I laugh at the thought and roll my eyes. "Bad planning is not something that I do, ever."

"Sure . . ." he mocks, and I swat my hand at him.

He grabs my wrist and wraps his fingers around it to stop my playful assault. A familiar warmth floods through my body, and I lock eyes with him. He lets go quickly and we both look away. The air fills with tension, and I stand up to put my shoes back on.

"You're going now?" he asks.

"Yeah . . . the mall closes at nine," I remind him.

"You're going alone?" He shuffles his feet awkwardly.

"Would you like to come?" I know this probably isn't the best idea, but if I want to at least try to move forward, then going to the mall together is fine. Right?

"Come shopping with you?"

"Yeah . . . if you don't want to, that's fine, too," I say awkwardly.

"No, of course I do. I just . . . wasn't expecting you to ask."

I nod, then grab my phone and purse. Hardin close on my heels, I go out into the living room.

"We're going to the mall for a while," Hardin tells his mom.

"Both of you?" she asks knowingly, and he rolls his eyes. As we hit the door, she yells over her shoulder, "Tessa, dear, if you want to leave him there, I won't complain."

I chuckle. "I'll keep that in mind," I say and follow him out.

WHEN HARDIN'S CAR STARTS, a very familiar piano melody fills the air. He hurries to turn the volume down, but it's too late. I give him a smug look.

"They grew on me, okay?" he says.

"Sure," I tease and turn the song back up.

If only things could go this way forever. If only this flirty getting along, this nervous middle ground that we are in, could last forever. But it won't. It can't. We have to actually discuss what has happened, and what will happen from here on out. I know we have so much to talk about, but we aren't going to solve this problem all at once, even if I force the issue. I want to find the right time, and take it slow until then.

Most of the drive is spent in silence, the music saying all of the things I wish we could say to each other. When we near the Macy's entrance, Hardin says, "I'll drop you off by the door," and I nod. I stand under the vent to warm up while he parks and hurries through the cold to me.

After nearly an hour of looking at baking dishes of all shapes and sizes, I decide to get Karen a set of cake pans. I know she probably has more than enough, but cooking and gardening seem to be her only hobbies, and I don't have time to think of anything better.

"Can we take this to the car and then finish shopping?" I ask Hardin and struggle to keep the large box in my hands.

"Here, I'll take it. Stay here," he says and takes the box from me.

As soon as he walks away, I walk over to the men's section, where hundreds of ties in large cases mockingly remind me of Landon's claim about them as an easy gift. I keep browsing, but I've never bought a "dad gift" before, so I have no idea what to get.

"It's so fucking cold out," Hardin says when he returns, shivering and rubbing his hands together.

"Well, maybe wearing a T-shirt in the snow isn't a good idea."

He rolls his eyes. "I'm hungry, are you?"

We make our way to the food court, where Hardin finds me a seat while he gets us some pizza from the only decent chain there. Minutes later, he joins me at the table with two plates piled full. I grab a slice and a napkin and take a small bite.

"How elegant of you," he teases when I wipe my mouth after I chew.

"Shut up," I say and take another.

"This is . . . nice. Isn't it?" he asks.

"What? The pizza?" I innocently ask back, even though I know he isn't talking about the food.

"Us. Hanging out. It's been a long time."

It does seem like so long . . . "It hasn't even been two weeks," I remind him.

"That's a long time . . . for us."

"Yeah . . ." I take a bigger bite so I can keep silent a little longer.

"How long have you been thinking about moving forward?" he asks.

I slowly finish chewing and take a long drink of my water. "A few days, I guess." I want to keep this conversation as light as I can in order to avoid causing a scene, but I do add, "There's still so much to talk about."

"I know there is, but I'm so . . ." His green eyes go wide as he focuses on something behind me. When I turn around, my stomach drops at the sight of red hair. Steph. And next to her, her boyfriend, Tristan.

"I want to go," I tell him and stand up, leaving the tray of food on the table.

"Tessa, you haven't gotten any other gifts. Besides, I don't think they even saw us."

When I turn back around, Steph's eyes meets mine, and the surprise on her face is evident. I can't tell if she's more surprised to see me, or that I'm with Hardin. Probably both.

"Yeah, she did."

The pair walk over to us, and I feel like my feet are bolted to the floor.

"Hey," Tristan says uncomfortably when they reach us.

"Hey," Hardin says and rubs the back of his neck.

I don't say anything. I look at Steph, then grab my purse from the table and begin to walk away.

"Tessa, wait!" she calls after me. The thick heels of her shoes smack against the hard tile as she hurries to catch up with me. "Can we talk?"

"Talk about *what*, Steph?" I snap. "How my first and basically only friend here let me be humiliated in front of everyone?"

Hardin and Tristan look at each other, obviously unsure whether to intervene.

Steph throws out her hands. "I'm sorry, okay! I know I should have told you—I thought he would tell you!"

"So that's supposed to make it okay, then?"

"No, I know it won't, but I'm really sorry, Tessa. I know I should have told you."

"But you didn't." I cross my arms.

"I miss you, I miss hanging out with you," she says.

"I'm sure you do miss having me as the focus of all of your jokes."

"It wasn't like that, Tessa. You are . . . were my friend. I know I fucked up, but I really am sorry."

Her apology catches me off guard. But I recover and say, "Well, I can't forgive you."

She frowns. And then her expression turns angry. "But you can forgive *him*? He's the one who started it all—and you forgave *him*. How fucked up is that?"

I want to snap at her, cuss her out even, but I know she's right. "I haven't forgiven him, I'm just . . . I don't know what I'm doing," I whine and put my hands over my face.

Steph sighs. "Tessa, I don't expect you to just let it go like that, but at least give me a chance. We could hang out, just the four of us. The group is all fucked up, anyway."

I look up at her. "What do you mean?"

"Well, Jace has been an even bigger dick since Hardin beat the shit out of him. So Tristan and I have been keeping our distance from everyone."

I look over to where Hardin and Tristan are watching us and then look back at Steph. "Hardin beat up Jace?"

"Yeah . . . last Saturday." She scrunches her brows. "He didn't say anything?"

"No . . ." I want to hear as much as I can before Hardin walks over and stops her from spilling, but she's eager to be on my good side, so she starts without my even having to ask.

"Yeah, well, it's because Molly told Hardin that Jace planned the whole . . . you know," she adds quietly, "telling you in front of everyone . . ." But then she laughs a little. "Honestly, he had it coming, and the look on Molly's face when Hardin basically pushed her off of him was priceless. I mean, seriously, I should have taken a picture!"

I'm pondering the fact that Hardin turned down Molly and beat up Jace that Saturday before he came to Seattle, when I hear Tristan say, "Ladies," almost as if in warning that Hardin's near.

Hardin joins me and takes my hand, and as Tristan starts to pull Steph away, she stays facing me for a moment and says with wide eyes, "Tessa, just think about it, okay? I miss you."

chapter thirty-two

TESSA

"You okay?" Hardin asks when they disappear.

"Yeah . . . I'm fine," I tell him.

"What did she say?"

"Nothing . . . just that she wants me to forgive her." I shrug, and we head off down the main throughway. I need to process everything that Steph just told me before I bring it up to Hardin. He must have been at one of their parties before he came to Seattle, and Molly must have been there. I can't deny it's a massive relief to hear Steph's take on things. It's almost funny that he had told me he slept with Molly that same night he was actually rejecting her. Almost. The relief and irony are quickly overshadowed by my guilt over kissing that stranger at the club while Hardin was pushing away Molly.

"Tess?" Hardin stops walking and waves his hand in front of my face. "What's going on?"

"Nothing. I was just thinking about what to get your dad." I'm a bad liar, and my voice gets more rushed than I'd like. "Does he like sports? He does, right? You two were watching that football game, remember?"

Hardin eyes me for a moment, then says, "The Packers, he likes the Packers." I am positive that he wants to ask more about Steph, but he stays quiet.

We go to a sporting goods store, and I stay fairly quiet as well and Hardin chooses a few things for his father. He refuses to let me pay, so I grab a key chain off the display case near the register and pay for it myself just to annoy him. He rolls his eyes and I stick my tongue out at him.

"You do know that you grabbed the wrong team, right?" he says when we exit the store.

"What?" I reach in and grab the small object.

"That's the Giants, not the Packers." He smirks, and I shove the key chain back into the bag.

"Well . . . good thing no one will know the good gifts are actually from you."

"Are we done yet?" he whines.

"No, I have to get something for Landon, remember?"

"Oh yeah. He mentioned that he wanted to try a new shade of lipstick. Maybe coral?"

I put my hands on my hips and face him. "You leave him alone! And maybe I should be getting you the lipstick, since you seem to know the exact shade," I tease. It feels good to be bickering with Hardin in a playful way instead of a let's-burn-the-house-down way.

He rolls his eyes, but I see a small smile appear before he speaks. "You should just get him hockey tickets. Easy and not too expensive."

"That's actually a good idea."

"I know," he says. "Too bad he doesn't have any friends to go with him."

"Um, I would go with him."

The way Hardin is teasing about Landon makes me smile because it is so different than before, there is no malice behind his tone now.

"I wanted to get your mom something, too," I tell him.

He gives me a funny, little, harmless look. "Why?"

"Because it's Christmas."

"Just get her a sweater or something," he says and gestures at a store meant more for old ladies.

Eyeing it, I say, "I'm terrible at buying gifts for people. What did you get her?"

The present he got me for my birthday was so perfect that I imagine the gift he chose for his mother must be equally thoughtful.

He shrugs. "A bracelet and a scarf."

"A bracelet?" I ask and pull him farther down the mall.

"No, I meant a necklace anyway. It's just a plain necklace that says *Mom* or some shit."

"How nice of you," I say as we walk back into Macy's. I look around, feeling confident. "I think I can find her something here . . . she likes those tracksuits."

"Oh God, please, no more tracksuits. She wears them *every* day."

I smile at his sour expression. "So . . . all the more reason to buy her another one."

As we look at several racks with various options, Hardin reaches out and feels the sheer fabric on one. I get a good look at his knuckles, and the scabs on them, bringing me back to the information Steph revealed.

I pretty quickly find a mint-green tracksuit that I'm sensing she'll like, and we wander off to find the register. En route, a sort of resolve takes over my frantic thoughts about Hardin, partly because I now know he wasn't actually sleeping with Molly while I was in Seattle.

As we get to the register and place the outfit on the counter, I suddenly turn to Hardin and say, "We need to talk tonight."

The cashier looks back and forth between Hardin and me, confusion evident in her eyes. I want to tell her it's rude to stare, but Hardin speaks before I get the courage.

"Talk?"

"Yeah . . ." I say and watch the cashier remove the security tag. "After we put that tree up that your mom got when you two went out yesterday."

"Talk about what, though?"

I turn to look at him. "Everything," I say.

Hardin looks terrified and the implications of that word hang heavy in the air. When the cashier scans the tracksuit's tag, a beep breaks the silence, and Hardin mumbles, "Oh . . . I'll go get the car."

As I watch the woman bag Trish's gift, I think, *Next year I'll make sure to get everyone amazing gifts to make up for my terrible gifts this year.* But then I think, *Next year? Who says there'll be a next year with him?*

BOTH OF US STAY SILENT during the ride back to the apartment, me because I'm trying to organize my thoughts about everything I should say, and him . . . well, I get the feeling he's doing the same. When we arrive, I grab the bags and rush through the freezing rain and into the lobby. I'd take the snow over this any day.

When we step into the elevator, my stomach grumbles. "I'm hungry," I tell Hardin when he looks down at me.

"Oh." He looks like he wants to say something sarcastic but decides against it.

The sensation is only heightened when we get inside the apartment and the smell of garlic takes over my senses, instantly making my mouth water.

"I made dinner!" Trish announces. "How was the mall?"

Hardin grabs the bags from my hands and disappears into the bedroom.

"It wasn't too bad. Not nearly as crowded as I'd thought it would be," I explain.

"That's good, I thought maybe you and I could put that tree up? Hardin probably won't want to help." She smiles. "He hates fun. But the two of us could do it, if you don't mind?"

I chuckle. "Yeah, of course."

"You should eat first," Hardin commands as he strides back into the kitchen.

I scowl at him and turn my attention back to Trish. Since my dreaded talk with Hardin is on the other end of my assembling the small tree with his mother, I'm in no particular rush. Besides, I need at least an hour to muster up enough strength to be able to say everything that I want to say. It's probably not the best idea to have such an important talk with his mother here, but I can't wait any longer. Everything that's going to be said needs to be said . . . now. My patience is waning; we can't stay in this in-between place much longer.

"Are you actually hungry now, Tessa dear?" Trish asks me.

"Yes, she is," Hardin answers for me over his shoulder.

"Yeah, I actually am," I tell her, ignoring her obnoxious son.

While Trish makes me a plate of chicken casserole with spinach and garlic, I sit at the table focusing on how delicious it smells. When she brings the plate over, I see it looks even better than it smells.

As she puts the plate in front of me, Trish says, "Hardin, you could take the pieces out of the tree out of box for us, make it a little easier?"

"Sure," he says.

She smiles at me. "I got a few ornaments, too."

By the time I've finished eating, Hardin has the branches slid into the slots and the tree assembled.

"That wasn't so bad, was it?" his mom says. When he grabs the box of ornaments, she goes over to him. "We'll help with those."

Completely full, I get up from the table, and ponder how putting together a Christmas tree with Hardin and his mother, in an apartment that was ours, is something I'd have never thought I'd be doing. Ever. I enjoy the feeling while we decorate, and in the end, though the ornaments seem randomly hung on the miniature tree, Trish looks very pleased.

"We should get a photo in front of it!" she suggests.

"I don't do pictures," Hardin grumbles.

"Oh, come on, Hardin, it's the holidays." She bats her lashes and he rolls his eyes at her for the hundredth time since her arrival.

"Not today," he replies.

I know it isn't fair of me, but I feel for his mother, so I look at him with big eyes and say, "Just one?"

"Fine, fuck. Just one." He stands next to Trish in front of the tree and I grab my phone to take a picture of them. Hardin barely smiles, but Trish's cheerfulness makes up for it. Still, I'm relieved when she doesn't suggest that Hardin and I take a picture together; we need to figure out what we're doing before we start romantic pictures in front of Christmas trees.

I get Trish's phone number and send a copy of the picture to her and Hardin, who walks back to the kitchen and makes himself a plate of food.

"I'm going to go wrap some gifts before it gets too late," I announce.

"Okay, see you in the morning, sweetie," Trish says and gives me a hug.

Going into the bedroom, I see that Hardin has already gathered the wrapping paper, bows, tape, and everything else I could possibly need. I hurry to start wrapping so we can have "the Talk" sooner rather than later. I really want to get it over with, but at the same time am afraid of how it will go. I know that I've made up my mind, but I'm not sure if I'm ready to admit it. I know how foolish it is of me, but I've been a fool since I first met Hardin, and that hasn't always been a bad thing.

I finish writing Ken's name on a gift tag just as he walks in.

"Done?" he asks.

"Yeah . . . I need to get those tickets printed for Landon before we talk."

He cocks his head back. "Why?"

"Because I need your help, and you're not helpful when we're fighting."

"How do you know we'll fight?" he asks.

"Because it's us." I half laugh, and he silently nods in agreement.

"I'll get the printer from the closet."

As he walks away, I turn on my laptop. Twenty minutes later we have two tickets to the Seattle Thunderbirds printed and wrapped in a small box for Landon.

"Okay . . . so any other distractions before we . . . you know, talk?" Hardin asks.

"No. I guess not," I reply.

We both go and sit on the bed, him against the headboard with his long legs stretched out, me with my legs tucked under me at the other end. I have no idea where to start or what to say.

"So . . ." Hardin begins.

This is awkward. "So . . ." I pick at my nails. "What happened with Jace?" I ask.

"Steph told you," he states flatly.

"Yeah, she did."

"He was running his mouth."

"Hardin, you have to talk to me or this isn't going to work."

His eyes go wide with indignation. "I *am* talking."

"Hardin . . ."

"Okay. Okay." He lets out an angry breath. "He was planning to try to hook up with you."

My stomach turns at the thought. Plus, that's not the reason for the fight that Steph told me at the mall. *Is Hardin lying to me again?* "So? You know that would never happen."

"That doesn't make a difference, even thinking about him touching you . . ." He shudders and continues: "And also, he's the one who . . . well. Molly, too, who planned to tell you about the bet in front of everyone. He had no fucking right to humiliate you like that. He ruined everything."

The momentary relief I feel that Hardin's story now matches Steph's is quickly replaced by anger over his attitude that if only I didn't know about the bet, everything would have been fine. "Hardin, *you* ruined it. They just told me about it," I remind him.

"I know that, Tessa," he says with annoyance.

"Do you? Do you know that, though? Because you haven't really said anything about it."

Hardin pulls his legs back with a sudden move. "Yes, I have—I was crying the other day, for fuck's sake."

I feel a scowl etch itself into my features. "You need to stop cursing at me so much, for one thing. And two, that was one time. That's really the only time you've said anything. And it wasn't much."

"I tried in Seattle, but you wouldn't talk to me. And you've been ignoring me, so when was I supposed to tell you?"

"Hardin, the point is, if we're going to even try to move past this, I need you to open up to me, I need to know exactly how you feel," I tell him.

His green eyes bore into me. "And when do I get to hear how you feel, Tessa? You're just as closed off as I am."

"What? No . . . No, I'm not."

"Yes, you are! You haven't told me how you feel about any of this. You just keep saying you're done with me." He waves his hands toward me. "But here you are. It gets a bit confusing."

I need a moment to think about what he just said. I've had so many thoughts jumbled in my head that I've forgotten to communicate any of them to him. "I have been so confused," I say.

"I'm not a mind reader, Tessa. What are you confused about?"

A lump forms in my throat. "This. Us. I don't know what to do. About us. About your betrayal." We've just started this conversation, and I'm already on the verge of tears.

A little harshly, he says, "What do you *want* to do?"

"I don't know."

He calls me out. "Yes, you do."

There are a lot of things that I need to hear him say before I can be sure of what I want to do. "What do *you* want me to do?"

"I want you to stay with me. I want you to forgive me and give me another chance. I know I've asked you too many times, but please, just give me one more chance. I can't be without you. I've tried, and I know you have, too. There isn't anyone else for either of us. If it's not us, it's nothing—and I know that you know that, too." His eyes are glassy when he finishes, and I wipe my tears away.

"You hurt me, so terribly, Hardin."

"I know, baby, I know I did. I would give anything to take that back," he says, then looks down at the bed with a strange expression. "Actually I wouldn't. I wouldn't change anything. Well, I would have told you sooner, obviously," he says. I snap my head up. He brings his up and stares right into me. "I wouldn't take it back, because we wouldn't have been together if I hadn't done such a fucked-up thing. Our paths would have never really crossed, not in the way that has bonded us together so tightly. Even though it's destroyed my life, without that stupid, evil bet, I wouldn't have had a life at all. I'm sure that makes you hate me even more, but you wanted the truth. And that's the truth."

Looking into Hardin through his green eyes, I don't know what to say.

Because when I think about it—really think about it—I know I wouldn't change anything either.

chapter thirty-three

HARDIN

've never been so honest with anyone before. But I want everything to be out on the table.

She starts crying and asks softly, "How will I know that you won't hurt me again?"

I could tell she was trying to hold her tears in the whole time, but I'm glad she can't anymore. I needed to see some emotion from her . . . she's been so cold lately. So unlike her. I used to be able to tell what she was thinking by her eyes alone. Now a wall is up, blocking me from reading her the way only I can. I pray to God that the time we spent together today will work in my favor.

That and my honesty. "You won't. Tessa, I can assure you that I will hurt you again. You will hurt me, too, but I can also assure you that I'll never keep anything from you or betray you again. You may say some shit that you don't mean, and God knows that I will, but we can work through our problems because that's what people do. I just need this one last chance to show you that I can be the man you deserve. Please, Tessa. Please . . ." I beg.

She stares at me with red eyes, chewing on the inside of her cheek. I hate to see her this way, and I hate myself for making her this way.

"You love me, don't you?" I ask, afraid of her answer.

"Yes. More than anything." She admits with a sigh.

I can't hide my stirrings of a smile. Hearing her say that she still loves me brings the life back into me. I've been so worried that she was going to give up on me, stop loving me and move on. I don't deserve her, and I know that she's aware of that.

But my mind is reeling, and she is being too quiet. I can't handle the distance. "What can I do, then? What do I need to do so we can get through this?" I ask desperately. I use too much emphasis—I know because of how she looks at me, like she's suddenly scared, or annoyed, or . . . I don't know what. "I said the wrong thing, didn't I." I bring my hands to my face and wipe the moisture from my eyes. "I knew I would, you know I'm not good with words."

I've never been this emotional in my entire life, and it doesn't feel good. I've never had to or even cared to express my emotions to anyone but I will do anything for this girl. I always fuck everything up, but I have to fix this, or try as hard as I can.

"No . . ." she sobs. "I'm just . . . I don't know. I want to be with you. I want to forget everything, but I don't want to regret it. I don't want to be that girl, the one who gets walked all over and treated like shit and just puts up with it."

I lean toward her and ask, "To who? Who are you worried will think that?"

"Everyone, my mother, your friends . . . you."

I knew that's what it was. I knew that she was more worried about what she *should* do rather than what she *wants* to do. "Don't think about anyone else. Who gives a shit what anyone else thinks? For once just consider what you want—what makes you happy?"

With big, round, beautiful, bloodshot, and crying eyes, she says, "You." And my heart leaps. "I'm so tired of keeping everything in. I'm *exhausted* by all of the things I haven't said and wanted to say," she adds.

"Then don't keep it in anymore," I tell her.

"You make me happy, Hardin. But you also make me miserable, angry, and—most of all—you make me insane."

"That's the point, isn't it? That's why we're so good together, Tess, because we are terrible for each other." She makes me insane, too, and angry, but happy. So happy.

"We are terrible for each other," she says with a small smile.

"We are," I repeat and return her smile. "I love you, though. More than anyone ever could, and I swear I will spend the rest of my life making this up to you if you just let me."

I hope she can hear the rawness in my voice, how badly I want her forgiveness. I need it—I need *her* like I've never needed anything before, and I know she loves me. She wouldn't be here if she didn't, though I can't believe I just said "the rest of my life"—that might freak her out.

When she doesn't say anything else, my heart breaks. And just before I feel more tears coming, I whisper, "I'm so sorry, Tessa . . . I love you so much—"

She catches me completely off guard when she darts across the space between us and climbs onto my lap. I bring my hands to her beautiful face, and she takes a deep breath, leaning her cheek into the palm of my hand.

She looks up at me. "I need it to be on my terms. I won't be able to make it through another heartbreak."

"Whatever it takes. I just want to be with you," I tell her.

"We have to take it slow, I shouldn't be doing this at all . . . If you hurt me again, I'll never forgive you, ever," she threatens.

"I won't. I swear it." I'd rather die than hurt her again. I still can't believe she's giving me another chance.

"I really have missed you so much, Hardin."

Her eyes close and I want to kiss her, I want to feel her lips hot against mine, but she just told me she wants to take it slow. "I missed you, too."

She rests her forehead against mine and I let out a breath that I didn't know I was holding. "We're really doing this, then?" I ask, trying not to sound as desperately relieved as I feel.

She sits up and I look into her eyes. The eyes that have haunted me every time I close my own for the last week. She smiles and nods her head. "Yeah . . . I guess we are."

My arms wrap around her waist and she leans into me once more. "Kiss me?" I practically beg.

She doesn't try to hide her amusement as she touches my forehead, brushing my hair back. God, I love when she does that.

"Please?" I say.

And she silences me by pressing her lips against mine.

chapter thirty-four

TESSA

My mouth immediately opens, and he doesn't miss the opportunity to slip his tongue into it. The metal of his lip ring is cool against my lips, and I run my tongue along its smooth surface. The familiar taste of him ignites me, like it always has. No matter how hard I fight it, I need him. I need to be close to him, I need him to comfort me, to challenge me, to annoy me, to kiss me, and to love me. My fingers tangle themselves in his hair, and I tug at the soft strands when his grip on my waist tightens. He said everything I wanted and needed to hear to feel better about my reckless decision to allow him back into my life . . . even though he never actually left. I know I should've held out longer, tortured him with waiting the way he tortured me with his lies, but I couldn't. This isn't the movies. This is real life—my life—and my life isn't complete or even tolerable without him. This tattooed, rude, angry boy has gotten under my skin and into my heart, and I know that no matter how hard I try, I can't get him out.

His tongue skims my bottom lip and I'm slightly embarrassed when a moan escapes my throat. When I pull away, we're both out of breath and my skin is hot and his cheeks are flushed.

"Thank you for giving me another chance," he pants and pulls me into his chest.

"You act like I had a choice."

He frowns. "You do."

"I know," I lie. But I haven't had a choice since I met him. I've been completely gone for him since the first time we kissed.

"Where do we go from here?" I ask him.

"That's up to you. You know what I want."

"I want to be like we were before . . . well, how we were without all the other stuff," I tell Hardin, and he nods.

"That's what I want, too, baby. I'll make this up to you, I promise."

Every time Hardin calls me baby my stomach flutters. The mixture of his raspy voice, his British accent, and the gentleness behind his tone makes for the most perfect combination.

"Please don't make me regret this," I beg him, and he takes my face into his hands once more.

"I won't. You'll see," he promises and kisses me again.

I know that Hardin and I still have things to sort out, but I feel so resolved now, so calm, so right. I'm worried about everyone's re-action, especially my mother's, but I'll deal with that when the time comes. The fact that I'm not spending Christmas with her for the first time in eighteen years in favor of Hardin and me being together again will only make things worse, but honestly I don't care. Well, I *care*, but I can't keep going to war with her over my life choices, and it's impossible to make her happy, so I'm done really trying.

I lean my head against Hardin's chest and he takes the end of my ponytail into his hands and twirls it between his fingers. I'm glad that I got all of the gifts wrapped; it was stressful enough buying them at the very last minute.

Shit. I didn't get Hardin a gift! Did he get me one? Probably not, but now that we're together again . . . or sort of for the first time . . . I'm afraid that he did and will feel bad that I didn't get him anything at all. Actually, what would I even get him?

"What's wrong?" he asks and moves his hand to my chin, tilt-ing my face to his.

"Nothing . . ."

"You aren't . . ." he starts, slow and unsure. "You're not . . . you know . . . changing your mind?"

"No . . . no. I just . . . I didn't get you a gift," I admit.

His face breaks into a smile, and his eyes meet mine. "You're worried about getting me a gift for Christmas?" He laughs. "Tessa, honestly, you've given me *everything*. You worrying about a Christmas gift is ridiculous."

I still feel guilty, but I love the confidence on his face. "You're sure?" I ask.

"Positive." He laughs again.

"I'll get you something really great for your birthday," I say, and he moves his hand back to my face. His thumb runs along my bottom lip, causing my lips to part, and I expect him to kiss me again. Instead, his lips touch down on my nose and then my forehead in a surprisingly sweet gesture.

"I don't really do birthdays," he tells me.

"I know . . . I don't either." This is one of the few things we have in common.

"Hardin?" Trish's voice calls as I hear a light tap on the door. He groans and rolls his eyes as I climb off his lap.

I give him a little frown. "It wouldn't kill you to be nicer to her—she hasn't seen you in a year."

"I'm not mean to her," he says. And, honestly, I know he believes that.

"Just try to be a little nicer, for me?" I bat my eyelashes dramatically, making him smile and shake his head.

"You're the devil," he teases.

His mom knocks again. "Hardin?"

"Coming!" he says and climbs off the bed. Opening the door, I see his mom, who looks completely bored.

"Do you two want to watch a movie, perhaps?" she asks.

He turns to me and raises his brow just as I say, "Yeah, we do" and climb off the bed.

"Fantastic!" She smiles and ruffles her son's hair.

"Let me change first," Hardin says and waves us out.

Trish holds her hand out to me. "Come on, Tessa, let's make some snacks."

As I follow his mom into the kitchen, I realize it's probably not a good idea for me to watch Hardin change anyway. I want to take things slow. Slow. With Hardin, I don't know if that's possible. I wonder if I should tell Trish that I've decided to forgive him, or least try to.

"Cookies?" she asks, and I nod and open the cabinets.

"Peanut butter?" I ask her and grab the flour.

She raises her eyebrows, impressed. "You're going to make them? I was okay with Break 'n Bake, but if you can make them homemade, so much the better!"

"I'm not the best cook, but Karen taught me an easy peanut butter cookie recipe."

"Karen?" she asks, and my stomach drops. I didn't mean to bring up Karen. The last thing I want to do is make Trish uncomfortable. I turn away to turn on the oven and hide my embarrassed expression.

"You've met her?"

I can't read her tone, so I tread carefully. "Yeah . . . her son Landon is my friend . . . my best friend, really."

Trish hands me some bowls and a spoon, asking in a purposely neutral manner, "Oh . . . what is she like?"

I level off flour in a measuring cup and add it to the large mixing bowl, all the while trying to avoid eye contact. I don't know how to answer her. I don't want to lie, but I don't know how she feels about Ken or his new wife.

"You can tell me," Trish prods.

"She's lovely," I admit.

She nods sharply. "I knew she would be."

"I didn't mean to bring her up, it just slipped out," I apologize.

She hands me a stick of butter. "No, honey, don't worry about it. I have no hard feelings toward that woman at all. Granted, I would love to hear that she's a dreadful troll." She laughs and relief washes through me. "But I'm glad Hardin's father is happy. I just wish Hardin would let go of his anger toward him."

"He has—" I begin, but stop abruptly when Hardin enters the kitchen.

"He has what?" she asks.

I look to Hardin, then back to Trish. It's not my place to tell her if Hardin hasn't. "What are you guys talking about?" he asks.

"Your father," she answers, and his face pales. I can tell by his expression that he didn't intend to tell her about his budding relationship with his father.

"I didn't know . . ." I try to tell him, but he puts his hand up to silence me.

I hate how secretive he is; this is a problem we will always have, I assume.

"It's fine, Tess. I've been . . . sort of spending a little time with him." Hardin's cheeks flush.

Without thinking, I walk over to stand next to him. I'd expected him to be angry with me and lie to his mother, but I'm glad that he proved me wrong.

"You have?" Trish gasps.

"Yeah . . . I'm sorry, Mum. I didn't go near him until a few months ago, I got drunk and trashed his living room . . . but then I stayed the night a few times and we went to the wedding."

"You've been drinking again?" Her eyes begin to water. "Hardin, please tell me you haven't been drinking again?"

"No, Mum, only a couple times. Not like before," he promises.

Not like before? I know Hardin used to drink way too much, but Trish's reaction makes it seem like it was worse than I was led to believe.

"Are you mad that I've been seeing him?" he asks, and I put my hand on his back to try to comfort him.

"Oh, Hardin, I would never be upset with you for having a relationship with your father. I'm just surprised, that's all. You could have told me." She blinks rapidly to avoid tears. "I have wanted you to let go of that anger for so long. That was a dark time in our lives, but we got through it, and it's in the past. Your father isn't the same man he was then, and I'm not the same woman."

"It still doesn't make it okay," he says quietly.

"No, it doesn't. But sometimes you have to choose to let things go, to move on. I really am happy that you've been seeing him. It's good for you. The reason I sent you here . . . well, one of the reasons, was for you to forgive him."

"I didn't forgive him."

"You should," she says sincerely. "I have."

Hardin leans on his elbows on the counter and drops his head while I rub my hand up and down his back. Noticing the gesture, Trish gives me a knowing smile. Even more than before, I admire her so much. She's so strong and loving despite the lack of emotion from her son. I wish she had someone in her life, the way Ken has Karen.

Hardin must have been thinking the exact same thing, because he drops his head and says, "But he lives in this big-ass house and has expensive cars. He has a new wife . . . and you're alone."

"I don't care about his house or his money," she assures him. Then she smiles. "And what makes you think I'm alone?"

"What?" He raises his head.

"Don't sound so surprised! I'm quite the catch, son."

"You're seeing someone? Who?"

"Mike." She blushes and my heart warms.

Hardin's mouth gapes. "*Mike?* Your neighbor?"

"Yes, my neighbor. He's a very nice man, Hardin." She laughs and looks at me knowingly. "And it's convenient having him live just next door."

Hardin waves that off. "For how long? Why didn't you tell me?"

"A few months, it's nothing serious . . . yet. Besides, I don't think I should be asking *you* for relationship advice," she teases.

"Mike, though? He's sort of a . . ."

"Don't you say a bad word about him. You're not too old for a spanking," she scolds with a wry grin.

He raises his arms playfully. "Fine . . . fine . . ."

He's much more relaxed than he was this morning. The tension between us has disappeared, mostly, and watching him joke with his mother makes me so happy.

Trish announces cheerfully, "Excellent! I'm going to go pick the movie—don't come in there unless you bring cookies." She smiles and leaves us alone in the kitchen.

I walk back over to the bowl of ingredients and finish mixing the cookie dough. When I lick a glob of it off my finger, Hardin oh-so-helpfully notes, "I don't think that's very sanitary."

I dip my finger back into the bowl, collecting the sticky dough and walk over to him. "Have some," I tell him. I hold up my hand and try to transfer the dough to his fingers, but he opens his mouth and wraps his lips around my finger. I gasp at the contact and try to convince myself this is just his method of removing the cookie dough . . . regardless of how he's looking at me with dark eyes. No matter how he's flicking his warm tongue over my finger. No matter how many degrees the temperature of the kitchen has seemed to have risen. No matter how my heart is beating out of my chest and my insides are igniting.

"I think that's enough," I croak and pull my finger from his mouth.

He gives me a wicked smirk. "Later, then."

* * *

THE PLATE OF COOKIES is devoured within the first ten minutes of the movie. I have to admit I'm proud of my newly acquired baking skills; Trish praises me and Hardin eats over half of the batch, which is praise in and of itself.

"Is it bad that these cookies are my favorite thing about America so far?" Trish laughs as she takes the last bite.

"Yes, very sad," Hardin teases her, and I giggle.

"You may have to make these every day until I leave, Tessa."

"Sounds good to me." I smile and lean into Hardin. One of his arms snakes behind me at my waist, and I fold my legs up so I can move even closer to him.

Trish falls asleep toward the end of the movie, and Hardin turns the volume down a bit so we can finish without waking her. By the end, I'm a sobbing mess and Hardin doesn't try to hide his humor at my despair. That was one of the saddest movies I've seen in my entire life; I have no idea how Trish fell asleep.

"That was terrible, amazing but terribly sad," I sob.

"Blame my mum. I requested a comedy, yet somehow we ended up with *The Green Mile*. I warned you." He moves his arm to my shoulder, pulling me closer and placing a gentle kiss on my forehead. "We can turn on *Friends* when we get to the room to get your mind off of him dy—"

"Hardin! Don't remind me!" I groan.

But he just chuckles before standing up off of the couch and pulling me by the arm to join him. When we get to the room, Hardin switches on the lamp and then the television.

When he goes over and locks the door, then turns to me with those bright green eyes and evil dimples, my insides quiver.

chapter thirty-five

HARDIN

'm going to change," Tessa tells me and disappears into the closet, tissue still in hand.

Her eyes are red from her breakdown during the movie. I knew it would upset her, though I have to admit that I was looking forward to her reaction. Not because I want her to be upset, but because I love how emotionally invested she becomes in things. She opens herself so fully to these fictional forces, whether in a movie or a novel, that she allows them to completely pull her in. It's captivating to watch.

She emerges from the closet in only shorts and her white lace bra.

Holy shit. I don't even try to be subtle with my staring.

"Do you think you could wear . . . you know, my shirt?" I ask her. I'm not sure how she'll feel about that, but I miss seeing her wearing my shirts to bed.

"I would love to." She smiles and pulls my used shirt off the top of the clothes hamper.

"Good," I state, trying not to seem too excited. But I watch the way her breasts spill out of the top of the lace as she lifts her arms.

Stop staring. Slow, she wants to go slow. I can go slow . . . slowly . . . in and out of her. Jesus, what the fuck is wrong with me? Just when I consider looking away, she reaches under the shirt and pulls her bra through one sleeve . . . *Christ.*

"Something wrong?" she asks and climbs onto the bed.

"No." I gulp and watch in awe as she pulls her hair out of the ponytail it was in. As it falls onto her shoulders in beautiful blond waves, she shakes her head slowly. She has *got* to be doing this on purpose.

"Okay . . ." she says and lies on top of the duvet. I wish she would get under it so she wouldn't look so . . . exposed.

She gives me a quizzical look. "Are you coming to bed?"

I hadn't realized that I was still standing by the door. "Yeah . . ."

"I know this is a little strange right now, you know, getting used to being together again, but you don't have to be so . . . distant," she says nervously.

"I know," I respond and join her on the bed, holding my hands low and in front of me, to hide things.

"It's really not as strange as I thought it would be," she says in a near whisper.

"Yeah . . ." I'm relieved to hear that; I was worried that it wouldn't be the same as before. That she would be guarded and not the Tess that I love so much. It's only been a few hours, but I hope things stay this way. It's so easy with her, so damn easy, yet difficult at the same time.

She lays a small hand on mine and leans onto my chest "You are being so weird. Tell me what's on your mind," she requests.

"I'm just glad you're still here, that's all." *And I can't stop thinking about making love to you*, I add silently. It's not just about getting off with Tessa like it always was before—it's much more. So much more. It's about being as connected and tied to her as I possibly can be. It's about her trusting me fully. My chest aches when I think about the trust she had for me but that I shattered.

"That's not all," she says, calling me out.

I shake my head in agreement, and she draws a line against my temple and down to the metal in my eyebrow with one finger.

"It's terrible what I'm thinking," I admit. I don't want her to think that she's an object to me, that I just want to use her. I really don't want to tell her what's on my mind, but I can't continue to keep things from her, I need to be honest with her now and always.

As she looks down at me, her worried expression pains me. "Tell me."

"I . . . well, I was thinking about . . . fucking . . . I mean *making love* to you."

"Oh," she says softly, her eyes wide.

"I know, I'm a dick," I groan, wishing I would've just lied.

"No . . . no, you're not." Her cheeks color red. "I was sort of thinking about the same thing." She takes her bottom lip between her teeth, taunting me further.

"You were?"

"Yeah . . . I mean it has been a while . . . well, not including Seattle, during which I was belligerently drunk."

I search her face for the judgment she's made about my lack of control when she came onto me last weekend, but there's none there. I see the embarrassment as she recalls the events in her mind. My boxers are growing uncomfortably tight as I remember them, too.

"I don't want you to think that I'm using you . . . because of everything," I explain.

"Hardin, out of all the things I'm thinking right now, that isn't one of them. Granted, it probably should be, but it's not."

I was afraid, so afraid that our intimate moments would be forever tainted by my foolishness. "You're sure? Because I don't want to fuck up again," I say.

She answers me by taking my hand and placing in in between her thighs.

Fuck. I grab her waist with my other hand and pull her toward me. Within seconds I'm hovering over her, one knee between her legs. I kiss her neck first, my mouth feverish and quick against her soft skin. She tugs my T-shirt up and lifts her back enough for me to pull it off. My tongue leaves a wet trail behind as I kiss over her collarbone and the swell of her breasts. Her hands pull at my shirt and my sweats simultaneously, and I help her, leaving me in only my boxers.

I want to touch every part of her body, every inch of skin, every curve, every angle. God, she is beautiful. As I lower myself to kiss her stomach, her fingers disappear into my hair, tugging at the roots. I nip at her skin. Her panties and shorts are tossed to the floor. My tongue caresses the skin over her hips.

I explore her body as if it's the first or last time, but she rushes me along with a "Hardin . . . please . . ."

I bring my mouth to her most sensitive area and slide my tongue across her slowly, savoring her taste as it consumes my senses.

"Oh God," she pants and pulls harder on my hair.

Her hips buck up off of the bed and she presses herself against my tongue. I pull back and she whines. I love that she's as desperate for me as I am for her. I quickly lean up and open the drawer on the nightstand, grabbing the foil packet and tear it open with my teeth.

She watches me and I watch her. I watch the way her chest rises and falls in anticipation. I push down my boxers and lean over to plant a small kiss on her cheek, my cock resting on her thigh for a couple of heartbeats.

I straighten up and put the condom on. "Stay still," I instruct.

She obliges and I climb back between her legs. The anticipation is exhilarating. I'm so hard that it hurts.

"You're always so ready for me, baby," I muse, collecting her moisture on my fingers before bringing them to her mouth to have her taste. She's shy but doesn't protest as she wraps her tongue around my finger. The sensation causes me to ease into her. The feeling is exquisite and one I have missed so, so much. "Christ," I curse as she moans in relief.

All of my previous heartache dissolves as I bury myself into her, filling her up completely. Her eyes roll back in her head, and I deliberately circle my hips slowly before pulling out and pushing back in repeatedly.

"More . . . please, Hardin." ·

Fuck, I love to hear her beg. "No, baby . . . I want to go slow this time." I rotate my hips again. I want to savor every second of this. I want it to be slow and I want her to feel how much I love her, how sorry I am for hurting her, and how I'm willing to do anything for her. I bring my mouth to hers and caress her tongue with mine. I groan when her fingernails dig into my biceps with a force sure to leave crescent marks in their wake.

"I love you . . . I love you so much," I tell her and increase my pace slightly. I know I'm torturing her with my teasing, slow movements.

"I . . . I love you," she moans, and her legs begin to shake, telling me she's almost there.

I would love to see what we look like in this moment, molded together yet so separated. The contrast of her smooth, clear skin and the black ink covering mine as she runs her hands up and down my arms must be quite the sight. It's dark meets light; it's chaotic perfection; it's everything I fear, want, and need.

Her moans become louder, and I bring my hand to her mouth so she can bite on it. "Shhh . . . let go, baby."

My thrusts quicken as her soft body goes rigid under mine and she calls my name into my hand. Within seconds I'm joining her, getting high off her. She's the perfect drug. "Look at me," I breathe. Her eyes meet mine and I'm done for. I spill out all of me, and her body relaxes, leaving us both a panting mess. I roll off the condom and toss it into the bin next to the bed.

When I move to climb off, she grabs my arms to stop me. I smile down at her and stay still. I use my elbow to prop me up and keep most of my weight off of her. Tessa's hand touches my cheek, she uses the pad of her thumb to draw small circles against my damp skin.

"I love you, Hardin," she says quietly.

"I love you, Tess," I respond and lay my head against her chest.

My eyes are heavy as I feel her breathing slow, and I fall asleep listening to the steady thrum of her heartbeat.

chapter thirty-six

TESSA

Hardin's head is heavy on my stomach when the sound of my phone vibrating on the table wakes me up. I lift him gently, as gently as I can, and retrieve the annoying object. The screen flashes with my mother's name, and I groan before answering it.

"Theresa?" my mother chimes through the receiver.

"Yes."

"Where are you, and what time will you be here?" she asks.

"I'm not coming there," I tell her.

"It's Christmas Eve, Tessa, I know you are upset over this thing with your father, but you need to spend Christmas with me. You shouldn't be at some hotel alone."

I do feel slightly guilty for not spending the holidays with my mother. She isn't the nicest woman, but I'm all she has. Still, I say, "I'm not driving all the way there, Mother. It's snowing out and I don't want to be there."

Hardin stirs and lifts his head. Just as I'm about to tell him not to speak, he opens his mouth. "What's wrong?" he says, and I hear my mother gasp.

"Theresa Young! What are you *thinking*?" she shouts.

"Mother, I'm not doing this right now."

"That's him, isn't it? I know that voice!"

This is a terrible way to wake up. I move Hardin off me and sit up, covering my naked body with the blanket. "I am getting off the phone now, Mother."

"Don't you dare hang—"

But I do hang up. And then put my phone on silent. I knew she would find out sooner or later; I was just hoping it would be later. "Well, she knows we're back to doing . . . us. She heard you, and now she's freaking out," I say and hold my phone up to him to show the two calls from her in the past minute.

He curls around behind me. "You knew she would, so really it's almost better that she found out this way."

"Not really. I could have told her instead of her just hearing you in the background."

He shrugs. "It's the same thing. She would've been mad either way."

"Still." I'm slightly annoyed by his reaction. I know he doesn't care for her, but she's still my mother, and I didn't want her to find out like this. "You could be a little nicer about the whole thing."

He nods and says, "Sorry."

I expected him to have a rude comeback, so that was a pleasant surprise.

Hardin smiles and pulls me back down to him. "Would you like me to make you some breakfast, Daisy?"

"Daisy?" I raise my eyebrow.

"It's early, and I'm not at my best to quote literature, but you're grumpy, so . . . I called you Daisy."

"Daisy Buchanan wasn't grumpy. And neither am I." I harrumph, but can't help smiling.

He laughs. "Yes, you are. And how do you know which Daisy I'm talking about?"

"There are only a few, and I know you well enough."

"Is that so?"

"Yes, and your attempt at insulting me failed miserably," I tease.

"Yeah . . . Yeah . . . Mrs. Bennet," he fires back.

"I assume that since you said *Mrs.*, you are talking about the mother, not Elizabeth, which means you are trying to call me obnoxious. Then again, you *have* been off this morning, so maybe you're saying I'm charming? I just don't know with you anymore." I smile.

"All right . . . all right . . . Christ." He laughs. "A man makes one bad joke around here and he's condemned."

My earlier irritation dissolves as we continue our banter and climb out of bed. Hardin says to stay in pajamas, since we aren't leaving the house. It's a strange idea to me, though. If I were at my mother's house, I would be expected to be dressed in my Sunday best.

"You could just wear that shirt." He points to his T-shirt on the floor.

I smile and pick it up, pulling it over me and putting on sweatpants. I don't remember hanging out with Noah in sweats, ever. I didn't wear much makeup until recently, but I was always dressed nicely. I wonder what Noah would have thought if I'd shown up to spend time with him dressed like this. It's funny, I always thought I was comfortable around Noah, thought I was myself around him because he knew me for so long, when in reality he doesn't know me at all. He doesn't know the real me, the me that Hardin has made me comfortable enough to show.

"Ready?" Hardin asks.

I nod and pull my hair back into a messy bun. I switch my phone off and leave it on the dresser, then follow Hardin out into the living room. The delicious scent of coffee fills the apartment, and we find Trish standing in front of the stove flipping pancakes.

She smiles and turns to us. "Merry Christmas!"

"It's not Christmas," Hardin says, and I shoot him a glare. He rolls his eyes, then smiles at his mother. I pour myself a cup of coffee and thank Trish for making breakfast. Hardin and I sit at the table while she tells us the story of how her grandmother taught her how to make this type of pancakes. Hardin listens intently and even smiles a little.

As we start to eat our breakfast of *delicious* raspberry pancakes, Trish asks, "Are we going to be opening gifts today? Since I assume you'll be at your mum's tomorrow?"

I don't know how to answer her exactly, and I start to fumble for words. "I am . . . actually I am . . . I told—"

"She's going to Dad's house tomorrow. She promised Landon that she would, and she's really the only friend he's got, so she can't cancel," Hardin interjects.

I'm thankful for the assist, but calling me Landon's only friend is kind of mean . . . Well, maybe I am. But he's my only friend as well.

"Oh . . . that's fine. Honey, you don't need to be afraid to tell me things like that. I have no problem with you spending time with Ken," Trish says, and I can't tell which one of us she's speaking to.

Hardin shakes his head. "I'm not going. I told Tessa to tell them we said no."

Trish stops midbite. " 'We'? They invited me?" Her voice is full of surprise.

"Yeah . . . They wanted both of you to come," I explain.

"Why?" she asks.

"I . . . don't know . . ." I say. Honestly, I don't. Karen is so kind, and I know she really wants to mend what is broken between her husband and his son, so that's the only explanation I have.

"I already said no. Don't worry about it, Mum."

Trish finishes her forkful and chews thoughtfully. "No, maybe we should go," she says at last, surprising both me and Hardin.

"Why would you want to go there?" Hardin asks and scowls.

"I don't know . . . the last time I saw your father was almost ten years ago. I think I owe it to myself and to him to see how he's turned his life around. Also, I know you don't want to be away from Tessa for Christmas."

"I could stay here," I say. I don't want to cancel on them, but I don't want Trish to feel like she has to go.

"No, really. It's fine. We should go—all of us."

"You're sure?" The worry in Hardin's voice is evident.

"Yeah . . . it won't be so bad." She smiles. "Besides, if Kathy taught Tessa how to make those cookies, imagine how good the food will be."

"Karen, Mum—her name's Karen."

"Hey, she's my ex-husband's new wife, who I'm spending Christmas with. I can call her whatever I want." She laughs and I join her.

"I'll tell Landon we're all coming," I say and go to grab my phone. I'd never have imagined that my Christmas would be spent with Hardin and his family—both sides of his family. The last few months have been anything but what I expected.

When I turn on my phone I have three voicemails, from my mother, I'm sure. I ignore them and dial Landon.

"Hey, Tessa, Merry Christmas Eve!" he greets me, cheery as ever. I can picture his warm smile.

"Merry Christmas Eve, Landon."

"Thanks! First things first—you're not calling to bail, are you?"

"No, of course not. Quite the opposite, actually. I was calling to make sure it was still okay if Hardin and Trish came over tomorrow?"

"Really? They want to?"

"Yeah . . ."

"Does this mean you and Hardin . . ."

"Yeah . . . I know I'm an idiot . . ."

"I didn't say that," he says.

"I know, but you're thinking it—"

"No. I am not. We can talk about it tomorrow, but you aren't an idiot, Tessa."

"Thank you," I tell him and mean it. He's the only person who won't have a negative opinion on this subject.

"I'll tell my mom they're coming. She'll be thrilled," he says before we hang up.

When I join Hardin and Trish back in the living room, they already have their presents on their laps, and there are two boxes on the couch that I assume are for me.

"Me first!" Trish says and tears the snowflake-printed paper off of a box. Her smile is huge as she takes out the tracksuit I got her. "I love these! How did you know?" She points to the gray one she's wearing.

"I'm not very good at buying gifts," I tell her.

She giggles. "Don't be silly, it's lovely," she assures me while opening the second box. After she has a moment to see what's inside, she squeezes Hardin tight and then holds up a necklace that says *Mom*, just like he told me. She seems to like the thick scarf he bought her as well.

I really wish I'd gotten Hardin something. I knew all along that I would go back to him, and I think he knew it, too. He hasn't mentioned that he got me one, and both of the boxes on my lap say they're from Trish, so that's a huge relief.

Hardin is next, and he gives his mother his best fake smile when he opens the clothes she bought him. One piece is a red long-sleeved shirt; I try to picture Hardin wearing anything other than black and white, but I can't.

"Your turn," he says to me.

I smile nervously and pull the sparkly bow off of the first gift. Clearly, Trish is better at choosing women's clothing than men's; the pastel-yellow dress in the box proves it. It's a light baby-doll style, and I love it.

"Thank you—it's beautiful," I say and give her a hug. I really appreciate her thinking of me. She just met me, but she's been so loving and welcoming that I feel as if I've known her much longer.

The second box is much smaller than the first, but the amount of tape used to wrap it makes it very difficult to open. When I finally tear through the packaging, I find a bracelet—a sort of charm bracelet unlike anything I've seen before. Trish is so thoughtful, just like her son. I lift it up and run my fingers along the rope-textured string to look at the charms. There are only three, each bigger than my thumbnail, two made from what looks like pewter, the other solid white . . . porcelain, maybe? The white charm is an infinity symbol, the ends shaped like hearts. Just like the tattoo on Hardin's wrist. I glance up at him, my eyes moving immediately to his tattoo. He shifts and I look back to the bracelet. The second charm is a music note, and the third, slightly larger than the other two, is in the shape of a book. When I turn the book charm in my fingers, I notice something written on the back. It says:

Whatever our souls are made of, his and mine are the same.

I look up at Hardin and swallow the tears threatening to form. His mother didn't get me this.

He did.

chapter thirty-seven

Hardin's cheeks are flushed. His lips hold a nervous smile as I stare at him quietly for a minute.

Then I practically jump over to where he sits on the easy chair. I nearly tackle him with my enthusiasm and my desire just to be close to this wild, crazy boy. Luckily, he's strong enough to keep us both from falling over. I hug him as tight as I can manage, causing him to cough, so I loosen my grip. "It's so . . . it's just perfect," I sob. "Thank you. It's so thoughtful, and just unbelievable." I press my forehead against his as I nestle into his lap.

"It's nothing . . . really," he timidly states, and I wonder at his casual tone—until Trish clears her throat from where she sits nearby.

I hurry off his lap. For a moment I forgot that we are not alone in the apartment. "Sorry!" I tell her and move back to my spot on the couch.

She gives me a knowing smile. "Don't apologize, dear."

Hardin stays quiet; I know he won't talk about the gift in front of Trish, so I change the subject for now. His gift was so incredibly thoughtful. He couldn't have picked a more perfect quote from any novel to engrave on that charm.

"Whatever our souls are made of, his and mine are the same"—it's so perfect for the way I feel about him. We are so different, yet we're exactly the same, just like Catherine and Heathcliff. I can only hope that we don't share the same fate as them. I would like to think that we've learned from their mistakes, somehow, and that we won't allow that to happen.

I slide the bracelet over my wrist and slowly rock my lower arm back and forth, letting the charms sway. I've never received anything like this before. I thought the e-reader was the best gift ever, but Hardin managed to outdo himself by giving me this bracelet. Noah always gave me the same thing: perfume and socks. Every single year. Then again, I gave him cologne and socks each year. That was our thing—our boring, routine thing.

I stare at the bracelet for a few more seconds before I realize that both Hardin and Trish are watching me. Immediately I get up and begin to clean the small mess of wrapping paper.

With a chuckle, Trish asks, "Well, lady and gent, what shall we do for the rest of the day?"

"I feel like taking a nap," Hardin tells her, and she rolls her eyes.

"A nap? This early? And on Christmas?" she mocks.

"It's not Christmas, for the tenth time," he says a bit harshly, but then smiles.

"You're obnoxious," she scolds and swats at his arm.

"Like mother, like son."

As they gently bicker, I get lost in thought and take the small pile of crinkled and torn paper and push it into the steel trash can. I feel even worse about not getting Hardin a gift than I did before. I wish the mall were open today . . . I have no idea what I'd get, but anything would be better than nothing. I look down at the bracelet again and run my finger over the infinity heart charm. I still can't believe that he would get me a charm to match his tattoo.

"Almost done?"

I jump in surprise from the sound and the tickle at my ear. Then I turn and smack Hardin. "You scared me!"

"Sorry, love," he says between chuckles. My heart leaps when he calls me "love." It's so unlike him.

I feel him smile against my neck, and he wraps his arms around my waist. "Join me for my nap?"

I turn and face him. "No. I'll keep your mom company. But," I add with a smile, "I *will* tuck you in." I don't really like to take naps unless I'm too exhausted to do anything else, and it would be nice to hang out with his mom and read or something.

Hardin rolls his eyes but leads me to our bedroom. He pulls his shirt over his head, and it falls to the floor. As my eyes travel over the familiar designs inked into his skin, he smiles at me. "You really like the bracelet?" he asks as he walks over to the bed. He tosses the decorative pillows onto the floor and I pick them up.

"You're so messy!" I complain. I put the pillows into the trunk and Hardin's shirt on the dresser before grabbing my e-reader and joining him by the bed. "But to answer your question, I do love the bracelet. It's really thoughtful, Hardin. Why didn't you say it was from you?"

He pulls me down and lays my head on his chest. "Because I knew you were already feeling bad about not getting me something." He lets out a laugh. "And that you would feel even worse after my amazing gift."

"Wow, so humble," I tease.

"Also, when I had it made for you, I had no idea if you would ever speak to me again," he admits.

"You knew I would."

"Honestly, I didn't. You were different this time."

"How so?" I look up at him.

"I don't know . . . you just were. It wasn't like the other hundred times you said you wanted nothing to do with me." Hardin's voice is light as he pushes my loose hair from my forehead with his thumb.

I concentrate on the rise and fall of his chest. "Well, I

knew . . . I mean, I didn't want to admit it, but I knew I would come back. I always do."

"I won't give you reason to leave again."

"I hope not," I say and kiss the palm of his hand. "Me, too."

I don't say anything else; there's nothing to say at the moment. He's sleepy, and I don't want to talk about me leaving him any longer. Within minutes he's asleep, breathing heavily. Hardin calling me Daisy this morning made me want to reread *The Great Gatsby*, so I scroll through my e-reader's library to see if Hardin already loaded it on there. And find that, of course, he has. Just as I'm about to get up and join his mother, I hear a woman's angry voice.

"Excuse me!"

My mother. I toss my e-reader to the end of the bed and get up. *Why the hell is she here?*

"You have no right to go in there!" I hear Trish yell.

Trish. My mother. Hardin. This apartment. Oh my Lord. This isn't going to go well.

The bedroom door crashes open to reveal my mother, looking sophisticated yet menacing in a red dress and black heels. Her hair is curled and pinned up to resemble a beehive, and her red lipstick is bright, too bright.

"How could you be here! After everything!" she yells.

"Mother . . ." I begin as she turns to Trish.

"And who the hell *are* you?" she asks, their faces close together.

"I'm his mother," Trish says sternly.

Hardin groans in his slumber and opens his eyes. "What the fuck?" are the first words out of his mouth when he spots the devil in the crimson dress.

My mother snaps her head back in my direction. "Let's go, Theresa."

"I'm not going anywhere. Why are you even here?" I ask her, and she huffs, putting her hands on her hips.

"Because I have already told you. You are my only child, and I will not sit back and watch you ruin your life over this . . . this *asshole*."

Her words light a fire under my skin, and I immediately go on defense. "Do *not* speak of him that way!" I shout.

"That 'asshole' is my son, missy," Trish says with hooded eyes. Underneath her humor is a woman clearly ready to go into the ring for her son.

"Well, your son is *ruining* and *corrupting* my daughter," my mother fires back.

"Both of you—get out," Hardin says and stands up from the bed.

My mother shakes her head and gives a toothy smile. "Theresa, grab your things, *now*."

Being ordered about makes me snap, "What part of *I am not leaving* do you not understand? I gave you the opportunity to spend the holidays with me, but you couldn't get over yourself long enough to allow it." I know I shouldn't be speaking to her this way, but I can't help it.

"*Get over myself?* You think just because you bought a few slutty dresses and learned to put on makeup, you suddenly know more than I do about life?" Although she's yelling, it's like she's laughing, too. Like my choices are a joke. "Well, you're wrong. Just because you gave yourself to this . . . this *filth* doesn't mean you're a woman! You are nothing but a little girl. A naive, impressionable little girl. Now grab your things before I do it for you."

"You will *not* touch her things," Hardin spits. "She isn't going anywhere with you. She's staying here with me, where she belongs."

My mother wheels toward him, all humor gone. " 'Where she belongs'? Where did she belong when she was staying in a damned motel because of what you did to her? You are no good for her—and she will not stay here with you."

"Mrs. White, these two are adults," Trish interjects. "Tessa is an adult. If she wants to stay, there is nothing—"

My mother's enraged eyes turn to meet Trish's equally hardened glare. This is a disaster. I open my mouth to speak, but my mother beats me to it.

"How can you defend this sinful behavior? After what he did to her, he should be locked away!" she screams.

"She has obviously chosen to forgive him. You need to accept that," Trish says coolly. Too coolly. She looks like a snake, one that slithers by so slowly you never see its attack coming. But when it does, you are done for. My mother is the prey, and right now I can't help but hope that Trish's bite is venomous.

"Forgive him? He stole her innocence as a *game*—a bet with his friends. And then bragged about it while she was here playing house!"

Trish's gasp overrides all sound in the air and silences everything for a second. Mouth agape, she looks at her son. "What . . ."

"Oh, you didn't know? You mean—surprise—the liar lied even to his own mother? Poor woman, no wonder you're defending him," my mother says, shaking her head. "Your son bet his friends—for money—that he could take Tessa's virginity. He even kept the evidence and flaunted it around the entire campus."

I'm frozen. I keep my eyes on our mothers, too afraid to look at Hardin. I can tell by the shift in his breathing that he hadn't thought I'd told my mother the details of his deceit. As for his mother, I didn't want her to know the terrible things her son has done. It was my embarrassment to share or not share with people.

"Evidence?" Trish's voice is shaky.

"Yes, evidence. The condom! Oh, and the sheets with Tessa's stolen virginity on them. God knows what he did with the money, but he was telling everyone every detail of their . . . intimacy. So now you tell me if I should make my daughter come with me or not." My mother raises her perfectly sculpted eyebrow to Trish.

I feel it the moment it happens. I feel the change in the room, the energy shifting. Trish is now on my mother's side of this. I try desperately to cling to the edge of the crumbling cliff that is Hardin, but I can see it all perfectly in the disgusted glare she gives her son. A look I can tell is nothing new. It's something she's had to use on him before, like a memory brought back as a facial expression. A look that all but says she believes, once again, every bad thing anyone's ever said about her son.

"How could you, Hardin?" she cries. "I had hoped you were different now . . . I hoped you had stopped doing things like this to girls . . . women. Have you forgotten what happened last time?"

chapter thirty-eight

It doesn't help. It doesn't help at all that my mother follows Trish into the living room and practically howls, "Last time? See, Theresa! This is exactly why you need to get away from him. He has done this before, I knew it! Prince Charming strikes again!"

I look over at Hardin, my fingers slipping from the edge. *Not again.* I don't think I can take any more. Not from him.

"It's not like that, Mum," Hardin finally says.

Trish gives him a look of utter disbelief and wipes under her eyes, even as her tears keep coming. "It sure sounds like it, Hardin. I honestly can't believe you. I love you, son, but I can't help you here. This is wrong, so wrong."

I never am able to find my voice in these situations. I want to speak, I need to, but an endless list of potential terrible things that Trish could be referring to as "last time" are running rapidly through my head, stealing my voice.

"I said it's not like that!" Hardin shouts, his arms out wide.

Trish turns and stares at me, hard. "Tessa, you should go with your mother," she says, and a lump rises in my throat.

"What?" Hardin says to her.

"You're no good for her, Hardin. I love you more than life itself, but I can't allow you to do this again. Coming to America was supposed to have helped you—"

"Theresa," my mother says. "I think we've have heard enough." She grabs hold of my arm. "It's time to go."

Hardin moves toward her and she steps back, gripping me tighter.

"Let go of her, now," he says through gritted teeth.

Her plum nails dig into my skin as I try to process the events of the last two minutes. I had not expected my mother to barge into the apartment—and I certainly didn't expect Trish to drop hints about yet another one of Hardin's secrets.

Has he done this before? To who? Did he love her? Did she love him? He said he had never been with a virgin before, he said he had never loved anyone before. *Was he lying?* The angry mask he wears makes it hard for me to decipher.

"You don't get to have a say in anything that concerns her any longer," my mother strikes back.

But, surprising everyone in the room, even myself, I slowly pull my arm from my mother's grip . . . and step behind Hardin. Hardin's mouth falls open, like he's unsure what I'm doing. Trish and my mother wear identical horrified expressions

"Theresa! Don't be stupid. Get over here!" my mother instructs.

In response, I wrap my fingers around Hardin's forearm and stay hidden behind him. I don't really understand why, but I do. I should be leaving with my mother, or forcing Hardin to tell me what the hell Trish is talking about. But, really, I just want my mother to go away. I need a few minutes, hours—some *time*— to comprehend what's going on. I just forgave Hardin. I just decided to forget everything and move on with him. Why must there always be some secret locked away that comes to a head at the worst possible time?

"Theresa." My mother takes another step toward me, and Hardin brings his arm back to wrap around me. To protect me from her.

"Stay away from her," he warns.

Trish steps forward. "Hardin. That is her *daughter*. You have no right coming between them."

"I have no *right*? *She* has no right coming into our apartment, into our fucking *bedroom*, uninvited!" he shouts. My grip on his arm tightens.

"That's not *her* bedroom, nor is this her apartment," my mother says.

"Yes. It is! See who she's standing behind? She's using me as a shield to block her from *you*." Hardin points a thick finger at her.

"She's just being foolish and doesn't understand what's best for her—"

But I interrupt her, finally finding part of my voice. "Stop speaking as if I'm not here! I'm right here, and I'm an adult, Mother. If I want to stay, I will," I announce.

With pitying eyes, Trish tries to appeal to me. "Tessa, honey. I think you should listen to your mother."

The sting of her dismissal burns my chest like a betrayal, but I don't know what she knows about her son.

"Thank you!" My mother sighs. "At least someone in this family is reasonable."

Trish shoots her a warning glare. "Missy, I don't agree with how you treat your daughter, so don't think that we're on the same team here, because we're not."

My mother shrugs a little. "Regardless, we both agree that you need to go, Tessa. You need to leave this apartment and not come back. We can transfer you to another school if need be."

"She can make up her own—" Hardin starts.

"He has poisoned your mind, Theresa—look at the things he's done to you. Do you know him *at all*?" my mother asks.

"I *know* him, Mother," I say through my teeth.

My mother turns her attention to Hardin. I don't know why she's not afraid of him, the way his chest is heaving up and down, the way his cheeks are flaring with anger, the way his fists are clenched into balls so tightly that his knuckles are white. He should intimidate her, but she's unfazed as she says, "Boy, if you care for her, even a little bit, you will tell her to go. You have done nothing but break her down. She isn't the same girl that I dropped off at college three months ago, and that's your fault. You didn't have to see her cry for days over what you did to her. You were probably partying with another girl while she was crying herself to sleep. You have destroyed her—how can you even live with yourself? You know you'll hurt her again sooner or later. So if you have one decent bone in your body, you'll tell her . . . tell her to come with me."

The silence in the room is chilling.

Trish stands silently staring at the wall, deep in thought, likely mulling over Hardin's past actions. My mother is glaring at Hardin, waiting for his response. Hardin is breathing so hard he may combust. And me, I'm trying to decide which will win the battle inside of me: my heart or my head?

"I'm not going with you," I finally say.

In response to my decision—my adult decision, one that I know will have consequences I will have to deal with, that will make me endure some very difficult things as I try to figure out whether I can be with the man I love or not—my mother rolls her eyes.

And I lose it.

"You aren't welcome here—don't ever come back!" I scream with a bloody rawness in my throat. "Who do you think you are, busting in here, and with the nerve to talk to him that way!" I push past Hardin and come face-to-face with her. "I want nothing to do with you! No one does! That's why you're alone after all these years—you are cruel and conceited! You will never be happy!" I take a breath and swallow, feeling just how dry my throat is.

My mother stares me down with full self-assurance, and

more than a little scorn. "I am alone because I choose to be. I don't have the need to be with someone; I'm not like you."

"Like *me*! I don't need to be with anyone! You basically *forced* me to be with Noah—I never felt like I had a choice in anything! You have always controlled me—and I am done. I am fucking *done*!" The tears erupt from me then.

My mother quirks her lips, like she's considering something in earnest, but her voice is full of sarcasm. "It's obvious that you have some codependency issues. Is this because of your father?"

My eyes sore, surely bloodshot, and filled with every evil I want to inflict on her, I stare at her. Speaking slowly at first, I feel myself frantically escalating as I say, "I hate you. I really hate you. You're the reason he left. Because he couldn't stand you! And I don't blame him—in fact, I wish he would have taken—"

And right then I feel Hardin's hand clamp over my mouth and his strong arms pull me back against his chest.

chapter thirty-nine

HARDIN

The whole time, I had just been thinking that her mum better not slap her again. I hadn't really considered Tessa going on the offensive like this.

Her face is red, and her tears are pouring down my hand.

Why does her mum always have to ruin shit? I can't blame her for being angry, regardless of how much I hate her. I *did* hurt Tessa. But I don't think I *ruined* her.

Have I?

I don't know what to do. I glance at my mum for help—the look she gives me lets me know that she hates me. I didn't want her to know what I did to Tess. I knew it would kill her, especially after what happened before.

But I'm not the same person I was then. This is totally different.

I love Tessa.

Through all the chaos I caused, I found love.

Tessa screams into my hand and tries to push me off of her, but she isn't strong enough. I know one of two things will happen if I don't keep her away: either her mum will slap her and I'll have to intervene, or Tessa will say something she'll regret forever. "I think you need to go now," I say to her mother.

Tessa is throwing a fit beneath my grip and keeps kicking her feet into my shins.

It's always so unsettling to see her angry—especially this

angry—although part of me is selfishly pleased that her anger isn't directed at me this time.

It will be soon . . .

I know her mother is right about me: I *am* terrible for her. I'm not the man Tessa thinks I am, but I love her too much to let her leave me again. I just got her back, and I will not lose her again. I just hope that she'll listen to me, listen to the entire story. Even then, I don't think it will matter. I know it's coming; there's no way she'll stay with me once she hears it. *Fuck, why did my mum have to say anything?*

I lead Tessa toward the bedroom. As we go, she twists so hard she spins us both around, so we're facing her mom again. With one last hateful glare, she makes her point and lunges, but I hold tight.

Pulling her into our room, I let go and quickly slam the door and lock it.

And she turns her poisonous glare at me. "Why did you do that! You—"

"Because you're saying things you know you'll regret."

"Why did you do that!" she yells. "Why did you stop me! I have so much shit to say to that bitch, it's not even . . . I can't even . . . !" She pushes her hands against my chest.

"Hey . . . hey . . . calm down," I say, trying to remember that she's displacing her anger at her mother toward me; I know she is.

I bring her face between my hands and gently move my thumbs across her cheekbones, making sure she keeps eye contact with me as her breathing slows. "Just calm down, baby," I repeat.

The redness disappears from her cheeks, and she nods slowly.

"I'm going to make sure she leaves, okay?" I say so low that it's almost a whisper.

She nods again and moves to sit on the bed. "Hurry up," she demands as I leave the room.

When I walk into the living room, Tessa's mother is there alone, pacing. She looks up at me sharply, like a jungle cat sensing prey. "Where is she?" she asks.

"She's not coming out. You are leaving, and you're not going to come back here. I mean it," I say through my teeth.

She raises an eyebrow. "Are you threatening me?"

"You can take it however you want, but you need to stay away from her."

This manicured woman, so put together and prim-looking, gives me a sly, hard look that I've only ever seen from people like those in Jace's crew. "This is all your fault," she says calmly. "You have brainwashed her; she doesn't think for herself anymore. I know what you are doing. I've been with men like you. I knew you were trouble since the day I laid eyes on you. I should have had Tessa change rooms and prevented all of this. No man is going to want her after this . . . after you. Look at you." She waves her hand in the air and turns toward the door.

I follow her out into the hallway. "That's the point, isn't it? That no man will want her, no man but me. She'll never be with anyone but me," I boast. "She will always choose me over you, over anyone."

She spins and takes a step toward me. "You are the devil, and I'm not going to just go away. She is my daughter, and she's too good for you."

I nod my head several times quickly, then look at her flatly. "I'll make sure to remember that when I'm burying myself into your daughter tonight."

As the words leave my lips, she gasps and reaches her hand up to smack me. I grab her wrist and push it back down gently. I would never hurt her or any woman, but neither am I going to let her hurt me.

I give her my best smile before I go back into the apartment and slam the door in her face.

chapter forty

HARDIN

I rest with my head against the door for a moment, and when I turn around, my mum is standing in the living room, staring at me with a mug of coffee in her hands, her eyes completely bloodshot.

"Where were you?" I ask.

"The bathroom," she says, her voice cracking.

"How could you tell Tessa to go? To leave me?" I say. I knew she would be disappointed, but that was too much.

"Because, Hardin"—she sighs, lifting her hands as if it's obvious—"you aren't good for her. You know you aren't. I don't want to see her end up like Natalie, or the others." My mum shakes her head.

"Do you know what will happen to me if she leaves me, Mum? I don't think you understand . . . I can*not* be without her. I know I'm not good for her, and I regret what I did every single time I look at her, but I *can* be good for her. I know I can be." I walk to the middle of the living room and start pacing back and forth.

"Hardin . . . are you sure you aren't just feeding into your own game right now?"

"No, Mum . . ." I lower my head to try and keep calm. "This isn't a game to me—not this time. I love her, I really love her." I look up at my good, kind mother, who I know has had to endure so much. "I love her more than I can even begin to tell you, because I don't even understand it myself. I never thought I could or would feel this way. All I know is that she's my only shot at happiness. If she leaves me, I'll never recover. I won't, Mum. She's the only chance I have to not be alone for the rest of my life. I don't know what the fuck I did to deserve her—nothing I know—but she loves me. Do you know how that feels to have someone love you despite all the fucked-up shit you do? She's way too good for me, and she loves me. I have no fucking clue why."

My mum wipes at her eyes with the back of her hand, making me pause for a moment. It's hard to go on, but I say, "She's always there for me, Mum. She always forgives me, even when she shouldn't. She always says the right thing. She calms me, but challenges me—she makes me want to be a better man. I know I'm a shitty person, I know that. I have done so much shit, but Tessa can't leave me. I don't want to be alone anymore, and I'll never love anyone again—she is it for me. I know it. She's my ultimate sin, Mum, and I'll gladly be damned for her."

I'm out of breath by the time I finish, and my mum's cheeks are wet. But she's also staring behind me.

I turn to find Tessa with her hands at her sides, her eyes wide and her cheeks just as wet as my mum's.

My mum blows her nose, then softly says, "I'm going to go out for a little while . . . give you two some privacy." She goes over to the door, grabs her shoes and coat, and heads out.

I feel kind of bad that there aren't many places for her to go on Christmas Eve, especially in the snow, but I need to be alone with Tessa right now. As soon as my mum is out the door, I pad across the room to her.

"What you said . . . just now . . . you meant it?" she asks through her tears.

"You know I did," I tell her.

The corners of her lips turn up, and she reaches across the small space between us to put her hand on my chest. "I need to know what you did."

"I know . . . just promise me that you'll try to understand . . ."

"Tell me, Hardin."

"And that you understand that I'm not proud of any of this."

She nods, and I take a deep breath as she leads us to the couch.

I really don't know where the fuck to start.

chapter forty-one

TESSA

Hardin's face pales. He rubs his hands over his knees. He runs his fingers through his hair. He looks up at the ceiling and then back down. He, somewhere deep inside, probably wishes these things would stall this conversation forever.

But finally, he begins. "I had a group of shitty friends back home. They were like Jace, I guess . . . We would do this thing . . . this game, I guess. We would pick a girl—pick a girl for one another, and see who could fuck their girl first."

My stomach drops.

"Whoever won would get the hottest chick the next week, and there was money involved . . ."

"How many weeks?" I ask, regretfully. I don't want to know, yet I have to know.

"Only five weeks went by before this girl—"

"Natalie." I say, connecting the dots.

Hardin looks over at the windows. "Yeah . . . Natalie was the last one."

"And what did you do to her?" I am terrified of his answer.

"The third week . . . James thought Martin was lying, so he came up with the idea of proof . . ."

Proof. That word will always haunt me. The bloodstained sheets pop into my mind, and my chest starts to hurt.

"Not the same type of proof . . ." He knows what I was thinking. "Pictures . . ."

My jaw drops. "Pictures?"

"And a video . . ." he admits and covers his face with his large hands.

Video? "You recorded sex with someone? Did she know?" I ask. But I know the answer even before he shakes his head. "How could you? How could you do that to someone?" I begin to cry.

The realization that I don't know Hardin at all hits me, and I have to swallow the bile rising in my throat. I scoot away from him instinctively, and I see pain flair up in his eyes.

"I don't know . . . I just didn't care. It was fun to me . . . Well, not exactly fun, but I didn't care." His honesty slices through me, and for once I long for the days when he kept everything from me.

"So what happened with Natalie?" My voice is coarse as I wipe the tears from my eyes.

"When James saw the video of her . . . He wanted to fuck her himself. And when she turned him down, he showed everyone the video."

"Oh my God. That poor girl." I feel so terrible for what they did to her, what Hardin did to her.

"The video spread so quickly that her parents found out before even a day had passed. Her family was really big in their church community . . . so the news didn't go well. They kicked her out of their house, and when word got around, she lost her scholarship to the private university she was going to that fall."

"You ruined her," I say quietly.

Hardin ruined this girl's life, the way he once threatened to ruin mine. Will I end up like her? Am I already just like her?

I look at him. "You said you'd never been with a virgin before."

"She wasn't a virgin. She had slept with one guy already. But that's why my mum sent me here. Everyone back home knew about it. I wasn't in the video. Well, I was fucking her in it, but I wasn't visible; only a few of the tattoos on my arms were." He grinds one fist into the palm of his other hand. "That's sort of what I'm known for there now . . ."

My head is spinning. "What did she say when she found out what you did?"

"She said she fell in love with me . . . and she asked if she could stay at my house until she found somewhere else to go."

"Did you let her?"

He shakes his head.

"Why?"

"Because I didn't want to. I didn't care for her."

"How can you be so cold about this? Do you not understand what you did to her? You led her on. You had sex with her and taped it. You showed your friends—and basically the school—and she lost her scholarship and family because of you! Then you don't even have the compassion to help her when *she had nowhere else to go*?" I shout and stand up. "Where is she *now*? What happened to her?"

"I don't know. I didn't care to find out."

The most chilling part of this whole thing is how casual and cold he is about it. This is nauseating. I see the pattern here, I see the similarities between Natalie and me. I was left with nowhere to go because of Hardin, too. I have no relationship with my mother because of Hardin. I fell for him while he was using me as part of some sick game.

Hardin stands up with me but keeps few feet of space between us.

"Oh my God . . ." My entire body begins to shake. "You recorded me—didn't you?"

"No! *Fuck* no! I would never do that to you! Tessa, I swear to God I did not."

I shouldn't, but part of me does believe that part, at least. "How many others?" I ask.

"How many others what?"

"Did you record?"

"Just Natalie . . . until I came here."

"You did it again! After everything you did to that poor girl, you did it again?" I scream.

"Once . . . to Dan's sister," he says.

Dan's sister? "Your friend Dan?" It makes sense now. "That's what Jace meant when you were fighting!" I had forgotten all about Dan and Hardin's fight, but Jace had hinted about some previous tension between the two of them.

"Why did you do that if he was your friend? Did you show everyone?"

"No, I didn't show anyone. I deleted it after I sent Dan a screen grab . . . I don't know why I did it, really. He was such a dick about telling me to stay away from her when he brought her around the first time that it made me want to fuck her just to piss him off. He's a true asshole anyway, Tessa."

"How do you not see how fucked up this is! How fucked up you are?" I yell.

"I know it is! I know that, Tessa!"

"I thought my bet was the worst thing you had done . . . but, oh my God, this is even worse."

Natalie's story doesn't hurt me nearly as bad as finding out about Hardin and Zed's bet, but it's worse by being more vile and revolting, and it makes me question everything I thought I knew about Hardin. I knew he wasn't perfect—far from it—but this is a whole new level of disgrace.

"This was all before you, Tessa—this is my past. Please let it stay that way," he pleads. "I'm not the same person now—you've made me a better person."

"Hardin, you don't even care about what you did to those girls! You don't even feel guilty, do you?"

"I do."

I cock my head and squint at him. "Only because now *I* know." When he doesn't argue, I reiterate my point. "You didn't care about them, about anyone!"

"You're right! I don't care—I honestly don't give a shit about anyone, except you!" he shouts back.

"This is too much, Hardin! Even for me . . . the bet, the apartment, the fights, the lies, getting back together, my mother, your mother, Christmas—it's too fucking much. I don't even get a breath between these . . . these *messes*. As soon as I get over one thing, another comes out. God knows what else you've done!" I start crying. "I don't know you at all, do I?"

"Yes, you do, Tessa! You do know me. That wasn't me—this is me. This is me now. I love you! I will do anything for you, for you to see that this is me, the man who loves you more than breathing, the man who dances at weddings and watches you sleep, the man whose day can't start until you kiss me, the man who would rather die than be without you. That's me, that's who I am. Please don't let this ruin us. Please, baby."

His green eyes are glossy, and I'm moved by his words, but it isn't enough. He steps toward me, and I back away. I need to be able to think. I raise my hand in front of me. "I need time. This is too much for me right now."

His shoulders lower, and he seems relieved. "Okay . . . okay . . . take time to think."

"Away from you," I explain.

"No—"

"Yes, Hardin. I can't think straight around you."

"No, Tessa, you're not leaving," he commands.

"You will not tell me what I will or will not do," I snap.

He sighs and wraps his fingers in his hair, tugging hard at the roots. "Fine . . . fine . . . Let me go, then. You stay here."

I want to argue, but I really don't want to leave. I've had enough of hotel rooms, and tomorrow is Christmas.

"I'll be back in the morning . . . unless you need more time," he says. He puts his shoes on and reaches for the key rack before realizing that his mother has taken his car.

"Take mine," I say.

He nods and walks toward me. "Don't," I say and bring my hands up in front of me. "And you're in your pajamas still."

He frowns and looks down, but walks into the bedroom and emerges two minutes later fully dressed. He stops to look me in the eyes. "Please remember that I love you, and I have changed," he says once more before leaving me alone in the apartment.

chapter forty-two

What the hell am I going to do?

I walk to the bedroom and sit on the edge of the bed. I'm sick to my stomach from all of this. I knew Hardin wasn't a good person before, and I knew there would be some more things that I wouldn't be happy to hear, but of all the things I thought Trish could be referring to, this never, ever crossed my mind. He violated that girl in a terrible, deplorable way, and he had no remorse—he still barely does.

I try to breathe in and out slowly as tears spill down my cheeks. The worst part to me is knowing her name. It's kind of fucked up, but if she was just some anonymous girl, I could almost pretend that she didn't exist. Knowing that her name is Natalie opens up too many thoughts. What does she look like? What did she plan to study in college before Hardin took her scholarship from her? Does she have any brothers or sisters? Did they see the tape? If Trish hadn't brought this up, would I have ever known?

How many times did they have sex? Did Hardin like it? . . . Of course he did. It's sex, and obviously Hardin was having a lot of it. With other girls. Lots of other girls. Did he stay the night with Natalie after? Why do I feel jealous of Natalie? I should feel sorry for her, not envy her for touching Hardin. I push this sick thought out of my mind and go back to thinking about the type of person Hardin really is.

I should have had him stay to talk it out; I always leave or, in this case, make him leave. The problem is that his presence washes away every ounce of restraint I should have.

I wish I knew what happened to Natalie after Hardin demolished her life. If she's happy now and leading a good life, I'd feel better, slightly. I wish I had a friend to talk about all of this with, someone to give me advice. Even if I did, I wouldn't divulge Hardin's indiscretion. I do not want anyone to know what he has done to these girls. I know how foolish it is to want to protect him when he doesn't deserve it, but I can't help it. I don't want anyone to think any worse of him, and mostly I don't want him to think any worse of himself than he already does.

I lie back against the pillows and stare up at the ceiling. I just got over . . . well, was *working on* getting over Hardin using me to win a bet—and now this? Natalie, plus four other girls, since he said she was week five. Then Dan's sister. This is a cycle with him, this is what he does—will he be able to stop doing it? What would have happened to me if he hadn't fallen in love with me?

I know that he loves me—he truly does love me. I know that.

And I do love him despite all the mistakes he makes, and has made in the past. I've seen changes in him, even in the course of the last week. He has never expressed his feelings about me the way he did today. I just wish that his beautiful declaration hadn't been followed by such an ugly revelation.

He said that I'm his only shot at happiness, I'm the only chance that he has to not spend the entirety of his life alone. What a heavy statement. What a true statement. No one will ever love him the way I do. Not because he's not worth loving, but because no one will ever know him the way that I do. Did. *Still do?* I can't decide, but I want to believe I know him, the true him. Who he is now is not the person he was just a few months ago.

Despite the pain he's caused me, he has also done a lot to prove himself to me. He has made a huge effort to be the person I need him to be. He can change; I've seen him change. Half of me thinks that it may be time for me to take some of the blame here—not for what he did to Natalie, but for being so hard on him when change takes time and nobody can erase their past. What he did was wrong, so incredibly wrong, but sometimes I forget that he's an angry, lonely man who up until now has never loved anyone. He loves his mother, in his manner, if not the same way that people usually love their parents.

The other half of me is tired. Tired of this cycle with Hardin. In the beginning of our relationship, it was a constant back-and-forth, with him being cruel, then nice, then cruel again. Now the cycle has evolved somewhat, but it's worse. Much worse. I leave him, then come back, then leave him again. I cannot keep doing this—*we* cannot keep doing this. If there's anything else that he's hiding, it will break me—I'm barely holding myself together now. I can't take any more secrets, any more heartache, any more breakups. I always used to have everything planned—every detail of my life was calculated, overanalyzed, until Hardin. He's completely turned my life upside down, often in a negative way. And yet he's also made me happier than I have ever been.

We need to be together and try to move past all of the terrible things he's done, or I need to end things and keep them that way. If I leave him, I need to move away from here, far away. I need to leave behind every reminder of my life with him or I'll never be able to move on.

And suddenly I realize the tears have stopped, telling me that my verdict is in. The pain that comes from considering leaving him is much worse than the pain he has caused me.

I can't leave him. I know I can't.

I know how pathetic that is, but there's no way I can be without him. No one will ever make me feel the way he does. No one will ever be him. He is it for me, just the way I am it for him. I shouldn't have had him leave. I needed time to think and I should take more time, but I'm already wanting him back. *Is love always like this? Is it always so passionate, yet so damn painful?* I have no experience to compare this to.

Hearing the front door open, I climb off the bed and rush into the living room. But I'm disappointed to find Trish instead of Hardin.

Trish hangs Hardin's keys on the rack and removes her snow-covered shoes. I'm not sure what to say to her since she told me to leave with my mother.

"Where is Hardin?" she asks as she walks into the kitchen.

"He left . . . for the night," I explain.

She turns to me. "Oh."

"I'm sure if you call him he'll tell you where he is, if you don't want to stay here . . . with me."

"Tessa," she says, clearly searching for words, but with sympathy on her face. "I'm sorry for what I said. I don't want you to think I have any ill feelings toward you—I don't. I was just trying to protect you from what Hardin can do. I don't want you to . . ."

"To end up like Natalie?"

I can see that the memory pains her. "He told you?"

"Yes."

"Everything?" I hear the doubt in her voice.

"Yes—the tape, the pictures, the scholarship. Everything."

"And you're still here?"

"I told him I needed time and space, but yes. I'm not going anywhere."

She nods, and we both sit down at the table across from each other. When she looks at me with wide eyes, I know what she's thinking, so I say, "I know he's done terrible things, deplorable things, but I believe him when he says that he's changed. He isn't that person anymore."

Trish puts one hand over the other. "Tessa, he's my son, and I love him, but you really have to think about this. He just did the same thing to you that he did before. I know that he loves you—

that's clear to me now—but I'm just afraid that the damage has been done."

I nod, appreciative of her honesty. But I tell her, "It hasn't. Well, damage has most certainly been done, but it's not irreversible. And it's *my* decision to figure out how to deal with his past. And if I hold his past against him, how will he move forward? Is he never deserving of love forever more? I know you probably think I'm naive and foolish to keep forgiving him, but I love your son, and I cannot be without him, either."

Trish softly clicks her tongue and shakes her head. "Tessa, I don't think you're either of those things. If anything, your forgiveness shows maturity and compassion. My son hates himself— always has—and I thought he always would, until you. I was mortified when your mum told me what he did to you, and for that I'm sorry. I don't know where I went wrong with Hardin. I tried to be the best mother that I could be, but it was so hard with his father not being around. I had to work so much, and I didn't give him the attention that I should have. If I had, maybe he would have more respect for women."

I know that if she hadn't already cried herself out today, she'd be crying now. The guilt in her is so thick, I just want to comfort her. "He's not this way because of you. I think it has a lot to do with his feelings about his father and the type of friends he has, both of which I'm trying to work on. Please don't blame yourself. None of this is your fault."

Trish reaches across the table, and I give her my hands. Taking them in hers, she says, "You are certainly the most kind-hearted person I've met in all of my thirty-five years."

I arch my brow. "Thirty-five?"

"Hey, just go with it. I can pass, right?" She smiles.

"Definitely." I laugh.

Twenty minutes ago I was just crying and on the verge of a breakdown, and now I'm laughing with Trish. The moment I decided to let Hardin's past be his past, I felt most of the tension leave my body.

"Maybe I should call him and tell him what I've decided," I say.

Trish tilts her head to the side and smirks. "I think he could use a little time to stir."

The idea of torturing him further isn't appealing, but he does need to really think about everything he's done. "I guess so . . ."

"I think he needs to know that there are consequences for bad choices." She gets a twinkle in her eye. "How about I make us dinner, and *then* you can put Hardin out of his misery?"

I'm happy to have her humor and guidance to bring me out of my sad confusion over Hardin's past. I'm willing to move beyond this, or at least try, but he needs to know this type of thing is not okay, and I need to know if there are any more demons from his past that are waiting to railroad me.

"What would you like?"

"Anything is fine. I can help," I offer, but she shakes her head.

"You just relax, as much as you can. You've had a long day, what with everything from Hardin . . . and your mum."

I roll my eyes. "Yeah . . . she's difficult."

She smiles and opens the refrigerator. " 'Difficult'? I was going to use another word, but she *is* your mother . . ."

"She's sort of a B-word," I say, not wanting to say the real word in front of Trish.

"Oh yeah, she's a bitch. I'll say it for you." She laughs, and I join in.

TRISH COOKS CHICKEN TACOS for dinner, and we make small talk about Christmas, the weather, and everything else except what is actually on my mind: Hardin.

Eventually, I feel like it's literally killing me not to call him and tell him to come home now.

"Do you think he's 'stirred' long enough?" I say, not admitting that I've been counting the minutes.

"No, but it's not my choice," his mother says.

"I have to."

I leave the kitchen to call Hardin. When he answers, the surprise in his voice is evident. "Tessa?"

"Hardin, we still have a lot to discuss, but I would like it if you could come home so we can talk."

"Already? Yeah—yeah, of course!" He rushes the words. "I'll be there shortly."

"Okay," I say and hang up. I don't have much time to go over everything in my head before he arrives. I need to stand my ground and make sure that he knows what he did is wrong but that I love him anyway.

I pace back and forth across the chilled concrete floor, waiting. After what seems like an hour, the front door opens, and I listen as his boots thud down the small hallway.

When he opens the bedroom door, my heart breaks for the thousandth time.

His eyes are swollen and bloodshot. He doesn't say anything. Instead, he walks over and places a small object in my hand. *Paper?*

I look up at him as he closes my fist around the folded-up paper. "Read it before you make up your mind," he says softly. Then, with a swift kiss to my temple, he goes into the living room.

chapter forty-three

TESSA

As I unfold the paper, my eyes widen in surprise. The entirety of the sheet is covered with black scribbles, front and back. It's a letter—a handwritten letter from Hardin.

I'm almost afraid to read it . . . but I know that I must.

Tess,

Since I'm not good with words when trying to relate my inner life, I may have stolen some from Mr. Darcy, whom you fancy so much. I write without any intention of paining you, or humbling myself, by dwelling on wishes which, for the happiness of both, cannot be too soon forgotten: and the effort which the formation and the perusal of this letter must occasion, should have been spared had not my character required it to be written and read. You must, therefore, pardon the freedom with which I demand your attention; your feelings, I know, will bestow it unwillingly, but I demand it of your justice . . .

I know that I've done so many fucked-up things to you, and that I in no way deserve you, but I'm asking—no, begging—you to please look past the things that I have done. I know I ask too much of you, always, and I'm sorry for that. If I could take it all back, I would. I know you are angry and disappointed by my actions, and that kills me. Instead of making excuses for the way I am, I'm going to tell you about me, the me that you never knew. I'm starting with the shit I remember—I'm sure there is more, but I swear not to purposely hide anything else from you from this day forth. When I was around nine, I stole my neighbor's bike and broke the wheel, then lied about it. That same year I threw a baseball through the living room window and lied about it. You know about my mother and the soldiers. My father left shortly after, and I was glad when he did.

I didn't have many friends because I was an asshole. I picked on kids in my year, a lot. Every day, basically. I was a dick to my mum—that was the last year I told her I love her. The teasing and being a dick to everyone continued until now, so I can't name all the instances, but just know it was a lot. Around thirteen, me and some friends broke into the drugstore down the road from my house and stole a bunch of random shit. I don't know why we did it, but when one of my friends got caught, I threatened him to make him take the blame for it, and he did. I smoked my first cigarette when I was thirteen. It tasted like shit, and I coughed for ten minutes. I never smoked again until I started smoking pot, but I'll get to that.

When I was fourteen I lost my virginity to my friend Mark's older sister. She was a whore and seventeen at the time. It was an awkward experience, but I liked it. She slept with all of our friends, not just me. After I had sex the first time I didn't do it again until I was fifteen, but after that I couldn't stop. I would hook up with random girls at parties. I always lied about my age, and the girls were easy. None of them cared about me, and I didn't give a fuck about them. I started smoking pot this same year and did it often. I started drinking around this time—me and my friends would steal liquor from their parents or from anywhere else we could. I started fighting a lot, too. I got my ass beat a few times, but most of the time I won. I was always so fucking angry—always—and it felt good to hurt someone else. I would pick fights with people all the time for fun. The worst one was with this boy named Tucker who came from a poor family. He wore the oldest, rattiest clothes, and I fucking tortured him for it. I would mark on his shirt with a pen just to prove how many times he wore it without washing it. Fucked up, I know.

So anyway, one day I saw him walking and I knocked him in the shoulder just to be a dick. He got angry and called me a dick, so I beat the shit out of him. His nose was broken, and his mum couldn't afford to even have him see a doctor. I still kept fucking with him afterward. A few months later his mum died, and he went into a foster home, a rich one, lucky for him, and he drove by me one day. It was my sixteenth birthday and he was in a brand-new car. I was angry at the time and wanted to find him just to break his nose again, but now that I think about it I'm happy for him.

I'll skip the rest of my sixteenth year because all I did was drink, get high, and fight. Actually that goes for seventeen, too. I keyed a few cars, busted some windows as well. When I was eighteen is when I met James. He was cool because he didn't give a fuck about anything, like me. We drank every day, our group. I would come home drunk every night and would puke on the floor, and my mum would have to clean it up. I would break something new almost every night . . . We had our own little gang of friends, and no one fucked with us. They knew better.

The games started, the ones I told you about, and you know what happened with Natalie. That was the worst of that, I swear. I know you are disgusted by me not caring about what happened to her. I don't know why I didn't care, but I didn't. Just now, when I was driving here to this empty hotel room, I was thinking about Natalie. I still don't feel as bad as I should, but I was thinking—what if someone did that to you? I nearly had to pull over to get sick even thinking about you being in Natalie's place. I was wrong, so wrong for doing that to her. One of the other girls, Melissa, got attached to me as well, but nothing came of it. She was obnoxious and loud. I told everyone that she had hygiene problems, down there . . . so everyone gave her shit about it, and she never bothered me again. I got arrested once for being drunk in public, and my mum was so angry she left me at the police station all night. Then when everyone found out about the Natalie shit, she had enough. I threw a fit when my mum mentioned sending me to America. I didn't want to leave my life back home no matter how fucked up it was—I was. But when I beat the shit out of someone in front of a crowd during a festival, Mum was done. I applied to WCU and got in, of course.

When I got here to America I fucking hated it. I hated everything. I was so upset that I had to be near my father that I rebelled even further, drinking and partying at the frat house all the time. I met Steph first. I hooked up with her at a party and she introduced me to the rest of her friends. Nate and I hit it off the best. Dan and Jace were dicks, Jace the worst. You already know about Dan's sister, so I'll skip that. There were a few girls that I fucked since then, but not as many as your imagination will have you think. I did sleep with Molly once after you and I kissed, but the only reason I did it was because I couldn't stop thinking about you. I couldn't get you out of my head, Tess. I kept thinking it was you the entire time. I had hoped that would help, but it didn't. I knew it wasn't you. You would have been better. I kept telling myself, if I only see Tessa one more time I will realize this is just a ridiculous fascination, nothing more. Purely lust. But every time I saw you I wanted more and more. I would think of ways to annoy you just so I could hear you say my name. I wanted to know what you were thinking of in class that made you stare at your book with a frown, I wanted to smooth the crease between your brows, I wanted to know what you and Landon whispered about, I wanted to know what you were writing in that damned planner of yours. I actually almost took it from you once, that day when you dropped it and I handed it to you. You probably don't remember, but you were wearing a purple shirt and that hideous gray skirt you used to wear almost every other day.

After that day in your dorm when I fucked up your notes and kissed you against the wall, I was in too deep to stay away. I thought about you constantly. My every thought was consumed by you. I didn't know what it was at first—I didn't know why I had become so obsessed with you. The first time that you stayed the night with me is when I knew, KNEW that I loved you. I knew that I would do anything for you. I know that sounds like bullshit now, after all that I've put you through, but it's true. I swear it.

I found myself daydreaming—me daydreaming . . . about the life that I could have with you. I pictured you sitting on the couch with a pen between your teeth and a novel on your lap, your feet on my lap. I don't know why, but I couldn't get the image out of my head. It tortured me, wanting you the way that I did and knowing you would never feel the same. I threatened anyone who tried to sit in that seat next to you, threatened Landon, to make sure that I could sit there, just to be near you. I would tell myself over and over that I was only doing all of this weird shit to win the bet. I knew that I was lying to myself, I just wasn't ready to admit it. I would do shit, like crazy shit, to fuel my obsession with you. I would mark lines in my novels that reminded me of you. Do you want to know the first one? It was, "He stepped down, trying not to look long at her, as if she were the sun, yet he saw her, like the sun, even without looking."

I knew I loved you when I was highlighting fucking Tolstoy.

When I told you I loved you in front of everyone, I meant it—I was just too much of a prick to admit it once you dismissed me. The day that you told me you loved me was the first time I felt like there was hope, hope for me. Hope for us. I don't know why I kept hurting you and treating you the way that I did. I won't waste your time with an excuse, because I don't have one. I just have all these bad instincts and habits, and I'm fighting against them for you. All I know is that you make me happy, Tess. You love me when you shouldn't, and I need you. I have always needed you and always will. When you left me just last week it nearly killed me, I was so lost. So completely lost without you. I went on a date with someone last week. I wasn't going to tell you, but I can't stand to chance losing you again. I wouldn't even call it a date, really. Nothing happened between us. I almost kissed her, but I stopped myself. I couldn't kiss her, I couldn't kiss anyone but you. She was boring, and nothing compared to you. No one is, no one ever will be.

I know it's probably too late for this, especially now that you know all of the fucked-up shit I've done. I can only pray that you will love me the same after reading this. If not, that's okay. I will understand. I know you can do better than *me. I'm not romantic, I won't ever write you poetry or sing you a song.*

I'm not even kind.

I can't promise that I won't hurt you again, but I can swear that I will love you until the day that I die. I'm a terrible person, and I don't deserve you, but I hope that you will allow me the chance to restore your faith in me. I am sorry for all the pain I have caused you, and I understand if you can't forgive me.

Sorry. This letter wasn't supposed to be this long. I guess I've fucked up more than I thought.

I love you. Always.

Hardin.

I SIT AND STARE at the paper in a daze, then reread it twice. I had no idea what I expected, but this was not it. How can he say he isn't romantic? The charm bracelet on my wrist and this beautiful, somewhat disturbing, but mostly beautiful letter shows otherwise. He even used the first paragraph of Darcy's letter to Elizabeth.

Now that he's bared himself to me, I can't help but love him more. He has done a lot of things that I would never do, terrible things that hurt many people—but the thing that matters most to me is that he doesn't do them anymore. He hasn't always done the right thing, but I can't ignore all the effort he's made to show me that he's changing, trying to change. That he loves me. I hate to admit it, but there is a sort of poetry to him never caring for anyone except me.

I stare at the letter a little longer until there is a knock at the bedroom door. Folding the sheet up, I put it in the bottom drawer of the dresser. I don't want Hardin to try to make me throw it away or tear it up now that I've read it.

"Come in," I say and walk over to the door to meet him.

He opens the door, already staring at the ground. "Did you . . ."

"I did . . ." I reach up and lift his chin to look at me, the way he usually does to me.

His bloodshot eyes are so wide and sad. "It was stupid . . . I knew I shouldn't have . . ." he begins.

"No, it wasn't. It wasn't stupid at all." I move my hand from under his chin, but he keeps his red eyes on mine. "Hardin, it was everything that I've been wanting you to say to me for so long."

"I'm sorry that I took so long, and that I wrote it down . . . It was just easier. I'm not good at saying things." The red of his weary eyes is beautiful against the vibrant green of his irises.

"I know you aren't."

"Did you . . . should we talk about it? Do you need more time, now that you know how fucked up I truly am?" He frowns and looks at the floor again.

"You aren't. You were . . . You've done a lot of things . . . bad things, Hardin." He nods in agreement; I can't stand to see him feel so bad about himself, even with his history. "But that doesn't mean you're a bad person. You've done bad things, but you aren't a bad person anymore."

He looks up. "What?"

I take his face between my hands. "I said you aren't a bad person, Hardin."

"You really think that? Did you read what I wrote?"

"Yes, and the fact that you wrote it proves that you aren't."

Confusion is clear on his perfect face. "How can you say that? I don't understand—you wanted me to give you space, and you read all that shit, and you still say that? I don't understand . . ."

I run my thumbs over his cheeks. "I read it, and now that I know everything that you've done, my mind hasn't changed."

"Oh . . ." His eyes become glossy.

The idea of him crying again, especially in front of me, pains me. He's obviously not getting what I'm trying to say.

"I already made my mind up while you were gone to stay. And after reading what you wrote, I want to stay more than ever. I love you, Hardin."

chapter forty-four

TESSA

Hardin takes my hands and holds them for a second before wrapping his arms around me as if I'll disappear should he let go.

As I said the words *I want to stay*, I realized how freeing this all is. I no longer have to worry that secrets from Hardin's past will come back to haunt us. I no longer have to wait for someone to drop a huge bombshell on me. I know everything. I finally know everything he's been hiding. I can't help but think of the phrase *Sometimes it is better to be kept in the dark than to be blinded by the light*. But I don't think that applies me to right now. I'm disturbed by the things he has done, but I love him and have chosen to not let his past affect us any longer.

Hardin pulls back and sits on the edge of the bed. "What are you thinking? Do you have any questions about anything? I want to be honest with you." I move to stand between his legs. He flips my hands over in his and traces small patterns on my palms as he searches my face for clues to how I am feeling.

"No . . . I do wish I knew what happened to Natalie . . . but I don't have any questions."

"I am done being that person—you know that, don't you?"

I've already told him I do, but I know he needs to hear it again. "I know that. I really do, babe."

His eyes dart to mine at the use of the word. "Babe?" He arches his eyebrow.

"I don't know why I said that . . ." I flush. I've never called him anything other than Hardin, so it does feel a little odd to call him "babe" like he does me.

"No . . . I like it." He smiles.

"I've missed your smile," I tell him, and his fingers stop their movements.

"I've missed yours, too." He frowns. "I don't make you smile enough."

I want to say something to remove that doubt from his face, but I don't want to lie to him. He needs to know how I feel. "Yeah . . . we need to work on that," I say.

His fingers move again, drawing little hearts on my palm. "I don't know why you love me."

"It doesn't matter why I love you, only that I do."

"The letter was stupid, wasn't it?"

"No! Would you stop with the self-loathing? It was wonderful. I read it three times straight. It really made me happy to read the things that you were thinking about me . . . about us."

He looks up, half smirking, half concerned. "You knew I loved you."

"Yes . . . but it was nice to know the small things, the way you remembered what I was wearing. Those types of things. You never say those types of things."

"Oh." He looks embarrassed. It is still slightly unnerving to have Hardin be the vulnerable one in our relationship. That role has always been mine.

"Don't be embarrassed," I say.

His arms wrap around my waist and pull me onto his lap. "I'm not," he lies.

I run one of my hands through his hair and wrap my other arm around his shoulder. "I think you are," I challenge softly, and he laughs, burying his head in my neck.

"What a Christmas Eve. It's been a long-ass day," he complains, and I can't help but agree.

"Way too long. I can't believe my mother came here. She is so unbelievable."

"Not really," he says, and I pull back to look at him.

"What?"

"She's not being unreasonable, really. Yeah, she goes about it the wrong way, but I can't blame her for not wanting you to be with someone like me."

Tired of this talk, and his notion that my mother is somehow right about him, I scowl at him and move off of his lap to sit next to him on the bed.

"Tess, don't look at me like that. I'm just saying that now that I've really thought about all the shit I've done, I don't blame her for worrying."

"Well, she's wrong, and we can stop talking about her," I whine. The emotional turmoil of the day—of the year, really—is making me tired and cranky. The year is almost over. I can't believe it.

"Okay, so what would you like to talk about?" he asks.

"I don't know . . . something lighter." I smile, convincing myself to be less cranky. "Like how romantic you can be."

"I am *not* romantic," he scoffs.

"Yes, you most certainly are. That letter was one for the classics," I tease.

He rolls his eyes. "It wasn't a letter, it was a note. A note that was only supposed to be a paragraph at most."

"Sure. A romantic note, then."

"Oh, would you shut up . . ." he groans comically.

I wrap a lock of his hair around my finger and laugh. "Is this where you annoy me to get me to say your name?"

He moves too quickly for me to respond, grabbing my waist

and pushing me back onto the bed, hovering over me with his hands on my hips. "No. I have since come up with other ways to get you to say my name," he breathes, his lips against my ear.

My entire body ignites with only a few words from Hardin. "Is that so?" I say in a thick voice.

But suddenly Natalie's faceless figure appears in my mind, causing my stomach to turn. "I think we should wait until your mother isn't in the other room," I suggest, partly because I clearly need more time to ease back into our relationship, but also because it was already awkward enough doing it once before while she was here.

"I can kick her out now," he jokes, but rolls off to lie next to me.

"Or I could kick you out."

"I'm not leaving again. Neither are you." The certainty in his tone makes me smile.

We are lying next to each other, both of us staring at the ceiling. "So this is it, then, we're done with the back-and-forth?" I ask.

"Yes, this is it. No more secrets, no more running away. Do you think you can manage not leaving me for a week at least?"

I push his shoulder with my arm and laugh. "Do you think you can manage to not piss me off for a week at least?"

"Yeah, probably not," he answers. I know that he's smiling.

As I turn my head to the side, sure enough: a huge grin covers his face. "You'll have to stay with me at my dorm sometimes, too. The drive is far."

"Your dorm? You aren't living in a dorm. You live here."

"We just got back together—do you really think that's a good idea?"

"You're staying here. We aren't discussing this any further."

"You are obviously confused, to be speaking to me that way,"

I say, then raise myself up on an elbow to look at him. I shake my head lightly and give a slight smile. "I don't really want to live in the dorm, I just wanted to see what you would say."

"Well," he says, lifting himself up and mirroring my actions, "I'm glad to see you're back to being annoying."

"I'm glad to see you're back to being rude. I was getting worried that after that romantic letter you had maybe lost your edge."

"Call me romantic one more time and I'll take you right here, right now, Mum or no Mum."

My eyes widen, and he laughs louder than I think I've ever heard him laugh. "I'm joking! You should see your face!" he bellows.

I can't help but laugh with him.

After we stop, he admits, "I feel like we shouldn't be laughing after all the stuff that happened today."

"Maybe that's why we *should* be laughing." This is what we do: we fight, then make up.

"Our relationship is sort of fucked up." He smiles.

"Yeah . . . just a little." It has definitely been a roller coaster.

"Not anymore, though, okay? I promise."

"Okay." I lean over and give him a quick kiss on the lips.

It isn't enough, though. It never is. I bring my lips back to his, and this time I let them linger. Both of our lips part at the same time, and he slips his tongue inside my mouth. My hands fist his hair, and he pulls me on top of him as his tongue massages mine. No matter how messed up our relationship has been, there is no denying our all-consuming passion. I start to move my hips, grinding down onto him, and I feel him smile against my lips.

"I think that's enough for now," he says.

Nodding, I shift and lay my head on his chest, reveling in the feeling of his arms wrapping around my back. "I hope tomorrow goes well," I say after a few minutes of silence.

He doesn't respond. And when I lift up my head, his eyes are closed and his lips are slightly parted in sleep. He must've been exhausted. Then again, so am I.

I climb off of him and check the time. It's past eleven. I pull his jeans off him, gently so not to wake him, then snuggle up next to him. Tomorrow is Christmas, and I can only pray that it goes much better than today.

chapter forty-five

HARDIN

"Hardin." Tessa's voice is soft. I groan and pull my arm from under her weight.

I grab the pillow and cover my face with it. "Not getting up yet."

"We slept late and we have to get ready." She snatches the pillow from me and tosses it onto the floor.

"Stay in bed with me. Let's cancel." I reach for her arm, and she rolls onto her side, molding her body to mine.

"We can't cancel *Christmas*." She laughs as she speaks and presses her lips against my neck. I rock into her, pushing my hips against hers, and she playfully pulls away. "Oh no you don't." Her hands push at my chest to keep me from rolling on top of her.

She climbs out of bed, leaving me alone. I have half a mind to follow her into the bathroom—not to do anything to her, just to be near her. Yet the bed is too warm, so I decide against it. I'm still reeling from the fact that she's still here. Her forgiveness and acceptance of me will never fail to surprise the fuck out of me.

Having her here for Christmas will be different, too. I've never really given a shit about holidays like this, but watching Tessa's face light up over some stupid tree with overpriced ornaments makes the whole thing a little more tolerable. My mum being here isn't too bad, either. Tessa seems to adore her, and my mum is almost as obsessed with my girl as I am.

My girl. Tessa is my girl again, and I'm spending Christmas with her—and my fucked-up family. What a difference from last year, when I spent Christmas Day wasted out of my mind. A few minutes later I force myself out of bed and find my way to the kitchen. Coffee. I need coffee.

"Merry Christmas," my mum says when I enter the kitchen.

"Same to you." I walk past her to the fridge.

"I made coffee," she says.

"I see that." I grab the Frosted Flakes from on top of the fridge and walk over to the coffeepot.

"Hardin, I'm sorry for what I said yesterday. I know that I upset you when I agreed with Tessa's mum, but you have to see where I was coming from."

The thing is, I *do* understand where she's coming from, but it's not her damn place to tell Tessa to leave me. After everything Tessa and I have been through, we need someone on our side. It feels like it's only her and me, fighting against everyone, and I need my mum to be on our side.

"It's just that she belongs with me, Mum, nowhere else. Only with me." I grab a towel to wipe up the excess coffee spilling over my mug. The brown liquid stains the white towel, and I can almost hear Tessa's voice scolding me for using the wrong towel.

"I know she does, Hardin. I see that now. I'm sorry."

"Me, too. I'm sorry for being a dick all the time. I don't mean to be."

She seems to be surprised by my words. I guess I don't blame her. I never apologize, regardless if I am right or wrong. It's my thing, I guess—being an asshole and not owning up to it.

"It's okay, we can move past it. Let's have a nice Christmas at your lovely father's house." She smiles, sarcasm clear in her voice.

"Yeah, let's move past it."

"Yes. Let's. I don't want today to be ruined because of that mess last night. I understand it better now, the whole situation. I know you love her, Hardin, and I can see you're learning to be a better man. She's teaching you, and that makes me so happy." My mum brings her hands to her chest, and I roll my eyes. "Really, I'm so happy for you," she says.

"Thanks." I look away. "I love you, Mum." The words taste odd coming out, but her expression makes it worth it.

She gasps. "What did you just say?" Tears immediately pool in her eyes from hearing the words I never say to her. I don't know what made me say it just now, maybe the way she truly only wants the best for me. Maybe the way she's here now, and she really has played such a big role in Tessa's forgiving me. I don't know, but the look on her face makes me wish I'd have said it sooner. She's dealt with a lot of shit, and she really has tried her best to be a good mum to me—she should have had the simple pleasure of hearing her only child say that he loves her more than once in the last thirteen years.

I was just so angry—still am—but it's not her fault. It never has been her fault.

"I love you, Mum," I repeat, a little embarrassed.

She pulls me into her arms and hugs me tighter, tighter than I usually allow.

"Oh, Hardin, I love you, too. So much, son."

chapter forty-six

TESSA

I decide to wear my hair straight, to try something different. But when I finish, it looks odd, so I end up curling it as usual. I'm taking too long to get ready, and it's probably getting close to time to leave. Perhaps I'm taking longer because part of me is stalling, nervous about how today will go.

I hope Hardin is on his best behavior, or at least tries to be.

I go with simple makeup, only wearing a little foundation, black eyeliner, and mascara. I was going to use eye shadow as well, but I've had to remove the messy line from my top eyelid three times before finally getting it right.

"You alive in there?" Hardin's voice calls through the door.

"Yes, I'm almost done," I reply and brush my teeth once more.

"I'm going to take a quick shower, but then we need to go if you want to be there on time," Hardin says when I open the door.

"Okay, okay, I'll get dressed while you shower."

He disappears into the bathroom, and I head for the closet, grabbing the sleeveless forest-green dress I bought to wear today. The dark-green material is thick, and the neckline is high. The bow covering my waist is much bigger than it looked when I tried it on the other day, but I'll have a cardigan over it anyway. I retrieve my charm bracelet from the dresser, and my stomach flutters as I read and reread the perfect inscription.

I can't decide on what shoes to wear; if I wear heels, I'll probably look too dressy. I go with black flats, and am pulling my white cardigan over the dress just as Hardin opens the door wearing only a towel tied around his waist.

Oh. No matter how many times I see him, I still lose my breath at the sight of him. Staring at Hardin's half-naked body, I do not understand how tattoos were not my thing before.

"Holy shit," he says as his eyes rake up and down my body.

"What? What?" I look down to see what's wrong.

"You look . . . incredibly innocent."

"Wait, is that good or bad? It's Christmas, I didn't want to look indecent." I suddenly feel unsure of what I chose to wear.

"Oh, it's good. Very good." His tongue snakes over his bottom lip, and I finally get it, blushing and looking away before we start something that we should not finish. Not right now, at least. "Thank you. What are you wearing?"

"What I always wear."

I look back at him. "Oh."

"I'm not dressing up to go to my dad's house."

"I know . . . maybe you could wear that shirt your mother got you for Christmas?" I suggest, even though I know he won't.

He barks out a laugh. "Not happening." He goes to the closet and pulls his jeans off the hanger, which falls to the ground, not that he notices such things. I decide not to say anything; instead I walk away from the closet as Hardin's towel falls to the floor.

"I'm going to go out there with your mom," I squeak out, trying to force myself not to look at his body.

"Suit yourself." He smirks, and I leave the room.

When I find Trish in the living room, she's wearing a red dress and black heels, much different from her usual tracksuit.

"You look so beautiful!" I tell her.

"You're sure? Is it too much, with the makeup and all?" she asks nervously. "It's not that I care, really—I just don't want to look bad when I see my ex-husband after all these years."

"Trust me, bad is the *last* thing you look," I tell her, which gets her to smile a little.

"You two ready?" Hardin asks when he joins us in the living room. His hair is still wet, but somehow it manages to look perfect. He's wearing all black, including the black Converses he wore in Seattle that I love.

His mother doesn't seem to notice the all-black attire, likely because she's still focusing on her own appearance. As we get into the elevator, Hardin looks at his mother as if for the first time, then asks, "Why are you so dressed up?"

She blushes a little. "It's a holiday, why wouldn't I be?"

"It just seems weird—"

I cut him off before he says something to ruin his mother's day. "She looks lovely, Hardin. I'm just as dressed up as she is."

During the drive, everyone is quiet, even Trish. I can tell she's anxious, and who could blame her? I'd be incredibly nervous, too. In fact, for different reasons, the closer we get to Ken's house, the more I feel it. I really just want a calm holiday.

When we finally arrive and park at the curb, I hear Trish gasp. "This is his *house*?"

"Yep. I told you it was big," Hardin says and turns off the car.

"I didn't think you meant *this* big," she says quietly.

Hardin hops out and opens his mother's door, since she's just sitting there in shock. I get out myself, and as we walk up the steps leading to the large house, I see the apprehension on his face. I take his hand in mine to try to calm him, and he looks down at me with a small but noticeable smile. He doesn't ring the doorbell—he just opens the door and walks inside.

Karen is standing in the living room with a beaming, welcoming smile that's so infectious it makes me feel a *little* better. Hardin walks through the foyer first with his mom, and I follow behind him, my hand still in his.

"Thank you all for coming," Karen says, approaching Trish,

since it's just understood Hardin's not one for introductions. "Hello, Trish, I'm Karen," she says and extends her hand. "It's so nice to get a chance to meet you. I really appreciate you coming." Karen appears completely calm, but I've gotten to know her well enough to know that's not really the case.

"Hi, Karen, it's nice to meet you, too," Trish says and shakes her hand.

Just then Ken enters the room and, doing a double take when he sees us, stops dead in his tracks and stares at his ex-wife. I lean into Hardin and hope that Landon told Ken we were coming.

"Hello, Ken," Trish says, her voice sounding stronger than it's been all morning.

"Trish . . . wow . . . hello," he stammers.

Trish, who I'm guessing is pleased by his reaction, nods her head once and says, "You look . . . different."

I've tried to imagine what Ken looked like back then—eyes likely bloodshot from liquor, forehead sweaty, face pale—but I can't seem to.

"Yeah . . . so do you," he says.

The awkward tension is making me dizzy, so I'm beyond relieved when Karen suddenly exclaims, "Landon!" and he joins us. Karen's clearly relieved to see the apple of her eye right now, and he looks the part, dressed in blue slacks and a white dress shirt with a black tie.

"You look beautiful." He compliments me and pulls me in for a hug.

Hardin's grip on my hand tightens, but I manage to pull my hand free and hug Landon back. "You look very nice yourself, Landon," I say.

Hardin hooks his arm around my waist and pulls me back over to him, closer than before. Landon rolls his eyes at Hardin, then turns to Trish. "Hello, ma'am, I'm Landon, Karen's son. It's great to finally meet you."

"Oh, please don't call me ma'am." Trish laughs. "But it's very nice to meet you, too. Tessa has told me a lot about you."

He smiles. "All good things, I hope."

"Mostly," she teases.

Landon's charm seems to ease some of the tension in the room, and Karen pipes up, "Well, you all are just in time. The goose is ready to be served in just a couple of minutes!"

Ken leads us to the dining room while Karen disappears into the kitchen. I'm not at all surprised to find the table perfectly set with their best china, polished silverware, and elegant wooden napkin rings. Platters of neatly arranged food cover the table. The main goose dish is surrounded by thick slices of oranges. A bundle of red berries rests atop the body. It's so elegantly arranged, and the smell makes my mouth water. A plate of roasted potatoes is directly in front of me. The scent of garlic and rosemary fills the air, and I admire the rest of the table. A large centerpiece full of flowers and ornaments sits in the middle, and each decoration echoes the same orange-and-berry theme. Karen is always an amazing host.

"Would anyone like a drink? I have some delicious red wine from the cellar," she says. Her cheeks flush red as she realizes what she just asked. Alcohol is definitely a sensitive subject with this crowd.

Trish smiles. "I would, actually."

Karen disappears, and we're so silent that when she pops the cork in the kitchen, it's a loud sound that feels like it bounces off the walls around us. When she returns with an open bottle, I consider asking for a glass to calm the uneasy feeling in my stomach, but then decide against it. The hostess returned, each of us takes a seat—Ken at the head of the table, Karen, Landon, and Trish on one side of him, Hardin and I on the other. After some "oohs" and "aahs" at the presentation, no one says a word as they fill their plates with food.

After we've all had a few bites, Landon makes eye contact with me, and I can tell he's debating whether or not to speak. I give him a small nod; I don't want to have to break the silence. I take a bite of goose, and Hardin puts his hand on my thigh.

Landon wipes his mouth with his napkin and turns to Trish. "So what do you think of America so far, Mrs. Daniels? Is this your first time here?"

She nods a couple of times. "Indeed, it is my first time here. I like it. I wouldn't want to live here, but I do like it. Are you planning on staying in Washington when you finish university?" She looks at Ken as if she was asking him instead of Landon.

"I'm not sure yet; my girlfriend is moving to New York next month, so it will depend on what she wants to do."

I selfishly hope he doesn't move out there anytime soon.

"Well, I'll be glad when Hardin finishes, so he can move back home," Trish says, and I drop my fork onto my plate.

All eyes focus on me and I smile apologetically before picking the utensil back up.

"You're moving back to England after you graduate?" Landon asks Hardin.

"Yeah, of course I am," Hardin answers rudely.

"Oh," Landon says, looking directly at me. Hardin and I haven't discussed any plans after college, but him going back to England never once crossed my mind. We will need to discuss this later, not in front of everyone.

"And you . . . how do you like America, Ken? Are *you* planning to live here permanently?" Trish asks him.

"Yes, I love it here. I'll be staying most definitely," he answers.

Trish smiles and takes a slow sip of her wine. "You always hated America."

"Yes . . . I *did*," he replies and half smiles back at her.

Karen and Hardin both shift uncomfortably in their seats, and I concentrate on chewing the bite of potato in my mouth.

"Does anyone have anything to talk about besides America?" Hardin rolls his eyes. I gently kick him under the table, but he doesn't acknowledge it.

Karen jumps in quickly, asking me, "How was your trip to Seattle, Tessa?"

I've definitely already told her about it, but I know that she's only trying to make conversation, so I tell everyone about the conference and my job again. That gets us through the meal at least, as everyone keeps asking me questions in a clear effort to stay on this safe, non-ex-wife-and-ex-husband topic.

Once everyone is done with the delicious goose and sides, I help Karen take the dishes to the kitchen. She seems to be distracted, so I don't probe her for conversation as we clean up the kitchen.

"Would you like another glass of wine, Trish?" Karen asks once we all move to the living room. Hardin, Trish, and I sit on one of the couches, Landon sits on the chair, and Karen and Ken sit on the other couch across from us. It feels as if we are on teams, with Landon acting as a referee.

"Yes, please. It's got a really great taste," Trish replies and hands over her empty glass for Karen to fill.

"Thank you, we got it in Greece this summer; it was such an amazing—" She stops midsentence. After a pause, she adds, "A nice place," before handing Trish back her glass.

Trish smiles and gives a little air salute. "Well, the wine is excellent."

At first I'm confused by this awkwardness, but then I realize that Karen has gotten the Ken that Trish never had. She gets trips to Greece and all over the world, a huge home, new cars, and most importantly she gets a loving and sober husband. I really applaud Trish for being so strong and forgiving. She's making a huge effort to be polite, especially given the circumstances.

"Anyone else? Tessa, would you like a glass?" Karen asks as

she finishes pouring one for Landon. I look toward Trish and Hardin.

"Only one, for the holiday," Karen adds.

I finally give in and reply, "Yes, please." I'm going to need a glass of wine if the day continues to be this awkward.

As she pours, I see Hardin nodding his head next to me several times. And then he remarks, "What about you, Dad? You want a glass of wine?"

Everyone looks at him with wide eyes and open mouths. I squeeze his hand to try to silence him.

But he continues with a wicked smirk. "What? No? C'mon, I'm sure you do. I know you miss it."

chapter forty-seven

TESSA

Hardin!" Trish snaps.

"What? I'm just offering the man a drink. Being social," he says.

I watch Ken, who I can tell is debating whether or not to take Hardin's bait, whether to let this become a full-blown argument.

"Stop it," I whisper to Hardin.

"Don't be rude," Trish tells him.

Ken finally reacts. "It's fine," he says and takes a drink of his water.

I look around the room. Karen's face has paled. Landon is staring at the large television on the wall. Trish downs her wine. Ken looks bemused, and Hardin is glaring at him.

Then he shows a simmering smile. "I know it's *fine.*"

"You are just angry, so go ahead and say what you please," Ken says. He shouldn't have said that. He shouldn't have treated Hardin's emotion in this area so trivially, like it was a young boy's opinion that merely had to be endured for a moment.

"Angry? I'm not angry. Annoyed and amused, yes, but angry, no," Hardin says calmly.

"Amused by what?" Ken asks. *Oh, Ken, just stop talking.*

"Amused by the fact that you're acting as if nothing ever happened, as if you weren't a massive fuckup." He points at Ken and Trish. "You two are being ridiculous."

"You're crossing the line here," Ken says. *Jesus, Ken.*

"Am I? Since when do you get to decide where the line is?" Hardin challenges him.

"Since this is my home, Hardin. That's why I get to decide."

Hardin is on his feet immediately. I grab his arm to stop him, but he shakes me off easily. I quickly set my glass of wine on the side table and get up. "Hardin, stop!" I beg and grab hold of his arm again.

Everything was going well. Awkward, but well. And then Hardin had to go and make a rude remark. I know he's angry at his father for his mistakes, but Christmas dinner is not the time to bring this up. Hardin and Ken had begun to repair their relationship, and if Hardin doesn't stop now, it will get much worse.

Ken stands up with an air of authority and asks, much like a professor might, "I thought we were moving past this. You came to the wedding?" They're only feet away from each other, and I know this will not end well.

"Moving past what? You haven't even owned up to anything! You're just pretending that it *didn't happen!*"

Hardin is yelling now. My head is swimming, and I wish I had never extended Landon's invite to Hardin and Trish. Once again I've caused a family argument.

"Today is not the day for us to be discussing this, Hardin. We're having a nice time, and you had to go and start a fight with me," Ken says.

Hardin asks, raising his hands in the air, "When *is* the day, then? God, can you believe this guy!"

"Not Christmas. I haven't seen your mother in years, and this is the time you choose to bring all of this up?"

"You haven't seen her in years because you fucking left! You left us with nothing—no fucking money, no car, nothing!" Hardin shouts and steps into his father's face.

Ken's face gets red with anger. And then he's yelling. "No

money? I sent money every month! A lot of money! And your mum wouldn't accept the car that I offered her!"

"Liar!" Hardin blows out a hard breath. "You didn't send *shit*. That's why we lived in that crap house and she worked fifty hours a week!"

"Hardin . . . he isn't lying," Trish interjects.

Hardin's head snaps around to his mother. "What?"

This is a disaster. A much bigger disaster than I saw coming.

"He sent money, Hardin," she explains. She puts her glass down and comes over to him.

"Where is the money, then?" Hardin asks his mother, disbelief clear in his tone.

"Paying your tuition."

Hardin points an angry finger at Ken. "You said *he* was paying the tuition!" he yells, and my heart aches for him.

"He is—with the money that I've saved over the years. Money that he sent us."

"What the fuck?" Hardin rubs his forehead with his hand. I move to stand behind him and thread my fingers through his free hand.

Trish puts a hand on her son's shoulder. "I didn't use all of it for your tuition. I paid the bills as well."

"Why wouldn't you tell me this? He should be paying it—and not with money that was meant to keep us fed, keep us in a *house* day to day." He turns to his father. "You still left us, whether you sent money or not! You just left without so much as a fucking call on my goddamned birthday."

Excess saliva pools in the corners of Ken's mouth, and he begins blinking rapidly. "What was I supposed to do, Hardin? Stay around? I was a drunk, a worthless drunk—and the two of you deserved better than what I could give you. After that night . . . I knew I had to go."

Hardin's body goes rigid, and his breathing comes in ragged breaths. *"Don't you speak of that night!* That happened because of *you!"*

When Hardin pulls his hand out of mine, Trish looks angry, Landon looks terrified, Karen . . . well, she continues crying, and I realize that I'm the one that's going to have to stop this.

"I know it did! You don't know how much I wish I could take that back, son—that night has haunted me for the last ten years!" Ken says hoarsely, clearly trying not to cry.

"It haunts *you*? I fucking *watched it happen*, you prick! I was there to clean up the fucking blood off the floor while you were still out getting shit-faced!" Hardin balls his fists.

Karen whimpers and covers her mouth before leaving the room. I don't blame her. I hadn't realized that I was crying until the warm tears hit my chest. I had a feeling something would happen today, but nothing like this.

Ken puts his hands in the air. "I know, Hardin! I know! There's nothing I can do to erase that! I'm sober now! I haven't had a drink in years! You can't hold that against me forever!"

Trish screams as Hardin lunges at his father. Landon rushes over to try to help, but it's too late. Hardin pushes Ken back against the china cabinet, the replacement for the one Hardin had broken months ago. Ken grabs Hardin's shirt and is trying to hold him back when Hardin's fist connects with his jaw.

I stand frozen, as always, as Hardin attacks his own father.

Ken manages to turn himself and Hardin around before Hardin can hit him again. Instead, Hardin punches through the glass cabinet door. Seeing the blood, I break out of my stupor and grab Hardin's shirt. His arm jerks back, knocking me into a table. A glass of red wine topples over, covering my white cardigan.

"Look what you did!" Landon yells at Hardin and rushes over to my side.

Trish is standing by the door, giving her son a murderous

glare, and Ken looks at his broken cabinet, then me, as Hardin stops his attack against his father and turns to face me.

"Tessa, Tessa—are you okay?" he asks.

I nod mutely from the floor, watching a trail of blood running off his knuckles and down his arm. I didn't get hurt; my sweater being ruined is too trivial to mention in the middle of this chaos.

"Move," Hardin snaps at Landon and takes his place next to me. "Are you okay? I thought you were Landon," he says and helps me up with his one bruised but unbloodied hand.

"I'm fine," I repeat and move away from his touch once I'm upright.

"We're leaving," he growls and goes to wrap his arm around my waist.

I move farther away from him. I look over at Ken as he uses the sleeve of his crisp white button-down to wipe the blood off his mouth.

"You should stay here, Tessa," Landon urges.

"Don't fucking start with me, Landon," Hardin warns, but Landon doesn't seem to be fazed. He should be.

"Hardin, stop it now," I snap. When he lets out a breath but doesn't argue, I turn to Landon. "I'll be fine." It's Hardin he should be worried about.

"Let's go," Hardin commands, but as he walks toward the door, he looks back to make sure that I'm behind him.

"I'm sorry . . . about all of this," I tell Ken as I follow Hardin.

Behind me, I hear him softly say, "It's not your fault, it's mine."

TRISH IS SILENT. Hardin is silent. And I'm freezing. The leather seats are ice-cold on my bare legs, and my wet cardigan isn't helping either. I turn the heat all the way up, and Hardin looks over at me, but I focus out the window. I can't decide if I should be angry with him. He ruined dinner and literally assaulted his father in front of everyone.

However, I feel for him. He has been through so much, and his father is the root of all his problems—the nightmares, the anger, the lack of respect for women. He never had anyone to teach him how to be a man.

When Hardin puts his hand on my thigh, I don't move it. My head is pounding, and I cannot believe the way everything escalated so quickly.

"Hardin, we have to talk about what just happened," Trish says after a few minutes.

"No, we don't," he responds.

"Yes, we do. You were way out of line."

"I was out of line? How can you forget everything he has done?"

"I have not forgotten anything, Hardin. I have chosen to forgive him; I cannot hold on to anger for him. But violence is always out of line. And even short of that, that type of anger will consume you—it will take over your life if you let it. If you hold on to it, it will destroy you. I do not want to live that way. I want to be happy, Hardin, and forgiving your father makes it much easier for me to be happy."

Her strength never ceases to amaze me, and Hardin's stubbornness doesn't either. He refuses to forgive his father for his past mistakes, yet he's quick to ask for my forgiveness at every turn. Hardin never forgives himself either, though. Irony at its finest.

"Well, I don't want to forgive him. I thought I could, but not after today."

"He didn't do anything to you today," Trish scolds him. "*You* provoked him about his drinking for no good reason."

Hardin removes his hand from my skin, leaving a smudge of blood behind. "He doesn't get a free pass, Mum."

"This isn't about free passes. Ask yourself this: What do you get out of being so angry with him? What does that get you besides bloody hands and a lonely life?"

Hardin doesn't answer. He just keeps staring straight ahead.

"Exactly," she says, and the rest of the ride is silent.

When we get back to the apartment, I head straight for the bedroom.

"You owe her an apology, Hardin," I hear Trish say somewhere behind me.

I pull my ruined sweater off and let it fall onto the floor. I slip my shoes off and push my hair from my face, tucking the strands behind my ears. Seconds later Hardin opens the bedroom door; his eyes go to the red-stained fabric on the floor, then up to my face.

He stands in front of me and takes my hands in his, his eyes pleading. "I'm so sorry, Tess. I didn't mean to push you like that."

"You really shouldn't have done that. Not today."

"I know . . . are you hurt?" he asks, wiping his wounded hands against his black jeans.

"No." If he had physically hurt me, we would have much bigger problems.

"I'm so sorry. I was in a rage. I thought you were Landon . . ."

"I don't like when you get that way, so angry." My eyes pool with tears as I recall Hardin's hand being cut open.

"I know, baby." He bends his knees slightly so he's eye level with me. "I would never hurt you purposely. You know that, don't you?" His thumb traces over my temple, and I nod slowly. I do know that he would never hurt me, physically at least. I have always known that.

"Why did you comment on his drinking in the first place? Things were going great," I say.

"Because he was acting like nothing happened. He was being this fucking pretentious prick, and my mum was just going along with it. Someone had to stand up for her." His voice is soft, confused, the polar opposite of how it was thirty minutes ago when he was screaming in his father's face.

My heart aches again; this was his way of defending his mother. The wrong way, but to Hardin it's his instinct. He pushes his hair from his forehead, blood staining his skin.

"Try to consider how he feels—he has to live with that guilt forever, Hardin, and you don't make it any easier. I'm not saying you shouldn't be angry, because that's a natural reaction, but you of all people should be more forgiving."

"I—"

"And you have to stop with the violence. You can't just go around beating people up every time you get pissed off. It's not right, and I don't like it at all."

"I know." He looks down at the concrete floor.

I sigh and take his hands in mine. "We need to get you cleaned up; your knuckles are still bleeding." I lead him to the bathroom to clean his wounds for what feels like the thousandth time since I met him.

chapter forty-eight

TESSA

Hardin doesn't even wince as I clean his wounds. I dip the towel back into the sink full of water, attempting to dilute the blood from the white fabric. He looks up at me as I stand over him. He's seated on the edge of the bathtub, and I stand between his legs. He holds his hands up once more.

"We need to get something to put on your thumb," I tell him as I twist the towel to wring out the excess water.

"It'll be fine," he says.

"No, look how deep it is," I scold him. "The skin is already mostly scar tissue, and you just keep tearing it back open."

He doesn't say anything; he just studies my face. "What?" I ask him.

I drain the pink water and wait for him to respond. "Nothing . . ." he lies.

"Tell me."

"I just can't believe you put up with my shit," he says.

"Me, either." I smile. I watch as a frown takes over his face. "It's worth it, though," I add, meaning it. He smiles, and I bring my hand to his face, running the pad of my thumb over the pit of his dimple.

His smile grows. "Sure it is," he says and stands up. "I need a shower." He removes his shirt before leaning down to turn the shower faucet.

"I'll be in the room, then," I tell him.

"Wait . . . why? Take one with me?"

"Your mother is in the other room," I explain quietly.

"So . . . it's only a shower. Please?"

I can't refuse him; he knows this. The smirk on his face as I sigh in defeat proves it.

"Unzip me?" I request and turn my back to him.

I lift my hair up, and his fingers find the zipper immediately. When the green fabric hits the floor, Hardin says, "I like that dress."

He removes his pants and boxers, and I try not to stare at his naked body as I slide the straps of my bra down my arms. When I'm completely naked, Hardin steps into the shower, holding his hand out for me. His eyes rake down my body and stop at my thighs with a scowl.

"What?" I try to cover myself with my arms.

"The blood. It's on you." He gestures to some faint red marks.

"It's fine." I grab the loofah and rub it against my skin.

He takes it from me and covers it with soap. "Let me." Hardin kneels, and I can't help the goose bumps that form on my skin at the sight of him on his knees in front of me. The loofah moves up and down my thighs, slowly circling around. The boy has a direct line to my hormones. He brings his face close to my skin, and I try not to squirm as his lips touch my left hip. He keeps one of his hands wrapped around the back of my thigh, holding me in place as he does the same to the right. "Hand me the shower-head," he says, breaking me from my perverted thoughts.

"What?"

"Hand me it, the showerhead," he says again.

I nod and lift the piece from its hook and hand it down to him. Looking up at me with a gleam in his eye and water dripping from his nose, he turns the head in his hand, pointing it directly at my stomach.

"What . . . what are you doing?" I squeak as he moves the object lower. The hot water pulses against my skin, and I watch in anticipation.

"Does that feel good?"

I nod.

"If you think it feels good now, let's see how it feels if we move it down, just a little lower . . ." Every cell in my body is awakened, dancing under my skin as Hardin teasingly tortures me. I jump as the water hits me, and Hardin smirks.

The water feels so good, much better than I'd ever have assumed it could. My fingers wrap into his hair, and I pull my bottom lip between my teeth to stifle my moans. His mother is in the other room, but I can't make him stop—it feels too good.

"Tessa . . ." Hardin probes for an answer.

"Same . . . stay there." I pant, and he chuckles, pressing the water closer to me to add more pressure. When I feel Hardin's soft tongue run across me just under the water, I nearly lose my balance. It's too much, his tongue lapping with the water pulsing and my knees shaking.

"Hardin . . . I can't . . ." I'm not sure what I'm trying to say, but when his tongue moves faster, I pull his hair, hard. My legs begin to shake, and Hardin drops the showerhead and uses both of his hands to hold me up.

"Fuck . . ." I curse quietly, hopeful that the noise of the shower will drown out my moans. I feel him smile against me before continuing to bring me over the edge. My eyes screw shut as I allow pleasure to take over my body.

Hardin pulls his mouth from mine long enough to say, "Come on, baby, come for me."

I do just that.

When I open my eyes, Hardin is still kneeling and his hand is wrapped around his cock. It's hard and heavy in his grip. Still catching my breath, I drop to my knees. I wrap my hand around his, stroking him.

"Stand up," I quietly instruct. His eyes lower and he nods, getting to his feet. I bring his length to my mouth, licking the tip of him.

"Fuck . . ." He sucks in a breath, and I lap my tongue around him. I wrap my arms around the back of his legs to keep my balance on the wet floor and take his cock down my throat. Hardin's fingers dig into my wet hair, holding me still as he moves his hips, thrusting into my mouth. "I could fuck your mouth for hours." He thrusts a little faster, and I groan. His dirty words make me tighten the suction of my lips around him, and he curses again. The animalistic way he's completely claiming my mouth is new. He has total control, and I love it.

"I'm going to come in your mouth, baby." He pulls at my hair a little more, and I can feel the muscles in his legs tighten under my hands, and he curses my name repeatedly as he relieves himself down my throat.

After a few ragged breaths, he helps me to my feet and kisses my forehead. "I think we're clean now." He smiles, licking his lips.

"I'd say so," I say with a ragged breath and grab the shampoo.

Once both of us are actually clean and ready to get out, I run my hands along his abs, tracing the skull pattern on his stomach. My hand creeps lower, but Hardin's fingers grip my wrist to stop me.

"I know I'm hard to resist, but my mum is just in the other room. Have some self-control, young lady," he teases, and I swat at his arm before climbing out of the shower and grabbing a towel.

"This, coming from someone who just used . . ." I flush, unable to finish the sentence.

"You liked it, didn't you?" He raises his eyebrow, and I roll my eyes.

"Go get my clothes from the room," I tell him in a bossy tone.

"Yes, ma'am." He wraps the towel around his waist and disappears from the steamy bathroom. I swipe my hand across the mirror after wrapping my soaking hair in a towel.

Today has been a hectic and very stressful Christmas. I

should probably call Landon later, but first I want to talk to Hardin about this moving-back-to-England-after-college idea. He's never mentioned it to me before.

"Here." Hardin hands me a pile of clothes and leaves me alone in the bathroom to get dressed. I'm amused to find the red lace bra and panties set along with the sweats and a clean black T-shirt. Clean, because the one from today is bloodied.

chapter forty-nine

TESSA

Our last night with Hardin's mom consists mostly of drinking tea and her telling embarrassing stories of when Hardin was little. That and about ten reminders that next year Christmas is in England, "No excuses."

The thought of celebrating Christmas with Hardin a year from now makes my stomach flutter. For the first time since we met, I can see a future with him. Not necessarily having children and getting married, but for once I feel secure enough about his feelings to be able to look a year ahead.

The next morning, when Hardin returns from dropping Trish off at the airport at far too early an hour, I wake up. I hear him drop his clothes onto the floor, and he climbs back into bed wearing only boxers. He wraps his arms around me once more. I'm still a little irritated with him from our earlier conversation, but his arms are cold, and I missed him during his absence from our bed.

"I go back to work tomorrow," I say after a few minutes, unsure if he's already fallen asleep or not.

"I know," he replies.

"I'm excited to get back to Vance."

"Why?"

"Because I love it there, and I've had the week off. I miss working."

"You're quite the overachiever," he mocks, and I know he's rolling his eyes even though I can't see his face.

Reflexively, this makes me roll my own eyes. "Sorry that I love my internship and you don't like your job."

"I do like my job, and I had the same job you have. I just left it for something better," he brags.

"Do you only like it more because you get to do it from home?"

"Yeah, that's the main reason."

"What's the other reason?"

"I felt like people thought I only got the job because of Vance."

This is not a huge revelation, but it's a much more honest answer than I expected from him. I expected a word or two about how the job sucked or was annoying.

"Do really you think people thought that?" I roll onto my back, and Hardin leans up on his elbow to look down at me.

"I don't know. No one said it, but I felt like they were thinking it. Especially after he hired me as an actual employee, not just an intern."

"Do you think he was upset when you left to work for someone else?"

He smiles a smile that appears especially bright in the half-lit bedroom. "No, I don't think so. His employees were constantly complaining about my supposed attitude anyway."

"*Supposed* attitude?" I tease.

He cups my cheek and dips his head down to kiss my forehead. "Yes, *supposed*. I am very charming. No attitude at all." He smiles against my skin. I giggle, and he smiles even more, pressing his forehead against mine. "What do you want to do today?" he asks.

"I don't know; I was thinking of calling Landon and going to the store."

He draws back a little. "For what?"

"To talk to him and see when he can meet up with me. I'd like to give him those tickets."

"The gifts are at their house. I'm sure they already opened them."

"I don't see them opening them without us being there."

"I do."

"My point exactly," I tease.

But Hardin's already turned serious with the mention of his family. "Do you think . . . What do you think about me apologizing . . . well, not apologizing . . . but what if I called him—you know, my dad?"

I know that I need to tread lightly when it comes to Hardin and Ken. "I think you should call him. I think you should try to make sure what happened yesterday doesn't ruin the beginning of the relationship you were forming with him."

"I guess . . ." He sighs. "After I hit him, I thought for a second that you were going to stay there and make me leave."

"You did?"

"Yeah, I did. I'm glad you didn't, but that's what I thought."

I lift my head off the mattress and plant a small kiss on his jawline instead of answering. I have to admit that I probably would have done just that had he not already come clean about his past. That changed everything for me. It changed the way I look at Hardin—not in a negative way, or a positive one, just a more understanding way.

Hardin looks past me toward the window. "I can call him today, I guess."

"Do you think that we could go to their house? I really want to give them their gifts."

Blinking back to me, he says, "We could just tell them to open them while you're on the phone. That's basically the same, only you won't have to see their fake smiles at your terrible presents."

"Hardin!" I whine.

He chuckles and lays his head on my chest. "I'm teasing; you give the best gifts. That key chain with the wrong sports team was killer." He laughs.

"Go back to bed." I swat at his messy hair.

"What did you need from the store?" he asks as he lies back down.

I forgot that I had mentioned that. "Nothing."

"No, no, you said you needed to go to the store. What was it, plugs or something?"

"Plugs?"

"You know to . . . plug yourself."

What? "I don't get it . . ."

"Tampons."

I blush. My whole body blushes, I'm sure. "Oh . . . no."

"Do you even have a period?"

"Oh my God, Hardin, stop talking about it."

"What? You're embarrassed to talk about your men-stru-ation with me?" When he lifts up his face to look at me, a huge grin is plastered across it.

"I'm not embarrassed. It's just inappropriate," I defend, highly embarrassed.

He smiles. "We've done quiet a few inappropriate things, Theresa."

"Don't call me Theresa—and stop talking about it!" I groan and cover my face with my hands.

"Are you bleeding now?" I feel his hand travel down my stomach.

"No . . ." I lie.

I have gotten away from exactly this situation before because we're always so on and off and it just never happened. Now that we're going to be around each other more steadily, I knew this would happen—I just was avoiding it.

"So you wouldn't mind if I . . ." His hand slips into the top of my panties.

"Hardin!" I squeal and smack his hand away.

He chuckles. "Admit it, then; say, 'Hardin, I'm on my period.'"

"No, I am not saying that." I know my face is a deep red by now.

"Come on, it's just a little blood."

"You're disgusting."

"Bloody amazing." He smiles, obviously proud of his ridiculous joke.

"You're obnoxious."

"You need to lighten up . . . learn to go with the flow." He laughs harder.

"Oh my God! Okay, if I say it, will you stop with the menstrual jokes?"

"I'm not making jokes. Period."

His laugh is contagious, and it feels great to be lying in bed laughing with Hardin, despite the subject of conversation. "Hardin, I'm on my period. I just started right before you got home. There, are you happy?"

"Why are you embarrassed by it?"

"I'm not—I just don't think it's something that women should discuss."

"It's not a big deal, I don't mind a little blood." He presses himself against me.

I scrunch my nose. "You're gross."

"I've been called worse." He smiles.

"You're in a good mood today," I point out.

"Maybe you would be, too, if it wasn't that time of month."

I groan and grab the pillow from behind me to cover my face. "Can we please talk about something else?" I say through the pillow.

"Sure . . . sure . . . someone's bloody panties are in a twist."
He laughs.

I pull the pillow from my face and hit him in the head with it
before climbing off the bed. I hear him laughing as he opens the
dresser, to find a pair of pants, I assume. It's early, only seven in
the morning, but I'm wide awake. I start a pot of coffee and make
myself a bowl of cereal. I can't believe Christmas is over; in a few
days the year will be over.

"What do you usually do to celebrate the New Year?" I ask
Hardin when he sits down at the table in white cotton drawstring
pants.

"Go out, usually."

"Go where?"

"Parties, or a club. Or both. Last year was both."

"Oh." I hand him the bowl of cereal.

"What would you like to do?"

"I'm not sure. I want to go out, I think," I answer.

He raises one eyebrow. "You do?"

"Yeah . . . don't you?"

"I don't really give a shit what we do, but if you want to go
out, *that* is what we shall do." He brings a spoonful of Frosted
Flakes to his mouth.

"Okay . . ." I say, unsure of where we'll go. I make myself another bowl. "Are you going to ask your father if we can stop by
today?" I ask him and take seat next to him.

"I don't know . . ."

"Maybe they could come here?" I suggest.

Hardin's eyes narrow. "I don't think so."

"Why not? You'd be more comfortable here, right?"

He closes his eyes for a moment before opening them again.
"I guess. Let me call them in a bit."

I finish my breakfast quickly and stand up from the table.

"Where are you going?" he asks.

"To clean, obviously."

"Clean what? The place is spotless."

"No, it's not, and I want it to be perfect if we're having guests over." I rinse my bowl and place it in the dishwasher. "You could help clean, you know? Since you're the one who makes most of the mess," I point out.

"Oh no. You're much better at cleaning than I am." He gestures at the cereal box.

I roll my eyes but give it to him. I don't mind cleaning, because, honestly, I like things a certain way, and Hardin's version of cleaning isn't actually cleaning. He just shoves things wherever they'll fit.

"Oh, and don't forget that we need to go to the store to get your plugs." He laughs.

"Stop calling them that!" I throw a dish towel at his face, and he laughs harder at my embarrassment.

chapter fifty

TESTA

After the apartment is clean to my standards, I go to the store to get tampons and a few things in case Ken, Karen, and Landon come over. Hardin tried to accompany me, but I knew he'd be teasing me about the tampons the entire time, so I made him stay home.

When I return, he's sitting in the same spot on the couch. "Have you called your father yet?" I ask from the kitchen.

"No . . . I was waiting for you," he replies, then wanders into the kitchen and sits down at the table with a sigh. "I'll call now."

I nod and sit across from him while he presses his phone to his ear.

"Uh . . . hey." Hardin says into the receiver. Then he sets the phone to speaker and places it on the table between us.

"Hardin?" Ken's voice is surprised.

"Yeah . . . um, look, I was wondering if you wanted to come over or something."

"Come over?"

Hardin looks up at me, and I can tell that his patience is already wearing thin. My hand moves across the table to rest atop his, and I nod in encouragement.

"Yeah . . . you, Karen, and Landon. We can exchange gifts, since we didn't yesterday. Mum's gone," he says.

"You're sure that's okay?" Ken asks his son.

"I just asked, didn't I?" Hardin says, and I squeeze his hand. "I mean . . . yeah, that's fine," he corrects, and I smile at him.

"Okay, well, let me talk to Karen, but I know she'll be thrilled. What time will be good for you?" Hardin looks at me. I mouth *two*, and he tells his father.

"Okay . . . well, we'll see you at two."

"Tessa will text Landon the address," Hardin says and hangs up the phone.

"That wasn't so bad, right?" I ask.

He rolls his eyes. "Sure."

"What should I wear?"

He gestures to my jeans and WCU T-shirt. "That."

"Definitely not. This is our Christmas."

"No, it's the day after Christmas, so you should wear jeans." He smiles, and his fingers tug at his lip ring.

"I'm not wearing jeans." I laugh and head to the bedroom to decide what to wear.

I'M HOLDING MY WHITE DRESS to my chest in front of the mirror when Hardin walks into the bedroom. "I don't know if wearing white is the best idea." He smiles.

"For God's sake, stop it!" I say.

"You're cute when you're embarrassed."

I grab my maroon dress from the closet. This dress holds a lot of memories for me; I wore it to my first frat party with Steph. I miss Steph despite all the anger I feel . . . felt toward her. I feel betrayed by her, but at the same time in a lot of ways she was right when she said it wasn't fair for me to forgive Hardin but not her.

"What's going on in that mind of yours?" Hardin questions.

"Nothing . . . I was just thinking of Steph."

"What about her?"

"I don't know . . . I miss her, sort of. Do you miss your friends?" I ask. He hasn't mentioned any of them since the letter.

"No." He shrugs. "I would rather spend my time with you."

I'm enjoying this honest Hardin, but I note, "You could still spend time with them, too."

"I guess. I don't know; I don't really care either way. Do you even want to be around them . . . you know, after everything?" His eyes focus on the floor.

"I don't know . . . but I'd be willing to try, at least, and see how it goes. Not Molly, though." I scowl.

He looks up mischievously. "But the two of you are such great friends."

"Ugh, enough about her. What do you think they'll do on New Year's Eve?" I ask. I don't know how it will be to be around everyone, but I miss having friends, or what passed for friends.

"There'll probably be a party. Logan is obsessed with New Year's . . . Are you sure you want to go out with them?"

I smile. "Yeah . . . if it blows up in my face, then we'll stay in next year."

Hardin's eyes widen when I mention next year, but I pretend I don't notice. I need our Christmas do-over to be peaceful today. I'm focusing on today.

"I need to make something for everyone to eat. I should have said three; it's already noon, and I'm not even ready." I rub my hands over my makeup-free face.

"Go ahead and get ready, I'll make something . . ." Hardin says, then smirks. "Just make sure you eat *only* what I put on your plate."

"Joking about poisoning your father, lovely," I tease. He shrugs and wanders off. I wash my face and apply light makeup before pulling my hair out of its ponytail and curling the ends. By the time I finish getting ready and get myself dressed, a wonderful garlic smell is coming from the kitchen.

When I join Hardin in the kitchen, I see he's laid out a couple of trays of fruit and vegetables and already set the table. I'm really impressed by what he's done, though I do have to fight the urge to rearrange a few things. I'm so glad that Hardin was willing to invite his father over to our apartment, and even more relieved that he seems to be in a really good mood today. Checking the clock, I see our company will be here in thirty minutes, so I begin cleaning up the small mess Hardin made while cooking and get the apartment spotless again.

I wrap my arms around his waist as he stands in front of the oven. "Thank you for doing all of this."

He shrugs. "It's nothing."

"Are you okay?" I ask and unwrap my arms and turn him to face me.

"Yeah . . . I'm fine."

"Are you sure you aren't a little nervous?" I ask. I can tell he is.

"No . . . well, just a little. It's just weird as fuck to have him coming here, you know?"

"I know. I'm really proud of you for inviting him." I press my cheek against his chest, and his hands move to my waist.

"You are?"

"Of course I am, ba—Hardin."

"What was that . . . what were you going to say?"

I hide my face. "Nothing." I don't know where this sudden urge to call him pet names comes from, but it's embarrassing.

"Tell me," he coos and lifts my chin to force me out of hiding.

"I don't know why, but I almost called you 'babe' again." I bring my bottom lip between my teeth, and his smile grows.

"Go ahead, call me it," he says.

"You'll make fun of me." I smile weakly.

"No, I won't. I call you 'baby' all the time."

"Yeah . . . but it's different when you do it."

"How so?"

"I don't know . . . it's, like, sexier or something when you do . . . more romantic. I don't know." I flush.

"You're awfully shy today." He smiles and plants a kiss on my forehead. "I like it, though. So go ahead and call me it."

I hug him tighter. "Okay."

"Okay what?"

"Okay . . . *babe*." The word tastes strange rolling off of my tongue.

"Again."

I let out a surprised squeak as he lifts me onto the cold countertop and stands between my legs. "Okay, babe!" I repeat.

His cheeks are a deeper shade of pink than usual. "I really love that. It's . . . what did you say? Sexy and romantic?" He smiles.

A sudden bravery makes me speak again. "Is it, babe?" I smile and bite my lip again.

"Yes . . . incredibly sexy." He presses his lips against my neck, and I shiver as his hands trail up my thighs.

"Don't think these will keep me out." His fingers draw circles on my black tights.

"They may not, but the . . . you know will."

A knock at the door makes me jump, and Hardin smiles and winks at me. As he walks to the door, he says over his shoulder, "Oh, baby . . . that won't *either*."

chapter fifty-one

HARDIN

When I open the door, my attention is immediately drawn to my dad's face. A deep purple bruise is clear on his cheek, and his bottom lip holds a small cut right down the center.

I nod as my greeting to them, not knowing what the hell to say.

"Your place is so lovely." Karen smiles, and the three of them stand by the door, unsure what to do.

Tessa saves all of us by walking into the room. "Come on in. You can put those by the tree," she says to Landon, gesturing to the bag of gifts in his arms.

"We brought the gifts you left at the house as well," my dad says.

The air is thick with tension—not an angry tension, exactly, but really damn awkward tension.

Tess smiles sweetly. "Thank you so much." She's so good at making people feel welcome. At least one of us is.

Landon walks to the kitchen first, followed by Karen and Ken. I reach for Tessa's hand, using her as an anchor for my anxiety.

"How was the drive?" Tessa tries to start conversation.

"It wasn't too bad; I drove," Landon answers.

The conversation flows from uncomfortable at first to somewhat relaxed as we eat. In between courses, Tessa squeezes my hand under the table.

"The food was excellent," Karen compliments, looking at Tessa.

"Oh, I didn't make it, Hardin did," Tessa tells her and places her hand on my thigh.

"Really? It was delicious, Hardin." Karen smiles.

I'd have been okay with Tessa taking the credit for the meal. Having four sets of eyes on me is making me want to vomit. Tessa applies more pressure to my leg, wanting me to say something.

I look at Karen. "Thanks," I say, and Tessa squeezes again, prompting me to offer Karen a really fucking awkward smile.

After a few seconds of silence, Tessa stands up and grabs her plate from the table. She walks into the kitchen, and I debate whether or not to follow.

"The food was really good, son. I'm impressed," my dad says, breaking the silence.

"Yeah, it's just food," I mumble. His eyes shift down, and I correct myself. "I mean, Tessa's the better cook, but thanks."

He seems pleased with my answer and takes a drink from his glass. Karen smiles awkwardly, staring at me with those weirdly almost comforting eyes of hers. I look away. Tessa joins us before anyone else has the chance to compliment the food.

"Well, should we open the gifts?" Landon asks.

"Yes," Karen and Tessa answer at the same time.

I stay as close to Tessa as possible as we go into the living room. My dad, Karen, and Landon sit on the couch. I reach for Tessa's hand and gently pull her to sit on my lap in the chair. I see her look toward our guests, and Karen tries to hide a smile. Tessa looks away, embarrassed, but doesn't move from my lap. I lean up a little more and wrap my arm tighter around her waist.

Landon stands and grabs the gifts. He passes them around, and I focus on Tessa and the way she gets excited over things like this. I love the way she's always so enthusiastic about everything, and I love the way she makes people comfortable. Even on "do-over Christmas."

Landon hands her a small box marked *From: Ken and*

Karen. When she tears the wrapping paper off, a blue box with *Tiffany & Co.* written in silver scroll on the front is revealed.

"What is it?" I ask quietly. I don't know shit about jewelry, but I know that brand is expensive.

"A bracelet." She extracts and dangles a silver chain-link bracelet in front of me. A small bow-shaped charm and a heart hang from the expensive metal. The shiny object makes the bracelet on her wrist, my gift to her, look like complete shit.

"Of course it is," I say under my breath.

Tessa frowns at me, then turns back to them. "It's beautiful; thank you both so much." She beams.

"She already . . ." I begin to complain. I hate that they got her a better gift than mine. I get it—he has money. Couldn't they have gotten her something else, anything else?

But Tessa turns back to me, silently begging me not to make shit any more awkward. I sigh in defeat and lean back against the chair.

"What's in yours?" Tessa smiles, trying to lighten my mood. She rests against me, kissing my forehead. She looks down at the box on the arm of the chair, hinting for me to open it. When I do, I hold the expensive contents up for her to see.

"A watch." I show her, trying to humor her the best I can.

Honestly, I'm still fucking irritated about the bracelet. I wanted her to wear *my* bracelet every day—I wanted it to be her favorite gift.

chapter fifty-two

HARDIN

Karen beams over the box of pans from Tessa. "I've been wanting this set all season!"

Tessa thought I didn't notice that she added my name to the small snowman-shaped tags, but I did. I just didn't feel like crossing it out.

"I feel like a jerk because I only got you a gift card when you got me these awesome tickets," Landon says to Tessa.

I have to admit that I'm happy for his impersonal present of a gift card for the e-reader that I got her for her birthday. If he had gotten something more thoughtful, it would have annoyed me, but with Tessa's caring smile, you'd think he bought her a fucking first-edition Austen novel. I still can't believe they got her an expensive bracelet; what show-offs. What if she wants to wear this new one instead of mine?

"Thank you for the gifts, they're great," my dad says and looks at me, holding up the key chain Tessa mistakenly chose for him.

I feel a little guilty for his busted face, but at the same time I find the weird coloring slightly amusing. I want to apologize for my outburst—well, I wouldn't say I *want to*, but I need to. I don't want to go backward with him. It was sort of okay to spend time with him, I guess. Karen and Tessa get on pretty well, and I feel obligated to give her the chance to have a motherly figure around, since it's my fault her and her mother are on such bad terms. It's good for me, in a fucked-up way, that they are, because it's one less person in the way of us being together.

"Hardin?" Tessa's voice says into my ear.

I look up at her and realize that one of them must have been talking to me.

"Would you want to go with Landon to the game?" she asks.

"What? No," I say quickly.

"Thanks, man." Landon rolls his eyes.

"I mean, I don't think Landon would want that," I correct myself.

Being decent is much harder than I thought it would be. I'm only doing this for her . . . Well, if I'm honest, it's a little for myself, as my mum's words that my anger will only give me busted hands and a lonely life keep repeating in my head.

"Tessa and I can go if you won't," Landon says to me.

Why is he trying to annoy me when I'm trying to be nice for once?

She smiles. "Yeah, I'll go with. I don't know anything about hockey, but I'll tag along."

Without thinking, I wrap my other arm around her waist and pull her against my chest. "I'll go." I give in.

Amusement is clear on Landon's face, and I can tell even with Tessa's back to me that she wears the same expression.

"I really like what you guys have done to the place, Hardin," my father says.

"It came decorated mostly, but thanks," I reply. I have come to the conclusion that it's less awkward when I'm punching him than when we're trying to avoid an argument.

Karen smiles at me. "It was really nice of you to invite us over."

My life would be easier if she was a hideous bitch, but of course she's one of the nicest people I have ever met. "It's nothing, really . . . after what happened yesterday, it's the least I can do." I know my voice sounds shakier and more strained than I want it to.

"It's okay . . . things happen," Karen assures me.

"Not really; I don't think that violence is a regular holiday tradition," I say.

"Maybe it will be from now on—Tessa can punch me out next year," Landon jokes in a lame attempt to lighten the mood.

"Maybe I will." Tessa sticks her tongue out at him, and I smile slightly.

"It won't happen again," I say and look at my dad.

My dad looks at me thoughtfully. "It was partly my fault, son. I should have known it wasn't going to go well, but I hope now that you let some of the anger out, we can get back to trying to develop a relationship," he says to me.

Tessa puts her small hands over mine to comfort me, and I nod. "Uh, yeah . . . cool," I say timidly. "Yeah . . ." I chew on the inside of my cheek.

Landon slaps his hands on his knees and stands. "Well, we should get going, but let me know if you really want to go to the game. Thank you both for having us over today."

Tessa hugs the three of them as I lean against the wall. I was nice enough today, but there's no way that I'm hugging anyone. Except Tessa, of course, but after my politeness today she should be giving me more than a hug. I stare at the way her loose dress hides her beautiful curves and literally have to talk myself down before I drag her to the bedroom. I remember the first time I saw her in that hideous dress. Well, back then it was hideous to me; now I sort of adore it. She came out of the dorm looking like she was getting ready to sell Bibles door-to-door. She rolled her eyes at me when I teased her as she climbed into my car, but I had no idea that she would make me fall in love with her.

I wave once more as our company leaves and let out a deep breath that I hadn't realized I was holding. *A hockey game with Landon—what the fuck have I gotten myself into?*

"That was so nice. *You* were so nice." Tessa praises me and immediately kicks off her high heels before lining them neatly by the door.

I shrug. "It was okay, I guess."

"It was better than okay." Tessa beams at me.

"Whatever," I state with an exaggerated grumpiness, and she giggles.

"I really love you. You know that, don't you?" she asks as she walks around the living room picking up after everyone. I tease her about her cleaning habits, but the place would be trashed if it were only me living here.

"So, the watch? You like it?" she asks.

"No, it's hideous, and I don't wear watches."

"I think it looks nice."

"What about your bracelet?" I hesitantly ask her.

"It's beautiful."

"Oh . . ." I look away. "It's fancy and expensive," I add.

"Yeah . . . I feel bad that they spent all that money on it when I won't really be wearing it. I'll have to wear it when they're around once or twice."

"Why won't you wear it?"

"Because I already have a favorite bracelet." She shakes her wrist back and forth, making the charms hit one another.

"Oh. You like mine better?" I can't hide my stupid smile.

She looks at me with a lightly chastising look. "Of course I do, Hardin."

I try to hold on to some of the little dignity I have left, but I can't help but scoop her up by the back of her legs. When she screams, I laugh loudly. I don't remember ever laughing this way in my entire life.

chapter fifty-three

TESSA

The next morning I wake up early, shower, and with my towel still wrapped around me, quickly start a pot of that elixir of life: coffee. As I watch it brew, an awareness bubbles up in me that I'm a little nervous to see Kimberly. I don't know what her reaction to Hardin and me getting back together will be. She's not judgmental, but flipping the situation around, I don't know what my reaction would be if it were her going through the same thing with Christian. She doesn't know all of the details, but she knows they're bad enough for me to keep them from her.

With a steaming mug in hand, I walk over to the large window in the living room. The snow is falling in thick clusters; I wish it would stop already. I hate driving in the snow, and most of the way to Vance is freeway.

"Morning." Hardin's voice startles me from the hall.

"Morning." I smile and take another sip of my coffee. "Shouldn't you be sleeping?" I ask him as he wipes the sleep from his eyes.

"Shouldn't you be dressed?" he retaliates.

I smile and walk past him toward the bedroom to get myself dressed, but he tugs on the towel and pulls it from my body, making me shriek and rush into the room. Hearing footsteps behind me, I lock the door. God knows what will happen if I let him in. My skin flames at the thought, but I don't have time for that right now.

"Nice, very mature," he says through the wood.

"I never claimed to be mature." I smile and pad to the closet, where I decide on a long black skirt and red blouse. Not my most flattering outfit, but it's my first day back and it's snowing. After I put light makeup on in the full-length mirror in the closet, all I have left to do is dry my hair. When I open the door, Hardin is nowhere to be found. I quickly half dry my hair before pulling it back into a secure bun.

"Hardin?" I grab my purse and take out my phone to call him.

No answer. *Where is he?* My heart begins to pound as I walk through the apartment. After a minute, the front door clicks open and he steps inside, covered in snow.

"Where were you? I was getting nervous."

"Nervous? Of what?" he asks.

"I don't know, really. That you were hurt or something?" I sound ridiculous.

"I was just scraping and starting your car for you so it's warm and ready when you get down there." He shrugs off his jacket and removes his soaked boots, leaving a puddle of slush on the concrete.

I can't hide my surprise. "Who are you?" I laugh.

"Don't start that shit or I'll go back down and slash your tires," he says.

I roll my eyes and laugh at his empty threat. "Well, thank you."

"I . . . I can drive you?" His eyes meet mine.

Now I really don't know who he is. He was polite for the most part yesterday, and now he's heating my car and offering to drive me to work—not to mention the way he laughed so hard last night that his eyes were brimming with moisture. Honesty really does look good on him.

". . . or not," he adds when I take too long to reply.

"I would love it," I say, and he puts his boots back on.

When we get downstairs and start pulling out of the lot, Hardin remarks, "Good thing your car is such shit, or someone could have stolen it while it was down here running."

"It is *not* shit!" I defend, eyeing the small crack in the passenger window. "Anyway, I was thinking next week when classes start back up we can drive to campus together, right? Your classes are around the same times as mine, and on the days I go to Vance, I'll just take my car and meet you back at home."

"Okay . . ." He stares ahead out the windshield.

"What?"

"I just wish you'd have told me what classes you were taking."

"Why?"

"I don't know . . . maybe I could've taken one with you instead of just you and Landon signing up together and becoming eternal study buddies."

"You've already taken French and American Lit, and I didn't think you'd be interested in World Religion."

"I'm not," he huffs.

I know this conversation isn't going to go anywhere, so when I see the big V on the Vance Building, I'm grateful. The snow has slowed, but Hardin pulls up close to the front door to minimize my exposure to the cold.

"I'll be here to get you at four," he says, and I nod before leaning across the small space to kiss him goodbye.

"Thank you for driving me," I whisper against his lips, touching them once more.

"Mm-hmm . . ." he mumbles, and I pull away.

When I step out of the car, Trevor appears only a few feet away, his black suit speckled with white snow. My stomach churns as he gives me a warm smile.

"Hey, long time no—"

"Tess!" Hardin calls my name and shuts the car door to walk around to my side. Trevor's eyes go to Hardin, then back to me, and his smile disappears. "You forgot something . . ." Hardin says, handing me a pen.

A pen? I raise my eyebrow.

He nods and wraps his arms around my waist, pressing his lips forcefully against mine. If we weren't in a parking lot—and I didn't feel like this was his sick way of marking his territory—I would melt under the aggressive manner with which his tongue parts my lips. When I pull away, his face holds a smug expression. I shiver and rub my hands over my arms. I should have worn a heavier jacket.

"Nice to see you. Trenton, was it?" Hardin says with false sincerity.

I know damn well he knows his name. He's so rude.

"Uh . . . yeah. Nice to see you, too," Trevor mumbles and disappears through the sliding doors.

"What the hell was that?" I scowl at Hardin.

"What?" He smirks.

I groan. "You're such a pig."

"Stay away from him, Tess. Please," Hardin commands, kissing me on the forehead to soften his harsh words.

I roll my eyes and stomp inside the building like a child.

"How was your Christmas?" Kimberly asks as I grab a donut and coffee. I probably shouldn't drink another cup, but Hardin's caveman act has annoyed me, and the smell of the coffee beans alone calms me.

"It . . ."

Oh, you know, I took Hardin back, then found out he made sex tapes with multiple girls, ruining one of their lives, but then I took him back again. My mother showed up at my apartment and caused a scene, so now she and I aren't speaking. Hardin's mother was in town, so we had to pretend we were together, even though we weren't, which basically brought us back together, and it was smooth

sailing until my mother told his mother about him taking my vir-
ginity for a bet. Oh, and Christmas? To commemorate that holiday,
Hardin beat the shit out of his dad and punched his hand through a
glass cabinet. You know, the usual.

". . . was great. How was yours?" I say, going with the short
version.

Kimberly dives into her amazing Christmas with Christian
and his son. The little boy cried when he saw the new bicycle
that "Santa" brought him. He had even called Kimberly "Mommy
Kim," which made her heart warm, but made her slightly uncomfortable at the same time. "It's strange, you know," she says.
"Thinking of myself as someone's guardian or whatever I am. I'm
not married, not even engaged, to Christian, so I don't know my
place with Smith."

"I think Smith and Christian are both lucky to have you in
their lives, whatever title you may have," I assure her.

"You're wise beyond your years, Ms. Young."

She smiles, and I rush to my office after glancing at the clock.
By the time lunch comes around, Kimberly's not at her desk.
When the elevator stops at the third floor, I silently scream as
Trevor steps into it.

"Hey," I say, my voice small.

I don't know why this is so uncomfortable. It's not like I was
dating Trevor or anything. We went on one date and I had a nice
time. I enjoy his company and he enjoys mine. That is all.

"How was your break?" he asks, his blue eyes shining under
the fluorescent lighting.

I wish people would stop asking me that today. "Nice. Yours?"

"It was nice—had a huge turnout at the shelter downtown,
fed over three hundred people." He beams proudly.

"Wow, three hundred people? That's incredible." I smile. He's
so kind, and the tension between us is somewhat diminished.

"It was really great; hopefully next year we'll have even more resources and we can feed five hundred." As we both step off the elevator he asks, "Are you going to lunch?"

"Yeah, I was going to walk over to Firehouse, since I didn't drive myself," I say, not wanting to discuss Hardin and me at the moment.

"You can ride with me if you want. I'm going to Panera, but I can run you by Firehouse first. You shouldn't walk in the snow," he offers politely.

"You know? Panera's good. I'll just come with." I smile, and we head to his car.

The heated seats in his BMW warm me up before we're even out of the parking lot. At the eatery, Trevor and I stay mostly silent while we order our lunch and sit down at a small table toward the back.

"I'm thinking about moving to Seattle," Trevor tells me as I dip a cracker into my broccoli soup.

"Really? When?" I ask loudly, trying to speak over the many voices of the lunch crowd.

"March. Christian has offered me a job there—a promotion to head of finance at the new branch—and I'm strongly considering taking it."

"That's really great news—congratulations, Trevor!"

He wipes the corners of his mouth with a napkin. "Thank you. I would love to run the entire finance department, and even more, I'd love to move to Seattle."

We talk about Seattle for the rest of the meal, and by the time we finish, all I can think is *Why can't Hardin feel the same about Seattle?*

When we get back to Vance, the snow has turned to freezing rain and the two of us rush into the building. I'm shivering by the time we reach the elevator. Trevor offers me his suit jacket, but I quickly decline.

"So you and Hardin are seeing each other again?" he finally asks, a question I had been waiting for.

"Yeah . . . we are working through things." I chew on my cheek.

"Oh . . . you're happy, then?" He looks down at me.

I look up at him. "Yeah."

"Well, I'm happy for you." He runs his hands over his black hair and I know he's lying, but I appreciate him not making this any more awkward than it already is. That's part of his goodness, too.

When we step off of the elevator, Kimberly's face holds a strange expression. I'm confused by the way she's looking at Trevor, until I follow her eyes to where Hardin is leaning against the wall.

chapter fifty-four

HARDIN

Really? *Really?*" I ask, my hands flying into the air dramatically.

Tessa's mouth falls open, but no words come out as she looks at fucking Trevor, then back to me. *Goddammit, Tessa.* Anger courses through me and I begin to envision the multiple ways I want to beat the shit out of this boy.

"Thanks for lunch, Tessa. See you later," Trevor calmly says before walking away.

When I look at Kimberly, she shakes her head in disapproval before grabbing a folder off her desk and leaving us alone. Tessa glares at her friend, and I almost laugh.

Tessa defends herself and walks toward her office. "We just got lunch, Hardin. I can have lunch with whoever I want to. So do not start with me," she warns.

As soon as we're both inside, I close and lock her door. "You know how I feel about him." I lean against the wall.

"You need to be quiet. This is my job."

"Internship," I correct her.

"What?" Her eyes open wide.

"You're not an actual employee, just an intern," I say.

"So we're back to this, then?"

"No, I was just stating a fact." I'm an asshole: another fact.

"Really?" she challenges.

I clench my jaw and stare at my stubborn girl.

"Why are you even here?" she asks me and sits down in her chair behind her desk.

"I came to take you to lunch so you didn't have to go out in the snow," I say. "But it seems like you know how to get other guys to help you out."

"It's not that big of a deal. We went to eat and came right back. You need to calm down with the jealousy."

"It's not jealousy." Of course it's jealousy. And fear. But I'm not admitting that.

"We are friends, Hardin. Let it go and come here."

"No," I whine.

"Please?" she begs, and I roll my eyes at my lack of self-control as I walk over to her. She leans against her desk and pulls me to stand in front of her. "I only want you, Hardin. I love you and I do not want to be with anyone else, only you." She stares at me with such intensity that I look away.

"I'm sorry that you don't like him, but you can't tell me who I can be friends with." When she smiles at me, I try to hold on to my anger, but feel it slowly slipping. *Damn, is she good.*

"I can't stand him."

"He's harmless. Really. Besides, he's moving to Seattle in March."

Ice fills my veins, but I try to remain neutral. "He is?" Of course fucking Trevor is moving to Seattle—the place Tessa wants to be. The place I am not moving to and never will. I wonder if she's thought about going with him? *No, she wouldn't. Would she?*

Fuck, I don't know.

"Yeah, so he won't be around. Please just leave him alone." She squeezes my hands.

I look down at her. "Fine; fuck, fine. I won't touch him." I sigh. *I can't believe I just agreed to let him get away with trying to kiss her.*

"Thank you. I love you so much," she tells me, her blue-gray eyes staring into mine.

"I'm still mad at him for trying to seduce you. And you for not listening to me."

"I know, now be quiet . . ." She licks her bottom lip. "Let me set you at ease?" she asks with a shaky voice.

What?

"I . . . I want to show you that I love only you." Her cheeks flush deep crimson, and her hands move to my belt as she stands on her toes to kiss me.

I am confused, angry—and incredibly turned on. She runs her tongue over my bottom lip. I groan immediately and lift her onto the desk. Her trembling hands fumble with my belt again, this time removing it. I lift the bottom of her ridiculously long skirt up to the tops of her thighs, thankful that she didn't wear tights today.

"I want *you*, babe," she breathes against my neck, wrapping her legs around my waist.

I moan at the way those words sound coming from her full lips, and I'm loving her sudden dominance as she takes control, tugging my jeans down my legs.

"Aren't you?" I ask, referring to her period. "Yeah . . . you aren't."

She blushes and takes my length into her hand. I hiss, and she smiles while pumping slowly, too slowly.

"Don't tease me." I groan and she works her hand faster as she sucks the skin on my neck. If this is her way of making amends to me, I welcome her to fuck up more often. As long as it doesn't involve her and another guy.

I pull her head back by her hair to look at me. "I want to fuck you."

She shakes her head no, and a shy smile plays on her lips.

"Yes."

"We can't." She looks toward the door.

"We have before."

"I mean . . . because of . . . you know."

"It's not so bad." I shrug. It really isn't as bad as people assume it is.

"Is that . . . normal?"

"Yes. It's normal," I decree, and her eyes widen. Despite how shy she's acting, her pupils are blown out, letting me know how bad she wants it, too. Her hand remains on me, slowly moving, and I spread her legs farther. I tug on the string of her tampon and dispose of it in the trash, then, moving her hand away, roll the condom on.

She climbs down, then bends over the desk, lifting her skirt up over her ass.

Fuck if this isn't the hottest thing I've seen in my entire life, despite the circumstances.

chapter fifty-five

TESSA

Anticipation builds as Hardin pushes the thick material of my skirt farther up my waist.

"Relax, Tess. Shut your mind off—it's not going to be any different than it usually is," Hardin promises.

I'm trying to hide my embarrassment as he slides into me; it doesn't feel any different. Well, if anything, it actually feels better. More daring. Doing something so out of my norm, so taboo, makes it all the more exciting. Hardin's hand runs down my spine, making me shiver in anticipation. His mood has totally shifted. Given his stance when I came out of the elevator, I had expected him to cause a much bigger scene.

"Are you okay?" he asks.

I nod, moaning in answer.

One of his hands digs into my hip as the other grips my hair, holding me in place. "You feel so good, so good, baby." His voice is tight as he slowly drags himself in and out of me.

Hardin's hand moves from my hair down to my breasts. He tugs at the neckline of my blouse, exposing my chest. His hand finds my nipple, tugging at it gently before he rolls it between his fingers. I gasp and arch my back as he repeats the action over and over.

"Oh God," I utter, then clamp my mouth shut. I'm aware that we are in my office, but I can't seem to worry in the way that I normally would. My thoughts begin with Hardin and end with pleasure. The reality of this and the taboo around our act isn't relevant to me right now.

"Feels good, doesn't it, baby? I told you, nothing different . . . well, nothing different-bad, at least." He moans and wraps his arm around my waist. I nearly slip from the edge of the desk as he changes positions, resting my back against the hard wood of my desk. "I fucking love you, you know that, don't you?" Hardin pants into my ear.

I nod, but I know that he needs more.

"Say it," he insists.

"I know you love me," I assure him. My body is tightening and he straightens his back, bringing his fingers to rub over my clit. I lean up, trying to watch his fingers work their magic on my body, but the sensation is too much.

"Come, baby, go on." Hardin picks up the pace and lifts one of my legs higher into the air.

His eyes roll back in his head. My release is so close, so intense, and so overpowering that I can't see anything but stars as I grip his inked arms. I press my lips together, hard, to keep from calling out his name as I come undone. Hardin's release isn't as composed: he leans down, burying his head in my neck, calling my name once before pressing his mouth into my skin to silence his voice.

Hardin pulls out, places a kiss on my ear. I stand up and adjust my clothes, figuring I should get to the restroom soon. *God, this is weird*. I can't deny that I enjoyed it, but it's hard to get past the idea that has been so ingrained in my mind.

"Ready?" he asks.

"For what?" I say, my breathing ragged.

"To go home."

"I can't go home. It's only two." I gesture to the clock on the wall.

"Call Vance's office on our way out. Come home with me," Hardin instructs and grabs my purse from my desk.

"Though you may want to replug yourself before we go." He pulls a tampon from my purse and taps me on the nose with it.

I swat his arm. "Stop saying that!" I groan, stuffing it back into my bag as he laughs.

THREE DAYS LATER, I'm waiting patiently for Hardin to pick me up, staring out the large glass windows in the lobby, thankful that it hasn't snowed of late. The only evidence of the snowfall from days before is the black sludge littering the dips in the sidewalk.

Much to my annoyance, Hardin has insisted on driving me to work every day since our fight over Trevor. I'm still surprised that I was able to calm him down the way that I did. I don't know what I would have done if he'd assaulted Trevor in the office; Kimberly would have been forced to call security, and Hardin surely would have been arrested.

Hardin was supposed to be here at four thirty and it's now five fifteen. Nearly everyone has left for the day, and multiple people have offered to give me a ride home, including Trevor, though he did say it from about ten dozen feet away. I don't want things to be awkward between us, and I would still like to be friends, despite Hardin's "orders."

Finally Hardin's car pulls into the lot, and I step outside into the chilling wind. It is warmer today than it has been, the bright sun adding a small amount of warmth, but not enough. "Sorry for being late, I fell asleep," he tells me as I climb into the warm car.

"It's okay," I assure him and stare out the window.

I'm slightly nervous about New Year's Eve tonight and don't want to add fighting with Hardin to my list of stressors today. We haven't decided what we are actually doing yet, which drives me insane—I want to know the details and have the entire night planned.

I've been debating whether or not to reply to the text messages that Steph sent me a couple days ago. Part of me really wants to see her, to show her and everyone that they did not break me—though they humiliated me, yes—and that I'm stronger than they think. That being said, the other half of me thinks it will be incredibly awkward to see Hardin's friends. I know they'll probably think I'm an idiot for being with him again.

I won't know how to act around them, and honestly I'm afraid that everything will be different when Hardin and I are not in our own small bubble. What if he ignores me the entire time, or what if Molly's there? My blood boils at the thought.

"Where do you want to go?" he asks.

I had earlier mentioned that I needed something to wear tonight, so I say, "The mall is fine. We need to decide where we're going so I know what to get."

"Do you really want to hang out with everyone, or just go out, the two of us? I'm still rooting for staying in."

"I don't want to stay in, we stay in all the time." I smile. I love staying in with Hardin, but he used to be out all the time, and sometimes I worry if I keep him in the house too much, he'll get bored with me.

When we arrive at the mall, Hardin drops me off at the entrance to Macy's and I hurry inside. By the time he joins me, I already have three dresses draped over my arms.

"What is that?" Hardin scrunches his nose at the canary-yellow dress on top. "That color is hideous," he says.

"You find every color hideous, apart from black, of course."

He shrugs at my truthful statement and runs his finger along the fabric of the gold dress underneath. "I like this one," he says.

"Really? That was the one I was unsure about. I don't want to stand out, you know?"

He arches his brow. "And you wouldn't be standing out in yellow?"

He has a point. I place the yellow dress back on the rack and hold up a white strapless, then ask, "What about this one?"

"You should try them on," he suggests with a cheeky smile.

"Pervert," I tease.

"Always." He smirks and follows me to the dressing room.

"You are not coming in here," I scold him and close the door to the stall, leaving just enough room to pop my head out.

He pouts before taking a seat on the black leather couch outside the dressing room. "I want to see each one," he calls when I close the door the rest of the way.

"Be quiet."

I hear him chuckle, and I want to open the door just to see his smile, but I decide against it. I put the white strapless dress on first and struggle to zip it up the back: tight. Too tight and short, way too short. Finally I get the thin fabric to zip, and I tug at the bottom of the dress before opening the door to the dressing room.

"Hardin?" I almost whisper.

"Holy shit." He practically gasps when he turns the corner and takes in the sight of me in the barely-there dress.

"It's short." I flush.

"Yeah, you aren't getting that," he says as his eyes move up and down my body.

"If I want to, I will," I say, reminding him that he will not tell me what to wear.

He glares at me for a moment before speaking. "I know . . . I just meant you shouldn't. It's too revealing for your taste."

"That's what I thought." I hum and look in the full-length mirror once more.

Hardin smirks, and I see him check out my bottom. "It *is* incredibly sexy, though."

"Next," I say and walk back into the dressing room.

The gold dress feels silky against my skin despite the entire dress being covered in tiny gold disks. It falls to the middle of my thighs, and the sleeves are quarter length. This is much more me, only a touch riskier than usual. The sleeves give the illusion of the dress being more conservative, but the way the material clings to my body and the short length say otherwise.

"Tess," Hardin whines impatiently from directly outside. I open the door, and his reaction makes my heart flutter.

"Christ." He swallows.

"You like it?" I chew my bottom lip. I feel pretty confident in the dress, especially after Hardin's cheeks turn pink and he shifts his weight from one foot to the other.

"Very much."

This is such a normal couple thing to be doing, trying on clothes for him at Macy's, it feels strange yet very comforting. I was terrified a few days ago when he found out about my dinner with Trevor in Seattle.

"I'm going to get this one, then," I say.

After finding a pair of thick and rather intimidating black pumps, we head to check-out. Hardin pesters me to let him pay, but I refuse, this time winning the battle.

"You're right, you really should be buying *me* something . . . you know, to make up for the lack of Christmas gifts I received," he teases as we exit the mall.

I swat at his arm, but he grabs my wrist before I can connect. His lips press a light kiss against my palm before he encases my hand in his and leads me to the car. *Holding hands in public is never our thing* . . . As soon as the thought crosses my mind, he seems to realize what we're doing and drops my hand. One step at a time, I suppose.

* * *

BACK AT THE APARTMENT, after I've declared for the eighth time that we should hang out with his friends, my nerves begin to get the best of me as I imagine the possibilities of how the night could turn out. But we can't hide from the world forever. How Hardin behaves around his old friends will really show me how he truly feels about me, about us.

When I shower, I shave my legs three times, staying under the hot water until it is no longer warm. When I get out, I ask Hardin, "What did Nate say about tonight?" I'm unsure what I want the answer to be.

"He texted to meet them at the house . . . my old house. At nine. They're having a big thing, apparently."

I glance at the clock: already seven. "Okay, I'll be ready."

I do my makeup and blow-dry my hair quickly. My hair is in tight curls, and I pin my bangs back as usual. I look . . . nice . . . *Boring. Boring.* The same as I always do. I need to look better than ever before for my comeback. This is my way of showing them that they didn't get the best of me. If Molly is there, she'll certainly be dressed to get attention, including Hardin's. And as much as I hate her, she *is* gorgeous. Molly's pink hair burning in the back of my mind, I grab my black eyeliner and draw a thick line across my top eyelid; for once the line is straight, blessedly. I do the same on the bottom and add more pink to my cheeks before pulling the bobby pin from my hair and tossing it in the trash.

Quickly, I retrieve the pin from the top of the trash. Okay, so maybe I'm not quite ready to throw it away yet, but I'll skip it tonight. I flip my head down and rake my fingers through my tight curls. The reflection in the mirror shocks me. She looks like she belongs in a nightclub, she looks wild and . . . sexy, even. The last time that I wore this much makeup was when Steph gave me a "makeover" and Hardin taunted me. This time, I look even better.

"It's eight thirty, Tess!" Hardin warns me from the living room.

I check the mirror one last time and take a deep breath before rushing to the bedroom to get dressed before Hardin can see me. *What if he thinks I look bad?* Last time he didn't care for my new and improved look. I shut off my doubtful thoughts and pull the dress over my head, zip it up, and step into my new pumps.

Maybe I should wear tights? No. I need to calm down and stop overthinking this.

"Tessa, we really need—" Hardin's voice gets louder as he comes into the room, but then stops midsentence.

"Do I look—"

"Yes, fuck yes," he practically growls.

"You don't think it's too much, all the makeup?"

"No, it's . . . um . . . it's nice, I mean . . . it's good," he stammers.

I try not to laugh at his apparent loss for words, something that never occurs with him. "Let's go . . . we need to go now or we won't make it out of this apartment," he mutters.

His reaction has given my confidence an extreme boost. I know it shouldn't, but it does. He looks flawless as usual, wearing a simple black T-shirt and snug black jeans. The black Converses I've quickly become fond of complete the look I know as "Hardin."

chapter fifty-six

TESSA

The Fray quietly sings about forgiveness as we pull up to Hardin's old fraternity house. The drive here was nerve-racking, and both of us stayed silent. Memories, mostly bad memories, flood my mind, but I push them back. Hardin and I are in a relationship now, a real one, so he'll be different now. *Won't he?*

Hardin stays close to me as we walk through the crowded house to the smoke-filled living room. Red cups are immediately placed in our hands, but Hardin discards his quickly before taking mine from me. I reach to take it back, and he frowns.

"I don't think we should drink tonight," he says.

"I don't think *you* should drink tonight."

"Fine, only one," he warns and hands me back the cup.

"Scott!" a familiar voice calls. Nate appears in the kitchen and pats Hardin's shoulder before giving me a friendly smile. I'd almost forgotten how cute he is. I try to picture what he'd look like without tattoos and piercings, but I can't seem to do it. "Wow, Tessa, you look . . . different," he says.

Hardin rolls his eyes and grabs my drink from my hand to take a sip. I want to take it from him, but I don't want to cause a fight. One drink won't hurt. I slide my phone into Hardin's back pocket so I can hold my cup more easily.

"Well . . . well . . . well . . . look who it is," a female voice says at the same time as a mop of pink hair steps around a big round guy.

"Great." Hardin groans as Molly the skank walks toward us.

"Long time no see, Hardin," she says with a sinister grin.

"Yep." He takes another drink from the cup.

Her eyes move to me. "Oh, Tessa! I didn't see you there," she says with obvious sarcasm.

I ignore her, and Nate hands me a new drink.

"Did you miss me?" Molly asks Hardin. She's wearing more than usual, which is to say she's still barely clothed. Her black shirt is ripped down the front, purposely, I assume. Her red shorts are incredibly short, with tears in the fabric going up the sides, revealing even more pale skin.

"Not so much," Hardin says without looking at her. I bring the cup to my lips to hide my smirk.

"I'm sure you did," she responds.

"Fuck off," he groans.

She rolls her eyes like it's all a game. "Jeez, someone is pissy."

"Come on, Tessa." Hardin grabs my hand and pulls me away. We walk to the kitchen, leaving an annoyed Molly and a laughing Nate behind.

"Tessa!" Steph squeals as she jumps up from one of the couches. "Damn, girl! You look so hot! Wow!" Then she adds, "I would actually wear that!"

"Thanks." I smile. It's a little awkward seeing Steph, but not nearly as bad as seeing Molly. I have honestly missed Steph and am hoping that tonight goes smoothly enough that we can explore the possibility of rebuilding our friendship.

She hugs me. "I'm glad you came."

"I'm going to go talk to Logan—stay right here," Hardin instructs before walking away.

Steph eyes him with humor. "Rude as ever, I see." She laughs loudly over the raucous music and partygoers' voices.

"Yeah . . . some things never change." I smile and gulp down the remainder of the sweet drink in my cup. I hate to think about it, but the taste of cherries reminds me of my kiss with Zed.

His mouth was cold and his tongue sweet. It seems like another world, another Tessa, who shared that kiss with him.

As if Steph can read my thoughts, she taps my shoulder. "There's Zed, have you seen him since . . . you know?" She points her zebra-print nail at a black-haired boy.

"No . . . I haven't seen anyone, really. Except Hardin."

"Zed felt like such an ass after everything. I almost felt sorry for him," she says.

"Can we talk about something else, please?" I beg as his eyes meet mine and I look away.

"Oh yeah, shit; sorry. Want another drink?" she asks.

I smile to minimize the tension. "Yes, definitely." I glance around the kitchen to where Zed was previously standing, but he's gone. I chew on the inside of my cheek and look back at Steph, who is staring into her cup. Neither of us knows what exactly to say.

"Let's go find Tristan," she suggests.

"Hardin . . ." I begin to say that he asked me to stay put. But he didn't ask, he demanded, which is annoying. I tip back my cup, gulping down the remainder of the cold drink. My cheeks are already getting warm from the alcohol running through me . . . My nerves are slightly calmer as I reach for yet another cup before following Steph into the living room.

The house is more crowded than I've ever seen it, and Hardin is nowhere to be found. Half of the living room has been taken over by a long card table filled with rows of red cups. Drunk college students throw Ping-Pong balls into the cups and then swallow the contents down. I'll never understand the need for them to play all sorts of games when they're intoxicated, but at least this one doesn't seem to involve kissing. I spot Tristan sitting on the couch next to a redheaded guy who I remember seeing here before. He was smoking a joint with Jace the last time I saw him. Zed is seated on the arm of the couch and says something to the group, causing Tristan's head to fall back from laughter. When

Tristan looks up at Steph walking toward him, he smiles. I've liked Nate's roommate from the first time I met him. He's sweet, and he seems to really care for Steph.

"How are things between the two of you?" I ask her before we approach them.

She turns her whole body to me and beams. "Great, actually. I think I love him!"

"Think? You guys haven't said it yet?" I gasp.

"No . . . God no. We've only been dating three months!"

"Oh . . ." Hardin and I said the words before we were dating at all.

"You and Hardin are different," she says quickly, only lending support to my suspicions that she can read my thoughts. "How are you two?" she asks, then looks past me.

"Good, we are good." It's great to be able to say, since we *are* good, for once.

"You two are really the oddest couple."

I chuckle. "Yeah, we are."

"It's a good thing, though. Could you imagine if Hardin were to find a girl like him? I would never want to meet her, that's for sure." She laughs.

"Me either," I say and join in her laughter.

Tristan waves to Steph, and she pads over to take a seat on his lap. "There's my girl." He gives her a swift kiss on the cheek, then looks at me. "And how are you, Tessa?"

"I am very well. How are you?" I ask. I sound like a politician. *Relax, Tessa.*

"Fine. Drunk as shit, but fine." He laughs.

"Where's Hardin? I haven't seen him," the boy with the red hair asks me.

"He's . . . well, I have no idea," I answer and shrug.

"I'm sure he's around here somewhere. I don't see him going far from you," Steph says to try and comfort me.

Actually, I don't mind that I haven't seen Hardin in a while, because the alcohol is making me less nervous, but I do wish he would return and hang out with me. These are all his friends, not mine. Except Steph, who I'm still deciding on. But right now she's the person that I know the best, and I don't want to stand here awkward and alone.

Someone bumps into me and I stumble forward slightly; luckily my drink is empty, so when the cup hits the already stained carpet, only a few drops of pink liquid dot the surface.

"Shit, sorry," a drunk girl stutters.

"It's fine, really," I respond. Her black hair is so shiny that it literally makes me squint. *How is that even possible?* I must be more intoxicated than I thought.

"Come sit down before you get trampled over," Steph teases, and I laugh before taking a seat on the edge of the couch.

"So did you hear about Jace?" Tristan asks.

"No, what about him?" The mention of his name makes my stomach turn.

"He got arrested, then just got out of jail yesterday," he explains.

"What? Really? What did he do?" I ask.

"He killed someone," the redhead answers.

"Oh my God!" I gasp, and everyone begins to laugh. My voice is much louder now that I'm on the verge of being intoxicated.

"He's just fucking with you; he got pulled over and had some pot on him." Tristan laughs.

"You are such a dick, Ed," Steph says, and swats the guy's arm, but I can't help but laugh at how quickly I believed him.

"You should have seen your face." Tristan laughs again.

Another thirty minutes go by with no sign of Hardin. I'm getting slightly annoyed by his absence, but the more I drink, the less I care. Some of that is due to the fact that Molly is within eyeshot, and I can see she's found herself a blond plaything for the night. His hand keeps snaking up her thighs, and they're both so drunk they look sloppy and ridiculous. Still, better him than Hardin.

"Who's up now? Kyle has obviously had enough," a guy with glasses says, gesturing to his drunken friend who is lying in the fetal position on the carpet.

I look over at the table lined with cups and put two and two together.

"I'll play!" Tristan shouts, gently pushing Steph off his lap.

"Me, too!" she chimes in.

"You know you aren't very good," Tristan teases her.

"I am, too. You're actually just mad that I'm better at it than you. But I'm on your team now, so there's no need to be intimidated." She bats her lashes playfully, and he shakes his head.

"Tess, you should play!" she yells over the music.

"Um . . . no, I'm okay." I have no idea what they're playing, but I know I would be terrible at it.

"Oh, come on! It'll be fun." She brings her hands into a praying motion to beg.

"What is it?"

"Beer pong, duh." She shrugs dramatically before bursting into drunken laughter. "You've never played, huh?" she adds.

"No, I don't like beer."

"We can use the cherry-vodka-sour mix instead. They literally have gallons made. I'll grab one from the fridge." She turns to Tristan. "Line up the cups, boy."

I want to protest, but at the same time I want to have fun tonight. I want to be carefree and let loose. Beer pong may not be so bad. It can't possibly be worse than sitting on that couch alone waiting for Hardin to come back from wherever the hell he is.

Tristan begins to put the cups back into a triangular formation that reminds me of bowling pins. "Are you going to play?" he asks.

"I guess. I don't know how, though," I tell him.

"Who wants to be her partner?" Tristan asks.

I feel foolish when no one speaks up. Great. *I knew this was—*

"Zed?" Tristan says, interrupting my thoughts.

"Er . . . I don't know . . ." Zed responds, not looking at me. He's been avoiding me the entire time that I've been here.

"Just one round, man."

Zed's caramel eyes flicker to me quickly before moving back to Tristan and giving in. "Okay, yeah, one game." He comes and stands next to me, and we both stay there silently as Steph fills the cups with the alcohol.

"These cups have been used all night?" I ask her, trying to hide my disgust at multiple mouths drinking from them.

"It's fine." She laughs. "The alcohol kills the germs!"

I notice Zed smile out of the corner of my eye, but when I look at him, he looks away. Yup, this is going to be a long game.

chapter fifty-seven

TESSA

Just toss it across the table into any of those cups, and they have to drink the cup that the ball lands into. Whichever team knocks out all the other's cups wins," Tristan explains.

"Wins what?" I ask.

"Uh, nothing. You just don't get drunk as fast because you don't have to drink as many cups."

I'm about to point out that a drinking game where the winner gets *less* to drink seems counter to the party mentality, when Steph shouts, "I'll go first!" She playfully rubs the small white ball against Tristan's shirt before blowing on it and tossing it across the table. It bounces off the lip of the front cup before rolling into the cup behind it.

"You want to drink first?" Zed asks.

"Sure." I shrug and lift the cup.

When Tristan tosses the next ball across the table, he misses. It falls to the floor, and Zed picks it up, dipping it into the lone glass of water on our side. So that's what that is for. It's hardly sanitary, but this is a college party . . . what do I really expect?

"Yeah, I'm the one who sucks," Steph taunts Tristan, who only smiles at her.

"You go first," Zed instructs.

My first attempt at playing beer—well, cherry-vodka-sour—pong seems to be going well, given that I make my first four shots in a row. My jaw hurts from smiling and giggling at my opponents, and my blood is singing from the liquor and the fact that I love to be successful at things, even college drinking games.

"You've played this before! I *know* you have!" Steph accuses me with a hand on her hip.

"No, I'm just skilled." I laugh.

" 'Skilled'?"

"Don't be jealous of my killer peer dong skills," I say, and everyone within a five-foot radius bursts into laughter.

"Oh Lord! Please do not say 'skills' again!" Steph says, and I hold my stomach while I try to stop laughing. This game was a better idea than I thought. The large amount of alcohol I've consumed helps, and I feel carefree. Young and carefree.

"If you make this, we'll win," I say to encourage Zed. The more cups he drinks, the more comfortable he seems to be around me.

"Oh, I'll make it," he boasts with a smile. The small ball cuts through the air and lands directly into Steph and Tristan's last remaining cup.

I squeal and jump up and down like an idiot, but I could care less. Zed claps his hands once, and without thinking, I wrap my arms around his neck in excitement. He stumbles back a little, but his arms reach my waist before we both pull away. It's a harmless hug—we've just won, and I'm excited. Harmless. Steph's eyes are wide when I glance over at her, making me look around the room for Hardin.

He's nowhere to be found, but so what if he was? He's the one who left me alone at this party. I can't even call or text him, because he has my phone in his pocket.

"I want a rematch!" Steph yells.

I look at Zed with wide eyes. "Want to play again?"

He looks around the room before answering. "Yeah . . . yeah . . . let's do another." He smiles.

Zed and I win for the second time, which causes Steph and Tristan both to playfully accuse us of cheating.

"You okay?" Zed asks as the four of us leave the table.

Two games of beer pong are enough for me; I'm sort of intoxicated. Okay, more than sort of, but I feel amazing. Tristan disappears with Steph into the kitchen.

"Yeah, I'm good. Really good. I'm having a great time," I tell him, and he laughs. The way his tongue rests behind his teeth when he smiles is so charming.

"That's good! If you excuse me, though, I'm going to go get some air," he says.

Air. I would love to breathe in air that isn't thick with cigarette smoke or the smell of sweat. It's hot in this house, too hot. "Can I come?" I ask.

"Um . . . I don't know if that's a good idea," he replies, looking away from me.

"Oh . . . okay." My cheeks flame in embarrassment.

I turn to walk away, but he gently grabs my arm. "You can come. I just don't want to start any trouble between you and Hardin."

"Hardin isn't here and I can be friends with whoever I want," I slur. My voice sounds funny, and I can't help but giggle at how weird it sounds.

"You're quite drunk, aren't you?" he asks and opens the door for me.

"A smittle—a small . . . a little." I laugh.

The crisp winter air feels amazing and refreshing. Zed and I walk through the yard and end up sitting on the broken stone wall that used to be my favorite spot during these parties. There are only a few people outside because of the cold. One of them is throwing up in the bushes a few yards away.

"Lovely," I groan.

Zed chuckles but doesn't say anything. The stone is cold against my thighs, but I have a jacket in Hardin's car if I need it. Not that I have any idea where he is. I can see his car is still here, but he's been gone for over . . . well, two beer-pongs-plus.

When I look over at Zed, he's staring off into the darkness. Why is this so awkward? His hand moves to his stomach, and he appears to be scratching the skin. When he lifts his shirt up slightly, I see a white bandage.

"What's that?" I ask nosily.

"A tattoo. I just got it done before I came here."

"Can I see it?"

"Yeah . . ." He shrugs his jacket off and sets it down next to him, then pulls back the tape and bandage.

"It's dark over here," he says, pulling out his phone to use the screen as a light.

"Clockwork?" I ask him.

Without thinking, I run my index finger across the ink. He flinches but doesn't move away. The tattoo is large, covering most of the skin on his stomach. The rest of his skin is covered by smaller, seemingly random tattoos. The new tattoo is a cluster of gears; they appear to be moving, but I'm going to say that's just the vodka.

My finger is still tracing his warm skin when I suddenly realize what I'm doing. "Sorry . . ." I squeak and jerk my hand away.

"It's fine . . . but, yeah, it's sort of like clockwork. See how the skin appears to be torn right here?" He points to the edges of the tattoo, and I nod.

He shrugs. "It's like when the skin is pulled back, what is underneath is mechanical. Like I'm a robot or something."

"Whose robot?" I don't know why I asked that.

"Society's, I guess."

"Oh . . ." is all I say. That's a much more complex answer than

I expected. "That's actually really cool; I get it." I smile, my head swimming from the alcohol.

"I don't know if people will get the whole concept. You're the only person so far that gets it."

"How many more tattoos do you want?" I ask.

"I don't know, I don't have any more room on my arms, and now my stomach, so I guess I'll stop when there isn't any room." He laughs.

"I should get a tattoo," I blurt.

"You?" He laughs loudly.

"Yeah! Why not?" I say with joke indignation. Getting a tattoo sounds like a good idea at the moment. I have no idea what I would get, but it sounds fun. Adventurous and fun.

"I think you drank way too much," he teases, rubbing his fingers over the tape to reattach the bandage to his skin.

"You don't think I could handle it?" I challenge.

"No, it's not that. I just . . . I don't know. I can't imagine you having a tattoo. What would you even get?" He tries not to laugh.

"I don't know . . . like a sun? Or a smiley face?"

"A smiley face? This is definitely the vodka talking here."

"Probably." I giggle. Then, when I'm quiet, I say, "I thought you were mad at me."

His expression changes from laughing to neutral. "Why did you think that?" he asks quietly.

"Because you avoided me until Tristan made you play beer pong."

He lets out a breath. "Oh . . . I wasn't avoiding you, Tessa. I just don't want to cause any problems."

"With who? Hardin?" I ask, though I already know the answer.

"Yeah. He made it clear that I need to stay away from you, and I don't want to fight him again. I don't want any more trouble between us, or with you. I just . . . never mind."

"He's getting better, sort of, anger-wise," I say awkwardly. I don't know if that's true, exactly, but I would like to think him not killing Trevor already says something.

He looks at me doubtfully. "*Is* he?"

"Yeah, he is. I think—"

"Where is he, anyway? I was surprised he let you out of his sight."

"I have *no* idea," I say and look around, as if that would help. "He went to talk with Logan, and I haven't seen him since."

He nods and scratches his stomach. "Weird."

"Yes, weird." I laugh, thankful that vodka seems to make everything much more amusing.

"Steph was really happy to see you tonight," he says as he puts a cigarette to his lips. A quick flick of his thumb brings a lighter flame to life, and soon the smell of nicotine invades my nostrils.

"I could tell. And I've missed her, but I'm still upset over everything that happened." The topic doesn't feel as heavy as it did before. I'm having a great time, even though Hardin isn't around. I laughed and joked with Steph, and for the first time it felt like I could put all of this behind me and move forward with her.

"You're brave for coming here," he tells me with a smile.

"Stupid and brave aren't the same thing," I joke.

"I mean it. After everything . . . you didn't hide away some-where. I probably would have."

"I did hide for a little while, but he found me."

"I always do." Hardin's voice startles me, and I grip on to Zed's jacket to prevent myself from falling off the stone wall.

chapter fifty-eight

HARDIN

My words are true. I do always find her. I usually find her doing things that drive me fucking mad, like hanging out with fucking Trevor or Zed.

I can't fucking believe that I came out here to find Tessa and Zed sitting on a wall talking about her hiding from me. This is *bullshit*. She latches on to Zed to steady herself as I stride across the frozen grass.

"Hardin," Tessa squeaks, clearly surprised by my presence.

"Yeah, Hardin," I say.

Zed scoots away from her, and I try to stay calm. Why the hell is she out here with Zed alone? I specifically told her to stay inside, in the kitchen. When I asked Steph where the hell Tessa was, all she said was "Zed." After five minutes of searching the entire fucking house—mostly the bedrooms—I finally looked outside. And here they are. Together.

"You were supposed to stay in the kitchen," I say, adding "babe" to soften my harsh tone.

"You were supposed to be right back . . . *Baby.*"

I sigh and take a deep breath before speaking again. I always react to every impulse that I get, and I'm trying not to do that anymore. But fuck if she doesn't make it difficult. "Let's go inside," I say and reach for her hand.

I need to get her away from Zed, and honestly, I need to get myself away from him as well. I've already beat the shit out of him once, and something in me wouldn't mind doing it again.

"I'm going to get a tattoo, Hardin," Tess tells me as I help her down from the wall.

"What?" *Is she drunk?*

"Yeah . . . you should see Zed's new tattoo, Hardin. It's so nice." She smiles. "Show him, Zed."

Why the fuck was Tessa looking at his tattoos, and how much did I miss? What else were they doing? What else was he showing her? He has wanted her since the first time he met her, just like I did. The difference being that I wanted to fuck her, and he actually liked her. But I won; she chose me.

"I don't . . ." Zed begins, visibly uncomfortable.

"No, no. Go on, show me, please," I say sarcastically.

Zed blows out some smoke and, to my horror and absolute fucking annoyance, lifts his shirt up. Moving the bandage aside, I see that the tattoo itself is actually pretty cool, but why he felt the need to show my Tessa this shit is beyond me.

Tessa beams. "Isn't it cool? I want one. I think we decided on a smiley face!"

She isn't serious. I pull my lip ring between my teeth to prevent myself from laughing at her. I look at Zed, who just shakes his head and shrugs. Some of my annoyance disappears at her ridiculous idea for a tattoo. "Are you drunk?" I ask her.

"Maybe." She giggles. *Great.*

"How much did you drink?" I ask. I had two drinks, but I can tell she's had more.

"I don't know . . . how much did *you* drink?" she teases, and lifts up the bottom of my shirt. Her cold hands rest against my hot skin, and I flinch before she nuzzles her head on my chest.

See, Zed, she's mine. Not yours, not anyone's, only mine.

Looking at him, I ask, "How much did she drink?"

"I'm not sure how much she drank before, but we just played two games of beer pong . . . with cherry vodka sour."

"Wait . . . we? You two played beer pong?" I ask through my teeth.

"Nope. Cherry-vodka-sour pong!" she corrects me with a laugh and brings her head up. "We won, too, twice! I made most of the shots. Steph and Tristan were both pretty good, but we beat them. Twice!" She holds her hand up like Zed should high-five it, and he begrudgingly does a sort of air-high-five from where he stands.

This is Tessa, the girl who is so used to being the best and smartest at everything that she's boasting over winning a game of beer pong.

I love every bit of it. "Straight vodka?" I ask Zed.

"No, it's the mix with only a little vodka, but she had a lot of it."

"And you brought her out here in the dark when you knew she was wasted?" I say, raising my voice.

Tessa brings her face close to mine, and I can smell the vodka and mix on her breath. "Hardin, please chill out. I'm the one who asked him if I could c-come outside with him. He told me no at first because he knew you'd act like . . . like *thissss*." She frowns and tries to remove her hands from my bare stomach, but I gently put them back against my skin. I wrap my arms around her waist, pulling her even closer to me.

Chill out? Did she really just tell me to chill out?

"And let'sss not forget if you wouldn't have left me, we c-could have been beer-pong partnersss," she adds, slurring.

I know she's right, but she's pissing me off. How could she play with Zed, of all people? I know he has feelings for her still. Nothing compared to what I feel, but I can tell by the way he's looking at her that he cares for her.

"Am I right, or am I right?" she asks.

"Okay, Tessa," I growl in an attempt to silence her.

"I'm going to go inside," Zed says, tossing his cigarette onto the ground before walking away.

Tessa watches him, then says to me, "You are so grumpy, maybe you should go back to wherever you ran off to." She tries to pull away from me again.

"I'm not going anywhere," I respond, purposely dodging her remark about my absence.

"Then stop being grumpy—because I'm having fun tonight." She looks up at me. Her eyes appear even lighter than usual with the black lines she colored around them.

"You couldn't have expected me to be happy to find you alone with that motherfucker."

"Would you rather me being out here with someone else?" She's awfully testy when she's drunk.

"No, you're missing the point here," I snap.

"There's no point. I didn't do anything wrong, so stop being an ass or I don't want to hang out with you," she threatens.

"Fine, I won't be a grouch." I roll my eyes.

"No rolling your eyes either," she scolds, and I take my arms away from her waist.

"Fine, no eye rolling." I smile.

"That's what I thought." She tries to fight her smile.

"You are quite bossy tonight."

"The vodka makes me brave."

I feel her hands move lower on my stomach. "So you want a tattoo, then?" I ask, moving her hands back up, but she defies my attempt and touches me even lower.

"Yep, maybe five." She shrugs her shoulders. "I don't know."

"You aren't getting a tattoo." I laugh, but I'm beyond serious.

"Why not?" Her fingers play at the hem of my boxers.

"Let's talk about it tomorrow when you're sober." I know this idea will not appeal to her when she's not drunk. "Let's go inside."

She slips her hand into my boxers and stands on her toes. I assume she's going to kiss my cheek, but she brings her mouth to my ear. I hiss as she squeezes me gently in her hand.

"I think we should stay out here," she whispers. *Fuck*.

"The vodka certainly makes you brave." My voice cracks, betraying me.

"Yes . . . and it makes me hor—" she begins to say, way too loud. I cover her mouth as a small group of drunk girls walks by.

"We need to get inside, it's freezing, and I don't think they would appreciate me fucking you in the bushes." I smirk, and her pupils dilate.

"But *I* would appreciate that very much," she says the moment my hand uncovers her mouth.

"Jesus, Tess, a few drinks and you become sex-crazed." I laugh, remembering Seattle and the filthy words that fell from her full lips. I need to get her inside before I take her up on her offer and drag her into the bushes.

She winks. "Only for you."

I can't hold in my laughter. "Let's go." I put my hand on her arm and pull her across the yard and into the house.

She pouts the entire time, and that makes my groin ache even more, especially when she pushes her bottom lip out. I could easily lean across and pull it between my teeth. Fuck, I'm just as bad as she is, and I'm not even drunk. Maybe a little high, but not drunk. She would be so mad if she'd found me upstairs; I didn't actually smoke, but I was in the room and they were making it a point to blow it in my face.

I pull her through the crowd and lead her into the least crowded room downstairs, which happens to the kitchen. Tessa leans her elbows on the island and looks up at me. How is it that she looks just as beautiful as she did when we left the apartment? All the other girls here look dreadful by now—after the first drink, their makeup begins to smear, their hair begins to tangle, and they look sloppy. Not Tessa. Tessa looks like a fucking goddess compared to them. Compared to anyone.

"I want another drink, Hardin," she says, but when I shake my head, she sticks her tongue out of her mouth like a child. "Please? I'm having fun, don't be a party pooper."

"Fine, one more, but you have to stop talking like a ten-year-old," I tease her.

"Okay, sir. I most sincerely apologize for my immature language. I will not repeat said indiscretion—"

"Or an old man," I say with a laugh. "But you can call me sir again."

"Fuck, well, okay, then. I'll fucking stop fucking talking like a motherfucking . . ."

But she doesn't finish her foul sentence because she and I are both laughing too hard.

"You're insane tonight," I tell her.

She giggles. "I know, it's fun."

I'm glad she's having fun, but I can't help the annoyance that I feel at her having had fun with Zed, not me. I'm going to keep my mouth shut, though, because I don't want to ruin her night.

She stands, taking a sip from her drink. "Let's go find Steph."

"You okay with her now?" I ask as I follow her. I don't know how I feel about that. Good? I suppose . . .

"I think so. There they are!" She points to Tristan and Steph sitting on the couch.

As we walk into the living room, a small cluster of guys sitting on the floor turns to look at Tessa. She's oblivious to their lustful stares, but I'm not. I shoot them a warning glare, and almost all of them turn away except a blond who slightly resembles Noah. He continues to stare as we walk by; I debate whether kicking him in the face would be a good idea or not. But I choose to take Tessa's hand in mine instead, for now at least.

Her head snaps back to look down at our joined hands,

and her eyes are wide. Why is she so surprised? I mean, yeah, hand-holding isn't something I feel comfortable doing usually, but I do it on occasion . . . don't I?

"There you two are!" Steph calls as we approach.

Molly is sitting on the floor next to a guy I recognize. I'm pretty sure he's a junior and his father owns some land in Vancouver, making him a trust-fund brat. The two of them look fucking stupid together, but I'm just glad she's leaving me alone for now. She is so damn annoying, and Tessa hates her.

"We were outside," I tell her.

"I'm bored," Nate says, stirring his finger through his beer.

I sit down at the end of the couch and pull Tessa onto my lap. Eyes dart to us, but I don't give a shit. I dare someone to say something about it. Within seconds, they all look away, except Steph, who stares a little too long before smiling. I don't return it, but I don't flip her off either, which is progress, right?

"We should play Truth or Dare," a voice suggests, and it takes a second to realize who the voice came from.

What the hell? I lean my head up to look at Tessa, who is still seated on my lap.

"Sure, like you want to play," Molly mocks her.

"Why would you suggest that? You hate those games," I say quietly.

She smirks. "I don't know, I think it could be fun tonight."

I follow her eyes to Molly, and I don't even want to know what is stirring in that pretty head of Tessa's.

chapter fifty-nine

HARDIN

Right as I whisper to Tessa, "I don't know if that's such a good idea," she turns around in my lap and puts her index finger over my lips to silence me.

Molly pipes up with a sly smile, "What's wrong, Hardin, afraid of a little dare . . . or is it the truth that you fear?"

What a fucking cunt. I'm about to reply, but I'm taken aback when Tessa growls, "You're the one that should be afraid."

Molly raises one brow. "Really?"

"Okay . . . okay . . . calm down, you two," Nate says.

As much as I'm enjoying watching Tessa put Molly in her place, I don't want Molly to take it too far. Tessa is a lot more fragile and sensitive than she is, and Molly will say anything she can to hurt Tessa.

"Who goes first?" Tristan asks.

Tessa's hand shoots up immediately. "Me."

Oh Lord, this is going to be a fucking disaster.

"I think that maybe I should go first," Steph interjects.

Tessa sighs but sits silently, bringing her cup to her lips. Her lips are reddish from the cherry drink, and for a moment I'm lost in thoughts of them being wrapped around me—

"Hardin, truth or dare?" Steph breaks me from my perverted thoughts.

"Not playing," I say and try to go back to my fantasy.

"Why not?" she asks.

The spell broken, I look at her and groan. "A, I don't want to. B, I've played more than enough lame-ass games."

"Isn't that the truth," Molly mutters.

"That isn't what he meant, back off," Tristan says to defend me.

Why did I ever fuck Molly, again? She's hot and was decent at giving blow jobs, but she's so damn annoying. The memory of her touching me makes me nauseous, and I give Steph a keep-it-moving hand motion in order to redirect my mind.

"Okay, Nate. Truth or dare?" Steph asks.

"Dare," he answers.

"Hmm . . ." Steph points to a tall girl wearing bright red lipstick. "I dare you to go kiss that blonde in the blue shirt."

Looking over, he whines, "Can't I kiss her friend instead?"

We all look at the girl next to the blonde, who has long, curly hair and deep brown skin. She's much prettier than the blonde, so for Nate's sake I hope Steph allows the change. But instead she laughs and says with authority, "Nope, Blondie it is."

"You are evil." He groans, and everyone laughs as he walks toward the girl.

As Nate walks back with red lipstick stains around his lips, I now get why Tessa usually despises these games. Daring one another to do stupid things like this is just pointless. I never minded before, but then again I've never wanted to kiss one person only. I never want to kiss anyone except Tessa ever again.

When Nate dares Tristan to drink a cup of beer that people have been using for an ashtray, I zone out. I take a lock of Tessa's soft hair between my fingers, slowly twisting it around. She covers her face with her hands as Tristan gags and Steph shrieks.

After a few more mindless dares, it's finally Tessa's turn. "Dare," she bravely says to Ed.

I glare at him, warning him that if he dares her to do anything inappropriate, I will not hesitate to jump across the table and choke him. He's a pretty cool and chill guy, so I didn't really think he would go too far, but I wanted to warn him anyway. "I dare you to take a shot," he says.

"Lame," Molly chimes in.

Tessa ignores her and downs the shot. She's already wasted— if she has much more, she'll be getting sick.

"Molly, truth or dare?" Tessa says, her voice much too smug. Everyone tenses. Steph looks at me questioningly.

Molly's eyes meet Tessa's, clearly surprised at Tessa's bold move. "Truth or dare?" Tess repeats.

"Truth," Molly answers.

"Is it true . . ." Tessa begins and leans forward, "that you're a whore?"

Gasps and chuckles fill the area. I bury my face in Tessa's back to muffle my laughs. Jesus, this girl is nuts when she's drunk.

"Ex*cuse me?*" Molly retorts, mouth agape.

"You heard me . . . is it true that you're a whore?"

"No," Molly says, her eyes now small slits.

Nate is still laughing, Steph looks amused yet worried, and Tessa looks like she's ready to pounce on Molly.

"It's called truth for a reason," Tess eggs her on. I gently squeeze her thigh and whisper to her to let it go. I don't want Molly to hurt her, because then I'll have to hurt Molly.

"My turn," Molly says.

"Tessa, truth or dare?" she asks. Here we go.

"Dare." Tessa smiles sadistically.

Molly fakes surprise, then sneers, "I dare you to kiss Zed."

I look up quickly at Molly's terrible face. "Fuck no," I say loudly. Everyone but her seems to shrink back a little.

"Why not?" Molly smirks. "It's familiar territory—she's done it before."

I sit up more, pulling Tessa against me as I move both of us.

"Not fucking happening," I growl at the little whore. I don't give a shit about this stupid-ass game, she isn't kissing anyone.

Zed's eyes are focused on the wall, and when Molly looks over at him, she sees she has no support there. "Fine, let's do truth, then," she says. "Is it true that you're a dumb-ass for getting back with Hardin after he *admitted* he fucked you for a bet?" she asks in a cheery voice.

Tessa's body goes rigid on my lap. "No, that's not true," she says, her voice small.

Molly stands up. "No, no, this is *Truth* or Dare, not little-girl make-believe. It is the *truth*—and you are a dumb-ass for it. You believe anything that comes out of his mouth. Not that I blame you, because I know all of the amazing things that mouth can do. Man, that tongue—"

Before I can stop her, Tessa is off of my lap and lunging toward Molly. Their bodies collide, Tessa pushing her back by her shoulders and grabbing on to them as they both fall back over Ed. Luckily for Molly, some other random kid breaks her fall. Unluckily for her, Tessa moves her hands from Molly's shoulders and grabs her hair.

"You fucking bitch!" Tessa screams, holding Molly's bright hair in her fists. She lifts Molly's head off of the carpet before slamming it back down. Molly yells and kicks her feet under Tessa's body, but Tessa has the advantage and Molly can't seem to gain any control over the situation. Molly's nails claw at Tessa's arms, but Tessa grabs her wrists and slams them down to her sides before raising a hand and slapping her across her face.

Holy shit. I jump off of the couch and hook my arm around Tessa's waist, yanking her off. I never in a million years thought I would be breaking up a fight between Tess and anyone, let alone Molly, who's all talk.

Tessa's body thrashes in my arms for a few seconds before she calms slightly and I'm able to drag her out of the living room. I tug at the ends of her dress to make sure it isn't hitched up; the last thing we need is for me to have to get into a fight, too. There are only a few people in the kitchen, and already they're talking about the fight in the living room.

"I will fucking kill her, Hardin! I swear!" she yells, moving out of my grip.

"I know . . . I know you will," I say, but I can't take her seriously, despite witnessing her savagery firsthand.

"Stop smirking at me," she huffs, out of breath. Her eyes are wide and shining, and her cheeks are red with anger.

"I'm not. I'm just really surprised at what happened." I bite down on my lip.

"I hate her so much! Like, *who the hell does she think she is?*" she shouts and bobs her head toward the others in the room, obviously trying to get Molly's attention.

"All right, Ortiz . . . let's get you some water," I say.

"Ortiz?" she asks.

"He's a UFC fighter . . ."

"UFC?"

"Never mind." I laugh and fill a glass of water for her. I check back in the living room to make sure Molly is nowhere to be found.

"My adrenaline is rushing like crazy," Tessa tells me.

The best part of fighting is the high from the adrenaline. It's addicting. "Have you ever been in a fight before?" I ask, even though I'm sure I know the answer.

"No, of course not."

"Why did you get into one just now? Who cares what Molly thinks about us being together."

"It's not that. That's not what made me mad."

"What was it, then?" I ask her.

She hands me the empty cup of water, and I refill it. "When she said that . . . about you and her," she admits, her face twisted in anger.

"Oh."

"Yeah. I should've punched her," she huffs out.

"Yes, but I think knocking her to the ground and slamming her head against the floor worked pretty well, too, Ortiz."

A small smile breaks from her lips, and she giggles. "I can't believe I just did that." She giggles again.

"You are so drunk." I laugh.

"I *am!*" she agrees loudly. "Drunk enough to slam Molly's head against the floor," she says, laughing again.

"I think everyone enjoyed the show," I tell her, snaking my arm around her waist.

"I hope no one is mad at me for causing a scene." There's my Tessa. Drunk as shit, yet still trying to be considerate of other people.

"No one is mad, baby. If anything, they'll be thanking you. This is the kind of shit these frat kids live for," I assure her.

"God, I hope not," she says and looks momentarily grossed out.

"Don't worry about it. Do you want to go find Steph?" I ask to distract her.

"Or we could do something else . . ." she says, hooking her fingers into the top of my jeans.

"You are never drinking vodka when I'm not around," I tell her, teasing but so serious.

"Sure . . . now let's go upstairs." She leans up and plants a kiss on my jaw.

"You're a bossy little thing, aren't you?" I smile.

"You aren't the only one who gets to be bossy all the time." She laughs and grips the collar of my shirt, pulling me down to her height. "At least let me do something for you," she purrs, nipping at my earlobe.

"You just got in a fight—your first fight, at that—and this is what you're thinking?"

She nods. Then she says in a low, slow voice that makes my pants feel even tighter, "You know you want to, Hardin."

"Okay . . . fuck . . . okay." I give in.

"Well, that was easy."

I grab her wrist and lead her upstairs.

"Has someone already taken over your old room?" she asks when we reach the second floor.

"Yeah, but there are plenty of empty rooms," I tell her and open the door to one of them. The two small beds are covered with black comforters, and there are shoes in the closet. I don't know whose room this is, but it's ours now.

I lock the door and take a few steps to meet Tessa. "Unzip me," she commands.

"Not wasting any time, I see—"

"Shut up and unzip my dress," she snaps.

I shake my head in amusement, and she turns around and lifts her hair. My lips brush over the nape of her neck as I slide the zipper down her back. Goose bumps appear on her soft skin, and I follow them down her spine with my index finger. Shivering a little, she turns around, sliding down the sleeves of her dress. The whole thing drops to her feet, revealing the hot-pink lace bra and panties that I absolutely fucking love. I can tell by the smile on her face that she knows this.

"Leave your shoes on," I practically beg.

She agrees with a smile and looks down at her shoes. "I want to do something for you first." In a swift motion, she tugs at my jeans, but frowns when they don't move. Her fingers quickly un-button the fly front and she pulls them down. I step backward toward the bed, but she stops me.

"No, ew. Who knows who has done what on that thing." She makes a disgusted face. "Floor," she demands.

"I guarantee that floor is much dirtier than the bed," I say. "Here, let me put my shirt down." I pull my shirt over my head and lay it on the floor, then sit down on top of it. Tessa joins me, straddling me. Her mouth latches on to the skin on my neck, and she rolls her hips, pushing herself against me.

Fuck. "Tess . . ." I breathe. "I'm going to finish before you start if you keep doing that."

She removes her lips from my neck. "What do you want me to do, Hardin? Do you want to fuck me or do you want me to bl—"

I cut her off with a kiss. I'm not wasting any time with foreplay. I want her—I need her—now. Within seconds, her panties lie on the floor next to her and I'm reaching for my jeans to grab a condom. I need to remind her about getting on birth control—I can't stand using a condom with her. I want to feel her, all of her.

"Hardin . . . hurry up," she begs and lies back on the floor, using her elbows to prop herself up, long hair trailing onto the floor behind her.

I crawl over to her, separate her thighs even farther with my knees, and move to slide into her. She loses balance on her elbows and falls back to the floor, grabbing on to my arms for leverage.

"No . . . I want to do it," she says, pushing me onto the floor and climbing on top of me. She whines as she lowers herself onto me, and it's the most delicious sound. Her hips roll slowly, circling, bouncing, torturing me. She covers her mouth with her hand, and her eyes roll back. When she rakes her nails down my stomach, I nearly lose it. I wrap my arm around her back and flip us over. I've had enough of her being in control—I can't handle it.

"What—" she begins.

"I'm the one in charge—the one with the control. Don't forget that, baby," I groan and slam into her roughly, moving in and out at a much faster pace than she was torturing me with.

She nods feverishly and covers her mouth again.

"When . . . we get home . . . I'll fuck you again, and you won't be covering your mouth . . ." I threaten, bringing her leg up to my shoulder. "Everyone will be able to hear you. Hear what I'm doing to you, what only I can do to you."

She moans again, and I place a kiss on her calf as she stiffens. I am close . . . too close, and I bury my head in her neck as I fill the condom. I rest my head on her chest until our breathing returns to normal.

"That was . . ." she breathes.

"Better than attacking Molly?" I laugh.

"I don't know . . . at least a close second," she teases and stands to get dressed.

chapter sixty

TESSA

Hardin helps me zip, up and I rake my fingers through my hair while he buttons his jeans. "What time is it?" I ask as he slides his shoes back on.

"Two minutes till midnight," he answers, after looking at the alarm clock on the small desk.

"Oh . . . well, we need to hurry and get downstairs," I tell him. I'm still beyond intoxicated, but now I'm relaxed and calm, thanks to Hardin. Drunk or not, I can't believe what happened with Molly.

"Let's go." He takes my hand, and we nearly make it to the staircase before everyone begins chanting.

"Ten . . . nine . . . eight . . ."

Hardin rolls his eyes.

"Seven . . . six . . ."

"This is stupid," Hardin complains.

"Five . . . four . . . three . . ." I begin chanting. "Do it with me," I say.

He tries not to smile, but is defeated as a huge grin spreads across his face. "Two . . . one . . ." I poke his cheek with my finger.

"Happy New Year!" everyone screams, including me.

"Yay for the New Year," Hardin says in a monotone voice, and I laugh as he presses his lips to mine. Part of me was worried that he wouldn't kiss me here, in front of everyone, but he is now. As my hands travel to his waist he grabs them to stop me. When he pulls away, his emerald eyes are shining. He is so beautiful.

"Aren't you worn out?" he jokes, and I shake my head.

"Don't flatter yourself. I wasn't coming onto you." I smile. "I really need to pee."

"Do you want me to come?"

"Nope. Be right back," I say, giving him a small kiss before walking to the bathroom. I should have had him come along; this is much more difficult than it is when I'm sober. Tonight has been so fun, even with the Molly drama. Hardin has surprised me by being calm, even with Zed, and he's remained in a good mood all night. After I wash my hands, I head back down the hall to find Hardin.

"Hardin!" a female voice calls.

I look over and see a familiar face: the girl with the black hair who bumped into me earlier. And she's walking toward Hardin. Being the nosy girl that I am, I stay back a few feet.

"I have your phone, you left it in Logan's room." She smiles, pulling Hardin's phone from her purse.

What? It's nothing, I'm sure. They were in Logan's room, which means most likely they were not alone. I trust him.

"Thanks." He grabs the phone from her, and she begins to walk away. Thank God.

"Hey!" he calls after her.

"Can you do me a favor and maybe not mention to anyone that we were in Logan's room together?" he asks.

"I never kiss and tell." She grins and walks off.

The hallway begins to spin. My chest immediately aches, and I quickly head for the stairs. Hardin notices me rushing by, and I watch as the color drains from his face, knowing he's been caught.

chapter sixty-one

HARDIN

I notice a flicker of gold a few feet away. I look past Jamie and see Tessa, whose eyes are wide and whose bottom lip starts trembling. She goes from deer in headlights to angry girlfriend quickly and takes off down the stairs *fast*.

What? "Tessa! Wait!" I yell after her. For someone as drunk as she is, she's really *flying* down those steps. Why must she always run from me?

"Tess!" I shout again, pushing people out of my way.

Finally, when I'm only a few feet from her in the entryway, she does something that nearly brings me to my knees. The blond asshole who was checking her out earlier whistles as she rushes by. As she stops in her tracks, her look makes me freeze, too. Grinning, she grabs a handful of the kid's shirt.

What the fuck is she doing? Is she going to . . .

She answers my thoughts by looking back at me before pressing her lips against his. I blink rapidly in an attempt to make this disappear. This isn't happening. She wouldn't do that, not Tessa, no matter how pissed off she is.

The kid, surprised by her sudden show of affection, quickly recovers and wraps his arms around her waist. Her mouth opens, and she moves one hand to his hair, tugging on it. I can't comprehend what's actually happening right now.

"Hardin! Stop!" she screams.

Stop what? When I blink again, I'm on top of the blond, and his lip is busted. I hit him already?

"Please, Hardin!" she screams again.

I climb off of him in a hurry before everyone crowds around us. "What the fuck?" the kid groans.

I want to kick him in his fucking head, but I've been trying to restrain myself. She had to go and fucking do this, mess up everything I've been working toward. I head for the door without bothering to see if she's following me.

"Why did you hit him?" her voice calls from behind me as I reach my car.

"Why do you *think*, Tessa? Maybe because I just watched you fucking make out with him!" I scream. I almost forgot what it feels like, this adrenaline rush and the familiar sting on my knuckles. I only got one hit in . . . I think, at least . . . so it's not so bad. But I want more.

She begins to cry. "Why do you care? You kissed that girl! Probably more than kissed! How could you?"

"No! You don't get to *fucking cry*, Tessa. You just kissed someone right in front of me!" My hand connects with the hood of my car.

"You did worse! I heard you tell that girl to stay quiet about you two in Logan's room!"

"You don't even know what you're talking about—I didn't fucking kiss anyone!"

"Yes, you did! She said she doesn't kiss and tell!" she screams, waving her arms around like an idiot. *Fuck, she is infuriating.*

"It's a fucking figure of speech, Tessa. She meant she wasn't going to tell anyone anything that we talked about—or that we were smoking pot!" I shout.

She gasps. "You were smoking pot?"

"No, I wasn't, actually, but who gives a shit! You just fucking cheated on me!" I tug at my own hair.

"Why did you leave me to hang out with her, then tell her not to say anything? It doesn't make any—"

"She's Dan's sister! I was telling her not to say anything because I was trying to apologize privately for what I did to her. I was going to tell you tomorrow when you weren't fucking belligerent! We were all in the room, me, her, Logan, and Nate. They were smoking a joint, and when they left I asked her to stay behind because I wanted to try to make shit right with her, for you." All my anger comes out through my eyes, I'm certain, when I say, "*I* wouldn't fucking cheat on you—you should know that!"

And like that, Tessa deflates. She's speechless. Damn right she is. She's fucking wrong, and I am fucking *mad*.

"Well . . ." she begins.

"Well *what*? You're wrong, not me. You didn't give me a chance to explain myself. Instead you acted like a child. An impulsive little child!" I scream, punching the hood again. She jumps from the noise, but I don't give a shit.

I should just go back inside, find the blond guy, and finish what I started. Punching my car doesn't give me the same satisfaction.

"I'm not a child! I thought you did something with her!" she shouts back at me through her tears.

"Well, I didn't! After everything I went through to get you to stay with me, do you think I'd cheat on you with a random chick at a party . . . or hell, with anyone?"

"I didn't know what to think." She throws her hands into the air again. I run my fingers through my hair, trying to calm myself.

"Well, that's on you, then. I don't know what the hell else to do to make you see that I love you." She kissed someone—she kissed another guy right in front of me. This feels worse than when she left me; at least I could blame myself then.

Her warm breath is creating puffs of smoke in the cold air. "Well, maybe if I wasn't so used to you keeping secrets, I wouldn't have been so ready to misunderstand!" she yells.

I look at her. "You're unbelievable. I honestly cannot even

look at you right now." The image of her kissing him won't stop playing over and over.

"I'm sorry for kissing him." She sighs. "It isn't that big of a deal."

"You're joking, right? Please tell me that you are, because if that had been me kissing someone else, you probably wouldn't have spoken to me again! But I forgot that since it's Princess Tessa, it's okay! No harm done!" I mock.

She crosses her arms with an indignation she doesn't deserve. "Princess Tessa? Really, Hardin?"

"Yeah, really! You cheated on me, right in front of me! I brought you here so you would know how much I care about you. I wanted you to know that I don't care what anyone thinks about us. I wanted you to have the best night you could have, and then you go and do this shit!"

"Hardin . . . I . . ."

"No! I'm not done." I pull out my keys. "You're acting as if this is no big deal! This is a huge deal to me. To see another man's lips on yours . . . is . . . I can't even explain how sick that makes me."

"I said—"

I lose it. I know I look wild and scary, but I can't help it. "Stop interrupting me for once in your goddamn life!" I shout. "You know what . . . it's fine. You can go back in there and ask your new boyfriend to give you a ride home." I turn and unlock the car door. "He looks a lot like Noah, and you probably miss him."

"What? What does Noah have to do with this? And I clearly do not have a type," she growls and gestures at me. "Though maybe I should."

"Fuck this," I spit and climb into the car, turning it on and leaving her standing out in the cold. When I get to the stop sign, I can't help but hit the steering wheel over and over.

If she doesn't call me within an hour, I'll know she went home with someone else.

chapter sixty-two

TESSA

Ten minutes later I'm still standing on the sidewalk. My legs and arms are numb, and I'm shivering. Hardin will come back any minute, there's no way he'll actually leave me here, alone. Drunk and alone.

When I go to call him, I remember that he has my phone. *Great.*

What the hell was I thinking? I wasn't thinking, that's the problem. We were doing so good, and I didn't even try to give him the benefit of the doubt. Instead I kissed someone. The memory makes me want to vomit on the sidewalk.

Why hasn't he come back yet?

I need to go inside. It's way too cold out here, and I want another drink. My buzz is starting to wear off, and I'm not ready to face reality. When I get inside, I head directly for the kitchen and pour myself a drink. This is why I shouldn't drink—I have no common sense when I'm drunk. I immediately assumed the worst of him and made a huge mistake.

"Tessa?" Zed's voice says from behind me.

"Hey." I groan and lift my head up from the cool counter and turn to face him.

"Um . . . what are you doing?" He half laughs. "Are you okay?"

"Yeah . . . I'm okay," I lie.

"Where's Hardin?"

"He left."

"He left? Without you?"

"Yep." I take a drink from my cup.

"Why?"

"Because I'm an idiot," I answer honestly.

"I doubt that." He smiles.

"No, really, I am this time."

"Do you want to talk about it?"

"No, not really." I sigh.

"Okay . . . well, I'll leave you alone," he says and begins to walk away. But then he turns back around. "It's not supposed to be so complicated, you know?"

"What?" I ask him and follow him to sit at a card table in the kitchen.

"Love, relationships, all that. It doesn't have to be so hard."

"Doesn't it, though? Isn't it always like this?" I have no reference except Noah. We never fought like this, but I don't know that I loved him. Not like I do Hardin. I dump my drink down the sink and grab a glass to fill with water.

"I don't think so. I've never seen anyone fight the way you two do."

"It's because we're so different, that's all."

"Yeah, I guess you are." He smiles.

By the time I check the clock again, it's been an hour since Hardin left me here. Maybe he isn't coming back after all. "Would you forgive someone if they kissed someone else?" I finally ask Zed.

"I guess it depends on the details."

"What if they did it right in front of you?"

"Hell, no. That's unforgivable," he says with a disgusted expression.

"Oh."

Zed leans toward me sympathetically. "He did that?"

"No." I look up at him with wide eyes. "*I* did."

"*You* did?" Zed is clearly surprised.

"Yeah . . . I told you I'm an idiot."

"Yeah, I hate to say it, but you are."

"Yep," I agree.

"How are you getting home?" he asks.

"Well, I keep thinking he's going to come back to get me, but he's obviously not going to." I bite my lip.

"I can take you if you want," he says. But when I look around uncertainly, he adds, "Or Steph and Tristan are probably upstairs . . . you know."

I look at him quickly. "Actually, can you take me now?" I don't want to dig myself in any deeper, but I'm beginning to sober up, thank goodness, and I just want to be home to try to talk to Hardin.

"Yeah, let's go," Zed says, and I down the last of my water before following him outside to his car.

WHEN WE'RE ONLY about ten minutes away from the apartment, I begin panicking over Hardin's reaction to Zed driving me home. I keep trying to force myself to sober up, but it doesn't work that way. I'm a lot less intoxicated than I was an hour ago, but I'm still drunk.

"Can I use your phone to try to call him?" I ask Zed.

He removes one hand from the steering wheel to dig into his pocket for his phone. "Here . . . shit, it's dead," he says, pressing the button on the top and revealing an empty-battery symbol.

"Thanks anyway." I shrug. Calling Hardin from Zed's phone probably isn't the best idea I've had. Not as bad as my idea to kiss a random guy in front of Hardin, but still not a good one.

"What if he isn't here?" I say.

Zed looks at me quizzically. "You have a key, don't you?"

"I didn't bring mine . . . I didn't think I would need it."

"Oh . . . well . . . I'm sure he'll be here," Zed says, but he sounds nervous.

Hardin would literally murder him if he found me at Zed's place. When we do arrive at the apartment, Zed parks and I scan the parking lot for Hardin's car. And it's parked in his usual spot, thank God. I have no idea what I would have done if he weren't here.

Zed insists on walking me up. As much as I think that will not end well, I don't know if I'm capable of getting myself up to the apartment alone in my intoxicated state.

Damn Hardin for leaving me at that party. Damn me for being an impulsive idiot. Damn Zed for being so sweet and fearless when he shouldn't be. Damn Washington for being so damn cold.

When we reach the elevator, my head begins to pound along with my heart. I need to go over what I'm going to say to Hardin. He'll be so mad at me, and I need to think of a good way to apologize without using sex. I'm not used to being the one to apologize for anything, because he's always the one who messes up. Being on this side of things doesn't feel good at all. It feels terrible.

We walk down the hallway, and I can't help but feel as if we're preparing to walk the plank. I just don't know whether it will be Zed or myself that drops down into the water.

I knock, and Zed stands a few feet behind me as we wait for the door to open. This was a terrible idea, I should've just stayed at the party. I knock again, this time louder. What if he doesn't answer?

What if he took my car and isn't even here? I didn't think of that.

"If he doesn't answer, can I go to your place?" I try to hold my tears back.

I don't want to stay at Zed's and make Hardin even more upset with me, but I can't really think of another option.

What if he doesn't forgive me? I can't be without him. Zed's hand touches my back, and he rubs up and down to soothe me. I can*not* cry, I need to be calm when he answers . . . if he answers.

"Of course you can," Zed finally replies.

"Hardin! Please open up," I quietly beg and rest my forehead against the door. I don't want to yell and cause a scene at nearly two in the morning; our neighbors probably have issues with us yelling enough already.

"I guess he's not going to answer." I sigh and lean up against the wall for a minute. Then, finally, as we turn to walk away, the door clicks open.

"Well . . . look who decided to show up," Hardin says as he stands in the doorway and eyes us. Something about his tone sends chills down my spine. When I turn to face him, his eyes are bloodshot and his cheeks are pink. "Zed! Pal! It's so nice to see you," he slurs. He's drunk.

My thoughts suddenly clear. "Hardin . . . have you been drinking?"

He looks at me imperiously, clearly unsteady. "What's it to you? You have a *new* boyfriend."

"Hardin . . ." I don't know what to say to him. He's obviously wasted. The last time I saw him this drunk was the night Landon called me to come to Ken's house. With his father's history of drinking, and the way Trish was so fearful that Hardin had began to drink again, my heart sinks.

"Thank you for bringing me home, I think you should go now," I politely say to Zed. Hardin is too drunk to be around Zed.

"Noooo-ho-ho . . ." Hardin exhales. "Come on in! Let's have a drink together!" He grabs Zed's arm and pulls him through the doorway.

I follow them in, protesting, "No, this is not a good idea. You're drunk."

"It's fine," Zed tells me, waving me off. It's almost like he has a death wish.

Hardin stumbles over to the coffee table, grabs the bottle of dark liquor standing on it, and pours the liquid into a glass. "Yeah, Tessa. Chill the fuck out." I want to yell at him for speaking to me that way, but I can't find my voice. "Here you go—I'll get another one. One for you, too, Tess," Hardin mumbles and walks into the kitchen.

Zed sits in the chair, and I take a seat on the couch. "I'm not leaving you here alone with him. Look how drunk he is," he whispers. "I thought he didn't drink?"

"He doesn't . . . not like this. This is my fault." I put my head in my hands. I hate that Hardin is drunk because of what I did. I wanted us to have a civil conversation so I could apologize for everything.

"No, it's not," Zed assures me.

"This one's . . . for you," Hardin says loudly as he bursts back into the room and hands me a glass half full of liquor.

"I don't want any more. I drank enough tonight." I take the glass from his hands and set it on the table.

"Suit yourself, more for me." He smiles at me something evil, not the same as the smile I've grown to adore. I'm honestly a little frightened. I know Hardin would never hurt me physically, but I don't like this side of him. I would rather him be screaming at me or punching a wall than sitting here drunk off his ass and being so calm. Too calm.

Zed gives a little "cheers" and brings his drink to his lips.

"This is just like old times, isn't it? You know, back before you wanted to fuck my girl," Hardin says, and Zed spits his drink back into the glass.

"It's not like that. You left her there, and I just brought her home," Zed says in a threatening tone.

Hardin waves his own drink in the air. "I'm not just talking about tonight, and you know it. Though I am pretty annoyed by you taking it upon yourself to bring her home. She's a big girl, she can fend for herself."

"She shouldn't *have* to fend for herself," Zed fires back.

Hardin slams his glass onto the table, and I jump. "That's not up to you! You wish it was, though, don't you?"

I feel like I'm in the middle of a gunfight, and I want to move, but my body won't allow it. I watch in horror as my Mr. Darcy begins to transform into Tom Buchanan . . .

"No," Zed responds.

Hardin sits down next to me but keeps his glassy eyes focused on Zed. I look down at the bottle, which is at least a fourth gone. I pray that Hardin has not consumed all of it tonight, within the last hour and a half.

"Yeah, it is. I'm not stupid. You want her; Molly told me everything you said before."

"Leave it alone, Hardin," Zed growls, only egging Hardin on. "Your first problem is talking to Molly."

" 'Oh, Tessa is so beautiful, Tessa is so sweet! Tessa is too good for Hardin! Tessa should be with me!' " Hardin mocks.

What?

Zed avoids looking at me. "Shut the fuck up, Hardin."

"Hear that, babe? Zed thought he could actually have you." Hardin laughs.

"Stop it, Hardin," I say and get up from the couch.

Zed looks humiliated. I shouldn't have asked him to drive me home. Did he really say those things about me? I had assumed the way he acted toward me had to do with shame over the bet, but now I'm not so sure.

"Look at her, I bet you're thinking about it right now . . . aren't you?" Hardin taunts him. Zed glares at Hardin and sets his drink on the table. "You will never have her, kid, so give it up. No one will have her except me, I'm the only one who will ever fuck her. The only one who will know how good it feels to have her—"

"Stop it!" I yell. "What the hell is wrong with you!"

"Nothing, I'm just telling him how it is," Hardin answers.

"You're being cruel," I tell him. "And disrespectful to *me*!" I turn to Zed. "I really think you should go." Zed looks at Hardin, then back to me. "I'm fine," I assure him.

I don't know what will happen, but I know it won't be as bad as what will occur if he stays. "Please," I beg.

Finally Zed nods. "Fine, I'll go. He needs to get his shit together. Both of you do."

"You heard her, get the fuck out. Don't be too sad, though, she doesn't want me either." Hardin takes another drink. "She likes those clean-cut pretty boys."

My heart sinks even lower, and I know I'm in for a long night. I don't know if I should be afraid, but I'm not. Well . . . a little, but I'm not leaving.

"Out," Hardin repeats, pointing, and Zed heads for the door.

Once Zed is no longer in the apartment, Hardin locks the door and turns to face me. "You're lucky I didn't beat his ass for bringing you here. You know that, don't you?"

"Yes," I agree. Arguing with him doesn't seem like a good idea.

"Why did you even come here?"

"I live here."

"Not for long." He pours more alcohol.

"What?" The air leaves my lungs. "You're going to kick me out?"

When the glass is full, he cocks one eye at me. "No, you'll leave on your own eventually."

"No, I won't."

"Maybe your new lover has room at his place. The two of you looked really nice together." The hateful way he's speaking to me takes me back to the beginning of our relationship, and I don't like it.

"Hardin, please stop saying those things. I don't even know him. And I'm incredibly sorry for what I did."

"I will say what I want, just the way you do whatever the fuck you want."

"I made a mistake, and I'm *sorry*, but that doesn't give you the right to treat me so cruelly and drink like this. I was so drunk, and I really thought something happened with you and that girl, I didn't know what to think. I'm so sorry, I'd never hurt you purposely." I say it all as fast as I can, with as much emphasis as possible, but he isn't listening.

"You are still talking?" he snaps.

I sigh and chew on my cheek. *Don't cry. Don't cry.* "I'm going to go to bed and we can talk when you aren't so drunk."

He doesn't say anything, he doesn't even look at me, so I take off my shoes and walk into the bedroom. As soon as I go to close the door, I hear glass shatter. When I rush into the living room, the wall is wet and glass litters the floor. I watch helplessly as he grabs the other two glasses and slams them against the wall. He takes one last swig from the bottle and then uses all of his strength to shatter it against the wall.

chapter sixty-three

TESSA

He grabs the lamp off the table, causing the cord to rip out of the wall before smashing it on the floor. Then he grabs a vase and breaks it against the brick. Why is his first instinct to break everything in sight?

"Stop it!" I scream. "Hardin, you're going to break all of our stuff! Please stop it!"

"This is your fault, Tessa! You fucking caused this!" he shouts back and grabs another vase. I scurry into the living room and snatch the object from his hand before he can break it.

"I know it is! Please just talk to me," I beg. I can't hold my tears back any longer. "Please, Hardin."

"You fucked up, Tessa, so badly!" His fist slams against the wall.

I knew this was coming, and honestly, I'm surprised it took this long. I'm thankful he chose the drywall to hit—the brick surely would have damaged his hand much worse.

"Just leave me alone, dammit! Go away!" He paces back and forth before slamming both palms against the wall.

"I love you," I blurt. I need to try to calm him, but he's just so drunk and intimidating.

"Well, you don't act like it! You kissed another fucking guy! Then you bring Zed to my fucking house!"

My heart lurches at the mention of Zed's name. Hardin humiliated him. "I know . . . I'm *sorry*." I fight the urge to call him out for being a hypocrite. Yes, I know what I did was wrong, so wrong—but I have forgiven him for hurting me repeatedly.

"You know how fucking crazy, how absolutely fucking mad it makes me to see you with anyone else, and you go and do this shit!" The veins in his neck are turning a deep purple, and he's beginning to resemble a monster.

"I said I'm sorry, Hardin." I speak as softly and slowly as I can manage. "What more can I say? I wasn't thinking clearly."

He tugs at his hair. "Sorry doesn't erase the image from my mind. It's all I can see."

I walk toward him and stand directly in front of him. He reeks of whiskey. "Then look at me, look at me." I put my hands on his face, directing his gaze.

"You kissed him, you kissed someone else." His voice is much lower than it was seconds ago.

"I know I did, and I'm so sorry, Hardin. I wasn't thinking. You know how irrational I can be."

"That's not an excuse."

"I know, baby, I know." I'm hoping those words will soften him.

"It hurts," he says, though his bloodshot eyes have lost their edge. "I knew better than to have a girlfriend, not that I ever wanted one, but this is what happens when people date . . . or get married. This type of shit is why I need to be alone. I don't want to go through this." He pulls away from me.

My chest aches because he sounds like a child, a lonely, sad child. I can't help but picture Hardin as a child, hiding away as his parents fight over his father's alcohol abuse. "Hardin, please forgive me. It won't happen again, I will never do anything like this again."

"It doesn't matter, Tess, one of us will. That's what people do when they love each other. They hurt each other, then break up or get divorced. I don't want that for us, for you."

I step closer to him. "That won't happen with us. We're different."

He shakes his head lightly. "It happens with everyone; look at our parents."

"Our parents just married the wrong people, that's all. Look at Karen and your dad." I'm relieved that he's being much calmer now.

"They'll get divorced, too."

"No, Hardin. I don't think they will."

"I do. Marriage is such a fucked-up concept: 'Hey, I sort of like you, so let's move in together and sign some paperwork promising to never leave each other, even though we won't stick to it anyway.' Why would anyone do that willingly? Why would you want to be tied down to one person forever?"

I'm not mentally prepared to process what he's just said to me. He doesn't see a future with me? He's only saying this because he's drunk. *Right?*

"Do you really want me to go? Is that what you want, to end this now?" I ask, looking straight into his eyes. He doesn't answer me. "Hardin?"

"No . . . fuck . . . no, Tessa. I love you. I love you so fucking much, but you . . . what you did was so wrong. You took every single fear that I have and brought them to life in one action." His eyes begin to water, and my chest begins to cave in.

"I know I did, I feel terrible for hurting you."

He looks around the room, and I can see in his eyes that everything we've built here was him trying to prove himself to me. "You should be with someone like Noah," he says.

"I don't want to be with anyone except you." I wipe my eyes.

"I'm afraid you will."

"Afraid I'll what? Leave you for Noah?"

"Not him exactly, but someone like him."

"I won't. Hardin, I love you. No one else, I love you. I love everything about you, please stop doubting yourself." It hurts me to think that he feels this way.

"Can you honestly tell me that you didn't start seeing me to piss off your mum?"

"What?" I say, but he just watches me and waits for an answer. "No, of course not. My mother has nothing to do with us. I fell in love with you because . . . well, because I didn't have a choice. I couldn't help it. I tried not to because of what my mother would think, but I never had a choice. I've always loved you, whether I wanted to or not."

"Sure."

"What can I do to make you see that?" After everything I've been through for him, how could he think me being with him is a way to rebel against my mother?

"Not kiss other guys, perhaps."

"I know you're insecure, but you should know that I love you. I have fought for you from day one, with my mother, Noah, everyone."

But something I've said strikes him wrong. " 'Insecure'? I'm not insecure. But I'm also not going to sit around and be played for a fucking fool."

With his sudden turn back to anger, I'm starting to get angry myself. "*You* are worried about 'being played'?" I know what I did was wrong, but he has done much worse to me. He really did treat me like a fool—and I forgave him.

"Don't start that shit with me," he growls.

"We've come such a long way, we've been through so much, Hardin. Don't let one mistake take that from us." I never thought I'd be the one begging for forgiveness.

"*You* did it, not me."

"Stop being so cold to me. You've done a lot of things to me, too," I snap.

Anger returns to his face, and he storms away from me, yelling over his shoulder, "You know what? I've done a lot of things, but you kissed someone right in front of me!"

"Oh, you mean like the night you had Molly on your lap and kissed her in front of me?"

He spins around quickly. "We *weren't together then*."

"Maybe not to you, but I thought we were."

"Doesn't fucking matter, Tessa."

"So you're saying that you aren't going to let this go, then?"

"I don't know what I'm saying, but you are getting on my nerves."

"I think you should go to bed," I suggest. Despite the glimpses of understanding that have appeared in the last few minutes, it's clear that he has his mind set on being cruel.

"I think you shouldn't tell me what to do."

"I know you're angry and hurt, but you can't talk to me that way. It's not right and I won't put up with it. Drunk or not."

"I am not hurt." He glares at me. Hardin and his pride.

"You just said you were."

"No, I didn't, don't tell me what I said."

"Okay, okay." I throw my hands up, giving in. I'm exhausted, and I don't want to pull the pin on the grenade that is Hardin. He walks over to the key rack and takes his key chain off while he stumbles to grab his boots. "What are you doing?" I rush over to him.

"Leaving, what does it look like?"

"You aren't leaving. You have been drinking. A lot." I reach for his keys, but he slips them into his pocket.

"I don't give a shit, I need more to drink."

"No! You don't. You had enough—and you broke the bottle." I try to reach for his pocket, but he grabs ahold of my wrist like he has done countless times.

This time is different because he's so angry, and for a second I begin to worry. "Let go," I challenge him.

"Don't try to stop me from leaving and I'll let go." He doesn't let up, and I try to appear unaffected.

"Hardin . . . you're going to hurt me."

His eyes meet mine, and he lets go quickly. When he raises

a hand, I flinch and slink back away from him, but he's only running it through his hair, I see.

His eyes flash with panic. "You thought I was going to hit you?" he nearly whispers, and I back away farther.

"I . . . I don't know, you're *so* angry, and you're scaring me." I knew he wouldn't hurt me, but this is the easiest way to get him back to reality.

"You should know I wouldn't hurt you. No matter how drunk I am, I wouldn't fucking touch you." He glares at me.

"For someone who hates your father so much, you sure as hell don't have a problem acting like him," I spit.

"Fuck you—I'm nothing like him!" he shouts.

"Yes, you are! You're drunk, you left me at that party, and you broke half our decorations in the living room—including my favorite lamp! You are acting like him . . . the old him."

"Yeah, well, you're acting like your mum. A spoiled snobby little—" he sneers and I gasp.

"Who *are* you?" I ask and shake my head. I walk away, not wanting to hear any more from him, and I know if we continue to argue while he's this drunk, it will not end well. He's taken his disrespect to a whole new level.

"Tessa . . . I'm . . ." he begins.

"Don't." I turn and spit before continuing to the bedroom. I can take his rude comments, I can take him yelling at me—because, hell, I dish it out right back to him—but we both need distance before one of us says something even worse.

"I didn't mean that," he says and follows me.

I close the bedroom door and lock it behind me. I slide my back down its smooth surface until I'm sitting on the floor, my knees pulled up to my chest. Maybe we can't make this work. Maybe he's too angry and I'm too irrational. I push him too far and he does the same to me.

No, that isn't true. We are good for each other *because* we push each other. Despite all the fights and tension between us, there's passion. So much passion that it nearly drowns me, pulling me under. And he's the only light, the only one to save me regardless of whether he's the one dooming me.

Hardin taps the wood softly. "Tess, open the door."

"Just go to sleep, please," I cry.

"Dammit, Tessa! Open this door now. I'm sorry, *okay*?" he shouts and begins to pound at the door.

Praying that he won't bust through the door, I force myself up off the floor and pad over to the dresser to dig through my bottom drawer. When I see the white of the paper, relief washes over me, and I go into the closet and close myself in there. As I begin reading Hardin's note to me, the pounding at the door is drowned out to the point of no longer existing. The ache in my chest dissolves along with my headache. Nothing exists except this letter, these perfect words from my imperfect Hardin.

I read it over and over until my tears stop along with the noise from the hall. I desperately hope that he didn't leave, but I'm not going out there to find out. My heart and my eyes are too heavy. I need to lie down.

Taking the letter with me, I drag my body to the bed, still wearing my dress. Eventually sleep comes to me, and I am free to dream of the Hardin that scribbled these words on a sheet of paper in a hotel room.

WHEN I WAKE UP in the middle of the night, I fold the letter up and place it back in my bottom drawer before opening the bedroom door. Hardin is asleep in the hallway, curled up in a ball on the concrete floor. Figuring I shouldn't wake him, I leave him alone to sleep off his intoxication, and go back to sleep.

chapter sixty-four

TESSA

Come the morning, the hallway is empty and the mess in the living room is completely cleared. Not one single piece of glass is left on the floor. The room smells of lemons, and the whiskey is no longer splattered across the wall.

I'm surprised Hardin even knew where the cleaner is stored.

"Hardin?" I call, my voice hoarse from all the yelling I did last night.

Getting no answer, I go over to the kitchen table, where an index card with his handwriting rests. *Please don't leave, I'll be back soon*, it says.

The thousand pounds of pressure lifts from my chest, and I grab the e-reader, make a cup of coffee, and wait for his return.

What feels like hours go by before Hardin finally comes back home. I have since showered, cleaned up the kitchen, and read fifty pages of *Moby-Dick*—and I don't even care for the book. Most of the time that has passed has been filled with me thinking of every possibility of his behavior and what he will say. The fact that he didn't want me to leave, so that is a good thing. Right? I sure hope so. The entire night is a blur, but I remember the key points.

When I hear the click of the front door, I instantly still. Everything I've been preparing to say to him vanishes from my mind. I set the e-reader down on the table and sit up on the couch.

When Hardin walks through the door, he's wearing a gray sweatshirt and his signature black jeans. He doesn't leave the house in anything except black and occasionally white, so the contrast today is a little strange, but the sweatshirt makes him look younger somehow. His hair is messy and pushed off his forehead, and his eyes have dark circles under them. In his hand is a lamp, different from the one he shattered last night, but very similar.

"Hey," he says and runs his tongue along his bottom lip before pulling his lip ring between his teeth.

"Hi," I mutter in return.

"How . . . how did you sleep?" he asks.

I stand up from the couch as he walks toward the kitchen. "Good . . ." I lie.

"That's good."

It is evident that we're both treading very lightly, afraid to say the wrong thing. He stands by the counter, and I stay near the fridge.

"I, um . . . I got a new lamp." He nods at his purchase before setting it on the counter.

"It's nice." I feel anxious, very anxious.

"They didn't have the one we had, but they—" he begins.

"I'm so sorry," I blurt out, interrupting him.

"Me, too, Tessa."

"Last night was not supposed to go that way," I say and look down.

"That is surely an understatement."

"It was a terrible night. I should have let you explain yourself before I kissed someone, it was stupid and immature of me."

"Yes, it was. I shouldn't have had to explain myself, you should have trusted me and not jumped to conclusions." He leans his elbows on the counter behind him, and I fiddle with my fingers, trying not to pick at the skin around my fingernails.

"I know. I'm sorry."

"I heard you the first ten times, Tess."

"Are you going to forgive me? You were talking about kicking me out."

"I wasn't talking about kicking you out." He shrugs. "I was just saying that relationships do not work."

A big part of me was praying that he wouldn't remember the things he was saying last night. He basically told me that marriage is for fools and that he should be alone.

"What are you saying?"

"Just that."

"Just that *what*? I thought . . ." I don't know what to say. I thought the new lamp was his way of apologizing and that he felt different this morning than he did last night.

"You thought what?"

"That you didn't want me to leave because you wanted to talk about it when you got home."

"We *are* talking about it."

A lump grows in my throat. "So what, then, you don't want to be with me anymore?"

"That isn't what I'm saying. Come here," he says, opening his arms.

I stay silent as I cross our small kitchen and step closer to him. He grows impatient, and when I get close enough he pulls me to his chest, wrapping his arms around my waist. My head lies on his chest, the soft cotton of his sweatshirt is still cool from the cold winter air. "I missed you so much," he says into my hair.

"I didn't go anywhere," I reply.

He pulls me closer. "Yes, you did. When you kissed that guy, I lost you momentarily; that was enough for me. I couldn't stand it, not even for a second."

"You didn't lose me, Hardin. I made a mistake."

"Please . . ." he begins to say, but corrects himself: "Don't do it again. I mean it."

"I won't," I assure him.

"You brought Zed here."

"Only because you left me at that party and I needed a ride home," I remind him. We haven't looked at each other so far during this conversation, and I want to keep it that way. I am fearless . . . well, slightly fearless without those green eyes piercing mine.

"You should have called," he says.

I continue staring beyond him. "You have my phone, and I waited outside. I thought you were coming back," I say.

He lifts me gently from his chest and holds me back slightly so he can look at me. He looks so tired. I know that I do, too. "I may have handled my anger poorly, but I didn't know what else to do." The intensity of his gaze causes me to move my eyes from his and stare at the floor.

"Do you care for him?" Hardin's voice is shaky when he lifts my chin to look at him.

What? He can't be serious. "Hardin . . ."

"Answer me."

"Not the way you're assuming."

"What does that mean?" Hardin is growing anxious, or angry, I can't tell. Maybe both.

"I care for him in a way, a friendly way."

"Nothing more?" Hardin's tone is pleading, begging me to assure him that I only care for him.

I cup his face with my hands. "Nothing more—I love you. Only you, and I know I did something very stupid, but that was only out of anger, and alcohol. It has nothing to do with me having feelings for anyone else."

"Why did you have him—of all people—bring you home?"

"He was the only one who offered." Then I ask a question I instantly regret: "Why are you so hard on him?"

"Hard on him?" he scoffs. "You're *not* serious."

"You were very cruel to humiliate him in front of me."

Hardin takes a step sideways so we're no longer standing face-to-face. I turn to stand in front of him, and he runs his fingers through his messy hair. "He should have known better than to come here with you."

"You promised to keep your temper at bay." I'm trying not to push him. I want to make up, not dive deeper into this argument.

"I have been. Until you cheated on me and left that party with Zed. I could've beat the shit out of Zed last night, and hell, I could still leave right now and do it," he says, raising his voice again.

"I know you could have, I'm glad you didn't."

"I'm not, but I'm glad you are."

"I don't want you to drink again. You're not the same person when you do." I can feel the tears coming, and I try to swallow them down.

"I know . . ." He turns away from me. "I didn't mean to get that way. I was just so pissed off and . . . hurt . . . I was hurt. The only thing I could think to do besides kill someone was drink, so I went down to Conner's and got the whiskey. I wasn't going to drink that much, but the images of you kissing that guy just kept coming, so I kept going."

I have half a mind to drive down to Conner's and yell at that old woman for selling Hardin alcohol, but his twenty-first birthday is exactly a month from today and the damage of last night has already been done.

"You were afraid of me, I saw it in your eyes," he says.

"No . . . I wasn't afraid of you. I know you wouldn't hurt me."

"You flinched. I remember that. Most of everything is a blur, but I remember that clear as day."

"I was just caught off guard," I tell him. I knew he wasn't going to hit me, but he was behaving so aggressively, and alcohol can make people do unspeakable things that they would never do sober.

He steps closer to me, almost closing the entire space between us. "I don't want you to ever . . . be *caught off guard* again. I won't drink like that ever again, I swear it." He brings his hand to my face and traces over my temple with his index finger.

I don't want to say anything in response, this whole conversation has been confusing and very back and forth. One second I feel that he's forgiving me, but the next I'm unsure. He's speaking in a much calmer tone than I expected, but his anger is just under the surface.

"I don't want to be that guy, and I definitely do not want to be like my father. I shouldn't have drunk that much, but you were wrong, too."

"I—" I start to say, but he silences me and his eyes get glassy.

"However, I have done a list of shit . . . an entire book of shit to you, and you always forgive me. I've done far worse than you, so I owe it to you to do my best to let it go and forgive you. It isn't fair to you for me to expect things from you that I can't return. I really am sorry, Tess, for everything last night. I was a fucking idiot."

"I was, too. I know how you feel about me with other guys, and I shouldn't have used that against you in anger. I'll try to think before I act next time, I'm sorry."

"Next time?" A small smile plays on Hardin's lips. He changes moods so quickly.

"So we are okay, then?" I ask.

"That's not only up to me."

I stare into his green eyes. "I want us to be."

"Me, too, baby; me, too."

Relief washes over me as I hear his words, and I lean into his chest once more. I know that a lot of things have purposely been left unsaid, but we have resolved enough for now. He places a kiss on the top of my head and my heart flutters. "Thank you."

He says with some humor in his voice, "Hopefully the lamp will make up for it."

Deciding to go with it, I smile and reply, "Maybe if you could have managed to get the same lamp . . ."

He looks down at me, equally amused. "I cleaned the entire living room." He smiles.

"You're the one who trashed it."

"Still, you know how I feel about cleaning." His arms wrap tighter around me, hugging me.

"I wouldn't have cleaned that mess, I would have left it there," I tell him.

"You? Please. No way."

"Yes, I would."

"I was afraid you wouldn't be here when I got home," Hardin says. I look up at him and he looks down at me.

"I'm not going anywhere," I tell him and pray that it's true.

Instead of speaking, he presses his lips to mine.

chapter sixty-five

W hat a way to begin the New Year," Hardin says when he pulls away from our kiss. He rests his forehead against mine.

My phone buzzes on the table, breaking the spell, and before I can grab it, Hardin already has it and is pressing it to his ear. When I get to my feet to try to take it from him, he steps back, shaking his head.

"Landon, Tess will have to call you back," he says into the small speaker. His free hand grips my wrist, and he pulls me close to him, my back to his chest. Seconds pass before he says, "She's otherwise occupied."

He pulls me with him as he walks into our bedroom. His lips brush my neck, and I shudder. *Oh.*

"Stop being annoying, you two need medication," Hardin says and ends the call before setting the phone on the desk.

"I have to talk to him about our classes," I say; my voice betrays me when he licks and sucks at the skin on my neck.

"You need to relax, baby."

"I can't—there's so much to do."

"I can help you." His voice is slow, slower than usual.

His grip on my hip tightens when he places his other hand across my chest to hold me still. "Remember that time when I fingered you in front of the mirror and made you watch yourself come?" he asks.

"Yes." I gulp.

"That was fun, wasn't it?" he purrs.

Heat makes its way through my body at the sound of his words. Not heat—*fire*.

"I can show you how to touch yourself the way that I touch you." He sucks harshly at my skin. I have now turned into a ball of electricity. "Do you want me to?"

The dirty idea sounds somewhat appealing, but way too humiliating to admit.

"I'll take your silence as a yes," he says and lets go of my waist, but takes my hand. I stay silent, nervously going over his words in my mind. This is beyond embarrassing, and I'm not sure how I feel about it.

He guides me to the bed and gently pushes me back onto the soft mattress. He climbs on top of me and straddles my legs. I assist Hardin in taking off my sweats, and he places a kiss on the inside of my thigh before sliding my panties off.

"Stay still, Tess," he instructs.

"I can't," I mewl as he softly bites my inner thigh. There's just no way. He chuckles, and if my brain were actually connected to the rest of my body right now, I would roll my eyes at him.

"Do you want to do this here or would you like to watch?" he asks and my stomach flutters. The pressure continues to build between my legs, and I attempt to squeeze them together to get some relief.

"No, no, baby. Not yet." He's torturing me. He pushes my thighs apart and puts more of his weight on me to keep them separated.

"Here," I finally answer, almost having forgotten he asked a question.

"Thought so." He smirks.

He's so cocky, but his words do things to me that I never thought possible. I can't get enough of him, even when he has me pinned to the bed with my legs spread open.

"I had thought about doing this before, but I was too selfish.

I wanted to be the only one to make you feel this way." He leans down and swipes his tongue along the bare skin between my hipbone and the top of my thigh.

My legs involuntarily try to stiffen, but he doesn't allow it. "Now, since I know exactly how you like to be touched, this will not take long."

"Why do you want to?" I squeak when he bites down on my skin again, then licks the sensitive skin.

"What?" He looks up at me.

"Why . . ." My voice is thick and shaky. "Why show me if you want to be the only one?"

"Because despite that, the thought of you doing it to yourself, in front of me . . . just, *fuck*," he breathes.

Oh. I need relief and soon; I hope he doesn't plan to torture me long.

"Besides, you can be a little uptight sometimes—and maybe this is just what you need." He smiles, and I try to hide my face in embarrassment.

If we weren't doing . . . this . . . I would say something back about him calling me uptight. But he's right, and like he said earlier, I'm otherwise occupied.

"Here . . . this is where you start." He surprises me by placing his cool fingers against me. A hiss escapes my lips from his cold touch. "Cold?" he asks and I nod. "Sorry." He chuckles, then slides his fingers inside of me without warning.

My hips buck off the bed, and I clamp my hand over my mouth to silence myself.

He smirks. "I just need to get them nice and warm."

As he moves his fingers slowly in and out a few times, the fire within me heats up. Then he removes them, making me feel empty and desperate. Suddenly he places them back where they previously were and I bite down on my lip.

"Now, don't go and do that, or we won't be able to finish your lesson."

I don't look at him. Instead, I swipe my tongue across my lip and bite down again.

"You're very testy today. Not a very good student," he teases.

Even while teasing he drives me crazy; how is it possible to be so seductive without even trying? This skill is surely something that only Hardin has mastered.

"Give me your hand, Tess," he instructs.

But I don't move. Embarrassment pools in my cheeks.

Then his hand grips mine, and he brings our hands down my stomach and to the top of my thighs.

"If you don't want to do it, you don't have to, but I think you'll like it," Hardin says softly.

"I do," I decide.

He smiles knowingly. "You sure?"

"Yeah, I'm just . . . nervous," I admit. I feel much more comfortable with Hardin than with anyone I've known in my entire life, and I know he won't do anything to make me uncomfortable, not in a malicious way at least. I am just overthinking this—people do it all the time. *Right?*

"Don't be. You'll like it." He bites down on the corner of his mouth, and I smile nervously. "And don't worry: if you can't get yourself off, I'll do it for you. It's no foreskin off my back."

"Hardin!" I groan in embarrassment and plop my head back down on the pillow. I hear him laugh lightly and say, "Like this."

He spreads my fingers. My heartbeat increases dramatically as he brings my hand . . . *there*. It feels so strange. Foreign and just strange. I'm so used to the way Hardin's hands feel on me, the way his fingers are rough and callused, the way they are long and slender, the way they know exactly how to touch me, how to . . .

"Just do this." Hardin's voice is thick with lust as he guides my fingers to the most sensitive spot. I'm trying not to think about what we're doing . . . *what I'm doing?*

"How does it feel?" Hardin asks.

"I . . . don't know," I mutter.

"Yes, you do. Tell me, Tess," he half demands and removes his hand from mine. I whimper at the loss of contact and begin to remove my hand. "No, keep it there, baby." His tone makes my hand snap back to the spot. "Continue," he commands lightly.

I gulp and close my eyes, trying to repeat what Hardin was doing. It doesn't feel nearly as good as when he does it, but it most certainly doesn't feel bad either. The pressure in my lower stomach begins to build again, and I screw my eyes shut, trying to pretend that it's Hardin's fingers that are making me feel this way.

"You look so hot touching yourself in front of me," Hardin says and I can't help but moan and continue to trace the pattern that he's shown my fingers.

When I open my eyes slightly, I see Hardin's hand rubbing over his jeans. Oh my God. Why is this so hot? This is something I thought people only did in naughty films, not real life. Hardin makes everything so hot, no matter how strange it is. His eyes are focused between my legs, and his teeth are digging into his bottom lip, making his silver ring stand up taut.

The second I feel he may catch me looking at him, I snap my eyes shut, I shut off my subconscious. This is a normal and natural thing, everyone does it . . . just not everyone has someone watching them, but if they had Hardin, they surely would.

"Such a good girl for me, always," he says into my ear, nipping at my earlobe. His breath is hot and smells of mint, and it makes me want to scream and melt into the sheets at the same time.

"Do it, too," I breathe, barely recognizing my voice.

"What?"

"Do what I'm doing . . ." I say, not wanting to use the word.

"You want that?" He sounds surprised.

"Yes . . . *please*, Hardin." I'm getting so close and I need this, I need to take some of the focus off of me, and honestly, seeing him rubbing himself just now did wicked things to me, and I want to see him do it again, that and more.

"Okay," he answers simply. Hardin is so confident when it comes to sex. I wish I was the same way.

I hear the zipper of his jeans, and I try to slow down the movements of my fingers; if I don't, this will be over very, very soon.

"Open your eyes, Tess," he demands, and I oblige.

His hand wraps around his bare length, and my eyes go wide at the perfect sight as I watch Hardin do something I never thought I would see anyone do.

He leans his head down again. This time he plants a single kiss on my neck before bringing his mouth back to my ear. "You like this, don't you? You like to watch me pleasure myself, you are so dirty, Tess, so fucking dirty."

My eyes never leave his hand between his legs. His hand moves faster as he continues talking to me. "I'm not going to last long watching you, baby. You have no idea how fucking hot this is." He groans and I do the same.

I no longer feel uncomfortable. I am close, so close, and I want Hardin to be close, too. "It feels so good, Hardin . . ." I moan, not caring how stupid or desperate I sound. It's the truth, and he makes me feel like it's okay to feel this way.

"Fuck. Say something else," he grits out.

"I want you to come, Hardin, just picture my mouth around you . . ." The filthy words tumble from my lips, and I feel the warmth on my stomach as he releases onto my flaming skin. That does it for me, and I come undone from my own doing and close my eyes as I repeat his name over and over.

When I open my eyes, Hardin is leaning up on his elbow next to me, and I instantly bury my face in his neck.

"How was it?" he asks, wrapping his arms around my waist to pull me close to him.

"I don't know . . ." I lie.

"Don't be shy, I know you liked it. So did I." He kisses the top of my head, and I look up at him.

"I did, but I still like it better when you do it," I admit and he smiles.

"Well, I would hope so," he says, and I lift my head up to plant a kiss over the indent of his dimple. "There are a lot of things I can show you," he adds, and when I flush again he reassures me, "One step at a time."

My imagination runs wild at the thoughts of all the things Hardin could show me—there are probably so many things I've never even heard of that he has done, and I want to learn them all.

He breaks the silence. "Let's get you a shower, my star pupil."

I lower my eyes at him. "You mean your *only* pupil?"

"Yeah, of course. Although maybe I should teach Landon next. He needs it just as bad as you," he teases and moves to climb off the bed.

"Hardin!" I shriek, and he laughs, a real laugh, and it is such a beautiful sound.

WHEN MY ALARM GOES OFF early Monday morning, I fly out of bed and head to the bathroom to take a shower. The water gives me energy, and my thoughts begin to travel back to my first semester at WCU. I had no idea what to expect, but at the same time I felt very prepared. I had every detail down. I thought I'd make a few friends and focus on extracurriculars, maybe join the literary club and a few more. I would spend my time in my dorm or at the library studying and preparing for my future.

Little did I know that just a few months later I would be living in an apartment with my boyfriend, who was not Noah. I had no idea what was coming when my mother pulled into the parking lot at WCU—even less so when I met the rude boy with the curly hair. I wouldn't have believed it if someone told me, and now I can't imagine my life without that crabby guy. Butterflies begin to dance in my stomach as I remember the way it felt to catch a glimpse of him on campus, to try to glance around the room to look for him in Literature, the way I'd catch him looking at me while the professor was speaking, the way he'd eavesdrop on Landon and me. Those days seem so long ago, ancient really.

I'm startled from my nostalgic thoughts as the shower curtain is pulled back to reveal a shirtless Hardin, his hair messy and falling over his forehead as he rubs his eyes.

He smiles, his speech drawn out and thick from sleep. "What are you doing in here so long? Practicing your lessons from yesterday?"

"No!" I squeak, flushing as the image of Hardin coming pops into my mind.

He winks. "Sure, babe."

"I wasn't! I was just thinking," I admit.

"About what?" He sits down on the toilet, and I close the curtain.

"Just about before . . ."

"Before what?" he asks, his tone full of worry.

"The first day of college and how you were so rude," I tease.

"Rude? I didn't even speak to you!"

I laugh. "Exactly."

"You were so annoying with your dreadful skirt and your loafer-wearing boyfriend." He claps with glee. "Your mum's face was priceless when she saw us."

My chest tenses at the mention of my mother. I miss her, but I refuse to take the blame for her mistakes. When she's ready to stop judging Hardin and me, then I'll talk to her, but if she doesn't do that, then she doesn't deserve my time.

"You were annoying with your . . . well . . . your attitude." I can't think of what to say, because he didn't speak to me the first time I met him.

"Remember the second time I saw you? You were in a towel and you were carrying those wet clothes."

"Yes, and you said you wouldn't look at me," I recall.

"I lied. I was certainly looking at you."

"It seems so long ago, doesn't it?"

"Yes, very long ago. It doesn't seem like those things actually happened; now it seems like it's always been us, you know what I mean?"

I pop my head around the curtain and smile. "I do, actually." It's true—but so odd to think about Noah being my boyfriend instead of Hardin. It doesn't sit right. I care for Noah so much, but both of us wasted years of our lives dating each other. I turn off the shower and push him to the back of my mind.

"Can you . . ." I begin to ask, but before I finish, Hardin tosses a towel over the top of the curtain.

"Thanks," I say while wrapping the cloth around my wet body.

Hardin follows me into our bedroom, and I get dressed as fast as possible while he lies on his stomach on our bed, his eyes never leaving me. I towel-dry my hair and get dressed. Hardin does a good job at distracting me with not so subtle gropes during the process.

"I'm driving you," he says and climbs off the bed to get himself dressed.

"We already had that established, remember?" I remind him.

"Shut up, Tess." He shakes his head playfully, and I smile a mock-innocent smile before heading back into the living room.

I decide to wear my hair straight for once. After I apply light makeup, I grab my bag and take another look inside to make sure everything I need is inside before meeting Hardin by the front door. Hardin carries my gym bag for yoga class, and I carry my bag full of everything else that I could possibly need.

"Go ahead," he says as we step out.

"What?" I turn to look at him.

"Go ahead and spaz," he says with a sigh.

I smile at him and tell him the intricate plans for the day, for the tenth time in twenty-four hours.

As he pretends to listen carefully, I promise him and myself that I'll be much more relaxed tomorrow.

chapter sixty-six

TESSA

Hardin parks as close to the coffeehouse as he can manage, but the campus is crowded since everyone has returned from Christmas break. He curses the entire time he circles each parking lot, and I try not to laugh at his annoyance. It's quite adorable.

"Give me your bag," Hardin says when I get out of the car.

I hand it to him with a smile and thank him for the thoughtful gesture. It's pretty heavy, manageable but heavy.

It feels strange being back on campus; so much has changed and happened since I was last here. The cold wind whips against my skin, and Hardin pulls a beanie over his head before zipping his jacket up all the way. We rush through the parking lot and down the street. I should have brought a thicker jacket, and gloves, and even a hat for myself. Hardin was right when he said I shouldn't wear the dress, but there is no way I am admitting that.

Hardin looks adorable with his hair hidden under the beanie, and his cheeks and nose are red from the cold. Only Hardin would look even more attractive in this harsh weather.

"There he is." He points to Landon as we walk inside the coffee shop.

The familiarity of the small space calms my nerves, and I smile as soon as I see my closest friend sitting at a small table waiting for me.

Landon smiles when he spots us, and when we get near he greets us. "Good morning."

"Morning," I chirp back.

"I'll get in line," Hardin mumbles and heads to the counter.

I didn't expect him to stay, or get my coffee, but I'm glad he does. We don't have any classes together this semester, and I'll miss seeing him since I've gotten used to seeing him all day.

"Ready for the new semester?" Landon asks when I take a seat across from him. The chair squeaks against the tile floor, drawing attention to us, and I smile apologetically before taking a good look at Landon.

He's tried a new hairstyle, pushing his hair up off his forehead—and it looks really good on him. As I look around the coffee shop, I begin to realize I probably should've just worn jeans and a sweatshirt. I'm the only person in the place who's remotely dressed up save for Landon in his light blue button-down shirt and khakis.

"Yes, and no," I tell him, and he agrees.

"Same. How are things . . ."—he leans across the table to whisper—"you know, between you two?"

I look over and see Hardin has his back to us, but the barista's face is in a deep scowl. She rolls her eyes as he hands her his debit card, and I wonder what he could have done to her to irritate her so much this early in the day.

"Good, actually. How are things with Dakota? It feels much longer than a week since we've seen each other."

"Good, she's preparing for New York."

"That is so amazing, I'd love to go to New York." I can't imagine what the city is like.

"Me, too." He smiles, and I want to tell him not to go, but I know that I can't. "I haven't made my mind up yet," he says, answering my thoughts. "I want to go and be close to her—we've lived so far for so long. But I love WCU and don't know if I want to be away from my mom and Ken to go to a huge city where I know absolutely no one, except her, of course."

I nod, and try to be encouraging despite myself. "You would

do amazing there—you could go to NYU and the two of you could get an apartment," I say.

"Yeah, I just don't know yet."

"Know what?" Hardin interrupts, setting my coffee in front of me but not sitting down. "Never mind. I've got to go, my first class begins in five minutes on the opposite side of campus," he says, and I cringe at the thought of running late on the first day of new classes.

"Okay, I'll see you after yoga. It's my last class," I tell him, and he surprises me by leaning down and planting a kiss on my lips, then my forehead.

"I love you, be careful being bendy," he says, and I get the feeling that if his cheeks weren't red from the cold, they would be now; his eyes shift to the floor when he remembers Landon is sitting across from us. Public displays of affection are definitely not his thing.

"I will. I love you," I tell him, and he gives Landon an uncomfortable head nod before walking toward the door.

"That was . . . weird." Landon lifts his eyebrows and takes a drink of his coffee.

"Yeah, it was." I laugh and rest my chin on my hand and sigh happily.

"We should get going to Religion," Landon says, and I grab my bag from the floor and follow him outside.

Luckily we don't have a long walk to our first class. I'm excited about World Religion. It should be very interesting and thought provoking, and having Landon there is an added bonus. When we enter the room, we aren't the first students to arrive, but the front row is completely empty. Landon and I sit down in the front center and take our books out. It feels good to be back in my element—academics has always been my thing, and I love that Landon feels the same.

We wait patiently as the room fills with students, most of

whom are obnoxiously loud. The compactness of the classroom doesn't help with the noise, either.

At last, a tall man who looks too young to be a professor strides in and immediately launches into his lesson. "Good morning, everyone. As most of you know by now, my name is Professor Soto. This is World Religion; you may get bored a few times, and I can promise you that you'll learn a heap of facts that you'll never actually use in the real world—but hey, what is college for?" He smiles and everyone laughs.

Well, this is different.

"So let's get started. There is no syllabus for this course. We will not be following a strict outline—that isn't my style . . . but you'll learn all that you need to know by the end date. Seventy-five percent of your grade will come from a journal that you'll be required to keep. And I know you're thinking: What does a journal have to do with religion? It doesn't per se . . . but in a way it does. In order to study and really understand any form of spirituality, you have to be open to the idea of anything and everything. Keeping a journal will help with that, and some of the things I'll have you write about will involve topics that people aren't comfortable with, topics that are very controversial and uncomfortable for some. But all the same, I have high hopes that everyone will leave this class with an open mind and maybe a little knowledge." He beams and unbuttons his jacket.

Landon and I both turn to look at each other at the same time. *No syllabus?* Landon mouths.

A journal? I reply silently.

Professor Soto takes a seat at the large desk in the front of the room and pulls a bottle of water from his bag. "You can talk amongst yourselves until the end of class, or you can go ahead and go for today and we'll begin the real work tomorrow. Just sign the roster so I can see how many flakes we had that didn't show for the first day," he announces with a playful grin.

The class howls and cheers before departing quickly, Landon shrugs at me, and we both stand up after the room is empty. We're the last to sign the attendance roster.

"Well, I guess this is cool. I can call Dakota for a little while between classes," he says and packs his things.

THE REST OF THE DAY goes by quickly, and I'm eager to see Hardin. I've sent him a few text messages, but he has yet to respond. My feet are killing me as I make my way to the athletic building; I hadn't realized how far of a walk it would be. The smell of sweat invades my nostrils as soon as I open the main door, and I hurry to the locker room labeled with a stick figure in a dress. The walls are lined with thin red lockers, the metal showing through the chipped paint job.

"How do we know which locker to use?" I ask a short brunette wearing a bathing suit.

"Just pick one and use the lock you brought," she says.

"Oh . . ." Of course, I didn't think to bring a lock.

Seeing my expression, she digs into her bag and hands me a small lock. "Here, I have an extra. The combination is on the back; I haven't removed the sticker."

I thank her as she walks out of the room. After I'm changed into a new pair of black yoga pants and a white T-shirt, I head out. As I walk down the hall to the yoga room, a group of lacrosse players pass by, several of them making a vulgar remark that I choose to ignore. All of them except one keeps moving.

"You trying out for cheer next year?" the boy asks, his deep brown, almost black eyes looking me up and down.

"Me? No, I'm just on my way to yoga class," I stammer. We are the only people in this hall.

"Oh, that's too bad. You would look phenomenal in a skirt."

"I have a boyfriend," I announce and try to move around him. He blocks me.

"I have a girlfriend . . . what does that matter?" He smiles and takes a step, cornering me.

He doesn't appear intimidating at all, but something about his cocky smile makes my skin crawl. "I need to get to class," I say.

"I can walk you . . . or you can skip and I could show you around." He puts his arm up on the wall next to my head, and I step backward with nowhere to go.

"Get the fuck away from her." Hardin's voice booms from behind me, and the creep turns his head to look at him.

He looks more intimidating than ever in long basketball shorts and a black T-shirt with the sleeves cut off to reveal his tattooed arms.

"I'm . . . sorry, man, I didn't know she had a boyfriend," he lies.

"Did you not hear me? I said get the fuck away from her." Hardin walks toward us, and the lacrosse player backs away quickly, but Hardin grabs hold of his shirt and slams him against the wall.

I don't stop him.

"Come near her again and I'll crack your skull against this wall. Do you understand me?" he growls.

"Ye-yes . . ." the guy stutters and rushes down the hall.

"Thank God," I say and wrap my arm around his neck. "Why are you here? I thought you didn't need any more PE classes?" I ask.

"I decided to take one. And good thing." He sighs and takes my hand into his.

"Which one?" I ask. I can't imagine Hardin being athletic at all.

"Yours."

I gasp. "You *didn't*."

"Oh, yes I did." His anger seems to be dissolved as he smiles at my horrified expression.

chapter sixty-seven

TESSA

Hardin makes it a point to walk slightly behind me, and I suddenly want to go back to the tenth grade when I would tie a sweater around my waist to hide myself.

His voice is quiet as he says, "You're going to need to get more of these pants."

I remember the last time I wore yoga pants in front of Hardin and the crude remarks he made, and those yoga pants weren't as tight as these. I laugh lightly and grab his hand to force him to walk next to me instead of behind me.

"You aren't seriously taking yoga." No matter how hard I try to picture Hardin posing, the image just won't come.

"Yeah, I am."

"You do know what yoga is, don't you?" I ask him as we walk into the room.

"Yes, Tessa. I know what it is, and I'm taking it with you," he huffs.

"Why?"

"It doesn't matter why—I just want to spend more time with you."

"Oh." I'm not convinced by his explanation, but I'm looking forward to seeing him try to do yoga, and the extra time with him doesn't hurt either.

In the center of the room, the instructor sits on a bright yellow mat. Her curly brown hair piled on top of her head and her flower-print shirt make a welcoming first impression.

"Where is everyone?" Hardin asks me as I grab a purple mat from the shelving unit on the wall.

"We're early." I hand him a blue one, and he examines it before tucking it under his arm.

"Of course we are." He smiles sarcastically and follows me to the front of the room.

I begin to lay my mat down directly in front of the instructor, but Hardin grabs my arm to stop me. "No way, we're sitting in the back," he says, and I see the instructor's face alight with a slight smile at his words.

"What? Sitting in the back of the class for *yoga*? No, I always sit in the front."

"Exactly. We're sitting in the back," he repeats and takes my mat from my hands to head to the back of the room.

"If you are going to be grumpy, you shouldn't stay," I whisper to him.

"I'm not grumpy."

The instructor waves and introduces herself to us as Marla when we take a seat on our mats, and afterward Hardin claims with certainty that she's high, which makes me giggle. This is going to be a fun class.

However, as the room fills with girls in tight yoga pants and tiny tank tops who all seem to glance or stare at Hardin, I get steadily less Zen. Of course he's the only male. Luckily, he doesn't seem to notice the heaps of female attention he's receiving. Either that, or he's just very used to it—that has to be it. He gets attention like this all of the time. It's not like I blame the girls, but he's my boyfriend and they need to look elsewhere. I know some of the girls are looking at him because of his tattoos and piercings; they must be wondering why the heck he's taking a yoga class.

"Okay, everyone! Let's get started!" the instructor calls through the room.

She introduces herself as Marla to everyone else and gives a short speech about why and how she got into teaching yoga.

"She's never going to shut up, is she?" Hardin groans after a few minutes.

"Eager to pose, are you?" I raise my brow.

"Pose what?" he asks.

"First we'll begin with a few stretches," Marla says just then.

Hardin sits still on the floor while everyone else mimics her actions. I can feel his eyes on me the entire time.

"You are supposed to be stretching," I scold him, and he shrugs but doesn't move.

Then, in a singsong voice, Marla calls Hardin out. "You in the back, join us."

"Erm . . . sure," he mumbles and uncrosses his long legs and stretches them in front and attempts to reach his toes.

I force myself to look toward the front of the room and away from Hardin to prevent the laughter that is fighting to surface.

"You're supposed to touch your toes," the blond girl next to Hardin says.

"Trying," he says with an overly saccharine smile.

Why did he even respond to her—and why am I so jealous? She giggles at him while the image of me slamming her head against the wall plays on repeat in my mind. I always lecture Hardin about his temper, but here I am planning this whore's murder . . . and calling her a whore even though I don't know her.

"I can't really see clearly, I'm going to move up," I tell Hardin.

He looks surprised as he speaks. "Why? I wasn't—"

"It's nothing, I just want to be able to see and hear what's going on," I explain and drag my mat a few feet, stopping directly in front of Hardin.

I sit down and finish stretching with the group. I don't have to turn around to see the look on Hardin's face.

"Tess," he hisses, trying to get my attention, but I don't turn around. "Tessa."

"Let's begin with the downward-dog pose—it's very simple and a basic one," Marla says.

I bend down, place my palms against the mat, and look at Hardin through the space between my stomach and the floor. He's standing still with his mouth open.

Once more Marla notices Hardin's lack of movement. "Hey, man, you thinking of *joining* us in yoga?" she asks jokingly. If she does it again, I won't be surprised if he curses her out in front of the entire class. I close my eyes and shift my hips so I'm bending over completely.

"Tessa," I hear him say again. "The-reeee-sa."

"What, Hardin? I'm trying to concentrate," I say, looking at him again.

He's now leaning over, attempting to do the pose, but his long body is bent at an awkward angle and I can't help but burst into laughter.

"Shut up, would you!" he snaps, and I laugh louder.

"You are terrible at this," I tease.

"You are distracting me," he says through his teeth.

"I am? How?" I love having the upper hand with Hardin, because it doesn't happen often.

"You know how, minx," he whispers. I know the girl next to him can hear us, but I don't care, I hope she does.

"Move your mat, then." I purposely stand up to stretch and bend back down into the pose.

"You move . . . you're the one toying with me."

"Teasing," I correct him, using his words from minutes ago against him.

"Okay, let's move into a halfway lift," Marla says.

I stand again then bend at my waist, putting my hands flat on my knees and making sure my back is at a ninety-degree angle.

"You've got to be kidding me." Hardin groans at the sight of my bottom practically right in front of his face. I turn around to look at him and see that he isn't remotely doing the pose correctly; he has his hands on his knees but his back is almost straight.

"Okay! Now for the forward fold," our instructor calls, and I bend down, folding my body.

"It's really like she wants me to fuck you right in front of everyone," he says, and I snap my head up to make sure no one heard him.

"Shhh . . ." I plead and hear him chuckle.

"Move your mat or I'll say everything that I'm thinking right now," he threatens, and I quickly stand up and move my mat back to its previous spot next to him.

"Thought so." He smirks.

"You can tell me those things later," I whisper, and he tilts his head to the side.

"Trust me, I will," Hardin promises and my stomach flutters.

He doesn't participate in much of the remainder of class, and the blonde ends up changing her spot halfway through, probably because Hardin won't stop talking.

"We're supposed to be meditating," I whisper back to him and close my eyes. The room is silent except for Hardin's quiet whispers.

"This is so fucking lame," he complains.

"You're the one who signed up for yoga."

"I didn't know how lame it was. I'm literally about to fall asleep right here."

"Stop whining."

"I can't. You had to go and get me all worked up, and now I'm stuck sitting cross-legged, meditating, with a hard-on in a room full of people."

"Hardin!" I hiss, louder than intended.

"Shhh . . ." Multiple voices attempt to silence me.

Hardin laughs, and I stick my tongue out at him, earning a dirty look from the girl to my right. Hardin and me taking yoga together is not going to work; I'm going to get kicked out or fail.

"We're dropping this class," he says when the meditation is over.

"You are, I'm not. I need a PE credit," I inform him.

"Great first day, everyone! I look forward to seeing you later this week. *Namaste*," Marla says, dismissing us.

I roll my mat up, but Hardin doesn't bother; he just shoves his onto the shelf.

chapter sixty-eight

TESSA

The girl who gave me her extra lock is nowhere to be found when I return to the locker room, so I just put the lock back on the handle, and if she doesn't claim it back tomorrow, then I'll continue to use it and pay her or something.

When I finish collecting my things, I meet Hardin back in the hall. He's leaning against the wall with one foot perched on the wall behind him. "If you'd taken any longer, I'd have barged in there," he threatens.

"You should have. You wouldn't have been the only guy in there," I lie and watch as his features change. I turn away from him, taking a few steps before he grabs my arm and spins me back around to face him.

"What did you just say?" he demands, eyes half closed and primal.

"Teasing." I smirk, and with a huff he lets go of my arm.

"I think you've done enough of that today."

"Maybe." I smile.

He shakes his head. "You clearly enjoy tormenting me."

"The yoga relaxed me and cleansed my aura." I laugh.

"Not mine," he reminds me as we walk outside.

The first day of the new semester went very well, even yoga, which ended up being amusing. Amusing is not my usual preference when it comes to academics, but having Hardin there was nice. My Religion class may be a problem because of the lack of structure, but I'm just going to try to go with the flow so I don't drive myself insane.

"I have some work to do for a few hours, but I'll be finished by dinnertime," Hardin tells me. He's been working a lot lately. "That hockey game is tomorrow, right?" he asks.

"Yes; you're still going, aren't you?"

"I don't know . . ."

"I need to know because if you flake then I'm going to go with him," I respond.

Landon would probably much rather I go with him, but the two of them could use some bonding time together. I know they'll never be friends really, but it would help tremendously if they got along better.

"Fine, fuck. I'll go . . ." He sighs and climbs into the car.

"Thank you." I smile and he rolls his eyes.

A half hour later, we pull into his usual spot in the parking lot of our apartment.

"How are your classes?" I ask him. "Hate them all except yoga?" I try to lighten up the mood.

"Yes, except yoga. Yoga was certainly . . . interesting." He turns to look at me.

"Really? How so?" I chew on my bottom lip in an attempt to appear innocent.

"I think it has something to do with a blonde." He smirks and I tense.

"Excuse me?"

"You didn't see the hot blonde next to me? You're really missing out, babe. You should see the way her ass looks in those yoga pants."

I scowl and open the car door.

"Where are you going?" he asks.

"Inside. It's cold in this car."

"Aw . . . Tess, are you jealous of the girl in yoga?" Hardin teases.

"No."

"Yes, you are," he challenges me, and I roll my eyes while I climb out of the car. I'm a little surprised when I hear his boots clomping on the concrete behind me. Pulling the heavy glass door open, I go inside and am at the elevator before I remember that I forgot my bag in the car.

"You're an idiot." He chuckles.

"Excuse me?" I look up at him.

"You think I'd be looking at some random blonde when you're there . . . when I can look at you? Especially in these pants, I am not looking and literally cannot look at anyone else. I was referring to you." He takes a long stride toward me, and I step back against the cold lobby wall.

I practically pout. "Well, I saw her trying to flirt with you." I don't like the way jealousy feels; it is the most obnoxious emotion possible.

"You silly girl." He takes one more step to bring his body to mine and then leads us into the elevator. Cupping my cheek, he forces me to make eye contact. "How can you not comprehend what you do to me?" he asks, inches away from my mouth.

"I don't know," I squeak when his free hand grabs mine and leads it down to his shorts.

"This is what you do." He shifts his hips so his erection fills my hand.

"Oh." My head is swimming.

"You'll be saying much more than 'oh'—" he begins, but is interrupted when the elevator stops at the next floor. "You've got to be kidding me," he groans when a woman and her three children step into the elevator.

I try to step away from him, but he wraps his arm around my waist, refusing to let me move. One of the children begins to cry, which makes Hardin huff in annoyance. I begin to imagine how humorous it would be if the elevator stalled and we were trapped inside with the crying child. Fortunately for Hardin, the doors open moments later and we step out into the hall.

"I literally despise children," he complains as we reach our apartment. When he unlocks the door, cold air flows out from the apartment.

"Did you turn the heat off?" I ask him when we walk inside.

"No, it was on this morning." Hardin walks over to the thermostat and curses under his breath. "It says it's eighty degrees in here when it's clearly not. I'll call maintenance."

I nod and grab the blanket from the back of the couch and wrap it around myself before sitting down.

"Yes . . . it isn't working and it's cold as fuck in here." Hardin speaks into the receiver. "Thirty minutes? No, that won't work . . . I don't give a shit, I pay a small fortune to live here, and I won't have my girlfriend freezing to death," he says, then corrects himself: "I won't have it freezing in here."

He glances over at me, and I look away. "Fine. Fifteen minutes. No longer," he barks into the phone and tosses it against the couch. "They're sending someone up to fix it," he tells me.

"Thank you." I smile at him, and he sits down next to me on the couch.

I open the front of the blanket and reach for him. When he scoots closer, I climb onto his lap and thread my fingers through his hair and tug lightly.

"What are you doing?" His hands rest on my hips.

"You said we have fifteen minutes." I brush my lips along his jaw and he shivers.

I feel his jaw move into a smile. "Are you coming onto me, Tess?"

"Hardin . . ." I whine to prevent him from teasing me further.

"I'm joking, now take your clothes off," he demands, but his hands lift the bottom of my shirt, contradicting his own command.

chapter sixty-nine

HARDIN

Goose bumps rise on her skin as my fingertips slide down her arms. I know she's cold, but I would like to think they're partly caused by me. My fingers wrap around her arms more forcefully when she shifts on my lap, pushing her hips down onto me to create the friction that I want and need. I have never wanted someone so much, so often.

Yes, I have fucked plenty of girls, but that was just about the thrill, about the bragging rights—it was never about being closer to them the way it is with Tess. With her, it's about the sensation, about the way these small bumps raise on her skin from my touch, the way she'll complain that having goose bumps makes her have to shave more frequently, and I will roll my eyes at her even though I find it humorous, the way she whimpers when I bring her lip between my teeth and it makes that noise when it snaps back, and, most importantly, the way that we're doing something that only her and I share. No one has or will ever be close to her in this way.

Her small fingers move to unclasp her bra as I suck on the skin just above the cup.

I stop her. "We don't have long," I remind her and she pouts, making me want her even more.

"Then hurry and get undressed," she softly demands. I love the way she's becoming more and more comfortable with me as the days pass.

"You know I don't have to be told twice." I wrap my hands

around her hips and lift her off, moving her over on the couch a bit.

I remove my shorts and boxers before gesturing for her to lie down. As I grab a condom from my wallet on the table, she slides her pants off—those damn yoga pants. I have never, in my entire twenty years of life, seen anything so sexy. I don't have a fucking clue what it is about them, maybe the way they cling to her thighs, showing every heavenly curve, or maybe because they display her ass perfectly—but either way they're going to have to become what she wears around the house at all times.

"You have really got to get on birth control; I don't want to use these anymore," I gripe and she nods, staring at my fingers while they roll the condom on.

I mean it, though: I'm going to remind her every morning.

Tessa surprises me by pulling my arm in an attempt to force me to sit down on the cushion next to her.

"What?" I ask, catching onto what she's doing, but I want to hear her say it. I love the innocence she possesses, but I know she's so much dirtier than she allows herself to admit—another trait that only I am aware of.

She glares at me, and time is short, so I decide not to taunt her. Instead, I sit down and immediately pull her onto me, wrapping my fingers in her hair and attaching my lips to hers. I swallow the moans and cries coming from her lips as I lower her onto me. We both sigh and her eyes roll back, nearly making me come on the spot.

"Next time will be slow, baby, but this time we only have a few minutes left. Okay?" I groan into her ear as she rotates her full hips.

"Mm-hmm . . ." she moans.

I take that as my cue to pick up the pace. My arms wrap around her back and pull her close to me so that our chests are touching, and I lift my hips at the same time she's rotating hers.

The feeling is indescribable; I can barely breathe as we both move faster. We don't have long and for once I'm desperate to finish quickly.

"Talk to me, Tess," I beg, knowing she will be shy, but hoping that if I slam into her hard enough, tug at the ends of her hair hard enough, she will gain the courage to speak to me in a way she has before.

"Okay . . ." She pants and I move faster. "Hardin . . ." Her voice is shaky, and she bites her lip to calm herself, turning me on even more. The pressure begins to build in my stomach. "Hardin, you feel so good . . ." She gains confidence, and I curse under my breath. "You are already whining and I haven't said anything," she boasts. Her smug tone brings me to the edge and pushes me over.

Her body trembles and stiffens, and I watch her climax. It's like she's just as—if not *more*—captivating each time she comes. This is why I cannot get enough of her and never will.

A knock at the door brings us both back from our postorgasm, almost sedated state, and she jumps off me in an instant. She grabs her shirt off the floor as I remove the spent condom, and pick up my clothes from the floor.

"Give me a minute," I call out. Tessa lights a candle and begins to rearrange the decorative pillows on our couch. "What is with the candle?" I ask as I dress and make my way toward the front door.

"It smells like sex in here," she whispers, despite the fact that the maintenance worker can't hear her.

She frantically runs her fingers through her hair; my only response is a chuckle and a shake of my head just before I pull open the door. The man on the other side of the door is tall, taller than me, and has a full beard. His brown hair touches his shoulders, and he looks to be at least fifty.

"Heat's out, right?" his raspy voice asks. He has clearly smoked too many cigarettes.

"Yes, why else would it be twenty degrees in this apartment?" I reply and watch as his eyes land on my Tessa.

Of course she would be bending over to retrieve her cellphone charger from the basket under the table. And of course she would be wearing the fucking yoga pants while doing so. And of course this greasy man with a damn beard would be checking out her ass. And of course she would stand back up and be oblivious to the entire exchange.

"Hey, Tess, why don't you go in the bedroom until it's fixed," I say. "It's warmer in there."

"No, I'm okay. I'll stay out here with you." She shrugs and sits down on the chair.

My patience is wearing thin, and when she lifts her arms behind her head to tie her hair up and she's practically giving this asshole a show, it takes everything in me not to drag her into the room.

I must be staring angrily at her, because she looks over at me and then says, "Okay . . ."—clearly puzzled. She gathers her schoolbooks in her arms and stalks into the bedroom.

"Fix the fucking heater," I snap at the old perv. He gets to work silently—and stays quiet—so he must be smarter than I assumed.

After a few minutes, Tessa's phone vibrates on the end table, and I take it upon myself to answer it when I see that the screen reads *Kimberly*. "Hello?"

"Hardin?" Kimberly's voice is so high-pitched, I have no idea how Christian can stand it. It must be her looks that drew him in. Probably in a club when he couldn't hear her very well.

"Yes. Lemme get Tess . . ."

I open the bedroom door to find Tessa lying across the bed with a pen between her teeth, her feet kicking in the air behind her.

"Kimberly is on the phone," I explain, tossing the cell on the bed next to her.

She snatches it up and says, "Hey, Kim! Is everything okay?" A few seconds pass before she says, "Oh no! That's terrible." I raise my brow at her, but she doesn't notice.

"Oh . . . okay . . . let me speak to Hardin about it. It'll only take a second, I'm sure it'll be fine." She removes the phone from her ear and covers the bottom with her hand. "Christian caught some sort of stomach flu and Kim needs to take him to the hospital. It's nothing too serious, but his babysitter isn't available," she whispers.

"So?" I shrug.

"They don't have anyone to watch Smith."

"Aaaaand you're telling me this because?"

"She wants to know if we can." She chews on the inside of her cheek.

There is no way in hell she's suggesting that she wants to babysit that child. "Can what?"

Tessa sighs. "*Babysit*, Hardin."

"Nope. Absolutely not."

"Why not? He's a good kid," she whines.

"No, Tessa, this isn't a day care. Not happening, tell Kim to buy him some Tylenol and some chicken soup and call it a day."

"Hardin . . . she's my friend and he's my boss—who is sick. I thought you cared for him?" she asks and my stomach turns.

Of course I like him, he was there for me and my mum when my father was fucking up, but that doesn't mean I want to watch his kid when I already have to go to a hockey game with Landon tomorrow. "I said no," I say, standing my ground. The last thing I need is some annoying kid with a Kool-Aid mustache messing up my apartment.

"Please, Hardin?" she begs. "They don't have anyone else. Pleeeease?"

I know she's going to say yes regardless; she's just entertaining me. I sigh in defeat and watch a smile grow on her face.

chapter seventy

HARDIN

Would you stop griping? You're behaving worse than he will—and he's five," Tessa scolds me, and I roll my eyes.

"I'm just saying, this is all you. He better not touch any of my shit. You agreed to this, so he's your problem, not mine," I remind her right as a knock at the door heralds their arrival.

Taking a seat on the couch, I let Tessa be the one to open the door. She glares at me but doesn't make the guests—*her* guests—wait long before plastering on her biggest and brightest smile and throwing the door to our place open wide.

Immediately Kimberly starts rambling, practically shrieking. "Thank you so much! You have no idea how much of a lifesaver the two of you are right now. I have no idea what we would have done if you couldn't watch Smith. Christian is so sick, he's throwing up everywhere, and we—"

"It's okay, really," Tess interrupts her, I assume because she doesn't want to hear the gory details of Christian's vomitousness.

"Okay, well, he's in the car, so I better get going. Smith is pretty independent, he mostly keeps to himself and will let you know if he needs anything." She moves to the left, revealing a small boy with dirty-blond hair.

"Hey, Smith! How are you?" Tessa says in a strange voice I've never heard her use before. This must be her attempt at baby talk, even though the kid's five. Only Tessa.

The boy doesn't say anything, just gives her a small smile and walks past Kimberly into the living room.

"Yeah, he doesn't talk much," Kimberly tells Tess, noticing the sad look on her face.

As humorous as it is that he didn't respond to Tessa, I don't want her to be upset, so the little shit better knock it off and be nice to her.

"Okay, I'm really leaving this time!" Kim smiles and closes the door after giving Smith one last wave.

Tessa bends down a bit and asks Smith, "Are you hungry?"

He shakes his head no.

"Thirsty?"

Same response, only this time he takes a seat on the couch opposite me.

"Do you want to play a game?"

"Tess, I think he just wants to sit here," I tell her and watch as her cheeks flush. I flip through the channels on the television, hoping to find something of interest to keep me occupied while Tessa is babysitting.

"Sorry, Smith," she apologizes. "I just want to make sure you're okay."

He nods rather robotically, and I realize that he actually looks an awful lot like his father. His hair is practically the exact color, his eyes are the same shade of green-blue, and I suspect that if he were to smile he would have the same dimples as Christian.

A few minutes of awkward silence pass during which Tessa stands next to the couch, and I can see her plans unraveling. She had assumed he would come in here full of energy and ready to play with her. Instead, he hasn't spoken a single word or budged from his spot on the couch. His outfit is as immaculate as I figured it would be, his small white tennis shoes look as if they have never been worn. When I glance up from his blue polo shirt, his eyes are on mine.

"What?" I ask.

He looks away quickly.

"Hardin!" Tessa groans.

"What? All I did was wonder why he was staring at me." I shrug and turn the channel from the garbage I'd accidentally stopped on. The last thing I want to watch is the Kardashians.

"Be nice." She glares at me.

"I am," I say and shrug my shoulders like *what's the big deal?*

Tessa rolls her eyes. "Well, I'm going to make dinner. Smith, do you want to come with me or sit with Hardin?"

I feel his gaze on me, but I choose not to look. He needs to go with her. She's the babysitter here, not me. "Go with her," I tell him.

"You can stay in here, Smith, Hardin won't bother you," she assures him.

He stays silent. Surprise. Tessa disappears into the kitchen, and I turn the television up louder to avoid any possible conversation with the rug rat, not that that is likely to happen anyway. I'm half tempted to go in the kitchen with her and make him sit alone in the living room.

Minutes pass and I begin to grow uncomfortable with him just sitting here. Why the hell isn't he talking or playing, or whatever the hell it is that five-year-olds do?

"So what's the deal? Why don't you talk?" I finally ask.

He shrugs.

"It's rude to ignore people when they're talking to you," I inform him.

"It's more rude to ask me why I don't talk," he fires back.

He has a slight British accent, not strong like his father's, but not completely watered down either. "Well, at least now I know you're able to speak," I say, kind of thrown off guard by his cheeky response and not really sure what to say to him.

"Why do you want me to talk so bad?" he asks, seeming much older than five.

"I . . . I don't know. Why don't you like to?"

"I dunno." He shrugs.

"Is everything okay in there?" Tessa calls from the kitchen. For a second, I consider telling her no, that the kid is dead or injured, but the humor is lost with the thought.

"Everything is fine!" I yell back. I hope she's finished soon, because I'm finished with this conversation.

"Why do you have those things in your face?" Smith asks, pointing to my lip ring.

"Because I want to. Maybe the better question is, why don't *you* have any?" I say to turn the tables on him, trying not to remember that he's a kid after all.

"Did they hurt?" he asks, ducking my question.

"No, not at all."

"They look like it." He half smiles.

He isn't so bad, I guess, but I still don't like the idea of babysitting him.

"Almost finished in here," Tessa calls out.

"Okay, I'm just teaching him how to make a homemade bomb out of a soda bottle," I tease, which causes her to poke her head around the corner to check on us.

"She's mental," I tell him, and he laughs, dimples showing.

"She's pretty," he whispers into cupped hands.

"Yeah, she is. Isn't she?" I nod and look up at Tess with her hair pulled up into some sort of nest on top of her head, her yoga pants and a plain T-shirt still on, and I nod again. She's beautiful, and she doesn't even have to try.

I know she can hear us still, and I catch a glimpse of her smile as she turns to finish her task in the kitchen. I don't get why she's smiling like that; so what if I'm talking to this kid? He's still annoying, like all the other half-sized humans.

"Yeah, really pretty," he agrees again.

"Okay, calm down, little dude. She's mine," I tease.

He looks at me with an O for a mouth. "Your what? Your wife?"

"No—fuck, no," I scoff.

"Fuck, no?" he repeats.

"Shit, don't say that!" I reach across the couch to cover his mouth.

"Don't say 'shit'?" he asks, shaking free of my hand.

"No, don't say 'shit,' or 'fuck.'" This is one of the many reasons I shouldn't be around kids.

"I know they're bad words," he tells me, and I nod.

"So don't say them," I remind him.

"Who is she if she isn't your wife?"

God, he's a nosy little shit. "She's my girlfriend." I should have never got this kid talking in the first place.

He folds his hands together and looks up at me like a little priest or something. "You want her to be your wife?"

"No, I don't want her to be my wife," I say slowly but clearly so he can hear me and maybe get it this time.

"Ever?"

"Never."

"And you have a baby?"

"No! Hell, no! Where do you get these things?" Just hearing them aloud is stressing me out.

"Why do—" he starts to ask, but I cut him off.

"Stop asking so many questions." I groan and he nods before grabbing the remote out of my hand and changing the channel.

Tessa hasn't checked up on us in a few minutes, so I decide to go into kitchen and see if she's almost finished. "Tess . . . are you almost done, because he's talking way too much," I complain, grabbing a piece of broccoli from the dish she's preparing. She hates when I eat before a meal is ready, but there is a five-year-old in my living room, so I can eat this damn broccoli.

"Yeah, just another minute or two," she answers without looking at me. Her tone is strange, and something seems off.

"You okay?" I ask her when she turns around with glassy eyes.

"Yeah, I'm fine. It was just the onions." She shrugs and turns the faucet on to wash her hands.

"It's okay . . . he'll talk to you, too. He's warmed up now," I assure her.

"Yeah, I know. It's not that . . . it's just the onions," she says again.

chapter seventy-one

HARDIN

The little shit remains mute and just nods when Tessa asks him cheerfully, "Do you like the chicken, Smith?"

"It's really good!" I say overenthusiastically, to soften the blow of the kid still not wanting to speak to her.

She gives me an appreciative smile but doesn't meet my eyes. The rest of the meal is eaten in silence.

While Tessa cleans up the kitchen, I head back into the living room. I can hear the small footsteps following me.

"Can I help you?" I ask and plop down on the couch.

"No." He shrugs, turning his attention to the television.

"Okay, then . . ." There is literally nothing on tonight.

"Is my dad going to die?" the small voice next to me suddenly asks.

I look at him. "What?"

"My dad, will he be dead?" Smith asks, though he looks pretty unfazed by the whole topic.

"No, he's just sick with food poisoning or something."

"My mom was sick and now she's dead," he says, and the little quaver in his voice makes me realize he's not immune to the worry, causing me to choke on my own breath.

"Erm . . . yeah. That was different." *Poor kid.*

"Why?"

Christ, he asks so many questions. I want to call for Tess, but something about the worried expression on his face stops me.

He won't even speak to her, so I don't think he would want me to bring her in here.

"Your dad is just a little sick . . . and your mum was really sick. Your dad will be fine."

"Are you lying?" He speaks well beyond his years, sort of the way I always have.

I suppose that is what happens when you're forced to grow up too quickly. "No, I would tell you if your dad was going to die," I say, and mean it.

"You would?" His bright eyes are shining, and I'm terrified that he may cry. I have no fucking idea what I would do if he cried right now. Run. I would run into the other room and hide behind Tessa.

"Yep. Now let's talk about something a little less morbid."

"What's morbid?"

"Something that's twisted and fucked up," I explain.

"Bad word," he scolds me.

"It's okay for me to say, because I'm an adult."

"Still a bad word."

"You said two of them earlier. I could tell your dad on you," I threaten.

"I'll tell your pretty girl on you," he counters, and I can't help but laugh.

"Okay, okay, you win," I say, gesturing for him to just stay put.

Tessa peers around the corner. "Smith, do you want to come in here with me?"

Smith looks at her, then looks back up at me and asks, "Can I stay with Hardin?"

"I don't—" she begins, but I interrupt.

"Fine." I sigh and hand the kid the remote.

chapter seventy-two

TESSA

I watch as Smith settles in on the couch, scooting slightly closer to Hardin. Hardin looks at him with caution but doesn't stop him or say anything about his proximity. It's ironic that Smith seems to like Hardin, when Hardin clearly despises children. Though since Smith feels in some ways more like a country gentleman from an Austen novel, he may or may not be included in that category.

Never, he said to Smith when asked about marrying me.

Never. He never plans on having a future with me. I knew this somewhere deep inside, but it still hurts me to hear him say it, especially the cold and confident way he said it, like it was a joke or something. He could have softened the blow, even just a little.

I don't want to be married right now, obviously, not for years. But it's the idea that it isn't even a possibility that hurts me, a lot. He says that he wants to be with me forever, yet he doesn't want to be married? Are we supposed to just be "boyfriend and girl-friend" forever? Am I okay with never having children? Will he love me enough to make this all okay, despite the future I had always envisioned for myself?

I honestly don't know, and my head is pounding thinking about it. I don't want to obsess about the future right now; I'm only nineteen. We've been getting along so well, and I don't want to ruin that.

After the kitchen is clean and the dishwasher is loaded, I check on Hardin and Smith once more before going into the bedroom to get my things ready for tomorrow. My phone rings as I lay out a long black skirt for tomorrow. Kimberly.

"Hey, is everything okay?" I ask after answering.

"Yeah, everything is okay. They're giving him some antibiotics and we should be getting sent home soon. It may be late, I hope that's okay," she says.

"Of course it is. Do what you need to do."

"How is Smith doing?"

"He's good—he's actually hanging out with Hardin," I tell her, still not believing it myself.

She laughs heartily. "*Really?* Hardin?"

"Yeah, tell me about it." I roll my eyes and make my way back into the living room.

"Well, that's unexpected, but it's good training for when you have little Hardins running around the house," she teases.

Her words tug at my heart, and I bite down on my lip. "Yeah . . . guess so." I want to change the subject before the lump in my throat grows any larger.

"Well, we'll be done soon, hopefully. Smith's bedtime is ten, but since it's already ten, just let him stay up until you want him to go to sleep. Thank you again," Kimberly says and hangs up.

I make a quick stop in the kitchen to pack a small lunch for tomorrow; I'll just bring leftovers from tonight.

"Why?" I hear Smith ask Hardin.

"Because they're trapped on the island."

"Why?"

"Their plane crashed."

"How come they're not dead?"

"It's a show."

"A stupid show," Smith says, and Hardin laughs.

"Yeah, I guess you're right." Hardin shakes his head in amusement, and Smith giggles. They look alike in some ways: the dimples, the shape of their eyes, and their smiles. I imagine that except for the blond hair and shade of eyes, Hardin looked much like Smith when he was younger.

"Is it okay if I go to bed, or do you want me to watch him?" I ask Hardin.

He looks at me, then at Smith. "Um . . . that's cool. We're just watching mindless television anyway," he says.

"Okay, good night, Smith. I'll see you in a bit when Kim is here to get you," I tell him. He looks over at Hardin, then back to me and smiles.

"Night," he whispers.

I turn to go back into the room, but I'm stopped by Hardin's fingers wrapping around my arm. "Hey, no good night to me?" He pouts.

"Oh . . . yeah. Sorry." I hug him and give him a kiss on the cheek. "Good night," I say, and he hugs me again.

"You sure you're okay?" he asks, pushing my shoulders back so he can look at me.

"Yeah, I'm just really tired, and he wants to hang out with you, anyway." I smile weakly.

"I love you," he tells me and kisses my forehead.

"I love you," I respond and hurry to the bedroom and close the door behind me.

chapter seventy-three

TESSA

The next day, the weather is nice, with no snow and minimal slush on the sides of the road. When I get to Vance, Kimberly is sitting at her desk, and she smiles at me as I grab my usual donut and coffee.

"I didn't even know you came last night. I fell asleep," I tell her.

"I know, Smith was sleeping, too. Thank you again," she says, and her phone rings.

My office feels strange after being on campus yesterday. Sometimes it seems as though I live a double life: one half a college student, one half full adult. I have an apartment with my boyfriend and a paid internship that honestly feels like a job, not an internship. I love both halves, and if I had to choose, I would choose the adult life, but with Hardin.

I dive into my work, and lunchtime comes quickly. After several duds, I hit upon a manuscript that is really captivating, and I find myself eating quickly so I can get back and finish it. I hope they find a cure for the main character's illness; I'll be heartbroken if he passes. The rest of the day goes quickly as I am completely withdrawn from the world and fully enveloped in the manuscript, which ends terribly sadly.

With tears staining my cheeks, I leave for the day and head home. I haven't heard from Hardin once since I left him asleep and grumpy in bed, and I can't stop thinking about his words from last night. I need a distraction from ruminations; sometimes I wish I could just shut my mind off the way other people seem to be able to do. I don't like that I overthink everything, but I can't help it. It's who I am, and now all I can think of is Hardin and me not having a future. Still, I really need to do something to get my mind off obsessing over this. He is who he is, and he doesn't want to ever get married or have children.

Maybe I should call Steph after I go to Conner's to get groceries and do a load of laundry since Hardin and Landon will be going to the hockey game tonight . . . God, I hope that goes well.

When I arrive at the apartment, I find Hardin reading in the bedroom.

"Hey, sexy. How was your day?" he asks as I walk in.

"It was okay, I guess."

"What's wrong?" Hardin looks up at me.

"The manuscript I read today was so sad, incredible but so heartbreaking," I say, trying not to get emotional again.

"Oh, it must have been good if you're still upset about it." He smiles. "I would hate to have been there the first time you read *A Farewell to Arms*."

I plop down next to him on the bed. "This was worse, so much worse."

He grabs hold of my shirt, pulling me to lay my head on his shoulder. "My sensitive girl." As he runs his fingers up and down my spine, the way he spoke the words he just uttered makes my stomach flutter. To be called "my girl" in any form makes me much happier than it should.

"Did you even go to classes today?" I ask him.

"Nope. Watching the mini-human wore me out."

"By 'watching,' you mean watching TV with him?"

"Same thing. I did more than you did."

"So you like him, then?" I'm not sure why I'm asking this.

"No . . . well, as far as annoying children go, he isn't at the top of the list, but I won't be planning any playdates soon." He smiles.

I roll my eyes but don't say anything else about Smith. "Are you ready for the game tonight?"

"No, I already told him I'm not going."

"Hardin! You have to go," I shriek.

"I'm teasing . . . he'll be here soon. You owe me for this shit, Tess." Hardin groans.

"You like hockey, though, and Landon is good company."

"Not as good of company as you." He kisses my cheek.

"You're in a good mood for someone who acts like they're being led to slaughter."

"If this goes badly, I won't be the one who is slaughtered."

"You better be nice to Landon tonight," I warn him.

He raises his hands in mock innocence, but I know better. A knock is heard at the door, but Hardin stays put. "He's your friend, you answer the door," he says.

I give him a look but go answer the door.

Landon is dressed in a hockey jersey, blue jeans, and tennis shoes. "Hey, Tessa!" he says with his usual friendly smile and a hug for a greeting.

"Can we get this over with?" Hardin says before I can even say hello.

"Well, I can see this will be a fun night." Landon jokes and runs a hand over his short hair.

"It'll be the best night of your entire life," Hardin teases him.

"Good luck," I tell Landon, who just chuckles.

"Oh, Tess, he's just showing off, trying to act like he isn't excited to spend time with me." Landon smiles, and it's Hardin's turn to roll his eyes.

"Well, this is too much testosterone for me, so I'm going to change and run some errands. You two have fun," I say, leaving the men to their little games.

chapter seventy-four

HARDIN

As Landon and I push our way through the crowd, I groan and ask, "Why the hell is it so crowded already?"

He gives me a look with a little attitude behind it. "Because you made us late."

"The game doesn't start for another fifteen minutes."

"I usually come an hour early," he explains.

"Of course you do. Even when I'm not with Tessa, I'm with Tessa," I complain. Landon and Tessa are literally the same person when it comes to their annoying need to be the first and best at everything they do.

"You should feel honored to be with Tessa," he tells me.

"Stop being a dick and we might actually enjoy the game," I tell him forcefully, but can't help the smile that appears on my face at his annoyance. "Sorry, Landon. I'm honored to be with her. Now, would you chill out?" I laugh.

"Sure, sure. Let's just get our seats," he says quietly, leading the way.

"WHAT THE HECK! Did you see that? How the heck did that count!?" Landon screams next to me. He's more energized than I've ever seen him. Still, even angry, he sounds like a pussy.

"C'mon!" he yells once more, and I bite my tongue in laughter.

I suppose Tessa was right: he isn't too terrible of company. Not my first choice, obviously, but not so bad.

"I hear that the more you yell and scream, the more likely they are to win," I tell him.

He ignores me and continues to yell and boo with the ebb and flow of the game. I alternate between paying attention and texting Tessa dirty things, and before I realize it, Landon's yelling "Yes!" when his team wins the game at the last second.

The crowd piles out of the arena, and I push my way through them. "Watch it," a voice behind me says.

"Sorry," Landon apologizes.

"That's what I thought," the voice says, and I turn around to find a nervous Landon and an asshole wearing the opposing team's jersey. Landon swallows but doesn't say anything else as the man and his crew continue to taunt him.

"Look how scared he is," another voice says, one of the asshole's friends, I presume.

"I . . . I . . ." Landon stammers.

Are you kidding me? "Fuck off, both of you," I snarl, and they both turn to look at me.

"Or what?" I can smell the beer on the tall one's breath.

"Or I will *shut* you up in front of everyone, and you'll be so humiliated it'll be on the game's highlight reel. That's what," I warn him, meaning every single word.

"C'mon, Dennis, let's go," the short one, the only one with some sense, says and tugs on his friend's jersey, and they disappear into the crowd. I grab Landon by the arm and pull him the rest of the way. Tessa will have my balls if I let him get beat up tonight.

"Thanks for that, you didn't have to do it," Landon says when we reach his car.

"Don't make it awkward, okay?" I grin, and he shakes his head, but I hear him laugh quietly to himself.

"Should I take you back to your apartment now?" he asks after several minutes of awkward silence while we wait to leave the crowded parking lot.

"Yeah, sure." I check my phone again to see if Tessa has responded; she hasn't. "Are you moving?" I ask Landon.

"I don't know yet, I really want to be closer to Dakota," he explains.

"So why doesn't she move here?"

"Because her career in ballet wouldn't work here; she has to be in New York City." Landon lets another car pass in front of his, despite the fact that we've barely moved in the line of traffic since we left our parking spot.

"And you are just going to give up your life and move for her?" I scoff.

"Yeah, I would rather do that than continue to be away from her. I don't mind moving, anyway. New York City would be an awesome place to live. It's not always about one person in the relationship, you know?" he says, looking sideways at me. *Fucker.*

"Was that supposed to be directed at me?"

"Not exactly, but if you think it was, maybe it is." A group of drunken idiots stumbles in front of the car, but Landon doesn't seem to mind that they're blocking us.

"Shut the hell up, would you?" I say. He's just being a dick now.

"Are you telling me you wouldn't move to New York to be with Tessa?"

"Yes, that is exactly what I'm telling you. I don't want to live in New York, so I won't be living in New York."

"You know I don't mean New York, I mean Seattle. She wants to live in Seattle."

"She'll be moving to England with me," I tell him. I turn the volume dial on his radio up in hopes of ending this conversation.

"What if she doesn't? You know she doesn't want to, so why would you force her to?"

"I'm not forcing her to do anything, Landon. She will move because we're supposed to be together and she won't want to be away from me, simple as that." I check my phone once more to try to distract myself from the irritation my lovely stepbrother is causing me.

"You're an asshole."

I shrug. "Never claimed that I wasn't."

I dial Tessa's number and wait for her to answer. She doesn't. *Great, fucking great.* I hope she's still at home when I get there. If Landon didn't drive so goddamn slow, we would be there by now. I stay silent, picking at the torn skin surrounding my fingernails. After what seems like three fucking hours Landon pulls up in front of my apartment.

"Tonight wasn't so bad, right?" he asks me as I get out of the car, and I chuckle.

"No, I guess it wasn't," I admit. Then I tease, "If you tell anyone I just said that, I will kill you."

Landon chuckles as he drives off. I let out a deep breath, very pleased that he didn't get his ass beat by those guys tonight.

When I walk into the apartment, Tessa is sound asleep on the couch, so I just sit and watch her for a bit.

chapter seventy-five

HARDIN

After watching Tessa sleep for a while, I gather her into my arms and carry her to our bedroom. She hugs on to my arms and rests her head against my chest. I gently lay her onto our bed and pull the covers up to her chest. I give her a soft kiss on the forehead and am about to turn and get myself ready for bed when she says something.

"Zed," she mumbles.

Did she just . . . ? I stare at her, trying to replay the last three seconds in my mind. She didn't say—

"Zed." She smiles, rolling onto her stomach.

What the fuck?

Part of me wants to wake her up and demand to know why she would call his name—twice—in her sleep. The rest of me, the paranoid and fucking fed-up part of me, knows what she'd say. Tessa will tell me that I have nothing to worry about, that they're only friends, that she loves me. Some of that may be true, but she just said his name.

Hearing that asshole's name fall from her lips on top of fucking Landon and his certainty about his future—it's too much. I'm not certain of anything, not in the way he is, and Tessa obviously isn't sure about me either. Otherwise she wouldn't be dreaming of Zed.

Grabbing paper and pen, I scribble out a note for her, leave it on the dresser, and head out into the night.

* * *

I TURN THE CAR toward the Canal Street Tavern. I don't want to go there in case Nate and the group are still there, but there's a place close by where I used to drink all the time. Gotta love the state of Washington and the dumb-asses that never ID college kids.

Tessa's voice plays in my mind, warning me not to drink again after the last time, but I don't give a shit. I need a drink. I hear Zed and Landon's voices next. Why does everyone around me think their opinions matter to me?

I'm not moving to Seattle—Landon and his shit advice can fuck off. Just because he wants to follow his girlfriend around doesn't mean that I want to. I can see it now: I pack my shit and move to Seattle with her, and two months later she decides she's had enough of my shit and she leaves me. In Seattle, it'll be her world, not mine, and I could be pushed out of it just as easily as I was brought in.

When I arrive at the bar, the music is low and there aren't many people inside. A familiar blonde stands behind the bar and looks at me with surprise, and interest, in her eyes.

"Long time, no see, Hardin. Miss me?" She grins and licks her full lips, remembering our nights together, I'm sure.

"Yeah, now give me a drink," I respond.

chapter seventy-six

TESSA

When I wake up, Hardin isn't in the bed. I assume he went for a coffee run or he's in the shower, so I check the time on my phone and force myself out of bed. Despite not having gone out last night, I'm feeling pretty tired, so I don't really make an effort with my appearance, just pulling on a WCU T-shirt and jeans. I'm tempted to wear yoga pants so I can tease Hardin when I see him, but I can't find them anywhere. Knowing him, he probably hid them or put them somewhere so no other guys can see me in them.

I look in my top drawer again, and when I close it, a piece of paper falls from the dresser.

Went out with my dad for breakfast, it says in Hardin's handwriting. I'm equally confused and happy about this. I really hope Hardin and Ken can continue to build their relationship.

Figuring that they're probably done, I try calling Hardin, but he doesn't answer. I shoot him a text message and head out to meet Landon at the coffee shop.

When I get there, Landon is sitting at a table, and gestures to the two drinks in front of him. "I already got yours," he says with a smile and lifts the paper cup to me.

"That was nice, thanks." The sweet yet bitter taste of the coffee wakes me up the rest of the way, but then I start getting anxious that I haven't heard back from Hardin.

"Look at us, looking like regular college students," Landon jokes, pointing at my shirt and then at his, which is identical to mine. I laugh and take another drink of the blessed coffee.

"Hey, where's Hardin today?" Landon grins. "He didn't walk you to class this morning."

I shrug. "I don't know. He left me a note that he left early to have breakfast with his dad."

Landon stops mid-drink and gives me a quizzical look. "Really?" Then after a moment, he nods and says, "Stranger things have happened, I guess."

His response only makes my mind fill with doubt. Hardin did go to breakfast with his father. *Didn't he?*

As Landon and I walk to class, and Hardin still hasn't responded to my previous or recent texts, an ache in my chest grows.

When we take our seats, Landon looks at me and asks, "Are you okay?" and I'm about to respond when I look up to see Professor Soto entering the room.

"Morning, everyone! Sorry I'm late, I had a late night last night." He smiles and shakes a leather jacket from his shoulders before throwing it across the back of his chair. "I hope everyone took the time to either purchase or steal a journal?"

Landon and I look at each other and pull out our journals. When I glance around, I see we're two of the only people to do so, and once again I'm amazed at just how unprepared college students are.

But Professor Soto continues undeterred and absently straightens his tie. "If not, take out a blank piece of paper, because we're going to use the first half of class to work on the first journal assignment. I haven't decided how many there will be exactly, but like I said, the journal will make up the majority of your grade, so you need to put in at least a little effort." He grins and sits, putting his feet on the desk. "I want to know your ideas on faith. What does it mean to you? There is literally no wrong answer here, and your personal religion doesn't make a difference.

You can take this in many different directions—do you yourself have faith in some higher power? Do you feel that faith can bring good things into people's lives? Maybe you think of faith in a completely different way altogether—does having faith in something or someone change the outcome of a situation? If you have faith that your unfaithful lover will stop being unfaithful, does that make a difference at all? Does having faith in God . . . or a number of gods, make you any better of a person than someone who doesn't? Take the topic of faith and do what you want with it . . . just do something," he says.

My mind is whirling with ideas. I used to go to church growing up, but I have to admit my relationship with God hasn't always been the strongest. Every time I try to press my pen to the first page of my journal, Hardin comes to mind. *Why haven't I heard from him? He always calls. He left a note, so I know he's safe—but where is he now? How long will it be before I hear from him?*

As each text remains unanswered, the panic inside of me grows. He has changed so much, improved his behavior.

Faith. Have I had too much faith in Hardin? If I continue to have faith in him, will he change?

Before I realize where the time has gone, I'm on my third page. Most of what I've written has gone straight from somewhere inside of me to the paper, leaving my mind and heart out of it. Somehow a weight has been lifted by writing about my faith in Hardin. Professor Soto calls the end of class, and I listen to Landon talk about his journal entry. He chose to write about faith in himself and his future. I wrote about Hardin without a thought. I'm not quite sure how I feel about that.

The rest of the day drags on miserably, since I haven't heard from Hardin. By one o'clock, I've called him three more times and sent eight more texts, but nothing. I feel bad about it—especially after having just written about faith and my feelings about him—

but my first thought is that I hope he isn't off doing something that will harm us.

My second thought is of Molly. It's funny how she always pops up in mind when there's trouble. Well, not funny, but persistent. She's like an apparition that appears in my head even though I know he wouldn't cheat on me.

chapter seventy-seven

HARDIN

"Do you want another cup of coffee?" she asks. "It'll help with the hangover."

"No, I know how to get rid of a hangover. I've had plenty," I growl.

Carly rolls her eyes. "Don't be a dick. I was just asking."

"Stop talking." I rub my temples. Her voice is annoying as hell.

"Charming as ever, I see." She laughs and leaves me alone in her small kitchen.

I'm a dumb-ass for even being here, but it's not like I had another option. Yes, I did, I'm just trying to not take the blame for my overreaction. I was harsh on Tessa and said some pretty fucked-up things, and now here I am in Carly's kitchen drinking fucking coffee this late in the afternoon.

"Do you need a ride back to your car?" she yells from the other room.

"Obviously," I respond, and she walks into the kitchen wearing only a bra.

"You're lucky that I brought your drunk ass home with me. My boyfriend will be arriving soon, so we need to go." She slides her shirt over her head.

"You have a boyfriend? Nice." This keeps getting better.

She rolls her eyes. "Yes. I do. It may be surprising to you that not everyone just wants an endless parade of fuck buddies."

I almost tell her about Tessa, but I decide against it, since it's none of her business. "I gotta piss first," I tell her and walk toward the bathroom.

My head is pounding and I'm angry at myself for coming here. I should be at home . . . well, on campus. I hear my phone buzzing on the counter and snap back around.

"Don't you dare answer that," I bark at Carly, and she takes a step back.

"I'm not! Man, you weren't this big of an asshole last night," she remarks, but I ignore her.

I follow Carly to her car, my head pounding with each step against the concrete. I shouldn't have drunk so much. I shouldn't have drunk at all. I look over at Carly as she rolls her window down and lights a cigarette.

How could she ever have been my type? She's not wearing a seat belt. She puts makeup on at stoplights. Tessa is so different from her, from any of the girls I've ever been with.

As we're driving back to the bar where I got shit-faced last night, I keep rereading the texts from Tessa, over and over again. This is terrible—she's probably really worried. My head's too foggy to think up a good excuse, so I just text her, I fell asleep in the car after drinking too much with Landon last night. Be home soon.

Something feels off, and I pause for a minute. But my whole brain is just rattled, so I hit send and watch the phone to see if she's replying. Nothing.

Well, I can't tell her about this, about staying at Carly's house. She'll never forgive me, she won't even hear me out. I know she won't. I can tell she's getting tired of my shit lately. I know she is.

I just don't have a fucking clue how to fix it.

Carly interrupts my rumination when she hits the brake and curses. "Aaagh, fuck. We have to go around—there's a wreck up there," she says, pointing to the cars blocking our way.

Glancing up, I see a middle-aged man standing with his

hands in his pockets while talking to a police officer. He points to a white car that looks . . . just like . . .

I panic. "Stop the car," I demand.

"What? Jesus, Hard—"

"I said *stop the goddamn car!*" Without thinking, I open the door as the car comes to a stop and rush over to the damaged cars. "Where's the other driver?" I ask the officer angrily and look around the scene.

The front end of the white car is badly damaged, and then I see the WCU parking pass hanging from the rearview mirror. *Fuck.* An ambulance is parked next to the police car. *Fuck.*

If something happened to her . . . if she isn't okay . . .

"Where's the girl? Someone fucking *answer me!*" I scream.

The cop gets an aggressively annoyed look on his face, but the other driver sees my anxiety and says softly, "There," and points to the ambulance.

My heart stops beating.

Wandering over in a daze, I see the ambulance doors are open . . . and Tessa is sitting on its back bumper, an ice pack on her cheek.

Thank God. Thank God it's only small.

I rush over to her, and the words start tumbling from my mouth. "What happened? Are you okay?"

Relief takes over her features when she sees me. "I had an accident." Above her eye is a small bandage, and her lip is swollen and split on the side.

"Can you go?" I ask rudely. "Can she go?" I ask the young EMT who's standing nearby.

The woman nods and walks away quickly. I reach for Tessa's ice pack and move it, revealing a knot the size of a golf ball. Her cheeks are stained with tears, and her eyes are swollen and red. I can already see the black eye forming under her delicate skin.

"Fuck—are you okay? Was it his fault?" I turn and try to find that asshole again.

"No, I ran into him," she says, wincing as she grabs the ice pack and puts it back on her skin. Then some of the relief leaves her eyes as she looks up at me and asks, "Where were you all day?"

"What?" I ask, honestly confused, between my hangover and seeing her like this.

With a colder look in her eyes, she says, "I said, 'Hardin, where were you all day?'"

I snap back to the situation. *Fuck.*

And right as I'm about to make an excuse, Carly walks up and smacks me on the ass. "Well, Mr. Dark and Moody, can I go? You can walk back to your car from here, right? I really need to get back home."

Tessa's eyes go wide. "Who are *you*?"

Fuck. Fuck. Fuck. Not this. Not now.

Carly smiles and gives Tessa a little nod. "I'm Hardin's friend Carly. Sorry about your accident." Then she looks at me. "Can I go now?"

"Bye, Carly," I snap.

"Wait," Tessa says. "He was with you last night at your place?"

I try to make eye contact with her, but she continues to stare at Carly, who says, "Yeah, I was just trying to take him back to his car."

"His car? Where's that?" she says, her voice shaking.

"*Bye*, Carly," I say again and glare at her.

Tessa stands up, though her knees buckle a little. "No—tell me where his car is."

I grab hold of her elbows in an attempt to stop her, but she pushes me away and then whimpers from the pain of the motion. "Don't touch me," she says through her teeth.

"Carly. Where is his car?" Tessa asks again.

Carly raises her hands and looks back and forth between Tessa and me. "At the bar where I work. Okay, I'm going now," she says and wanders off.

"Tess . . ." I plead. *God, why am I such a fuckup?*

"Get away from me," she replies. Her cheek goes in a little; I can tell she's biting down on it to keep her tears at bay. Now that she's standing here, staring off in the distance and trying to appear emotionless, I'm missing the days of her constant crying.

"Tessa, we have . . ." I begin, but my voice cracks. Now I'm the emotional one, and for once I don't care. The panic from seeing the front end of her car smashed still courses through me, and I don't want anything other than to hold her right now.

She still doesn't look at me. "Go. Now. Or I'll tell the officer to make you."

"I don't give a fuck about them—"

Her eyes whip back toward me with a vengeance. "No—I'm done listening to you! I'm not sure what happened last night, but all morning I knew—somehow *knew*—you were with someone else. I was just trying to force myself not to believe it."

"We can work this out," I beg. "We always have."

"Hardin! Do you not *see* that I was just in an accident?" she yells and starts crying, prompting the EMT to walk back over. "Actually, you probably can't tell, your version of reality is so warped. You write me a note last night about going out with your dad this morning, *then* you text me that you fell asleep drunk in your car after drinking with Landon. With *Landon*! You must think I'm stupid enough to believe anything—even things that contradict each other." She glares at me. "Of course, you're a walking bundle of contradictions, so, yeah, I can see how you might mistakenly think the rest of reality is, too."

The realization of just how stupid I was fills me, and I can't speak for a moment. I'm so stupid, so very, very stupid. And not just because I couldn't keep my stories straight.

The EMT takes that moment to put a hand on Tessa's shoulder and says, "Is everything okay over here? We need to get you to the hospital, just to check everything out."

Wiping her tears from her cheeks, Tessa looks dead at me and says to her, "Yes. I'm ready. I'm ready to leave now."

chapter seventy-eight

HARDIN

I crack open my fourth beer and spin the cap on the glossy wooden surface of our coffee table. When is she going to be here? *Is* she going to be here?

Maybe I should just text her and tell her that I *did* have sex with Carly, just to end both of our miseries.

A loud knock on the door breaks me from my plotting.

Here we go. I hope she's alone. I grab my beer, take another swig, and head for the door. The knocking quickly shifts to pounding, and I swing open the door to find Landon. Before I can react, his hands grip the collar of my T-shirt and he slams me against the wall.

What the fuck? He's much stronger than I ever expected, and I'm astounded by his aggressive behavior.

"What the hell is wrong with you!" he yells. I didn't know his voice could even get that loud.

"Get the fuck off of me!" I push back, but he doesn't move. Fuck, he's strong.

He lets go of me and for a second I think he's going to punch me, but he doesn't. "I know that you slept with another girl and you caused her to wreck her car!" He gets in my face again.

"I suggest you lower your fucking voice," I snap.

"I'm not afraid of you," he says through his teeth.

The alcohol makes me indignant, when I should be ashamed. "I already beat your ass before, remember," I say as I go back to the couch and sit.

Landon follows me. "I wasn't as angry with you then as I am now." He lifts his chin higher. "You can't just go around hurting her all the time!"

I wave him off. "I didn't even sleep with that girl. I just slept over at her house, so mind your own damn business."

"Oh, wow! Of course you're drinking!" He gestures at the empty beer bottles on the table and the one in my hand. "Tessa is all banged up and has a concussion because of you, and here you are getting drunk. You're such a prick!" he practically screams.

"That wasn't my fucking fault and I tried to talk to her!"

"Yes, it *was* your fault! It was your damn text message that she was trying to read when she crashed. A text that she knew right away was a lie, might I add."

The breath is knocked out of me. "What are you talking about?" I choke.

"She was so anxious to hear from you all day, she grabbed her phone as soon as she saw your name."

This is my fault. How did I not put it together? I cause these injuries to her. I hurt her.

Landon continues to stare at me. "She's done with you—you know that, don't you?"

I look up at him, suddenly weary. "Yeah. I know." I reach for my beer. "And you can leave now."

But he snatches the bottle from my hand and walks into the kitchen.

"You're really fucking pushing it," I warn him and jump up.

"You're being an idiot and you know it. You're here getting shit-faced while Tessa's hurt, and you don't even care!" he yells.

"Stop yelling at me! Fuck!" I twist my fingers into my hair, tugging at the roots. "I do care. But she isn't going to believe anything I say!"

"Do you blame her? You should have just come home, or how about this, never left at all?" he says and pours my beer down the drain. "How can you be so uncaring? She loves you so much." He goes to the refrigerator and hands me a bottle of water.

"I'm not uncaring. I'm just sick of waiting for some shit to happen. You were babbling on and on about your fucking perfect love life and making sacrifices, blah, blah. Then Tess goes and says his damn name." I roll my head back, staring at the ceiling for a moment.

"Whose name?" he asks.

"Zed. She said his name in her sleep. Clear as day, like she wanted him to be there instead of me."

"In her sleep?" he asks, and I can hear the sarcasm in his voice.

"Yes. Sleeping or not, she said his name instead of mine."

He rolls his eyes. "You do realize how ridiculous this sounds, don't you? Tessa said Zed's name while she was sleeping, so you go out and get drunk? You're making a big deal out of this for no reason."

The water bottle crunches and collapses in my hand from my grip.

"You don't even—" I start, but then hear keys and the sound of the front lock turning and opening.

I turn around and see her come through the door. *Tessa.*

. . . and Zed. Zed next to her.

I can't see straight as I get up and move toward them. "What the fuck is this shit?" I scream.

Tessa takes a step back, stumbles, and catches herself on the wall behind her. "Hardin, stop!" she yells at me.

"No! Fuck this! I'm sick of you coming around every time shit goes down!" I say and shove my hands against Zed's chest.

"Stop it!" Tessa yells again.

"Please," she says, then looks at Landon. "What are you doing here?" she asks him.

"I . . . I came to talk to him."

I nod sarcastically. "*Actually*, he came here trying to fight me."

Tessa's eyes nearly pop out of their sockets. "What?"

"I'll tell you later," Landon says.

Zed is breathing hard and he's staring at her. How could she bring him here after everything? Of course she'd go running to him. The man of her *dreams*.

Tessa turns to Zed and puts a gentle hand on his shoulder. "Thanks for bringing me home, Zed. I really appreciate it, but it's probably best you go."

He eyes me. "Are you sure?" he asks.

"Yes, I am. Thank you so much. Landon's here, and I'll be going to his parents' place tonight."

Zed nods in agreement—*like he gets enough of a say to agree to anything!*—then turns and leaves. Tessa closes the door behind him.

I can't control my anger as Tessa turns to me with a scowl on her face. "I'm getting my clothes." She walks into the bedroom.

I follow her, of course.

"Why did you call him for a ride?" I shout behind her.

"Why did you go drinking with this Carly girl? Oh, wait, you were probably complaining how *needy* and *full of expectations* your girlfriend is," she snaps.

"Oh, let me guess how quick you were to unload to Zed about how fucked up I am," I growl back at her.

"No! I didn't tell him anything, actually. I'm sure he already knows it."

"Are you going to let me explain my side of this?" I ask her.

"Sure," she remarks, attempting to pull her suitcase from the top shelf in the closet. I move to help her.

"Move," she snaps, obviously out of patience with my bullshit.

I step back and let her get the case down. "I shouldn't have left last night," I tell her.

"Really?" she sarcastically says.

"Yes, really. I shouldn't have left and I shouldn't have drunk so much—but I didn't cheat on you. I wouldn't do that. I only slept at her house because I was too drunk to drive—that's it," I explain.

She crosses her arms and gets that classic mad-girlfriend pose. "Then why lie?"

"I don't know . . . because I knew you wouldn't believe me if I told you."

"Well, cheaters usually don't admit when they cheat."

"I didn't cheat on you," I tell her. She sighs, obviously not convinced.

"It's really hard to believe you when you blatantly lie all the time. This time isn't any different."

"I know. I'm sorry for lying before, about everything, but I wouldn't cheat on you." I put my arms in the air.

She neatly places a folded shirt in her suitcase. "Like I said, cheaters don't admit they cheated. If you didn't have anything to hide, you wouldn't have lied."

"It's not that big of a deal, I didn't do anything with her," I say, defending myself as she adds another article of clothing.

"So what if I got wasted and stayed the night at Zed's house? What would you do?" she asks me, and the thought nearly sends me over the edge.

"I'd fucking kill him."

"So it's not a big deal when you do it, only if it were me?" She calls me out on my double standard. "None of this even matters— you made it clear that I'm only temporary in your life," Tessa says. She walks out of the room and into the bathroom across the hall to get her toiletries. She really is going with Landon to my father's house. This is bullshit. She isn't temporary to me, how could she even think that? Probably because of all the shit I said to her last night and my lack of words today.

"You know I'm not going to let this go," I tell her when she zips her suitcase.

"Well, I'm leaving."

"Why? You know you'll be back." My anger speaks for me.

"That's exactly why I'm leaving," she says, her voice shaky as she grabs her suitcase and leaves the room without looking back.

When I hear the front door slam shut, I lean my back against the wall and slide to the floor.

chapter seventy-nine

TESSA

Nine days. Nine days have gone by without a single word from Hardin. I didn't think it was possible for me to go a single day without speaking to him, let alone nine. It feels like one hundred, honestly, though each hour does hurt microscopically less than the prior one. It hasn't been easy, not even close to that. Ken made a call to Mr. Vance asking that I be allowed to take the rest of the week off, which only meant missing one day anyway.

I know I'm the one who left, the one who walked away, but it kills me that he hasn't even tried to get in touch with me. I have always given more in the relationship, and this was his chance to show me how he truly feels. I guess in a way he's showing me—it's just that what he feels is the opposite of what I had desperately wanted. Needed.

I know that Hardin loves me, I do. However, I also know that if he loves me as much as I thought he did, he would have made it a point to show me by now. He said he wasn't going to let this go, but he did. He let it go, and he let me go. The part that scares me the most is that the first week I was walking around completely lost. I was lost without Hardin. Lost without his witty comments. Lost without his crude remarks. Lost without his assurance and his confidence. Lost without the way he'd sometimes draw circles on my hand while holding it between his, the way he'd kiss me for no reason and smile at me when he thought I wasn't looking. I don't want to be lost without him; I want to be strong. I want my days and nights to be just the same whether

I'm alone or not. I'm beginning to suspect I may always be alone, as dramatic as the thought seems; I wasn't happy with Noah, yet Hardin and I didn't work. Maybe I'm like my mother in that way. Maybe I'm better off alone.

I didn't want it to be over this way, so cut-and-dried. I wanted to talk about everything, I wanted him to answer my calls so we could come to some sort of agreement. I just needed space, I needed a break from him to show him that I'm not his doormat. It backfired on me because he obviously doesn't care as much as I thought he did. Maybe this was his plan all along: get me to break up with him. I've known a few girls who go that route when leaving their boyfriends.

During the first day I did expect a call, text, or hell, I really expected Hardin to come bursting through the door screaming at the top of his lungs and causing a scene while his family and I sat in the dining room in silence, no one quite sure what to say to me. When that didn't happen, I lost it. Not crying-in-the-corner, feeling-sorry-for-myself lost it. I mean I lost myself. Every second I lived in anticipation of Hardin coming back to grovel for my forgiveness. I almost gave in that day. I almost went back to the apartment. I was ready to tell him to hell with marriage, I don't care if he lies to me every day and doesn't respect me, as long as he never leaves me. Thankfully, I snapped out of that and salvaged some respect for myself.

Day three was the worst. Day three was when the realization really began to hit me. Day three was when I finally spoke after three days of near silence, having only muttered a simple yes or no to Landon or Karen during their awkward attempts to engage me in conversation. The only sounds that actually came out were a strangled sob and a choppy explanation through tears of why my life would be better, easier, without him that even I didn't believe. Day three was when I finally looked in the mirror at my dirty and bruised face, my eyes swollen to the point of barely opening. Day three was when I fell to the floor, finally praying to God to make the pain disappear. No one can handle this pain, I told Him. Not even me. Day three I called him, I couldn't help myself. I told myself that if he answers we would work it out and both come to a compromise, apologizing profusely and promising to never leave each other again. Instead, I got his voicemail after two rings, proving that he rejected the call.

Day four, I slipped and called him again. This time he had the courtesy to let it ring to voicemail instead of pressing ignore. Day four was when I realized how much more I actually care for him than he does me. Day four was when I spent the entire day in bed reliving the few times he actually told me how he felt about me. I began to realize that most of our relationship and how I portrayed his feelings for me in my mind was just that . . . in my mind. I began to realize that while I was thinking we could do this, we could make this work forever, he wasn't thinking about me at all.

That was the day I decide to join the ranks of normal teenagers and had Landon show me how to download music onto my phone. Once I started, I couldn't stop. Over one hundred songs were added, and headphones were put in my ears and barely removed for almost twenty-four hours. The music helps a lot. To hear about other people's pain reminds me that I'm not the only one to suffer in life. I'm not the only one who loved someone who didn't love them enough to fight for them.

Day five was when I finally showered and attempted to go to class. I went to yoga, hoping that I could handle the memories it would evoke. I felt strange walking around in a sea of cheery college students. I used all the energy I had in hoping that I wouldn't run into Hardin on campus. I was past the stage of wanting him to call. I managed to drink half of my coffee that morning, and Landon told me that the color was coming back into my cheeks. No one seemed to notice me, and that was exactly what I wanted.

Professor Soto assigned us to write down our biggest fears when it comes to life and how they relate to faith and God. "Are you afraid to die?" he asked us. *Aren't I already dead?* I answered silently.

Day six was a Tuesday. I began to speak in sentences, broken sentences that usually didn't relate to the subject at hand, but no one had the heart to call me out on it. I returned to Vance. Kimberly couldn't meet my eyes for the first part of the day, but she finally attempted to have a conversation, which I couldn't bring myself to participate in. She mentioned a dinner, and I reminded myself to ask her again when I can think straight. The day was spent staring at the first page of a manuscript that, no matter how many times I read and reread it, wouldn't soak in. I ate that day, more than just the rice or a banana I had in the days before. Karen made a ham—I only noticed because it reminded me that she made one for the dinner Hardin and I had here in the beginning. The images from that night, the picture of him sitting next to me and holding my hand under the table, sent me back into my tragic state, making me spend the night in the bathroom vomiting up the small bit of food I had consumed.

As day seven dragged on I began to imagine what would happen if I didn't have to feel this pain anymore. What if I just disappeared? The thought terrified me—not because of my death, but because my mind was capable of going to such a dark place. That thought snapped me out of my downward spiral and brought me to the closest thing to reality my mind can handle. I changed my shirt and vowed to never step foot in Hardin's bedroom again, no matter what happened. I began to look up apartments that I could afford close to Vance, and online classes at WCU. I enjoy academics too much to close myself off and take online classes, so I ultimately decided against it, but I found a few apartments to look into.

Day eight I smiled, briefly, but everyone noticed. Day eight was the first morning that I grabbed my usual donut and coffee when I arrived at Vance. I kept it down and even went back for more. I saw Trevor, who told me I looked beautiful despite my wrinkled clothes and hollow eyes. Day eight was the shift, day eight was the first day that only half of my time was spent wishing that things had gone differently between Hardin and me. I heard Ken and Karen discussing Hardin's birthday in a few days, and I was surprised to only feel a slight burn in my chest at the sound of his name.

Day nine is today.

"I'll be downstairs!" Landon calls through the door of "my" bedroom.

No one has even mentioned me leaving, or where I would go if I did. I'm grateful for it, but at the same time I know my presence will eventually be a burden. Landon keeps assuring me that I can stay as long as I need to, and Karen reminds me how much she enjoys my company multiple times a day. But at the end of the day, they're Hardin's family. I want to make a move forward, decide where I should go and where I should live, and I'm no longer afraid.

I cannot, and refuse to, spend another day crying over a dishonest boy with tattoos who doesn't love me anymore.

When I see Landon downstairs, he's taking a large bite of a bagel; a dab of cream cheese rests in the corner of his mouth and his tongue darts out to retrieve it. "Morning." He smiles, his cheek full and eyes wide.

"Morning," I repeat and pour a glass of water.

He continues to stare at me while I sip my water. "What?" I finally ask him.

"You . . . well . . . you look great," he says.

"Thank you. I decided to shower and come back from the

dead," I joke, and he smiles slowly as if he's unsure about my mental state. "Really, it's fine," I assure him, and he takes another bite of his bagel, finishing it.

I decide to put one in the toaster for myself and try not to notice Landon staring at me like I'm an animal in a zoo.

"I'm ready whenever you are," I tell him after finishing my breakfast.

"Tessa, you look so gorgeous today!" Karen exclaims when she enters the kitchen.

"Thank you." I smile at her.

Today's the first day that I've taken the time to get ready, really ready and presentable. The last eight days I have gone far away from my usual neat appearance. Today I feel like myself. My new self. My "After Hardin" self. Day nine is my day.

"That dress is flattering." Karen compliments me again.

The yellow dress that Trish got me for Christmas fits well and it's very casual. I'm not going to make the same mistake as last time and attempt to wear heels to classes, so my Toms it is. Half of my hair is pinned back, with a few loose curls tapering over my face. My makeup is subtle, but I think it suits me well. My eyes burned slightly as I dragged the brown liner underneath my eye . . . makeup surely wasn't on my list of priorities during my downward spiral.

"Thank you so much." I smile again.

"Have a great day." Karen smiles, clearly surprised but very pleased at my return to the real world.

This must be what it's like to have a caring mother, someone to send you off to school with kind and encouraging words. Someone unlike my mother.

My mother . . . I have dodged all calls from her, and thankfully so. She was the last person I wanted to speak to, but now that I can breathe without wanting to rip my heart from my chest, I actually want to call her.

"Oh, Tessa, will you be riding with us to Christian's house on Sunday?" Karen asks just as I reach the door.

"Sunday?"

"The dinner they're having to celebrate their move to Seattle?" she tells me as if I should know this already. "Kimberly said she told you about it? If you don't want to go, I know they'll understand," she assures me.

"No, no. I want to go. I'll ride with you." I smile. I am ready for this. I can be in public, in a social setting, without cracking. My subconscious is mute for the first time in nine days, and I thank her before following Landon outside.

The weather mirrors my mood, sunny and somewhat warm for the end of January. "Are you going on Sunday?" I ask him once we get in the car.

"No, I'm leaving tonight, remember?" he replies.

"What?"

He looks at me with a wrinkled brow. "I'm going to New York for the weekend. Dakota is moving into her apartment there. I told you a few days ago."

"I'm so sorry, I should've paid more attention to you instead of making it all about me," I tell him. I can't believe how selfish I've been to not even pay attention to him telling me about Dakota's move to New York.

"No, it's okay. I only briefly mentioned it, anyway. I didn't want to rub it in your face when you were . . . well, you know."

"A zombie?" I finish for him.

"Yes, a very scary zombie," he jokes, and I smile for the fifth time in nine days. It feels nice.

"When will you be back?" I ask Landon.

"Monday morning. I'll miss Religion, but I'll be there right after."

"Wow, that's exciting. New York will be incredible." I would love to escape, to get out of here for a while.

"I was worried about going and leaving you here," he tells me, and guilt fills me.

"Don't be! You already do way too much for me; it's time I do things for myself. I don't want you to ever think about not doing something for yourself because of me. I'm so sorry that I made you feel that way," I tell him.

"It's not your fault, it's his," he reminds me, and I nod.

My headphones go back into my ears, and Landon smiles.

IN RELIGION, PROFESSOR SOTO chooses the subject of pain. For a moment I swear he's done it on my behalf, to torture me, but when I begin to write about how pain can cause people to turn to or away from their faith and God, I'm thankful for this torture. My entry ends up being filled with thoughts about how pain can change you, how pain can make you much stronger, and in the end you don't need faith as much. You need yourself. You need to be strong and not allow pain to push you or pull you into anything.

I end up going back to the coffeehouse before yoga to acquire more energy. On my way back to yoga I pass the environmental studies building and my mind goes to Zed. I wonder if he's in there now. I assume he is, but I don't have a clue about his schedule.

Before I can overthink it, I go inside. I have a little time before my class begins, and it's less than a five-minute walk from here.

I look around the large lobby of the building. Just like I might have expected, large trees fill most of the massive space. Sticking to the theme, the ceiling is mostly skylights, giving the illusion that it's almost nonexistent.

"Tessa?"

I turn, and indeed, there is Zed, wearing a lab coat and thick safety goggles on top of his head that push his hair back.

"Hey . . ." I say.

He smiles. "What are you doing in here? Did you change your major?"

I adore the way his tongue hides behind his teeth when he smiles, I always have. "I was looking for you, actually."

"You were?" He seems astounded.

chapter eighty

HARDIN

Nine days.

Nine days have gone by without speaking to Tessa. I didn't think it was possible for me to go a single day without speaking to her, let alone nine fucking days. It feels like one thousand, and each hour is more painful than the last.

When she left the apartment that night, I waited and waited to hear her footsteps rush through the door, and I waited for her voice to begin screaming at me. It didn't come. I sat on the floor waiting and waiting. It never came. She never came.

I finished the beer in my fridge and smashed the evidence against the wall. The next morning when I woke up and she was still gone, I packed my shit. I got on a plane to get the fuck out of Washington. If she was going to come back, it would have been that night. I needed to get out of there and get some space. With alcohol on my breath and stains on my white T-shirt, I left for the airport. I didn't call my mum before I got there; it's not like she had anything going on anyway.

If Tessa calls me before I get on the flight, I'll turn around. But if not, then too bad, I kept thinking. She had her chance to come back to me. She does every other time, no matter what I do, so why is this time so different? It's not like I did anything, really; I lied to her, but it was a small-ass lie and she overreacted.

If anyone should be pissed off, it's me. She brought Zed to my fucking house. On top of that, Landon comes barging in like the fucking Hulk and slams me into the wall? What the actual fuck.

This whole situation is utterly fucked up and it's not my fault. Well, maybe it is, but she can come crawling back to me, not the other way around. I love her, but I'm not making the first move.

Day one was spent mostly on the airplane sleeping off my hangover. I got many dirty looks from snobby-ass flight attendants and assholes in business suits, but I could give a fuck less. They don't mean shit to me. I took a cab to my mum's and nearly choked the driver. Who charges that much for a fucking ten-mile cab ride?

My mum was shocked and happy to see me. She cried for a few minutes, but thankfully she stopped when Mike appeared. Apparently the two of them have begun to move her things into his house, and she plans on selling hers. I don't give a shit about that house, so it's no skin off my back. That place is full of shit memories with my drunk asshole of a dad.

It's nice to be able to think these things without Tessa's influence. I would feel slightly guilty being rude to my mum and her boyfriend if Tessa were here with me.

So thank God she isn't.

Day two was exhausting as shit. I spent the entire afternoon listening to my mum talk about her plans for the summer and dodged her questions about why I'm home. I kept telling her if I wanted to talk about it I would. I came here for some goddamn peace, and all I get is more annoyance. I ended up at the pub down the street by eight. A pretty brunette with the same color eyes as Tessa smiled at me and offered me a drink that night. I declined somewhat politely, my kindness only coming out because of the color of her eyes. The longer I stared at them, the more I realized they weren't the same as Tessa's. They were dull and held no life behind them. Tessa's eyes are the most intriguing shade of gray that appears blue at first glance, until you really look at them. They're nice, as far as eyes go. *Why the fuck am I sitting at a pub thinking about eyeballs? Fuck.*

I saw the disappointment in my mum's eyes when I stumbled

through the door after two in the morning, but I did my best to ignore it, mumbling a shit apology before forcing my way up the stairs.

Day three was when it started. Small thoughts of Tessa kept sneaking in at the most random times. While watching my mum hand-wash the dishes, I thought of Tessa loading the dishwasher constantly, making sure there was never a single dirty dish lying in the sink.

"We're going to the fair today. Would you like to come?" my mum asked.

"No."

"Please, Hardin, you're here visiting, and you've barely spoken to me or spent any time with me."

"No, Mum." I dismiss her.

"I know why you're here," she said softly.

I slammed my cup down on the table and stormed out of the kitchen.

I knew she would catch on that I was running, hiding really, from reality. I'm not sure what type of reality there is without Tessa, but I'm not ready to deal with the shit, so why does she have to pester me about it? If Tessa doesn't want to be with me, then to hell with her. I don't need her—I am better off alone, the way I had planned to be all along.

Seconds later my phone rang, but I ignored the call as soon as I saw her name. Why did she call me? To tell me she hates me or she needs her name off the lease, I was sure.

Goddammit, Hardin, why did you do that? I kept asking myself. I didn't have a good enough answer.

Day four began the worst way possible.

"Hardin, go upstairs!" she's begging. No, not this again. One of the men slaps her across her face and she looks at the staircase; her eyes meet mine and I scream. Tessa.

"Hardin! Wake up, Hardin! Please wake up!" my mum screamed and shook me awake.

"Where is she? Where's Tess?" I choked, sweat soaking my skin.

"She isn't here, Hardin."

"But they . . ." It took me a moment to collect my thoughts and realize it was only a nightmare. The same nightmare I've had my entire life, only this time it was so much worse. My mother's face was replaced with Tessa's.

"Shhh . . . it's okay. It was only a dream." My mum cried and tried to hug me, but I gently pushed her arms back.

"No, I'm fine," I assured her and told her to leave me alone.

I lay awake for the rest of the night trying to get the image out of my head, but I couldn't.

Day four continued just as it started. My mum ignored me all day, which I thought I would want but it turned out I was sort of . . . lonely. I began to miss Tessa. I kept finding myself looking next to me to talk to her, to wait for her to say something that was sure to make me smile. I wanted to call her, my finger traced over that green button over one hundred times, but I couldn't bring myself to do it. I can't give her what she wants, and that isn't going to be good enough for her. It's better this way. I spent the afternoon looking up how much it would cost me to move my shit back here to England. This is where I'm going to end up anyway, so I might as well get it over with.

We would never work, Tessa and me. I always knew we wouldn't last. We couldn't. It wasn't possible for us to be together always. She's too damn good for me and I know it. Everyone knows it. I see the way people turn to stare at us everywhere we go, and I know they're wondering why that beautiful girl is with me.

I had been staring at my phone while downing a half bottle

of whiskey for hours before I turned off the light and fell asleep. I thought I heard the buzzing of my phone on the nightstand, but I was too drunk to sit up and answer. The nightmare came again; this time Tessa's nightgown was soaked in blood and she cried for me to go away, to leave her there on that couch.

Day five I woke up to a flashing red light on my phone indicating that yet again I'd missed her call, only this time it wasn't intentional. Day five was when I stared at her name on the screen before looking at picture after picture of her. When did I take so many? I hadn't realized how many pictures I had snapped without her paying any mind.

While looking through the pictures, I kept remembering the way her voice sounds. I never liked American accents—they bore me and they're annoying—but Tessa's voice is perfect. Her accent is perfect, and I could listen to her speak all day, every single day. Will I ever hear her voice again?

This one's my favorite, I thought at least ten times while looking through the photos. I finally settled on a picture of her lying on her stomach on the bed, her legs crossed in the air and her hair down, tucked behind her ear. She had her chin resting on one of her hands and her lips slightly parted as she took in the words in front of her on the screen of her e-reader. I snapped the picture the moment she caught me staring, the exact moment that a smile, the most beautiful smile, appeared on her face. She looked so happy to be looking at me in this picture. Does . . . well, *did* she always look at me that way?

That day, day five, was when the weight appeared on my chest. A constant reminder of what I'd done, and most likely lost. I should have called her that day while staring at her pictures. Did she stare at my pictures? She only has one to this day, and ironically I found myself wishing I'd have allowed her to take more. Day five was when I threw my phone against the wall in hopes of smashing it, but only cracked the screen. Day five was when

I desperately wished she would call me. If she called me, then it would be okay, everything would be okay. We'd both apologize and I'd go home. If she was the one to call me, then I wouldn't feel guilty for coming back into her life. I wondered if she was feeling the same way I was. Was every day getting harder for her? Did every second without me make it harder for her to breathe?

I began to lose my appetite that day. I just wasn't hungry. I missed her cooking, even the simple meals that she would make for me. Hell, I missed watching her eat. I missed every goddamn thing about that infuriating girl with kind eyes. Day five was when I finally broke down. I cried like a bitch and didn't even feel bad about it. I cried and cried. I couldn't stop. I tried desperately, but she wouldn't leave my mind. She wouldn't leave me alone; she kept appearing, she kept saying she loved me, and she kept hugging me, and when I realized it was my imagination, I cried again.

Day six I woke with swollen and bloodshot eyes. I couldn't believe the way I'd broken down the previous night. The weight on my chest had magnified, and I could barely see straight. Why was I such a fuckup? Why did I continue to treat her like shit? She's the first person who has ever been able to see me, inside of me, the real me, and I treated her like shit. I blamed her for everything, when in reality it was me. It was always me—even when I didn't seem to be doing anything wrong, I was. I was rude to her when she tried to talk to me about things. I yelled at her when she called me out on my bullshit. And I lied to her repeatedly. She has forgiven me for everything, always. I could always count on that, and maybe that's why I treated her the way I did, because I knew I could. I smashed my phone under my boot on day six. I went half the day without eating. My mum offered me oatmeal, but when I tried to force myself to eat it, it nearly came back up. I hadn't showered since day three, and I was a fucking wreck. I tried to listen as my mum told me the few things she needed me to get from the store, but I couldn't hear her. All I could think of was Tessa and her need to go to Conner's at least five days a week.

Tessa once told me I ruined her. Now, as I sit here trying to focus, trying to just catch my breath, I know that she was wrong. *She* ruined *me*. She got inside me and fucked me up. I had spent years building those walls—my entire life, really—and here she came in and tore them down, leaving me with nothing but rubble.

"Did you hear me, Hardin? I made a small list in case you didn't," my mum said, handing me the frilly piece of stationery.

"Yes." My voice was barely audible.

"Are you sure you're okay to go?" she asked.

"Yeah, I'm good." I stood up and tucked the list into my dirty jeans.

"I heard you last night, Hardin, if you want to—"

"Don't, Mum. Please don't." I nearly choked on my words. My mouth was so dry and my throat was aching.

"Okay." Her eyes were full of sadness as I walked out of the house to head to the store just down the road.

The list only consisted of a few items, yet I couldn't remember any of them without digging the damn paper out of my pocket. I managed to corral the few things: bread, jam, coffee beans, and some fruit. Looking at all the food in the store made my empty stomach turn. I took an apple for myself and began to force myself to eat it. It tasted like cardboard, and I could feel the small pieces hitting the pit of my stomach as I paid the elderly woman at the cash register.

I walked outside and it began to snow. The snow made me think of her, too. Everything made me think of her. My head was aching with a headache that refused to go away. I rubbed my fingers over my temples with my free hand and crossed the street.

"Hardin? Hardin Scott?" a voice called from the other side of the street. No. It couldn't be.

"Is that you?" she asked again.

Natalie.

This couldn't be happening, I kept thinking as she walked toward me with her hands full of shopping bags.

"Erm . . . hey," was all I could say, my mind frantic, my palms already beginning to sweat.

"I thought you moved?" she asked.

Her eyes were bright, not lifeless like I remembered as she cried and begged for me to let her stay at my house when she had nowhere to go.

"I did . . . I'm only visiting," I told her, and she set her bags on the sidewalk.

"Well, that's good." She smiled.

How could she be smiling at me after what I had done to her?

"Uh . . . yeah. How are you?" I forced myself to ask the girl whose life I ruined.

"I'm good, really good," she chirped and ran her hands over her swollen belly.

Swollen belly? Oh God. No, wait . . . the time line didn't add up. Holy shit, that scared me for a second.

"You're pregnant?" I asked, hoping that she was so I hadn't just insulted her.

"Yeah, six months along. And engaged!" She smiled again, holding her small hand up to show me a gold ring on her finger.

"Oh."

"Yeah, it's funny how things work out, isn't it?" She tucked her brown hair behind her ear and looked into my eyes, which were circled with blue rings from lack of sleep.

Her voice was so sweet that it made me feel a thousand times worse. I couldn't stop picturing her face as she caught all of us watching her on the small screen. She'd screamed, literally screamed, and ran from the room. I didn't follow her, of course. I just laughed at her, laughed at her humiliation and her pain.

"I'm really sorry," I blurted. It was strange, weird, and necessary. I expected her to call me names, to tell me how fucked up of a person I am, to punch me, even.

What I didn't expect was for her to wrap her arms around me and tell me she forgave me.

"How can you forgive me? I was so fucked up. I ruined your life," I said; my eyes were burning.

"No, you didn't. Well, you did at first, but in a way, it all worked out in the end," she said, and I nearly vomited on her green sweater.

"What?"

"After you . . . well, you know . . . I had nowhere to go, so I found a church, a new church since mine exiled me, and that's where I met Elijah." Her face instantly lit up at the mention of his name.

"And now here we are nearly three years later, engaged and expecting. Everything happens for a reason, I guess? Sounds cheesy, huh?" She giggled.

The sound reminded me that she was always such a sweet girl. I just hadn't given a shit; her kindness made it easier to prey on her.

"I suppose it does, but I'm really glad you found someone. I've been thinking about you lately . . . you know . . . what I did, and I felt like shit about it. I know you're happy now, but that doesn't excuse what I did to you. It wasn't until Tessa that I—" I cut myself off.

A little smile tweaked her lips. "Tessa?"

I nearly passed out from the pain. "She's, um . . . well . . . she's . . ." I stutter.

"She's what? Your wife?" Natalie's words cut straight to the core as her eyes searched my fingers for a band.

"No, she was . . . she was my girlfriend."

"Oh. So you date now?" she half teased; she could sense my pain, I was sure.

"No . . . well, only her."

"I see. And now she's not your girlfriend anymore?"

"Nope." I brought my fingers to my lip ring.

"Well, I'm sorry to hear that. I hope things work out for you, the way they have for me," she said.

"Thank you. Congratulations on the engagement and . . . baby," I said uncomfortably.

"Thank you! We expect to marry this summer."

"So soon?"

"Well, we've been engaged for two years." She laughed.

"Wow."

"It was fast, soon after we met," Natalie explained.

I felt like an asshole as soon as the words left my mouth, but I asked: "Aren't you too young?"

But she just smiled. "I'm nearly twenty-one, and it doesn't make sense to wait. I've been fortunate enough to find the person I want to spend my life with at a young age—why waste any more time when he's right in front of me asking that I do just that. I'm honored that he wants to make me his wife; there's no greater expression of love than that." As she explained, I could hear Tessa's voice saying the words instead.

"I guess you're right," I told her and she smiled.

"Oh, there he is! I have to go—I'm freezing and pregnant, not a good combination." She laughed before picking her bags up off the sidewalk and greeting a man in a sweater vest and khakis. His smile when seeing his pregnant fiancée was so bright that I swore it lit up that dreary day in England.

Day seven was long. Every day has been long. I kept thinking of Natalie and her forgiveness; it couldn't have come at a better time. Sure, I looked like hell and she knew it, but she was happy and in love. Pregnant, at that. I didn't ruin her life the way I thought I had.

And I thank God for that.

I spent the whole day in bed. I couldn't even bring myself to open the damned blinds. My mum and Mike were out all day, so I was left alone to sulk in my misery. Each day got worse. I constantly thought about what she was doing, who she was with. Was she crying? Was she lonely? Had she returned to our apartment to find me? Why hadn't she called me again?

This isn't the pain I had read about in novels. This pain isn't just in my mind, this pain isn't physical. This is a soul-aching pain, something that is ripping me apart from the inside out, and I don't think I can survive it. No one could.

This must be how Tessa feels when I hurt her. I can't imagine her fragile body withstanding this type of pain, but clearly she's stronger than she appears. She has to be to put up with me. Her mum once told me that if I really cared about her I would leave her alone; I would hurt her anyway, she said.

She was right. I should have left her alone then. I should have left her alone from that first day she walked into that dorm room. I promised myself that I would rather die than hurt her again . . . this is what this is. This is dying, this is worse than dying. It hurts worse. It has to.

I spent day eight drinking, the entire day. I couldn't stop. With each drink I prayed that her face would leave my mind, but it wouldn't. It couldn't.

You have to get your shit together, Hardin. You have to. I have to. I really do.

"Hardin . . ." *Tessa's voice sends chills down my spine.*

"Babe . . ." *she says.*

When I look up at her, she's sitting on my mum's couch with a smile on her face and a book in her lap.

"Come here, please," she whines as the door opens and a group of men step inside. No.

"There she is," says the short man who torments my dreams each night.

"Hardin?" Tessa begins to cry.

"Get away from her," I warn them as they close in on her. They don't seem to hear me.

Her nightgown is ripped off as she's thrown to the floor. Wrinkled and dirt-stained hands travel up her thighs as she whimpers my name.

"Please . . . Hardin, help me." She looks to me, but I'm frozen.

I am immobile and unable to help her. I am forced to watch as they beat her and violate her until she's lying on the floor silent and bloodied.

My mum didn't wake me, no one did. I had to finish it, all of it, and when I woke up my reality was worse than any nightmare.

DAY NINE is today.

"Did you hear about Christian Vance moving to Seattle?" my mum asks me as I push the cereal around the bowl in front of me.

"Yeah."

"That's exciting, isn't it? A new branch in Seattle."

"I suppose it is."

"He's having a dinner party on Sunday. He thought you'd be there."

"How do you know?" I ask her.

"He told me, we talk from time to time." She looks away and refills her coffee mug.

"What for?"

"Because we can—now eat your cereal." She scolds me like a child, but I don't have the energy to come up with a snappy remark.

"I don't want to go," I tell her and force the spoon to my mouth.

"You may not see him again for a while."

"So? I barely see him now anyway."

She looks as if she has something else to say, but she keeps quiet.

"Have you got any aspirin?" I ask, and she nods before disappearing to retrieve some.

I don't want to go to a stupid fucking dinner party celebrating Christian and Kimberly leaving for Seattle. I'm tired of everyone always talking about Seattle, and I know Tessa will be there. The pain at the idea of seeing her tackles me and nearly knocks me out of the chair. I have to stay away from her, I owe it to her. If I can stay here for a few more days, weeks even, we can both move on. She'll find someone like Natalie's fiancé, someone much better for her than me.

"I still think you should go," my mum says again as I swallow the aspirin, knowing they won't help.

"I can't go, Mum . . . even if I wanted to. I would have to leave first thing in the morning and I'm not ready to leave."

"You mean you aren't ready to face what you left," she says.

I can't hold it in any longer. I bury my face in my hands as I let the pain take over, I let it drown me. I welcome it, and hope it kills me.

"Hardin . . ." My mum's voice is quiet and comforting as she hugs me and I shake in her arms.

chapter eighty-one

TESSA

The moment Karen leaves to take Landon to the airport, I instantly feel it. I feel the loneliness creeping in, but I have to ignore it. I have to. I'm fine by myself. I walk downstairs to the kitchen after my stomach's refusal to stop growling reminds me how hungry I am.

Ken is leaning against the kitchen counter, tearing back the foil wrapper on a light blue frosted cupcake. "Hey, Tessa." He smiles, taking a small bite. "Grab one."

My grandmother used to tell me that cupcakes are food for the soul. If I need anything, it's something for my soul.

"Thank you." I smile before licking a stripe across the top.

"Don't thank me, thank Karen."

"I will." This cupcake tastes incredible. Maybe it's because I've barely eaten in the last nine days, or maybe it's because cupcakes truly are good for the soul. Regardless of the reason, I finish it in less than two minutes.

After the glow of the treat washes away, I can feel that the pain is still present, steady as my heartbeat. But it's no longer overwhelming me, no longer pulling me under.

Ken surprises me by saying, "It'll get easier, and you'll find someone who is capable of loving another person besides themselves."

My stomach churns from his sudden subject change. I don't want to backtrack, I want to move forward.

"I treated Hardin's mum terribly. I know I did. I would leave for days at a time, I would lie, I would drink until I couldn't see straight. If it weren't for Christian, I don't know how Trish and Hardin would ever have made it through . . ."

With his words, I remember my anger toward Ken when I heard about the origin of Hardin's nightmares. I remember wanting to slap him right across his face for ever letting anything hurt his son in that way, so when he says this, it stirs my stored anger. I ball my fists.

"I will never be able to take any of that back, no matter how hard I wish that I could. I wasn't good for her and I knew it. She was too good for me and I knew that, too. So did everyone else. Now she has Mike, who I know will treat her the way she deserves to be treated. There's a Mike for you, too, I know it," he says, looking at me in a fatherly way. "My son hopefully will be lucky enough to find his Karen later in life when he grows up and stops fighting everything and everyone along the way."

At the mention of Hardin with "his Karen," I swallow and look away. I don't want to imagine Hardin with anyone else. It's way too soon. I do wish that for him, though; I would never wish for him to be alone for the rest of his life. I just hope he finds someone who he loves as much as Ken loves Karen so that he can have a second chance to love someone more than he loved me.

"I hope he does, too," I finally say.

"I'm sorry that he hasn't contacted you," Ken says quietly.

"It's okay . . . I stopped expecting it a few days ago."

"Anyway," he says with a sigh, "I better get upstairs to my office. I have some phone calls to make."

I'm glad he's excusing himself before we get any deeper into the conversation. I don't want to talk about Hardin anymore.

WHEN I PULL UP in front of Zed's apartment building, he's waiting outside with a cigarette behind his ear.

"You smoke?" I ask and crinkle my nose.

He seems puzzled as he climbs into my small car. "Oh, yeah. Well, sometimes. And you saw me smoke that night at the frat house, remember?" He pulls the cigarette from behind his ear and smiles. "I found this one in my room."

I laugh a little. "Yeah, after the beer pong and Hardin yelling at us that night, I guess the smoking thing slipped my mind." I give him a smile but then realize something. "But wait, so not only do you plan to smoke, you plan to smoke an old cigarette?"

"I guess so. You don't like cigarettes?"

"No, not at all. But hey, if you want to smoke, you can. Well, not in my car, obviously," I say.

His fingers move to the door, and he presses one of the small buttons. When the window is half down, he tosses the cigarette out the window.

"Then I won't smoke." He smiles and rolls it back up.

As much as I despise the habit, I have to admit there was something about the way he looked with his hair styled nearly straight up, his dark sunglasses, and his leather jacket that made that cigarette look stylish.

chapter eighty-two

HARDIN

Here you go," my mum says when she walks into my old bedroom.

She hands me a small porcelain cup on a saucer, and I sit up from the bed. "What is it?" I ask, my voice hoarse.

"Warm milk and honey," she says as I take a sip. "Remember when you were little and I used to make it when you were sick?"

"Yeah."

"She'll forgive you, Hardin," she tells me, and I close my eyes.

I finally moved on from sobbing to dry-heaving to numbness. That's all it is, is numb. "I don't think so . . ."

"She will, I saw the way she looked at you. She's forgiven you for much worse, remember?" She brushes the matted hair away from my forehead, and I don't flinch away for once.

"I know, but this time isn't like that, Mum. I ruined everything that I spent months building with her."

"She loves you."

"I can't do it anymore, I can't. I can't be who she wants me to be. I always fuck everything up. That's who I am and always will be, the guy who fucks everything up."

"That's not true, and I happen to know that you're exactly what she wants."

The cup shakes in my hand and I nearly drop it. "I know you're only trying to help, but, please . . . just stop, Mum."

"So what, then? You're just going to let her go and move on?"

I set the cup down on the side table before answering. I sigh.

"No, I couldn't move on if I wanted to, but she has to. I have to let her move on before I do any more damage."

I have to let her end up like Natalie. Happy . . . happy after everything I did to her. Happy with someone like Elijah.

"Fine, Hardin. I don't know what else to say to convince you to step up and apologize," she snaps.

"Just go. Please," I beg.

"I will. But only because I have faith in you that you'll do the right thing and fight for her."

The small cup and platter are thrown against the wall and shattered into small pieces as soon as she closes the door behind her.

chapter eighty-three

TESSA

After we have lunch at a little nondescript strip mall, we head back toward Zed's place. As we pass the campus, I finally have the courage to ask him the question I've always wanted to ask.

"Zed, what do you think would've happened if you had won?"

He's clearly caught by surprise, but he recovers after looking at his hands for a minute. "I don't know. I've thought about that a lot."

"You have?" I look at him, and his caramel eyes meet mine.

"Of course I have."

"What did you come up with?" I tuck my hair behind my ear, waiting for his answer.

"Well . . . I know I would've told you about it before I let it get that far. I always wanted to tell you. Every time I saw the two of you together, I wanted you to know." He gulps. "You have to know that."

"I do know it," I barely whisper, and he continues.

"I like to think that you could've forgiven me since I would have told you before anything happened, and we'd have gone out on dates, proper dates. Like the movies or something, and I would have had fun. You would have smiled and laughed, and I wouldn't have taken advantage of you. And I like to think that you'd eventually have fallen for me, the way you did for him, and when it was right we would have . . . and I wouldn't have told anyone. I wouldn't have given anyone a single detail about it. Hell, I wouldn't have even hung around any of them anymore because

I'd have wanted to spend every second with you, making you giggle the way you do when you think something is really funny . . . it's different from your regular laugh. That's how I know when I'm really entertaining you or you're faking it to be polite." He smiles, and my heart begins to race.

"And I would have appreciated you and not lied to you. I wouldn't have mocked you behind your back or called you names. I wouldn't have cared about my reputation and . . . and . . . I think we could have been happy. *You* could have been happy, all the time, not just sometimes. I'd like to think—"

I cut him off by grabbing the collar of his jacket and bringing my lips to his.

chapter eighty-four

TESSA

Zed's hand immediately moves to my cheek, causing the skin on the back of my neck to rise, and he pulls my arm to bring me to him. I hit my knee on the steering wheel as I climb across and mentally curse at myself for nearly ruining the moment, but he doesn't seem to notice and wraps his arms around my back, bringing me flush against his chest. My arms latch around his neck, and our mouths move in sync.

His mouth is foreign to me; it's not like Hardin's. His tongue doesn't move the same, it doesn't trace mine, and he doesn't trap my bottom lip between his teeth.

Stop it, Tessa. You need this, you need to stop thinking about Hardin. He's surely in bed with some random girl, Molly even. Oh God, if he's with Molly . . .

You could have been happy all the time, not just sometimes, Zed just said.

I know he's right—I would have been much better off with him. I deserve this. I deserve to be happy. I've suffered enough and dealt with enough of Hardin's bullshit, and he hasn't even tried to talk to me about it. Only a weak person would run back to someone who has trampled on them repeatedly. I can't be that weak, I have to be strong and move on. Or try at least.

I feel better right now, in this moment, than I've felt in the last nine days. Nine days doesn't sound like a long time until you spend it counting every single second of misery waiting for something that doesn't come. With Zed's arms around me, I can finally breathe. I can see the light at the end of the tunnel.

Zed has always been so kind to me and he's always been there. I wish he had been the one I fell for instead of Hardin.

"God, Tessa . . ." Zed moans and I tug at his hair.

I kiss him harder.

"Wait . . ." he says into my mouth, and I pull away slowly. "What is this?" He looks into my eyes.

"I . . . I don't know?" My voice is shaky and I'm out of breath.

"Me, either . . ."

"I'm sorry . . . I'm just emotional, and I've been going through a lot, and what you said to me just now made me . . . I don't know, I shouldn't have done that." I look away from him and climb off of his lap, getting back into the driver's seat.

"It's nothing to be sorry for . . . I just don't want to get the wrong idea, you know? I just want to know what this means to you," he tells me.

What does *this mean to me?* "I don't think I can answer that, not yet. I—"

"Thought so," he says, his voice slightly angry.

"I just don't know . . ."

"It's fine, I get it. You still love him."

"It's only been nine days, Zed, I can't help it." I keep managing to make new messes, each one bigger than the last.

"I know, I'm not saying that you can or will stop loving him. I just don't want to be your rebound. I just started dating someone—I haven't dated anyone since I met you, and I finally met Rebecca. Then, when I drove you home and saw the way you reacted to me dating someone, I started thinking . . . I know I'm an idiot, but I started thinking you didn't want me to move on or something." I look away from his handsome face and stare out the window.

"You aren't my rebound . . . I wanted to kiss you just now; I just don't know what I'm thinking or doing. Nothing's made sense to me for the last nine days, and I finally stopped thinking about him when I kissed you and it felt amazing. I felt like I could do this. I could get over him, but I know that it's not fair for me to use you that way. I'm just confused and irrational. I'm sorry for making you cheat on your girlfriend; that wasn't my intention. I just—"

"I don't expect you to move on so soon. I know how deep his claws are into you."

He has no idea.

"Just tell me one thing," Zed says and I nod. "Tell me that you'll at least try to allow yourself to be happy. He hasn't even called you, not once. He's done so much shit to you and he hasn't even tried to fight for you. If that were me, I'd be fighting for you. I would have never let you go in the first place." He reaches across and tucks an errant lock of hair behind my ear. "Tessa, I don't need an answer right now, I just need to know that you're ready to try to be happy. I know you aren't ready for any type of relationship with me, but maybe someday you will be."

My mind is racing, my heart is racing and aching all at once, and the air has been sucked out of the car. I want to tell him that I *can* try and I *will* try to allow myself this, but the words won't come. That small smile that Hardin has on his face in the mornings when I finally get him to wake up after complaining about my alarm clock, the way his raspy morning voice says my name, the way he tries to force me to stay in bed with him and I end up squealing and running from the room, the way he likes his coffee black just like me, the way I love him more than anything in the entire world and I wish he could be different. I wish he could be exactly the same, only different—it doesn't make sense to me, and I know it won't make sense to anyone else, but that's the way it is.

I wish I didn't love him as much as I do. I wish he hadn't made me fall in love with him.

"I get it. It's okay," Zed says, and he tries his best to smile but fails miserably.

"I'm sorry . . ." I say, and mean it more than he could ever know.

He climbs out of the car and shuts the door behind him, and I'm left alone, again.

"Fuck!" I scream and hit my hands against the steering wheel, reminding me of Hardin once again.

chapter eighty-five

HARDIN

I wake up soaked in my own sweat again. I had forgotten how miserable it was to wake up this way nearly every night. I had thought the sleepless nights were a thing of the past, but now the past is haunting me yet again.

I glance at the clock: it's six in the morning. I need sleep, real sleep. Uninterrupted sleep. I need her, I need Tess. Maybe if I close my eyes and pretend that she's here, I'll be able to go back to sleep . . .

I close my eyes and try to imagine her head on my chest as I lie on my back. I try to remember the way her hair always smells like vanilla, the way she breathes heavily in her sleep. For a moment I feel her, feel her warm skin against my bare chest . . . I'm officially going fucking crazy.

Fuck.

Tomorrow will be better, it has to be. I've been thinking that for the last . . . ten days now. If I could just see her one more time, it wouldn't be so bad. Just once. If I saw her smile one more time, I could live with myself for letting her go. Will she be at Christian's party tomorrow? Seems pretty likely . . .

I stare at the ceiling and try to imagine what she'd be wearing if she was to go. Would she wear the white dress that she knows I love so much? Will her hair be curled and tucked behind her ear or will she pull it back? Will she wear makeup even though she doesn't need to?

Goddammit.

I sit up and get out of bed. There is no way I can go back to sleep. When I get downstairs, Mike is sitting at the kitchen table, reading the paper.

"Good morning, Hardin," he says to me.

"Hey," I mumble back and pour myself a cup of coffee.

"Your mum is still asleep."

"You don't say . . ." I roll my eyes.

"Your mum is really happy to have you here."

"Yeah, sure. I've been a dick the entire time."

"Yeah, that's true. But she was glad to have you open up to her. She's always been so worried about you . . . until she met Tessa. Then she wasn't so worried anymore."

"Well, guess she'll have to be worried again." I sigh. Why is he trying to have a fucking heart-to-heart with me at six in the fucking morning?

"I wanted to bring something to your attention," he says and turns to me.

"Okay . . . ?" I eye him.

"Hardin, I love your mum and I intend to marry her."

I spit my coffee back into my cup. "*Marry* her? Are you mad?"

He raises a brow. "And why would my intention to marry her be mad?"

"I don't know . . . she's already been married . . . and you're our neighbor . . . her neighbor."

"I can take care of her the way she should have been taken care of her entire life. If you don't approve, I'm sorry, but I thought I'd let you know that when the time is right, I'll be asking her to spend her life with me, officially."

I don't know what to say to this man, the man who has lived next door to me my entire life, the man who I've never seen angry, not even once. He loves her, I can tell, but this is too weird for me to comprehend right now.

"Okay then . . ."

"Okay then," he echoes back and then looks behind me.

My mum walks into the kitchen with her robe wrapped tight around her and her hair in a mess on her head. "What are you doing up, Hardin? Are you going back home?" she asks.

"No, I couldn't sleep. And *this* is home," I tell her and take another drink of coffee. This is my home.

"Hmm . . ." she sleepily replies.

chapter eighty-six

TESSA

I'm getting sucked back in, back under. The memories that I shared with Hardin tug at my feet, attempting to pull me under the water.

I roll the windows down in an attempt to get some air. Zed is so sweet to me, he's understanding and kind. He's dealt with a lot for me and I've always brushed him aside. If I could just stop being foolish, I could try with him. I can't even imagine being in a relationship right now, or really anytime soon. But maybe with time I could. I don't want Zed to break up with Rebecca because of me if I can't give him an answer, or even a hint of an answer.

As I drive back to Landon's house, I'm more confused than ever.

If I could just talk to Hardin, just see him once more, I could get closure. If I could hear him say that he doesn't care, if he would be cruel to me just one last time, I could give Zed the chance, give myself the chance.

Before I can stop myself, I grab my phone and press the button that I've been avoiding since day four. If he ignores me, I can move on. We are officially over if he doesn't answer my call. If he tells me that he's sorry and that we can work on it . . . no. I put the phone back on the seat. I've come too far to call him again, to break down again.

But I need to know.

The line goes straight to voicemail. "Hardin . . ." The words leave my lips at a frantic rate. "Hardin . . . it's Tessa. I . . . well, I need to talk to you. I'm in my car and I'm so confused . . ." I begin to cry. "Why haven't you even tried to contact me? You just let me leave, and here I am pathetically calling you and crying into your voicemail. I need to know what happened to us. Why was this time different—why didn't we fight it out? Why didn't you fight for me? I deserve to be happy, Hardin," I sob and hang the phone up.

Why did I just do that? Why did I break down and call him? I'm such an idiot—he's probably going to listen to it and laugh. He'll probably let whatever girl he's hooking up with listen to the message, and they'll laugh and laugh at my expense. I pull into a deserted parking lot to gather my thoughts before getting into another accident.

I stare at the phone and breathe in and out in order to stop crying. Twenty minutes go by and he still hasn't returned my call, or even texted me.

Why am I sitting in a parking lot at ten at night crying and calling him? I've fought myself for the last nine days to get myself to be strong, yet here I am falling apart, again. I can't let this happen. I pull out of the parking lot and drive back to Zed's apartment. Hardin is obviously too busy to be bothered with me, and Zed is here, honest and always here for me. I park next to his truck and take a deep breath. I have to think of myself first and what I want.

As I race up the stairs to Zed's door, I'm at peace with myself.

I bang on the door, shifting back and forth waiting for it to open. What if I'm too late and he doesn't answer the door? I'll get what I deserve, I suppose. I should've known better than to kiss him in the middle of all of this.

When the door opens I nearly stop breathing. Zed is wearing only black gym shorts, his inked chest exposed.

"Tessa?" He gapes, clearly surprised.

"I . . . I don't know what I can give you, but I want to try," I tell him.

He runs his hand over his black hair and takes a deep breath. He's going to reject me, I know it.

"I'm sorry. I shouldn't have come . . ." I can't handle any more rejection.

I turn toward the stairs and take two at a time before a hand hooks my arm and Zed turns me around to face him.

He doesn't say anything at all; he just takes my hand in his and leads me back up the stairs and inside his apartment.

Zed is calm, so quiet and understanding as we sit on his couch, him on one side and me on the other. He's completely different from what I'm used to with Hardin. When I don't want to talk, he doesn't push me to talk. When I can't think of an explanation for my actions, he doesn't call me out. And when I tell him that I'm not comfortable sleeping in his bed with him, he brings me the softest blanket and a somewhat clean pillow and lays them on his couch.

THE NEXT MORNING when I wake up, my neck is killing me. Zed's old couch isn't the most comfortable, but I slept well, considering.

"Hey," he says when he walks into the living room.

"Hey." I smile.

"Did you sleep okay?" he asks me, and I nod.

Zed was incredible last night. He didn't even blink when I asked to sleep on the couch. He listened to me talk about Hardin and how it had all gone wrong. He told me how he cares for Rebecca but now doesn't know what to do because he's always thought about me, even after meeting her. I felt guilty for the first hour while crying to him, but as the night went on, the tears turned to smiles, which shifted to laughs. My stomach literally hurt from laughing about stupid memories from our childhoods by the time we decided to go to bed.

It's nearly two in the afternoon now, the latest I think I've ever slept, but that's what happens when you stay up until seven in the morning.

"Yes; you?" I stand and fold the blanket he lent me. I vaguely remember him draping it over me while I drifted off to sleep.

"Same." He grins and sits on the couch. His hair is wet, and his skin is glistening like he just got out of the shower.

"Where should I put this?" I ask him, referring to the blanket.

"Wherever; you didn't have to fold it." He laughs.

My mind goes to the closet in the apartment and how Hardin shoves random things in there just to drive me insane.

"Do you have anything going on today?" I ask him.

"I worked this morning, so no."

"Already?"

"Yeah, from nine to noon." He smiles. "I basically only went in to fix my truck."

I forgot that Zed works as a mechanic. I don't really know much about him at all. Except that he has pretty good stamina if he can sleep two hours and then work like that.

"Environmental studies prodigy by day, grease monkey by night?" I tease, and he chuckles.

"Something like that; what are your plans?"

"I don't know. I need to get something to wear to my boss's dinner party tomorrow." For a moment I think about asking Zed to come along, but that would be wrong. I'd never do that; it would make everyone uncomfortable, including myself.

Zed and I had come to an agreement that we weren't going to push anything. We're just going to spend time together and see where it goes. He isn't going to push me to move on from Hardin; we both know that I need more time before I can consider dating anyone. I have too much to figure out—like finding somewhere to live, for starters.

"I can come along if you want? Or maybe we could see a movie later?" he asks nervously.

"Yeah, either one is fine." I smile and check my phone.

No missed calls. No text messages. No voicemails.

Zed and I end up ordering pizza and hanging out for the majority of the day until I finally leave to go back to Landon's to take a shower. On my way back I stop by the mall right before it closes and happen upon the perfect red dress with a square neckline; it rests just above my knees. It's not too conservative but not too revealing either.

By the time I get back to Landon's, there is a note on the counter next to a plate of food that Karen put aside for me. Her and Ken went to a movie and will be back soon, it says.

I'm relieved to have the place to myself even though when they're there, I don't really notice because the house is so large. I take a shower and put on pajamas before lying down and forcing myself to catch up on my sleep.

My dreams shift back and forth between green- and golden-eyed boys.

chapter eighty-seven

TESSA

Eleven days. It's been eleven days since I've heard from Hardin, and it hasn't been easy.

But Zed's company has surely helped.

Tonight is the dinner party at Christian's, and all day I've become increasingly afraid that being around the familiar faces there will remind me of Hardin and knock at the walls that I've been building. All it will take is one small crack and I'll no longer be protected.

Finally, when it's time to go, I take a deep breath and check myself one last time in the mirror. My hair is the same way it always is, down and curled in loose waves, but my makeup is darker than usual. I slide Hardin's bracelet over my wrist; even though I know I shouldn't be wearing it, I feel naked without it. It's such a part of me now, the way he is . . . was. The dress looks even better today than it did yesterday, and I'm grateful that I've gained back the few pounds that I lost during the first few days of barely eating.

"I just want it back the way it was before. And I just want to see you back at my front door . . ." The music plays as I grab my small clutch purse. After one more beat, I pull the buds out of my ears and place them inside.

When I meet Karen and Ken downstairs, they're dressed to a T. Karen is in a long blue-and-white-patterned gown, and Ken is wearing a suit and tie.

"You look so lovely," I say to her, and her cheeks flush.

"Thank you, dear, so do you." She beams.

She is so sweet. I'm going to miss seeing her and Ken so often when I have to leave.

"I was thinking that sometime this week we could go out to the greenhouse and work a little?" she asks me as we walk to the car, my nude heels clanking loudly on the concrete driveway.

"I would love to," I tell her and climb into the back of their Volvo.

"This will be so much fun. We haven't been to a party like this in a while." Karen takes Ken's hand in hers and places it on her lap as he pulls out of the driveway.

Their affection doesn't make me envious, it reminds me that people can actually be good to each other.

"Landon will be home from New York late tonight. I'll be picking him up at two a.m.," Karen says excitedly.

"I can't wait for him to be back," I say. And I really mean it—I've missed my best friend, his words of wisdom, and his warm smile.

CHRISTIAN VANCE'S HOUSE is exactly how I had imagined it would be. Extremely modern in style, the entire structure is nearly transparent, beams and glass appearing to be the only things securing it to the hill. Every decoration and detail is styled to blend into a perfect theme throughout the entire interior. It's amazing, and reminds me of a museum in the way that nothing in it looks like it's even been touched before.

Kimberly greets us at the front door. "Thank you guys so much for coming," she says, pulling me into her arms.

"Thank you for inviting us." Ken shakes Christian's hand. "Congratulations on the big move."

I lose my breath at the sight of the water just out the back windows. Now I understand why most of the house is glass—the house sits on a large lake. The water outside seems endless, and the setting sun makes the whole panorama even more breathtaking as it reflects off the lake, nearly blinding me. That the house is on a hill and the yard is slightly sloped creates the illusion that you're floating on top of the water.

"Everyone's in here." Kimberly leads us to their dining room, which, like the rest of the house, is perfect.

None of this is my style—I prefer more old-fashioned decor—but Vance's place really is exquisite. Two elongated, rectangular dinner tables fill the space, each full of multicolored flowers and small bowls with floating candles inside for each place setting. The napkins are folded into the shape of flowers, a silver ring holding them in place. It's beautiful. So elegant and colorful, it looks like something straight from a magazine. Kimberly really has gone all out for this party.

Trevor is sitting at the table closest to the window along with a few other faces I recognize from the office, including Crystal from marketing and her soon-to-be husband. Smith is seated two chairs down and has his face buried in some sort of handheld video game.

"You look beautiful." Trevor smiles at me and rises from his seat to greet Ken and Karen.

"Thank you. How are you?" I ask.

His tie is the exact same shade of blue as his eyes, which are bright and beaming. "Great, ready for the big move!"

"I bet!" I say, but am really thinking, *If only I were able to move to Seattle now* . . .

"Trevor, it's nice to see you." Ken shakes his hand, and I look down when I feel a slight tug at my dress.

"Hi, Smith, how are you?" I ask the little boy with shining green eyes.

"Okay." He shrugs. Then, in a quiet voice, he asks, "Where's your Hardin?"

I don't know what else to say, and the way Smith called him "my Hardin" stirs something in me. The stone wall is already beginning to chip away, and I've only been here for ten minutes. "He's, um . . . he's not here right now."

"He's coming, though?"

"No, I'm sorry. I don't think he is, honey."

"Oh."

It's a terrible lie and one that anyone who knows Hardin would see through, but I tell the little guy, "But he did say to tell you hello," and I ruffle his hair a little. Now Hardin has me lying to children. Great.

Smith half smiles and sits back down at the table. "Okay. I like your Hardin."

Me, too, I want to tell him, *but he's not mine.*

Within fifteen minutes, twenty more people arrive, and Christian has turned on his super-high-tech stereo system. With only a click of a button, a soft piano melody spreads through the house. Young men in white-collared shirts begin to circle the room with trays of appetizers, and I help myself to something that looks like a small piece of bread topped with tomatoes and sauce.

"The Seattle office is breathtaking—you should see it," Christian says to a small group of us. "It's right on the water; it's two times larger than our office here. I can't believe I'm finally expanding."

I try to appear as interested as I can as a waiter hands me a glass of white wine. Well, I *am* interested—I'm just distracted. Distracted by the mention of Hardin and the idea of Seattle. As I stare out the glass wall at the water, I imagine Hardin and me moving into an apartment together amid the excitement of a new city, a new place, and new people. We would make new friends and start a new life there, together. Hardin would work for Vance again and he'd brag all day and night about how he makes more money than me, and I would fight him to be allowed to pay the cable bill.

"Tessa?"

I'm brought out of my pointless daydream by the sound of Trevor's voice. "Sorry . . ." I stutter and realize it's just the two of us now, and he's beginning or finishing a story that I wasn't even aware he was telling.

"As I was saying, my apartment is close to the new building and right in the middle of downtown—you should see the view." He smiles. "The Seattle skyline is so beautiful, especially at night."

I smile and nod. I bet it is. I bet it really, really is.

chapter eighty-eight

HARDIN

*W*hat the fuck am I doing?

I keep pacing back and forth. This was a stupid fucking idea to begin with.

I kick a stone across the driveway. What am I expecting to happen . . . that she'll run into my arms and forgive me for all the shit I have done to her? She'll suddenly believe that I didn't sleep with Carly?

I look up at Vance's gorgeous house. Tessa probably isn't even in there, and I'll look like an idiot showing up uninvited. Actually, I'll look like a dumb-ass either way. I should just leave.

Besides, this shirt is fucking itchy, and I hate dressing up. It's only a black button-up shirt, but still.

Seeing my father's car, I walk up the driveway a little bit and look inside. In the backseat is that hideous purse that Tessa brings along to every single function she attends.

So she's inside, she's in there. My empty stomach flutters at the idea of seeing her, of being close to her. *What would I even say?* I don't know. I have to explain how my days have been complete hell since I left for England and how I need her, I need her more than anything. I have to tell her that I'm an asshole and I can't believe that I fucked up the one good thing in my life, her. She's everything to me, she always will be.

I'll just go inside and get her to leave with me so we can talk—*I'm nervous, fuck am I nervous.*

I'm going to throw up. No. But if there were food in my stomach, I'm sure I would. I know I look like complete shit; I wonder if she does. Not that she ever could, but has it been as hard for her as it's been for me?

I finally reach the front door, but then turn back around. I hate being around people as it is, and there are at least fifteen cars in this driveway. Everyone will stare at me, and I'll look like a goddamned fool, which is exactly what I am.

Before I can talk myself out of it, I spin around and quickly ring the doorbell.

This is for Tessa. This is for her, I keep reminding myself when Kim opens the door with a surprised smile.

"Hardin? I didn't know you'd be here," she says. I can tell she's trying her hardest to be polite, but there's an anger coming to the surface, probably because she'll feel defensive of Tessa.

"Yeah . . . me either," I reply.

Then a new emotion—pity. It seeps into her eyes when she takes in my appearance, which is probably even worse than I imagine, since I just got off the plane and came straight here.

"Well . . . come inside, it's freezing out," she offers and waves me inside.

For a moment I'm stunned by the way Vance's house is decorated like a fucking work of art; it doesn't even look like anyone lives here. It's cool and all, but I like older things, not so Modern Art.

"We're just getting ready to eat," she tells me as I follow her into a dining room with glass walls.

And that's when I see her.

My heart stops, and a pressure lands on my chest that is so overwhelming it nearly chokes me. As she listens to someone telling her a story or something, she smiles and slides her hand across her forehead to push her hair back. The reflection of the setting sun behind her makes her glow—literally—and I can't move.

I hear her laugh, and for the first time in ten days I can

breathe. I've missed her so much, and she looks phenomenal—she always does—but the red dress she's wearing and the sun hitting her skin, the smile on her face . . . why is she smiling and laughing?

Shouldn't she be crying and shouldn't she look like hell? She giggles again, and my eyes finally discern who she's talking to, who's making her forget me.

Fucking Trevor. I hate that bastard so fucking much—I could walk over there and throw him through that glass window and no one would be able to stop me. Why the fuck is he always around her? He's a fucking twit, and I'm going to fucking kill him.

No. I need to calm down. If I hurt him right now, Tessa will never listen to me.

I close my eyes for a few seconds and talk myself down. If I stay calm she'll listen, and she'll leave here with me so we can go home, where I'll beg for her forgiveness, and she'll tell me she still loves me, and we'll make love and everything will be okay.

I continue to watch her; she looks animated as she begins to tell a story. The hand that isn't holding the glass of wine moves around as she talks and smiles. My heart races as I spot the bracelet on her wrist. She's still wearing it—she's still wearing it. That's a good sign; it has to be.

Fucking Trevor watches her intently, his expression holding an adoration for her that makes my blood boil. He looks like a love-sick puppy, and she's feeding right into it.

Has she moved on already? With him?

It would break me if she did . . . but I couldn't blame her, really. I haven't returned her calls. I haven't even bothered to purchase a new phone yet. She probably thinks I don't care, that I've moved on already, too.

My mind travels back to that quiet street in England, to Natalie's swollen belly, to Elijah's adoring smile for his fiancée. Trevor is looking at Tessa that same way.

Trevor is her Elijah. He's her second chance to have what she deserves.

The realization hits me like a ton of bricks. I need to leave. I have to get out of here and leave her alone.

It now makes sense to me why I ran into Natalie that day. I saw the girl I hurt tremendously so I wouldn't make the same mistake again with Tessa.

I have to leave. I have to get out of here before she sees me.

But the moment I admit this to myself, she looks up and her eyes meet mine. Her smile vanishes, and the glass of wine slips from her hand and shatters on the hardwood floor.

Everyone turns to look at her, but she stays focused on me. I break eye contact, and see Trevor looking at her, confused but ready to spring into action to help her.

Tessa blinks a few times, and her eyes travel to the floor. "I'm so sorry," she says frantically and bends down to try to gather the pieces of broken glass.

"Oh, please—it's okay! I'll grab a broom and some paper towels," Kimberly calls and hurries off.

I need to get the fuck out of here. I turn, ready to run. And nearly trip over a little person. I look down and see Smith, who's staring at me blankly.

"Thought you weren't coming," he says.

I shake my head and pat him on the head. "Yeah . . . I was just leaving."

"Why?"

"Because I shouldn't be here," I tell him and look over my shoulder. Trevor has grabbed the little brush from Kimberly and is helping Tessa gather the shards of glass and toss them into a small bag. There has to be some symbolism behind this, behind watching him help her pick up the pieces. Fucking metaphors.

"I don't like it either." Smith groans, and I look back at him and nod.

"Stay?" he asks innocently. Hopefully.

I look back and forth between Tessa and the kid. I don't feel as annoyed with the little guy as I once did. I don't think I have the energy to be annoyed with him.

A hand suddenly falls on my shoulder. "You should listen to him," Christian says and squeezes a little. "At least stay until after dinner. Kim has put a lot of effort into tonight," he adds with a warm smile.

I look over to where his girlfriend in her simple black dress wipes a towel across the mess Tessa made because of me. And of course, Tessa is right beside her, apologizing more than she probably needs to.

"Fine," I agree and give Christian a nod.

If I can make it through this dinner, I can make it through anything. I'll just swallow the pain that comes from watching Tessa be so complacent without me. She appeared unaffected until she saw me, and then, when she did, sadness took over her beautiful face.

I'll act the same, act like she isn't killing me with every blink of her eyes. If she's under the impression that I don't care, she'll be free to move on and finally be treated the way that she deserves.

Kimberly finishes cleaning up right as one of the waiters rings a little dinner bell. "Well, now that the show's over, it's time to eat!" she says with a laugh and sweeps her arms to guide people to the tables.

I follow Christian to a table, then pick a seat at random, not paying attention to where Tessa and her "friend" are. I play with the silverware a little, until my father and Karen come over and greet me.

"I didn't expect to see you here, Hardin," my father says.

I sigh as Karen takes the seat next to me. "Everyone keeps saying that," I say. I don't allow myself to look up from the table to find Tessa.

"Have you spoken to her?" Karen asks me almost inaudibly.

"No," I reply.

I stare at the small printed swirl pattern on the tablecloth and wait for the waiters to bring out the food. Chickens, whole fucking chickens are brought out on large platters. Bowl after bowl of sides are placed in a row along the table. Finally, I can't help but look up to find her. I look to my left, but then am surprised to find that she's sitting almost directly across from me . . . next to fucking Trevor, of course.

She's absentmindedly pushing an asparagus spear across her plate repeatedly. I know she doesn't like them, but she's too polite to not eat something someone else has prepared for her. I watch her as she closes her eyes and brings the vegetable to her mouth, and I almost smile when she tries her best to not appear disgusted as she washes the bite down with water, then pats her lips with a napkin.

She catches me staring at her, and I immediately look away. I can see the pain behind her blue-gray eyes. Pain that I've caused. Pain that will only stop if I stay away from her and let her move on.

All our unspoken words float in the air between us . . . and she directs her attention back to her plate.

I don't look up again during the sumptuous meal, of which I barely take five bites. Even when I hear Trevor talking to Tessa about Seattle, I keep my eyes averted. For the first time in my life I wish I was someone else. I would give anything to be Trevor, to be able to make her happy, and not hurt her.

Throughout the meal, Tessa answers his questions briefly, and I know she's thankful when Karen begins to talk about Landon and his longtime girlfriend in New York.

The sounds of a fork against a glass ring through the room, and Christian stands up and says, "If I could have everyone's attention, please . . ." He taps it one more time, then chuckles and adds, "I better stop before I break it," giving Tessa a whimsical look.

Her cheeks flush, and I have to press my hands down against my thighs to hold myself in the chair and not tackle him to the ground for embarrassing her. I know he's only teasing, but it's still a dick move.

"Thank you all so much for coming, it means the world to me to have everyone that I love here with us. I am beyond proud of the work that everyone in this room has done, and I couldn't possibly be making this move without you all. You're the best team I could ever hope for. Who knows—maybe next year we'll even be opening an office in Los Angeles or even New York, so I can drive you all batshit crazy with the planning again." He nods at his own joke, but beams with ambition.

"Don't get ahead of yourself," Kimberly says and smacks his butt.

"And you, especially you, Kimberly. I wouldn't be anywhere without you." His tone changes drastically, altering the air in the room as well. He takes her hands in his and moves to stand in front of where she sits. "After Rose died, I was living in complete darkness. The days came and went in a blur, and I never thought I would be happy again. I didn't think I was capable of loving anyone else; I had accepted that it would just be Smith and me. Then one day this bubbly blonde crashes into my office, ten minutes late for her interview and with the most hideous coffee stain on her white blouse—and that was it for me. I was captivated by her spirit and your energy." He turns to Kimberly. "You gave me life when I had none left in me. No one could ever replace Rose, and you knew that. But you didn't try to replace her—you welcomed her memory and helped me get my life back. I only wish I had met you sooner, so I wasn't miserable for so long first." He laughs a little, trying to draw back on the emotionality of the moment, but he fails.

"I love you, Kimberly, more than anything, and I would love to spend the rest of my life repaying you for what you have given me." He bends down on one knee.

Is this some kind of fucking joke? Is everyone I know suddenly deciding to get married or is this some fucked-up cosmic joke on me?

"This wasn't a celebration party, this was an engagement party." He smiles at the object of his affection. "Well, that is, if you say yes."

Kimberly squeals and begins to cry. I look away from them as she practically screams her acceptance.

I can't help but look at Tessa as she claps her hands to her face and wipes at her tears. I know she's doing her best to smile for her friend in this joyful moment, to pretend they're tears of happiness. But really, I can tell that she's only pretending. She's overwhelmed, having just listened to her friend hear everything that she once wished she would hear from me.

chapter eighty-nine

TESSA

My chest aches as I watch Christian wrap his arms around Kimberly and lift her off the floor in a loving embrace. I'm so happy for her, I really am. It's just that it's hard to sit and watch someone get something that you wanted, no matter how happy you are for them. I would never want to take even an ounce of her happiness away, but it's hard to watch as he kisses both her cheeks and slides a gorgeous diamond ring onto her finger.

I stand up from my seat, hoping that no one will notice my absence. I make it to the living room before the tears fall in earnest. I knew this would happen, I knew I would break. If he wasn't here, I could handle it, but it's too surreal, too painful, to have him here.

He came here to taunt me, he had to have. Why else come, but not speak to me at all? It doesn't make sense: he's avoided me for the past ten days, then he shows up here, where he knew I would be. I shouldn't have come. I should have at least driven myself so I could leave right now. Zed won't be here until . . .

Zed.

Zed is coming to pick me up at eight. Looking at a sleek grandfather clock, I see it's seven thirty already. Hardin will kill him, literally, if he sees him here.

Or maybe he won't, maybe he doesn't care at all.

I find the restroom and close the door behind me. It takes me a moment to realize the light switch is a touch-screen panel on the wall. This house is too damn high tech for me.

I was absolutely humiliated when I dropped the wineglass. Hardin seems so indifferent, like he could care less about me being here or how awkward for me his presence really is. Has it even been hard for him? Did he spend days crying and lying in bed the way I did? I have no way to know, and he isn't giving off the heartbroken impression.

Breathe, Tessa. You have to breathe. Ignore the knife lodged in your chest.

I wipe my eyes and look at my reflection. My makeup hasn't smudged, thank goodness, and my hair is still perfectly curled. My cheeks are slightly flushed, but in a way it makes me look better, more lively.

When I open the door, Trevor is leaning against the wall with concern clear in his features. "Are you okay? You ran out of there pretty fast." He takes a step toward me.

"Yeah . . . I just needed some air," I lie. A stupid lie, at that; it doesn't even make sense to rush to the bathroom for air.

Lucky for me, Trevor is a gentleman and would never call me out on my lie the way Hardin would. "Okay, they're serving dessert now, if you're still hungry," he says and escorts me back down the hallway.

"Not really, but I'll have some," I respond. I practice regulating my breathing, and find that it helps settle me some. I'm thinking about what to do about the impending Zed-Hardin meet-up when I hear Smith's small voice coming from a room we pass by.

"How do you know?" he asks in his little, clinical manner.

"Because I know everything," Hardin replies.

Hardin? Hanging out with Smith?

I stop and wave Trevor on. "Trevor, why don't you go on. I . . . um . . . I'm going to talk to Smith."

He looks at me questioningly. "Are you sure . . . I can wait," he offers.

"No, I'm fine." I politely dismiss him. He gives a little nod and wanders off. Leaving me free to impolitely eavesdrop.

Smith says something I don't get, and Hardin replies, "I do, though, I know everything." His voice is as calm as ever.

I lean against the wall next to the door as Smith asks, "Will she die?"

"No, man. What is with you always thinking everyone's going to die?"

"I don't know," the little boy tells him.

"Well, it's not true, not everyone dies."

"Who dies?"

"Not everyone."

"But who, Hardin?" Smith presses.

"People, bad people, I guess. And old people. And sick people—oh, and sad people sometimes."

"Like your pretty girl?"

My heart races.

"No! She won't. She's not sad," Hardin says, and I put my hand over my mouth.

"Yeah, huh."

"No, she's not. She's happy, and she won't die. Neither will Kimberly."

"How do you know?"

"I already told you how I know, it's because I know everything." His tone has changed since the mention of my name.

I hear a dismissive little laugh from Smith. "No, you don't."

"Are you okay now? Or are you going to cry more?" Hardin asks.

"Don't tease."

"Sorry, are you done crying, though?"

"Yeah."

"Good."

"Good."

"Don't mock me. It's rude," Hardin says.

"You're rude."

"So are you—are you sure you're only five?" Hardin asks.

Which is exactly what I've always wanted to ask the kid. Smith is so mature for his age, but I guess he has to be, considering what he's been through.

"Pretty sure. Do you want to play?" Smith asks him.

"No, I don't."

"Why?"

"Why do you ask so many questions? You remind—"

"Tessa?" Kimberly's voice startles me and I nearly scream. She puts a reassuring hand on my shoulder. "Sorry! Have you seen Smith? He took off, and Hardin, of all people, went after him." She looks confused yet touched by that.

"Um, no." I hurry down the hallway to avoid the humiliation of being caught by Hardin. I know he heard Kimberly call my name.

When I get back to the dining room, I approach the small group that Christian is speaking with and tell him how much I appreciate him inviting me, and I congratulate him on his engagement. Kimberly appears moments later, and I hug her goodbye before doing the same with Karen and Ken.

I check my phone: ten minutes till eight. Hardin is occupied with Smith and obviously has no intention of speaking to me, and that's fine. That's what I need, I don't need him to apologize and tell me that he's been miserable without me. I don't need him to hold me and tell me we'll find a way to work this out, to fix everything he has broken. I don't need that. He won't do it anyway, so it's pointless to need it.

It hurts less when I don't need it.

By the time I reach the end of the driveway, I'm freezing. I should've worn a jacket—it's the end of January and it's just begun to snow. I don't know what I was thinking. I hope Zed gets here soon.

The icy wind is unforgiving as it whips my hair around and makes me shiver. I wrap my arms around me in an attempt to keep warm.

"Tess?" I look up, and for a moment I think I'm imagining the boy in all black walking toward me in the snow.

"What are you doing?" Hardin asks me, drawing even closer.

"I'm leaving."

"Oh . . ." He rubs his hand over the back of his neck like he always does. I stay quiet. "How are you?" he asks and I'm baffled.

"How *am* I?" I turn to look at him.

I try to keep my cool as he stares at me with a completely neutral expression. "Yeah . . . I mean, are you . . . you know, okay?"

Should I tell him the truth or lie . . . ? "How are you?" I ask, my teeth chattering.

"I asked first," he responds.

This is not how I had envisioned our first encounter. I'm not entirely sure what I thought would happen, but this isn't it. I thought he would be cursing me out and we would be in a screaming match. Standing in a snow-dusted driveway, asking each other how we're doing, is the last thing I imagined. The lanterns hanging in the trees lining the driveway make Hardin appear to be glowing, like an angel. Obviously an illusion.

"I'm fine," I lie.

He looks me up and down slowly, making my stomach leap and my heart pound. "I see that." His voice carries over the wind.

"And now, how are you?"

I want him to say he's doing terribly. But he doesn't.

"Same. Fine."

Quickly I ask, "Why haven't you called me?" Maybe this will evoke some emotion from him.

"I . . ." He looks at me and then down at his hands before running them through his snow-covered hair. "I . . . was busy." His answer is the wrecking ball that takes down the rest of my wall.

Anger overpowers the bone-crushing hurt that is threatening to take over at any moment. "You were 'busy'?"

"Yeah . . . I was busy."

"Wow."

"Wow what?" he asks.

"You were busy? Do you know what I've been going through the last eleven days? It's been hell, and I felt pain that I didn't know I could endure, and at times I didn't think I could. I kept waiting . . . waiting like a fucking idiot!" I scream.

"You don't know what I've been doing either! You always think you know everything—but you don't know shit!" he yells back, and I walk to the very end of the driveway.

He's going to lose it when he sees who's picking me up. Where the hell is Zed, anyway? It's five minutes after eight.

"Tell me, then! Tell me what was more important than fighting for me, Hardin." I wipe the tears from under my eyes and beg myself to stop crying.

I'm so sick of crying all the time.

chapter ninety

HARDIN

When she starts to cry, it becomes much harder to keep a neutral face. I don't know what would happen if I told her that I've been through hell, too, that I felt pain that I wasn't sure I could endure either. I think she'd run into my arms and tell me it's okay. She was listening to me talk to Smith, I know she was. She's sad, just the way the obnoxious little boy claimed, but I know how this ends. If she forgives me, I'll just come up with some other fucked-up thing to do to her next. It's always been that way, and I don't know how to stop it.

The only option here is giving her a chance to be with someone much better for her. I believe that deep fucking down she wants someone who is more like her. Someone with no tattoos, no piercings. Someone without a fucked-up childhood and anger issues. She thinks that she loves me now, but one day, when I do something even more fucked up than I already have, she'll regret ever speaking to me. The more I look at her crying in this driveway with the snow falling down around her, the more I know that I'm not good for her.

I'm Tom and she's Daisy. Lovely Daisy, who is corrupted by Tom, and she's never the same after. If I beg for her forgiveness right now, on my knees, in this snowy driveway, she'll be the awful Daisy for eternity, all of her innocence will be gone and she'll end up hating me, and herself. If Tom had left Daisy at the first moment of her uncertainty, she could have had a life with the man she was destined to be with, a man that would have treated her the way she deserved to be treated.

"It's none of your concern really, is it?" I say and watch as my words rattle her to her core.

She should be inside with Trevor, or back home with Noah. Not with me. I'm no Darcy, and she deserves one. I can't change for her. I will find a way to live without her, just the way she must live without me.

"How could you even say that? After everything we've been through, you just toss me aside and don't even have the decency to give me an explanation?" she cries.

Headlights appear at the end of the dark street, casting her into silhouette and creating new shadows across the land.

I'm doing this for you! I want to shout. But I don't. I just shrug my shoulders.

Her mouth opens, then closes as a truck stops in front of us.

That truck . . .

"What is he doing here?" I croak.

"Picking me up," she says with such offhand finality that the news nearly brings me to my knees.

"Why would . . . why is he . . . what the *fuck*?" I pace back and forth. I had been trying to push her away from me and trying to let her move on so she could be with someone like herself— not fucking Zed, out of all people.

"Have you . . . have you been seeing that piece of shit?" I say, glaring at her. I'm aware of how frantic I sound, but I don't give a shit as I step past Tessa and walk over to where his truck is stopped. "Get out of the goddamn car!" I shout.

Zed surprises me by climbing out and leaving the engine running. He's such a fucking idiot.

"Are you all right?" he has the nerve to ask her.

I get up in Zed's face. "I knew it! I knew you were waiting for your moment to swoop in and make a move on her! Did you think I wouldn't find out?"

He looks at her and she looks at him. *Holy fucking shit, this is really happening.*

"Leave him alone, Hardin!" she insists . . .

And I snap.

One of my hands wraps around the collar of Zed's jacket. The other connects with his jaw. Tessa screams, but it's barely a whisper, lost in the wind and my rage.

Zed stumbles back, holding his jaw. But then he quickly steps back up toward me. He and his death wish.

"Did you think I wasn't going to find out! I fucking told you to stay away from her!" I move to hit him again, but this time he blocks me and manages to nail me right in the jaw.

Anger mixes with the adrenaline of being in a fight for the first time in weeks. I've missed this feeling, the energy flowing through my bloodstream, getting me high.

I hit him in the ribs. This time he falls to the ground, and I'm on top of him in seconds, pummeling him again and again. I'll give him credit: he's managed to get in a few punches. But he has no way to overpower me.

"I was there . . . and you weren't." He eggs me on.

"Stop it! Stop, Hardin!" Tessa pulls on my arm, and reflexively I knock her backward onto the driveway.

Immediately, I snap out of my rage and turn to her as she backs away on her hands and knees and then stands and puts her arms straight out, as if to ward me off. *What the fuck did I just do?*

"Don't you fucking go near her!" Zed yells behind me. He's by her side in no time, and she's staring at him, not bothering to even look at me.

"Tess . . . I didn't mean to do that. I didn't know it was

you, I swear! You know how I see red when I'm angry . . . I'm so sorry. I . . ."

She stares straight through me. "Can we just go, please?" she asks calmly, and my heart leaps . . . until I realize that she's talking to him, to Zed.

How the fuck did this happen?

"Yes, of course." Zed drapes his jacket over her shoulders and opens the passenger seat of his truck for her and helps her inside.

"Tessa . . ." I call again, but she doesn't acknowledge me as she buries her face in her hands and her body is racked with sobs.

I point a finger at Zed and threaten, "This isn't over."

He nods and goes around to the driver's side before looking at me again. "I think it is, actually." He smirks and climbs inside his truck.

chapter ninety-one

TESSA

'm so sorry that he pushed you like that," Zed tells me as I swipe the warm cloth across his busted cheek. The skin is cut and just won't stop bleeding.

"No, it's not your fault. I'm sorry you keep getting dragged into this." I sigh and dip the cloth back into his sink.

He had offered to take me back to Landon's instead of following our previous plan of seeing a movie, but I didn't want to go back to Landon's. I didn't want Hardin to show up there and cause a scene

He's probably there destroying Ken and Karen's entire house right now. God, I hope not.

"It's cool. I know how he is, I'm just glad he didn't hurt you. Well, worse than he did." He sighs.

"I'm going to apply pressure to this, so it may hurt," I warn him.

He closes his eyes as I press the cloth to his skin. The cut is deep—it looks like it may scar, even. I hope not; Zed's face is too perfect to have a scar like this, and I certainly don't want to be the cause of it.

"Done," I say, and he smiles despite the fact that his mouth is swollen as well. *Why am I always cleaning up wounds?*

"Thank you." He smiles again as I rinse off the bloodstained towel.

"I'll send you a bill," I tease.

"Are you sure you're okay, though? You hit the ground pretty hard."

"Yeah, I'm a little sore, but I'm fine." The events from tonight took a drastic turn for the worse when Hardin followed me outside. I had a feeling he wasn't too hurt by me leaving him, but I thought he would be more affected than he was. He said he was busy and that's why he hadn't called me. Even though I thought he wouldn't care as much as I did, I thought he loved me enough to care a little. Instead, he acted as if nothing had even happened, as if we were friends having a casual conversation. That is, until he saw Zed and lost it. If anything, I thought seeing Trevor would anger him and he would try to start a fight in front of everyone, but he couldn't have cared less. Which is kind of strange.

Regardless of how brokenhearted I am, I know Hardin wouldn't hurt me purposely, but this is the second time something like this has happened. The first time I was quick to excuse his behavior. I was the one who convinced him to go to his father's for Christmas, and he just couldn't handle it. Tonight was his fault—he shouldn't even have been there.

"Are you hungry?" Zed asks me as we leave his small bathroom for the living room.

"No, I already ate at the party," I say; my voice is still hoarse from my excessive, embarrassing sobbing on the way to Zed's apartment.

"Okay, we don't have much anyway, but I could order you something if you want, so just let me know if you change your mind."

"Thank you." Zed is always so incredibly sweet to me.

"My roommate will be here in a little while, but he won't bother us. He'll probably crash as soon as he gets in."

"I really am sorry that this keeps happening, Zed."

"Don't apologize. Like I said, I'm just glad I was there for you. Hardin seemed pretty angry when I got there."

"We were already fighting." I roll my eyes and take a seat on the couch, wincing from the soreness. "Go figure."

All of my bruises and cuts from my automobile accident just healed, and now I'm going to have another, from Hardin. The back of my dress is dirty and ruined, and my shoes are scuffed down the sides. Hardin really does ruin everything that he comes in contact with.

"Do you need some clothes to sleep in?" Zed asks, handing me the old blanket I slept with a few nights ago.

I'm slightly apprehensive about borrowing Zed's clothes. That's something I share with Hardin, and I've never worn anyone else's clothing.

"I think Molly has some stuff here . . . in my roommate's room. I know that's probably awkward . . ." He half smiles. "But I'm sure they're better than sleeping in that dress."

Molly is much thinner than me, and I almost laugh. "I can't fit in her clothes, but thank you for thinking I could."

Zed seems to be confused by my answer; his cluelessness is adorable. "Well, I have some clothes you can wear," he offers, and I nod before I allow myself to overthink it. I can wear whoever's stuff I want, Hardin doesn't own me—he didn't even care enough to try to explain himself to me.

Zed disappears into his bedroom and returns moments later with his hands full of clothing. "I grabbed a few different things, I don't know what you like." There's something behind his tone that makes me think he'd really like to get to that stage with me. The one where you know what the other likes. The stage I'm at with Hardin. *Was* at. Whatever.

I grab a blue T-shirt and a pair of plaid pajama bottoms. "I'm not picky." I give him a thankful smile before I go into the bathroom to change.

To my horror, the plaid thing that I thought was pants is in fact a pair of boxers. Zed's boxers. Oh God. I unzip my dress and pull the large T-shirt over my head before considering what to do about the boxers.

The shirt is smaller than Hardin's shirts are; it barely hits the top of my thigh and it doesn't smell like Hardin. Of course it doesn't, it's not Hardin's. It smells like laundry soap with the smallest hint of cigarette smoke. The smell is nice somehow, though not as nice as the familiar scent of the boy that I miss.

I pull the boxers up my legs and look down. They aren't too short. In fact, they're sort of baggy, tighter than Hardin's would be, but not too tight. I'll just walk to the couch and cover myself with the blanket as fast as I can.

I'm incredibly embarrassed to be wearing them, but it would be even more embarrassing to make a big deal out of it after everything Zed has been through tonight because of me. His poor face holds the proof of Hardin's anger, a big bloody reminder of why Hardin and I would never work. Hardin only cares for himself, and the only reason he lost it when he saw Zed is his pride. He doesn't want me, but he doesn't want me to be with anyone else either.

I leave my dress folded on the bathroom floor; it's already dirty and ruined anyway. I'll try the dry cleaners, but I'm not sure if it can be saved. I really loved that dress, too, and it cost me a decent amount of money—money that I sorely need once I find my own apartment.

I walk as fast as I can, but when I reach the living room, Zed is standing next to the television. His eyes go wide as they rake up and down my body. "I . . . uh, I was putting something . . . I was putting, trying to find a movie . . . to watch. Or something for you to watch, I mean," he stammers, and I sit on the couch and pull the blanket over me.

His fumbled words and the look in his eyes make him appear younger and more vulnerable than usual.

He laughs nervously. "Sorry, I was trying to say I was turning the TV on so you could watch it."

"Thank you," I say and smile as he takes a seat on the other end of the couch. He rests his elbows on his knees and stares forward.

"If you don't want to keep hanging out with me, I understand," I say to break the silence.

He turns to face me. "What? No, don't think that." His eyes pour into mine. "Don't worry about me, I can handle it. A couple beatings aren't going to make me stay away from you. The only thing that will is if you tell me to. You want me to, then I will. But until you tell me to go, I'm here."

"I don't. Want you to go, that is. I just don't know what to do about Hardin. I don't want him to hurt you, again," I tell him.

"He's a pretty violent guy. I know what to expect, I guess. Don't worry about me, though. I just hope that after seeing who he really is tonight, you'll distance yourself from him."

Sadness creeps in at the thought, but I say, "I am, I definitely am. He doesn't care anyway, so why should I?"

"You shouldn't. You're too good for him, anyway; you always have been," he assures. I scoot closer to him on the couch, and he lifts my blanket and gets under it, too, before pressing a button to turn on the television. I love the ease between us; he doesn't say things just for the single purpose of pissing me off, and he doesn't hurt my feelings on purpose.

"Are you tired?" I ask him after a bit.

"Nah, you?"

"A little."

"Go to sleep, then. I can go to my room."

"No. Actually, you can stay out here until I fall asleep?" My tone is more asking than telling.

He looks at me, relief and happiness in his eyes. "Yeah, sure. I can do that."

chapter ninety-two

HARDIN

I pound my fist onto the trunk of my car and scream to let out some of my anger.

How did that happen? How did I push her to the ground? He knew what was going to happen the moment he stepped out of that truck, and he ended up getting his ass beat again. I know Tessa—she's going to pity him and blame herself for his ass-beating, and then she's going to think she owes him something.

"Fuck!" I scream even louder.

"What are you yelling about?" Christian appears in the snowy driveway.

I look over at him and roll my eyes. "Nothing." The only person that I will ever love just left with the person I despise the most in the world.

Vance looks at me with bemusement for a second. "Obviously something," he quips and takes a big sip of his drink.

"I don't really feel like having a fucking heart-to-heart right now," I snap.

"Such a coincidence—neither do I. I'm just trying to figure out why there's an asshole screaming in my driveway," he says with a smile.

I nearly laugh at that. "Fuck off."

"I take it she didn't accept your apology?"

"Who says I gave an apology, or a reason to need one?"

"Because you're you, and on top of that, you're a man . . ." He salutes me and downs the rest of what's in his glass. "We always have to apologize first. It's the way it is."

Letting out a hard breath, I say, "Yeah, well, she doesn't want my apology."

"Every woman wants an apology."

I can't get the image of her looking to Zed for comfort out of my mind. "Not mine . . . not her."

"Fine, fine, fine," Christian says, flapping his hands down. "Are you coming back inside?"

"No . . . I don't know." I shake the snow from my hair and push it back off my forehead.

"Ken . . . your dad and Karen are getting ready to leave."

"And I give a shit . . . why?" I reply, and he chuckles.

"Your language never ceases to surprise me."

I give him a grin. "What? You curse just as much as I do."

"Exactly." He puts his arm around my shoulders. And I surprise myself by letting him lead me back inside.

chapter ninety-three

TESSA

I can't sleep. I've been waking up every thirty minutes to check my phone to see if Hardin's tried to contact me. Of course there's nothing. I check my alarm again. I have classes tomorrow, so Zed's going to take me back to Landon's early enough to get ready and get to school on time.

When I try to close my eyes again, my mind races, remembering the way the dream Hardin pleaded with me to come home. Hearing it, dream or not, still kills me. After tossing and turning on the small couch, I decide to do what I should have done at the beginning of the night.

When I push Zed's bedroom door open, I immediately hear his light snoring. He's shirtless and lying on his stomach, with his arms folded under his head.

I'm waging an internal war with myself as he stirs in his sleep. "Tessa?" He sits up. "Are you okay?" He sounds panicked.

"Yeah . . . I'm sorry for waking you up . . . I was just wondering if maybe I could sleep in here?" I ask timidly.

He looks at me for a second before saying, "Yeah, of course." Shifting his body a little, he makes sure there is plenty of room for me to lie down.

I try to ignore the fact that his bed doesn't have a sheet on it. He's a college boy, after all; not everyone is as neat as I am. He slides a pillow across the mattress, and I lie down next to him, the distance between us being less than a foot.

"Do you want to talk about anything?" he asks.

Do I? I wonder. But I say, "No, not tonight. I can't make out the mess that is inside of my head."

"Is there anything I can do?" His voice is so soft in the darkness.

"Scoot closer?" I request, and he does just that.

I'm nervous as I turn on my side to face him. His hand moves up to my cheek, and he rubs his thumb back and forth. His touch is warm and gentle. "I'm glad you're here with me, and not him," Zed whispers.

"Me, too," I respond, having no clue if I mean it or not.

chapter ninety-four

HARDIN

Landon's developed quite the attitude since the night he attempted to assault me. He threw a tantrum at the airport when he saw me standing at the baggage claim and realized I was here to pick him up instead of his mum. Karen had agreed to allow me to pick her son up, maybe because she didn't want to go out after Vance's party, or maybe because she pities me. I'm not sure either way, but I'm glad she did.

For his part, Landon is flat-out annoyed, claiming that I'm the biggest asshole he's ever met, and refusing to get into the car with me at first. It took me nearly twenty minutes to convince my lovely stepbrother that riding with me had to be better than walking thirty miles in the middle of the night.

After a few miles of driving in silence, I pick up the conversation where we agreed to let it die back in the terminal. "Well, I'm here, Landon, and I need you to tell me what I should do. I'm split. Right down the fucking middle."

"Between what and what?" he asks.

"Between leaving here and going back home to England to ensure that Tessa has the life that she deserves, and driving over to Zed's and fucking murdering him."

"Where does she fit into the latter of those?"

I look at him and shrug. "I would make her come with me after I murder him."

"That's the problem here. You think you can make her do whatever you want, and look where that got you."

"I didn't mean it like that. I just mean . . ." I know he's right, so I don't even try to finish that thought. "But she's with Zed—I mean, how did that even happen? I can't fucking see straight thinking about it." I groan, rubbing my temples.

"Well, maybe I should drive, then?"

Landon is so fucking annoying.

"Hardin, she stayed the night with him Friday and hung out with him all day Saturday."

My vision literally goes black. "What? So . . . she's just . . . so she's dating him?"

Landon traces a pattern on the window. "I don't know if she's dating him . . . but I do know that when I talked to her Saturday she said she'd laughed for the first time since you deserted her."

I scoff. "She doesn't even *know* him." I can't believe this shit's happening.

"Not to be a jerk, but you can't ignore the irony of the fact that you were so obsessed with her being with someone like her, but she ends up seeing someone just like you," Landon says.

"He's nothing like me," I say and try to focus on the road before I end up breaking down in front of Landon. I stay quiet the rest of the ride to my father's house.

"Did she cry at all?" I finally ask when I pull up to the driveway.

Landon looks at me incredulously. "Yes, for a week straight." Then he shakes his head. "Man, you have no idea what you've done to her, and you didn't even care. You're still only thinking about yourself."

"How can you say that when I've done this for her? I've kept myself away so that she can move on. I don't deserve her, you told me that yourself, remember?"

"I do, and I still mean it. But I also think she should be the one to decide what she deserves," he says with a huff and gets out of my car.

* * *

JACE TAKES A PUFF from his joint, then looks at it intensely. "I haven't really been doing shit lately, just hanging out. Tristan barely comes around anymore; he's stuck up Steph's ass."

"Hmm," I murmur. I take a sip from my beer and look around his shit apartment. I don't even know why I came here in the first place, but I didn't know where else to go. I'm sure as hell not going back to that apartment tonight. I can't believe Tessa is with Zed—*what the actual fuck.*

And Landon wouldn't call Tessa and trick her into coming back to my father's house no matter how many times I tried to force him to. He's a dick.

Still, I have to admit I admire his loyalty, but not when it stands in the way of what I want. Landon said I should allow Tessa to make the choice whether she wants to be with me or not, but I know what she'd choose. Well, I thought I did.

I was completely blindsided by Zed picking her up and having spent almost the entire weekend with her.

"What's going on with you?" Jace asks me, his pot smoke blowing right in my face.

"Nothing."

"I must say I was pretty surprised to have you show up at my door tonight after what happened the last time I saw you," he reminds me.

"You know why I'm here."

"Do I?" he taunts.

"Tessa and Zed. I know you know about it."

"Tessa? Tessa Young and Zed Evans?" He smiles. "Tell me."

He needs to wipe that goddamned smile off his face.

After I meet him with silence, he shrugs. "I don't know anything about it, honest." He takes another drag, and small flakes of the white paper fall onto his lap, not that he seems to notice.

"You're never honest." I take another sip.

"Yes, I am. So they're fucking?" He raises a brow.

I nearly choke on my breath from his question. "Don't fuck-ing go there. Have you seen them together?" I breathe in and out slowly.

"Nope, I don't know anything about them." Jace puts his joint in the ashtray. "I thought he was dating some high school chick."

I stare at a pile of dirty laundry in the corner of the room. "So did I."

"So she ditched you for Zed?"

"Don't mock me, I'm not in the mood."

"You came here asking questions. I'm not mocking you," Jace sneers.

"I heard they were together on Friday, and I wanted to know who was there."

"I don't know. I wasn't, though. Don't you two live together or some shit?" He takes his wannabe-hipster glasses off and places them on the table.

"Yes. Why do you think I'm so pissed about this shit with Zed."

"Well, you know how he's after what you—"

"I *know*." I hate Jace, I really do. And Zed. Couldn't Tessa have chosen Trevor to move on with? Holy shit, I never thought I would consider her being with Trevor a positive.

I roll my eyes and fight the urge to knock Jace through his coffee table. This is getting me nowhere, none of this is—the drinking, the anger, none of it.

"You're sure you don't know shit, because if I find out you do, I will kill you. You know that, don't you?" I threaten, meaning every word.

"Yes, dude, we all know how psychotic you are over this chick. Stop being such a dick."

"I'm just warning you," I tell him, and he rolls his eyes.

Why did I start hanging out with him in the first place? He's a fucking slime ball, and I should have let our so-called friendship end with me beating his ass.

Jace gets up and does a slow stretch. "Well, man, I'm going to bed now. It's four a.m. You can crash on the couch if you want."

"No, I'm good," I say and head for the door.

It's four in the morning, and it's cold outside, but I'll never be able to sleep knowing she's with Zed. At his apartment. What if he's touching her? What if he spent this entire weekend touching her?

Would she fuck him to spite me?

No, I know her better than that. This is a girl who still blushes each time I slide her panties down her thighs. However, Zed can be pretty convincing, and he could have her drinking. I know she can't handle alcohol—two drinks and she starts cursing like a sailor and trying to unfasten my belt.

Fuck, if he gets her drunk and touches her . . .

I make a U-turn right in the middle of the intersection and hope there are no cops around, especially since they'll smell the beer on my breath.

Fuck this staying-away-from-her shit. I may have been a dick to her, and I have treated her like shit—but Zed is far worse than me. I love her more than he, or any other man, possibly could. I know what I had now. I know what the fuck I had to lose—and now that I've lost it, I need it back. He can't have her, no one can. No one except me.

Goddammit. Why didn't I just apologize to her at the party? That's what I should have done. I should have dropped to my knees in front of everyone and begged for her to forgive me, and we could be in our bed together right now. Instead I argued with her, and accidentally knocked her over when I was so mad I couldn't tell who was who.

Zed is a fucking prick. Who the fuck does he think he is, picking her up from that party? Is he serious?

My anger is getting the best of me again. I need to calm down before I get there. If I stay calm she'll speak to me, I hope.

By the time I get to Zed's door, it's four thirty in the morning. I stop and stand still for a few minutes in an attempt to calm myself down. Finally, I knock and wait impatiently.

Just as I'm about to turn my knocking into pounding, the door swings open, revealing Tyler, Zed's roommate, who I've spoken to a few times when they had parties here.

"Scott? What's up, man?" he slurs.

"Where's Zed?" I push past him, not wasting any time.

He rubs his eyes. "Dude, you know it's like five in the morning, right?"

"Nope, only four thirty. Where . . ." But then I notice the folded-up blanket on the couch. Neatly folded: a Tessa indicator. It takes a moment for my brain to connect to the fact that the couch is empty.

Where is she if she's not on the couch?

Bile rises in my throat, and I lose the ability to breathe for the hundredth time tonight. I storm across the apartment, leaving a confused Tyler in my wake.

When I open Zed's bedroom, it's dark, near pitch black. I pull my phone from my pocket and switch on its flashlight. Tessa's blond hair is sprawled out on the pillow under her, and Zed is shirtless.

Oh my fucking God.

When I find the light switch and flip it on, Tessa stirs and rolls over onto her side. My boot hits the edge of a desk with a loud thud. She scrunches her eyes shut and then opens them slightly to find the source of disruption.

I try to think of what to say as I process the scene in front of me. Tess and Zed in bed, together.

"Hardin?" she whines, and a frown takes over as she appears to wake up. She looks over to Zed before she looks up at me, clearly shocked. "What . . . what are you doing here?" she asks frantically.

"No, no. What are *you* doing here! In bed with him?" I try my best not to shout, my fingernails digging into my palm.

If she fucked him, I'm done, completely and utterly fucking done with her.

"How did you get in here?" she asks, her face full of sadness.

"Tyler let me in. You're in his bed? How could you be in his bed?"

Zed rolls over onto his back and wipes his eyes, then he pops up and sits ready, eyeing me where I stand in the doorway. "What the hell are you doing in my room?" he demands.

Don't, Hardin. Stay still. I have to stay fucking still or someone will end up in the hospital. That someone is Zed, but if I'm going to get her away from him, I have to stay as calm as possible.

"I came to get you, Tessa. Let's go," I say and reach my hand out, even though I'm across the room.

Her brow furrows. "Excuse me?"

Here comes the infamous Tessa attitude . . .

"You can't just come to my apartment and tell her to leave." Zed moves to get out of bed, and I see he's only in loose gym shorts that sag down to show his boxers.

I don't think I can stay calm.

"I can, and I just did. Tessa . . ." I wait for her to get off the bed, but she doesn't move.

"I'm not going anywhere with you, Hardin," she tells me.

"You heard her, man. She's not coming with you," Zed taunts me.

"I wouldn't start that shit right now. I'm trying with every fucking fiber of my being not to do anything that I'll regret, so just shut the fuck up," I growl.

He throws his arms wide in challenge to me. "It's my apartment, my bedroom at that—and she doesn't want to go with you, so she's not. If you want to fight me, then go ahead. But I'm not going to force her to go if she doesn't want to." When he finishes, he gives her the fakest concerned expression I've ever seen.

I let out an evil laugh. "That's the plan, though, isn't it? You get me mad enough so I beat your ass, and she'll feel bad for you, and I'll be the monster who everyone is afraid of? Don't buy into this shit, Tessa!" I shout.

I can't stand the fact that she's still sitting in his bed, and even more I can't stand the fact that I can't beat the shit out of him for it because that's exactly what he wants.

Tessa sighs. "Just go."

"Tessa, listen to me. He isn't who you think he is, he's not Mr. Fucking Innocent."

"And how's that?" she challenges.

"Because . . . well, I don't know—*yet*. But I know he's using you for something. He just wants to fuck you—you *know* this," I tell her, struggling to keep hold of my emotions.

"No, he doesn't." She says it flatly, but I can see she's getting angry.

"Dude, you should just go—she doesn't want to leave. You're making a fool out of yourself."

When the words leave his busted lip, my body starts to shake. I have way too much anger that I need to let out.

"I warned you—to *shut the fuck up*. Tessa, stop being difficult and let's go. We need to talk."

"It's the middle of the night, and you—" she begins, but I cut her off.

"Please, Tessa."

Her expression changes as she hears my words, and I have no idea why. "No, Hardin, you can't just come here and demand that I leave with you!"

Zed shrugs and nonchalantly says, "Don't make me call the cops, Hardin."

And that's it. I take a step toward him, but Tessa jumps up off the bed and steps between us. "Don't. Not again," she begs, her eyes staring directly into mine.

"Then come with me. You can't trust him," I tell her.

Zed scoffs. "And she can trust *you*? You blew it, just face it. She deserves better than you, and if you would just let her be happy—"

"Let her be happy? With you? As if you actually want a relationship with her? I know you only want to get in her pants!"

"That's not true! I care about her and I could treat her better than you ever did!" he shouts back in my face, and Tessa presses her palms against my chest.

I know it's stupid, but I can't help but revel in her touch, the way her hands feel against me. I haven't felt her touch in so long.

"Both of you stop, please! Hardin, you have to go."

"I'm not leaving, Tessa. You're too naïve, he could give a shit about you!" I yell in her face.

She doesn't even blink. "And you do? You were 'too busy' to call me for eleven days! He was there when you weren't, and if . . ." she shouts, and continues shouting something at me, but right then I notice her clothing.

Is she? She isn't . . .

I take a step back to find out for sure. "Are those . . . what the hell are you wearing?" I stammer and begin to pace back and forth.

She looks down, seeming to have forgotten her attire.

"Are those his fucking *clothes*?!" I nearly scream. My voice cracks and I tug at my hair.

"Hardin . . ." She tries to speak.

"Indeed they are," Zed answers for her.

If she's wearing his clothes . . . "Did you fuck him?" I croak, tears threatening to spill at any given moment.

Her eyes go wide. "No! Of course not!"

"Tell me the truth right fucking now, Tessa! Did you fuck him?"

"I already answered you!" she shouts back.

Zed stands back and watches with a worried look on his bruised face. I should have done more damage.

"Did you touch him? Oh my fucking God! Did he touch you?" I'm frantic and I don't give a shit. I can't handle this; if he touched her I couldn't stand it, I wouldn't be able to.

I turn to Zed before either of them can answer. "If you touched her at all, I swear to fucking God I don't give a shit if she's here or not, I'll—"

She steps between us again, and I see fear in her eyes.

"Get out of my apartment *now* or I'm calling the police," Zed threatens me.

"The police? You think I give a flying—"

"I'll go." Tessa's voice is soft in the middle of the chaos.

"What?" Zed and I say in unison.

"I'll go with you, Hardin, only because I know you won't leave unless I do."

And I feel relief. Well, a little. I don't give a fuck why she's coming, only that she is.

Zed turns to her, almost pleading. "Tessa, you don't have to go; I can call the cops. You don't have to leave with him. This is what he does, he controls you by frightening you and everyone around you."

"You're not wrong . . ." She sighs. "But I'm exhausted, and it's five in the morning, and we do have stuff to talk about, so this is the easiest way."

"It doesn't have to—"

"She's coming with me," I tell him, and Tessa shoots me a glare that would surely kill me dead if it could.

"Zed, let me just call you tomorrow. I'm so sorry that he came here," she tells him softly, and at last he nods, finally understanding that I've won. He's fucking sulking, and she better not fall for it.

Actually, I'm really surprised she's agreeing to come with me so easily . . . but she does know me better than anyone else, so she was right when she said I wouldn't leave until she came with me.

"Don't apologize. Be careful, and if you need anything, don't hesitate for a moment to call me," he says to her.

It must suck to be a little bitch and not be able to do shit about me showing up at his apartment in the middle of the night and taking Tessa with me.

Tessa doesn't speak a word as she walks out of his bedroom and stalks to the bathroom across the hall.

"Don't come near her again. I've already warned you before, and you haven't gotten the hint yet," I say when I reach the bedroom door.

Zed glowers at me, and if it weren't for Tessa calling my name from the living room, I would have snapped his neck.

"If you hurt her, I swear to God I will make it the last time!" he says loud enough for her to hear as we walk through the door and out into the snow.

chapter ninety-five

HARDIN

High heels and his fucking boxers. It's a ridiculous pairing, but I assume she doesn't have other shoes, which may be a sign that she didn't plan on staying the night. But, still, she did, and I'm fucking disgusted that she was in his bed. I can't stand to look at her in those clothes. This is the first time that I don't want to look at her. Her red dress is in her arms and I know she's freezing.

I tried to give her my coat, but she just snapped at me to shut up and take her to my father's place. I don't even mind her anger toward me; in fact, I welcome it. I'm so relieved and so damn happy that she left with me at all. She could curse me out the entire drive and I'd enjoy every word falling from her full lips.

I'm angry, too, angry at her for running to Zed. Angry at myself for trying to push her away. "I have so much to tell you," I say as we pull onto my father's street.

With an icy glare she holds her ground, though. "I don't want to hear it. You had your chance to talk to me for the past eleven days."

"Just hear me out, okay?" I beg.

"Why now?" she asks and looks out the window.

"Because . . . because I miss you," I admit.

"You miss me? You mean you're jealous that I was with Zed. You didn't miss me until he picked me up tonight. You are fueled by jealousy, not love."

"That's not true, that doesn't have anything to do with it." Okay, it *does* have a lot to do with it, but I do miss her, regardless.

"You didn't talk to me all evening, then you came outside and told me you were too busy to talk to me. That's not what you do when you miss someone," she points out.

"I was lying." I lift my hands into the air.

"*You? Lying?* No way." Her eyes close, and she shakes her head slowly.

God, she's feisty tonight. I take a deep breath to make sure that I don't say something that will make this worse. "I don't have a phone, for starters, and I went home to England."

Her head snaps to look at me. "You what?"

"I went to England to clear my head. I didn't know what else to do," I explain.

Tessa turns down the volume on the radio and crosses her arms in front of her chest. "You didn't answer my calls."

"I know. I ignored them, and I'm so sorry for that. I wanted to call you back, but I couldn't bring myself to, and then I got drunk and broke my phone."

"Is that supposed to make me feel better?"

"No . . . I just want you to be happy, Tessa."

She doesn't say anything; she looks out the window again and I reach for her hand, but she pulls away. "Don't," she says.

"Tess . . ."

"No, Hardin! You can't just show up eleven days later and hold my hand. I'm sick of going around in circles with you. I'm finally at a point where I can go an hour without crying, then you pop up and try to pull me back under. You've done this to me since the day I met you, and I'm sick of giving in to it. If you cared about me, you would have explained yourself." She's trying her hardest not to cry, I can tell.

"I'm trying to explain myself now," I remind her, my annoyance growing as I pull into my father's driveway.

She tries to open the door, but I hit the locks.

"You aren't seriously trying to lock me in the car with you. You already basically forced me to leave Zed's house! What's wrong with you!" she begins to shout.

"I'm not trying to lock you in the car." I am, though. However, in my defense, she's stubborn and doesn't like to listen to anything I have to say.

She presses the unlock button and climbs out.

"Tessa! Goddammit, Tessa, just listen to me!" I shout into the wind.

"You keep telling me to listen, but you haven't been saying anything!"

"Because you won't shut up long enough for me to!"

We always end up in a screaming match. I need to let her yell at me and just take it, otherwise I'll say something I regret. I want to bring up Zed and the fact that she's in his fucking clothes, but I have to keep my temper under control. "I'm sorry, okay, just give me two minutes to talk without interrupting me. Please?"

She surprises me by nodding and crossing her arms to wait for me to speak.

The snow is really coming down, and I know she's freezing, but I have to talk to her now or she may change her mind.

"I went to England after you didn't come back that night. I was so pissed off at you that I couldn't see straight. You were being so damned difficult, and I just . . ."

She turns away from me and starts to walk up the snowy driveway toward the house. Dammit. I'm shit at apologies.

"I know it's not your fault. I lied to you and I'm sorry!" I shout, hoping she'll turn around.

She does. "This isn't only about you lying, Hardin. There is so much more than that," Tessa says.

"Then tell me, please."

"It's about you not treating me the way I should be treated. I never come first with you—it's always about you. Your friends, your parties, your future. I don't get to make any decisions about anything, and you made me feel like a fool when you said I was being crazy about marriage. You weren't listening to me—it isn't about marriage, it's about the fact that you haven't even thought of what I want for myself and my future. And yes, I would like to be married someday, not anytime soon, but I need security. So stop acting like I'm into this relationship more than you. Let's not forget that you were drunk and stayed out all night with another woman." She's out of breath by the time she finishes speaking, and I take a few steps toward her.

She's right, and I know she is. I just don't know what to do about it.

"I know, I thought if it were just the two of us there, you would . . ." I stutter.

"I would *what*, Hardin?" Her teeth are chattering, and her nose is red from the cold.

I pick at the dried scabs on my knuckles. I don't know how to say what I feel without sounding like the world's most selfish asshole. "You would be less likely to leave me," I admit . . . and wait for her horrified response.

It doesn't come.

Instead she begins to cry. "I don't know what else I could have done to show you how much I loved you, Hardin. I kept coming back every time you hurt me, I moved in with you and I forgave you for every unthinkable thing you did to me, I gave up my relationship with my mother for you, and you're still so insecure." She quickly wipes her tears away.

"I'm not insecure," I tell her.

"See?" she cries. "That's why this would never work. You always let your ego get in the way."

"I don't let my ego get in the way of shit!" I snap. "If anything, my ego is pretty fucked right now because I just found you in Zed's bed."

"You're really going to go there right now?"

"Hell, yes I am, you're acting like a . . ." I stop myself as she flinches from the words that she knows will follow. I know it's not her fault that he got under her skin—he's good at that—but it still fucking hurts me that she stayed with him.

She throws her arms out in challenge. "Go ahead, Hardin, call me names."

She's the most infuriating woman in the entire world, but fuck if I don't love her even at her most difficult. When I stay silent and try to tamp down my anger, she clicks her tongue. "Well, that's some improvement, but I'm going inside. I'm cold and have to be up in an hour to get ready for school."

She walks toward the house, and I follow her up the driveway, waiting for her to remember that she left her purse in my father's car. Which is here, but locked.

After looking at the door for a moment, she says, mostly to herself, I assume, "I'll have to call Landon. I don't have a key."

"You can come home," I suggest.

"You know that's not a good idea."

"Why not? We just need to figure this all out." I pull at my hair with one hand. "Together," I clarify.

"Together?" Tessa repeats, half laughing.

"Yes, together. I've missed you so much. I've been through hell without you . . . and I hope you've missed me, too."

"You should have reached out to me. I'm exhausted by this, we do this too much."

"We can do it, though. You're too good for me, and I fucking know it. But please, Tessa, I'll do anything. I can't go through another day like this."

chapter ninety-six

TESSA

My heart aches as the words leave his mouth. He's too good at this. "You always do this. You say the same things over and over, yet nothing changes," I say.

"You're right," he admits, looking directly into my eyes. "It's true. Yeah, I'll admit the first few days I was just so mad, and I didn't want to be anywhere near you because you were overreacting—but then, as I began to realize this could be it, it terrified me. I know I haven't treated you the way I should have, I don't know how to love anyone other than myself, Tess. I'm trying as hard as I can—*okay*, I haven't been trying as hard I could. But I will from now on—I swear it."

I look at him. I've heard those words too many times. "You know you've said that before."

"I know, but this time I mean it. After I saw Natalie, I—"

Natalie? My stomach drops. "You *saw* her?"

Does she still love him? Or hate him? Has he truly ruined her entire life?

"Yeah, I saw her and I spoke to her. She's pregnant."

Oh God.

"I haven't seen her in *years*, Tessa," he says sarcastically, reading my mind. "She's also engaged, and she's happy, and she told me that she forgives me and was saying how she's happy to be getting married because there's no greater honor or some shit, but it was really eye-opening for me." He steps toward me again.

My legs and arms are numb from the cold air, and I'm furious at Hardin, more than furious. I'm enraged and heartbroken. He keeps going back and forth, and it's exhausting. Now he's here in front of me talking about marriage, and I don't know what to think.

I shouldn't have even left with him. My mind was made up earlier: I would get over him if it was the last thing I did.

"What are you saying?" I ask.

"That now I realize how lucky I am to have you, to have you stick by me through all the shit I put you through."

"Well, you are. And you should've realized that before. I've always loved you more than you love me and—"

"That's *not true*! I love you more than anyone has ever loved another person. I went through hell, too, Tessa. I've been sick, literally, without you. I've barely eaten, I know I look like shit. I was doing this for you so you could move on," he explains.

"That doesn't even make any sense." I push my damp hair away from my face.

"Yes, it does. It does make sense. I thought if I stayed out of your life, you could move on and be happy without me, with your own Elijah."

"Who's Elijah?" *What is he talking about?*

"What? Oh, Natalie's fiancé. See, she found someone to love and marry her; you can, too," he tells me.

"But that someone's not you . . . is it?" I ask him.

A few seconds pass and he doesn't say anything. His expression is puzzled and frantic as he tugs at his hair for the tenth time in the last hour. Slivers of orange and red light are beginning to appear behind the large houses on the block, and I need to get inside before everyone wakes up and I have to shame-walk past them in boxers and high heels.

"I didn't think so." I sigh, not allowing any more tears to be shed for him, not until I'm alone, at least.

Hardin stands in front of me with a completely blank expres-

sion as I pull up Landon's number and ask him to open the door
for me. I should have known that Hardin was only going to fight
enough to get me out of Zed's apartment. Now that he actually
has the perfect opportunity to tell me everything I need to hear,
he's standing there in silence.

"COME ON, IT'S FREEZING," Landon says and closes the door behind me.

I don't want to push my problems on Landon right now. He
only got home from New York a few hours ago, and I need to not
be selfish.

He grabs the blanket that hangs over the back of the chair
and drapes it over my shoulders. "Let's go upstairs before they get
up," he suggests, and I nod.

My entire body and mind are numb from the snow and Hardin. I glance at the clock as I follow Landon up the stairs; it's ten
till six. I need to get into the shower in ten minutes. It's going to
be a long day. Landon opens the door to the room I've been staying in and turns the light on as I walk over to sit on the edge of
the bed.

"Are you okay? You look like you're freezing," he says, and I
nod. I'm grateful for him not asking what I'm wearing and why.

"How was New York?" I ask, but I know my voice comes out
monotone and uninterested. The thing is, I *am* interested in my
best friend's life, I just have no emotions left to show.

He gives me a little look. "You sure you want to talk about this
right now? It can wait until coffee o'clock, you know."

"I'm sure," I say and force a smile.

I'm used to this back-and-forth with Hardin; it still hurts, but
I knew it was coming. It always does. I can't believe he went to
England to get away from me. He said he had to clear his head,
but I should be the one clearing mine. I shouldn't have stayed

outside and talked to him for so long. I should have had him drive me here and come right inside the house instead of listening to him. The words he said only made me more confused. I thought for a moment he was going to say he does see and want a future with me, but when it came time for him to say just that, he let me walk away again.

When he admitted that he wanted to take me away to England so I couldn't leave him, I should have run for the hills, but I know him too well. I know he doesn't believe he's worthy of anyone loving him, and I know that in his mind that made sense to him. The problem is that's not a normal thing to do—he can't just expect me to give up everything and be trapped with him in England. We can't be there just because he's scared that if we're not, I'll leave him.

He has a lot of things he needs to work out on his own, and so do I. I love him, but I have to love myself more.

"It was nice, I loved it. Dakota's apartment is really awesome, and her roommate is really nice," Landon starts off by saying. And all I can think is that it must be so nice to have an uncomplicated relationship. Memories of Noah and me watching endless hours of movies flash through my mind; nothing was ever complicated with him. But maybe that's why it didn't last. Maybe that's why I love Hardin so much: because he challenges me and we have so much passion between us that it nearly crushes us both.

After he tells me some more details, I pick up on his excitement over New York City. "So are you moving there?" I ask.

"Yeah, I think I am. Not until the semester ends, but I really want to be near her. I miss her a lot," he tells me.

"I know you do. I'm happy for you, I really am."

"I'm sorry that you and Hardin . . ."

"Don't be. It's done. I'm done. I have to be. Maybe I should come to New York with you." I smile, and his face lights up with the warm smile I adore so much.

"You could, you know."

I always say this. I always say I'm done with Hardin, then I go back to him; it's an endless cycle. So in this moment, I make a decision: "I'm going to talk to Christian Tuesday about Seattle."

"Really?"

"I have to," I tell him, and he nods in agreement.

"I'm going to get dressed, so you can take a shower. I'll meet you downstairs when you're ready."

"I missed you so much." I stand and hug him as tight as I can. Tears spill down my cheeks, and he hugs me tighter.

"I'm sorry, I'm just a mess now. I have been since he came into my life," I cry and pull away.

He frowns but doesn't say anything as he heads to the door. I gather my clothes in my arms and follow him into the hallway to head to the bathroom.

"Tessa?" he says as he reaches his bedroom door.

"Yeah?"

Landon looks at me with great sympathy in his eyes. "Just because he can't love you the way you want him to doesn't mean he doesn't love you with everything he has," he says.

What does that even mean? I process his words as I close the bathroom door and start the shower. Hardin loves me, I know he does, but he continues to make mistake after mistake. I continue to make the mistake of putting up with it. Does he love me with everything he has? Is that enough? As I pull Zed's T-shirt over my head, there's a knock at the door.

"Hang on, Landon, I need one second," I call and pull the shirt down to cover my stomach.

But when I open the door, it's not Landon. It's Hardin, and his cheeks are stained with tears and his eyes are bloodshot.

"Hardin?"

His hand cups my neck, and he pulls me to him. His mouth moves against mine before I can resist.

chapter ninety-seven

HARDIN

I can taste my tears and the hesitation on her lips as I bring her body against mine. I press my palm against the small of her back and kiss her harder—it's a feverish and purely emotional kiss, and I could pass out from the relief of feeling her mouth on mine.

I know it won't be long before she pushes me away, so I take in every movement of her tongue, every barely audible gasp falling from her lips.

All of the pain from the last eleven days nearly evaporates when her arms wrap around my waist, and in this moment, more than ever, I know that no matter how much we fight, we will always find a way back to each other. Always.

After I watched her walk back into the house, I sat in my car for a second before finally growing some fucking balls and coming after her. I've let her slip away too many times, and I can't take the chance of this being the last day I see her. I lost it—I couldn't help but cry as Landon closed the door behind her. I knew that I had to come after her, I had to fight for her before someone else takes her away from me.

I'll show her that I can be who she wants me to be. Not completely, but I can show her how much I love her and that I won't allow her to walk away so easily, not anymore.

"Hardin . . ." she says and gently presses her hand against my chest and pushes me back, breaking our kiss.

"Don't, Tessa," I beg her. I'm not ready for it to end yet.

"Hardin, you can't just kiss me and expect everything to be

okay. Not this time," she whispers, and I fall to my knees in front of her.

"I know, I don't know why I let you walk away again, but I'm sorry. So sorry, baby," I tell her, hoping the use of the word will help my cause. I wrap my arms around her legs, and her hands move to my head, caressing and running her fingers through my hair. "I know I always fuck everything up and I know I can't treat you the way that I have been. I just love you so much that it overwhelms me, and I don't know what the fuck to do half the time, so I just say things on impulse and don't think of how the words affect you. I know I keep breaking your heart, but please . . . please let me fix it. I'll put it back together and I won't dare to break it again. I'm sorry, I'm always sorry, I know. I'll get a fucking shrink or something. I don't care, just . . ." I sob into her legs.

I grab hold of the waistband of the boxers and slide them down.

"What are you . . ." She stops my hands.

"Please, just take them off. I can't stand you wearing them, please . . . I won't touch you, just let me take them off," I beg, and she lifts her hands from mine, returning them to my hair as I slide the boxers to the floor and she steps out of them.

Her hand moves under my chin to lift up my head. Her small fingers caress my cheek, then move up to wipe away the tears from my eyes. Her face holds a confused expression, and she watches me carefully, as if she's studying me.

"I don't understand you," she tells me, still swiping her thumb across my tearstained cheeks.

"I don't either," I agree, and she frowns.

I stay in this position, kneeling in front of her, begging for her to give me one last chance even though I've blown through more chances than I deserve. I register that the bathroom has filled with steam, and her hair is sticking to her face, and moisture is beginning to pool on her skin.

God, she's beautiful.

"We can't keep going back and forth, Hardin. It's not good for either of us."

"It's not going to be that way anymore; we can get through this. We've gotten through worse, and I know now how quickly I can lose you. I took you for granted, and I know that. I'm only asking for one more chance." I take her face between my hands.

"It's not that simple," she tells me; her bottom lip begins to quiver, and I'm still trying to stop my tears.

"It's not supposed to be simple."

"It's not supposed to be this hard either." She begins to cry with me.

"Yes; yes, it is. It'll never be easy with us. We are who we are, but it won't always be this hard. We just have to learn to talk to each other without fighting every time. If we'd been able to have a conversation about the future, it wouldn't have turned into this big fucking mess."

"I tried, but you wouldn't have it," she reminds me.

"I know." I sigh. "And that's something I have to learn. I'm a mess without you, Tessa. I'm nothing. I can't eat, sleep, or even breathe. I've been crying for days straight, and you know I don't cry. I just . . . I need you." My voice is breaking and cracking, and I sound like a fucking idiot.

"Stand up." She hooks her arm under mine to try to pull me up.

Once I'm on my feet, I stand directly in front of her. My breath is ragged, and it's hard to breathe in here, with the steam filling every inch of the bathroom.

Her eyes pour into mine as she takes in my confession. If it wasn't for the fact that I'm crying, she wouldn't believe me. I know she's battling with herself, I can tell by the look in her eyes. I've seen it before.

"I don't know if I can; we keep doing this over and over. I

don't know if I can set myself up for it again." She looks down at the ground. "I'm sorry."

"Hey, look at me," I plead and tilt her head up so her eyes meet mine.

She averts her eyes, though. "No, Hardin. I need to get in the shower, I'm going to be late."

I capture a single tear from just below her eye and nod.

I know that I've put her through hell and no one in their right mind would take me back again after the bet, the lies, and my constant need to fuck everything up. She's not *like* anyone else, though; she loves unconditionally, and she puts everything she has into loving me. Even now, when she's turning me away, I know she loves me.

"Just think about it, okay?" I ask her.

I'll give her space to think about it, but I'm not going to give up on her. I need her too fucking much.

"Please?" I say when she doesn't respond.

"Okay," Tessa finally whispers.

And my heart leaps.

"I'll show you—I'll show you how much I love you and that this can work. Just don't give up on me yet, okay?" I wrap my hand around the doorknob.

She bites down on her bottom lip, and I let go of the knob to close the small space between us. When I reach her she looks up with cautious eyes. I want to kiss her lips again, to feel her arms wrapped around me, but instead I plant a single kiss on her cheek and step away from her.

"Okay," she repeats, and I head out of the door.

It takes every bit of self-discipline I possess to walk out of the bathroom, especially when I turn around and she's pulling the T-shirt over her head to expose her creamy skin, which I haven't laid eyes on in what seems like years.

I shut the door behind me and lean against the frame, closing my eyes to stop myself from crying again. *Fuck.*

At least she said she'd think about it. She seemed so apprehensive, though, like it pained her to think of being with me again. I open my eyes when Landon's bedroom door opens, and he steps into the hall wearing a white polo and khakis.

"Hey," he says to me as he slings his bag over his shoulder.

"Hey."

"Is she okay?" he asks.

"No, but I hope she will be."

"Me, too. She's stronger than she knows."

"I know she is." I use my shirt to wipe my eyes. "I love her."

"I know you do," he says, which surprises me.

I look up at him again. "How do I show her that? What would you do?" I ask him.

A pained look flashes in his eyes, but quickly disappears before he answers. "You just have to prove to her that you'll change for her; you have to treat her the way she deserves to be treated and give her the space she needs."

"It's not that easy to give her space," I tell him. I can't believe I'm talking to Landon about this shit, again.

"You have to, though, or she'll just fight back against you. Why don't you try to show her in a nonsuffocating way that you'll fight for her? That's all she wants. She wants you to make an effort."

"A 'nonsuffocating' effort?" I don't suffocate her.

Okay, maybe I do, but I can't help it, there is no lukewarm for me: I either push her away or hold her too close. I don't know how to balance the two.

"Yeah," he says, like I wasn't being sarcastic.

But since I need his help, I shake the attitude off. "Could you explain what the hell you mean? Give me an example or something."

"Well, you could ask her out on a date. Have you guys ever even been on an actual date?" he asks.

"Yeah, of course we have," I say quickly.

Haven't we?

Landon arches an eyebrow. "When?"

"Um . . . well, we went to . . . and there was this time we . . ." I'm drawing a blank here. "Okay, so maybe we haven't," I conclude.

Trevor would have taken her on dates. Has Zed? If he has, I swear to fucking . . .

"Okay, so ask her out. Not today, though, because that's too soon for even you two."

"What's that supposed to mean?" I snap.

"Nothing, I'm just saying you need some space. Well, *she* does; otherwise you're going to push her away even more than you already have."

"How long should I wait?"

"A few days, at least. Try to act like the two of you just began dating, or you're trying to get her to date you. Basically try to make her fall in love with you again."

"You're saying that she doesn't love me anymore?" I harshly remark.

Landon rolls his eyes. "No. Jeez, would you stop with the pessimism all the time?"

"I'm not a pessimist," I bark, defending myself. If anything, this is the most optimistic I've been in a long time.

"Okay . . ."

"You're an asshole," I tell my stepbrother.

"An asshole that you keep asking for relationship advice from," he brags with an annoying smile.

"Only because you're the only friend I have that has an actual relationship, and you happen to know Tessa better than anyone—except me, of course."

His smile grows. "You just called me your friend."

"What? No, I didn't."

"Yes; yes, you did," he says, clearly pleased.

"I didn't mean friend-friend, I meant . . . I don't know what the hell I meant, but it sure wasn't 'friend.' "

"Sure." He chuckles, and I hear the water turn off behind the door.

He's not so bad, I guess, but I'll never tell him that.

"Should I ask to drive her to campus today?" I follow him down the stairs.

He shakes his head at me. "What part of *nonsuffocating* do you not get?"

"I liked you better when you kept your mouth shut."

"I liked you better when you . . . well, I never liked you," he says, but I can tell he's teasing.

I never thought he liked me, actually. I thought he hated me for the terrible things I've done to Tessa. But here he is, my only ally in this mess I made for myself.

I reach out my arm and push him lightly, which makes him laugh, and I almost join him until I spot my father at the bottom of the stairs watching us like we're an act in a circus.

"What are you doing here?" he asks and takes a drink from his coffee mug.

I shrug. "I brought her home . . . well, here."

Is this her home now? I hope not.

"Oh?" my father says and looks to Landon.

Probably too pointedly, I say, "It's fine, Dad. I can bring her wherever I want to. You can stop trying to play protector and re-member which one of us is your actual child."

Landon gives me a look as we walk downstairs, and the three of us walk into the kitchen. I grab some coffee, aware of Landon's eyes still on me.

My dad grabs an apple from the wire fruit basket on the island and begins a fatherly lecture. "Hardin, Tessa has become a part of this family in the last few months, and this is her only place to go when you . . ." He trails off as Karen enters the kitchen.

"When I what?" I ask.

"When you mess up."

"You don't even know what happened."

"I don't have to know the whole story; all I know is she's the best thing that's ever happened to you and I'm watching as you make the same mistakes that I did with your mother."

Is he fucking serious? "I'm nothing like you! I love her and I would do anything for her! She's everything to me—which is nothing like you and my mum!" I slam the mug down, spilling coffee on the counter.

"Hardin . . ." Tessa's voice is behind me. *Dammit.*

To my surprise Karen jumps to my defense. "Ken, you leave the boy alone. He's doing his best."

My father's eyes immediately soften as he turns to his wife. Then he looks back at me. "I'm sorry, Hardin, I just worry about you." He sighs, and Karen rubs her hand up and down his back.

"It's fine," I say and look at Tessa standing in her jeans and WCU sweatshirt. She looks so innocently beautiful with her damp hair hanging around her makeup-free face. If Tessa hadn't appeared in the kitchen, I'd have told him how big of an asshole he is and how he needs to learn to mind his own goddamn business.

I grab a paper towel and wipe it over the counter to clean up the pool of coffee on their expensive-ass granite countertop.

"Are you ready?" Landon asks Tessa, and she nods, still staring at me.

I really want to take her, but I should go home and sleep or shower, lie on the bed and stare at the ceiling, clean the place . . . hell, anything but sit here and chat with my father.

Her eyes finally leave mine, and she leaves the room. When I hear the front door close, I let out a deep breath.

As soon as I walk away from my father and Karen, I hear them start talking about me, of course.

chapter ninety-eight

TESSA

I know what I should have done: I should have told Hardin to go away, but I couldn't. He rarely shows emotion, and the way he was on his knees in front of me broke the pieces of my already-shattered heart into smaller bits. I told him that I'll think about it, about giving us another try, but I don't know how this is going to work.

I'm so conflicted right now, more confused than ever, and annoyed with myself for almost giving in to him wholesale. But on the other hand, I'm proud of myself for stopping things before they went too far. I need to think of myself here, not only him—for once.

As Landon drives, my phone buzzes in my lap and I check the screen.

It's Zed. Are you okay?

I take a deep breath before responding. Yeah, I'm fine. I'm on my way to campus with Landon. I'm sorry about last night, it was my fault that he came there.

Hitting send, I turn my attention back to Landon. "What do you think will happen now?" he asks.

"I have no clue. I'm still talking to Christian about Seattle," I say.

Zed writes back: No it's not. It's his fault. I'm glad you're okay. Are we still on for lunch today?

I had forgotten about our plans to meet in the environmental studies building for lunch. He wanted to show me some sort of flower that glows in the dark that he helped to create.

I want to keep my plans with him—he's been so kind to me through everything—but now that I kissed Hardin this morning, I don't know what to do. I was just sleeping at Zed's last night, then there I am kissing Hardin this morning. *What's happening to me?* I don't want to be that girl; I still feel some guilt over what happened with Hardin while I was still with Noah. In my defense, Hardin came in like a wrecking ball—I had no choice but to gravitate to him as he slowly destroyed me, then built me back up, then destroyed me again.

Everything that's happening with Zed is totally different. Hardin hadn't spoken to me in eleven days, and I had no idea why. I was left to assume he didn't want me anymore, and Zed has always been there for me. Since the beginning he's always been sweet. He tried to end the bet with Hardin, but Hardin wouldn't have it—he had to prove he could bag me regardless of Zed's protestations to stop the disgusting game.

There's been bad blood between Hardin and Zed since I met them. I'm not sure why—because of the bet, I started assuming recently—but it's been evident since the first time I hung out with the two of them. Hardin claims that Zed only wants to get in my pants, but honestly, that's a little hypocritical of him to say. And Zed hasn't done a single thing to even hint that he's trying to sleep with me. Even before I knew about the bet and I kissed him at his apartment, he never made me feel like I had to do anything I didn't want to.

I hate when my thoughts go back to that time. I was so clueless, and they both played me. But there's something behind Zed's caramel eyes that shows kindness, while behind Hardin's green eyes all I see is anger.

Yeah. Noon's good, I respond to Zed.

chapter ninety-nine

TESSA

'm not sure how I feel today. I'm not exactly happy, but not miserable either. I'm confused as hell, and I miss Hardin already. Pathetic, I know. I can't help it. I'd been away from him so long and almost had him out of my system, but one kiss and he's coursing through my veins again, overwhelming every last bit of sense I had left.

Landon and I wait for the crosswalk light to change, and I realize I'm really glad I wore a sweatshirt today, because the cold weather is just not letting up.

"Well, looks like it's time to make those calls to NYU," he says and pulls out a list of names.

"Whoa! NYU," I say. "You would do great there. That's incredible."

"Thank you. I'm a little nervous that I won't be accepted for the summer semester and I don't want to take the summer off."

"Are you insane? Of course they'll accept you, for any semester! You've got a perfect GPA." I laugh. "And you've got a chancellor for a stepfather."

"I should have you call them *for* me," he jokes.

We go our separate ways and arrange to meet in the parking lot at the end of the day.

My stomach is in knots as I approach the large environmental studies building and pull open the heavy double doors. Zed is sitting on a concrete bench in front of one of the trees in the lobby. When his eyes find me, a smile instantly takes over his face and he stands to greet me. He's dressed in a white long-sleeved shirt and jeans, the material of his shirt so thin that I can see the swirls of ink below the fabric.

"Hey." He smiles.

"Hey."

"I ordered a pizza, it should be here any minute," he tells me, and we sit back down on the bench and talk about our day so far.

After the pizza is delivered, Zed leads me back to a room full of plants that appears to be a greenhouse. Rows and rows of different types of flowers that I've never seen before fill the small space. Zed walks over to one of the small tables and takes a seat.

"That smells so good," I tell him while I sit across from him.

"What, the flowers?"

"No, the pizza. Well, the flowers are okay, too." I laugh.

I'm starving, I didn't have a chance to eat breakfast this morning and I've been up since Hardin barged into Zed's apartment to get me.

He takes a slice of pizza and places it on a napkin for me. Then he grabs his own and folds it in half, the way my father used to do. Before taking a massive bite, he asks, "How did everything go last night . . . well, this morning, I guess."

I begin to feel uneasy watching him, and the smell of the flowers reminds me of the hours I used to spend in the greenhouse behind my childhood home, escaping from my drunk father screaming at my mother.

I look away from him and finish chewing before answering him. "It was a disaster at first, as always."

"At first?" He tilts his head and licks his lips.

"Yeah, we fought like we always do, but it's sort of better now." I'm not going to tell Zed about Hardin breaking down and falling onto his knees in front of me; it's too personal and only for Hardin and me to know.

"What do you mean?"

"He apologized."

He gives me a look I don't like much. "And you fell for it?"

"No, I told him I wasn't ready for anything yet. I just told him I'd think about it." I shrug.

"You aren't really going to, are you?" Disappointment is clear in his voice.

"Yeah, I'm not going to dive right back into anything, and it's not like I'm moving back into that apartment."

Zed puts his slice down on his napkin. "You shouldn't even be giving him a minute of your time, Tessa. What more does he have to do to you to make you stay away from him?" He stares at me as if I owe him an answer.

"It's not like that. It's not that simple to just cut him out of my life. I said I'm not dating him or anything, but we've been through a lot together and he's been having a really hard time without me."

Zed rolls his eyes. "Oh, drinking and getting high with Jace is his version of having a hard time, then?" he tells me, and my stomach drops.

"He hasn't been hanging out with Jace. He was in England." *He really was in England, wasn't he?*

"He was just at Jace's place last night, just before he showed up at my place."

"He was?" Of all people, I never thought Hardin would hang out with Jace again.

"It seems a little shady that he would hang out with someone who had such a big part in everything when he seems to hate *me* being near you."

"Yeah . . . but you were in on it, too," I remind him.

"Not in telling you; I had nothing to do with when they embarrassed you in front of everyone. Jace and Molly set the whole thing up—and Hardin knows that, that's why he beat Jace's ass. And you know, I wanted to tell you the whole time; it was always more than a bet for me, Tessa. But to him it wasn't. He proved that when he showed us the sheets."

My appetite is lost and I feel nauseous. "I don't want to talk about this anymore."

Zed nods and puts up a gentle hand. "You're right. I'm sorry for bringing all of that up. I just wish you would give me half the chances you give him. I'd never do things like hang out with Jace if I were in Hardin's position, and on top of that, Jace always has random girls over there—"

"Okay," I interrupt him. I can't listen to any more about Jace and girls at his apartment.

"Let's talk about something else. I'm sorry if I hurt your feelings just now. I really am. I just don't understand. You're too good for him, and you've given him so many chances. But I won't bring it up again unless you want to talk about it." He reaches across the table and puts his hand on top of mine.

"It's okay," I say. But I can't believe Hardin would be hanging out with Jace after we got into that fight in the driveway. That's the last place I thought he would be.

Zed stands up and walks over to the door. "Come on, let me show you something." I stand and follow him. "Wait there," he says when I reach the middle of the room.

The light shuts off and I'm expecting pitch black. Instead my eyes are greeted with neon green, pink, orange, and red. Each row of flowers glows with a different color, some of them brighter than others.

"Whoa . . ." I half whisper.

"Neat, isn't it?" He asks.

"Yes, very." I walk down the row slowly, taking in the sight.

"We basically engineered them, then altered the seeds to glow like this." Suddenly he's behind me. "Watch this." His hand moves to my arm and he guides my hand to touch a petal of a glowing pink flower. This flower isn't glowing as bright as the rest—that is, until my fingertip touches it and it comes to life. I jerk my hand back in surprise and hear him chuckle behind me.

"How is that even possible?" I ask in amazement.

I love flowers, especially lilies, and these man-made blooms look similar to them—they're officially my new favorite.

"Anything's possible when science is involved," he says, his face lit up by the flowers and his smile bright.

"How nerdy of you," I tease, and he laughs.

"*You* aren't in any position to call me nerdy," he teases back, and I laugh.

"True." I touch the flower again and watch it glow once more. "This is incredible."

"I thought you'd like it. We're working on doing the same with a tree; the problem is that trees take much longer to grow than flowers. But trees live much longer; flowers are too fragile. If you neglect them, they wilt and die." His tone is soft, and I can't help but compare myself to the flower, and get the feeling he's doing the same.

"If only trees were as pretty as flowers," I remark.

He moves to stand in front of me. "They could be, if someone made them that way. Just the way we took ordinary flowers and turned them into this, the same could be done with a tree. If it was given the right type of attention and care, it could glow like these flowers, but be much stronger." I stay silent as he brings his thumb to my cheek. "You deserve that type of attention. You deserve to be with someone who makes you glow, not who burns out your light."

Then Zed leans in to kiss me.

I take a step back and smack into a row of flowers; thankfully none fall as I steady myself. "I'm sorry, I can't."

"You can't *what*?" He raises his voice slightly. "Let me be the one to show you how happy you could be?"

"No . . . I can't kiss you, not right now. I can't go back and forth between the two of you. I was in your bed last night, then I kissed Hardin this morning, and now . . ."

"You kissed him?" He gapes, and I'm grateful for the room being dark except for the glow from the flowers.

"Well, he kissed me, but I let him before I pulled away," I explain. "I'm confused, and until I know what I'm going to do, I can't go around kissing everyone. It's not right."

He doesn't say anything.

"I'm sorry if I'm leading you on or making you think—"

"It's fine," Zed says.

"No, it's not. I shouldn't have brought you into the middle of this until I could think straight."

"It's not your fault. I'm the one who keeps coming around. I don't mind being led on, as long as you'll have me around. I know we could be good together, and I have all the time in the world to wait for you to see it, too," he says and walks over to turn the light on.

How can he always be so understanding?

"I wouldn't blame you if you hated me, you know?" I tell him and sling my bag over my shoulder.

"I would never hate you," he says, and I smile.

"Thank you for showing me this—it's incredible."

"Thanks for coming. Let me at least walk you to class, though?" he offers with a smile.

BY THE TIME I get to the locker room to change and grab my mat, I arrive at yoga class only five minutes early. A tall brunette has taken my spot in the front, and I'm forced to sit in the back row closest to the door. I had planned on telling Zed that I'd never be able to feel the same way about him that I do about Hardin, that I was sorry for kissing him, and that we could only be friends, but he just kept saying all the right things. When he told me about Hardin being at Jace's last night, it totally caught me off guard.

I always think I know what to do until Zed starts talking. The smoothness of his voice and the kindness behind his eyes always flusters me and messes with my thoughts.

I need to call Hardin when I get back to Landon's and tell him about my lunch with Zed, and ask him why he was at Jace's . . . I wonder what Hardin's doing now? Did he go to classes at all today?

Yoga class was exactly what I needed to clear my head. When the class is dismissed, I feel much better. I roll up my mat and head out of the room, then suddenly hear "Tessa!" as I reach the locker room.

When I turn around, Hardin jogs up to meet me and runs his hands over his hair. "I, um . . . I wanted to talk to you about something . . ."

He sounds off, like he's . . . *nervous*?

"Right now? I don't think this is the place . . ." I don't want to hash out all of our problems in the middle of the athletic building.

"No . . . it's not that." His voice is high-pitched. He's nervous; this can't be good. He's never nervous.

"I was wondering . . . I don't know . . . Never mind." He flushes and turns around to walk away. I sigh and turn to go inside to change.

"Would you *go out with me!*" he yells . . . practically screams, really.

I can't hide my surprise as I turn around. "What?"

"Like a date . . . you know, like, I could take you on a date? Only if you want to, of course, but it could be fun, maybe? I'm not sure, really, but I would . . ." He trails off, and I decide to end his humiliation as his cheeks flush a deep crimson.

"Sure," I answer, and he looks down at me.

"Really?" His lips turn to a smile. A nervous smile.

"Yeah." I don't know how this will go, but he's never asked me on a date before. The closest thing to a date was when he took me to the stream and then to eat afterward. But that was all a lie and it wasn't an actual date. It was Hardin's way of getting into my pants.

"Okay . . . When do you want to? I mean, we could go right now? Or tomorrow or later in the week?"

I don't remember ever seeing him this nervous before; it's adorable, and I try not to laugh. "Tomorrow?" I suggest.

"Yeah, tomorrow's good." He smiles and captures his bottom lip between his teeth. The air between us is awkward, but in a good way.

"Okay . . ."

I find myself feeling flustered, like I used to get the first few times I was around him.

"Okay," he repeats.

He turns on his heel and walks away quickly, nearly tripping over a rolled-up wrestling mat. As I walk into the locker room, I burst into laughter.

chapter **one hundred**

HARDIN

Landon startles, then huffs, "What are you doing here?" as I burst into my father's office.

"I came to talk to you."

"About what?" he asks, and I sit in the large leather chair behind the hideously expensive oak desk.

"Tessa, what else?" I roll my eyes at him.

"She told me you asked her out already—looks like you really gave her some space."

"What did she say?" I question.

"I'm not going to tell you what she says." He slides a piece of paper into the fax machine.

"What are you doing, anyway?" I ask him.

"Faxing my transcripts to NYU. I'm going there next semester."

Next semester? *What the fuck?* "Why so soon?"

"Because I don't want to waste any more time here when I could be with Dakota."

"Does Tessa know?" I know this will hurt her. He's her only real friend. I find myself sort of reluctant for him to go . . . sort of.

"Yeah, of course she knows, she was the first person I told."

"Anyway, I need some help with this date shit."

"Date shit?" He smiles. "How nice."

"Are you going to help me or not?"

"I guess." He shrugs.

"Where is she, anyway?" I ask him. I had walked past the

room she's been staying in, but the door was closed and I didn't want to knock. Well, I *wanted* to knock, but I'm trying my hardest to give her space. If her car hadn't been in the driveway, I'd be freaking the fuck out, but I know she's here. Well, I sure fucking hope so.

"I don't know; she's with that Zed guy, I think," Landon says and my heart drops. I jump up to my feet in seconds.

"Joking! I'm joking. She's in the greenhouse with my mum," Landon says, looking at me with playful scorn.

I don't care, though, I'm just relieved to know that my paranoid thoughts were getting the best of me. "That's not funny. You're a dick," I spit, and he chuckles. "Now you're definitely helping me," I tell him.

AFTER LANDON GIVES ME some advice, he calls it a day and escorts me to the front door. On the way, I ask, "Has she been driving herself to Vance?"

"Yeah, she missed a few days when she was . . . well, you already know."

"Hmm . . ." I lower my voice as we walk past the room that's Tessa's for now. I don't want to think of how I hurt her, not right now. "Do you think she's in there?" I ask quietly.

He shrugs. "I don't know; probably."

"I should just . . ." I turn the doorknob, and it opens with a small creak. Landon shoots me a glare, but I ignore him as I peer inside.

She's lying on the bed with papers and textbooks scattered all around her. Her jeans are still on along with a sweatshirt; she must've been really exhausted to have fallen asleep while she was studying.

"Are you done being a creep now?" Landon hisses in my ear.

I flip the light switch off and step out of the doorway, pulling the door closed behind me. "I'm not being a creep. I love her, okay?"

"I know, but you clearly don't understand the concept of giving her some space."

"I can't help it. I'm so used to being with her and I've been through hell the last nearly two weeks without her. It's hard for me to stay away from her."

We walk down the stairs in silence, and I hope I didn't sound too desperate. Then again, it's only Landon, so I don't really give a fuck anyway.

I HATE GOING to the apartment now that Tessa isn't there. For a second I consider calling Logan and going by the frat house, but deep down I know that's a bad idea. I don't want any problems to occur, and they always do. I just really don't want to go back to that empty apartment.

I do anyway. I'm so damn tired. I haven't slept properly in ages, it seems.

As I lie down in our bed I try to envision her arms around my waist and her head on my chest. It's hard to imagine spending my life this way. If I never get to hold her again, if I never get to feel the warmth of her body next to mine . . . I have to do something. I have to do something different, something that will show her and show myself that I can do this.

I can change. I have to, and I fucking will.

chapter
one hundred and one

TESSA

By the time I take a shower and dry my hair, it's already six and the sky is long since dark. I knock on Landon's bedroom door, but there's no answer. I don't see his car in the driveway, but he's been parking in the garage lately, so he may still be here.

I have no idea what to wear because I don't know where we're going. I can't stop looking out the window, waiting anxiously for Hardin's car to appear in the driveway. When the bright flash of headlights finally does appear, my stomach turns.

Most of my anxiety is dissolved when Hardin steps out of the car in the black button-up shirt he wore to the dinner party. Is he wearing dress pants? Oh my God, he is. And dress shoes, shiny black dress shoes. Wow. Hardin dressed up? I feel underdressed, but the way he's looking at me dissolves my unease.

He really is going all out for this. He looks so handsome, and he even styled his hair. It's pushed back, and I can tell he used something to keep it that way, because it doesn't fall down onto his forehead as he walks, the way it usually does.

He flushes. "Erm . . . hi?"

"Hi." I can't stop staring at him. *Wait* . . . "Where are your piercings?" The metal rings are gone from his eyebrow and lip.

"I took them out." He shrugs.

"Why?"

"I don't know . . . you don't think I look better this way?" He looks into my eyes.

"No! I loved the way you looked before . . . and now, too, but you should put them back."

"I don't want them back in." He walks to the passenger side of his car to open the door for me.

"Hardin . . . I hope you didn't take them out because you thought I'd like you better this way, because it's not true. I love you either way. Please put them back in."

His eyes light up at my words, and I look away before climbing into the car. No matter how mad at him I am, I never want him to feel like he has to change his appearance for me. I was judgmental when I saw his rings for the first time, but I grew to love them. They're part of him. "It's not really like that, honestly. I've been thinking about taking them out for a while anyway. I've had them forever, and they're sort of annoying. Besides, who the hell will hire me for a real job with that shit in my face?" He buckles his seat belt and looks over to me.

"People would hire you; it's the twenty-first century. If you like them . . ."

"It's not that big of a deal. I sort of like the way I look without them, like I'm not hiding anymore, you know?" I stare at him again and take in his new look.

He looks exquisite—he always does—but it's sort of nice to not have any distractions on his perfect face.

"Well, I think you look perfect either way, Hardin; just don't think that I want you to look a certain way, because I don't," I tell him and mean it.

When he looks at me he gives me such a shy smile that I forget what I wanted to yell at him about.

"Where are you taking me, anyway?" I ask him.

"To dinner. It's a really nice place." His voice is shaky. Nervous Hardin is my new favorite Hardin.

"Have I heard of it?"

"I don't know . . . maybe?"

The rest of car ride is quiet. I hum along to the Fray songs that Hardin has obviously taken a strong liking to, and Hardin stares out the windshield. He keeps rubbing his hand over his thigh as he drives—a nervous action, I can tell.

When we arrive at the restaurant, it looks fancy and very expensive. All of the cars in the parking lot cost more than my mother's house, I'm sure.

"I meant to open the door for you," he tells me when I open the door to get out.

"I can shut it back and you can reopen it?" I offer.

"That hardly counts, Theresa." He smiles his smug smile, and I can't help the butterflies in my stomach that appear when he calls me by my real name.

It used to drive me crazy, but I secretly loved every time he would say it to annoy me. I love it almost as much as I love the way he says "Tess."

"We're back to 'Theresa,' I see?" I smile back at him.

"Yes; yes, we are," he says and takes my arm. I can see his confidence growing with each step we take toward the restaurant.

chapter
one hundred and two

HARDIN

Do you know of another place you think you might like instead?"
I ask her when we get back to the car. The man at the fancy
restaurant I made reservations at claimed that my name wasn't on
the list. I kept my cool, careful not to ruin the night. He was such
a fucking prick. My fingers grip the steering wheel.

Calm. I need to relax. I look over at Tessa and smile.

She bites her lip and looks away.

Was that creepy? That was creepy.

"Well, that was awkward." My voice is unsteady and oddly
high-pitched. "Do you have anything in particular you want, since
we've apparently moved on to Plan B now?" I ask her, wishing I
could think of another nice place to take her. One that might actually let us in.

"No, not really. Just somewhere with food." She smiles.

She's being really cool about this, and I'm glad. It was humiliating to be turned away like that. "Okay . . . McDonald's, then?" I
tease just to hear her laugh.

"We may look a little silly in McDonald's."

"Yeah, a little," I agree.

I have no fucking idea where to go now. I should've come up
with a backup plan ahead of time. This night is already spiraling,
and it hasn't even started yet.

We pull up to a stoplight, and I look around. A crowd of people fills the parking lot next to us. "What's going on over there?" Tessa asks, trying to peer around me.

"I don't know, there's an ice-skating rink or some shit," I tell her.

"Ice skating?" Her voice raises the way it does when she's getting excited.

Oh no . . .

"Can we?" she asks.

Fuck. "Go ice skating?" I ask innocently, like I'm unsure of what she means.

Please say no. Please say no.

"Yeah!" she exclaims.

"I . . . I don't . . ." I've never ice-skated in my life and never intended to, but if this is what she wants to do, then it won't kill me to try . . . maybe it will, but I'll do it anyway. "Sure . . . we can."

When I look over, I can tell she's surprised—she never expected me to agree to it. Hell, I didn't either.

"Wait . . . what'll we wear? I only have this dress and some Toms. I should have worn jeans, it would have been so fun," she says, almost pouting.

"We could always run to the store and get you some clothes? I have some in my trunk that I could wear," I tell her. I can't believe I'm going through all this shit to go ice skating.

"Okay." She beams. "The trunk full of clothes comes in handy! Actually . . . Why *do* you keep those clothes in there, anyway? You've never told me."

"It was just a habit. When I'd stay with girls . . . I mean, when I would be out all night, I'd need different clothes in the morning, and I never had them, so I just started keeping them in my trunk. It's pretty convenient," I explain.

Her lips are pursed slightly, and I know I shouldn't have mentioned the other girls, even if they were before her. I wish she knew how it was then, how I would fuck them with no emotion. It wasn't the same. I didn't touch them the way I do her, I didn't study every inch of their bodies, I didn't revel in their shallow breathing and try to match mine to theirs, I didn't desperately wait for them to say they loved me while I moved in and out of them.

I didn't let them touch me in our sleep; if I even stayed in the same bed as them, it was because I was too drunk to move. It wasn't anything like it is with her, and if she knew that, maybe knowing about them wouldn't bother her. If I were her, I . . . Thoughts of Tessa fucking anyone else cloud my mind and make me nauseous.

"Hardin?" she says quietly, bringing me back to reality.

"Yeah?"

"Did you hear me?"

"No . . . sorry. What did you say?"

"You passed Target already."

"Oh, shit, sorry. I'll turn around." I pull into the next parking lot and turn the car around. Tessa has an obsession with Target that I'll never understand. It's just like M&S back in London, only more expensive, and the employees are annoying as shit in their stupid red polos and khaki pants. But she always tells me, *Target has great quality and a lot to choose from.* I can't say she's wrong, but "big box stores" are still one of the things in America that make me feel most like the foreigner that I am.

"I'll just run inside and get something," Tessa says when I park the car.

"Are you sure? I can come." I want to go with her, but I can't insist on my presence, not tonight.

"If you want to . . ."

"I do," I answer before she can finish.

* * *

WITHIN TEN MINUTES she has her basket nearly full of crap. She ended up getting a gigantic sweatshirt and some sort of spandex pants—she swears they're not spandex, that they're leggings, but damn if they don't look like spandex to me. I try to stop picturing her in them as she grabs gloves, a scarf, and a hat. She acts like we're going to fucking Antarctica; then again, it *is* pretty damn cold outside.

"I really think you should get some gloves, too. The ice is really cold, and when you fall your hands will freeze," she says again.

"I'm not going to fall . . . but sure, I'll get gloves if you insist." I smile, and she returns it as she tosses a pair of black gloves into her basket.

"Do you want a hat?" she asks.

"No, I have a beanie in the trunk."

"Of course you do." She pulls the scarf out of the basket and hangs it back up.

"No scarf?" I ask her.

"I think I'll be okay with all of this." She points to the basket.

"Yeah, I'd say so," I tease, but she ignores me and walks to the sock section. We're going to be in this damn store all night.

Finally, Tessa says, "Okay, I'm done, I think."

At the register, she tries to argue with me over paying for her stuff like she always does. But this is a date that I asked her on, so there's no way in hell I'm letting her pay. To that sentiment, she just rolls her eyes a few times and takes out her purse and hands over her last bills to the clerk.

Is she running low on money? If she was, would she tell me? Should I ask her? Fuck, I'm thinking way too much into this.

By the time we get back to the lot where the skating is, Tessa's ready to jump out of the car, but we need to change first. I change my clothes; she keeps her head turned and stares out the window the whole time. Afterward, I tell her "We can find a bathroom for you to change in."

But she just shrugs. "I was just going to change in the car so I don't have to carry my dress around."

"No, there are too many people. Someone will see you undress." I look around at the area of the parking lot where we are and it's pretty empty, but still . . .

"Hardin . . . it's *fine*," she says with a little annoyance.

I should've stolen that stress ball I saw on my father's desk last night. "If you insist," I huff, and she tears the tags off of her new clothes.

"Can you help me unzip this before you get out?" she asks me.

"Erm . . . yeah." I reach across the center console, and she lifts her hair up to allow me access to the zipper. I have unzipped this dress countless times, but this is the first time that I won't be able to touch her as she slides it down her arms.

"Thank you. Now wait outside," she instructs.

"What? It's not like I haven't—" I start to say.

"Hardin . . ."

"Fine. Hurry up." I get out of the car and close the door. What I just said was rude, I realize. I open the door quickly and lean down. "Please," I add and close it again.

I can hear her laughing inside the car.

Minutes later she climbs out and her hands comb through her long hair before she pulls a purple beanie down over her head. When she joins me on the other side of the car, she looks . . . cute. She always looks beautiful and sexy, but something about the giant sweatshirt, hat, and gloves makes her look even more innocent than usual.

"Here, you forgot your gloves," she says, handing them to me.

"Good thing. I wouldn't have made it without them," I mock, and she nudges me with her elbow. She's so goddamned cute.

There are so many things I want to say to her, but I don't want to say something wrong and ruin the night.

"You know, if you wanted to wear such a large sweater, you

could've worn one of mine and saved yourself twenty bucks," I say, and she grabs my hand but lets go quickly.

"Sorry," she mutters, and her cheeks flush.

I want to grab her hand again, but I'm distracted by a short woman greeting us. "What size skates?" the lady asks in a deep voice.

I look down at Tessa, and she answers for both of us. The woman returns with two pairs of ice skates, and I cringe. There is no way in hell this is going to go well.

I follow Tess to a bench nearby and remove my shoes. She has both of her ice skates on before I have half of my foot in one. Hopefully she'll get bored easily and want to leave.

"You okay over there?" she mocks me as I finally lace up the second skate.

"Yes. Where do I put my shoes?" I ask her.

"I'll take them." The short woman appears out of nowhere. I hand her my shoes and Tess does the same with hers.

"Ready?" she asks, and I stand up.

I grip the railing immediately. *How the fuck am I going to do this?*

Tessa fights a smile. "It gets easier when you're moving on the ice."

I sure fucking hope so.

It doesn't get easier, though, and I fall three times within five minutes. Tessa laughs each time, and I have to admit that if I didn't have the gloves, my hands would be ice by now.

She laughs and reaches her hand out to me to help me up. "Remember like thirty minutes ago when you said you weren't going to fall?"

"What are you, some sort of professional ice skater?" I ask her as I climb to my feet. I hate ice skating more than anything right now, but she is beyond amused.

"No, I haven't been in a while, but my friend Josie and I used to go a lot."

"Josie? I've never heard you talk about any friends from back home."

"I didn't have many. I spent most of my time with Noah growing up. Josie moved before my senior year."

"Oh." I don't know why she wouldn't have many friends. So what if she's a little OCD and prudish and she obsesses over novels . . . she's nice, sometimes too damn nice, to everyone. Except me, of course, she gives me shit constantly, but I do love that about her. Most of the time.

Thirty minutes later, we haven't even lapped around the rink once because of my fine footwork.

"I'm hungry," she says at last and looks over to a food stand with dancing lights on top.

I smile. "But you haven't fallen and pulled me down with you so you're lying perfectly on top of me and staring into my eyes, like the movies."

"This is so not like the movies," she reminds me and heads toward the exit.

I wish she had held my hand while we skated; if I could manage to stay on my feet, that is. All the happy couples seem to be mocking us as they circle around me holding hands.

The second I leave the rink, I remove the horrendous skates and find the tiny lady and get my damn shoes back.

"You really have a future in sports," Tess teases me for the thousandth time when I join her at the food stand, where she's eating a funnel cake and wiping flakes of powdered sugar off her purple sweatshirt.

"Ha ha." I roll my eyes. My ankles still hurt from that shit. "I could have taken you somewhere else to eat; funnel cakes aren't exactly a nice dinner," I tell her and look at the ground.

"It's fine. I haven't had one in so long." She has eaten all of hers and half of mine.

I catch her staring at me again; her face holds a thoughtful expression as she studies my face. "Why do you keep staring at me?" I finally ask, and she looks away.

"Sorry . . . I'm just not used to the piercings being gone," she admits, staring again.

"It's not that different." Without realizing it, I find I've moved my fingers to my mouth.

"I know . . . it's just weird, though. I was so used to seeing them."

Should I put them back in? I didn't remove them only for her sake—it's true what I told her. I do feel like I was hiding behind them, using the small metal rings to block people out. Piercings intimidate people and make them far less likely to talk to me or come near me at all, and I feel like I'm getting past that stage of my life. I don't want to keep people out, especially not Tessa. I want to pull her in.

I got them done when I was only a teenager, forging my mum's signature and getting wasted before stumbling into the shop. The dumb-ass could smell the booze on me but did the piercings anyway. I don't regret getting them at all; I'm just over them.

I don't feel that way about my tattoos, though. I love them and I always will. I'll continue to cover my body in ink, expressing thoughts that I can't bring myself to actually say. Well, that's not really the case, seeing as they are random shit that have no meaning whatsoever, but they look all right, so I don't give a fuck.

"I don't want you to change," she tells me, and I look over at her. "Not physically. I only want you to show me that you can treat me better and not try to control me. I don't want you to change your personality either. I only want you to fight for me, not turn yourself into someone you think I want to be with."

Her words tug at the edges of my heart, threatening to tear it open. "I'm not," I tell her.

I'm trying to change for her, but not that way. This was for me, and for her.

"Taking them out was just a step in all of this. I'm trying to be a better person, and the piercings remind me of a bad time in my life. A time I want to move on from," I tell her.

"Oh," she nearly whispers.

"You liked them, then?" I smile.

"Yes, very much," she admits.

"I could put them back?" I offer, but she shakes her head.

I'm much less nervous now than I was two hours ago. This is Tessa, my Tessa, and I shouldn't be nervous.

"Only if you want to."

"I could put them back in when we . . ." I stop myself.

"When we what?" She tilts her head to the side.

"You don't want me to finish it."

"Yes, I do! What were you going to say?"

"Fine, have it your way. I was going to say I could always put them back in and fuck you if they turn you on that much."

Her horrified expression makes me laugh, and she looks around to make sure no one heard me. "Hardin!" she scolds me, between bouts of red-faced laughter.

"I warned you . . . Plus I haven't made any perverted comments at all tonight, I should be allowed one."

"True," she agrees with a smile and takes a drink of her lemonade.

I want to ask her if that means she could see herself having sex with me again since she didn't correct me, but I get the feeling this isn't the right time. It's not only because I want to feel her again, it's because I genuinely miss her so fucking much. We're getting along pretty well, especially for us. I know a lot of it's because I'm not being a dick for once. It's not that hard, really. I just have to think before I say shit.

"Your birthday is tomorrow. What do you have planned?" she asks me after a few moments of silence.

Shit.

"Well, um . . . Logan and Nate are sort of throwing me a party. I wasn't going to go, but Steph said they went all out and spent a shitload of money, so I figured I would at least drop by there. Unless . . . you wanted to do something? I won't go," I tell her.

"No, it's okay. I'm sure the party will be much more fun."

"You could come?" And because I know her answer, I add, "No one even knows what's going on between us—except Zed, of course."

I need to not focus on why Zed knows my fucking business.

"No, thanks, though." She smiles, but it doesn't meet her eyes.

"I really don't have to go."

If she wants to spend my birthday with me, then Logan and Nate can fuck off.

"No, really, it's fine. I have stuff to do anyway," she says and looks away.

chapter
one hundred and three

TESSA

D o you have plans for the rest of the night?" Hardin asks as he pulls into his father's driveway.

"No, just studying and going to sleep. Wild night." I smile at him.

"I miss sleep." He frowns, running his index finger along the ridges on the steering wheel.

"You haven't been sleeping?" Of course he hasn't. "Are you . . . have you been . . ." I begin.

"Yeah, every single night," he tells me, and my heart aches.

"I'm sorry." I hate this. I hate those nightmares for haunting him. I hate that I'm the only elixir, the only thing to make them stay away.

"It's fine. I'm fine," he says, but the dark circles under his eyes beg to differ.

Inviting him up would be a terribly stupid idea. I'm supposed to be thinking about what to do with my life from this point forward, not spending the night with Hardin. It's so awkward that he's dropping me off at his father's house; this is exactly why I need to get my own place.

"You could come up? Just to get some sleep. It's still early," I offer, and his head snaps up.

"You'd be okay with that?" he asks, and I nod before I let my thoughts invade.

"Sure . . . only to sleep, though," I remind him with a smile, and he nods.

"I know, Tess."

"I didn't mean it like that . . ." I try to explain.

"I got it," he huffs.

Okay . . .

There is a distance between us that's both uncomfortable and necessary at the same time. I want to just reach over and push the lone strand of hair that's fallen onto his forehead, but that would be too much. I need this distance, just like I need Hardin. It's very confusing, and I know inviting him up won't be helpful to clearing up that confusion, but I just really want him to be able to sleep.

I give him a small smile, and he stares at me for a second before shaking his head. "You know, I better not. I've got some work to do and—" he begins.

"It's fine. Really," I interrupt and open the car door to escape my embarrassment.

I shouldn't have done that. I'm supposed to be distancing myself and here I am being rejected . . . again.

When I reach the door I remember I forgot my dress and heels in Hardin's car, but he's already backing out of the driveway by the time I turn around.

AS I WIPE THE MAKEUP from my face that night and get ready for bed, my mind replays our date over and over. Hardin was so . . . nice. Hardin was nice. He was dressed up and he didn't get into a fight, he didn't even curse anyone out. This is major progress. I begin to giggle like an idiot as I remember him falling on the ice; he was so irritated, but it was so funny to watch him fall. He's so tall and lanky and his legs kept wobbling in the skates. It was definitely one of the funniest things that I've ever seen.

I'm not sure how I feel about Hardin's piercings being removed, but he told me over and over that he wanted to keep them out, so it's not up to me. I wonder what his friends will say about it.

My mood shifted slightly when he told me about his birthday party. I don't know what I assumed he would be doing for his birthday, but partying wasn't it. I'm an idiot, though, because this is his *twenty-first* birthday, after all.

I want to spend it with him more than anything, but something bad happens every single time I go to that damn frat house, and I don't want to continue the cycle, especially when we're in such a fragile state as it is. The last thing I need is to drink and make things worse. I'd like to get Hardin something for his birthday, though. I'm terrible at gifts, but I'll think of something. I stop by Landon's room but he doesn't answer when I knock; when I open the door he's asleep and I decide to go to bed myself.

I open the bedroom door and nearly jump out of my skin when I'm confronted with a figure sitting on the bed. I drop my toiletry bag on the dresser . . . then realize it's Hardin and I calm down. As I watch, he awkwardly crosses his ankles in front of him.

"I . . . I, um, I'm sorry for being a dick down there, I wanted to stay." Hardin runs his fingers through his unruly hair.

"I asked you, too," I remind him and cross over to the bed.

He sighs. "I know and I'm sorry. Can I please stay? I had such a good time tonight just being around you, and I'm so tired . . ."

I contemplate this for a few moments. I wanted him to stay. I miss the comfort of having him in my bed, but he was just saying that he had things to do.

"What about your work?" I raise a brow.

"It can wait," he says, looking distressed.

I sit next to him on the bed and grab the pillow, covering my lap with it.

"Thank you," Hardin says, and I scoot closer. He's still a magnet to me; I can't seem to stay even feet away from him.

I look over at him, and he smiles, then quickly looks down at the floor. My body has a mind of its own, and I lean into him, wrapping my hand around his. His hands are cold, his breathing heavy.

I've missed you, I want to say. *I want to be close to you,* I want to confess.

He squeezes my hand gently and I rest my head on his shoulder. One of his arms wraps around my back, holding me close.

"I had a really nice time tonight," I tell him.

"Me too, baby. Me too."

Being called "baby" makes me want to be even closer to him. I look up at him to find his eyes resting on my mouth. Instinctively, my head tilts up, bringing my mouth closer to his. When I close the space between us and press my lips to his, he leans back on his elbows and I climb onto his lap. I feel one hand resting on my lower back, pushing my body further onto his.

"I missed you," he says, then sweeps his tongue over mine. I miss the cold of the metal ring, but my body is heated by my need for him, making everything else irrelevant.

"I missed you, too." I wrap my fingers into his hair and kiss him harder. My other hand snakes down to touch the hard muscles under his shirt, but he stops me, leaning up with me still on his lap.

He smiles, not without chagrin. "I think we should keep it PG." His cheeks are flushed and his breath heavy against my face.

I want to protest, to tell him that I need his touch, but I know he's right. Sighing, I climb off of his lap and lie down on the far side of the bed.

"I'm sorry, Tess. I didn't mean . . ." he trails off.

"No, you're right. Really, it's okay. Let's get some sleep." I smile, my body still reeling from the contact.

He lies across from me, keeping to his side of the bed with a pillow shoved between us, reminding me of our earlier days. He falls asleep fast, his peaceful snores filling the air, but when I wake up in the middle of the night, Hardin is gone. Instead, a note on his pillow has taken his place.

Thank you again, had to get some work done, it says.

THE NEXT MORNING I text Hardin as soon as I wake up to wish him a happy birthday and get dressed while I wait for a reply. I wish he would have stayed, but, in the light of day, I'm a little relieved to not have to deal with the awkward morning-after-a-first-date thing.

With a sigh I put my phone into my bag and head downstairs to meet Landon, to tell him I'm going to miss half the day today in order to get Hardin a birthday present.

chapter
one hundred and four

HARDIN

It's gonna be sick, man," Nate tells me as he climbs onto the stone wall at the end of the parking lot.

"Sure it will," I remark. I move out of the way of Logan's cigarette smoke and sit next to Nate.

"It will, and you better not bitch out, because we've had this planned for months," Logan tells me.

My legs swing back and forth, and for a second I think of pushing Logan off the stone wall for all the shit he gave me about taking my piercings out.

"I'm coming. I already told you I was."

"Are you bringing her?" Nate asks, obviously talking about Tess.

"Nah, she's busy."

"Busy? It's your twenty-first birthday, dude. You took your rings out for her, she needs to be there," Logan remarks.

"Whenever she comes, shit always goes down anyway. And for the last fucking time, I didn't take them out for her." I roll my eyes and trace the cracks in the concrete.

"Maybe you should have her beat Molly's ass again—that was priceless." Nate chuckles.

"That was so funny; she's funny when she's drunk, too. And when she cusses it's so funny. It's like hearing my Nan cuss." Logan laughs along with Nate.

"Would you two just shut the fuck up about her, already? She's not coming."

"All right, calm down, would you?" Nate asks with a smile.

I wish the two of them hadn't put together a party for me, because I wanted to spend my birthday with Tessa. I don't really give a shit about birthdays, but I wanted to see her. I know she doesn't have shit to do, she just doesn't want to be around my friends—not that I blame her.

"Is something going on with you and Zed?" Nate asks as we head to class.

"Yeah, he's a dick and won't stay away from Tessa. Why?"

"I'm just wondering because I saw Tessa going into the environmental-whatever-the-fuck-it's-called building and I thought it was weird . . ." Nate tells me.

"When was this?"

"Like two days ago. Monday, I think."

"Are you . . ." But I stop midsentence because I know he's serious.

Goddammit, Tessa, what part of "stay the fuck away from Zed" do you not understand?

"You don't care if he comes, though, right? Because we already told everybody and I don't want to uninvite anyone," Nate says; he's always been the nice one out of our group.

"I don't give a shit. He's not the one fucking her, I am," I tell him and he laughs. If he only knew what was actually going on.

Nate and Logan leave me in front of the athletic building, and I have to admit I'm anxious to see Tessa. I wonder how she wore her hair today and if she'll be in those pants that I love so much.

What the fuck? It still blows my mind the way I think about the dumbest shit. Months ago, if you'd told me I'd be daydreaming about the way some girl was wearing her hair, I would have knocked your teeth out. And yet here I am hoping that Tessa's pulled hers back so I can see her face.

* * *

LATER, I CAN'T BELIEVE I'm back at the frat house again. It feels like ages ago that I lived here. I don't miss it at all, but I don't exactly love living in that apartment alone either.

This year has been fucking insane. I really can't believe I'm twenty-one now and will be finished with university next year. My mum kept crying on the phone earlier about how I'm growing up too quickly, and I ended up hanging up on her because she just wouldn't stop. In my defense, I was somewhat polite about it, acting as if my phone was about to die the whole conversation.

The house is packed, the street is lined with cars, and I wonder who the fuck-all these people are that are here for my birthday. I know the party isn't totally for me. It's just an excuse to throw a big-ass party, but still. Just as I begin to wish Tessa were here, I spot Molly's hideous pink hair and I'm glad Tessa didn't come.

"There's the birthday boy." She smiles and walks into the house before me.

"Scott!" Tristan calls from the kitchen; he's already been drinking, I can tell.

"Where's Tessa?" Steph asks.

All of my friends are standing in a small circle basically staring me down as I try to think of something on the spot. The last thing I need is for them to know I'm trying to persuade her to come back to me.

"Wait . . . more importantly, where the hell are your rings?" Steph puts her hand under my chin and tilts my head to examine me like I'm a fucking lab rat.

"Get off," I groan and pull away from her.

"Holy shit! You're turning into one of them," Molly says and points to a group of preppy douche bags across the room.

"No, I'm not." I glare at her.

She cackles and presses on: "Yes, you are! She told you to take them out, didn't she?"

"No, she didn't, I took them out because I fucking felt like it. Mind your own damn business," I snap, and she rolls her eyes.

"Whatever you say." She walks away, thank God.

"Ignore her. Anyway, is Tessa coming?" Steph asks me, and I shake my head. "Well, I miss her! I wish she would hang out more." She takes a drink from her red cup.

"Me, too," I say under my breath and fill a cup with water.

Much to my misery, the music and voices get louder as the night goes on. Everyone is wasted before eight o'clock. I still haven't decided if I want to drink or not. I went a long time without drinking until that night at my father's when I destroyed all of Karen's china. I used to go through these lame-ass parties without drinking . . . well, for the most part. I barely remember my early college days, bottle after bottle, slut after slut—it's a blur, and I'm glad. Shit didn't make sense before Tessa came around.

I find a spot on the couch next to Tristan and zone out to thoughts of Tessa while my friends play another dumb-ass drinking game.

chapter
one hundred and five

TESSA

Hey, the text from Hardin reads.

The butterflies that appear in my stomach are ridiculous.

How's your party? I send, and shove another handful of popcorn into my mouth. I've been staring at the screen of my e-reader for two hours straight, and I need a break.

Lame. Can I come over? he responds.

I nearly jump off the bed. I made the decision earlier after spending hours finding a decent gift for him that my "space" can wait until after his birthday. I don't care how needy or pathetic that is. If he chooses to spend time with me over his friends, I'll take it. He really is trying and I need to acknowledge that; granted, we need to discuss his not wanting a future with me and how that will affect my career.

But that can wait until tomorrow.

Yeah, how long until you'll be here? I write.

I dig through the dresser and grab a blue sleeveless shirt that Hardin once told me looks nice on me. I'll have to wear jeans; otherwise I'll look like an idiot sitting in this bedroom in a dress. I wonder what he'll be wearing. Will his hair be pushed back like it was yesterday? Was his party boring without me and he wanted to see me instead? He really is changing and I love him for it.

Why am I so giddy?

Thirty minutes.

I rush to the bathroom to brush the popcorn kernels from my teeth. I shouldn't be kissing him, should I? It *is* his birthday . . . one kiss won't be so bad, and let's be honest: he deserves a kiss for all the effort he's put into this so far. One kiss won't hurt anything I'm trying to do.

I touch up my makeup and run the hairbrush through my hair before pulling it into a ponytail. I clearly have no sense of judgment where Hardin is involved, but I'll scold myself tomorrow. I know he doesn't do much for birthdays, but I want this one to be different—I want him to know that his birthday is important.

I grab the gift I bought and begin to wrap it quickly. The paper I bought is covered in music notes and would make a good book cover. I'm getting nervous and sidetracked even though I shouldn't be.

Okay, see you soon, I send, and head downstairs after scribbling his name on the small gift tag.

Karen is dancing to an old Luther Vandross song, and I can't help but laugh when she turns around with flushed cheeks. "Sorry, I didn't know you were there," she says, clearly embarrassed.

"I love this song. My father used to play it all the time," I tell her, and she smiles.

"He has good taste, then."

"He did." I smile at the somewhat decent memory of my father twirling me around the kitchen . . . before the sun fell and he gave my mother a black eye for the first time.

"So what are you up to tonight? Landon's at the library again," she tells me, though I already knew.

"I was actually going to see if you could help me make a cake or something for Hardin. It's his birthday and he's going to be here in about a half hour." I can't help but smile.

"He is? Well, of course, we can make a quick sheet cake . . . or actually, let's do a two-layer circle cake. What does he like better, chocolate or vanilla?"

"Chocolate cake and chocolate icing," I tell her. No matter how much I feel I don't know him sometimes, I know him better than I think I know myself.

"Okay, get the pans out for me?" she asks, and I jump to it.

Thirty minutes later I'm waiting for the cake to cool the rest of the way so that we can ice it before Hardin gets here. Karen has dug out some old candles; she could only find a one and a three, but I know he'll find humor in that.

I walk to the living room and look out the window to see if he's here yet, but the driveway is empty. He's probably just running a little late. It's only been forty-five minutes.

"Ken'll be home in an hour or so, he had a dinner with some colleagues. Being a terrible person, I claimed to have a stomachache. I just hate those dinners." She laughs and I giggle as I attempt to smooth the chocolate icing along the edges of the cake.

"I don't blame you," I tell her and place the numbers on the top of the cake.

After arranging them to say thirty-one, I decide to have them say thirteen instead. Karen and I laugh at the corny candles and I struggle with the thick icing to write Hardin's name below the candles.

"It looks . . . nice," she lies.

I cringe at my terrible icing skills. "It's the thought that counts. Or at least it better be . . ."

"He'll love it," Karen assures me before heading upstairs so Hardin and I can have some privacy when he gets here.

It's now been an hour since he texted, and I'm sitting in the kitchen alone waiting for him to show. I want to call him, but if he isn't coming he should be the one to call me and tell me.

He'll come. It was his idea to come, anyway. He will come.

chapter
one hundred and six

HARDIN

For a third time, Nate tries to hand me his cup. "C'mon, man. Just one drink, it's your twenty-first birthday, dude—it's illegal *not* to!"

Because it will get me out of here smoother, I finally relent. "Fine, one drink. But that's it."

Smiling, he pulls his cup back and grabs the bottle of liquor out of Tristan's hand. "Okay, then. At least have a proper one," he says.

I roll my eyes before taking a swig of the dark liquid. "All right, that's all. Now you can leave me alone," I tell him, and he nods in agreement.

I head to the kitchen to get another cup of water, and Zed, of all fucking people, stops me. "Here," he says, handing me my phone. "You left it on the couch when you got up."

Then he wanders back into the living room.

chapter
one hundred and seven

TESSA

After two hours, I leave the cake on the counter and head upstairs to take my makeup off and change back into my pajamas. This is what happens every single time I let myself give him another chance. Reality smacks me in the face.

I really thought he was coming; I'm so foolish. I was downstairs baking him a cake . . . God, I'm an idiot.

I grab my headphones before I allow myself to cry again. The music pours into my ears as I lie back on the bed and do my best to not be too hard on myself. He acted so different last night—mostly in a good way, but I do miss his perverted and rude remarks that I always pretend to hate but secretly love.

I'm glad Landon didn't come to say hello when I heard him get home. I was still holding a little hope and I would have looked even more ridiculous, not that he'd ever tell me that, of course.

I reach over and turn off the light on the nightstand, then turn down the music slightly. If this were a month ago, I would jump into my car and drive to that stupid house and ask him why the hell he stood me up, but it's now, and now I just don't have it in me to fight him. Not anymore.

* * *

I'M WOKEN UP by my phone ringing in my ears, and the noise coming through my headphones startles me.

It's Hardin. And it's almost midnight. *Don't answer it, Tessa.*

I literally have to force myself to ignore his call and shut off my phone. I reach over and set the alarm clock on the nightstand and close my eyes.

Of course he'd be drunk, dialing me after standing me up. I should have known better.

chapter
one hundred and eight

HARDIN

Tessa isn't answering my calls, and it's pissing me off. It's my damn birthday for fifteen more minutes, and she doesn't answer the phone?

Yeah, I probably should have called her sooner, but still. She hasn't even responded to my text from hours ago. I thought we had a nice time yesterday, and she even tried to get me naked. It killed me to say no, but I knew what would happen if we went there. I don't need to take advantage of her right now, even though I really fucking want to.

"I think I'm going to go," I tell Logan, prompting him to unwrap himself from the dark-skinned brunette he's obviously taken a liking to.

"Nah, you can't leave yet, not until—oh, there they are!" he calls and points.

I turn around to see two girls in trench coats coming toward us. *No fucking way.*

The crowded living room bursts into clapping and cheering.

"I don't do strippers," I tell him.

"Oh, come on! How'd you even know they were strippers?" He laughs.

"They're in fucking trench coats and high heels!" This is so fucking stupid.

"Come on, man, Tessa won't care!" Logan adds.

"That's not the point," I growl, even though it is. It's not the only point, but it's the biggest.

"Is this the birthday boy?" one of the girls says.

Her bright red lipstick is giving me a headache already. "No, no, no. I'm not," I lie and bolt out the door.

"Come on, Hardin!" a few voices call.

Hell no, I'm not turning around. Tessa will lose her shit if she thought I was around strippers. I can practically hear her screaming at me about it now. I wish she'd answered when I called. I try to call her one more time as Nate attempts to call my other line. I'm not going back in there, no way in hell. I've participated in the birthday festivities long enough.

I bet she's mad at me right now for not calling her earlier, but I never know when I should call and when I shouldn't. I don't want to push her, but I don't want to give her too much space either. It's a difficult line to walk, and I have no fucking balance.

I check my phone one more time, and see that the *Hey* I sent her is the last message sent or received. Looks like it's me and that lonely-ass apartment again.

Happy fucking birthday to me.

chapter
one hundred and nine

TESSA

I wake up to a strange alarm, and it takes me a few seconds to re-member I shut my phone off last night because of Hardin. Then I remember how I'd sat at the kitchen counter, my excitement dying a little with each passing minute, only to have him never show up at all.

I wash my face and get myself ready for the long drive to Vance; the one thing I really miss about the apartment is the shorter drive. And Hardin. And the bookshelves that cover the wall. And the small but perfect kitchen. And that lamp. And Hardin.

When I walk downstairs, Karen is the only one in the kitchen. My eyes go directly to the cake with the number thirteen in can-dles and the stupid scribble that used to say *Hardin* but now has shifted as a result of sitting out all night and looks like it says *Hell*.

Maybe it does.

"He wasn't able to make it," I tell her without meeting her eyes.

"Yeah . . . I deduced." She gives me a sympathetic smile and wipes her glasses on her apron.

She's the perfect housewife, she's always cooking or clean-ing something, but more than that, she's so kind and she loves her husband and family, even her rude stepson, dearly.

"It's fine." I shrug and fill a mug with coffee.

"You know you don't always have to be fine, honey."

"I know. But it's easier to be fine," I tell her, and she nods.

"It's not supposed to be easy," she tells me, and I nearly laugh at the irony of her using the words that Hardin always uses against me.

"Anyway, we're thinking of taking a trip to the beach next week. If you want to come, that would be lovely." One of the things I love about Landon's mother is that she never pushes me to talk about anything.

"The beach? In February?" I ask.

"We have a boat that we like to take out before it gets too warm. We go whale watching, and it's really neat; you should come."

"Really?" I've never been on a boat before, and the thought terrifies me, but whale watching does sound interesting. "Yeah, okay."

"Great! We'll have a really nice time," she assures me, and heads into the living room.

I finally turn my phone back on when I get to Vance. I need to stop turning it off when I'm angry. I can just ignore Hardin's calls next time. If something happened with my mother and she couldn't get ahold of me, I'd feel terrible.

Kimberly and Christian are leaning into each other in the hall when I step off of the elevator. He whispers something into her ear and she giggles before he tucks her hair behind her ear and smiles widely as he kisses her, both of them still smiling.

I hurry to my office to call my mother, figuring it's time, but she doesn't answer. The manuscript I begin to read pisses me off within the first five pages. When I skim through the last few pages, I see *I do* and sigh. I'm sick of the same old story: girl meets boy, boy loves her, one problem gets in the way, they make up, get married, have kids, the end. I toss the pages into the trash without reading further. I feel bad for not giving it much of a chance, but it's not working for me.

I need a realistic story, where there are real problems, more than one fight, and even a breakup. A real one. People hurt each other and keep coming back for more . . . including me, of course. I realize this now.

Christian walks past my office and I take a deep breath before getting up to follow him. I smooth my skirt and try to practice what to say to him about Seattle. I hope Hardin didn't ruin my chance to go.

"Mr. Vance?" I knock lightly at his door.

"Tessa? Come on in," he says with a smile.

"Sorry for bothering you, but I was wondering if you have a few minutes to talk about something?" I ask, and he waves for me to sit down. "I was wondering about Seattle, if there's any chance that I could transfer there? I understand if it's too late, but I'd really like to go, and Trevor mentioned it to me and I was just thinking that it could be a really great opportunity for me if—"

Christian raises his hand and laughs, stopping me. "You really want to go?" he asks with a smile. "Seattle's a much different place from here." His green eyes are soft, but I get the feeling he isn't convinced.

"Yeah, I'm positive. I really would love to go . . ." I would. I honestly would. Wouldn't I?

"And Hardin? Would he be coming along?" He pulls at the knot on his tie, loosening the printed material around his neck.

Should I tell him that Hardin refuses to go? That his place in my future is as unsure as it could be and he's stubborn and paranoid? Instead I go with "We're still discussing."

Vance meets my eyes. "I would love to bring you to Seattle with us." Then after a beat he adds, "Hardin, too. He can tag along, maybe even get his old job back," Christian says, then laughs. "If he can keep his mouth shut."

"Really?"

"Yes, of course. You should have spoken up sooner." He plays with his tie a little longer before completely removing it and laying it on his desk.

"Thank you so much! I really appreciate it," I say and mean it.

"Do you have any idea when you'll be ready to go? Kim, Trevor, and myself will be leaving in about two weeks, but you can join us whenever you're ready. I know you have to transfer colleges. I'll work with you as much as I can."

"Two weeks should be good," I answer before I can think about it.

"Great, this is just great. Kim will be happier than ever." He smiles and I watch his eyes shift to the picture of Kimberly and Smith on his desk.

"Thank you again, this means so much to me," I tell him before leaving his office. Seattle. Two weeks. I'm moving to Seattle in two freaking weeks. I'm ready.

Aren't I?

Of course I am, I've been waiting for this moment for years. I just never expected it to happen so soon.

chapter
one hundred and ten

TESSA

I wait outside of Zed's apartment, hoping he won't be too much longer. I really need to talk to him, and he said he was on his way home from work. I stopped to grab a coffee on my way to kill some time. After waiting a few minutes, he pulls up, his truck blaring something amazingly loud. When he climbs out of it, he looks so good dressed in black jeans and a red T-shirt with cutoff sleeves that I'm momentarily distracted from my purpose.

"Tessa!" he says with a big smile and invites me inside. After getting me another coffee and himself a soda, we go into the living room.

"Zed, I have something to tell you, I think. But I want to tell you something else first," I say.

He puts his hands behind his head and leans against the back of the couch. "Is it about the party?"

"You went?" I ask, putting my news on hold. I sit down on the chair across from the couch.

"Yeah, for a while, but once those strippers showed up, I left." Zed rubs the back of his neck. My breath is lost.

"Strippers?" I croak, sitting my cup of coffee on the table before I drop the hot liquid onto my lap.

"Yeah, everyone was so wasted, and on top of that they had strippers. That's not my thing, so I got out of there." He shrugs.

I was baking Hardin a cake and planning to spend his birthday with him while he was getting wasted with strippers?

"Did anything else happen at the party?" I ask, changing the subject again. I can't get the strippers out of my head. How could Hardin stand me up for that?

"Not really, it was just the typical party. Have you talked to Hardin?" he asks, his eyes focused on his can of soda as his finger pushes the tab back and forth.

"No, I . . ." I don't want to admit that he stood me up.

"What were you going to say?" Zed questions.

"He said he was going to come over but he didn't show."

"That's low." He shakes his head.

"I know, and you know what the worst part is? That we had a really good time on our date and I thought he was really going to start putting me first." Zed's eyes are full of sympathy when I look at him.

"Then he chose a party over going to see you," he adds.

"Yeah . . ." I really don't know what else to say.

"I think that really shows what type of person he is and that he isn't going to change. You know?" *Is he right?*

"I know. I just really wish he'd talked to me about it or told me he just didn't want to come over instead of leaving me sitting there for hours waiting on him." My fingers play with the edges of the table, picking at the peeling wood.

"I don't think you should talk to him about it; if he thought you were worth his time, he would have showed and not left you waiting."

"I know you're right, but this is the main problem in our relationship. We don't talk about things, we both jump to conclusions that lead to yelling and one of us leaving," I say. I know Zed is only trying to help, but I really want Hardin to explain to me, to my face, why hanging out with strippers was more important than me.

"I thought you didn't have a relationship anymore?"

"We do . . . well, we don't, but . . . I don't even know how to explain it." I'm mentally exhausted and Zed's presence sometimes confuses me even more.

"It's your choice, I just wish you wouldn't waste any more time on him." He sighs and gets up from the couch.

"I know," I whisper and check my phone for a message from Hardin. There isn't one.

"Are you hungry?" Zed asks me from the kitchen, and I hear his empty can hit the trash.

chapter
one hundred and eleven

HARDIN

This apartment is so goddamned empty.

I hate sitting here without her. I miss her legs resting on my lap as she studies and I steal unnoticed glances at her while pretending to work. I miss the way she would obnoxiously poke my arm with her pen until I snatched it from her and held it above her head, and then she'd act so annoyed, but I knew she was only bugging me to get me to pay attention to her. The way she would climb on my lap to retrieve the object always led to the same thing, every time, which was obviously a good thing for me.

"Fuck," I say to myself and set my binder down. I haven't gotten shit done today, or yesterday, or the past two weeks really.

I'm still pissed that she didn't respond to me last night, but more than anything I just want to see her. I'm pretty sure she'll be at my father's house, so I should just go by there and talk to her. If I call her she may not answer and that will make me more anxious, so I'll just stop by.

I know I'm supposed to be giving her space, but, really . . . fuck space. It's not working for me and I hope it's not working for her either.

By the time I get to my father's house, it's almost seven and Tessa's car isn't here.

What the fuck.

She's probably at the store or library with Landon or some shit. I'm proven wrong when I see Landon sitting on the couch with a textbook on his lap. Great.

"Where is she?" I ask him as soon as I enter the living room.

I almost sit down next to him but I decide to stand. That would be weird as fuck to just sit down with him.

"I don't know, I haven't seen her yet today," he responds, barely looking up from his studies.

"Have you talked to her?" I ask him.

"No."

"Why not?"

"Why would I? Not everyone stalks her," he says with a smile.

"Fuck off," I huff.

"I really don't know where she is," Landon tells me.

"Well, I'll wait here . . . I guess." I walk into the kitchen and take a seat at the counter. Just because I sort of like him a little more now doesn't mean I'm going to sit there and stare at him while he does his homework.

There's a blob of chocolate on a plate in front of me with candles reading *thirteen*. Is this thing supposed to be someone's birthday cake?

"Who's shit cake is this in here?" I yell. I can't make out the name, if that's what the white icing was supposed to be.

"It's *your* shit cake," Karen answers me. When I turn around, she's giving me a sarcastic smile.

I didn't even see her come in. "Mine? It says 'thirteen.'"

"Those were the only candles I had and Tessa really got a kick out of them," she tells me. There's something behind her voice that sounds off. Is she mad or something?

"Tessa? I'm confused."

"She made that for you last night while she was waiting for

you to get here," she says, then turns her attention to the chicken she's now carving.

"I didn't come here."

"I know you didn't, but she was expecting you." I stare at the hideous cake and feel like a complete ass. Why would she make me a cake without even asking me to come over? I'll never understand that girl. The longer I stare at the cake she made, the more charming it becomes. I'll admit it's not easy on the eyes, but it may have been yesterday before it sat out all night.

I can picture her laughing to herself as she pushed the wrong-numbered candles in the top of the chocolate cake. I can picture her licking the cake batter off of the spoon and scrunching up her nose as she wrote out my name.

She made me a fucking cake and I went to that party. Could I be more of an asshole? "Where is she now?" I ask Karen.

"I have no idea, I'm not sure if she'll be here for dinner."

"Can I stay? For dinner?" I ask her.

"Of course you can, you don't have to ask." She turns around with a smile.

Her smile is a true testament to her character; she must think I'm an asshole, but she still smiles and welcomes me to stay for dinner.

BY DINNERTIME I'm going fucking crazy. I'm fidgeting in my seat, looking out the window every few seconds, about to call her a thousand times until she answers. Fucking crazy.

My father is talking to Landon about the upcoming baseball season and I really wish both of them would shut the fuck up.

Where the hell is she?

I pull my phone out to finally text her as I hear the front door open. I'm on my feet before I realize it and everyone looks up at me.

"What?" I snap and head to the living room.

Relief washes over me when she practically stumbles in with books and what looks like a poster board in her hands.

As soon as she sees me, the objects begin to topple to the floor. I rush over to help her pick them up.

"Thanks." She takes the books from my hands and starts to walk up the staircase.

"Where are you going?" I ask her.

"To put my stuff away . . ." She turns to answer but then turns back around.

I would normally start cussing at her, but I'm hoping to find out what's wrong with her without yelling, for once. "Are you going to eat dinner?" I call after her.

"Yeah," she answers simply, without turning around.

I bite my tongue and head back to the dining room.

"She'll be down in a minute," I say, and I swear I catch Karen smiling, but it disappears when I look at her.

Minutes feel like hours before Tessa finally takes a seat next to me at the table. Hopefully her sitting next to me is a good sign.

A few minutes later, I realize it's not a good sign, since she hasn't spoken to me once and she's barely eating the food on her plate.

"I got all my paperwork squared away for NYU. I still can't believe it," Landon says, and his mum smiles with pride.

"You won't be getting the family rate," my father jokes, but only his wife actually laughs.

Tessa and Landon—both being the polite suck-ups they are—smile and attempt fake laughs, but I know better.

Once my father brings the conversation back to sports, I find my opening to talk to Tessa. "I saw that cake . . . I didn't know . . ." I begin to whisper.

"Don't. Not right now, please." She frowns and gestures to the other people in the room.

"After dinner?" I ask and she nods.

It drives me insane as she picks at her food; I really just want to shove her forkful of potatoes into her mouth. This is why we have issues, because I daydream about force-feeding her. The dining room is filled with my father trying to bring us all together through small talk and shitty attempts at jokes. I ignore him the best I can and finish my dinner.

"It was really good, honey," my father praises Karen as she begins to clean up the table. He looks at Tessa, then back at his wife. "When you're done with that, why don't I take you and Landon out to Dairy Queen. Haven't been there in a while . . ."

Karen nods with false enthusiasm, and Landon pops up to help her.

"Can we talk, please?" Tessa surprises me by asking when she stands up.

"Yeah, of course." I follow her upstairs and into the room she's been staying in.

I can't tell if she's going to scream at me or cry when she closes the door behind me.

"I saw the cake . . ." I decide to speak first.

"Did you?" She sounds almost uninterested and she takes a seat on the edge of the bed.

"Yeah . . . it was . . . nice of you."

"Yeah . . ."

"I'm sorry for going to the party instead of asking you to spend time with me."

She closes her eyes for a few seconds and takes a deep breath before opening them again. "Okay," she says in a monotone voice.

The way she's staring out the window with no emotion on her face gives me the chills. She looks as if someone has sucked the life out of her . . .

Someone has.

Me.

"I really am sorry. I didn't think you wanted to see me; you said you were busy."

"How could you think that? I waited for you as 'I'll be there in thirty minutes' turned into two hours." She still sounds so emotionless, and the hair on the back of my neck is standing up from it.

"What are you talking about?"

"You said you said you'd be here, and you weren't. Simple as that." I really wish she'd scream at me.

"I didn't say I'd be here. I asked you if you wanted to come to the party and then I even texted and called you last night, but you didn't answer to either."

"Wow. You must've been really drunk," she says slowly, and I move to stand in front of her.

Even though I'm right here, she doesn't look at me. She stares off into space, and it's really unsettling. I'm used to her fire, to her stubbornness, to her tears . . . but I'm not used to this.

"What do you mean? I called you—"

"Yeah, at midnight."

"I know I'm not as smart as you, but I'm really fucking confused right now," I tell her.

"Why did you change your mind? What made you not come?" she asks.

"I didn't know I was supposed to be here. I texted you and said 'hey,' but you never responded."

"Yes, I did, so did you. You said you weren't having fun and you asked if you could come over."

"No . . . I didn't." Was she drunk that night?

"Yes, you did." She holds her phone in the air and I grab it from her.

Lame. Can I come over?

Yeah, how long until you'll be here?

Thirty minutes.

What the fuck?

"I didn't send those, that wasn't me." I try to replay the night. She doesn't say anything, she only picks at her fingernails. "Tessa, if I had thought for a second that you were waiting on me, I would have been here with you."

"You're honestly telling me you didn't text me, when I just showed you proof that you did?" She almost laughs.

I need her to yell at me; at least when she's yelling I know she cares. "Did I not just say that?" I bark.

She stays silent. "Who did, then?"

"I don't know . . . shit, I don't know who . . . Zed! That's who it fucking was—it was Zed." That fucker handed me my phone from where he was sitting on the couch; he must have been texting Tessa acting like he was me so she would be waiting on me.

"Zed? You're really trying to blame Zed for this?"

"Yes! That's exactly what I'm doing. He sat down on the couch right after me and handed me my phone. I know it was him, Tessa," I tell her.

Her eyes flash with confusion and for a second I know she believes me, but she shakes her head. "I don't know . . ." She seems to be talking to herself.

"I wouldn't tell you I was coming and not show, Tess. I've been trying hard, so damn hard, to show you that I can change. I wouldn't stand you up like that, not anymore. That party was so fucking boring anyway, and I was miserable without you there—"

"So, *were* you?" She raises her voice and stands from the bed.

Here we go.

"Were you miserable while there were strippers there?" she yells.

Fuck. "Yes! I didn't even stay after they got there! Wait . . . how do you know about the strippers?"

"Does that *matter*?" she challenges me.

"Yes! It matters; it was him, wasn't it? It was Zed! He's filling your head with all this bullshit to make you turn on me!" I yell back at her. I fucking knew he was up to something. I just didn't know he'd stoop that low. He texted her from my phone and then deleted the messages. Is he really that fucking stupid that he would fuck with my relationship again? I'm going to find that little shit—

"He is not!" she yells, interrupting my rage.

Oh my fuck. "Okay, then, let's call your precious fucking Zed and ask him." I grab her phone again and pull up his name . . . in her favorites list. Goddamn, I want to smash her phone against the goddamn wall.

"Do not call him," she growls at me, but I ignore her.

He doesn't answer. Of fucking course.

"What else did he tell you?" I am fucking fuming.

"Nothing," she lies.

"You're a terrible liar, Tessa. What else did he tell you?"

She glares at me with her arms crossed, and I await her answer.

"Huh?" I press.

"That you were hanging out with Jace the night I was at his house." My anger is threatening to get the best of me. "You wanna know who hangs out with Jace, Tess? Fucking Zed, that's who. They hang out all the time. I went there to ask him about you two since you want to fucking shack up with him all of a sudden."

"Shack up with him? I wasn't shacking up with anyone! I stayed there those times because I like his company and he's always so kind to me! Unlike you!" She steps toward me.

I wanted her to yell at me and now she won't stop, but it's much better than her sitting there like she didn't give a shit.

"He's not as sweet as you think he is, Tessa! How can you not see that! He's feeding you all this bullshit to get to you. He wants to fuck you, that's all. Don't flatter yourself and think he . . ." I stop myself. I meant the part about Zed but not the rest. "I didn't mean that last part," I say, trying to stoke the anger in her instead of the sadness.

"Sure you didn't." She rolls her eyes.

I can't believe we're having this fight over Zed. This is such bullshit; I told her to stay away from him, but being the stubborn girl she is, she doesn't listen to shit I say.

At least she said she wasn't shacking up with him when she stayed with him those times . . . *times?*

"How many times did you stay at his house?" I ask her, praying I heard her wrong.

"You already know this." She's getting angrier as the seconds pass, and so am I.

"Can we just try to talk about this calmly, because I'm this fucking close to losing my shit and that won't be good for anyone." I pinch my fingers together to prove my point.

"I tried that, and you—"

"Would you just shut up for two seconds and listen to me!" I yell and run my fingers through my hair.

And surprisingly, she does the exact opposite of what I thought she was going to do when she walks over to the bed, sits down on it, and shuts her damn mouth.

I DON'T REALLY KNOW what to say or how to begin, because I didn't expect her to actually listen to me.

I move toward her and stand in front of where she's sitting on the bed; she looks up at me with an unreadable expression, and I pace back and forth for a few seconds before stopping to talk.

"Thank you." I sigh in relief and frustration. "Okay . . . so this is all just twisted around and fucked up. You thought I asked to come over and then I stood you up; you should know by now that I wouldn't do that."

"Should I?" she interrupts.

I don't know how I expect her to know that by now, when I have done so much shit. "You're right . . . but be quiet," I say, and she rolls her eyes.

"My party fucking sucked, and I wouldn't have even gone if you didn't want me to. I didn't drink at all—well, actually I did have one drink, but that's all. I didn't talk to any other girls, I barely spoke to Molly, and I sure as hell wasn't hanging out with strippers. Why the fuck would I want anything to do with a stripper when I have you?"

Her eyes soften slightly, and she's no longer glaring at me like she wants to chop my fucking head off. It's a start.

"Not that I have you . . . but I'm trying to have you again. I don't want anyone else. More importantly, I don't want you to want anyone else either. I don't know why you would run to Zed, anyway. I know he's nice to you blah blah blah . . . but he's full of shit."

"He hasn't done anything to make me think that, Hardin," she insists.

"He texted you from my phone pretending to be me, he purposely told you about the strippers—"

"You don't know that he texted me, and I'm actually glad to have learned about the strippers."

"I would have told you if you'd answered when I called you. I had no idea what was going on. I didn't know you made me a cake or that you were waiting on me. It's already hard enough to get you to see that I'm trying here, but then he has to come in between us and plant these ideas in your head."

She stays silent.

"So where do we go from here, Tess? I need to know, because this back-and-forth shit's killing me and I can't give you space any longer." I kneel down in front of her, and her eyes meet mine as I wait for an answer.

chapter
one hundred and twelve

TESSA

I don't know what to do or say to Hardin at this point.

Part of me knows he isn't lying to me about the texts, but I don't think Zed would do that to me. I just got finished talking to him about everything with Hardin, and he was so kind and understanding.

But this is Hardin.

His voice is low and slow, but he presses: "Can you give me an answer?"

"I don't know, I'm tired of the back-and-forth, too. It's so exhausting and I can't do it anymore, I really can't," I tell him.

"But I didn't do anything; we were fine until yesterday, and none of this is my fault. I know it usually is, but not this time. I'm sorry I didn't spend my birthday with you. I know I should have, and I'm sorry," Hardin says.

He rests his palms on his thighs as he sits in front of me on his knees, not begging like before but just waiting.

If he's telling the truth about not sending the texts, which I believe he is, then this really is just a misunderstanding.

"When will it stop, though? I've had enough of all of it. I had such a great time when you took me out, but then you wouldn't even stay until morning." It's been bothering me that he left like that, but I hadn't fully realized it, I guess.

"I didn't stick around because—per Landon, who I *also* consulted—I'm trying to give you space. I'm shit at it, obviously, but I thought if I gave you a little space you would have time to think about all of this and it would be easier for you," he tells me.

"It's not easier for me, but it's not all about me. It's about you, too," I tell him.

"What?" he questions.

"It's not only about me. I mean, this has to be exhausting for you, too."

"Who gives a shit about me? I just want you to be okay and for you to know that I'm really trying here."

"I do."

"You do what? Believe that I'm trying?" he asks.

"That, and I give a shit about you," I tell him.

"So what are we doing, Tessa? Are we okay now? Or at least on the road to being okay?" He lifts his hand and brings it to my cheek.

He looks at me for approval and I don't stop him.

"Why are we both so crazy?" I whisper as his thumb runs over my bottom lip.

"I'm not. You surely are, though." He smiles.

"You're crazier than me," I tell him, and he inches closer and closer.

I'm irritated at him for yelling at me and for making me wait for him last night even though he supposedly had nothing to do with it, I'm upset that we can't seem to get along, but more than all of that I miss him. I miss the closeness between us. I miss the way his eyes change when he looks at me.

I have to admit my faults and the role I played in all of this mess. I know how stubborn I am, and it doesn't help anything when I assume the worst about him when he's trying, I know he is. I'm not ready to be in a relationship with him, but I have no reason to be upset with him over last night. I hope not, at least.

I don't know what to think, but I don't want to think right now.

"No," he whispers, his lips mere centimeters from mine.

"Yes."

"Shut up." He presses his lips against mine with extreme caution. They barely touch mine as he uses both hands to cup my cheeks.

His tongue grazes along my bottom lip, and I lose my breath. I open my mouth slightly to try to get some air, but there doesn't seem to be any—there's nothing, only him. I tug at his shirt to bring him off of his knees, but he doesn't budge as he continues to kiss me slowly. His torturous pace is driving me mad, and I move from my spot at the end of the bed down to meet him on the floor.

Both of his arms wrap around my waist, and mine do the same to his neck. I try to push him back to climb on top of him, but once again he doesn't budge.

"What's wrong?" I ask.

"Nothing, I just don't want to take it too far."

"Why not?" I tell him, keeping our lips touching.

"Because we have a lot to talk about; we can't jump into bed without resolving anything."

What? "But we aren't on the bed, we're on the floor." I sound desperate.

"Tessa . . ." He pushes me back again.

I give up. I scramble to my feet and sit back on the bed, and he stares at me with wide eyes.

"I'm just trying to do the right thing, okay? I want to fuck you, believe me I do. God, I do. But—"

"It's fine. Stop talking about it," I beg.

I know it's probably not the best idea, but I didn't necessarily think we were going to sleep together. I just wanted to be closer to him.

"Tess."

"Just stop, okay? I get it."

"No, you don't, obviously," he says in frustration and moves to his feet.

"This is never going to be fixed, is it? This is how it will always be with us. Back and forth, up and down. You want me, but when I want you, all you do is push me away," I say, willing myself not to cry.

"No . . . that's not true."

"It seems like it. What do you want from me? You want me to believe that you're trying to prove that you can change for me, but then what?"

"What do you mean?"

"What's after that?"

"I don't know . . . we haven't even gotten to that point yet. I want to continue to take you out and make you laugh instead of cry. I want you to love me again." His eyes are glossing over, and he's blinking rapidly.

"I do love you, always," I assure him. "But it takes more than that, Hardin. Love doesn't conquer all, the way the novels make you believe. There are always so many complications, and they're overpowering the love that I have for you."

"I know. Things are complicated, but they won't always be. We can't get along with one another for even a day, we yell and fight and give each other the silent treatment like five-year-olds, we do things out of spite and we say the wrong things. We sure as hell complicate things when they don't need to be complicated, but we can figure it out somehow."

I don't know where we go from here. I'm glad that Hardin and I are having a somewhat civil discussion over everything that has happened, but I can't ignore the fact that he wouldn't support me going to Seattle.

I was going to tell him, but I'm afraid if I do he'll say something to Christian again, and honestly, if Hardin and I are going to continue trying to rebuild our relationship or whatever it is that we're doing, it will only complicate it more.

If we're truly able to make this work, it won't matter if I'm here or two hours away. I was raised better than to let a man dictate my future, no matter how deep my love for him is.

I know exactly what will happen: he'll lose his temper and storm out of here to find Christian, or Zed. Most likely Zed.

"If I pretend that the last twenty-four hours didn't happen, will you promise me something?" I ask him.

"Anything," he answers quickly.

"Don't hurt him."

"Zed?" he asks, anger coloring his voice.

"Yes, Zed," I clarify.

"No, fuck no. I'm not promising that."

"You said—" I begin.

"No, don't even start that shit. He's causing a bunch of shit between us, and I'm not going to sit back and allow it. Fuck no." He paces back and forth.

"You don't have any proof that he did what you say, Hardin, and fighting him isn't going to solve anything. Just let me talk to him and—"

"No, Tessa! I already told you I don't want you near him. I'm not going to tell you again," he growls.

"You don't get to tell me who I can talk to, Hardin."

"What more proof do you need? Was him texting you from my phone not enough?"

"It wasn't him! He wouldn't do that."

I don't think he would, at least. Why would he?

I'm going to ask him about it either way, but I just don't see him doing that to me.

"You are literally the most naïve person I've ever met, and it's really fucking infuriating."

"Can we please stop arguing?" I sit back down on the bed and hold my head in my hands.

"Agree to stay away from him."

"Agree to not fight him, again," I fire back.

"You'll stay away if I don't fight him?"

I don't want to agree, but I don't want Hardin to fight him either. This is all giving me a headache. "Yes."

"When I say stay away from him, I mean no contact with him at all. No texts, no going by the science building, nothing," he says.

"How did you know I went there?" I ask him. Did he see me?

My heart begins to race at the thought of Hardin seeing Zed and me in the greenhouse full of glowing flowers.

"Nate told me he saw you."

"Oh."

"Is there anything else you need to tell me while we're on the topic of Zed? Because once this conversation is over, I don't want to hear another word about him," Hardin says.

"No." I lie.

"You're sure?" he asks again.

I don't want to tell him, but I have to. I can't expect honesty from him when I don't give the same in return.

I close my eyes. "I kissed him," I whisper, hoping that he didn't hear me. But when he knocks the books off the desk, I know he did.

chapter
one hundred and thirteen

I open my eyes and look up at Hardin from the bed, but he isn't looking at me. I feel like he's barely registering that I exist. His eyes are focused on the books he pushed to the floor as he clenches his fists at his sides.

To bring him back to me from wherever he is, I say it again. "I kissed him, Hardin."

Instead of looking at me, he taps his fists against his forehead in frustration, and my mind scrambles for an explanation. "I . . . you . . . why?" he mumbles.

"I thought you forgot about me . . . that you didn't want me anymore, and he was there and . . ." My explanation isn't fair, and I know it. But I don't know what else to say. My feet won't move toward him like my mind wants them to, and I remain on the bed.

"Stop saying that shit! Stop fucking saying he was there. I swear to God, if I hear that one more fucking time . . . !"

"Okay! I'm sorry, I'm so sorry, Hardin. I was so hurt and confused, he was saying all the things that I was so desperate for you to say and—"

"What was he saying?"

I don't want to repeat anything that Zed said, not to Hardin. "Hardin . . ." I hold on to the pillow as an anchor.

"Now," he demands.

"He was just saying what would have happened if he had won the bet, if we had dated instead."

"And what was that like?"

"What?"

"What was that like, hearing that bullshit? Is that what you want? You want to be with him instead of me?" His anger is boiling and I can tell he's trying his hardest to keep the lid on it, but the steam is pressing and pressing.

"No, that's not what I want." I climb off the bed and take a cautious step toward him.

"Don't. Don't come near me." His words pierce me, pinning me to where I am.

"What else did you do with him? Did you fuck him? Suck his dick?"

I'm so thankful that the house is empty and they can't hear Hardin's foul accusations.

"Oh my God! No! You know I didn't. I don't know what I was thinking when I kissed him. I was just being stupid, and I was at such a bad place with you abandoning me."

"Abandoning you? You're the one who fucking left me, and now I find out you were flaunting yourself around campus like a fucking whore!" he screams.

I want to cry but this isn't about me, it's about him and how hurt and angry he must be. "I didn't mean it that way. Don't call me names." I squeeze the back of the desk chair.

Hardin turns his back to me, leaving me alone in my guilt. I can't imagine how I would feel if he had done this during the worst time in my life. I hadn't thought about how he'd feel when I did it, though; I had only assumed he was doing the same.

I don't want to continue to push him. I know the way his temper gets too heated for him to control, and he's been trying his best to do so.

"Do you want me to leave you alone for now?" I weakly ask.

"Yes."

I didn't want him to agree for me to leave him be, but I do what he asks and head out of the bedroom. He doesn't turn around.

I'm unsure what to do with myself as I lean against the wall in the hallway. In a sick way I'd rather him be screaming at me, pinning me against the wall, and demanding me to tell him why I did what I did instead of staring out of the window and asking me to leave the room.

Maybe that's what's wrong with us: we both crave the drama of disagreements. I don't believe that to be true; we have come a long way since the beginning of our relationship, even if we've fought more than we've had peace. Most of the novels that I've read led me to believe quarrels come and go in the blink of an eye, a simple apology will bandage any problem and everything will be worked out within minutes. The novels lie. Maybe that's why I'm so enamored with *Wuthering Heights* and *Pride and Prejudice*; both are incredibly romantic in their own way, but they reveal the truth behind blind love and promises of forever.

This is the truth. This is a world where everyone makes mistakes, even the incredibly naïve girl who is usually the victim of a boy's insensitivity and temper. No one is truly innocent in this world, no one. The people who believe themselves to be perfect are the worst ones of all.

A crash from within Hardin's room frightens me, and I bring my hand to my mouth as I hear another and another. He's destroying the room. I knew he would. I should stop him from breaking more and more of his father's property, but honestly, I'm afraid to. I'm not afraid that he'll hurt me physically—I'm afraid of the words he'll say while he's in this state. I can't be afraid, though, I can handle it.

"Fuck!" he screams, and I step into the room. I'm half thankful that Ken took Karen and Landon out for dessert, but I almost wish someone was here to help me stop him.

In Hardin's hand is a piece of wood, the leg of a chair, I realize when I see the chair lying on its side at Hardin's feet. He tosses the dark wood away, and his eyes glow an angry green when he sees me.

"What part of *leave me the fuck alone* do you not get, Tessa?"

I take another breath and let his angry words bounce off of me. "I'm not leaving you alone." My voice doesn't come out as strong as I intended.

"If you know what's good for you, you will," he threatens.

I take a few steps forward to meet him and stop less than a foot away. He tries to back up, but he's blocked by the wall.

"You won't hurt me." I call him out on his empty threat.

"You don't know that, I've done it before."

"Not purposely. You wouldn't be able to live with yourself if you did, I know that."

"You don't know anything!" he yells.

"Talk to me," I calmly say. My heart is in my mouth as I watch him close his eyes and open them again.

"I don't have anything to say to you, I don't want you." His voice is labored.

"Yes, you do."

"No, Tessa, I don't. I don't want shit to do with you. He can have you."

"I don't want him." I try not to let his harsh words penetrate me.

"You obviously do."

"No, I only want you."

"Bullshit!" He slams his open palm against the wall. It startles me, but I stay still. "Get out, Tess."

"No, Hardin."

"Don't you have anything better to do? Go find Zed. Go fuck him, for all I fucking care—I'll do the same, believe me, Tessa. I will leave here and fuck every girl I lay eyes on."

Tears spring to my eyes, but he doesn't pay any mind. "You're saying these things out of anger, you don't mean them."

His eyes search the room for something, anything, left to break. He hasn't left much unscathed. Luckily, the things that have been demolished are mostly mine. The poster board I brought home for Landon's biology assignment . . . the suitcase full of books has been dumped out and my novels are scattered across the carpet. Some of my clothes have been pulled from the dresser, and the chair, of course, has been knocked to the floor and broken.

"I don't want to look at you . . . go," he says gruffly, but softer than before.

"I'm sorry for kissing him, Hardin. I know it hurts you, and for that I'm sorry." I look up at him.

Silently he studies my face. I jump slightly when his thumb wipes away the tears staining my cheeks.

"Don't be afraid," he whispers.

"I'm not," I say in an equally hushed tone.

"I don't know if I can get past this." He breathes heavily.

My knees nearly buckle at the thought. I don't think there has ever been a time since we declared our love for each other that I've had to consider Hardin being the one to end things over an infidelity. My kiss with the stranger on New Year's was nothing like this; he was pissed off and I knew he would let me have it, but deep down I knew he wouldn't hold on to it for too long. This time, though, it was with Zed, whom he had had a rocky friendship with because of me; they've been in several fights, and I know it drives Hardin insane for me to even speak to Zed.

I don't think getting back into a full-blown relationship with Hardin is a good idea at this moment, but our problems have shifted from uncertainty over the future to this. Unwanted tears spill from my unfaithful eyes, and his frown deepens.

"Don't cry," he coaxes, his fingers expanding and resting against my cheek.

"I'm sorry," I breathe; a single tear falls onto my lips, and I lick it away. "Do you love me still?" I have to ask.

I know he does, but I'm desperate and needy for the words.

"Of course I do, I always will." He comforts me in a soothing voice.

It's a strangely beautiful sound, really: the way his exasperated breathing is heavy and loud but his voice is calm and soft, like an image of angry waves crashing against the shore with no sound.

"When will you know what you want to do?" I ask him, afraid of the answer.

He sighs and presses his forehead against mine as his breathing begins to slightly slow down. "I don't know; it's not like I can be without you."

"I can't either," I whisper to him. "Be without you."

"We can't seem to get our shit together, can we?"

"No, not at all." I almost smile at our calm exchange of words after his tantrum only minutes ago.

"We can try?" I offer, and I attempt to lean into him, nervously waiting for him to stop me.

"Come here." His fingers press into the skin on my arms, and he brings me to his chest.

It feels heavenly, like visiting home after being away for so long, and the scent of him as I bury my face into his T-shirt calms my heart.

"You won't go near him again," he says into my hair.

"I know." I agree without thinking.

"This doesn't mean I'm over it, I just miss you."

"I know," I repeat, nuzzling further into him. His heartbeat is solid and rapid against my ear.

"You can't go around kissing people every time you're angry. It's fucked up and I won't have it. You would lose your shit if I did that."

I lift my head from Hardin's chest to look at his hostile face.

My fingers unwrap from around the thin material of his T-shirt and I thread them through his soft curls.

His gaze is harsh, but the way his lips are parting slowly lets me know he won't stop me when I tug at his hair to bring his face down to mine. If it weren't for his height, this would be much easier. Hardin sighs into the kiss; tightening his grip around my waist, his fingers move to my hips and back around me again.

My tears are mixed with his harsh breathing into the most lethal combination of love and lust. I love him a thousand times more than I lust for him, but the two mix and intensify as he removes his mouth from mine to trail his warm lips down my jaw and neckline. He bends at his knees to get better contact with my skin, and I can barely stand on my feet as he bites down softly just above where my collarbone would show if I were as thin as society wanted me to be.

I begin to walk back toward the bed and tug at his shirt when he tries to protest. He gives in with a huff and a firm kiss to my neck; we reach the bed and stop to look at each other.

I don't want either of us to speak and ruin what we've started, so I grab ahold of the hem on my shirt and pull it up over my head. His breathing is deepening again, this time out of need, not anger.

When my shirt hits the floor, I reach in front of me to undress him. He lifts his own shirt, and as my nervous but quick fingers fumble with his belt and tug his jeans down his legs, he grows impatient and uses the leg I'm not holding to push them to the floor.

I climb back onto the bed as he does the same, his fingers constantly running along my bare skin. Hardin shifts his weight as his lips find mine again, his tongue pushing through my lips slowly as he hovers over me, using his arms to support his weight.

I can feel him getting hard just from our kissing, so I lift my hips slightly off of the bed to meet his in order to create friction between us. He groans and tugs his boxers down with one hand, leaving them at his knees. My hand immediately grips his length, and he hisses into my ear. My hand pumps slowly up and down him. I lean down, tracing my tongue over the tip of his cock, wanting to elicit more sounds from him. I lift my head back up to face him and wrap my hand around him again.

"I love you," I remind him as he moans into my neck.

He moves one hand to my chest and tugs carelessly at the cups of my bra to expose my breasts to him.

"I love you," he finally says.

"Are you sure you want to do this? What with everything going on, and we aren't together right now . . ." he explains, and I nod.

"Please," I beg.

His mouth meets my chest, and his hands travel behind my back to unclasp my bra so he can remove it fully. His fingers are cold against my hot skin, but his tongue is warm and needy as he flicks it over my nipple, grazing the skin with his teeth.

I tug at his hair, and I'm rewarded with a low moan as his mouth moves to my other breast.

chapter
one hundred and fourteen

HARDIN

One look at her while she's undressing and I'm ready to bury myself inside of her. I know all of our issues haven't been resolved, but I need this, *we* fucking need this.

I push my jeans down over my ankles and climb back onto the bed to meet her, the infuriating girl who has stolen every ounce of me, body and soul, and I never want it back. I don't even care what she does with it. It's hers. I'm hers.

I'm already hard just from looking at her naked body. I tear my mouth away from her beautiful tits just long enough to grab a condom from the dresser. She lies down on her back, legs spread open.

"I want to be able to see you," I tell her.

She tilts her head to the side slightly in confusion, so I gently hold on to her arms and pull her on top of me. Her body feels so damn good on top of mine; she was made for me.

Tessa's thighs part farther, and she moves her hips, rubbing her wetness against my hard cock. I'm already fucking anxious and ready, but this, the way she glides over my length with a teasing roll of her hips, is driving me fucking crazy.

I reach my hand down between us and rub my thumb over her clit. She gasps and wraps her hand around the back of my neck.

She lowers herself down onto me, and we both hiss as I enter her. Fuck, I've missed this. I've missed us.

"You feel so good with me filling you." I praise her and watch as her eyes roll back in pleasure. Her hips begin to move in slow circles as I take in the sight in front of me. She's beautiful and so damn sexy, exquisite really. I've never seen anything or anyone like her. Her chest is full, pushing out each time her hips move. I love watching her ride me.

She's getting better and better at this, being on top. I can remember the first time she tried. She wasn't bad, but she was so nervous the entire time. Right now she's taking full control, and it couldn't be any fucking better. She's getting more and more comfortable in her body, and that makes me happy. She's fucking sexy, and she should own it.

I lift my hips from the bed and meet her movements. She moans, her eyes widening.

"Feels good, doesn't it, baby? You're fucking amazing," I encourage her.

I gently tug at Tessa's arm to bring her down to me. As much as I want to look at her as her body owns mine, I want to kiss her even more. My mouth finds hers, and I love the way she whimpers into my kiss.

"Tell me how it feels," I say into her mouth and cup her ass, pushing my cock deeper inside of her.

"Good . . . so good, Hardin," she whimpers. Her hands rest on my chest to support her weight.

"Move faster, baby." I reach up and take one of her tits in my hand. I squeeze, and she fucking loves it.

"Mm-hmm . . ." she agrees.

Seconds later she winces and stills. Her eyes meet mine.

"What's wrong?" I try to sit up with her against my chest without removing myself from her.

"Nothing . . . it just felt . . . deeper or something. I can feel you so much deeper." She flushes, her voice soft with wonder.

"Good or bad?" I lift my hand to push her hair back behind her ear.

"Oh, it's good," she says as her eyes roll back.

I have fucked this girl so many times now and she's still basically clueless about all things sex, except giving me head. She's great at that.

I move her hips again in an attempt to find that spot, the spot that will have her screaming my name in seconds. I love the way she looks when she rolls her hips; the shape of them is beyond fucking perfect. Her nails dig into my bare chest, and I know that I've found the spot. She covers her mouth with her hand and bites down on her palm to quiet herself as I lift my hips to meet her movements, to thrust faster in and out of her.

"I'm going to make you come this way," I breathe.

She's too perfect. Her eyes screw closed and her movements grow slower.

"You're going to come now, aren't you? You're going to come for me, baby?"

"Hardin . . ." She moans my name, and it's the perfect answer.

"Holy shit." I can't help but curse as her back arches and her blue-gray eyes close again. The fingernails on the hand she isn't using to cover her mouth dig into my chest, and I feel her tighten around me. Fuck, she feels so good. I change the pace and move slower, but I'm sure to hit as deep inside of her as I can with each thrust of my hips.

I know how much she loves hearing my voice while I fuck her, and she screams into her hand when I let out an "Oh God" and spill into the condom.

"Hardin . . ." she whines and lays her head on my chest in a panting mess.

"Baby," I say, and she looks up at me with a sleepy smile.

I match my breathing to hers and run my fingers through the mess of blond hair sprawled across my chest. I'm still pissed at her, and at Zed, but I love her and I'm trying to prove to her that I'm changing for her. I can't deny that our communication is one thousand times better than it used to be.

She's going to be pissed at me at least one more time because of Zed, but he needs to know that she's mine and that if he fucking touches her again, he's dead.

chapter
one hundred and fifteen

TESSA

I lie on top of Hardin's chest to catch my breath. Both of our bare chests are moving slowly up and down in our postcoital bliss. It doesn't feel as foreign as I had believed it would, not at all. I was desperately missing being intimate with him; I know that making love so soon, before anything has been determined, may not have been the best idea, but right now, as his fingers trail up and down my spine, it sure feels like it.

I can't stop picturing the way his body looked underneath mine as he lifted his hips off the mattress to fill me completely. We've slept together many times, but this time goes down as one of the best. It was so intense and sincere and full of want—no, need—for each other.

Hardin's temper got the best of him only a short while ago, but as I stare up at him his eyes are closed and his lips are slightly upturned.

"I know you're staring at me, and I have to take a piss," he finally says, and I can't help but giggle. "Up you go." He lifts my body at my hips to lay me beside him.

Hardin's hands run through his hair and he pushes the loose fringe back to bare his forehead while he retrieves his clothing from the floor. He remains shirtless and disappears from the room, leaving me to get myself dressed. My eyes dart to his worn

T-shirt on the floor, and out of habit I bend down to pick it up but then drop it again. I don't want to push things or make him angry, so I should just stick to my own clothing for now.

It's nearly eight, so I go ahead and pull on a pair of loose sweats and a plain T-shirt. The wreckage from Hardin's outburst covers the floor, so I take it upon myself to begin putting everything back in its place; the clothes from my drawers are my first task. Hardin enters the room as I'm zipping my suitcase full of novels.

"What are you doing?" he asks. He holds a glass of water and a muffin in one of his large hands.

"Just straightening up," I say quietly.

I'm slightly nervous that we'll slide back into fighting again, so I'm unsure of how to behave. "Okay . . ." he says, placing the glass and snack on the dresser before walking over to me.

"I'll help," he offers and picks up the broken chair from the floor. We work in silence to get the room back to its normal state. Hardin grabs the suitcase and walks toward the closet with it, nearly tripping over a decorative pillow from the bed.

I don't know if I should speak first and I'm not sure what to say; I know he's still angry, but I keep catching his eyes on me, so he must not be too angry.

He steps out from the closet holding a small bag and a medium-sized box. "What's this?"

Oh no. "Nothing." I hurry to my feet in an attempt to take the items from him.

"Are these for me?" he asks with a curious expression.

chapter
one hundred and sixteen

HARDIN

N o," she lies and stands up on her toes to try to reach for the box in my left hand. I lift it higher.

"The tag right here says my name," I point out, and she looks down.

Why is she so embarrassed?

"I just . . . well, I got you a few things before, but now they seem so silly; you don't have to open them."

"I want to," I tell her and sit down on the edge of the bed. I really shouldn't have broken that hideous chair.

She sighs and keeps her position on the other side of the room as I pull at the taped edges of wrapping paper. I'm slightly irritated by the amount of tape she used for this one box, but I'll admit I'm a little . . .

. . . *excited*.

Not excited, exactly, but happy. I can't remember the last time I received a birthday gift from anyone, even my mum. I made it a point at a young age to despise birthdays, and I was such an asshole over whatever ridiculous gift my mum would buy me that she just stopped buying them before I was sixteen.

My father would send some shitty card with a check inside every year, but I'd get a kick out of burning the damn thing. I even took a piss on the one that arrived on my seventeenth birthday. When I finally get the box open, there are multiple things inside.

First is a tattered copy of *Pride and Prejudice*, which, when I take it in my hands, prompts Tessa to walk over and grab it from me.

"This is stupid . . . just ignore this one," she says, but obviously that's the last thing I'm going to do.

"Why? Give it back to me," I demand, holding my hand out.

When I stand to my feet, she seems to remember that she obviously isn't going to win this battle, so she places the book back in my hands. As I skim through the pages, I notice bright yellow markings throughout the entire thing.

"You know how you told me about highlighting Tolstoy?" she asks, her cheeks as red as they've ever been.

"Yeah?"

"Well . . . I sort of did that, too," she admits, and her eyes meet mine.

"Really?" I ask her and open to a page that's nearly covered in markings.

"Yeah. Mostly this book, though; you don't have to reread or anything. I just thought . . . I'm terrible at giving gifts, I really am."

She's not, though. I would love to see the words in her favorite novel that remind her of me. This is the best gift anyone could have possibly given me. These are the simple things, the things that give me hope that somehow we can make this work, the fact that both of us were doing the same thing, reading Jane Austen, when neither of us was aware of the other.

"You're not," I tell her and sit back on the bed.

I tuck the novel under my leg to keep her from trying to take it from me again. A low chuckle leaves my mouth when another item from the box is revealed.

"What's this for?" I ask with a grin, holding up the leather binder.

"Your work, that thing you use, is tearing at the seams and it's so unorganized. See, this one has tabs for each week—or subject, you can decide." She smiles.

This gift is humorous because I always take note of the way she cringes when I shove papers into my old binder. I refuse to let her organize it for me despite her multiple attempts, and I know that drives her insane. I don't want her to see what's inside.

"Thanks." I laugh.

"That one wasn't really a birthday gift. I got it a while ago and I was going to just toss your old one, but I never found an opportunity," she admits with a laugh.

"That's because I kept it by my side. I knew what you were up to," I tease. The small bag is left to open, and once again I'm laughing at her choice.

Kickboxing is the first word I catch on the small ticket.

"It's a week's worth of kickboxing at the gym by our . . . your apartment." She smiles, clearly proud of her witty gift.

"And why do you think I'd be interested in kickboxing?"

"You know why."

To let out some of my anger is the obvious reason she got this. "I've never done it before."

"It could be fun," she says.

"Not as fun as kicking the shit out of someone without padding," I tell her, and she frowns.

"I'm teasing," I say and grab the CD that's still left in the bag. My inner asshole wants to tease her for buying a CD when I could easily download the album. I'll enjoy hearing her hum along to it; I'm assuming it's the second one by the Fray.

I'm sure she already knows each word to every song and she'll be delighted to explain the meaning of them to me as we drive and listen.

chapter
one hundred and seventeen

TESSA

S tay with me tonight?" Hardin asked, his eyes scanning my face. I nod eagerly.

So now that he's pulling his shirt over his head, I grab at it greedily and bring it to my chest. He watches me as I change, but stays silent. Our relationship is so confusing—it always is—but now especially. At the moment, I'm not sure who holds the upper hand. Earlier I was upset with him for standing me up on his birthday, but now I'm pretty convinced he had nothing to do with that, so I'm back where I was days ago when he so sweetly took me ice skating.

He was so upset with me over Zed, but now I can barely tell how he felt, given the smiles and sarcastic humor he keeps throwing at me. Maybe his anger is overpowered by the fact that he missed me and he's happy that I'm no longer upset with him? I don't know the reasoning, but I know better than to question it. I do wish he'd let me talk about Seattle. How will he react? I don't even want to tell him, but I know that I have to. Will he be happy for me? I don't think so; actually, I know he won't be.

"Come here." He coaxes me onto his chest as he lies back on the bed. His hand finds the remote to the television on the wall, and he flicks through channel after channel before pausing on some sort of historical documentary.

"How was it seeing your mom?" I ask him a few minutes later.

He doesn't respond, and when I look up at his face, he's fast asleep.

IT'S HOT. WAY TOO HOT, when I come back to consciousness. Hardin is lying on top of me, nearly all his weight pinning me down to the mattress. I'm on my back and Hardin's on his front, his head on my chest; one of his arms is wrapped around my waist and the other stretched across the space next to him. I've missed sleeping this way and even waking up sweating from Hardin's body blanketing mine. When I glance at the clock, I see that it's seven twenty—my alarm is set to go off in ten minutes. I don't want to wake Hardin, he looks so serene; a soft smile plays on his sleeping lips. He usually frowns, even in his sleep.

In an attempt to move him without waking him up, I lift his arm from around my waist.

"Mm-hmm . . ." he whines as his eyes flutter and his body stirs, gripping me tighter.

I stare at the ceiling and debate whether or not to just roll him off of me.

"What time is it?" he asks, his voice thick with sleep.

"Almost seven-thirty." I tell him quietly.

"Dammit. Can we play hooky today?"

"No, but *you* can." I smile and gently run my fingers over his hair, massaging his scalp softly.

"We could go to breakfast?" He turns his face to look at me.

"You drive a hard bargain, but I can't." I really want to, though. He slides his body down slightly so his chin rests just under my chest. "Did you sleep well?" I ask him.

"Yes, very. I haven't slept like that since . . ." He trails off.

I feel so happy suddenly and smile wide. "I'm glad you got some sleep."

"Can I tell you something?" He doesn't seem quite awake yet; his eyes are glossy and his voice is raspier than ever.

"Of course." I go back to massaging his scalp.

"When I was in England, at my mum's, I had a dream . . . well, nightmare."

Oh no. My heart sinks. I knew his nightmares had come back, but it still hurts me to hear about it.

"I'm sorry those dreams came back."

"No, they didn't just come back, Tess. They were worse." I swear that I feel his body shiver, but his face holds no emotion.

"Worse?"

How could they possibly be worse?

"It was you, they were . . . doing it to you," he says, and ice replaces the warm blood in my veins.

"Oh." My voice is weak, pathetic.

"Yeah. It was . . . it was so fucked up. It was so much worse than before because I'm used to the ones with my mum, you know?"

I nod and bring my other hand to his bare arm to caress it like I'm doing to his scalp.

"I didn't even try to sleep after that. I purposely stayed awake because I couldn't bear to see it again. The thought of someone hurting you drives me mad."

"I'm so sorry." His eyes are haunted, and mine are full of tears.

"Don't pity me." He reaches up and captures the tears before they fall.

"I'm not. It makes me upset because I don't want you to be hurt. I don't pity you." It's true, I don't pity him. I feel terrible for this broken man who has nightmares about his mother being violated and abused, and the thought of my face replacing Trish's kills me. I don't want those thoughts tainting his already anguished mind.

"You know I would never let anyone hurt you, don't you?" His eyes meet mine.

"Yes, I do, Hardin."

"Even now, even if we never get back to where we were before. I'd kill anyone who even tried, okay?" His tone is clipped yet soft.

"I know," I assure him with a small smile.

I don't want to appear alarmed by his sudden threats, because I know that he means them in a loving way.

"It was nice to sleep." He lightens the mood slightly, and I nod in agreement.

"Where do you want to go for breakfast?" I ask him.

"You said no, that you—"

"I changed my mind. I'm hungry."

After his being so open with me about his nightmares, I want to spend the morning with him; maybe he'll continue the open line of communication. I usually have to fight him for any type of information, but he confessed this willingly and that means the world to me.

"So easily persuaded by my pathetic story?" He raises a brow.

"Don't say that." I scowl.

"Why not?" He sits up and climbs off of the bed.

"Because it's not true. It wasn't *what* you told me that changed my mind, but *that* you shared that with me. And don't call yourself pathetic. That's certainly not true." My feet hit the floor as he pulls his jeans up over his legs. "*Hard*in . . ." I say when he doesn't reply.

"*Tes*sa . . ." He mocks me in a high-pitched voice.

"I mean it, you shouldn't think of yourself like that."

"I know," he says quickly, abruptly ending the conversation.

I know Hardin is far from perfect and he has his flaws, but so does everyone else, especially me. I wish he was able to see past his flaws; maybe that would help resolve his issues about the future.

"So anyway, do I have you all day or just for breakfast?" He bends down to push his foot into his shoe.

"I like those shoes, I've been meaning to tell you." I point to the solid black tennis shoes he's putting on.

"Um . . . thanks . . ." He laces them and stands back up. For someone with such a big ego, he's terrible at accepting compliments. "You still didn't answer me."

"Just breakfast. I can't miss all my classes." I pull his shirt over my head and replace it with one of my own.

"Okay."

"I just need to pull my hair back and brush my teeth," I say after I'm finished getting dressed. As I begin to scrub my tongue, Hardin knocks at the door.

"Come in," I mumble through the paste in my mouth.

"It's been a while since we've done this," he tells me.

"Had sex in the bathroom?" I ask. *Why did I just say that?*

"Nooooo . . . I was going to say 'brushed our teeth together.'" He laughs and opens one of the packs of toothbrushes from the cabinet. "However, if bathroom sex is something you want . . ." Hardin teases, and I roll my eyes.

"I don't know why I said that, it was the first thing that came to my mind." I have to laugh at my stupidity and quick tongue.

"Well, that's good to hear." He dips the brush under the faucet and doesn't say another word. After both of us brush our teeth and I attempt to comb my hair into a ponytail, we head downstairs. Karen and Landon are in the kitchen, talking over bowls of oatmeal.

Landon gives me a warm smile; he doesn't seem too surprised by seeing Hardin and me together. Karen doesn't either. If anything, I think she looks . . . pleased? I can't tell, because she brings her coffee cup to her mouth to hide her smile.

"I'm taking Tessa to campus today," Hardin tells Landon.

"Okay."

"Ready?" Hardin turns to me, and I nod.

"I'll see you in Religion." I tell Landon before Hardin drags me, literally, out of the kitchen.

"What's the rush?" I ask him once we're outside.

He grabs my bag from my shoulder as we walk down the driveway. "Nothing, but I know you two; if you start talking, we'll never make it out of there, and when you add Karen into the mix, I'd starve to death before you shut up." He opens the car door for me before walking around to open his own and climb in.

"True." I smile.

We debate over IHOP or Denny's for at least twenty minutes before deciding on IHOP. Hardin claims that they have the best French toast, but I refuse to believe it until I eat it.

"It'll be ten to fifteen minutes before you can be seated," a short woman with a blue scarf around her neck tells us when we walk inside.

"Okay," I say at the same time that Hardin says, "Why?"

"We're busy and there aren't any tables open at the moment," she explains sweetly. Hardin rolls his eyes and I pull him away from her to sit at the bench in the entryway.

"It's nice to see you're back," I tease.

"What's that mean?"

"I just mean you've still got your edge."

"When didn't I?"

"I don't know, when we went on our date and a little last night."

"I trashed that bedroom and cussed you out," he reminds me.

"I know, I'm trying to make a joke."

"Well, try making a good one next time," he says, but I see the glint of a smile appear.

When we're finally seated, we give our order to a young guy

with a beard that seems to be a little too long for someone who's working as a waiter. After he walks off, Hardin complains and swears that if he finds a hair in his food, he's going to lose it. "Just had to show you that I still have my edge," he reminds me, and I giggle.

I love that he's trying to be a little nicer, but I also love his attitude and the way he doesn't care what people think of him. I wish more of those qualities would rub off on me. He runs through a list of other things that are bothering him about the place until our food arrives.

"Why can't you just miss the entire day?" Hardin asks as he shovels a forkful of French toast into his mouth.

"Because . . ." I begin. Oh, you know, because I'm transferring to another campus and I don't want to complicate things by losing any participation points before I transfer in the middle of the semester.

"I don't want to lose my A's," I tell him.

"This is college, no one goes to class," he tells me for the hundredth time since I met him.

"Aren't you excited about yoga?" I laugh.

"No. Not at all."

We finish breakfast, and the mood is still light as Hardin drives toward the campus. His phone vibrates on the console but he ignores it. I want to answer for him but we're getting along so well. The third time it rings, I finally speak up.

"Aren't you going to answer that?" I ask him.

"No, it'll go to voicemail. It's probably my mum." He lifts the phone to show me the screen.

"See, she left a voicemail. Can you check it?" he asks.

My curiosity gets the best of me and I snatch the phone from his hands.

"Speakerphone," he reminds me.

"You have seven new voicemails," the robotic voice announces as he parks the car.

He groans. "This is why I never check them."

I press the numeral one to listen to them. *"Hardin? . . . Hardin, it's Tessa . . . I . . . "* I try to press the end button but Hardin grabs the phone from my hand.

Oh God.

"Well, I need to talk to you. I'm in my car and I'm so confused . . . " My voice is hysterical and I want to jump out of the car.

"Please turn it off," I beg him but he shifts the phone into his other hand so I can't reach it.

"What is this?" he asks, staring at the phone.

"Why haven't you even tried? You just let me leave and here I am pathetically calling you and crying into your voicemail. I need to know what happened to us? Why was this time different, why didn't we fight it out? Why didn't you fight for me? I deserve to be happy, Hardin." My idiotic voice fills the car, trapping me inside.

I sit in silence and stare down at my hands in my lap. This is humiliating; I had nearly forgotten about the voicemail and I wish he hadn't heard it, especially not now.

"When was this?"

"While you were gone."

He lets out a deep breath and ends the call. "What were you confused about?" he asks.

"I don't think you want to talk about it." I pull my lip between my teeth.

"Yes, I do." Hardin unbuckles his seat belt and turns to face me.

I look up at him, and try to think of how to phrase this. "That hideous voicemail is from the night . . . the night I kissed him."

"Oh." He turns his face away from me.

Breakfast went so well, only to be ruined by my stupid voicemail that I left in the middle of an emotional tidal wave. I shouldn't be held accountable.

"Before or after you kissed him?"

"After."

"How many times did you kiss him?"

"Once."

"Where?"

"My car," I squeak.

"Then what? What did you do after you left this?" He holds the phone in the air between us.

"Went back to his apartment." As soon as the words leave my mouth, Hardin rests his forehead against the steering wheel.

"I . . ." I begin.

He raises his finger to silence me. "What happened at his apartment?" He closes his eyes.

"Nothing! I cried and we watched television."

"You're lying."

"No, I'm not. I slept on the couch. The only time I slept in his room was the time you showed up there. I haven't done anything with him except kiss him, and a few days ago when I met him for lunch, he tried to kiss me and I pulled away."

"He tried to kiss you *again*?"

Shit. "Yes, but he understands the way I feel about you. I know I made a huge mess of all of this and I'm sorry for even spending time with him. I don't have a good reason or excuse but I'm sorry."

"You remember what you said, right? That you'll stay away from him?" His breathing is controlled, too controlled, as he lifts his head from the wheel.

"Yes, I remember." I don't like the idea of being told who I can be friends with, but I can't say I wouldn't expect the same from him if the roles were reversed, which they have been a lot lately.

"Now that I know the details, I don't want to talk about it

again, okay? I mean it . . . like I don't even want to hear his fucking name come out of your mouth." He's trying to stay calm.

"Okay," I agree and reach across to grab his hand in mine. I don't want to talk about it anymore either; we've both said all we can say about the subject, and going back over it will only cause more unnecessary problems for us and our already damaged relationship. It's sort of a relief to be the cause of the problem this time, because the last thing Hardin needs is another reason to despise himself.

"We better get to class," he finally says.

My heart sinks at his cool tone, but I keep my mouth shut as he withdraws his hand from mine. Hardin walks me to the philosophy building, and I scan the street for Landon but don't see him. He must be inside already.

"Thank you for breakfast," I say and take my bag from Hardin's hand.

"It's nothing." He shrugs, and I attempt a smile before turning to walk away.

A hand presses into my arm, and even before his mouth forcefully presses against mine, he's claimed me in the way only he can.

"I'll see you after class. I love you," he breathes and withdraws, leaving me panting and smiling as I head inside.

chapter
one hundred and eighteen

HARDIN

I listen to that voicemail for the fifth time as I walk down the campus sidewalk. She sounds so miserable and upset. In a fucked-up way it makes me happy to hear it, to hear the anguish and pure sadness in her voice as she cries into my ear. I wanted to know if she was as miserable without me as I was without her, and here is the proof that she was. I know I forgave her quickly for kissing that asshole, but what else was I supposed to do? I can't be without her, and we've both done some fucked-up shit—not only her.

This is his fault, anyway; he knew how fucking vulnerable she would be when we split. I know he fucking knew that: he saw her crying and shit, then he goes and kisses her a week after she left me? What kind of fucking dickhead does that?

He took advantage of her, of my Tessa, and I won't fucking have it. He thinks he's so smooth and he gets away with shit, but not any fucking more.

"Where's Zed Evans?" I ask a short blond girl sitting by a tree near the environmental studies building.

Why the fuck is there a giant-ass tree in the middle of this stupid-ass building, anyway?

"In the plant room, number two eighteen," she informs me with a shaky voice.

I finally reach the room with "218" printed on the door and open it before I can think about my promise to Tessa. I wasn't actually going to leave him alone anyway, but hearing how distraught she was on the night she was with him made it ten times worse for him.

THE ROOM IS FULL of rows of plants. Who would want to mess with this shit all day for a living?

"What are you doing here?" I hear him before I lay eyes on him.

He's standing next to a large box or some shit; when he steps out I take a step toward him.

"Don't play fucking stupid, you know exactly what I'm doing here."

He smiles. "No, sorry, I don't. The study of botany doesn't require psychic powers."

He mocks me with those dumb fucking goggles on his head. "You actually have the nerve to be a smug asshole about it?"

"About what?"

"Tessa."

"I'm not being a dick at all. You're the one treating her like shit, so don't get pissed when she runs to me because of it."

"Are you that fucking stupid to mess with what is mine?"

He backs away and walks down the aisle next to me. "She isn't yours. You don't own her," he challenges.

I reach across the boxes of plants to wrap my hand around his neck—and slam his face into the metal barrier between us. I hear a crisp snap, so I already know what happened. But when he lifts his head up and shouts "You broke my fucking nose!" while struggling to get out of my grip, I have to admit that the amount of blood pouring from his face *is* a little alarming.

"I already warned you over and over for fucking months now to stay away from Tessa, but then what do you do? You fucking kiss her, have her sleep in your goddamn bed?" I stride down the aisle to get to him again.

His hand is covering his broken nose as blood pours down his face. "And I already fucking told you that I don't give a fuck what you've got to say," he snarls, taking a step toward me. "You just broke my fucking nose!" he yells again.

Tessa is going to fucking kill me.

I should just leave now. He deserves to get his ass beat, again, but she's going to be furious.

"You've done worse shit to me, you keep messing with my girl-friend!" I shout back.

"She isn't your girlfriend, and I haven't even begun to mess with her yet."

"Are you actually fucking threatening me right now?"

"I don't know, am I?"

I take another step toward him, and he surprises me by swinging on me. His fist connects with my jaw and I stagger back-ward, knocking into a wooden box of plants. They crash to the ground, and as I recover, he swings again in a fury, but this time I'm able to block him and stumble to the side.

"You thought I was just a bitch, didn't you?" He grins a de-ranged and bloody grin and continues to walk toward me. "You really thought you were a badass, didn't you?" He laughs, pausing to spit blood onto the white tile floor.

My fingers wrap around the material of his lab coat, and I push him into another row of plants; the plants and our bodies hit the ground. I climb on top of him, making sure not to let him be in control. Out of the corner of my eye I see him raise his arm, but by the time I realize what's happening, he's slammed one of the small pots against the side of my head.

My head jerks and I blink rapidly to restore my vision. I'm stronger than him, but it seems he's a better fighter than he had led me to believe.

But there's no way in hell I'm letting him get the best of me.

"I already fucked her, anyway," he chokes as I grab hold of his hair and slam his head into the floor. At this point I don't give a fuck if I kill him or not.

"No, you didn't!" I scream.

"Yes, I did, she was . . . nice and t-tight, too." His voice is strangled and choppy, spitting out its venom with my hands still on his face.

My fist snaps his head to the side and he half screams from the pain, and for a brief moment I consider gripping his broken nose between my fingers to cause him even more. His feet kick frantically under me to try to lift my body from his. Images of Zed touching Tessa are fueling me, pushing me further than I've ever been pushed before.

His hands grip my arms, trying to lift my body from his. "You will never fucking touch her again," I say and bring a hand to his throat. "If you think you're going to take her from me, you're fucking wrong."

I tighten my grip around his neck. His bloody face is turning red and he tries to speak, but I only hear broken gasps for air.

"What the hell is going on in here?" a male voice shouts behind me.

When I turn my head around to see who the voice belongs to, Zed attempts to wrap his hands around my neck. Not fucking happening. Another punch to his cheek is all it takes for his arms to drop to the floor next to his sides.

A hand wraps around my arm, and I shove it off. "Call campus security!" the voice says, and I hurry to climb off of Zed.

Fuck. "No, don't," I say and stumble to my feet.

"What's going on? Get out of here! Go wait in the other room!" the middle-aged man yells, but I don't move. I assume he's a professor. *Fuck*.

"He came in here and attacked me," Zed says, then starts to cry. He literally starts to *cry*.

His hand is covering his swollen and crooked nose as he stands to his feet. His face is bloody, his lab coat is splattered with red, and his smug smile has evaporated.

With an air of authority, the man points at me and commands, "Stand against the wall until the police arrive! I mean it, don't move an inch!"

Fuck, the campus police are coming. I'm so fucking screwed. Why the fuck did I come here in the first place? I promised to stay away from him if she would.

Now that I've broken another one of my promises, will she break hers?

chapter
one hundred and nineteen

TESSA

When my pen presses to the paper, I have every intention of writing about my grandmother and how she dedicated her life to Christianity, but somehow Hardin's name appears in black ink.

"Ms. Young?" Professor Soto's voice says gently, though loudly enough for everyone in the first row to hear.

"Yes?" I look up, and my attention is immediately brought to Ken. *Why is Ken here?*

"Tessa, I need you to come with me," he says, and the annoying blonde behind me makes an "oohhh" sound like we're back in the sixth grade. She most likely doesn't even know who he is, that Ken is the chancellor of the college.

"What's going on?" Landon asks Ken as I get to my feet and begin to gather my things.

"We can talk about it outside." Ken's voice is unsteady.

"I'm coming," Landon says and stands as well.

Professor Soto looks at Ken. "Is that okay with you?"

"Yes, he's my son," he tells him and our teacher's eyes go wide.

"Oh, I'm sorry. I didn't know that; she's your daughter?" he asks him.

"No," Ken says tersely. He appears panicked, which is starting to scare me.

"Is Hardin . . ." I begin to ask, but Ken guides me out the door with Landon behind me.

"Hardin's been arrested," Ken tells us as soon as we get outside.

I can't breathe. "He's *what*?"

"He's been arrested for fighting, and for vandalizing campus property."

"Oh my God" is the only thing I can think to say.

"When? How?" Landon asks.

"About twenty minutes ago. I'm trying my best to keep this matter within the campus jurisdiction, but he isn't making it easy." Ken hurries across the street, and I nearly have to run to catch up with him.

My mind is racing: *Hardin, arrested? Oh my God. How could he get arrested? Who did he fight?*

But I already know the answer to that question.

Why couldn't he just keep his cool, for once? Is Hardin okay? Will he go to jail? Real jail? Is Zed okay?

Ken unlocks his car's doors, and the three of us get inside.

"Where are we going?" Landon asks.

"To campus security."

"Is he okay?" I ask.

"He's got a cut across his cheek and another on his ear, or so I've heard."

"You 'heard'? You haven't seen him yet?" Landon asks his stepfather.

"No, I haven't. He's throwing a fit, so I knew it would be better to get Tessa first." He nods his head in my direction.

"Yeah, good idea," Landon agrees, and I stay quiet.

A cut across his head and face? I hope he isn't in pain. Oh my God, this is all so crazy. I should have just agreed to spend the entire day with him. If I had, he wouldn't have even been on campus today.

* * *

KEN ZOOMS DOWN several backstreets, and within five minutes we're parking in front of the small brick building that houses campus security. There's a No Parking sign directly in front of where he parks, but I suppose parking wherever you like is one of the perks of being the chancellor.

The three of us hurry inside the building, and my eyes immediately start scanning for any sign of Hardin.

But I hear him first . . . "I don't give a fuck, you're nothing more than a douche bag with a fake badge! You're basically a mall cop, you fucking prick!"

I follow his voice and turn down the hall in pursuit of him. I hear Ken and Landon on my heels, but all I care about is getting to Hardin.

I come to where several people are gathered . . . and see Hardin pacing back and forth inside a small cell. *Holy shit*. His arms are behind his back in handcuffs.

"Fuck you! All of you!" he yells.

"Hardin!" His father's voice booms from behind me.

My angry boy's head snaps to the side, to where I'm standing, and his eyes go wide immediately. His face is split open just below his cheekbone, and his skin is sliced from his ear to the back of his head, his hair matted with blood.

"I'm trying to contain this, and you aren't helping!" Ken barks at his son.

"They have me trapped in here like some fucking animal. This is bullshit. Call whoever you need to call and get them to unlock this shit!" Hardin yells, attempting to tear his hands from the cuffs.

"Stop it," I say to him and scowl.

Immediately, his demeanor changes. He calms a little, but is no less angry. "Tessa, you shouldn't even be here. What kind of genius fucking idea was it to bring her?" Hardin hisses at his father and Landon.

"Hardin, stop it now. He's trying to help you. You need to calm down," I say through the bars. This doesn't feel real, talking to him while he's literally in a cell in handcuffs. This can't be real. But then again, this is what happens in the real world. You get arrested if you assault someone, on campus just as anywhere else.

As he looks at my eyes, I imagine he sees the pain I feel for him right now. I want to think that's why he finally gives in, and softly nods and says, "Okay."

"Thank you, Tessa," Ken says. Then he warns his son, "Give me a few minutes to see what I can do—in the meantime you need to stop yelling. You're making this worse for yourself when you're already in a load of trouble."

Landon looks to me, then to Hardin, before following Ken back down the narrow hallway. I hate this place already; everything is too white and black, too small, and it smells like bleach.

The campus security officers that sit behind the desk are immersed in their own conversation at the moment, or at least they've begun pretending to be since the chancellor of the school showed up to deal with his son.

"What happened?" I ask Hardin.

"I got arrested by campus security," he huffs.

"Are you okay?" I ask him, desperately wanting to reach through and wipe his face.

"Me? Yeah, I'm fine. It's not so bad as it looks," he answers, and examining him, I can see he's right. I can tell from here that the cuts aren't deep. His arms have light red streaks on them, mixing with the black ink to form a rather terrifying sight.

"Are you upset with me?" His voice is soft, a thousand degrees from where it was moments ago while he was screaming at the police.

"I don't know," I answer honestly.

Of course I'm upset with him, because I know who he fought . . . well, it isn't hard to guess. But I'm also worried about him, and I want to know what happened that led him to be in all of this trouble.

"I couldn't help it," he says, as if that justifies his actions.

"I told you before I wouldn't visit you in a jail cell, remember?" I frown, looking around the cell he's in.

"This doesn't count, it's not a real cell."

"It looks real to me." I tap on the metal bars to prove my point.

"It's not an actual jail; this is just a bullshit holding cell until they decide to involve the real police," he says loud enough for the two officers to look up from their conversation.

"Stop it. This isn't a joke, Hardin. You could be in a lot of trouble."

Hearing that, he rolls his eyes.

That's the problem with Hardin: he hasn't quite realized that his actions have consequences.

chapter
one hundred and twenty

TESSA

"Who started it?" I ask, trying my best not to jump to conclusions like I normally do.

Hardin tries to meet my eyes, but I look away. "I went to find him after I walked you to class," he says.

"You promised me that you'd leave him alone."

"I know."

"So why didn't you?"

"He was pushing it—he started provoking me, saying that he fucked you." He looks at me with a wild desperation. "You aren't lying about that, are you?" he asks, and I nearly lose it.

"I'm not answering that question again. I already told you that nothing happened between us, and here you are in a freaking jail cell asking such a thing," I say with frustration.

He rolls his eyes and sits down on the small metal bench inside the holding cell. He's really pissing me off.

"Why did you go find him? I want to know."

"Because he needed his ass beat, Tessa. He needs to know that he isn't to come near you again. I'm sick of his fucking games and the way he thinks he has some sort of fucking chance with you. I did this for you!"

I cross my arms over my chest. "How would you feel if I'd been the one to go find him today after I told you I wouldn't? I

thought we were both trying to make this work, and here you blatantly lied to my face. You knew you weren't going to hold up your
end of the deal, didn't you?"

"Yeah, I did, okay? It doesn't matter now, what's done is
done," he huffs like an angry child.

"It matters to me, Hardin. You keep getting yourself in trouble
when it's not necessary."

"It's very necessary, Tess."

"Where's Zed now? Is he in jail, too?"

"This isn't jail."

"Hardin . . ."

"I don't know where he is, nor do I give a shit, and neither do
you. You aren't going near him."

"Stop being like this! Stop telling me what I can and can't
do—it's really pissing me off."

"Are you cursing at me?" he says with an amused smirk.

Why does he think this is funny? It's anything but funny. I
begin to walk away from him, and the smile disappears from his
lips.

"Tessa, come back," he says, making me turn around.

"I'm going to find your father to see what's going on."

"Tell him to hurry up."

I growl at him, literally, as I walk away. He thinks just because
his father is the chancellor, he's going to get out of this easily, and
honestly, I really hope he does. But it's still nerve-racking how
lightly he's taking the whole thing.

"What the fuck are you looking at?" I hear him say to a cop,
and I rub my fingers over my temples.

I find Ken and Landon standing next to an older man with
gray hair and a mustache. He's wearing a tie and black dress
pants, and the way he's holding himself gives me the feeling that
he's important. When Landon notices me standing in the hall, he
walks over to me.

"Who's that?" I ask him quietly.

"He's the provost."

"That's the vice chancellor, right?"

Landon looks worried. "Yeah."

"What's going on? What are they saying?" I try to hear the two men talking, but I can't make out anything.

"It's . . . well, it's not looking good. There was a lot of damage done to the lab that Zed was in—I'm talking thousands of dollars' worth of damage. On top of that, Zed has a broken nose and a concussion. Someone drove him to the hospital."

My blood begins to boil. Hardin didn't just push Zed around. He seriously injured him!

"Also, Hardin shoved a professor to the floor. There's a girl who's in Zed's class that already wrote a statement saying Hardin came in there looking for Zed specifically. It's looking really bad right now. Ken's trying his best to keep Hardin out of jail, but I don't know if that's going to happen." Landon sighs, running his fingers through his hair. "The only thing that can keep him out of jail is if Zed decides to not press charges. Even then I don't know what'll happen."

My head is spinning.

"Expulsion," I hear the gray-haired man say, and Ken rubs his hand over his chin.

Expulsion? Hardin can't get expelled from school! Oh my God, this is a mess.

"He's my son," Ken says quietly, and I take a sly step closer to them.

"I know he is, but assaulting a professor and damaging school property isn't something we can just brush aside," the man says.

Damn Hardin and his temper. "This is a disaster," I tell Landon, and he nods sullenly.

I want to throw myself on the floor and cry, or better yet, I want to stomp over to Hardin's cell and punch him in his face. Neither of those things will help.

"Maybe you should talk to Zed about not pressing charges?" Landon suggests.

"Hardin will freak out if I go anywhere near him." Not that I should even listen to him, since he doesn't listen to me.

"I know," Landon replies, "but I don't know what else to suggest at this point."

"I guess you're right." I look back at Ken, then down the hall, to where Hardin is.

Hardin is my first priority, but I do feel awful for what he did to Zed, who I hope is going to be okay. Maybe if I go talk to him he'll decide not to press charges, which would at least eliminate one problem.

"Where is he? Do you know?" I ask Landon.

"I think I overheard them say he's at Grandview Hospital."

"Okay. Well, I'll go there first."

"Do you need a ride back to your car?"

"Shit. I didn't drive."

Landon digs his hand into his pocket and hands me his keys. "Here. Just drive carefully."

I smile at my best friend. "Thanks."

I have no idea what I would do without him, but since he's leaving soon, I guess I'll have to find out. The thought saddens me but I push it back; I can't think about Landon's leaving right now.

"I'll go talk to Hardin and let him know what's going on."

"Thank you again." I wrap my arms around Landon's neck in a tight hug.

Just as I reach the door Hardin's voice booms down the hall. "Tessa! Don't you fucking dare go find him!" he screams. I ignore him and open the double doors.

"I mean it, Tessa! Come back in here!"

The cold air drowns out his loud voice as I walk outside. How dare he tell me what to do like that? Who does he think he is? He's made a huge mess because he can't control his temper and jealousy. I'm trying to help clean up this mess. He's lucky I didn't slap him for breaking his promise to me. God, he's so frustrating.

WHEN I ARRIVE at Grandview, the woman at the nurse's station doesn't want to give me any information on Zed. She won't confirm if he's here now or tell me if he's been here at all.

"He's my boyfriend and I really need to see him," I tell the young bottle blonde.

She obnoxiously pops her chewing gum and twirls a lock of her hair between her fingers. "He's your boyfriend? The kid with all the *tattoos*?" She laughs, obviously not believing me.

"Yes. He is." My tone is clipped, nearly threatening, and I'm surprised at how intimidating I actually manage to sound.

It must work, because she shrugs and says, "Go down the hall and make a right. First door on the left," before wandering off.

Well, that wasn't too hard. I should be more forceful more often. I do as she told me and approach the first door on the left. It's closed, so I knock lightly before entering. I hope she told me the right room.

Zed is sitting on the edge of a hospital bed. He's shirtless, wearing only jeans and socks. His face.

"Oh my God!" I can't help but blurt out as I take in his appearance.

His nose is broken; I already knew that, but it looks so bad. It's so swollen and both his eyes are black. His chest is covered in bandages; the set of stars inked just below his collarbones is the only thing not covered in bandages or cuts.

"Are you okay?" I walk over to the bed. I hope he's not angry with me for coming here, to the hospital; this is my fault, after all.

"Not really," Zed says timidly. He lets out a deep breath and ruffles his hair before opening his eyes. He pats the bed next to him and I walk over to sit beside him.

"I'm so sorry for this. Will you tell me what happened?"

Zed's caramel eyes meet mine and he nods. "I was in the lab—not the one I showed you, but our plant tissue lab—and he came in there and started telling me to stay away from you."

"Then what?"

"I told him he doesn't own you and he slammed my head against a metal bar." I flinch at his words, looking at his nose.

"Did you tell him you slept with me?" I ask, unsure whether I believe this or not.

"Yeah. I did. I'm really sorry for saying that, but you have to understand he was attacking me, and I knew that was the only way to get to him. I feel like such an asshole for saying it. I'm really sorry, Tessa."

"He promised me that he'd stay away from you if I did, too," I tell him.

"Well, looks like he broke another promise, didn't he?" he says pointedly.

I stay quiet for a minute and try to put the fight together in my head. I'm angry at Zed for telling Hardin we slept together, but I'm glad he admitted it and apologized. I don't know which of these boys to be more angry with. It's hard to be angry at Zed as he sits here with so many injuries that I basically caused, and despite all of that he's still being so kind to me.

"I'm sorry that this keeps happening because of me," I tell him.

"It's not your fault. It's mine, and his. He just views you as some sort of property, and it pisses me off. You know what he said to me? He said that I should know better than to 'fuck with what's his.' That's how he talks about you when you aren't around, Tessa." His voice is soft and calm, totally unlike Hardin's.

I don't like the way Hardin seems to think he owns me either, but it bothers me when someone else says it. Hardin doesn't know how to handle his emotions and he's never been in a relationship before. "He's just territorial."

"You can't really be defending him right now."

"I'm not, that's not what I'm doing. I don't know what to think. He's in jail . . . well, in a holding cell on campus, and you're in the hospital. This is just too much for me. I know I shouldn't be complaining but I'm so sick of this drama all the time. Every time I feel like I can breathe, something else happens. It's drowning me."

"*He's* drowning you," Zed corrects me.

It's not only Hardin that's drowning me. It's everything: it's this college, my so-called friends who betrayed me, Hardin, Landon leaving me, my mother, Zed . . .

"I did this to myself, though."

Zed says, not without a little annoyance, "Stop blaming yourself for his mistakes. He does this shit because he doesn't care about anyone but himself. If he cared about you, he'd have stayed away from me like he promised. He wouldn't have stood you up on your birthday . . . I could go on for ages."

"Did you text me from his phone?"

"What?" He presses his palm to the bed to shift his body closer to mine. "Fuck." He hisses from the pain.

"Do you need something? I can call a nurse?" I offer, momentarily distracted.

"No, I'm getting ready to leave here. They should be finishing up my discharge papers. Now, what were you saying about me texting you?" he asks.

"Hardin seems to think you're the one who texted me on his birthday pretending to be him so I thought he was coming but he didn't know he was supposed to."

"He's lying. I would never do that. Why would I?"

"I don't know, he thinks you're trying to make me hate him or something."

Zed's gaze is too intense, I have to look away. "He's doing a pretty good job of that on his own, isn't he?"

"No, he's not," I counter. No matter how angry I am with him and how confused Zed's words are making me, I want to defend Hardin.

"He's only saying that so you'll think I'm some sort of villain when I'm not. I've always been there for you when he wasn't. He can't even keep a simple promise to you. He came in there and attacked me—and a professor! He kept on saying he was going to kill me, and I really believed him. If Professor Sutton hadn't come in, he would have. He already knows he can take me, he's done it multiple times." Zed shivers and stands to his feet. He grabs his green T-shirt from the chair and lifts his arms to pull it on. "Shit." He drops it to the floor.

I hurry to my feet to help him and grab the shirt from the ground.

"Lift as much as you can," I say and he brings his arms straight forward in front of him to aid me in dressing him.

"Thank you." He tries to smile again.

"What hurts the most?" I ask, assessing his swollen face again.

"Rejection," he timidly answers.

Ouch. I look down at my hands and begin to pick at my fingers.

"My nose," he then offers as a gesture to soften the moment. "When they had to set the broken bone."

"Are you going to press charges against him?" I finally ask what I came here to ask.

"Yeah."

"Don't, please." I stare into his eyes.

"Tessa, you can't do this. It isn't fair."

"I know. I'm sorry, but if you press charges he'll go to jail, to real jail." The thought sends me into a panic again.

"He broke my nose and I have a concussion; if he'd hit my head against that floor again, it would've killed me."

"I'm not saying that's okay, but I'm begging you. Please, Zed. We are leaving anyway. I'm transferring to Seattle, and Hardin will be gone, too."

Zed looks at me with worry. "He's coming with you?"

"No—well, yes. You won't have to worry about him any-more. If you don't press charges, you won't have to hear from him again."

Zed looks at me through swollen eyes for a few seconds. "Fine." He sighs. "I won't press charges against him, but please promise me that you'll really think about this. All of this; think of how much easier your life would be without him, Tessa. He at-tacked me for no reason, and here you are cleaning up his mess, as always," he says, utterly irritated

I don't blame him, though. I'm using the feelings he has for me against him, to persuade him to not press charges against Hardin.

"I will, thank you so much," I tell him and he nods.

"I wish I had fallen in love with someone who could love me back," he says so quietly that I barely hear him.

Love? Zed loves me? I know he has feelings for me . . . but he loves me? His fight with Hardin—the reason he's in the hospital right now—is my fault. But he loves me? He has a girlfriend and I'm so back and forth with Hardin. I look over at him and pray it's the pain medication speaking, not really him.

chapter
one hundred and twenty-one

HARDIN

'll see you at home, Tessa," Landon says as Tessa and I climb out of my dad's car and walk toward mine.

I look back at him and mumble a nice "fuck you" under my breath.

"Leave him alone," she warns and disappears into my car.

When I get inside, I turn the heat up and look at her with thankfulness in my eyes. "Thanks for coming home with me, even if it's just for the night."

Tessa just nods and leans her cheek against the window.

"You okay? I'm sorry about today, I—" I begin.

She sighs, cutting me off. "I'm just tired."

Two hours later, Tessa is fast asleep on the bed, her arms hugging my pillow and her knees curled up to her chest. She's breathtaking even when she's exhausted. It's still too early for me to go to sleep, so I go into the closet and grab the copy of *Pride and Prejudice* she gave me. Bright yellow marker covers much more of the book than I expected, so I lie next to her once again and begin to read the marked passages. One catches my eye:

"There are few people whom I really love, and still fewer of whom I think well. The more I see of the world, the more am I dissatisfied with it; and every day confirms my belief of the inconsis-

tency of all human characters, and of the little dependence that can be placed on the appearance of merit or sense."

This one is certainly from our earlier days. I can picture her now, annoyed and flustered, sitting on her tiny bed in that dorm with a highlighter and novel in hand.

I glance over at her and chuckle lightly at her expense. Flipping through the pages, I see a pattern here; she despised me. I knew that then, but being reminded of it is pretty damn strange:

"An unhappy alternative is before you, Elizabeth. From this day you must be a stranger to one of your parents. Your mother will never see you again if you do not marry Mr. Collins, and I will never see you again if you do."

Her mother and Noah.

"Angry people are not always wise."

Isn't that the truth . . .

"I have not the pleasure of understanding you."

I didn't understand my own damn self and still don't, really.

"I could easily forgive his pride, if he had not mortified mine."

She did this the day I told her I loved her and took it back. I know she did.

"I must learn to be content with being happier than I deserve."

Easier said than done, Tess.

"To be fond of dancing was a certain step toward falling in love."

The wedding. I know it. I remember the way she beamed up at me and pretended not to be in pain as I stepped all over her shoes.

"We all know him to be a proud, unpleasant sort of man; but this would be nothing if you really liked him."

This still applies. Landon would say some shit like this to Tessa, he probably has before.

"Till this moment I never knew myself."

I'm not sure which of us this applies to more.

" 'There is, I believe, in every disposition a tendency to some par-

ticular evil, a natural defect, which not even the best education can overcome.'

" *'And your defect is a propensity to hate everybody.'*

" *'And yours,' he replied with a smile, 'is willfully to misunderstand them.' "*

Each part holds more truth than the last as I skip back to the front section of the familiar novel.

"She is tolerable, but not handsome enough to tempt me, and I am in no humor at present to give consequence to young ladies who are slighted by other men."

I had once told Tessa she wasn't my type—what a fucking idiot I was. I mean, look at her: she's everyone's type, even if they're too damn stupid to see it at first. My hands work the pages, and my eyes skim over countless marked lines that relate to the two of us and how she feels about me. This is the best gift I'll ever receive, that's for damn sure.

"You have bewitched me, body and soul."

One of my favorite lines, I used it on her once when we first moved into this place. She scrunched up her nose at my corny use of the line, laughed at me, and tossed a piece of broccoli at me. She's always throwing shit at me.

"But people themselves alter so much, that there is something new to be observed in them forever."

I have changed for the better, for her, since I met her. I'm not perfect, fuck, nowhere near, but I could be one day.

"How little of permanent happiness could belong to a couple who were only brought together because their passions were stronger than their virtue."

I don't like this one at all. I know exactly what was going through her mind as she highlighted it. Moving on . . .

"A lady's imagination is very rapid; it jumps from admiration to love, from love to matrimony in a moment."

At least it isn't just Tessa's mind that does this crazy shit.

"Only the deepest love will persuade me into matrimony."

She left the rest of the sentence out, the part that says *"which is why I shall end up and old maid."*

Only the deepest love can persuade me into matrimony. Hmm . . . I'm not sure even that will do it for me. There is no possible way that there is a love deeper than what I feel for this girl, but it doesn't change my opinion on marriage. People don't get married for the right reasons anymore, not that they ever did. In the past it was for status or money, and now it's only to be sure you won't be lonely and miserable—two things nearly every married person still feels anyway.

I place the book on the bedside table before I switch off the light and lay my head flat on the mattress. I want to take my pillow back, but she's holding it too tight and I don't want to be a dick.

"Would you please just stop being so stubborn and come to England with me? I can't be without you," I whisper to her in her sleep, running my thumb along the warm skin of her cheek.

I'm looking forward to getting some sleep again, real sleep with her next to me.

chapter
one hundred and twenty-two

TESSA

When I wake up, Hardin is sprawled across the bed, one arm covering his face and the other hanging over the edge of the mattress. His T-shirt is soaked in sweat, and I feel disgusting. With a quick kiss to his cheek, I hurry to the bathroom.

When I return from my shower, Hardin's awake, like he's been waiting for me. He leans up on his elbow. "I'm afraid to be expelled," he says. His voice startles me, but his confession startles me even more.

I sit next to him on the bed, and he doesn't even try to tear the towel from around my body. "You are?"

"Yeah. I know it's stupid . . ." he begins.

"No, it's not stupid. Anyone would be afraid, I know I would be. It's okay to be afraid."

"What will I do if I can't go to WCU anymore?"

"Go to another college."

"I want to go back home," he says, and my heart sinks.

"Please don't," I say quietly.

"I have to, Tess. I can't afford university if my dad isn't the chancellor."

"We could find a way."

"No, this isn't your problem."

"Yes, it is. If you go to England, we'll never see each other."

"You have to come, Tessa. I know you don't want to, but you have to. I can't be away from you again. Please just come." His words are so full of emotion that I can't seem to find mine.

"Hardin, it's not that easy."

"Yes, it is. It's easy—you could get a job doing exactly what you're doing now and possibly make even more money and go to an even better university."

"Hardin . . ." I focus my eyes back on his bare skin.

He sighs. "You don't have to decide right now."

I almost tell him that I'll pack my bags and go to England with him, but I can't.

For now, I'll stay the coward that I am and push the news of Seattle back another day while I roll onto my side and he gathers me in his arms.

For once, he's gotten me to crawl back into bed with him in the morning. Comforting him is more of a priority than my routine.

"THE OWNER, DREW, seems like a dick, but he's pretty cool," Hardin informs me as we approach the small brick building.

A bell sounds above my head when Hardin opens the door for me and we walk inside. Steph and Tristan are already there. Steph is seated on a leather chair, and Tristan is looking through what appears to be . . . a book of tattoos?

"Took you long enough!" Steph kicks her leg out as Hardin and I walk by and he grabs her boot in his hand before it touches me.

"Already being annoying, I see . . ." He rolls his eyes and attempts to lead me over to Tristan, but I pull my hand from his and stand near Steph.

"She's fine with me," she tells him, and he scowls at her but doesn't say anything in return.

Hardin stands next to Tristan about twenty feet away, grabs a black book like the one Tristan has in his hands, and flips through the pages.

"I haven't seen you in here before." The guy looks up at me while he wipes the surface of Steph's bare stomach with a towel.

"I've never been here before," I reply.

"Name's Drew. I own the place."

"Nice to meet you. I'm Tessa."

"Are you getting any work done today?" He smiles.

"No, she's not." Hardin answers for me, wrapping his arm around my waist.

"She's with you, Scott?"

"Yes, she is." Hardin pulls me closer. He's obviously doing this for show. He said that Drew seems like an asshole, but I don't get that vibe from him at all. He seems really nice.

"Cool. Cool. About time you got a girlfriend." Drew laughs. Hardin relaxes a little but keeps his arm around me. "So why don't you get something done, hombre?"

A buzzing noise fills the space, and I look down at Steph's stomach to watch in amazement as the tattoo gun drags slowly across her skin. Drew wipes the excess ink off with a towel and continues.

"I might, actually," Hardin tells him.

I look up at Hardin, and his eyes meet mine. "Really? What do you want to get?" I ask him.

"I don't know yet, something on my back." Hardin's back is virtually the only part of his body that is completely ink-free.

"Really?"

"Yeah." He rests his chin on top of my hair.

"Speaking of getting work done, where the fuck are your rings?" Drew asks, dipping the gun into a small plastic cup full of black ink.

"I'm over them." Hardin shrugs.

"If he messes this up because you won't stop talking to him, you're paying for the whole thing." Steph looks at Hardin, and I laugh.

"I'm not going to pay for that shit," Hardin and Drew say in unison.

Tristan finally joins us and pulls a chair over to sit by Steph; he takes her hand in his. I look over at the small and freshly inked cluster of birds drawn into Steph's skin. It's sort of lovely, actually, the placement of them. Drew gives her a mirror so she can get a better look.

"I love it!" She smiles, handing the mirror back to Drew before sitting up.

"What are you going to get, Hardin?" I ask him quietly.

"Your name." He smiles.

Shocked, I step back from him with my jaw on the floor.

"You wouldn't want that?" he asks.

"No! Gosh no, that's . . . I don't know, that's insane," I whisper.

"Insane? Not really, it's just showing you that I'm committed to you and don't need a ring or marriage proposal to stay that way."

His voice is so clear that I'm no longer sure if he's joking. How did we go from joking to commitments and marriage in less than three minutes? This is how it always is with us, so I suppose I should be used to it by now.

"Ready, Hardin?"

"Sure." Hardin steps away from me and pulls his shirt over his head.

"A quote?" Drew speaks my exact thoughts.

"I just want it across the top of my back; it's 'I never wish to be parted from you from this day on.' Just make it like an inch in height, do it in your cool freehand," Hardin instructs and turns his back to face Drew.

I never wish to be parted from you from this day on . . .

"Hardin, can we talk about this for a second, please?" I ask him.

I swear he knows about my plans to go to Seattle and he's taunting me by getting this tattoo. The line he chose is perfect but cruelly ironic, considering I've been withholding telling him about my move to Seattle.

"No, Tess, I want to do it," he says, dismissing me.

"Hardin, I really don't think—"

"It's not a big deal, Tessa, it's not my first tattoo," he jokes.

"I just—"

"If you don't shut up, I'll have your name and Social Security number printed across my entire back," he threatens with a laugh, but I get the feeling he would actually go through with it to prove his point.

I stay quiet to try to think about what to say. I should just blurt it out right now before the gun touches his clear skin. If I wait . . .

The now-familiar buzz of the gun sounds, and black ink litters Hardin's back.

"Now, come over here and hold my hand." He smirks, holding out his hand to me.

chapter
one hundred and twenty-three

HARDIN

Tessa shyly grasps my hand, and I pull her closer to me.

"Stop moving," Drew snaps.

"My bad."

"Does it hurt?" she softly asks.

The innocence in her eyes astounds me, to this day. She was on her knees last night, and twenty hours later she's speaking to me the way she would speak to a wounded child.

"Yes, really fucking bad," I lie.

"Really?" Worry flashes over her features.

I love the feeling that comes with the needle transferring the ink to my skin; it's no longer painful, it's relaxing.

"No, baby, it doesn't hurt," I assure her, and Drew, being the dick he is, makes gagging noises behind my back.

Tessa giggles, and I put my middle finger in the air. I didn't mean to call her baby just now, in front of Drew, but I don't really give a fuck what he thinks, and I know for a fact he's head over heels for the girl he just had a baby with a few months ago, so he can't say shit to me.

"I still can't believe you're doing this," she says as Drew spreads the ointment over the new tattoo.

"It's already done," I remind her, and she looks worried as she stares at her phone screen.

I hope Tess doesn't make too big of a deal out of this tattoo; it's not that serious. I have a shitload of tattoos. This one is for her, and I'm hoping she's excited about it. I know I am.

"Where the fuck are Steph and Tristan?" I look out the windows of the shop in an attempt to spot Steph's bright-ass hair.

"We can go next door and find them?" Tessa suggests after I pay Drew and promise to come back and let him give me an entire back piece.

I nearly knock his teeth out when he suggests giving Tessa a sleeve or belly piercing.

"I think I would look cool with my nose pierced." She smiles as we walk outside.

I laugh at the thought and bring my arm around her waist as a bearded man stumbles past us. His jeans and shoes are dirty, and his thick sweatshirt is stained with liquid. From the smell of it, I assume vodka.

Tessa stops next to me, and the man does the same. I gently pull her behind me. If this homeless drunk thinks he's coming any fucking closer to her, I will fucking. . . .

What she says next is so spoken so softly that it comes out as a whisper, and I watch in confusion as all the color drains from her face.

"Dad?"

If you don't like spoilers, don't read this chapter!

TESSA

Hardin, it's so cold in here." I bury my feet under his sprawled legs, and he flinches, sucking air in between his teeth.

Wiggling my toes under his warm legs, I laugh when he winces and tugs his shorts down between my cold feet and his skin.

"You were just hot fifteen minutes ago and had me turn on the air." Hardin smiles, reaches for my feet, and lifts them onto his lap.

I close my eyes as his warm hands begin to rub. His thumb presses into the heel of my foot, and the instant relief is heavenly. My feet have officially given up on me lately.

"Are you complaining?" I raise my brows to question him.

He shakes his head, smiling at me.

"Me?" He taps his hand against his chest. "Never."

"Mm-hmm. Right," I tease, and he moves his fingers along the arch of my foot, pressing gently as he goes.

"I'm so over my feet being swollen," I groan. "They're better than yesterday, but my skin is still just so tight."

I roll my ankles, feeling my skin pull with the movement. I haven't been on my feet much except walking from my bed to the shower, and now to the couch, where Hardin and I have decided to camp out for the entire Sunday. I nearly couldn't believe it when he closed his work binder, put it up on the shelf with a grin so cheeky that it was beyond suspicious, and agreed to spend the day with me, on the couch, no work, no e-mails, no phones. Just us. I know a round of edits on his latest manuscript is due and a stack of interviews is piling up in his e-mail, but today is my day with him, without either of us leaving our little budding family bubble.

Sitting here on our couch and doing absolutely nothing has been something that I've been dying to have as the world pulls my Hardin in so many directions the more people begin to know his name. It's equal parts terrifying and gratifying.

"Come on out, little one. Finish cooking in there and come on out." Hardin's voice is as soft as his fingers as they lift the bottom of my shirt up, inch by inch.

I watch him carefully, taking in the way his eyes just scream with panic and peace all at once as he touches my stomach. No matter how many times I feel him touch where our baby is, my skin still breaks into goose bumps at the sight of his inked hand comforting our baby. It's nearly too much for me and my heart.

"Cooking? Seriously, Hardin?" I laugh at his choice of words.

"Well, that's what it's doing." He shrugs his shoulders.

"It." I roll my eyes. "You're just so eloquent. Where did you learn how to use words?"

He grins. "My use of words seems to be working out just fine for me." He eyes the little stack of books on the coffee table with his name printed on their covers.

"So I've been told."

"Speaking of eloquent," he begins.

As he's talking, I reach over and lift a cotton ball off his black shirt.

"I need your help with another interview."

"Another one?" I tease him.

He nods, and his hair falls down over his forehead. It's nearly dry from our hour-long shower.

"Your hair takes so long to dry," I unconsciously say, wrapping a dark strand around my finger, letting it curl and bounce back across his forehead. He brushes it away, hating the feel of his hair touching him after going weeks with it shorter than usual. I was beyond relieved that it was growing out from when he let me give him a (disastrous) trim, and I didn't want him to touch it.

"Are you trying to seduce or distract me, Theresa?"

"Neither." I laugh with him. "My brain is all over the place, as usual."

"Pleeeeze, Tess," he whines. "Even my publicist asked me to ask you to help. She says the interviews you do for me make me much more likable. Don't you want the public to like me?"

"Not the way your publicist likes you." I frown at the thought of her.

She is great at her job. But she is very much an opportunist, and I don't like the way I instinctively feel around her. Something is off, but I can't bring myself to interfere with another woman's job based on my gut feeling. And Hardin really does need the help with his image now that strangers on the Internet judge everything he says and does. Sometimes having our entire personal life out there for people to dissect really fucking sucks.

"She does not like me." He rolls his eyes, kissing the top of my stomach. I shiver.

"Shh, I don't care. We're not eighteen anymore," I remind myself, and to my annoyance and pleasure, he laughs and kisses my belly again.

"Don't worry, Tess, you two are the only girls I'll ever be able to tolerate," he says against my skin.

He traces his index finger along a deep purple line stretching from my hip to the center of my stomach. I fight the bubble of insecurity and try to replace it with the comfort of knowing that someone loves every bit of me, that he revels in the changes I'm going through, that I can read his mind after all we've been through, and I can tell everything he's thinking with one look. Some days are easier than others, but recently it's gotten much harder since Hardin's career has bloomed and he is surrounded by an ever-increasing number of successful and stunning women. Their dresses get tighter and heels get higher while my entire body changes every week.

Because of the complications with our last pregnancy, my doctor advised me not to work anymore. Honestly, even though I'd never endanger my pregnancy, it feels like another part of my identity that I'm losing. I never imagined myself to be a stay-at-home mom, especially given that my mother had been drilling into my head since birth that I must always work and never, ever depend on anyone else. Hardin, though not always dependable in the past, has become an exception to my mother's rule.

"What are you thinking about?" Hardin asks me, catching my hand just as I drift off into a current of my own thoughts, and I feel myself flushing.

I sigh. "Oh, just trying to decipher my role in modern society as a mother and a woman. The usual," I add with another sigh.

Hardin's lips turn into a soft frown, and his fingers stop their tracing. "That's it?"

I nod.

"Do you want to talk about it? Not that I'm an expert on anything to do with . . . well, anything at all, but if you want to talk about it I—"

I cover his mouth with my hand and shake my head. I don't want to talk about it. There's nothing he can really say to make me feel better. He's already going above and beyond, but some things you just have to work out yourself. And this is one of those things.

"No, not really. I'd rather talk about your interviews and how great I am at doing them for you."

Hardin reads my face. First my eyes, then my mouth. He finds what he's looking for and smiles.

"Deal." He backs off.

God, how I love this man and who he's growing up to be.

"Anyway, I have to agree with my publicist and save my public image. I don't want to be known as the 'sad boy' or the dickhead I was when I was a kid."

"You're not even thirty. You're still a kid."

"Not all of us were forty by the time we were twelve, my love." He slides one of his hands between my thighs and playfully squeezes my leg. "You're just so good at everything, Tess. Being a mum, being a wife, a scholar really. A true force to be reckoned with. A—"

I shut him up by covering his mouth again. "Okay, okay. Now you're just sucking up. And I'm no one's wife, mister."

He shakes his head and licks my hand with his tongue. A half scream from me later and he's gone from a covered mouth to his mouth on mine. He talks to me through his soft display of affection.

"I don't need to suck up anymore. I'd say I've secured myself here nicely." He gently taps his fingertips across my stomach like they're lightly kissing the keys of a piano.

"Secured yourself?" I pretend to be offended, hanging my mouth open.

"Mm-hmm. Quite literally." His smile grows as I roll my eyes.

"I wouldn't get too comfy. I'm sure the city is full of toe heaters and blanket fetchers."

"A blanket fetcher? Oh god." He directs his attention to our growing baby. "Okay, now you really must come out. You're turning your mother into a tyrant who makes up her own words to demean me. Do you hear me?" He taps on my belly.

"Hello?" He taps again.

My adoration of him is somehow still growing with time. Even though I always feel like there couldn't possibly be any more room inside of me to love him, there always is.

A beat of silence bounces between us as he groans. "Oh god, now she's not listening either. Lord help me."

Nervousness fills my stomach at his sincere certainty that our little bean is going to be a girl. Not that I know for sure that he's wrong or care what the sex of the baby is. It's more the fear that the pregnancy won't last long enough to find out or that once the baby has a gender, it will have a name. It's the immense fear that it will feel so much more agonizing if we lose another child. Hardin says it was the most pain we would ever have to feel for the rest of our lives and that he would make sure of it. As if it were that simple, as if the gods or the universe had ever listened to our prayers before. We aren't special, and we had been reminded of that too often. I let Hardin stay in that hopeful state because that's how he's coping with his fear.

Hardin has been the happy, positive, nothing-can-go-wrong one during all of this. Even during the first trimester (of hell), which we both spent on edge and full of anxiety. He hid it better than I did. I spent the days, and Hardin spent his nights, wondering if the curse that seemed to have been cast upon us had been lifted, or if we should expect another punishment, another loss. I'm still not sure and I still haven't taken a full breath since the second little line appeared on the third pregnancy test.

"We have no idea if it's a boy or a girl," I remind him, my voice cracking a little. I reach for the cup of water on the table, and Hardin grabs it and hands it to me.

He notices my change in demeanor—of course he does—and he pulls me onto his lap and sets the water back on the side table.

"I know what you're thinking. Don't worry, Tess."

"How can I not?" I ask him, leaving his eyes to look at the baby between us.

"I know it's easier said than done. It just makes me fucking crazy thinking you're being so hard on yourself and not allowing yourself to have any happiness. You deserve to be happy, Tess. You have done everything by the book, and this baby is here and will be here and will be sitting with us on this hideous couch you forced me to buy. And when that's happening, I don't want you to miss any of it, because you deserve to feel that joy of bringing another life into the world and knowing that she will have a much better upbringing than her mummy and dad had."

I wish I could just believe his words the second I hear them, but unfortunately my brain doesn't work that way, and lately most of the happiness I feel turns into worry no matter what I do.

There are about one hundred sixty-eight days left of my pregnancy, and getting through each one is a little victory here in the Scott house—well, town house. Landon made us a wall calendar for Christmas, full of bad pictures of Hardin, which made everyone's—except Hardin's—year, and each morning, we mark the day before off with a big happy circle, instead of with an X.

The rows of circles make me feel accomplished as each day passes. We aren't safe yet. During the last pregnancy, I got too comfortable and let the chance of risk leave my mind too often. I don't want to do that this time. I can't handle losing this baby too. We know her too well. The baby knows our voices and our laughter and watches corny romance movies with us. The baby is already such a part of our family, we can't handle another loss. Hardin says we can if it comes to that, that we can handle anything, but I'm just not seeing his optimism these days. Oh, the tables have absolutely turned since I met this man years ago.

"I'm positive it's a girl. Only two more weeks and you'll see."

"Fourteen more circles," I say to him. It feels so close but so far. "What if you're wrong?" I ask.

He moves his hands to the side of my face, and the light catches on the patches of scar tissue on the bends of his knuckles. His thumb touches my cheek, just above the corner of my mouth.

"It wouldn't be the first time I was wrong."

"Understatement of the year."

His smile grows. "The century."

He kisses me. His lips are cold, opposite of his fevered hands moving up and down my thighs, slowly rocking my body against his. His shorts move up with the movements until the hem of his black briefs is visible. My body overrides my mind, and I relax as he effectively turns my brain off and gifts me with peace as he kisses down my jaw to my neck.

"Are you still cold, Tess?" he asks, the tone of his voice completely changed from seconds ago.

I shake my head and wrap one arm around the back of his neck, burying my fingers in his thick black hair. Now dripping with honey, I feel him kissing me again.

"It's almost off," I tell him, knowing he understands that I'm referring to my brain and the whirl of doubt circling around in there. "Kiss me harder," I beg him, and he does, so intimately that every thought leaves my head and all I can see or smell or feel or touch is Hardin.

He kisses me like we don't have anywhere to be. He kisses me like I'm the only place he's ever been and the only place he will ever be. The way I can feel his heart beating in his chest for me and for our baby voids out everything else. Everything except the buzzing coming from his phone on the table. I kiss him and pull at his hair to drown out the phone vibrating against the glass.

"Ignore it," he tells me, pulling my lower lip between his. He bites down hard enough that I can't stop the groan falling from my lips even if I tried.

He licks at the tender spot and lifts my shirt over my head.

The moment the shirt hits the cushion beside me, a pounding knock bangs at the door. His hands move to my back to hold me still.

"Who the fuck?" Our door buzzer goes off as Hardin growls in frustration.

"Hardin!" a female voice yells on the other side of the door. I know her voice immediately.

"Why didn't you pick up? Answer your phone. You're already late!" his publicist screeches from outside.

I climb off him and hand him his phone. Three missed calls from her and a calendar pop-up reminding him of dinner with someone named Carlton Santos, whoever that is.

Hardin grabs my T-shirt and hands it to me with a look of apology already written on his face.

"Hang on," he says when she knocks again.

He looks at me to make sure I'm dressed, then pulls open the door.

"What the hell are you doing here?" he asks her.

She looks flustered, her cheeks are flushed, and she seems a little out of breath. Her long hair is even a little disheveled compared to its usual pin-straight style.

"We have a dinner tonight. Right now, with Mr. Santos from Unified One; you know, the company you're asking to sponsor your launch party and benefit. The man who we're asking to drop tens of thousands of dollars to—"

"I didn't know about this?" he tells her.

She looks like she could cry. I feel bad for her at the moment, even though I know she's here to take him away from our little bubble. Will he go?

"I put it into your calendar and I told you about it the other day when I called," she defends herself.

It's not lost on me that she hasn't acknowledged me being in the room at all.

"You know I barely listen when you talk," he tells her. She isn't fazed by his rudeness. "And I never check that fucking calendar."

"Well, he's waiting at Masa right now with his daughter, who's a fan of yours. Luckily he agreed to come to Brooklyn for you, so we don't have far to go," she says, checking her phone.

Hardin looks at me, waiting for my reaction. I can tell he's genuinely not sure what to do.

"It's fine," I say, knowing this is bigger than me and my little bubble on a Sunday night.

"See, she's fine. Let's go." She smiles at me for probably the first time since I met her a while ago.

"Don't talk to her," Hardin tells her as he stands in front of me.

"Are you sure you're okay with this? I'm so sorry. I didn't know I had this . . . I was going to be here with you all night, I swear it," he tells me, desperately seeking my approval.

"Do you want to come? You should come," he offers, and I fully notice the way the woman's expression changes. Maybe she doesn't want a fan of his to have her experience ruined by the reminder of him having a baby on the way, or maybe the man would be less likely to donate to Hardin's foundation if I were there? I don't know, but it sure does feel like another punch to my already fragile mental state.

"No, no. It's fine. I'm tired anyway," I lie, knowing damn well I was wide-awake two minutes ago and had an entirely different plan for our night away from the world.

"We have more Sundays before the baby." I smile, wanting to take some of the pressure off him.

"I'm sorry," he whispers into my ear, and kisses me there.

"Shh, don't be." I beg my voice not to expose the heavy disappointment washing over me.

I wonder if it will always be this way. A call, a dinner, a

signing, an event, always demanding his attention. My thoughts are incredibly selfish, but I'm too disappointed to care and I have the rest of the night to wallow in it.

"I'm not changing." He turns to her and squeezes my hands, then lets go of them and walks to the door.

She doesn't say anything as he slips his sneakers on and runs his fingers through his messy hair. Instead of acknowledging him, she's watching me. Her stare makes me uneasy, and I get the feeling that she thinks she's gaining more than a donation for Hardin's charity as she follows him out the door of our home. As the door shuts, my brain cracks open, and all the poisonous thoughts Hardin swept away come crashing over me as the sound of their footsteps dissolves down the hall.

acknowledgments

Here we are again, the second book over already. Two down, two to go. I am going to try to make it through this without turning into a blubbering mess like I did while writing the first book's acknowledgments. (Not likely, but it's worth a try.)

First, I want to thank my husband, who continued to support me while I spent hours and hours writing and tweeting and writing and tweeting and then writing again.

Next are my Afternators (I think we decided on this name—hah!). You all mean the world to me, and I still can't believe how lucky I am to have you supporting me. (Here come the tears.) Every single tweet, every comment, every random selfie you send me, every secret you share with me has made us into the family we are now. Those of you who were here from the beginning (Wattpad days), we have a bond that can never be explained. We will be the ones who remember how it felt the first time Harry and Tess kissed. You know how nerve-racking it was waiting for updates—you remember commenting things like OMH HARTYSH SHJD, and we all know exactly what it means. I could never thank you enough, and I hope Hardin has the same place in your heart as our Harry.

I owe so much to Wattpad. I have no idea where my life would be right now if I hadn't found the platform. Ashleigh Gardner, you are always there for me for all my random questions and life advice. You have become a friend to me, and I'm so thankful to have you in my corner. Candice Faktor, you always support me and fight for the vision behind After, and I owe you so much for that. Nazia Khan, you make my life easier every single day, and I'm lucky to have you as a friend. Wattpad was my first home and will always be my favorite place to write.

Adam Wilson, the world's most fabulous and witty editor, you are next, my friend. I know that I drive you insane with my fandom references, Twilight references, and every other random thing I bother you with. You had your work cut out for you taking on After (and me), and you have made this into the easiest, most enjoyable experience. (Even if you sent me work during a 1D concert lol.) Thank you for everything. Two more to go!

Gallery Books, thank you for believing in me and my story. You made my dreams come true! Kristin Dwyer, you always have my back and help keep me sane! A huge thank-you goes out to the proofreaders and production folks working on this series: Steve Breslin and crew, I know you had your work cut out for you, and you are incredible!

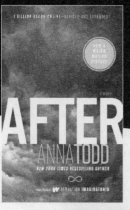
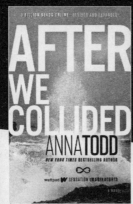